LOON LAKE

"HYPNOTIC . . . *LOON LAKE* tantalizes long after it has ended."

—*Time*

"Doctorow's most prodigious work—wonderfully brave, enthralling, THE BEST AMERICAN BOOK I have read in years."

—*Susan Sontag*

"A FASCINATING, TANTALIZING novel . . . It's so rich . . . The experience of reading it was exhilarating."

—*The New York Times Book Review*

"A GENUINE THRILLER . . . a marvelous exploration of the complexities, even contradictions of the American Dream . . . Not under any circumstances would we reveal the truly shattering climax."

—*Dallas Morning News*

"COMPELLING . . . BRILLIANTLY DONE."

—*St. Louis Post-Dispatch*

"ONE DAZZLING SOLO PERFORMANCE AFTER ANOTHER . . . Anatomizes America with insight, passion and inventiveness."

—*Washington Post Book World*

LOON LAKE

"A WONDERFUL BOOK . . . It may very well be a MASTERPIECE. I read the book virtually in one night. I have been rereading it ever since. I cannot forget it . . . a most scintillating, moving experience."
—*Chicago Sun-Times*

"UNPREDICTABLE and ASTONISHING. It's tough and sad and triumphant and frightening and haunting. It's the kind of book you should be sure your friends read, too, because you're going to want to talk about it with them."
—*The Bulletin*

"ONE OF THE GLORIES OF OUR LITERATURE, AND WE MUST ALWAYS LISTEN TO HIM."
—*Fort Worth Star Telegram*

"A HAUNTING and POWERFUL book."
—*The Toledo Blade*

"As COMPELLING as the wilderness that embraces it and as SIGNIFICANT as the America from which it springs . . . the story is a whopping good one."
—*St. Louis Globe-Democrat*

"HIGHLY INTERESTING for its . . . intrinsic picturesqueness and dramatic power."
—*The Chicago Tribune*

E.L.DOCTOROW

LOON LAKE

BANTAM BOOKS
TORONTO · NEW YORK · LONDON · SYDNEY

LOON LAKE

*A Bantam Book / published by arrangement with
Random House*

PRINTING HISTORY

*Random House edition published September 1980
5 printings through August 1980*

*A Special Fall 1980 offer (Dual Main Selection)
of Book-of-the-Month Club*

Serialized in PLAYBOY *magazine October 1980*

The poem "Loon Lake" originally appeared in the
KENYON REVIEW

*Portions of the work originally appeared in somewhat
altered form in* PLAYBOY *magazine*

A limited first edition of this book has been privately printed

Bantam Export edition / October 1981

Bantam edition / December 1981

Grateful acknowledgment is made to the following for permission to reprint previously published material: Chappell Music Company: Lyrics from "Five Hundred Miles" by Hedy West. Copyright © 1961 & 1962 by Friendship Music Corp. All rights controlled by Unichappell Music, Inc. (Rightsong Music, Publisher). International Copyright Secured. All rights reserved. Used by permission. Peer International Corporation: Lyrics from "Wabash Cannon Ball" by A. P. Carter. Copyrights 1933 & 1939 by Peer International Corporation. Copyrights renewed. Used by permission. All rights reserved. Shapiro, Bernstein & Co. Inc.: Lyrics from "Exactly Like You" by Dorothy Fields. Copyright MCMXXX Renewed by Shapiro, Bernstein & Co. Inc., New York, N.Y. 10022. Used by permission. All rights reserved.

ISBN 0–553–20027–5

Published simultaneously in the United States and Canada

Bantam Books are published by Bantam Books, Inc. Its trademark, consisting of the words "Bantam Books" and the portrayal of a rooster, is Registered in U.S. Patent and Trademark Office and in other countries. Marca Registrada. Bantam Books, Inc., 666 Fifth Avenue, New York, New York 10103.

TO HELEN HENSLEE

They were hateful presences in me. Like a little old couple in the woods, all alone for each other, the son only a whim of fate. It was their lousy little house, they never let me forget that. They lived on a linoleum terrain and sat in the evenings by their radio. What were they expecting to hear? If I came in early I distracted them, if I came in late I enraged them, it was my life they resented, the juicy fullness of being they couldn't abide. They were all dried up. They were slightly smoking sticks. They were crumbling into ash. What, after all, was the tragedy in their lives implicit in the profoundly reproachful looks they sent my way? That things hadn't worked out for them? How did that make them different from anyone else on Mechanic Street, even the houses were the same, two by two, the same asphalt palace over and over, streetcars rang the bell on the whole fucking neighborhood. Only the maniacs were alive, the men and women who lived on the street, there was one we called Saint Garbage who went from ash can to ash can collecting what poor people had no use for—can you imagine?—and whatever he found he put on his cart or on his back, he wore several hats several jackets coats pairs of pants, socks over shoes over slippers, you couldn't look at his face, it was bearded and red and raw and one of his eyes ran with some yellow excrescence oh Saint Garbage. And three blocks away was the mill where everybody in Paterson made the wages to keep up their wonderful life, including my father including my mother they went there together and came home together and ate their meals and went to the same bed together. Where was I in all of this, they only paid attention to me if I got sick. For a while there I got sick all the time, coughing and running fevers and wheezing, threatening them with scarlet fever or whooping cough or diphtheria, my only power was in suggesting to them the terrible consequence of one mindless moment of their lust. They clung to their miserable lives, held to their meager rituals on Sundays going to Mass with the other suckers as if some monumental plan was working out that might be personally painful to them but made Sense because God had to make Sense even if the poor dumb hollow-eyed hunkies didn't know what it was. And I despised that. I grew up in a dervish spin of health and sickness and by the time I was fifteen everything was fine, I knew my life and I made it work, I raced down alleys and jumped fences a few seconds before the cops, I stole what I needed and went after girls like prey, I went looking for trouble and was keen for it, I was keen for life, I ran down the street to follow the airships sailing by, I climbed firescapes and watched old women struggle into their corsets, I joined a gang and carried a penknife I had sharpened like an Arab, like a Dago, I stuck it in the vegetable peddler's horse, I stuck it in a feeb with a watermelon head, I slit awnings with it, I played peg with it, I robbed little kids with it, I took a girl on the roof with it and got her to take off her clothes with it. I only wanted to be famous!

And the coal trucks releasing their fearsome anthracite down the sliding chutes to the dark basements, and Ricco the Sweet Potato man putting into your hand a hot orange potato in a half sheet of the *Daily News* for three cents, the filthy black snow lying banked in the streets, the wind smelling of soot and machine oil blowing down Mechanic Street and you are holding your hands on the sweet heat, cupping it holding it up to your red face. The taking humbly, almost unconsciously of goodness by little kids who took it all, the rage of parents, the madness of old women in the dank stairwells, murder, robbery, threat in the sky, the unendurable prison of schoolrooms. In the five-and-ten was the cornucopia of small tin cars with wind-up keys made in Japan and rubber cops on motorcycles, and rubber chiefs in sidecars from Japan there were tin autogyros and tin DC-3s! You went for the small things, the molded metal car models that would fit in your palm, you watched the lady in her green smock and the eyeglasses looping from a black string around her neck, and when she turned, out came the white hand like a frog's tongue, like a cobra's, and down the aisles you went, another toy of goodness, bright-painted toy of gladness in your pocket.

But I was alone in this, I was alone in it all, alone at night in the spread of warmth waking to the warm pool of undeniable satisfaction pissed from my infant cock into the flat world of the sheet and only when it turned cold and chafed my thighs did I admit to being awake, mama, oh mama, the sense of real catastrophe, he wet the bed again—alone in that, alone for years in all of that. I don't remember anyone's name, I don't remember who the gang members were, I don't remember the names of my schoolteachers, I was alone in all of it, there was some faculty of being alone I was born with, in the noise of life and clatter of tenement war, my brain was alone in the silence of observation and perception and understanding, that true silence of waiting for conclusions, of waiting for everything to add up to a judgment, a decision, that silence worse than the silence of the deaf and dumb.

And then one day I am caught breaking the lock on the poorbox, the fat priest in his skirts grabbing my neck with a hand like pincers, not the first time slapping my head with his flat hand and giving me the bum's rush back to the sacristy behind the stone Christs and Marys and the votive candles flickering like a distant jungle encampment and I conceive of what a great vaulting stone penitence this is, with its dark light quite deliberate and its hard stone floors and its cathedral carved space intimating the inside of the cross of man the glory of God, the sin of existence, my sin of existence, born with it stuck with it enraging them all with it God the Father the Son and That Other One really pissing them off with my existence I twist turn kick the Father has balls they don't cut off their own balls they don't go that far the son of a bitch—spungo! I aim truly and he's no priest going down now with eyes about to pop out of his head, red apoplectic face I know the feeling Father but you're no father of mine he is on his hands and knees on the stone he is gasping for breath You want your money I scream take your fucking money and rearing back throw it to heaven run under it as it rains down pennies from heaven on the stone floor ringing like chaos loosed on the good stern Father. I run through the money coming down like slants of rain from the black vaults of heaven.

I lived in New York for a couple of months. It seemed to me at first an incredibly clean place with well-dressed people and washed cars and bright-painted red-and-yellow streetcars and white buildings. It was a stone city then, and in midtown the skyscrapers were white stone and the sanitation men went around pushing big cans on two-wheeled carts and they'd stop here and there and sweep the gutters, that seems incredible to me now, they wore white jackets and white pants and military style caps of khaki. And in Central Park, which I thought of as the country, the park men came along with broomsticks with a nail on the end of them and impaled cigarette wrappers and ice cream wrappers on these sticks and then wiped the sticks off in these burlap bags they carried over their shoulders. The park was glorious and green. The city hummed with enterprise. It was a wonderful city! I thought, a place where things happened and where everyone was important even streetsweepers just from being there not like Paterson where nothing mattered because it was Paterson where nothing important could happen where even death was unimportant. It had size it had magnitude, it gave life magnitude it was one of the great cities of the world. And it went on, it was colossal, miles of streets of grand famous stores and miles of streetcar tracks, great ships bassoing in the harbor and gulls gliding lazily over the docks. I rode the clattering elevated trains that rocked and careened around the corners and when the weather was cold I stayed aboard making complete circles around the city keeping warm on the rush seats set over the heaters. I got to know the city. It calmed me down. Off on its edges you could always get a place to flop, there were still shanties on the hillsides below Riverside Drive, there were mission houses where you could get a bed down at the Bowery and be fumigated and there was a whole network of welfare places where you could get soup and bread if you weren't proud. But I looked for work, I tried to stay clean and present myself at employment agencies crowds of pushing shoving men staring at jobs described in chalk on blackboards at employment agencies it was very difficult to persuade yourself you and not any of a hundred others were the man for the job.

One day I got wise. I saw a fat kid delivering groceries. He was wearing an apron over his clothes and pushing a cart, one of those wooden carts with giant steel-banded wheels. The name and address of the grocery was painted on the slats. His arms full, he went down the steps to the trade entrance of a brownstone, rang the bell and disappeared inside. The cobra strikes! I raced down the street clattering the cart over the cobblestones, I tore around the corner, I went down a side street made dark by the gridwork shadows of industrial firescapes and dark green iron fronts, I felt like Charlie Chaplin, turning one way, braking, doing an about face, scooting off another way, I think I was laughing, imagining a squad of Keystone

Kops piling up behind me, I thought of the fat kid's face, even if he knew where to look he couldn't catch me. I sat down for a while in an alley and caught my breath. Eventually, like the most conscientious grocery boy in the world, I trundled my cart back the way I had come and delivered every last one of the orders. Each bag and box had a bill stuck inside with the name and address of the customer. I took tips and cash receipts. I was polite. I pushed my cart back to Graeber's Groceries Fancy Fruits and Vegetables and found Graeber himself loading up another cart grumbling and saying things in German and making life hell for his clerks. No fat kid among them. Graeber was angry, suspicious, skeptical. He didn't believe I found the cart abandoned at a tilt in an alley. And then I turned over into his hands the cash receipts. To the penny.

And that's how I came to be a grocery delivery boy in the rich precincts of Murray Hill. I wore the long white apron and pushed the wooden cart and I earned three dollars a week and tips.

At one home in Gramercy Park I made the acquaintance of a maid she had an eye for me she liked my innocent face. She was an older woman, some kind of Scandinavian wore her hair in braids. She was no great shakes but she had her own room and late one night I was admitted and led up all the flights of this mansion and brought to a small bathroom top floor at the back. She sat me in a claw-foot tub and gave me a bath, this hefty hot steaming red-faced woman. I don't remember her name Hilda Bertha something like that, and she knows herself well before we make love she pulls a pillow over her head to muffle the noise she makes and it is really interesting to go at this great chunky energetic big-bellied soft-assed flop-titted but headless woman, teasing it with a touch, watching it quiver, hearing its muffled squeaks, composing a fuck for it, the likes of which I like to imagine she has never known.

Come with me
Compose with me
Coming she is coming is she

She was very decent really and for my love gave me little presents, castoff sweaters and shoes, food sometimes. I tried to save as much of my wages as I could. My luxuries were cigarettes and movies. I liked to go to the movies and sit there you could see two features and a newsreel for a dime. I liked comedies and musicals and pictures with high style. I always went alone. In my mind was the quiet fellow trying to see himself, hear what he sounded like. He fitted himself out in movie stars he discarded them. I was interested in the way I instantly knew who the situation called for and became him. For Graeber, who wore a straw hat and a bow tie, a stubblehead German with an accent you better not laugh at, I was the honest young fellow who wanted to make something of himself. For Hilda the maid I was the boy who thought he was lucky to have her. When I went along after work with my tips in my pocket I was John D. Rockefeller. I came to make the distinction between the great busy glorious city of civilization on the one hand, and the meagerness or pretense of any one individual I looked at on the other. It was a matter of the distance you took, if you went to the top of the Empire State Building as I liked to do seeing it all was thrilling you had to admire the human race making its encampment like this I could hear the sound of traffic rising like some song to God and love His Genius for shining the sun on it. But down on the docks men slept in the open pulled up like babies on beds of newspapers, hands palm on palm for a pillow. Not their dereliction, that wasn't the point, but their meagerness, for I saw this too as I stood at the piers and watched the ocean liners sail. I watched the well-dressed men and women going up the gangways, turning to wave at their friends, I saw the stevedores taking aboard their steamer trunks and wicker hatboxes, I saw the women wrapping their fur collars tighter against the chill coming up off the water, the men in sporty caps and spats looking self-consciously important, I saw their exhaustion, their pretense, their terror, and in these too, the lucky ones, I understood the meagerness of the adult world. It was an important bit of knowledge and no shock at all for a Paterson mill kid. Adults were in one way or another the ones who were done, finished, living past their hope or their purpose. Even the gulls sitting on the tops of the pilings had more class. The gulls lifting in the wind and spreading their wings over the Hudson.

I distinguished myself from whomever I looked at when I felt the need to, which was often, I felt I could get by make my way whatever the circumstances. I would sell pencils on the sidewalk in front of department stores I would be a newsboy I would steal kill use all my cunning but never would I lose the look in my eye of the living spirit, or give up till that silent secret presence grew out to the edges of me and I was the same as he, imposed upon myself in full completion, the same man with all men, the one man in all events—

I remember this roughneck boy more whole than he knew. Going down the dark stairs of the mansion on Gramercy Park one night trusted to let myself out by the drowsy spent maid, I lifted a silver platter a silver creamer and teapot and a pair of silver candlesticks from the dining room. Even now I see the curved glass cabinet doors in the streetlight coming through the French windows. I hear my breathing. I catch sight of my own face in the salver. Loot-laden I tiptoed over the thick rug I half walked half ran through the streets clutching my lumpy lumberjacket. I had a room on the West Side in a rooming house fifty cents a night no cooking. In the morning going to work from across the wide cobblestone street the cars going past, the streetcars ringing their bells horns blowing trucks ratcheting along with chain-wheel drive I see in Graeber's Groceries Fancy Fruits and Vegetables an officer of the law in earnest conversation with my employer.

Come with me
Compute with me
Computerized she prints out me

Commingling with me she becomes me
Coming she is coming is she
Coming she is a comrade of mine

Sometimes around those fires by the river a man would talk a war veteran usually who had a vision of things, who could say more than how he felt or what was so unfair or who he was going to get someday. And invariably he was a socialist or a communist or an anarchist and he'd call you brother or comrade this fellow and he was always contemplative and didn't seem to mind if anyone listened to him or not. Not that he was wise or especially decent or kind or even that he was sober but even if none of these in those fitful flashes of lucidity like momentary flares of a dying fire he'd say why things were as they were. I liked that. It was a kind of music, I lingered by the edges of the city with the hobos and at night that grand and glorious civilization now had walls all around it we were on the outside looking up at this immense looming presence, a fortress now it was a kind of music to point to the walls and suggest why they would come down. And if you didn't have a true friend, someone in the world as close to you as you were to yourself, this kind of music was interesting to hear. At night you smelled the river in daylight you didn't, I smelled the river scum and felt the mosquitoes and followed the shadows of the great rats who butted right through the tarpaper shacks and dove into the shitholes, and some poor tramp on Sterno would suddenly present with incredible grace an eloquent analysis of monopoly capitalism. It would go on two three minutes he'd take a swig eyes would roll up in his skull and he'd pass out falling backward into the fire and he'd roast his brains if we didn't pull him out his hair smoking his singed burned hair. Wide awake again he'd tell us more.

But it was here I also learned about California. In California you could eat the oranges off the trees, along the seaside boulevards the avocados fell when they were ripe and you found them everywhere and peeled them and you ate them on the seaside boulevards. When you were sleepy you slept on the sand and when you were hot you went wading in the warm Pacific surf and the waves lit up at night off the shore with their own light. And off beyond the waves was a gambling ship.

I decided to go to California.

Armed only with his unpronounceable last name, he went down to the freight yards to begin his journey. He confuses this now in his mind with the West Side slaughtering plant such atomized extract of organic essence, such a perfumery of disembowelment, that in the fetid blood spumed viscera mist above the yards helplessly flew flights of gulls schools of pigeons moths bats insect plagues all swirling round and round in a great squawking endlessly ejaculative anguish.

I found a door that slid open, got it wide enough to slip through, climbed in, pulled the door almost shut behind me stood in the darkness breathing triumph. The car lurches again, almost stops, begins to roll, I was thrown into something that moved. I look around my private car my eyes accustoming themselves to the darkness, soot and pungent cinder begins to flow through the boards, that railroad tang, my eyes see all around the perimeter of my private car a cargo of youths. We are the shipped manufacture of this nation there must have been thirty or forty of us in that car gradually my eyes made out fifty sixty sitting on the floor by the dawn in eastern Pennsylvania at a siding in the chill frosted morning a hundred of us jumped and ran when the bulls came shouting ahead from the engine. Later alone in the tall weeds of another crossing a toot and leisurely around the bend bell-clanging another stately red ball my chance I make for it all around me from the weeds a thousand like me leap I thought I was alone.

I let it go. All my gaunt brothers in my own rags carrying my roped valise hopped the freight. I watched it go. I put up my collar pulled my cap down on my head stuck my hands in my pockets and headed north up the road.

Come with me
Compute with me
Computerized she prints out me

Commingling with me she becomes me
Coming she is coming is she
Coming she is a comrade of mine
Comrades come all over comrades
Communists come upon communists
Hi. Hi.

We are here to complete our fusion
We are here to create confusion
Do you confuse coming with confession?
Do you fuel for nuclear compression?
I'm for funicular ascension.

Decline all word temptation
Define all worldly tension
Deride all prayerful intervention

Computer nukes come pray with me
Before the war, the war, after the war
Before the war, the war after the war, the war
before the war disestablishes human character.

Computer data composes World War One poet
Warren Penfield born Indianapolis Indiana
City of Indians in the Plains Wars after the peace
City of Indians going about their business
Indian poets in headbands walking on grid streets
Secure in their city of Indian architecture of cool concrete
Bernard Cornfield Investors Overseas Securities

Data linkage escape this is not emergency
Before the war before the last war
A boy stood on the dirt street in Ludlow Colorado.
The wind of the plain blew the coal dust under his
eyelids.   The wind blew the black dust down the canyons of the Sangre de Cristo.   The clothesline stretching across the plain the miner's cotton swung its arms and
legs wildly in the wind.   A miner's wife stepped from a
tent with an infant girl suspended from her hands.   She
held the child beyond the edge of the wood sidewalk over
the dirt the dust blowing back along the ground like
hordes of microscopiccreatures running.   The infant's
girl's dress raised under her arms she hung from her knees
and underarms so as to have her hairless child's fruit
expressed for the purpose indicated by the mother's sibilant sound effects punctuated with foreign words of encouragement.   The boy standing there happening to be
there remained to watch shamelessly and the beautiful
little girl turned upon him a face of such outrage that he
immediately recognized her, willing white neck companion
of the old monk it's you, and with then saintly inability to
withstand life she closed her eyes and allowed the thin
stream of golden water to cascade into the dust where
instantly formed minuscule tulips.   He beheld the frui-
tion of a small fertile universe.

When the nights were bad, when the uncanny sounds in the woods kept him awake, when the crack of a twig in the pine forest was inexplicable or some distant whimpering creature sounded in his mind like a child being fucked he swore it was still better than going with the red ball. Whowhoo. Better to take alone whatever came. Soft web of night threads across the face. Something watching breathing in the dark a few feet away. He had heard of people having a foot cut off for the dollar in their shoe. It was still better. It was still better to take alone whatever came. Better to die in the open. Whowhoo. Lying in a city mission flop in the great stink of mankind was worse. Arraigned in the ranks of the self-deluding in their bunkbeds was worse.

It was the bums of the commonest conversation who angered him the most, the casuists of misfortune who bragged about the labels inside their torn filthy coats, or swore there was some brand of alcohol they wouldn't be so low as to drink. Or the ones who claimed to be only temporarily down on their luck, en route to some glorious destination not where they had a job waiting or a family, but where they were *known,* where what they were did not have to be proved.

I didn't want these mockeries to my own kingship of consciousness, with all the conquests of my life still to come. How could I hope or scheme however idly in a flophouse with a hundred others, a thousand others, a hundred thousand others where the dreams rise on the breath and dissolve one another in a precipitate element not your own—and you are trapped in it, a dark underwater kingdom fed by springs of alcoholic piss and sweat, in which there live and swim the vilest phantoms of God.

And strangely enough each morning I woke up still alive. In the lake villages and the small towns of old mills, I was moved along by the constable but a shade more gently. I didn't feel like a tramp when I asked for work. I even had a certain distinction. We were like birds or insects, pestilential, when we buzzed or flocked in great numbers, but one sole specimen could be tolerated with a certain scientific interest. Sometimes I washed dishes for a meal. Sometimes I stole my food. Sometimes I found a day's work at some farm.

Then in one town, walking down the main street in a manner that suggested I had someplace to go, I saw coming out of the drugstore three midgets and a heavyset dwarf who huddled over them like their father. They took their quick little steps down the street, all talking at the same time, the muscular torso of the dwarf jolting from side to side with each step. I followed them. Even when they noticed me following them I followed them. They led me to the edge of town. In a grass lot between two stands of trees was the Hearn Bros. carnival, a traveling show of tattered brown tents, old trucks, kiddy rides and paint-peeled wagons. I heard the growl of a big cat.

Ah, what I felt standing there in the sun! A broken-down carnival—a few acts, a few rides and a contingent of freaks. But the sight of it made me a boy again. I was going backward. Those ridiculous bickering midgets had called up my love for tiny things, my great unslaked child's thirst for tiny things, as if I had never held enough toys that were small to my small hand. Holy shit a carnival! I knew it was for me as sure as I knew my own face in the mirror.

I hung around. I made myself useful. They were still putting it together. I helped lay the wooden track for the kiddy cars. I heaved-ho the tent ropes, I set the corral poles for the pony ride. There were three or four tired stiffs doing these things. I recognized them for what they were, everyone of them had a pint of wine in his pocket, they were no problem at all. I thought the Hearn Bros. were lucky to have me.

But nothing happened. Nobody paid attention. At dusk the generator was cranked, and the power went on with a thump. The string lights glowed, the Victrola band music came out of the loudspeakers, the Wheel of Fortune went ratatat-tat, and I saw how money was made from the poor. They drifted in, appearing starved and sucked dry, but holding in their palms the nickels and dimes that would give them a view of Wolf Woman, Lizard Man, the Living Oyster, the Fingerling Family and in fact the whole Hearn Bros. bestiary of human virtue and excellence.

The clear favorite was Fanny the Fat Lady. She sat on a scale that was like a porch swing. Over her head a big red arrow attested to six hundred and eight pounds. Someone doubted that. She responded with an emphatic sigh and the arrow fluctuated wildly, going as high as nine hundred. This made people laugh. She was dressed in a short jumper with a big collar and a bow in her hair, just like Shirley Temple. Her dyed red hair was set in waves over her small skull. The other freaks did routines or sold souvenirs and pamphlets of their life stories. Not the Fat Lady. She only sat and suffered herself to be gazed on, her slathered legs crossed at the ankles. I couldn't stop looking at her. Finally I caught her attention, and her little painted mouth widened like the wings of a butterfly as if it were basking on some pulpy extragalactic flower. The folds of her chins rising in cups of delicate hue, her blue eyes setting like moons behind her cheeks, she smiled at me and unsmiled, smiled and unsmiled, sitting there with each arm resting on the base of a plump hand supported by a knee that was like the cap of an exotic giant white mushroom.

I realized she was slow-witted. Behind her and off to the side was a woman who was keeping an eye out, maybe a relative, a mother, an aunt. This woman looked at me with the alert eyes of the carney.

And as I went about I saw those eyes everywhere behind the show, alert carney eyes on the gaunt man with a white shirt and tie and sleeve garters, on the girl in the ticket booth, on the freaks themselves staring out from their enclosures. What were they looking for? Life! A threat! An advantage! I had that look myself. I recognized it, I knew these people.

But I wasn't getting anywhere with them. By midnight the crowd had thinned out. The lights were blinked in warning and the generator was turned off. The last of the rubes drifted back into the hills. They held Kewpie dolls. They held pinwheels.

I saw the acts going into their trailers to find some supper or drink some wine. I sat across the road with my back against a tree. I wanted a job with the carney. It seemed to me the finest possible way to live.

A while later a truck came along running without headlights and it turned into the dark lot. I sat up. I heard the truck doors slam. A few minutes later an old car and three men got out and walked into the carney. Other men arrived on foot, in jalopies. A few lights had gone back on. I crossed the road. There was some kind of renewed commerce, I didn't understand. I saw the belly dancer standing in the door of her trailer her arms folded a man at the foot of the steps tipped his cap. I saw the girl who sold tickets outside her booth she was looking into a hand mirror and primping her hair. At the back end of the lot in the shadow of the trees a line of men and boys outside a trailer. I went there and got on the end of the line. A man came out and talked in low tones to the others. I heard something moaning. Another man went in. From the trailer came these sounds of life's panic, shivers and moans and shrieks and crashings and hoarse cries, the most awesome fuckmusic I had ever heard. I got closer. I hadn't seen before sitting on a chair at the foot of the trailer steps that same woman attendant from the afternoon who kept a close and watchful eye on the crowd in front of Fanny the Fat Lady.

I led her from the trailer to the tent in the afternoon and back to her trailer at the end of the night. She placed her hand on my shoulder, and walking behind me at arm's length with a great quivering resettlement of herself at each step, she made her stately trustful way down the midway.

Once she hugged me. She was surprisingly gentle I did not share the popular lust for her I was embarrassed and maybe frightened by that mountainous softness I pulled away. Right away I saw I'd made a mistake. Fanny had a cleft palate and on top of that the sounds she made were in Spanish but I could tell her feelings were hurt. I moved to her and let her hug me. She put her warm hand on the small of my back. I thought I felt the touch of an astute intelligence.

She was truly sensitive to men, she had a real affection for them. She didn't know she was making money, she never saw the money. She held out her arms and loved them, and it didn't matter what happened, if they came in the folds of her thighs or the creases in the sides of her which spilled over the structure of her trunk like down quilts, she always screamed as if they had found her true center.

I decided that between this retarded whore freak and the riffraff who stood in line to fuck her some really important sacrament was taken, some means of continuing with hope, a ritual oath of life which did not wear away but grew in the memory of her around the bars and taverns of the mountains, catching her image in the sawdust flying up through the sunlight in the mill yards or lying like the mist of the morning over the clear lakes.

On the other hand it was common knowledge in the carney that fat ladies were the biggest draw.

I got along with all the freaks, I made a point to. It was as if I had to acclimate myself to the worst there was. I never let them see that I had any special awareness of them. I knew it was important not to act like a rube. After a while they stopped looking at me with the carney eyes and forgot I was there. Some, the Living Oyster for instance, were taken care of by members of their families who lived with them and probably got them their jobs in the first place. There was about them all, freaks and family, such competence that you almost wondered how normal people got along. There was a harmony of malformation and life that could only scare the shit out of you if you thought about it. The freaks read the papers and talked about Roosevelt, just like everyone else in the country.

But with all of that they lived invalid lives, as someone in the pain of constant hopeless bad health, and so their dispositions were seldom sunny.

The Fingerlings were mean little bastards, they were not really a family but who could tell? They all had these little pug faces. They used to get into fights all the time and only the dwarf could do anything with them. They used to torture Wolf Woman. What she had done to arouse their wrath I never knew. They liked to sneak up on her and pull out tufts of her hair. "That's all right," they screamed, scuttling out of her way. "Plenty more where that came from!"

And every day the rubes paid their money to see them and then went off and took a chance on Fortune's wheel.

I had great respect for Sim Hearn. He was the owner of the enterprise. He was pretty strange himself, a tall thin man who walked with a stoop. Even the hottest days of the summer he wore an old gray fedora with the brim pulled way down, and a white-on-white shirt with a black tie and rubber bands around the sleeves above the elbows. He had stick arms. He was always sucking on his teeth, alighting on a particular crevasse with his tongue and then pulling air through it. *Cheeup cheeup!* If you wanted to know where Hearn was on the lot, all you had to do was listen. Sometimes you'd be doing your work and you'd realize it was you he was watching, the *cheeup cheeup* just behind your ear, as if he'd landed on your shoulder. You'd turn and there he'd be. He'd point at what he wanted done with his chin. "That," he'd say. He was a stingy son of a bitch even with his words.

I was fascinated by him. Sucking his teeth and never speaking more than he had to gave him an air of preoccupation, as if he had weightier matters on his mind than a fifth-rate carney. But he knew his business, all right. He knew what towns to skip, he knew what games would go in one place but not another, and he knew when it was time to pull up stakes. We were a smooth efficient outfit under Sim Hearn. He'd go on ahead to find the location and make the payoff. And when we drove into town he'd be waiting where we could see him sitting behind the wheel of his Model A with one arm out the window, the rubber band around the shirt sleeve.

His real genius was in freak dealing. Where did he get them? Could they be ordered? Was there a clearing house for freaks somewhere? There really was—a theatrical agency in New York on lower Broadway. But if he could, Sim Hearn liked to find them himself. People would come up to him and he'd go with them to see what was hidden in the basement or the barn. If he liked what he saw, he named his terms and didn't have to pay a commission. Maybe he had dreams of finding something so inspiring that he'd make his fortune, like Barnum. But to the afflicted of the countryside, he was a chance in a million. I'd go to work one morning and see some grotesque I hadn't seen before, not necessarily in costume at show time but definitely with the carney. Sometimes they didn't want to display themselves in their own neighborhoods. Sometimes Hearn's particular conviction of their ability was lacking or maybe he hadn't figured out how best to show them. They required some kind of seasoning, like rookie ballplayers, to give them their competence as professionals. One would be around awhile and disappear just as another would show up, I think they were traded back and forth among the different franchises of this mysterious league.

But when a new freak was introduced, that evening everyone would shine, the new one would tone them all up in competitive awareness, except for Fanny, secure and serene in her mightiness.

Herewith bio the poet Warren Penfield.
Born Indianapolis Indiana August 2 1899.
Moved at an early age with parents to southern
Colorado.   First place Ludlow Consolidated Grade
School Spelling Bee 1908.   Ludlow Colorado Boy of
the Year 1913.   Colorado State Mental Asylum 1914,
1915.   Enlisted US Army Signal Corps 1916.   Vale-
dictorian US Army Semaphore School Augusta Georgia.   Assigned First Carrier Pigeon Company Seventh
Signal Battalion First Division, AEF.   Saw action
Somme Offensive pigeons having the shit shot out of them
feathers falling over trenches blasted in bits like snowflakes
drifting through the concussions of air or balancing on the
thin fountain of a scream.   Citation accompanying Silver Star awarded Warren Penfield 1918: that his company
of pigeons having been rendered inoperable and all other
signal apparatus including field telephone no longer available to him Corporal Penfield did stand in an exposed
position lit by flare under enemy heavy fire and transmit
in extended arm semaphore the urgent communication of

his battalion commander until accurate and redemptive fire from his own artillery indicated the message had been received.   This was not true.   What he transmitted via full arm semaphore under enemy heavy fire was the first verse of English poet William Wordsworth's Ode Intimations of Immortality from Recollections of Early Childhood as follows quote There was a time when meadow grove and stream the earth and every common sight to me did seem apparelled in celestial light the glory and the freshness of a dream.   It is not now as it hath been of yore—turn wheresoe'er I may by night or day the things which I have seen I now can see no more endquote

So informed Secretary of Army in letter July 4 1918, medal enclosed.   Incarceration US Army Veterans Psychological Facility Nutley New Jersey 1918.   First volume of verse *The Flowers of the Sangre de Cristo* unpaged published by the author 1918.   No reviews.   Cross-country journey to Seattle Washington 1919.   Trans-Pacific voyage 1919.   Resident of Japan 1919–1927. Second volume of verse *Child Bride in a Zen Garden* unpaged published in English by Nosaka Publishing Company, Tokyo, 1926.   No reviews.   Deported Japan undesirable alien 1927.   Poet in residence private mountain retreat Loon Lake NY 1929–1937.   Disappeared presumed lost at sea on around-the-world airplane voyage 1937.   No survivors.   Third volume of verse *Loon Lake* unpaged published posthumously by the Grebe Press, Loon Lake NY 1939.   No reviews.

Y ou are what? said Jack Penfield, leaning over the table to hear better. His brow lowered and his mouth opened, the face was poised in skeptical anticipation of the intelligence he was about to receive. Or had he received it? In his middle age he no longer wanted to be the recipient of good news of any kind. And if some was forthcoming he quickly rendered it ineffective, almost as if it were more important that the world be grimly consistent at this point than that it would offer a surprise. You are what?

The boy of the year, his son said.

What does that mean?

Oh Warren, his mother said, isn't that fine. She sat down beside her son, pulling the wooden chair next to his, and she faced her husband across the table. He would have to work on both of them now.

I don't know, Warren said. You get a certificate and five dollars at the spring ceremony.

Jack Penfield leaned back in his chair. I see. He got up and went to the mantel and took his pipe and tobacco tin and came back to the table and fixed up for a while while they watched. The large flat fingers tamped the tobacco in the bowl. The hand of the lifelong miner with its unerasable lines of charcoal in the knuckles and under the nails. He lit his pipe. You know, he said, when I come up this evening there was a man with a rifle on Watertank Hill.

Please Jack his wife said.

What you going to do with the money lad?

I don't know.

That's moren a day's wages. Are you proud?

I don't know.

You won't make four dollars when you come below. Did you know that?

Yes.

If there still is a mine. Are there any other english-speaking there aren't are there?

I don't think so.

Well then you had to be boy of the year didn't you.

Please Jack.

Didn't you.

I suppose.

The only one they can call up to the platform and trust to say thank you properly. No polack wop or damned greek knows to say thank you for makin me boy of the year does he?

I don't know.

And your ma's going to find a clean shirt for you that day won't she. And she'll comb her hair back and put the comb in it and go with the tears of thanks in her eyes for the company school and the company supply and the company house and the company boy of the year.

You poison everything Neda Penfield said. You make everything bad, you make a child feel bad for being alive. There's nothing worse than that. There's no evil worse than that.

But he minded less than his mother thought he did. He wanted his father to talk this way. It was very helpful to him. The consistency of their positions was all he asked, that his pa be unyielding and full of anger, that his ma be enraged or worse frightened by her husband's spiritual tactlessenss. Warren knew they were poor and lived lives the color of slag. He knew there was nothing beautiful in Ludlow but he was eager to get up each morning and test the day. He knew the real evil was his own, the eye and ear that took in everything and suffered nothing. He accumulated meaningless useless data that nevertheless bewitched him. The thick bulbed vein in his father's hand, for instance, in contrast to the thin greenish vein in his mother's. The characteristic smell of the house and the privy were noted and recorded. There were certain objects he liked very much. His mother's tortoise-shell comb, the teeth broken off in several places. The coal stove, whose shape was like a naked woman, her long neck disappearing through the roof. He liked to see underwear drying on the line the wind animating it to a maniac dance. Sometimes he thought of the flapping long johns as a desperate signaling of imprisoned or tortured people. He was absorbed by the sun rising and the sun setting or the rain when it fell from rock to rock. He was excited by any kind of violence, a parent hitting a child a man hitting a woman. When he happened to see such things he would be suffused with a weird heat. His heart would beat furiously and then he'd feel sickened and would feel like throwing up. Until he broke into a cold sweat. Then he would feel all right again. He listened now with eyes downcast but in some contentment to their argument, enjoying the words of it, the claims and counterclaims, agreeing with each in turn they were so well matched and spoke so well the images that flew through his mind on their words.

I got out of bed and rolled my clothes and shoes into a bundle. I grabbed the money from the bureau. I unlatched the door quietly and closed it behind me. There were no other guests at the Pine Grove Motor Court. A thin frost lay on the window of her car. The wind blew.

I threw the bills into the wind.

I found a privy up the hill behind the cabins and next to it an outdoor shower, the kind you pumped the water for yourself. I stood in the shower of cold spring water and looked up at the swaying tops of the pine trees and I watched the sky turning gray and heard through the water and the toneless wind the sounds of the first bird waking.

I dried myself as best I could and put on my clothes. Shivering, stipple-skinned, I struck off through the woods. I had no idea where I was going. It didn't matter. I ran to get warm. I ran into the woods as to another world.

All morning I went up and down the hills of timber. Sometimes I'd hear the sound of a truck or a car and it would shock me. I'd veer off to get as deep in the woods as possible. It was difficult to keep my sense of direction, difficult to put life behind me. I'd come along into a clearing and find the remains of a fire or an empty wine bottle. Traces of human life everywhere: stone fences, old trails, dirt roads grown over. I found a busted inner tube, yellowed sheets of newspaper with dates on them from the early summer.

But I saw no one: any stiff in his right mind would get out of the Adirondacks before autumn.

By the late morning I was so hungry I changed course and went downhill till I found a paved road. I walked along the tree line for several miles and came to a country store with a gas pump and some chickens in a coop. Stood in the trees and waited to see a black Model A or perhaps a carney truck or even a state police car. The odds were against it, but I was not thinking odds. The carney was a territory in my mind. It loomed out further than I had gone or maybe could go.

There were no cars. I slid down the embankment of loose earth behind the store and went around front and stepped in the door like any customer. I had my savings of the summer, twenty-six dollars, in my shoes; in my wallet I carried three dollars more. I bought a loaf of wax-papered bread, some slices of baloney, a bottle of Grade A milk and a package of Luckies. The store lady, short and wide and with thick dirty eyeglasses, treated me as if it were the most normal thing in the world for someone to come along from nowhere, as maybe it was.

I went down the road till it curved out of sight of the store, and then I ran back up into the woods and found a tree in a spot of sun and sat there and made my lunch. Then I went to sleep for a while, while the woods were still warm, but it was a mistake because I suffered terrible dreams of indistinct shapes and shadows and awful sounds of violence. Someone was crying, sobbing, and it turned out to be me. I jumped up and got going again.

I went deeper and deeper into the woods and sometime at the height of the afternoon wandered into a stand of ancient pine with a porous forest floor of brown pine needles that was so soft you couldn't hear your own footsteps. It was dark in here, there was an umber twilight

in lieu of the day, and there seemed to be no usual busy
life at all, no birds, no insects, just this dark place of
unnatural quiet. Looking up, I could hardly find anything
green. Yet it was not threatening, the solitude was so
complete, the stillness so perfect that I felt as if I had
come into some vast, hushed cathedral of peace. Not even
a Father. I stopped walking and stood very still and
listened for I don't know what. And then, right in my
tracks I sat down and for a while was as still as everything else.

I thought of Fanny the Fat Lady's warm hand on the
small of my back.

By early afternoon I was traveling again on roads, only
jumping off to the side when I heard a car coming, or
taking to the woods in order to skirt a town. I went along
that day with no destination in mind, no plan of action
except to follow the rise, and go for the altitude. I had no
food left and did not feel I needed any. I came out to a
broad plateau and looking out ahead of me realized I had
gone past the region of towns and now, for my arrogance,
had no hope of supper unless I found a farmhouse somewhere.

The open ground was uncultivated, mile after mile. I
was on a crumbling two-lane road with grass growing in
the cracks and this suggested to me the unlikelihood of a
ride coming along. Still I kept going.

And then with the sun turning red as it dropped toward
the evening, I saw to my left, perhaps fifty yards into an
open space of tall weed and tangled brush, a single-track
railroad embankment. Behind the embankment was a
curved outcropping of shiny flaked rock. I got up on the
embankment for a professional survey: I had happened
upon a one-track spur line of some sort. I figured that as
it curved in an arc around the rock hill, there was a fair
chance it would be going slowly enough to hop. Coming
down from the roadbed, I found a bare patch of ground
spotted with oil. And beside the charred remains of a fire
I saw a flask of clear glass and a lady's shoe with the heel
torn off. So others had stopped here in their great study
of the outdoors—it was a station of sorts.

I gathered a great bundle of kindling, but I was too tired to build a fire. I lay on my back with my hands behind my head and I watched the sky. The sun had gone down but the sky was still blue, a very pale blue, with a few high clouds still golden with sunlight. Soon I was lying in the dusk and feeling the chill of the evening but the sky was sunlit and blue and so far away in its warmth that I felt I was looking at it from a grave.

I fell asleep that way and sometime during the night was aroused by a train whistle. I lay there listening for it again in case I had only been dreaming. Again I heard it, this time somewhat closer. I stood up and tried to pound some circulation into my stiff hulk. The train was coming without question now. I had no idea what time it was, the sky was black, starless. I thought I could hear the locomotive. I moved toward the embankment and waited. I could hear the engine clearly now and knew it was moving at a slow speed. The first I saw of it was a diffuse paling of the darkness along the curve of the embankment. Suddenly I was blinded by a powerful light, as if I had looked into the sun. I dropped to my knees. The beam swung away from me in a transverse arc and a long conical ray of light illuminated the entire rock outcropping, every silvery vein of schist glittering as bright as a mirror, every fern and evergreen flaring for a moment as if torched. I rubbed my eyes and looked for the train behind the glare. It was passing from my left to my right. The locomotive and tender were blacker than the night, a massive movement forward of shadow, but there was a passenger car behind them and it was all lit up inside. I saw a porter in a white jacket serving drinks to three men sitting at a table. I saw dark wood paneling, a lamp with a fringed shade, and shelves of books in leather bindings. Then two women sitting talking at a group of wing chairs that looked textured, as if needle-pointed. Then a bright bedroom with frosted-glass wall lamps and a canopied bed and standing naked in front of a mirror was a blond girl and she was holding up for her examination a white dress on a hanger.

Oh my lords and ladies and then the train had passed through the clearing and I was watching the red light disappear around the bend. I hadn't moved from the moment the light had dazzled my eyes. I'd heard of private railroad cars but was not prepared. I was under the impression I would see it again if I waited. I waited. I heard it going down the track and listened until I couldn't hear it anymore. Into my vacated mind flowed all the English I never knew I'd learned at Paterson Latin High School. Grammar slammed into my brain. In an instant this vision of incandescent splendor had left me more alone and terrified than I knew it was possible to be.

I got a fire going and made it as large as I could, I threw everything I could find into it, it was a damn bonfire and I crouched beside it trying to get warm I made an involuntary sound in my throat for my dereliction, my loneliness, the callow hopes of my life. Who did I think I was? Where did I think I was going? What made me think it was worth anything to stay alive?

The fire blazed up. I wanted to get in it.

At the first light of the morning I climbed the embankment and set out down the tracks in the direction the train had gone.

Compare the private railroad car sitting on the Santa Fe siding one night in 1910 in front of the mine near Ludlow Colorado whose collapsed entry was being dug away by rescue crews. Late at night by the glow of torches they began to bring out the dead hunky miners, some so impregnated by coal dust they looked like ancient archaeological finds of considerable significance. Some had been blown to pieces and were assembled on the cold ground by thoughtful colleagues who matched the torn halves of pants legs or recognized what head went with what trunk. The boy followed these deliberations and remarked on the sepulchral interest of assembling pieces of bodies matching and discarding, trying this arm here that foot there on the dark ground, the chill of the October night on the slag hills, the black mineral mountains looming darker than the night sky, the boy noticing the darkening stains around the bodies as blood blacker than coalwater. Some miners were brought out intact, uninjured and looking only slightly stunned to have breathed all the available air until there was no more.

Some faces had the look of irritability that comes when something small has gone wrong. Others had eyes rolled into their heads in exasperation others had sorrowed into death and by some curious self-embalmment of the skin left the tracks of their tears like shining falling stars through their grizzled faces. The rescue work was commanded from the private railroad car, a property like the mine and like the miners of the Colorado Fuel and Iron Company, and in the car a self-sufficient unit with bedrooms kitchen small library and a row of partners' desks were three or four officers of the firm some in gartered shirt sleeves efficiently dealing with the wives making settlements pushing waivers across their desks proffering pens matching the tally sheets to the employment records and in general dealing so efficiently with the disaster that the mine would be back in action within the week. The only thing that threatened this work performance was the occasional embittered woman who would come in screaming and tearing her hair and cursing them in her own language. They would nod to one of the private peace officers and the troublesome woman would be removed. Gradually in his inspection of the disaster the boy found his way into the car and in the moment before he was ejected he observed one of the company officers, a stolid man impassively wiping the spittle from his cheek. The brass plate at his desk informed the boy of F. W. Bennett Vice President for Engineering. Warren felt the rough hand of the armed guard on his neck and then the coolness of the night air as he flew from the top of the rail-car step to the graveled ground. His knee was embedded with bits of stone as the miners had been peppered with coal fragments, so he understood that feeling. To understand what it meant to be buried alive in a mountain he sat later with his eyes closed in the night and his hands over his ears and he held his breath as long as he could.

Every day to school she wore her faded dress of flowers, horizontal lines of originally cheery little tulips row upon row. It came below her knees and there the cast off shoes, boots practically, hook-and-eye boots all cracked and curled, there the boots began, and so nothing of her was uncovered except the neck above the high collar of frazzled lace, and the wrists and the hands and the incredible face that struck my heart like a jolt every time I raised my eyes to look at it.

Migod. When it was possible to feel that way.

Wasn't it. I used to wake up before dawn and wait impatiently for the light to come into the window so that I could jump out of bed and get ready for school. I would sit on the front wooden step and wait for her to come down the canyon. She would smile when she saw me.

Were you her best friend?

We were each other's only friend. Her English was very bad. The theory of the teacher with all these immigrant kids was that if you spoke English loudly enough they would eventually understand. They all sat there with their immense eyes and watched her every move. They never smiled, even when she scratched her head with her pencil and her wig moved up and down on her forehead. She taught them the pledge of allegiance phonetically.

I would like to have known you then.

You would not believe it, Lucinda, but I was very sensual.

I believe it.

No, you're smiling. But I was, I really was. I lived in such an alerted state that even the daylight sifting through a cloud would give me enormous shuddering response. My friend and I used to play after school in the hills above town. The sun would go down behind the Black Hills but we'd see it to the east still on the plains, moving away from us on the flat plains, racing away in a broad front like an army losing territory on a map. In the shadow in some gully or behind some rock she'd lie in my arms and look at me with her dark eyes, frightened and speechless by our strange intimacy, frightened but not spooked. She could say my name but not much else. She rolled the *rr*'s. Wadden.

Light me a cigarette, will you?

Is this boring?

No, it makes me sad, though. I know what happened.

I have in my life just three times seen faces in dark light, at dusk, or at dawn, or against a white pillow in which the fear of life was so profoundly accurate, like an animal's perfect apprehension, that it encompassed its opposite and became the gallantry to break your heart.

Go on.

One day I remember late in the summer, before we all had to leave Ludlow for the flats, we were playing up there at some run-off. Some black-water run-off falling off the rocks somehow, so filthy with coal dust that just putting your hand in it was enough to dye yourself black. She didn't want to get her one and only dress wet, she'd get a beating for that, so she tied it up around her waist and hunkered there by the stream to play. She wasn't as old as I. She was a younger person. She wore nothing underneath. It was very lovely. Because I had become still she became still. She let me touch her. She let me run my hand over her small back. I could feel the bones in her ass. I could feel the heat under her skinny thighs.

Was this when you became lovers?

Perhaps so. I mean I know we were at one time or another, I remember that it happened, but I don't remember the experience of it. What is that up ahead, Lucinda? It looks very dark.

It's nothing. A line squall.

Heave said his father and they swung the wooden chest up on the wagon bed. Now make it fast. He pushed up with his hands landed lightly on one knee and stood up beside the chest and worked it firmly between the bureau and the slatted side gate. He glanced up the canyon. They were coming along steadily now, mule-drawn wagons like his own or the two-wheeled handcarts which required the woman to throw her entire weight stiff-armed on the handle to keep it from rising and the man around the front braking with his bootheels dug into the ground.

She was nowhere in sight.

The sky was heavy almost black, it felt like evening although it wasn't yet noon. A fine drizzle misted on the skin and made everything slippery to hold. Each drop of rain seemed to contain a seed of coal dust. If you rubbed the water on the back of your hand it smeared black. Hey his father shouted keep your wits boy! He nearly fell backward as a cardboard box hit him in the chest. He grabbed it. His mother came out of the house with her arms full of pots and pans. His parents went in and out of the door bringing him things which he found a place for on the wagon bed. Gradually he realized he was constructing the model of a city. Seen from a distance, the boxes and headboards and chairs and chests were the skyline of some glorious Eastern city, the kind he had seen in the rotogravure, New York maybe, or St. Louis.

I have a comment here: I note the boy Warren Penfield's relentless faculty of composition. Rather than apprehend reality he transforms it so that in this case, for example, in the eviction of the striking miners from the Colorado Fuel Company's houses, the pitiful pile of his family's belongings on the wagon bed is represented as a vision of high civilization. No wonder his father is angered by his constant daydreaming. Jack Penfield perceives it as mental incompetence. How he wonders will his son survive the harshness of this life when he the father and she the mother are no longer there to protect him? As to book learning, Warren can do that passably well, but as to plain good sense the character of his mind is not reassuring.

Neda Penfield takes a different view but not without some irritation that the boy doesn't give her more support for it. Her view is that he is a rare soul, a finer being either than herself or her husband. By some benign celestial error he was born to them and to their life of slag who would more properly have been the child of a wealthy family going to the finest schools and with every material and intellectual advantage. He gives her qualms of course but she nourishes a private and barely articulated conviction that he is not deficient only latent, that his strength is there but still wrapped up in itself still to unfold in its fullness when the time is ripe. When will the time be ripe? His hands and feet are large and clumsy, he looms next to her sometimes like a giant he is at that stage of life when the largeness of him seems to wax and wane according to his own rhythms of confidence. She is aware as mothers are of the changes in him the manhood beginning to shine and she is comforted. But the wisdom of him has still to appear. Sometimes the light will hit his amber eye and she will feel ill at ease, as if she is living with two men rather than a man and a boy. Perhaps Jack

Penfield feels this too and anticipates the revolt of his son, the loosening of his power over him, the freeing of his son from himself till he has nothing but himself and then inevitably he will be subjected to his son's power over him. Yet he is secretly proud too and likes the boy's good looks. Warren is gentle and distracted as ever only his ears and elbows and wrists and ankles show the power of him still to come.

Neda Penfield would like Warren to win some sort of scholarship and go away to the city to study. She wants this desperately even though she knows her life with her husband then would be hell. Jack Penfield wants Warren in the mines. He wants him in the mines to establish such rage that he will finally be in contact with the circumstances of his life, he will wake up to it. And then see what happens, then see what glorious flights of power and genius the boy has in him perhaps to become an organizer a great union orator a radical a leader of men out of their living graves of coal. Let the boy work in a crouch for ten hours hacking coal in the chilling blackness of the earth, crouching with his feet in brackish water, not knowing which bite of the pick will bring the roof down on him. Let him work for his three tons a day and bring them up to be short-weighted by the company. Then my son will justify me and sanctify my name and fulfill the genius of my line.

The wagon loaded, Warren gives a hand up to his father and after a moment the two of them teetering on the gate, he nimbly leaps down and suffers the inspection of his work. The father pushes this adjusts that but says nothing, which is the highest approval. Together they tie everything in a web of stout rope, Warren running around from one side of the wagon to the other hauling tight looping knotting and he thinks of a wonderful bridge with granite towers and steel suspension cables what bridge is that.

And then his mother comes out of the house her hands empty but for a summer straw hat, a wide-brimmed straw with a round crown, and not seeing any place to put it she

places it on her head. It is such a gallant gesture, so
incongruous with the rain and the state of their fortunes
that the two men look at her startled and she pulls her
shoulders back and defies them with her glance, her face
peculiarly shadowed by the brim as if the sun was oddly
proven, but they wouldn't laugh because both have perceived in one shimmering instant before the fact of her
wearing that hat is established, the still alive girl and the
undefeated kingdom of their family.

She took her place on the bench and looked straight
ahead over the mule's rump. Jack Penfield went into the
house and came out with the last thing, his new bolt-
action Savage whose stock was oiled smooth and whose
barrel was blue steel, and he placed this across his lap as
he sat up behind the mule and took the reins.

And so with a lurch of the wheels they turned into the
traffic of wagons winding down through the canyons. In
front of the Colorado Supply Company two sheriff's deputies stood on the porch to watch the procession. They
had Winchesters cradled in their arms. Some of the families passing them made loud remarks. Some of them sang
their union song. Most of them looked straight ahead and
went on down the street into the descent of the prairie,
too cold or too realistic to bother with the trappings of
the spirit.

The rain was changing its nature, getting heavy turning
hard, and Warren sitting cross-legged on top of a bureau
felt the sting of ice, like steel pellets. He held out his hand
and received a particle of hail. He put up his denim
collar. He was facing forward but for some reason swiv-
eled on his rump and looked back at the street just as the
wagon behind picked up the pace to fill in the slack in the
parade and it was she in her dress of tulips faded sitting
up on her wagon on a stool like a princess borne in her
palanquin, her body moving forward and back, her head
moving in the lag of her body's rhythm and he smiled and
raised his hand and she smiled and raised hers, and they
stared at each other their bodies gently bending and
straightening in the rhythm of the mules' pace, the wheels
creaking in the mud the traces rattling like ancient music

of fanfares and the two of them staring at each other like royal lovers in a procession toward their investiture under the hardening rain through the canyon of slag going down to the plains.

Thinking about that girl standing in front of the mirror and holding up the white dress on the train gliding past me out of sight, I came along the track before I even knew it into the main street of a mountain village.

It was noon on the church tower. A pretty lakeside village with a general store a gas pump a white hotel with rocking chairs on the porch, a bait-and-tackle shop. I wanted to keep going but there was a cop on the corner. Casually I crossed the street and went into a diner and ordered the baked ham and brown beans in a crock and coffee. When I finished I ordered the same thing again. The waitress smiled and the chef himself looked out through the porthole of the kitchen door to see this prize customer.

I got out of that village without trouble resuming my walk just beyond the station crossing, following the rails that forked off into a narrower cut of trees. The track went through some woods circled around a small mountain lake and then it started up a grade a long slow winding grade, I was not already in love with her but in her field of force, what I thought I felt like was some stray dog following the first human being it happened to see.

In the late afternoon I came to a miniature station house of creosoted brown logs complete with ticket window and potbellied stove. It was empty. Out the back door was the sidetracked private railroad car.

I climbed aboard. Each room had a narrow door with brass handle opening onto the corridor going down one side along the windows.

Here was the room of grand appointments where the men were drinking a card table of green baize and leather with receptacles for poker chips, a bar with bottles and glasses in fitted recesses, a Persian rug of rich red tone, paneling of dark wood, books in the shelves The Harvard Classics. A faint odor of cigar smoke. I brushed the tassels of the lampshades with the back of my hand.

Everything in this room, unlit and still, seemed more awesome than from the distance of the night, for it was quite clearly owned. That was the main property of the entire car, not that it was handsome or luxurious but that it was owned.

In the girl's bedroom I sat on the plump mattress newly made up with fresh sheets thick quilt of satiny material there was no sign of her of course not a thread not a bobby pin but as I thought about it the faintest intimation of a scent, a not unfamiliar scent, I inhaled deeply, a variety common enough to have previously informed the nostrils of a derelict somewhere before in his wandering one summer night in the carney perhaps.

The afternoon light came through the window at a low angle between the trees it suddenly faded the car darkened I left. Outside, the sky was showing stars as it does earlier than you think it should in the last of the summer.

I was so blue. I was sorry I'd found the car, if I hadn't found it I could have thought about it for the rest of my life. If any. But now I felt let-down stupid at a loss what to do. The breeze had a chill and I supposed I couldn't do better going back as I'd come, so I followed the one road from the small station as it ran uphill into the woods.

Long before I got there, probably from the moment I left the village, I'd been on private property. They were the same hills and forest and stone of the natural world, they looked like the Adirondacks, but I was walking in fact on a map of fixed color, crimson perhaps.

The road inclined gradually around the side of a mountain, one side dropping away to show the darkening sky.

And then, below, a broad lake came into view, a lake glittering with the last light of the day. I stopped to look at it. Something was moving, making a straight line of agitation, like a tear, in the surface.

A moment later a bird was rising slowly from the water, a bird large enough to be seen from this distance but only against the silver phosphorescence of the water. When it rose as high as the land it was gone.

The rest of my survey I made in darkness, by the light of stars. I had come on some isolated reservation, and its center was a cluster of buildings on the mountain over-looking this same lake: a lodge of two stories, and several smaller outbuildings, barns, stables, garages. Even in darkness I could tell that the buildings, like the little station house at the bottom of the trail, were uniformly of log construction.

My vantage point was from the land side, a rise in an enormous rolling meadow beside a tennis court fenced in wood and mesh. I did not try to move closer to see in detail what was in the light of the lodge windows, all ablaze everywhere, as if great crowds were inside. I knew there were no crowds. The wind amplified in gusts the strains of a dance band. When the song was over, it began again. It was a Victrola record of a tune I recognized, "Exactly Like You."

The perverse effect of this music and the lighted windows was of a repellent and desolate isolation.

Now the wind came up stronger across the meadow, it was off the lake and carried the water's chill. I looked up to the treetops of the wood behind me and saw them

prancing and bucking in the way of a hard life of eminence. I was fixed by my own pride from going to the
back door of this establishment and asking for a place to
stay or a meal. I didn't know if I had the stamina for a
night on these grounds, but it was as if I was reflecting
the clear arrogance of whoever owned this place and
traveled to it by imperial railroad, for I was goddamned if
I would ask him or them for anything.

I didn't want her to see me like this!

I remember squatting behind the little tennis shack and
keeping myself company with my cigarettes. I smoked
one after another and made a community around their
glow.

Now I'll tell what I don't remember. I don't remember
the sound they must have made, the uncanny sound as it
separated itself from the wind in the trees, of group
exertion, breath chuffing across twenty or thirty hanging
tongues, yelps of murderous excitement. Was the moon
out? I rose from my crouch seeing something like an
earthwave coming toward me, as if the ground were
advancing in a sort of rolling quaking upheaval. This
gradually distinguished itself as the furred musculature of
shoulders and chests and legs, and I think now I must
have seen the face of the lead dog, flung into moonlight,
its maddened red eyes like the tracers of those launched
fangs. If I didn't see it I've dreamed it a thousand times.

Goddamnit, if city boys knew any animals at all it was
dogs. But these were like nothing I'd ever seen. Not that I
had the leisure for contemplation. I held up my forearm
and his teeth tore it like a piece of paper. Together we
rammed into the side of the tennis shack. And then the
others were up, tossing themselves at me in their fury but
with great inefficiency, they turned on each other snarling
for getting in each other's way though they were effective
enough to my pain and screaming terror. I was kicking at
them and flinging them off going for the throat trying to
tear my throat out, I was kicking and waving my arms
and fists and howling like a dog myself and knowing that
if I went down I faced something more than the end of
my life—shit—the extenuated appreciation of its end,

piecemeal, my life taken from me chunk by chunk drop by drop every nerve shrieking.

I think I can imagine some faint memory of the odor of those dogs, feel the closeness of their life, their wild heartbeat! I hear their snorts and the snaps of teeth on air, I remember the toothtumblers lock once the flesh is found, the quick release and regrip down to the bone.

I recall without difficulty the intimate apprehension of prey in the jaws of a maniac life beyond all appeal.

Somehow I was vaulted or inspired upward in some acrobatic backward tumble through the unframed shack window. I took one of the dogs with me, slamming it fixed in my wrist against the inner wall of the shack while the heads of the others appeared outside the window, a fountain of faces leaping and falling back in rage in frustration. But then one gripped the sill with its paws and began to pull itself up till its own weight would get it inside, I grabbed a tennis racquet hanging in its press and swung toward that head down on those paws. The dog fell out of sight and the other, who had come in with me, stunned loose from its slam against the wall, I now caught on the back with the racquet edge in its heavy press and broke its spine. They were not uniformed pedigreed hounds, they were every kind and make, and this one, a smaller mongrel, I lifted howling and threw to the others.

Things immediately got quiet. I heard the yelps and moans and grunts of appeasement, the soft sound of flesh being fanged. The small moonlit square of night I saw from the floor of the shack was peaceful with stars. Maybe I heard human voices, or the firing of a rifle or a gun, but I'm not sure. I lay there and as the blood flowed from me I lost consciousness.

Adirondacks.
Region first known for wilderness industries trapping
hunting.   Earliest roads were logging trails out came
the great trees chained to sledges.   In the winter blocks
of ice were sawn from the frozen lakes and carried in
procession on funicular tracks uphill to the railroad depots
for shipment to the cities.   In early spring the tapping
of the huge sugar maples and the sap houses sweet blue
smoke hanging over the green valleys.   In summer the
natives grew small corn and picked wild berries and grilled
trout on open fires by the edge of rock rivers.   But one
summer after the May flies painters and poets arrived who
paid money to sit in guide boats and to stand momentous-
ly above the gorges of rushing streams.   The artists and
poets patrons seeing and hearing their reports bought vast
tracts of the Adirondacks very cheaply and began to build
elaborate camps there thus inventing the wilderness as
luxury.   Loon Lake a high mountain retreat cratered as
purely cold and clear in the mountains as water cupped in
your hands.

In the morning the old man, Bennett, gave them all woolen ponchos and took them for a speedboat ride on the lake. She sat up front between him and Tommy. Tommy put his arm around her but she preferred to lean forward in the lee of the windshield where she avoided the wind if not the cold space it left as it blew by.

The little flag in the stern flapped like a machine gun. In the back seat there was no protection at all and they were truly unhappy. The cigarette was whipped out of Buster's mouth and taken in the air over the wake by a black-and-white bird, some sort of gull. She saw that, having turned to smile back at them, her knee just touching the old man's pants leg, and Buster, looking startled, saw it too. It seemed to fall away into the sky. He faced her stupidly, his mouth still open and a piece of cigarette paper pasted on his lower lip.

She knew Bennett was showing off for her, rearing the mahogany speedboat through the waves as if it were Buck Jones' Silver. The sky was very low and the tops of the hills around the lake were shrouded in clouds. The clouds drifted through the trees and she was startled by that intimacy. She thought clouds should stay up in the sky where they belonged.

They had come to the closed end of the lake. The old man throttled down and the boat settled flatter in the water. There were marshes here and dead striplings poking out of the water. He headed straight for the trees and she felt Tommy clench up until a notch appeared in the shoreline. They went into a channel at slow speed and rode serenely by a beaver lodge of wet dark sticks and mud. The old man pointed it out.

She imagined the beaver pups inside their lodge lying on shelves just out of reach of the wavelets lapping their feet.

Then they were out in an even bigger lake with the hills somewhat farther away and a broad stretch of sky higher over everything. It turned out the old man owned this lake too. She wondered if he trained the crazy bird who came down from the sky for a cigarette.

Later, in the boathouse, Buster was so relieved at having survived travel on water that he told everyone about the bird.

That was a loon, the old man said, a kind of grebe. They all respectfully considered this intelligence.

You knew that didn't you Buster, Tommy said.

They put their ponchos back on the wall pegs and reclaimed their fedoras. There were other speedboats in the boathouse, each in its own berth. There were racks with wooden canoes. It was a brown log boathouse with casement windows in the same style as the big house up the hill.

There was a man there to take care of everything.

Bennett led the way. She noted how easily he moved up the path, his back straight, beautiful white hair. These people knew as no one else how to take care of themselves. He was dressed for the outdoors, with boots and a red plaid flannel shirt.

She held Tommy's arm and enjoyed the warmth of the land on her back. It looked as if the sun might burn through the clouds. She felt good. She felt like dancing. She watched her own feet walking in their strap shoes. They were grown-up-looking feet. She was arm in arm with Tommy, pulling him in close, trying to match strides up the hill. She watched his small black wing-tipped shoes pacing along, their shine ruined, and the cuffs of his pin-stripe flapping dust from the ground.

Up ahead the party was met by a fat guy. He saw her and stood as if struck by lightning. He had been coming down to the lake but turned now with another glance at her over his shoulder and ran along behind the old man.

She held Tommy's arm, held him back and let them all go out of sight up the hill.

You've got to be joking, Tommy said.

She rubbed against him. She kissed him and ran her tongue over his lips and leaned back from him holding her groin against him and looking into his eyes right there in the mountains of the Adirondacks.

Well the kid's impressed, Tommy said.

She nodded while looking into his eyes. The tip of her tongue appeared in the corner of her mouth. He disengaged her arms and stood back from her.

That's how much you know, he said.

It's who she is, thinks Warren, definitely, now dressed in flimsies and struggling with the torments of her class but it's her, the same girl, returned to my life, changed in time, true, changed in place, changed let us be honest in character, but how can I doubt my feelings they are all I have I have spent my life studying them and of them all this is the indisputable constant, the feeling of recognition I have for her when she appears, the ease with which she comes to me regardless of the circumstances, for I have no particular appeal to women, only to this woman, and so the recognition must be mutual and it pushes us toward each other despite our differences, and our inability to understand each other's language, and here it has happened again though I am indisputably older fatter and more ridiculous as a figure of love than I have been before. Always I am older. Always we do not understand each other. Always I lose her. Oh God who made this girl give her to me this time to hold let me sink into the complacencies of fulfilled love, let us lose our memories together, and let me die from the ordinary insubstantial results of having lived.

What he intuits from the coolness of her conversation or the moods that come over her is that she did not expect to find herself in her present situation. She is not devious and did not plan this. She seems to take each day as it comes and is clearly forged in her being by the race of men she's had to deal with. In short, they are equals. The realization sends him to the bottle with a shaking hand.

Naturally she would think he was part of the old man's retinue. It was a natural assumption. At drinks that evening they're alone. Can I tell you a story? he says. Outside, the rain is heavy, the kind of rain that tamps down the wind. Smoke from the big fireplace drifts into the room like a wisp of cloud come in from the mountains.

I've lived here for six years. I'm a poet and the Bennetts are my patrons. But I found this place on my own and when I came here it was to kill him.

The old man?

Yes.

She has to this point only half listened but now he is rewarded by her direct gaze. She sips her Manhattan. She is wearing pleated linen slacks and a thin blouse half buttoned. She likes to show herself.

I swear to the lordourgod I will make her see who I am.

People I loved died because of the policies of one of his companies. He owns lots of companies.

You know what he's worth?

Worth? What can it matter. I haven't got a dime myself, he says conscientiously, as if he'd made it his life's achievement. Millions, billions, the power over people. So I was going to kill him. I got through the dogs with just a tear or two and introduced myself out on that

terrace there through the dining room one morning with
my knife in my pocket.

She turns and looks through the big bay windows. She
turns back.

But you didn't, she says.

One night when the dogs are in the neighborhood he
takes two wineglasses and a bottle of his table red and
closes his door and half walks half runs over to her cottage.

I thought you might need some company, he says.

He follows her inside. She wears a robe. She is barefoot.
He realizes she answered the door without breaking stride.
She is pacing the room. Her arms are folded across her
breasts.

The doors to her terrace are closed and locked. The curtain is pulled shut. The room smells of cigarettes. He pours
the wine.

Later they are sitting on the floor beside the bed. He has
been telling her about his life. He has recited some of his
work. She has listened and smoked and held out her
glass for wine.

Listen, he says holding his hand up, forefinger pointed.
The dogs are gone. She smiles and accepts this as something he's done. Sitting Indian style, she leans forward
and touches his face. Her robe has fallen open over her
thighs like a curtain rising. He kisses her hand as it is
withdrawn. I've loved three times in my life, he says.
Always the same person.

I don't know what that's supposed to mean, she says.
But I see I've got a live one here.

Then she is lying on the floor in his arms reading his
face with judicious solemnity, her eyes gathering up the
dim light of the room so widely open that he feels himself
pouring into them. Because her spirit is strong he is

surprised by the frailty of her. She is a small person. Her breasts are full and her thighs rather short. He can feel her ribs. Her buttocks are hard with a thin layer of sweet softness over them, like a child's ass. Her mons hair feels lightly oiled. He touches her cunt. She closes her eyes. A queer bitter smell comes off her body. He kisses her soft open mouth and it's just as he knew, she is here and he's found her again.

Like many large overweight men he has surprising agility. She is obviously entranced. But the lack of practice is too much for him.

She says with characteristic directness: Is that the whole show?

He laughs and one way or another maintains her interest. Eventually he is ready again. Later he will try to remember the experience of being in her and will find that difficult. But he'll remember them lying on their backs next to each other and the feel of the hard nap of the carpet on his sweaty skin. He'll remember that when he turned on his side to look at her the silhouette of her body in the dark was like a range of distant hills.

Yes, she said, as if their fucking had been conversation, sometimes nothing else will do but to drive as flat out hard and fast as you can.

Annotated text *Loon Lake* by Warren Penfield.
If you listen the small splash is beaver.
As beaver swim their fur lies back and their heads
      elongate
and a true imperial cruelty shines from their eyes.
They're rodents, after all.
Beaver otter weasel mink and rat
a rodent specie of the Adirondacks
and they redistrict the world.
They go after the young trees and bring them
      down—
whole hillsides collapse in the lake when
      they're through.
They make their lodges of skinned poles,
      mud and boughs
like igloos of dark wet wood
and they enter and exit under water and build
      shelves
out of the water for the babies.
And when the mahogany speedboat goes by

trimmed with silver horns
in Loon Lake, in the Adirondacks,
the waves of the lake inside the beaver lodge
     lap gently
against the children's feet in the darkness.

Loon Lake
was once the destination of private railroad cars
rocking on a single track
through forests of pine and spruce and hemlock
branches and fronds brushing the windows
     of cut glass
while inside incandescent bulbs flickered
in frosted-glass chimneys over double beds
and liquor bottles trembled in their recessed
     cabinet fittings
above card tables of green baize
in rooms entered through narrow doors
     with brass latches.

If you step on a twig in a soft bed of pine needles
under an ancient stand of this wilderness
you will make no sound.
All due respect to the Indians of Loon Lake
the Adirondack nations, with all due respect.
What a clear cold life it must have been.
Everyone knew where he stood
chiefs or children or malcontents
and every village had its lover whom no one wanted
who sometimes lay down because of that
with a last self-pitying look at Loon Lake
before intoning his death prayers
and beginning the difficult business of dying by will
on the dry hummocks of pine needles.
The loons they heard were the loons we hear today,
cries to distract the dying
loons diving into the cold black lake
and diving back out again in a whorl of clinging
     water
clinging like importuning spirits

fingers shattering in spray
feeling up the wing along the rounded body of the
thrillingly exerting loon
taking a fish
rising to the moon streamlined
its loon eyes round and red.
A doomed Indian would hear them at night
    in their diving
and hear their cry not as triumph or as rage
or the insane compatibility with the earth
attributed to birds of prey
but in protest against falling
of having to fall into that black water
and struggle up from it again and again
the water kissing and pawing and whispering
the most horrible promises
the awful presumptuousness of the water
squeezing the eyes out of the head
floating the lungs out on the beak which clamps
    on them
like wriggling fish
extruding all organs and waste matter
turning the bird inside out
which the Indian sees is what death is
the environment exchanging itself for the being.
And there are stars where that happens too in space
in the black space some railroad journeys above
    the Adirondacks.

Well, anyway, in the summer of 1936
a chilling summer high in the Eastern mountains
a group of people arrived at a rich man's camp
in his private railway car
the men in fedoras and dark double-breasted suits
and the women in silver fox and cloche hats
sheer stockings of Japanese silk
and dresses that clung to them in the mountain air.
They shivered from the station to the camp
in an open carriage drawn by two horses.
It was the clearest night in the heavens

and the silhouettes of the jagged pines on the
    mountaintop
in the moonlight looked like arrowheads
looked like the graves of heroic Indians.
The old man who was their host
an industrialist of enormous wealth
over the years had welcomed to his camp
financiers politicians screen stars
European princes boxing champions and
conductors of major orchestras
all of whom were honored to sign the guest book.
Occasionally for complicated reasons
he received persons strangely undistinguished.
His camp was a long log building of two stories
on a hill overlooking Loon Lake.
There was a great rustic entrance hall
with a wide staircase of halved logs
and a balustrade made of scraped saplings
a living room as large as a hotel lobby
with walls papered in birch bark
and hung with the mounted heads of deer and elk
and with modern leather sofas with rounded corners
and a great warming fireplace of native stone
big enough to roast an ox.
It was a fine manor house lacking nothing
with suites of bedrooms each with its own
    shade porch
and the most discreet staff of cooks and maids and
    porters
but designated a camp because its décor was
    rough-hewn.

Annotate old man who was their host as follows: F
(Francis) W (Warren) Bennett born August 2 1878
Glens Falls New York.　　　Father millionaire Augustus
Bennett founder of Union Supply Company major outfitter
army uniforms and military accessories hats boots Spring-
field rifles insignia saddles ceremonial swords etc to Army
of the United States during Civil War.　　　FW Bennett a

student at Groton thence Massachusetts Institute of Technology Boston graduating with a degree in mine engineering.   Bought controlling interest Missouri-Clanback
Coal Company St Louis upon graduation.   Took con-
trol Missouri & Western Railroad 1902.   Founding
partner Colorado Fuel Company with John C. Osgood
Julian Kleber John L Jerome.   Surviving partner associate of John D. Rockefeller Colorado Fuel and Iron
Company, vice president of engineering.   Immense
success Colorado and Missouri speculative coal-mining
ventures suggested use of capital abroad.   Took over
National Mexican Silver Mining Company.   Founder
Chilean-American Copper Company.   Board of Directors James Steel Co., Northwest Lumber Trust, Balti-
more, Chicago & Albuquerque RR Co., etc.   Trustee
Jordan College, Rhinebeck N.Y.   Trustee Miss Morris'
School for Young Women, Briarcliff Manor NY.   Member Knickerbocker, Acropolis, New York; Silks, Saratoga
Springs; Rhode Island Keel, Newport.   Marriages Fan-
ny Teale Stevens, no issue; Bootsie van der Kellen, no
issue; Lucinda Bailey, no issue.   Died 1967 Lausanne
Switzerland.

And this party of visitors were really romantic
        gangsters
thieves, extortionists and murderers of the lower class
and their women who might or might not be whores.
The old man welcomed them warmly
enjoying their responses to his camp
admiring the women in their tight dresses and red
        lips
relishing the having of them there so out of place
at Loon Lake.
The first morning of their visit
he led everyone down the hill
to give them rides in his biggest speedboat
a long mahogany Chris-Craft with a powerful inboard
that resonantly shook the water as she idled.
He handed them each a woolen poncho with a hood

and told them the ride was fast and cold
but still they were not prepared when under way
he opened up the throttle
and the boat reared in the water like Buck Jones'
    horse.
The women shrieked and gripped the gangsters' arms
and spray stinging like ice coated their faces
while the small flag at the stern snapped like
    a machine gun.
And one of the men lipping an unlit cigarette
felt it whipped away by the wind.
He turned and saw it sail over the wake
where a loon appeared from nowhere
beaked it before it hit the water
and rose back into the sky above the mountain.

Annotate boat reared in the water like Buck Jones' horse
as follows: Buck Jones a cowboy movie star silents 1920s
and talkies early 1930s.   Others of this specie: Tom
Mix, Tim McCoy, Big Boy Williams.   Buck Jones'
horse palomino stallion named Silver.   Others of this
specie: Pal Feller Tony.

The old man rode them around Loon Lake,
    its islands
through channels where beaver had built their lodges
and everything they saw the trees the mountains
the water and even the land they couldn't see
    under the water
was what he owned. And then he brought them in
    throttling down
and the boat was awash in a rush of foam
like the outspread wings of a waterbird coming
    to rest.
Two other mahogany boats of different lengths
were berthed in the boathouse
and racks of canoes and guide boats upside down
and on walls paddles hanging from brackets

and fishing rods and snowshoes for some strange
 reason
and not a gangster there did not reflect
how this dark boathouse with its canals
and hollow-sounding deck floors
was bigger than the home his family lived in
when he was a kid, as big as the orphan's home
 in fact.
But one gangster wanted to know about the lake
and its connecting lakes, the distance one could
 travel on them
as if he was planning a fast getaway.

Just disappearing around the corner out of sight
was the boathouse attendant.
And everyone walked up the hill for drinks and lunch.
Drinks were at twelve-thirty and lunch at one-thirty
after which, returning to their rooms,
the guests found riding outfits laid across their beds
and boots in their right sizes all new.
At three they met each other at the stables
laughing at each other and being laughed at
and the stableman fitted them out with horses
and the sensation was particularly giddy when
 the horses
began to move without warning ignoring them
 up there in the saddle
threatening to launch with each bounce
 like a paddle ball.
And so each day, the best gangster among them
 realized,
there would be something to do they could not do
 well.

The unchecked walking horses made for the woods
no one was in the lead, the old man was not there.
They were alone on these horses who took this wide
 trail
they seemed to know.

They were busy maintaining themselves
    on the tops of these horses
stepping with their plodding footfall
through the soft earth of the wide trail.
By and by proceeding gently downhill they came
to another shore of the lake, of Loon Lake,
and the trees were cut down here, the cold sun shone.
They found themselves before an airplane hangar
with a concrete ramp sloping into the water.
As the horses stood there the hangar doors slid open
there was a man pushing back each of the steel doors
although they saw only his arm and hand and
    shoetops.
And then from a gray cloud over the mountain
beyond the far end of the lake an airplane appeared
and made its descent in front of the mountain
growing larger as it came toward them
a green-and-white seaplane with a cowled engine and
    overhead wing.
It landed in the water with barely a splash
taxiing smartly with a feathery sound.
The horses nickered and stirred, everyone held on
and the lead gangster said whoa boy, whoa boy
and the goddamn plane came right out of the water
up the ramp, water falling from its pontoons
the wheels in the pontoons leaving a wet track on
    the concrete
and nosed up to the open hangar
blowing up a cloud of dirt and noise.
The engine was cut and the cabin door opened
and putting her hands on the wing struts a woman
    jumped down
a slim woman in trousers and a leather jacket and
    a silk scarf
and a leather helmet which she removed showing
    light-brown hair cut close
and she looked at them and nodded without smiling
and that was the old man's wife.

Annotate old man's wife as follows: Lucinda Bailey Bennett born 1896 Philadelphia PA.   Father US Undersecretary of State Bangwin Channing under McKinley. Private tutoring in France and Switzerland.   Miss Morris' School for Young Women.   Brearley.   Long Island School of Aviation practicing stalls tailspins stalled glide half-roll snap roll slow roll rolling eight wingovers Immelmann loops.   Winner First Women's Air Regatta Long Island New York to Palm Beach Florida 1921. Winner Single-Engine National Women's Sprints 1922– 1929.   First woman to fly alone Long Island–Bermuda.   Woman's world record cross-country flight Long Island to San Diego 1932, twenty-seven hours sixteen minutes.   First woman to fly alone Long Island to Newfoundland.   Winner Chicago Air Meet 1931, 1932, 1933.   Glenn Curtiss National Aviatrix Silver Cup 1934.   Lindbergh Trophy 1935.   Member President's Commission on the Future of Aviation 1936. Honorary Member US Naval Air Patrol 1936. Lost on round-the world flight over the Pacific 1937.

She strode off down the trail toward the big house
and they were not to see her again that day
neither at drinks which were at six-thirty
nor dinner at seven-thirty.
But her husband was a gracious host
attentive to the women particularly.
He revealed that she was a famous aviatrix
and some of them recognized her name from
        the newspapers.
He spoke proudly of her accomplishments
the races she won flying measured courses
marked by towers with checkered windsocks
and her endurance flights some of which
were still the record for a woman.
After dinner he talked vaguely of his life

his regret that so much of it was business.
He talked about the unrest in the country
and the peculiar mood of the workers
and he solicited the gangsters' views over brandy
on the likelihood of revolution.
And now he said rising I'm going to retire.
But you're still young said one of the gangsters.
For the night the old man said with a smile
I mean I'm going to bed. Good night.
And when he went up the stairs of halved
    tree trunks
they all looked at each other and had nothing to say.
They were standing where the old man had left them
in their tuxes and black ties.
They had stood when he stood the women had stood
    when he stood
and quietly as they could they all went to their rooms,
where the bedcovers had been turned back and
    the reading lamps lighted.
And in the room of the best gangster there
a slim and swarthy man with dark eyes, a short man
very well put together
there were doors leading to a screened porch
and he opened them and stood on the dark porch
and heard the night life of the forest and the lake
and the splash of the fish terrifyingly removed
    from Loon Lake.
He had long since run out of words
for his sickening recognition of real class
nervously insisting how swell it was.
He turned back into the room.
His girl was fingering the hand-embroidered initials
in the center of the blanket.
They were the same initials as on the bath towels
and on the cigarette box filled with fresh Luckies
and on the matchbooks and on the breast pockets
    of the pajamas
of every size stocked in the drawers
the same initials, the logo.

Annotate reference the best gangster there as follows:
Thomas Crapo alias Tommy the Emperor.   Born Hoboken New Jersey 1898.   Hoboken Consolidated
Grade School 1917.   New Jersey National Guard
1914–1917.   Rainbow Division American Expedition-
ary Force 1917–1918.   Saw action Château-Thierry.
Victory Medal.   Founder Brandywine Importing Company 1919.   Board of Directors Inverness Distribution
Company.   Founding partner Boardwalk Amusement
Company 1920.   President Dance-a-dime Incorporated.   Founder Crapo Industrial Services Incorporated, New York, Chicago, Detroit.   Patron Boys
Town, March of Dimes, Police Athletic League New
York, Policeman's Benevolent Society Chicago.   Present whereabouts unknown.

Annotate reference his girl as follows: Clara Lukács born
1918 Hell's Kitchen New York.   School of the Sisters
of Poor Clare, expelled 1932.   S.S. Kresge counter
girl (notions) 1932–1934.   Receptionist Lukács West
29th St Funeral Parlor 1934.   Present whereabouts
unknown.

The gangster's girl was eighteen
and had had an abortion he knew nothing about.
She found something to criticize, one thing,
the single beds, and as she undressed
raising her knees, slipping off her shoes
unhooking her stockings from her garters
she spoke of the bloodlessness of the rich
    not believing it
while the gangster lay between the sheets
    in the initialed pajamas
arranging himself under the covers
    so that they were neat and tight

as if trying to take as little possession of the bed
    as possible
not wanting to appear to himself to threaten anything.
He locked his hands behind his head and ignored the girl
and lay in the dark not even smoking.

But at three that morning
there was a terrible howl
from the pack of wild dogs that ran in the mountains—
not wolves but dogs that had reverted
when their owners couldn't feed them any longer.
The old man had warned them this might happen
but the girl crept into the bed of the gangster
and he put his arm around her and held her
so that she would not slip off the edge
and they listened to the howling
and then the sound nearer to the house
of running dogs, of terrifying exertion
and then something gushing
in the gardens below the windows.
And they heard the soft separation
together with grunts and snorts and yelps
of flesh as it is fanged and lifted from a body.
Jesus, the girl said
and the gangster felt her breath on his collarbone
and smelled the gel in her hair, the sweetness of it,
and felt the gathered dice of her shoulders
and her shivering and her cold hand on his stomach
underneath the waistband.

In the morning they joined the old man
on the sun terrace outside the dining room.
Halfway down the hill a handyman pushing a wheelbarrow
was just disappearing around a bend in the path.
I hope you weren't frightened, the old man said,
    they took a deer.
And he turned surprisingly young blue eyes
    on the best gangster's girl.
Later that morning she saw on the hills in the sun
all around Lake Loon

patches of color where the trees were turning.
She went for a walk alone and in the woods saw
in the orange and yellowing leaves of deciduous trees
the coming winter
imagining in these high mountains
snow falling like some astronomical disaster
and Loon Lake as the white hole of a monstrous
    meteor
and every branch of the evergreens all around
described with snow, each twig each needle
balancing a tiny snowfall precisely imitative of itself.
And at dinner she wore her white satin gown
with nothing underneath to ruin the lines.
And the old man's wife came to dinner this night
clearly younger than her husband, trim and neat
with small beautifully groomed hands and still young
    shoulders and neck
but brackets at the corners of her mouth.
She talked to them politely with no condescension
and showed them in glass cases in the game room
trophies of air races she had won
small silver women pilots
silver cups and silver planes on pedestals.
Then still early in the evening she said good night
and that she had enjoyed meeting them.
They watched her go.
And after the old man retired
and all the gangsters and their women stood around
in their black ties and tuxes and long gowns
the best gangster's girl saw a large Victrola
    in the corner
of the big living room with its leather couches
and grand fireplace
the servants spirited away the coffee service
and the gangster's girl put on a record
and commanded everyone to dance.
And they danced to the Victrola music
they felt better they did the fox trot
and went to the liquor cabinet and broke open
some Scotch and gin and they danced and smoked

the old man's cigarettes from the boxes on the tables
and the only light came from the big fire
and the women danced with one arm dangling
      holding empty glasses
and the gangsters nuzzled their shoulders
and their new shoes made slow sibilant rhythms
on the polished floors
as they danced in their tuxes and gowns of satin
at Loon Lake, at Loon Lake
in the rich man's camp
in the mountains of the Adirondacks.

He was a whistling wonder with his face and arms and legs in bandages and bandages crisscrossed like bandoliers across his chest. Every now and then they looked in on him with the same separation of themselves from the sight as rubes looking at the freaks. They all wore green.

They told him the dog packs were well known in the region, several of them told him that, as if it were a consolation. He had difficulty speaking through his pain and swollen tissue, so that they could not be exactly sure what he thought of them and their fucking dogs.

The elderly country doctor was eager to see what complication might set in to try him beyond the resources of his medicine.

There were pills for the pain but I took as few as I could. It seemed important to me to stay awake, to know what was going on. Maybe I thought the dogs would come back. The room was damp. There was a small window high on the wall. I was in the basement of one of the log buildings I'd seen and it seemed to me not a very safe place to be. Also it was as bad as the original event to dream of it again drugged in a kind of dream prison and struggling for consciousness. Pain was better. It came in spasms and with the sharp point of imprinted teeth, it tore along in clawing sweeps down my chest and seemed sometimes to raise the bandages from the skin. I tried to consider it objectively, like a scientist sitting in a white coat looking through a microscope. Ahh, peering at each little cellpoint of pain. Remarkable!

And since I was in pain, I thought of my mother and father. I thought of myself bedridden in Paterson. They look at me lying there flushed and wheezing, a boy impossibly exercised just by the act of living, and go off to work at their machines.

A man looked in on me each morning and made a grunt of disgust or scorn just like my father had although heavyset not at all like my thin and gaunt father but in the same role, with the same wordless eloquence. He wore a kind of uniform of dark green shirt and matching pants.

And for my mother a woman in pale green uniform and white shoes and opaque brown hose with a thick seam down the back. An impassive porky being with hands that worked at high speed setting down trays pounding pillows carrying off urinals while she thought her own thoughts.

I could tell that each of them felt badly used to be taking care of some tramp who had wandered onto the grounds. It was an affront to the natural order which made service to people bearable because they were higher than you, not lower.

I responded with a pride of my own which asked for nothing and gave as little indication of need as possible. And I never thanked them for anything. As I felt better I grew contemptuous as if, coming into this province of wealth, I had adopted its customs. Or perhaps it was more serious, perhaps it had been injected in the saliva of the dogs.

On the other hand I had only the word of these people that the dogs didn't belong to the owner of this place. And even if they didn't, they certainly ran to his advantage. My rage flared as if it were the last wound to be felt and the slowest to heal.

As time went on I understood that I lay in a room of the staff house where perhaps fifteen or twenty people lived who wore the green livery, forest-green for the outdoor workers, the paler shade for the indoor. They all looked somewhat stolidly alike, as if related.

I was alert to find a friend and I did. She was a girl of the pale green set, a young maid in the big house who shyly looked in on me, advancing each time a little farther into the room until finally she showed up in mid-morning one day when everyone else was working. She had seen we were the same age and that was enough.

Her name was Libby. She didn't think of not answering any question that occurred to me.

This place was called Loon Lake. It was the domain of the same F. W. Bennett of the Bennett Autobody Works. Did I know the name? He was very rich. He owned thirty thousand acres here and it was just one of his places. He owned the lake itself, the water in the lake, the land under the water and the fish that swam in it.

"But not the dogs," I said.

"Oh no," she said, "those are wild-running, those dogs. It's the fault of the people who own them and can't feed them anymore. And then they go off and forage and breed wild and hunt in packs."

"The people?"

"The dogs. All through the mountains it's like that, not just here. Does it hurt?" she asked.

"It don't tickle."

A tremor went through her. She held her arms as if she was cold.

"Tell me, does your F. W. Bennett have a wife?"

"Oh, sure! She's famous. The Mrs. Bennett who wins all the air races. Her picture's in the papers. Lucinda Bennett?"

"Oh, her," I said. "The one with the blond hair?"

"No, she's a brunette." Libby touched her own hair, which was brunette too. Like all her features it was ordinary. She was possessed of a sort of plain prettiness that caused you to study her and wish this feature or that might be better.

"Brunettes are my favorite," I said.

She blushed. She was a simple innocent person, she granted me her own youthful face on the world without knowing who I was or where I came from. In five minutes I had her whole history. Her uncle, one of the groundskeepers, had gotten her the job. She made twelve dollars a week plus room and board. She was fervent in her gratitude. She spoke in what I could tell was the communal piety of the staff. How nervously lucky they would have to feel, how clannish in their good fortune exempt in these mountains from an afflicted age. Mr. Bennett and Mrs. Bennett came or went separately or together or had guests or didn't, but the place was maintained all year round including the dead of winter.

"Don't you get lonely up here?" I said.

She thought a long time. "Well, I send six dollars to my father in Albany."

Not realizing this was enough for me to feel chastened, she frowned and cast about in her mind for justification. "You'd be surprised who comes here," she said. She brightened "You get to see famous people."

"Who?"

"Why, big politicians, and prime ministers from England. And Jeanette MacDonald? She was here in the spring! She's beautiful. I saw her clothes. She gave me five dollars!"

"Who else?"

"Oh well, I never saw him, it was before I came. But Charlie Chaplin."

"Sure," I said. "On roller skates."

She looked then suddenly frightened. Who would doubt her word? She turned and left the room, and I thought to myself well that's that. But a short while later she re-

turned, softly closing the door behind her. She held a
large leatherbound book to her chest and looked at me
over the gilt edge with bright excited eyes. "I better not
get caught," she said.

It was the Loon Lake guest book. She fixed the pillows
so I could pull myself up and she sat on the side of the
bed and opened the book to a page marked "1931." Her
index finger ran down a list of signatures and stopped and
she turned her eyes on me as I saw whose signature it
was: Charles Chaplin had made an elegant scrawl, and
next to it, where there was a space for comment, he had
written: "Splendid weekend! Gay company!"

Vindicated, Libby watched with pleasure as I became
absorbed by all the names, right up to the present:
signatures of movie stars, orchestra leaders, authors, sen-
ators, all famous enough to be recognized by me, but also
signatures I recognized only vaguely, or only sensed as
names of magnitude, like the name F. W. Bennett, names
that had been given to things, names painted on the big
signs over factories or carved in the stone over the en-
trances of office buildings. I couldn't stop looking at
them. I felt I could learn something, that there was
something here, some powerful knowledge I could use.
But it was in code! If only I could understand the significance of the notations, I'd have what I needed I'd know
what I'd always dreamed of knowing—although I
couldn't have said what it was. I touched the signatures,
traced them trying to feel the ink. It was some mysterious
system of legalities and caste and extended brilliant endeavor—all abbreviated into these names and dates of
proud people from all over the world who had come here
to this secret place in the mountains.

I became aware of this girl Libby in her pale green
uniform. She sat very close to me, the starched front of her
uniform rose and fell with her breathing. When I glanced
up from the book I found her face near mine, her head
bowed and her eyes on the page, but her consciousness all
directed to me. Her full lower lip was impressed into a
suggestion of voluptuousness by her front teeth. She had

thick wavy hair. What sweet appropriate modesty of being. Her trust was part of it, or so I understood—the willingness of the others of us to find a place and live our lives within it, making our trembling alliances and becoming famous and powerful to each other.

I turned back to the book. Some of the people there were such big shots they needed only one name to identify themselves. Leopold, one of them had written. Of Belgium.

I said to Libby, "Hey, how long have I been here, anyway?"

"We were taking off the summer covers and putting the rugs down," she said. "It was that night. I never hope to hear what I heard that night."

"Well, when was it, please?"

"Two weeks ago."

"Wasn't someone here then? Didn't you have visitors?"

She looked at me and then looked away. She glanced at the book. She wanted it back.

"I saw the train, Libby. People were on it. Is anyone here now?"

She shook her head.

"Well, how come I don't see anything that recent in the guest book?"

She was silent a long while. I knew I was extending her loyalty. I gazed at her and waited for my answer. She looked discouraged. "Not just anyone gets to sign," she said finally.

"Is that right?" I said. She wouldn't look at me now.

"I think someone's calling you, Libby."

"Where?" She went to the door, opened it and listened. I leaned over with a painful lunge to the bedside stand. In the little drawer was a fountain pen. I unscrewed the cap, shook a blot on the floor, spread open the guest book and signed my name with a flourish.

"What are you doing!" Libby said. Her hand was on her cheek and she stared at me in horror.

"Joe," I wrote. "Of Paterson. Splendid dogs. Swell company."

I fell back on the pillow. By signing the guest book, did I mean to be going on my way? I felt the pretense, as well as any other, washed away in a wave of weakness and despair.

The girl grabbed the book and ran.

She had a friend, as it turned out, a man who lived on the grounds as a kind of permanent houseguest. He came to look at me later that day, peering in the door with an expression of wonder very odd in a full-grown middle-aged adult.

He was a large heavy man. He was bearded. His hair was overgrown and unkempt. His eyes were blue and set in a field of pink that suggested a history of torments and conflicts past ordinary understanding. His weight and size seemed to amplify the act of breathing, which took place through his mouth. His nose looked swollen, a web of fine purple lines ran up his cheeks from the undergrowth, and all the ravage together told of the drinker.

He said his name was Warren Penfield. He wanted to speak about moral responsibility.

He padded around the room in a pair of old tennis sneakers. He wore baggy trousers belted below his stomach, and an ancient tweed jacket with patches at the elbow. Beneath the jacket was what seemed to be a soft graying tennis shirt part of the collar folded under he didn't seem to be aware of this.

"I can understand your feeling better than you can, young man. I spend my life understanding feelings, yes, my own and others, that's what I do, that's what poets do, that's what they're supposed to do."

"You're a poet?"

"I'm the poet in residence here," he said, drawing himself up slightly trying to tuck his shirt in glancing then at me from the corner of his eye.

I thought I would never know the end of the subtle luxuries with which the wealthy provided themselves.

"So I can understand your feelings. But I also under-

stand poor Libby's, good God she's one of the few decent
people around here, and now she's in fear for her job. Do
you realize what it would mean for her to lose her job? Of
course I'll do what I can, the Bennetts aren't here right
now, fortunately, I'll think of something, yes, I'll speak to
Lucinda, I suppose I can, but that's not the point. You
should have realized the girl was responsible for anything
you did. She was nice to you, she made you her friend,
she shared something she knew, and that's how you
repaid her."

I liked him enormously. I was smiling I was admitted
into his realm of moral concern without passport creden-
tials references of any sort. There I was a hobo boy lying
on this cot in this weird place suppurating, for all he
knew, in my dereliction, not a pot to pee in, and he was
trying to recall me to my honor. He assumed I had it!

He saw me smiling and started to smile too. Then we
were laughing.

"Of course it was wicked, a good wicked joke, God
knows I can enjoy a joke at his expense. I wish there were
more of them. Incidentally, he himself is not totally de-
void of humor, you know."

"Who?"

"Bennett. I've studied him a long time. He's a very
capable human being. Quite charming at times. The mistake most people make is to jump to conclusions before
they even meet him."

"Well, I'll try not to," I said and we laughed again.

At that moment my mother-keeper came in, took my
tray, gave Penfield a dirty look, and left.

"Dreadful woman," he said. "They all are. Except for
Libby, of course. They despise me. I'm more than they
are but I have no place as they have. They play all sorts
of tricks on me, I have to beg for my meals. But when the
Bennetts are here they'll invite me to dine and then I'm
served like I'm the king of England."

I saw that he suffered from this, as from everything, in
a state of expressive self-magnifying complaint.

"Well, I suppose I should go. How do you feel, by the
way?"

"Lousy."

He pulled up his jacket sleeve and showed me on the inside of his left arm a pale scar from the wrist to the elbow. "You're not the only one, I want you to know. They treed me seven years ago when I came here one night—just like you."

One morning on his bed at the foot a folded suit of dark green. He dressed in it and looked for the first time into the hallway outside the room where he had been since he was carried there on some door was a mirror and there he was thin pale-faced boy pale as a sheet, with a sparse stubble on the rim of the jaw, a head of uncombed hair looking too big for the body, and a hunch as if he were still flinching from the teeth, from the snarling face of the mountainous night.

Something has leaked out through the stitches and some of the serious intention of the world has leaked in: like the sense of high stakes, the desolate chance of real destiny.

There was a distant railroad track with telephone poles regularly spaced down the side of my neck over the clavicle across the breastbone. There was another spur line on either arm and the right leg.

I had no feeling in the fourth finger of my right hand.

Thus I found myself on a brilliant morning raking leaves in the shadow of the great sprawling lodge house of the auto magnate F. W. Bennett. I was not to consider myself employed, however. My Loon Lake parents would as frankly have sent me on my way but they did nothing without the approval of their employer, who was still to return.

I felt weak in the knees, I couldn't have gone anywhere anyway. I was glad to hold on to the rake.

The lodge house was two stories on the land side, three on the lake side—the land dropped precipitously from the crest of the hill—and its walls were logs, uniformly brown, set with casement windows and crowned with a wood shingle roof of many angles and regularly spaced dormers. The trees oak maple elm, and though it was still September, a heavy leaf fall everywhere behind the meadow of my encounter, a burning wood of orange and gold and behind this on a distant mountain, ageless stands of evergreen against the bright blue sky.

As the morning advanced the sun was warm on my back. The air was sweet. I felt better. I was one of three or four workmen. A small truck with slat sides moved slowly among us to receive our leaves. We moved around to the back of the house and swept the leaves from two terraces, the upper with tables and chairs for dining, the lower with cushioned wooden wheeled lounge chairs for the view and the sun.

The lake out there a definite mountain lake, a water cupped high in the earth, its east and west shores hidden from view by intervening hills, its south shore across the water filled with pine and spruce that rose up straight on the mountainside in a kind of terror.

The lake glittered with fragments of sun, and flying over it were a couple of large black-and-white loons, big as swans. There was a boathouse down at the water in the same style as the main house. A dock going around the boathouse. A swimming float fifty yards out.

Between the terraces and the water line was a steep hillside garden of wild things, and through its paths we raked away the unwanted leaves from the bushes and plants.

I looked back up the hill to the house and felt the

imposition of an enormous will on the natural planet. Stillness and peace, not the sound of a car or a horn or even a human voice, and I felt Loon Lake in its isolation, the bought wilderness, and speculated what I would do if I had the money. Would I purchase isolation, as this man had? Was that what money was for, to put a distance of fifty thousand acres of mountain terrain between you and the boondocks of the world?

The man made automobile bodies, and they were for connection, cars were democracy we had been told.

The wind rose in a sudden gust about my ears, and as I looked back to the lake, a loon was coming in like a roller coaster. He hit the water and skidded for thirty yards, sending up a great spray, and when the water settled he was gone. I couldn't see him, I thought the fucker had drowned. But up he popped, shaking and mauling a fat fish. And when the fish was polished off, I heard a weird maniac cry coming off the water, and echoing off the hills.

A while later I followed the workers going along the hillside with their rakes through the trees past the stables to the staff house for lunch. The people of the light and dark green ate in a sort of bunkhouse dining room with long tables and benches. The food was put out on compartmented metal trays as in a cafeteria.

Fifteen, twenty of them looking at me as I hesitated with my tray and then slid into a place next to Libby, who smiled and looked with some satisfaction to the rest of the table. I was inspected by a heavyset man with thick black eyebrows I took to be the uncle she had mentioned. I gave back a clear-eyed friendly face don't worry I'm no threat not me. After that I was ignored. I studied them all covertly: there were two, possibly three families of Bennett servants here. They did not make conversation. I had a palpable feeling of the politics of the place, the suspicious credential I had as a victim of the dogs. It wasn't enough to crack their guild. They seemed confident of that.

Well, screw them, they couldn't even understand that I wanted no part of it. When I was strong enough, a day or two, I'd be on my way down the railroad track and leave it to them to work out why. I still had the dollars I'd come with, stained brown with my blood but no less negotiable. Nobody here, not even Libby, knew my full name or had asked where I came from or where I'd been going.

The force of self-distinguishing which I found so foolish among stiffs and hobos was what I ran on. When you are nobody and have nothing, you depend on your troubles for self-respect. I had paid heavily for the bed and board. I wasn't one of them, I was a paying guest.

I finished and walked out while they were still drinking their coffee. I'd be damned if I'd lift a rake or anything else. What could they do, fire me? I stood on the porch and thought about leaving right away, immediately.

And it was at this moment that I saw over the rise to the meadow two people on the tennis court—one of them a girl with blond hair.

I fixed my eyes on her and walked forward already confirmed in expectation by the agonized heave of my heart.

Mr. Penfield the resident poet, an absurd roundish figure in white shorts and a shirt stretched dangerously by an enormous belly, was showing from his side of the net the proper form of the forehand. Once twice three times he stroked the air. His lithe student, trim in a tennis dress, watched him while holding her racquet on her shoulder.

Penfield now hit a ball to her. Careless of all his advice, she swung at it with a great wild lunge and poled it far over the fence across the meadow. I saw tennis balls lying like white flowers everywhere.

He reached into a round basket for another ball and hit it gently, and again she took a furious swing and the ball flew over the fence. Once more he hit to her and she spun herself around missing the ball entirely. He said something to her. She glared at him, dropped the racquet and left the court.

She strode across the grass toward the main house. She tossed her visor away unpinned her hair fluffing it to the

breeze ignoring him as he stood on the court and called
after her in a voice half reproach half apology, "Clara!
Clara!"

But she went over the crest of a slope and descended by
degrees until only her head could be seen moving toward
the house. Mr. Penfield hurriedly collected the tennis balls
lying about the court. I did the same thing in the grass. We
met at the court gate. His large bleary face gazed upon
mine.

"She can't bear to be taught," he said, admitting me
with a stunning lack of ceremony to his thoughts. "All I
said was 'Take a level swing, don't worry about hitting
hard.'" He looked again in the direction she had gone.
He smiled. "But what game can it be, after all, in which
one doesn't hit one's hardest!"

He thrust into my hands the racquet and pail of balls
and hurried off after her, moving lightly on the balls of
his feet with that ability of some fat people to be quick
and graceful. I stepped onto the court and picked up her
racquet. I took everything to the shack not even thinking
of it as the site of my grisly misfortune. I had forgotten
misfortune. I headed back to the staff house, from one
moment to the next, a worried probationary in my dark
green shirt and pants no thought further from my mind
than leaving. I wanted a job! Their job! Just as they knew
I did. I would take up the rake or any other tool they had
in mind oh God it was Clara, that was her name, Clara the
girl on the train, no question about it, twice now the sight
of her had stopped my heart.

I didn't know what would happen in my life but I knew whatever it was it would have to do with her, with Clara. I thought even having her name was an enormous inroad of intelligence. Was she a Bennett? But wouldn't they know their games, weren't they trained to their tennis and their riding? This one, so blazingly beautiful and pissed-off, knew nothing, this one standing pigeon-toed and swinging stiff-armed at balls so incredibly breath-takingly awkward and untrained—no, she was not a relation. Was she a guest? If so, where were the others, she had come with a train, maids in waiting! an entourage! but they were nowhere about, only the resident poet Penfield ambled after her like her pet bear. Was she related to Penfield?

I would do anything be anything to know her and know about her. Dressed in dark green, a spy! I worked to show them how worthy I was, how useful, to show them how I admired what *they* were and how I wanted to be like them and one of them. How much time did I have? Only until the big man arrived, I had only that time to prove I shouldn't be thrown out on my ass.

Of course I couldn't express to Libby even the most idly curious question about this princess living on the grounds. But she had loved showing me the guest book and I thought from her same peasant identification with Bennett wealth she would enjoy the wonder on my face as she secretly showed me the main house, where they lived and had their lives and Charlie Chaplin and the one-named kings sat down to dinner.

The Bennetts not at home there was a bending of the rules: on Saturday night two Loon Lake station wagons pulled out leaving a skeleton staff.

On Sunday afternoon with the sun coming through the trees at low angles to light the rooms, through rectangles of sun along dark corridors, Libby and I tiptoed about the vast upstairs with its hall alcoves of casement windows and window seats and bookshelves and its suites of rooms, each with its generous shade porch, and Adirondacks chairs and sofas.

Whatever empty room I saw led my mind to the next room, the next turn in the corridor, everywhere the light off the lake cast its silvery shimmer on the walls or in my eyes as we passed open doorways.

One wing was closed off. "We can't go there," Libby said.

"Why not?" I asked, casual as I could be.

"It's the Bennetts' wing, where they stay."

"Is someone there?"

"No. But I wouldn't feel right about it. Rose and Mary take care of it," she said.

She led me down a back stair through a kitchen with two black steel ranges and pantries of provisions and several iceboxes each crowned with its humming cylindrical motor.

Through a room of glass cabinets filled with sets of china and drawers of silver service.

Through the hexagonal dining room, three walls of glass and a table hexagonal in shape to seat thirty people.

To the huge living room, the grandest room of all, with tan leather couches built into the walls, the walls hung with the heads of trophy. There were two different levels of game tables and racks of magazines and clusters of stuffed chairs all looking out enormous windows to the lake.

I found myself tiptoeing, with a sense of intrusion, my chest constricted—and something else—the thinnest possibility of destructive intent, some very fine denial on my part to submit to awe. "Of course this is just one of their places," Libby said. "Can you imagine?"

One or two steps up and we were in the entrance hall. The walls were of dark rough wood. We stood under a chandelier made from antlers. I gazed up a wide curved staircase of halved logs polished to a high shine, with balusters of saplings. I gazed at this as at the gnarled and swirling access to a kingdom of trolls.

"Don't you love roughing it?" I said to Libby, running her up the staircase. "What!" she cried, but laughing too, entirely subject to my mood. In the long upstairs corridor I placed her hand on my arm and strolled with her as if we were master and mistress. I led her into one of the suites and flinging open the glass doors of the porch, I extended my arm and said, "Let us enjoy the view that God in his wisdom has arranged for us, my deah." She swept past me giggling in the game and we stood in the sun side by side looking over the kingdom.

"Do you mind if I smoke, old girl?" I said in my best imitation of wealthy speech. "No? Why, thank you, I think I'll light up one of these monogrammed cigs with my initials on them."

She was animated with pleasure, how easily she could be made to live! I kissed her to show her how the wealthy kissed, their noses so high in the air that their lips never met, only their chins. Then of course I kissed her properly. She was confused, she drew back blushing, she had thought it her secret that she was sweet on me.

Whatever I wanted from poor Libby I couldn't explain what I was doing solely to gain it. We had the run of the house and pretended to be masters. For those few minutes the upstairs maid and the hobo boy were the Bennetts of Loon Lake.

Libby took my hand and showed me a storage room where F. W. Bennett kept his stock of outfits that he provided his guests as gifts: riding habits and boots, tennis flannels, bathing suits, a goddamn haberdashery.

I stood in front of a full-length mirror and took off my greens and put on a pair of tan tweed knickers with pleats, ribbed socks, brown-and-white saddle shoes, my size, a soft white shirt, and a white sweater with an argyle design of large gold and brown diamonds across my chest.

I was stunned by the magnificent youth that looked back at me from the mirror. All the scars and deeper marks of hard life were covered in fine fashion. The face, a bit gaunt but unlined, the hair I combed back hastily with my fingers. He made a passing aristocrat! Well, I thought, so a lot of the effect comes from the outside, doesn't it? I might be a Bennett son!

And then I felt again my child's pretense that those two gray sticks in Paterson were not really my parents but my kidnappers! Who knew whose child I was!

I dreamed of recognition from her from Clara. It was her nearness that made me so crazy, and bold with Libby. So feverish so happy.

And as for Bennett I thought, He is no more aware of me than of some unfortunate prowler mauled by the wild dogs. But here I am, wearing his clothes, wandering freely through his house. Here I am, Mr. Muck-a-muck, and you don't even know it!

Then Libby came back from the female supply store and she was wearing jodhpurs and a silk blouse and a riding helmet perched none too securely on her thick hair and she wobbled in a pair of shiny boots too wide in the shank for her thin legs.

"You look swell, Libby," I said. She turned around with little shaky steps and gave me all the dimensions. Her gray eyes shone, her mouth stretched in her tremulous overbitten smile. I danced her out of there down the corridor doing a fast fox trot full of swirls while I hummed the tune I had heard the night I came, "Exactly Like You," Libby laughing and worrying at the same time, telling me to hush, looking back over her shoulder, giggling, falling against me every other step, brushing my cheek with her lips. And the light lay like a track along the carpet and shone in golden stations of the open doors.

There being no sign of her in the main house I knew she was staying in the smaller lodge perhaps a hundred yards west, into the woods and halfway down the hill to the lake.

I think I must have spent some while calculating how to get there, figuring out a pretext and then a script for the conversation we would have. But one evening, during the staff meal, one of the woodfolk, a grandmotherly one, said to me, "That Penfield called. You're to go over to the cottage."

"Who, me? What for?"

"How should I know?" she said. "I'll be glad when you're gone and them with you."

I finished my meal as slowly as I could, feigning the attitude of the workingmen of dark green. I washed my tray and lit a cigarette and sauntered back to my room.

I latched the door and changed from my work clothes to the knickers and shirt and sweater and ribbed socks and saddle shoes. Poor Libby, all happiness drained like the color in her face when I told her I was keeping these things. Shouldn't she have known that the fellow who'd write in the guest book would do that? Anyway, she understood the firm basis of our relationship, that whatever trust she placed in me I would betray.

And as for Mr. Penfield I knew in my bones I didn't have anything to fear from him. He had a way of canceling himself out if you let him talk long enough.

I washed my face and combed my hair and got out of the staff house without being seen.

Already dark on the path, the first stars coming out. Joe drew a sharp breath and tried to calm himself. He was trembling. He had followed her, navigating by her star, and by that means had been sleeping in a bed and eating well and indulging his self-regard for several weeks. An edited view but fervently held.

In his mind, his feelings were enough. He didn't need intentions, plans, the specificity of hope. Presenting his heart was enough.

"Here he is—and look at him!" Penfield said at the door. He held a bottle of red wine in one hand and a glass in the other. "Come in, come in!"

It was a low-ceilinged cottage with a living room and kitchen and stone hearth all in one. I tried not to look at her she was sitting on the sofa Indian style wearing a robe of white satiny material and it had fallen open across her thighs. I tried not to look she was not looking at me but taking a mighty pull from her wineglass head up neck beautiful pulsing neck.

"Here he is, Clara—Joe of Paterson, the man I wanted you to meet." A glass was put in my hand.

"Miss Clara Lukaćs," he said.

Pointing me at a chair, he crossed his ankles and sank his bulk down on the floor at her feet.

They were both facing me and to my right and their left a fire was going in the fireplace. The light flared and dimmed on their faces as some kind of wavering attention, I thought, especially from her she had not asked to meet me how absurd to have thought that. I sensed some purpose not entirely complimentary in the summons. Yet

Penfield was smiling amiably indicating to me to drink and so I did, with the odd conviction that I had never tasted wine before. I had ridden the cars with the bums of three states worked with freaks and was wicked and shameless but in this moment it was my inexperience that shone.

What was the conversation? Mostly his, of course, the brilliant singsong of the failed poet, but how could I have been listening with the attention such beautiful words demanded, people from my world didn't talk with such embellishment such scrollwork. I had never before met someone who admitted to the profession of poet but believed it by the way he spoke. I kept my eyes on his face but it was her I looked at, this restless cat of inattention sitting quite still and staring into her wine careless of exposed limbs the inner thigh the rounded knee small cream cracked hummock of the underknees she sat quite still but her mind pacing from one wall to another, an expression on her small fair face of grief or petulance I couldn't tell. But how she felt was of overriding importance to me, how she felt!—then and every moment after—was my foremost concern, what I lived by. This was her quality and I think she was unconscious of it, that her presence occupied great moral space around her though she was surprisingly small, a small-boned slight thing with narrow shoulders. There was nothing stately about her except the alarming size of her moods. I studied her face with a fervent rush of recognition, a fair skin with a rouge of chapped cheeks, quick green eyes prominent upper lip everything framed in marcelled bleached blond hair I had friends playing as a child with such faces in Paterson I heard the fluent yowl of injustice from this face.

Mr. Penfield speaking of injustice explained how much more modest were his own rooms over the stables than this full cottage in the rustic log style. On the other hand he wrote well there he said in his way of negating his every point of view by obliging himself to express its opposite.

Then he recites some lines about the place, about Loon
Lake. The glass in one hand, the bottle in the other, he
sits with legs outstretched he is in his dirty sneakers with
no socks his tweed jacket with the elbow patches his
tennis shirt with the soft collar turned under on one side,
he produces a deep melodious voice for his lines not his
normal voice I was embarrassed by this sudden access to
performance but she was not. She paid attention to his
poetry as she had not to his conversation. But no audience was as responsive to Mr. Penfield's words as he was.
His red eyes grew large with a film of tears.

I augment my memory with the lines actually printed in
a private edition, the last of his three privately published
volumes all recording different times of his life in the
different places the same person. "The loons they heard
were the loons we hear today"—in his deep reader's
chant—"cries to distract the dying loons diving into the
cold black lake　　and diving back out again in a whorl
of clinging water　　clinging like importuning spirits
　　　　fingers shattering in spray　　feeling up the wing
along the rounded body of the　　　　thrillingly exerting
loon　　beaking a fish　　rising to the moon streamlined　　its loon eyes round and red."

And I, resonantly attuned to her, alive to the firelit
moment—somewhere I had gotten at great cost, with the
scars to show it, from such profound effort, the kind of
unceasing insistence on my life's rights that was only now
so exhausting in my release from it. As this absurd fat
drunkard sang his words they seemed the most beautiful I
had ever heard. But perhaps any words would have done.
I heard them and I didn't hear them, I had no idea he
had just written them I thought they were from some
book already done, I heard the feeling they inspired in
me, that I was living at last! That it was the way it should
be, I was feeling Penfield's immense careless generosity,
the boon of himself which granted me without argument
everything I was struggling for, all of it assumed in the
simple giving of words, so moving to this scruffy boy.

It was the moment of dangerous specification of everything I thought worth wanting. After the loon flew off whose red eyes were much like his own he cleared his throat and he poured wine all around although I'd barely sipped mine. He emptied the bottle on his turn and struggled to his feet for another bottle which he uncorked while continuing to speak and again he sat down with the new bottle as attached to his hand as the old.

I tried not to look at her. I saw the glance from under her brows toward the ceiling, the impatience, and then I began to feel the force of the occasion which was that somehow I was enlisted to help divert, distract or pacify Clara Lukaćs. That was the meaning of the self-dramatization of the man, that we were in some overburdened instant, with our backs to it, grounding our heels, digging in.

And then he was telling us about the war, of all things, a veteran, migod, would he bring out the poppies? But soon we were inside his images, listening like children, the mule-drawn caissons sinking in the mud, the troops in greatcoats and tin helmets riding the mules' backs, kicking their boots sharply against the mules' flanks, the bracing of backs on six-foot wheels, spokes like baseball bats tires of steel, each soldier alone and miserable inside his coat, charred trees beside the road the sky showing through city hall, gusts of acrid air blowing from the front, and here is Corporal Penfield riding the signal wagon, flag tubes strapped to his back like quivers, a helmet tilting over his eyes because the strap is too loose, and on his lap the crate covered with a khaki blanket shifts perceptibly, the pigeons whirring with each dull boom lighting the sky like lightning miles ahead.

He was dangling a medal. He had taken it from his pocket. He handed it to me. The colors of the ribbon had bled, there was thread and lint attached to it, but it was a Silver Star and it was his.

I leaned forward put it in her hand leaning forward over the bear rug between us, our hands grazed I felt the heat of her hand.

And there in our minds as we looked at the palpable

proof was Signal Corporal Penfield during the battle of the Somme dispatched urgently to semaphore the artillery to drop some heavy stuff on the encircling Huns.

"The field telephone didn't work, there wasn't even a damn pigeon left." He paused to wet his throat. "So I took the old semaphore flags and went up to the top of a hill where I could be seen, because even though it was night the star shells were like the Fourth of July and it was brighter than day. I could see out over no man's land. I sent my message"—here he lifted his arms, attached to the glass and bottle and did a half-hearted pantomime—"and a while later the artillery came in on target, and that's what I got the medal for."

"You're a hero," she said, smiling. She dropped the medal in his lap and then raised her glass to her lips.

"No, but, love, you haven't heard the end." He dropped his chin to his chest. "I was so terrified I didn't send the message I was supposed to. What I semaphored was the first verse of a poem."

"What?" I said.

" 'There was a time when meadow, grove, and stream, The earth, and every common sight,   To me did seem   Apparelled in celestial light, The glory and the freshness of a dream,' and so on," he said. "And a while later the shells came in on target. It was very strange."

She was laughing. "In the war—in the battle?"

"Surely you know it," he said. "The Intimations Ode? Didn't you have it in school?"

"But why?"

"I don't know why. Maybe I thought I was going to die. Maybe it seemed to me the only appropriate thing *to* say. Anyway, after I got the medal I wrote a letter to the Secretary of the Army returning it and telling him it was more properly William Wordsworth's."

"But it wasn't a medal for poetry," I said, and immediately felt like a fool.

"Apparently not, Joe of Paterson. Apparently not. I had to go for psychiatric tests. They pinned the medal on my bathrobe. They kept me under observation for ninety days in Nutley, New Jersey."

"Where?" she said, happily laughing. He looked up at her, victorious in her amusement. "Oh, Warren, you old fuck, where?" She threw back her head and laughed and laughed, I gazed at her throat, her neck, it was a moment in which I could look at all of her as she sat in her white satin robe, she bending forward now in her laughter, the robe unfolding like unfolding wings so that I could see her breasts.

Then I realized Penfield was looking at me, with his head lowered, with raised eyebrows, a characteristic expression, I knew at once, full of sadness, full of self-acknowledgment, and as she reached out and touched his head he too began to giggle, he was in love with her, and soon they were both laughing and I was laughing, but trying not to for some reason, feeling badly that I laughed, feeling ashamed.

I hadn't realized how drunk they were. A few moments later, in silence, she put her glass down and reached out, holding his head in her arms. He looked up at her, and behind her shingle of hair he kissed her, his hand with the bottle going up involuntarily, another semaphore, and I heard her sob, and then both of them were crying.

I tried to leave, but they wouldn't allow it. All at once they were very physical with me, placing themselves on either side of me and leading me back to the middle of the room. Penfield went to stoke up the fire. She led me to my chair and pressed my shoulders firmly with her small hands and then sat across from me and studied me solemnly. Until this moment her primary awareness had been of Penfield, she had not quite acknowledged me, as if one person at a time, and only one, could occupy her mind. She was always to be this way, intense and direct with whatever she fixed upon, and whatever the affront to those on the periphery. It was not snobbishness or anything like that—she was in fact reckless of her self-interest in a situation, and that I think was the center of her force and effect. She knew nothing about courtesy in the sense of not being subject to it. She blazed through her feelings and suffered the consequences.

I began to realize as we talked that she was no older than I was. I was stunned—I was not yet twenty— I equated power and position in the world with age.

"You live here?" she said. "How do you stand it?" I rubbed my palms on my knickers. I looked with alarm at Warren Penfield, who said, "Clara, he's my surprise for you," and came back to his place on the floor.

She had a throaty voice with a scratched quality. Her diction was of the street. "Whats 'at mean!" She gazed at me, her eyes widening, and I was certain, as if a chasm were opening around me, that she was as fraudulent in this place as I was. I drank off my wine.

"You remember the night you heard the dogs?" the poet said to her, and leaned forward to refill my glass. "Joe here is taking each day as it comes—like you, Clara."

I saw realization light her eyes. She went to the fire and sat down before it with her back to us. I don't remember much of what happened after that. I drank more than I should have. The fire looming her shadow across the low-ceilinged room. Later we heard the rain falling, a heavy rain that seemed to do something to the draught. Wood smoke came into the room on gusts. At this point we were all standing, I had removed my shirt, and she was tracing the scars on my chest and arms and neck with her fingertips.

I could smell her, the soap she used, the gel of her hair. The firelight flared on our faces as if we were standing with the poet in his war.

"He told me it was a deer, that they took a deer," she said. "That was a lie."

"Yes," Penfield said, watching her fingers.

"What class," Clara said. Tears were suddenly coming down her cheeks.

"I could help you leave," Penfield said. His eyes closed and he began moving his head from side to side like someone in mourning. "I can get you out of here. We can leave together." His sentences became a hum, a soft keening, as if he were listening to some private elegy and had no hope of an answer from her.

"That son of a bitch," she said with the tears streaming. "I wouldn't give him the satisfaction."

Certain contracts having quietly been made in mountains certified convicts having mislaid their companions.

I direct you eight hundred Mercator miles west to the autobody works on the flat landscape.   Dawn whitening the frost on the corrugated shed roofs the smokeless stacks the endless chain-link fence the first trolley of the morning down Division Street discharges workers in caps and open jackets but not workers.   The pickets roused from their sleep huddled by steel-drum fires the cops awakened in their cars rubbing their misted windshields the second trolley of the morning tolls down Division Street discharges workers or workers at first glance but somehow not resembling the strikers grouping uneasily in front of the main gates of the autobody works.   The cops make calls from phoneboxes on the corners.   The third trolley of the morning grinding its flanged wheels on Division Street stopping the arrivals stepping down now seen in the light their expressions of newly purchased loyalty appearing as an unaccustomed cause in their shrewd appraising eyes the insignia of their dereliction, jackets with pockets of pints shoes tied around with rope, medals of filth, mercenaries with callused fingers discovering the cobblestones pried so easily by ones and twos and hefted as many as until the tracks of the trolleys of Division Street stand up from unpaved beds.   Open trucks arrive filled with the faces not of workers.   This army can take the city apart and put it back together if it so wishes or perhaps wrap the electrified lines stringing the utility poles overhead around each individual striker until he may go self-powered into eternity.

Cops start patrol-car engines drive quietly away.   Certain black sedans now arrive between arrivals of the crowded streetcars and trucks some men in overcoats appearing among the seeming workers resembling only slightly now the pickets with the eyes of lepers staring at them no saints present on this wet gray morning to kiss them, so numerous now they do not even have to look at whom they will face when they walk over them into the plant and throw the switches.   And primly planning the action deploying forces is a slim and swarthy man in overcoat and pearl-gray fedora a dark-eyed man short but very well put together friend of industrialists, businessman who keeps his word and capable of a gracious gesture under the right conditions.   Only now, as with a gloved hand he beckons one of the strikers an aged man with white hair and rounded shoulders who has called out brothers don't do this to your brothers to meet him between the lines alone in no man's land does a small snapshot of rage light his brain.   He impassively demonstrates the function of the cobblestone a sudden event on the workingman's skull who has met him surprised now at the red routes of death mapped on his forehead turning to share this intelligence with his brothers hand lifted too late as the signal for the engagement to begin.

And then the life quickened, suddenly the people in green were scurrying about purposefully, there even seemed to be more of them, and I knew without being told that the master of Loon Lake, Mr. F. W. Bennett, was in place.

One morning I was mucking out the stables. Two horses were made ready for riding. The wide doors swung open admitting a great flood of light, the horses were led out, and I caught a glimpse of her in jodhpurs, velvet riding jacket, she was fixing the strap of her riding helmet. The doors closed. I climbed over the stall gate and ran to a window. A bay flank and a shiny brown boot moved through my field of vision. I heard a man's voice, a quiet word of encouragement, and then she, on her lighter mount, passed my eyes, the boot not quite secure in the stirrup.

I ran to the doors and put my eyes to the crack: the back and head of white hair were all I could see of Bennett before Clara's figure loomed up on her fat-assed horse, she didn't roll with its footfalls but took each one bumping, her black riding helmet slightly askew.

And then horses and riders passed behind some trees and were gone.

I raked shit.

In the evening I went to Mr. Penfield's rooms and we listened to the scraps of dance music carried from the main house on the wind.

"I suppose I'll be out of here tomorrow," I said.

"What?" He had been staring into his wineglass.

"When it comes to his attention."

"You can't be sure, Joe of Paterson. I have made a great study of the very rich. The one way they are accessible is through their whim." He swallowed some wine. "Yes. I have not told you this, but six or seven years ago when I came up here at night along the track, as you did, I knew where I was going. I had traced Frank Bennett to Loon Lake and I intended to kill him."

"I have the idea myself," I said. He didn't seem to hear me.

"Mr. Bennett was amused. I was invited to remain on the grounds and write my poetry. Yes. And now you see me."

"I do," I said. "I see you."

"I know what you think. You think living this way year after year and not going anywhere, not doing anything, I have lost my perspective. It's true! It's true. So that everything that happens, every, oh God"—his eyes go heavenward, he swallows some wine—"small thing, is monumentally significant. I know! I lie in wait like a bullfrog lying in wait for whatever comes along for his tongue to stick to. Yes. That's the only part of me that moves, my tongue."

He dropped his chin on his chest and stared at me with his bleary red eyes. "You want to hear me croak?"

"What?"

He emitted the sound of a bullfrog, never had I heard such a blat of self-disgust I didn't want to. It was not one night like this but several I remember, sitting in his living room over the stables, piles of books on the floor, a desk covered with papers, composition notebooks the kind I used in school, clumps of dust on the floors, ashtrays filled to overflowing, ashes on the carpet, on the window seat, he drifts back and forth back and forth between the wine bottles and the window, and all the while Miss Clara Lukaćs dances rides swims dines in the provinces of Loon Lake, mysteriously advanced now to the rank of its mistress.

"I don't think it's a small thing," I said. "I think it is monumentally significant."

"Yes," he says, and he pulls his chair closer to mine, "this is not the first acquaintance. And it has nothing to do with who I am or the way I look, it's always the same—the immediate recognition I have for her when she appears, and the ease with which she comes to me whatever circumstances I'm in, whatever I've become. Because I have no particular appeal to women and I never have, except to this woman, and so the recognition must be mutual and it pushes us toward each other even though we don't talk the same language. And so, you see, now again, even though I'm indisputably fatter and more ridiculous as a figure of love than I ever was. And even though" his eyes brimmed—"she is faithful to nothing but her own life."

I didn't know what he was talking about.

He struggled out of his chair and ran to his bookshelves, and not finding what he wanted, he disappeared into a closet from which came the sounds of crashing and falling things.

He stumbled out with a book in his hand. He blew the dust off. "I want you to have this," he said, "my first published work, my first thin volume of verse"—he smiled unsmiled—"*The Flowers of the Sangre de Cristo.*" He did not hand me the book but examined it closely. "I printed it on a hand press and bound it myself in Nutley. It was my project for recovery, you see. The signatures in this one are out of order. But no matter, no matter."

He pressed the volume on me now and looked in my eyes as if hoping to see the wisdom that would flow into them from the book.

"Just a minute," he said. He ran back into the closet

there was a terrible crash I jumped up but he came out coughing in a cloud of chalky dust waving his second published work. "This one too," he said, slamming the closet door. He swallowed a great draught of wine and slumped back in his chair wheezing from the exertion.

I held the two slim volumes, the second included a Japanese woodprint as frontispiece. "Don't read them now, don't ask me to watch you as you read them," he said.

I held the books, I could not help granting him the authority he craved as profound commentator on his own life—he was an author! Never mind that he published his books himself, I was impressed, nobody I ever knew had written a book. I held them in my hand.

Apart from everything else and despite the shadows of the wishes in my mind the vaguest shadows of the implementation of the wishes, I am moved to be so set up in the world with such a distinguished friend. I know he is a posturing drunk, how could I not recognize the type, but he has made me his friend, this poet, and I have a presence in the world.

He tells me his one remaining belief.

"Who are you to doubt it," he says angrily, "a follower of trains in the night!"

I don't doubt it I don't. I have listened to his life, heard it accounted indulged improved incanted and I believe it all. It is a life that goes past grief and sorrow into a realm, like the life of a famous gangster or an explorer, where sudden death is the ordinary condition. And somehow I'm invited to engage my instinct not to share his suffering but to marvel at it, a life farcically set in the path of historical and natural disaster it comes to me as entertainment—

The war before the war before the war
Before the rise of the Meiji emperor
Before the black ships—

his great accomplishment was his own private being the grandness and the depth of his failed affections each of

his representations of himself at the critical moments of
his past contributed to the finished man before me

Child Bride in a Zen Garden by Warren Penfield
In a poem of plum blossoms and boats poled down
     a river
Behind a garden wall the sun lighting its pediment
     of red tile
A fourteen-year-old girl aches for her husband.
One bird whistles in the foliage of a tree
     that stands on crutches.
Small things are cherished, a comb a hand mirror
a golden carp in a pool eight inches deep.
Curved wooden footbridges of great age
     connect the banks of ponds.
But everywhere we know on the map are mountains
with vertical faces, and thunderous waterfalls,
escutcheons of burning houses, and suicidal armies,
history clattering in contradistinction
to the sunlight melting itself in the bamboo grove.

Oh the fifty-three stations of the Tokaido.
On the embankment above the rice paddy
travelers crouch under slants of rain.
Messengers run with their breechcloths flapping.
Merchants beat their donkeys. Boats with squared sails
make directly for shore. Paper lanterns
slide down the waves.
Rain like the hammers of sculptors
works the curved slopes of water.
When the sky clears at sunset fifty-three
prefecture officials arrive in the stations of the Tokaido.
Fifty-three women are prepared for them.
Sunlit legends will be made tonight.
Beans are picked from the gardens, plump fowl
slaughtered, and in castles above the road

unemployed warriors duel the firelight.
They weep they curse they raise wine cups to honor.
Saints of the wrong religion go unrecognized
in the darkness beyond the lighted windows of the inns.
And at the end of the Tokaido
at the top of an inaccessible mountain
the emperor himself, a self-imperator,
a self impersonating a self in splendor
sits in his empty room, its walls painted with long-legged
        waterbirds,
its floor cushioned with ministers lying face down
        attending him.
The emperor is lacquered, his sword is set with suns,
while in another room
doctors dispute the meaning of his stool.

Oh compact foreign devils flesh of rice
Everywhere we are smaller than the landscape.
I sit on the wood promenade overlooking my garden
and I am the real emperor. The small twisted tree
is very old and has a name. The rocks, like islands
in the sea of raked gravel, have names. The gravel waves
break upon the rocks.
A girl with suncast eyes cries on the other side
        of the ancient wall.
I cross the gravel sea and spy on her through the gate.
Her blue-black hair is undressed, like a child's.
She sits on a bed of moss,
her bowed neck as long as a lady's of the court.
The words rise and fall in my throat
growling and humming and making tunes.
I am breaking the laws of my religion.
She is alert now to the aviary of our language
and stares at me with her wet mournful eyes,
the track of one tear surmounting the pout of her lip
and disappearing in the corner of her mouth.
I speak and she shifts to her knees,
places her hands flat upon her thighs.

The soles of her feet are pale. She listens.
She is as still as the fieldmouse
in the talons of the hawk.

Oh the fifty-three stages of the Tokaido!
The old monk and the girl
clamber up the rock path. Along the path
falls a stream so vertically on rocks that the water,
broken into millions of drops,
bounces pachinko pachinko like pellets of steel.
We find a ledge overlooking the ocean.
I aspire to goodness. I aspire
to the endless serenity of the realized Buddha.
In the sun on the rock ledge I remove her clothing.
I remove my clothing she averts her eyes.
We hunker in the hairless sallow integument of our kind.
Her haunches are small and muscular.
Her thighs are slender.
Her backbone is as ordered as the stones of a Zen garden.
I see reflected in the polished gray rock under her
the entrance to her life. It is like the etching of a fig.
Raising my hand in the gesture of tenderness,
I see her chin lift in trust,
and at that moment I fling myself at her
and she falls into the sea.
She falls in a slow spiral, wobbling like a spent arrow.
I feel her heart beating in my chest.
I feel all she is, her flesh and bone,
her terror in the sky.

The field of his accomplishment was his own private being, the grandness and depth of his failed affections. Each of his representations of himself at the critical moments of this past contributed to the finished man before me. He proved everything by his self-deprecation, his sighs, his lachrymose pauses, his prodigious thirst for wine, and he proved it in the scene or two with Clara, when, at an hour he somehow always knew, he would get me to help him over to her cottage not five minutes since she had come in herself, her make-up and hair and dress all showing the use of the evening, and she in some sort of sodden rage. What excited Mr. Penfield was the idea of rescue. He wanted to save her, take her away, carry her off. It was the pulsating center of his passion. And she seemed now not to understand, as if they spoke different languages, hers being Realism.

"War-rin," she would say, "do I have to spell it out?"

"Oh God," he'd cry, lifting his eyes, "oh God who made this girl, give her to me this time to hold, let me sink into the complacencies of fulfilled love, let us lose our memories together and let me die from the ordinary insubstantial results of having lived!"

"Goddamnit," Clara shouted, and then, appealing to me, the audience, a role I embraced as I would any she chose, "what does he want from me? Oh Jesus! Joe," she'd say when, invariably, he broke down, "why did you bring him? Take him home. Get this fucking drunk out of here."

Another night or the one after, I went over to her cottage alone. I supposed it was midnight. No light on. It didn't matter. I sat in the shadow of her porch and I folded my arms and waited. A strong wind blowing over the mountains and sounding in the trees around the cottage. The trunks of the pine trees swayed and creaked. I sat with my back to the door and drew up my knees. I might be hearing her in her rut, singing somewhere with the wind going past an open window. That was all right. That was all right. If the poet could have her on her terms and the rich man on his, I could have her on mine. My revelation. Maybe she traveled like a princess on a private train, maybe poets thought they recognized her, but I knew her accent, she was an Eastern industrial child, she had come off streets like my streets she was born of the infinite class of nameless workers my very own exclusive class. Jesus, I had pressed against girls like her in the hallways, I had bent them backward on the banister, I had pulled their hair I had lifted their skirts I had rubbed them till they creamed through their underpants.

I reached over my head and tried the doorknob. Open. I decided to wait for her in comfort. I turned on a light. The wood smoke lay under the low ceiling. The hearth was cold. I put in some paper and kindling and got a fire going and stood with my back to the fire.

The green livery had as little regard for her as they did for Penfield. The place was a mess. I saw traces of our first party. Dirty dishes in the little alcove kitchen. Not that she'd care. I looked in her bedroom. Her clothes everywhere, stockings twisted and curled like strips of bacon, step-ins in two perfect circles on the floor as if disengaged in a meditative moment, or flung across a lampshade as if drop-kicked.

Poor Mr. Penfield. I knew what he couldn't possibly know. I knew what made his sympathies obsolete. Clara and Bennett had had breakfast together on the morning after he arrived. I managed to be raking leaves at the foot of the terrace wall under their line of sight. It was a bright windy morning and the clouds actually were below us over the lake and drifting through the trees on the mountains. "I think clouds should stay in the sky where they belong," Clara said, "don't you?" And Bennett had laughed.

Clara held a relentless view of the world. There were no visible principles. Every one of her moods and feelings was intense and true to itself—if not to the one before or the one after. She lightened and darkened like the times of the day.

I smoked a cigarette from the monogrammed cigarette box. Clearly, in my aspiration it was FWB I would have to contend with. FWB, the man who was paying for everything. Conceivably this gave him an advantage.

I mashed out the cigarette, stretched out on my back before the fire, put my hands under my head and closed my eyes.

I slept in that position for several hours. I remember coming awake with the fire out and sunlight glowing on the windows. The silhouettes of branches and leaves wavered on the log wall and a reddish gold light filled the room. I heard the sound of an airplane. It grew louder and then with a rise in pitch it receded and grew faint. I lay there and it got louder again and finally so close and thunderous that the cups rattled in the sink. Then the sound receded once more, the pitch of the engine rising. I went to the window: a single-engine plane with pontoons was banking over the mountain on the other side of the lake. I watched it, a seaplane with a cowled engine and an overhead wing. As it banked, its dimensions flared and I saw a smartly painted green-and-white craft zooming over the water and then lifting its nose and banking off again, the sun flashing on its wings. It was very beautiful to see. Again it was coming around. I ran outside. I watched several runs, each one was different in speed or angle of descent, it looked as if the pilot was practicing or doing tests. You didn't often see airplanes this close.

And then as the show continued here was Clara Lukács coming through the woods from the main house. She wore a white evening gown. She carried her shoes in her hand. She peered up through the trees, she turned, she walked backward, she stopped, she stood on her toes. She moved through patches of light and shade, and reaching the little clearing in front of the cabin, she took me in with a glance and turned to see the plane in its run.

It was very low this time. It drifted down the length of the lake and then dropped below the tree line.

"Are *you* here?" Clara said. She passed into the house and I followed. She stood in the middle of the room with her hands on her hips, and realizing she still held her shoes, she flung them away. At this moment the phone rang. It was in the bedroom and she ran in as if she was going to attack it.

"What!" I heard her shout by way of greeting. A pause. "Yeah, well, I wouldn't count on it!" she said and slammed the phone down.

I waited a minute. When she didn't come out, I moved to the doorway. She was sitting on the edge of her bed in some distraction slipping off one shoulder strap, then the other, shrugging her gown to her waist. Losing all volition, she dropped her hands in her lap and sat hunched over without glamour or grace. Her hair was matted and tears streamed down her cheeks.

She had no degrees of response, she lived hard, and the effect of her crying on my heart was calamitous. Her eyes were swollen almost immediately, her breasts were wet with her tears. Her looks collapsed as if they were a pretense.

"Hey," I said. "Come on. Come on."

After a while she stood up and let the gown fall to her ankles. She had nothing on underneath. She was big-breasted for such a thin narrow-shouldered girl. She stepped out of the gown and went into the bathroom and a moment later I heard the shower running. Her behind was small and firm, if a bit on the flat side. The prominence of her backbone made me smile. It made me think of the scrawny backs on sunburned little girls who came to the carnival in their bathing suits and convened at the cotton candy.

While she showered I found a percolator and put up some coffee. She came out wrapped in a white bath towel with a big maroon *FWB* monogrammed on the front. She accepted a mug of coffee and sat on the couch with her legs folded under her and held the mug with both hands as if for warmth. She had washed her hair, which lay about her head in wet curls, she was no longer crying but the exercise had left her eyes glistening and as she looked at me I wondered how I could have found anything to criticize. I had never in my life seen a woman more beautiful.

"This place is getting on my nerves," she said. "How do I get out of here?"

"I'll take care of it, leave it to me," I said without a moment's hesitation. Without a moment's hesitation. She glanced at me as she sipped her coffee. I waited for my justice. I wondered if I had taken her too literally if she would laugh now crack my heart with her laughter. But she said nothing and seemed satisfied enough by my assurance. Sun filled the room. She put her cup on the floor and curled up on the sofa with her back to me.

Drops of water glittered in her hair. After a while I realized she had gone to sleep.

I ran out of there determined not to be amazed. I should concentrate on what I was going to do next. Amazement would set me back. I wanted to sing, I was exhilarated to madness. But the way to bring this off was to think of my brazen hopes as reasonable and myself as a calm practical person matter-of-factly making a life for himself that was no more than he deserved.

Then Bennett himself was suddenly in full force in my life like a storm that had arrived.

I found myself that same morning with three or four of the groundkeepers, each of us with a pick or shovel on our shoulders, we were hurrying to a site in the woods off the main bridle path. Bennett was waiting. He was standing on a hill of some sort. His horse was tethered to a tree along the trail. "Come up here," he called.

We climbed up the face of an enormous boulder imbedded in the ground. "I've always wondered about this," he said. "I want it exposed."

The foreman of us, an older man long in the Bennett service, took off his cap and scratched his head. "You want us to dig this rock up?" he asked.

"Dig around it," Bennett said. "You see here? This is the top of it, we're standing on top of it. That's what this rise is. I want the whole thing uncovered, I don't know why it's here."

The workmen had trouble believing what he wanted. Bennett didn't get mad. Instead, he took one of the picks and started going at it himself. "You see?" he called out, breathing hard between swings of the pick. "Work it away, like this. You see that, how it extends? Goes all the way over here."

"Here, Mr. Bennett," the foreman said. "Don't you be doing that. You, you," he said to us. "Get to work."

So we started digging out a boulder that might be the size of a dirigible. Bennett watched each of us to see that we understood.

"That's the way," he said. "That's what I want."

He was sturdy and vigorous. Moved around a lot. A short wide-shouldered man with a large head. His hair was white but very full and combed as I combed mine, to a pompadour. He was well tanned. Blue eyes. A handsome blunt-faced old bastard in a riding outfit.

I had expected someone older, more restrained.

He climbed down off the rise and for several minutes crashed around in the woods nearby to see if he could find another rock like it. "You see," he shouted, "it's the only one. Damnedest thing!" he called out as if we were all colleagues on some archaeological expedition.

Then he mounted his horse and rode off in the direction of the stables. As soon as he was out of sight the foreman leaned on his shovel, took off his cap and wiped his forehead with the back of his hand. "Jesus Mary and Joseph," he said.

We all sat down on the boulder.

But a while later two more diggers came along flushed from their dens, and soon there were a half-dozen of us standing shirtless in the woods swinging our picks and shovels at this mountainous stone.

It was interesting to me how the impulse of the man transformed into the hard work of the rest of us. By our digging we suggested something really important was going on, someone passing by would look at us and think it was serious—we ourselves were proof of the seriousness of the thing.

I had expected not to like F. W. Bennett. But he was insane. How could I resist that? There was this manic energy of his, a mad light in his eye. He was free! That was what free men were like, they shone their freedom over everyone.

I didn't want to think what he did with Clara. I could not dream that she could matter to him in any way at all that I would recognize. I swung my pick. All the intelligence I had of him, from his house and his lands and his train and his resident poets, had not prepared me for the impersonal force of him, the frightening freedom of him.

In the late afternoon we knocked off work, having unearthed the boulder to its southern polar slope. It sat now in an enormous trench at the bottom of which were packed several other stones. It looked as if it weighed several tons. On the way back we stopped in front of the main house to report these findings. Bennett stood on his front porch. He was very pleased. "We'll take it as far down as it goes, boys," he said. "And tomorrow we'll look for markings. I want to see if it has markings."

Apparently as he gazed at these dirty and sweat-stained workmen he saw in the face of one something that might have been disbelief.

"You, Joe," he said to me, "you think it's just a rock, don't you?"

I was so stunned that he knew my name I didn't know what to say.

"Come inside. I want you to see something." He turned and went in the house.

Someone reached over and took the pick from my shoulder. I heard a snicker. I followed F. W. Bennett into his front hall and went past the stairway of halved logs to the sunken living room.

There was a shimmering light on the ceiling, a reflection of the lake. But the floor was in shadow. In one corner, on a table, was a book with line drawings of primitive stone monuments: in all cases one large boulder rested on three or four smaller ones.

"You see?" he said. "I'm not as crazy as you think. They put down these megaliths, or dolmens, for their fallen chiefs."

He strode around the room lecturing me on the burial practices of ancient Indian tribes of New England. He compared them to the ancient burial practices of the Western desert tribes. Indoors he seemed older. He was vigorous and moved constantly but his voice was somewhat hoarse, it suggested age.

I stood in my filthy dark greens wondering how I was going to get out of there.

A maid came in holding a phone on a long cord. She brought it to his side and held it for him on her palm while he picked up the receiver. "Yes?" He continued to move about, and the maid in her light green uniform followed him dutifully where he went, dealing with the cord so that it wouldn't snag on the furniture. He was getting information. He asked short questions—How many? What time?—and listened to lengthy answers. I looked out the bay wall of windows. The late afternoon shadows made the lake a brilliant dark blue water.

On the terrace a woman was arranging flowers in a vase. I realized I was looking at Lucinda Bailey Bennett, the aviatrix. The small shock of seeing someone famous.

"You don't know how to work cameras, by any chance?"

The phone was gone. Bennett was talking to me.

"I've got all this equipment here but I can't get the hang of it myself," he said. "I want to take proper pictures of the excavation and send them out to see if I'm right."

"I don't know anything about cameras," I said.

"I thought you were smart . . . Well," he said, "I wanted to take a look at you, anyway, to see if you belong with me on a permanent basis. What's *your* opinion?"

"You mean a job?" I said.

"That's what I mean. You think you ought to be hired?"

I swallowed. "No," I said.

"No?" He seemed amused.

"I couldn't live here," I said. "It's not for me."

He laughed out loud. "You seemed to have adapted

well enough. From what I understand you've made the place your own."

Something outside had caught his eye. He stepped onto the terrace, closing the glass doors behind him, and stood calling down the hill to somebody at the boathouse.

My muscles were tight and my hands clenched. I tried to loosen up.

Mrs. Bennett glanced through the window to where I was and said something to her husband. He turned to her smiling and said something back and she looked again in at me briefly, a half smile on her face. She was a very elegant, honest-looking lady, very well composed, with brown hair cut short, no make-up or anything like that, she wore a loose sweater and a longish skirt and low-heeled shoes. I thought you would not be able to tell, if you didn't know, that this slim handsome woman with her flowers knew how to fly the hell out of airplanes.

And then it came to me he was telling her who the boy inside was. The one and only Joe of Paterson. She was so elegant I realized that what I had written in anger and pride was from another point of view pathetic. I felt betrayed, like a child who gives out his most precious secret and hears it laughed about.

I turned to leave. I thought how powerful this Bennett was if I could be made to feel so bad from just a moment or two of his attention.

"Just a minute, Joe," he called. "I'm not finished with you."

He went past me into the front hall and then down the corridor of the other wing of the house. He opened a door and beckoned to me.

A large room filled with books, cabinets with silver cups, photographs of Mrs. Bennett standing in front of airplanes, Mr. Bennett in a railroad engineer's cap waving from the controls of a steam locomotive, photographs of cars and horses and presidents and governors and film stars. There were globes on stands and big dictionaries on lecterns, a ticker-tape machine under glass—a whole life of glory was in this room.

Bennett sat down behind his desk and took a manila folder out of a drawer and studied the papers in it for several minutes while I stood before him.

Without looking up, he said, "Are your injuries healed?"

"I suppose."

"Have you been in touch with your parents?"

"My parents?"

"They signed a waiver," he said, removing a document from the folder. "You mean you haven't talked to them? I am not at fault for the injuries you incurred on my property. They received two hundred and fifty dollars."

"How do you know my parents?"

"We looked through your billfold. You might have been on your way out."

I was too stunned to speak.

"They haven't called or written to see how you're getting along?" He shoved a paper along the desk and I saw at the bottom the shaky signature of my father. "I'm not lying to you," Bennett said. "By rights that's your money."

I shook my head.

"You don't want to work for me. Fine. You can go home and if you're smart you can use that money to make money. Buy something and sell it for profit. Anything, it doesn't matter. Some of the great fortunes in this country were built from less."

I pictured my father in the kitchen, coming to terms with this legal paper that had to be signed. Finding my school pen somewhere in a drawer and the bottle with Waterman's ink. Testing the penpoint on the oilcloth that covered the table and then rubbing the ink off with his thumb before it dried. My mother standing at the sink, washing the dishes, disguising the moment of the waiver in their lives as one more ordinary moment.

"No," I said. "It's theirs."

"I'll tell you," Bennett said. "I always respect a man's decision. Never try to argue him out of it. You're not staying here and you're not going home. That leaves you back on the road, doesn't it? Back on the bum. Well, I say why not, if that's what you want. But be sure you can handle it. Just be sure you've got the guts. So that if you have to steal or take a sap to someone's head for a meal, you'll be able to. Every kind of life has its demands, its tests. Can I do this? Can I live with the consequences of what I'm doing? If you can't answer yes, you're in a life that's too much for you. Then you drop down a notch. If you can't steal and you can't sap someone on the head when you have to, you join the line at the flophouse. You get on the bread line. If you can't muscle your way into the bread line, you sit at the curb and hold out your hand. You're a beggar. If you can't whine and wheedle and beg your cup of coffee, if you can't take the billy on the bottoms of your feet—why, I say be a poet. Yes"—he laughed at the thought—"like old Penfield, find your level. Get in, get into the place that's your nature, whether it's running a corporation or picking daisies in a field, get in there and live to it, live to the fullness of it, become what you are, and I'll say to you, you've done more than most men. Most men—and let me tell you, I know men— most of them don't ever do that. They'll work at a job and not know why. They'll marry a woman and not know why. They'll go to their graves and not know why."

He was standing at the window gazing out with his hands behind his back, gently slapping the back of one hand into the palm of the other. "I've never understood it, but there it is. I've never understood how a man could give up his life, give it up, moment by moment, even as he lives it, give it up from the second he's born. But there it is. Bow his head. Agree. Go along. Do what everyone's doing. Let it leach away. Sign it away. Drink it away. Sleep it away."

He was standing at the window meditating, eclipsing the window light so that the dark bulk of him was apparent. He was stocky and short-legged with a large head, like a mountain troll. "Well," he said, "you're brash enough. Where are you going?"

"I don't know. As far as I can get."

He came back to his desk and wrote something on a piece of paper. "You happen to need something—this is a private number, not to be given out, you understand?"

He folded the paper and handed it to me. He gave me a quick glance, one eyebrow arching over the lighted eye of shrewdness. "But don't leave until I've got my dolmen," he said, turning and picking up his telephone.

The first chance I had I hurried to Penfield's. He was the only one who could help me with Clara's escape. That was his word, escape. Clara would leave because she was dislodged by the returning wife, Clara would leave because with unforgivable haste she'd been removed from the cozy confidences of Loon Lake's master bedroom. But it wouldn't do to tell him that. He thought he was in torment for her sake. He brooded about rescuing her. That's the way poets are, I said to myself. They see what no one else can see, and what is clear to everyone else they don't see.

I found him in bed. His breath rasped. His skin was a strange pink-gray color and it shone in a glaze of perspiration. He stared at me mournfully from his pillows, his blue and bloodshot eyes swimming in helplessness.

Oh God. That was all I needed.

I went out and found Libby in the staff house.

"I'll have nothing to do with you," she said.

"It's not me, Libby. It's Mr. Penfield. Something's wrong with him. I think he needs a doctor."

She looked at me with suspicion. She went ahead of me to the stables and ran up the stairs to keep as much distance between us as she could.

She took one look at the poet and without troubling to remove herself from his hearing said, "There's nothing wrong with him, he just likes to carry on."

"What do you know, Libby?" he cried out, stung.

"I know what a hollow leg is," she said. "Look at this place, it's enough to make anyone sick."

"Get out, get out!" Penfield shouted. "Will everyone torture me? Am I to die with the scorn of servants in my ears?"

She ignored him and with a great flurry went into action, picking up papers books dirty socks.

"Go away," he shouted. "Don't touch a thing, damnit, you're disrupting everything!"

She straightened his bedcovers and plumped up his pillows while he shouted at her to leave him alone.

Furious with both of us, she marched out.

"Joe, there's a bottle of wine under the window seat," Mr. Penfield said.

I wondered what was wrong with me to be so gullible to the claims of this man. He lived here at Loon Lake sloshing in self-pity, the best aspect of him, his gift for poetry, put to the use of unsound notions. Obviously this was the solution of his life. I couldn't change that if I tried. Nobody could.

I handed him the bottle and a glass. He sat up.

"Mr. Penfield, I've got to tell you something," I said, pulling a chair to his bedside. "But I need some information first. Who is Clara? Who were those people who came with her on the train?"

"Tommy Crapo," he said.

"Who?"

"Tommy Crapo. The industrial consultant." He drank off a half-glass of wine. "Don't you read the newspapers? Don't you look at the tabloids? Tommy Crapo who has his picture taken on night-club banquettes with beautiful women."

Color was coming back to his face. He emptied the glass and lay back on his pillows.

"Is he in the rackets?"

"Mr. Crapo is a specialist in labor relations. Yes. I think that's a fair description."

"Does he work for Bennett? Does he knock heads for Bennett?"

He stared at the ceiling. A moment passed. "Why do you ask? You think I should get Miss Lukács away from here, don't you?"

"Well, she's ready."

"What?" He was not used to being taken at his word. He was not equipped for action.

"Miss Lukács is ready to get out of here," I said.

"What?"

"She's ready to make her escape."

I have committed many sins in my life. This precise sin—the sin against poets—is without absolution.

He was out of bed and struggling into a worn maroon robe that had a few tassels left on the belt. I could hear each breath he took. He got on his knees to look under the bed for his slippers. He found them, stood, stepped into them, and then went slapping across the floor, back and forth from one corner of his apartment to another without purpose or intent but busy with agitation.

I sat him down in his reading chair and brought him a cigarette and lit it for him, he held it between thumb and forefinger, his hand shaking.

"What did she say?" he asked.

"She wants me to get her away."

"You?"

"She thinks if you leave together, you'll be too easy to follow. Like a hot car."

"What?"

"Crapo doesn't know me from Adam."

"Crapo is back?"

"He's on his way, Mr. Penfield."

"I see. I see."

"Miss Lukács says once she's safe she can get in touch with you."

"She said that?"

"I've worked out a plan but I need money and I need a car."

"Yes, yes, so that's the way it happens. I see. I see." He was not fooled, he was not a fool, the large protuberant eyes stared through me. "Yes, yes. To be absolutely realistic I'm not in the picture. That's all right, it's just, I'm reconciled. The two young ones. Yes."

He kept talking this way.

I had the uncanny feeling that he was translating what I told him into another language. Yet I could hear everything he said. He rose, he seemed to gain strength, he strode back and forth from the window to the door. "Yes, of course, there is more than I knew. Yes. I want this for her. It's just. I put my faith in you, Joe. Yes, take her away from here. Two young people! It's right. Yes, it's the only way."

"I'll need money and a car," I said.

"Of course. Leave it to me. I'll help you. I'll get you both out. You'll see, you'll see. I have resources. Yes. You'll find Warren Penfield comes through. I have resources. I have allies."

He seemed joyful. He clapped his hands together and glanced heavenward to express his joy. In this moment he would rather have died than reveal his anguish.

As I was leaving he stood at the door and pulled back the sleeve of his robe. "Look here, Joe," he said. He held up his right arm. "The sign of the wild dog! Right?" He gave me a wan but demonstrably brave smile. I had to smile back. I rolled up my sleeve and showed my arm.

"That's right," he said. "You know what two men do who share the sign of the wild dog?" He touched his forearm to mine so that they crossed. "That's right," he said in a husky voice. "My pain is your pain. My life is your life."

Data linkage escape this is not an emergency
Come with me compound with me

A tulip cups the sun quietly in its color
Dixie cups hold chocolate and vanilla
Before the war after the war or
After the war before the war
A man sells me a Dixie cup for a nickel in a dark
candy store.   The boy stands on the sidewalk in the
sun   licking the face of Joan Crawford free of ice
cream.   A boy enjoys ice cream from a wooden spoon
in the sun before the war in front of the candy store on
the corner while he waits for the light to change.   At
this moment several things happen.   A horse pulling
the wagon of a peddler of vegetables trots by smartly gold-
en balls of dung dropping from the base of its arched
tail.   Then there was a whirring in my ears and over
the top of Paterson Grade School Three a monumental
dirigible nosed into view looming so low I could see the
seams of its paneled silver skin and human shadows on the
windows of its gondola.   It was not sailing straight
through its bow but shouldering the wind shuddering dip-
ping and rising in its sea of air.   It soared over the
roof of a tenement and disappeared.   At the same time
the traffic light turned green and I crossed from sun to
shade noting that the not unpleasant odor of fresh horse
manure abruptly ceased with the change of tempera-
ture.   In front of the shoe repair on Mechanic Street at
the sidewalk's edge between a Nash and a Hudson parked
at the curb a baby girl was suspended from her mother's
hands her pants pulled down.   It was desired of this
child that she relieve herself there and then schoolchildren
going past in bunches peddlers at their cars mothers pushing strollers and an older boy with ice cream stopping
shamelessly to watch.   And this beautiful little girl
turned a face of such outrage upon me that I immediately
recognized you Clara and with then saintly inability to
withstand life you closed your eyes and allowed the thin
stream of golden water to cascade to the tar which was
instantly black and shone clearer than a night sky.

In the morning hacking away at the Indian-chief monument, I saw him going down the bridle path, going right by without so much as a glance at the strange work on the rock, walking a few steps, running, walking again hurriedly, on the trail through the woods.

I waited five minutes and then I dropped my shovel and sauntered off. "Where you going!" someone called behind me. I raised my hand to show I knew what I was doing and that I'd be right back.

This was the trail the riders took to get to another shore of the lake, a mile down from the main house. It was hoed regularly to keep it soft—I had done some of that myself. It went through stands of towering pine and over small clearings where the grass was turning tan and gold in the autumn, and then it dropped down into an area where the leaves were falling like snowflakes. I felt the same turning season in me.

Where the trail cornered, along the shore of the wide lake, was an airplane hangar with a concrete ramp. Mr. Penfield sat on the ramp with his arms around his knees. He was looking at the water. The wind had whipped up a small white chop. Wavelets slapped at the concrete. He didn't seem to notice Lucinda Bailey Bennett coming out of the hangar and walking toward him. She pulled a big red trainman's handkerchief from the pocket of her overalls and wiped her hands.

I ducked around through the underbrush and came within a few feet of them. I could see inside: an engine was suspended from pulleys. A man was guiding it to a workbench.

"What do you do, Lucinda," said Mr. Penfield in a petulant tone. "Paint the innards like a new toy?"

"No, old bear. When I'm through, its innards will be

dark and oiled, and refitted to tolerances that will take me to the top of the sky." She stuffed her handkerchief into the pouch of her overalls. "Why are you sulking? I thought you loved me."

"Since I gave up manhood to live here, I make no claims of that sort on anyone."

She smiled. "That's not the report I have."

"Oh, Lucinda," he said with a groan, and he turned to look up at her.

"So much suffering." She touched the back of her hand to his temple. "Poor Warren."

"How much better for me if when I came here my throat had been ripped out."

She sighed. "Yes," she said, "I suppose so."

After a moment she turned back and he lifted himself grunting to his feet. He lumbered after her. "Forgive me," he called.

"Oh, Warren, it's such a bore when you whine." She went into the hangar.

"Yes," he cried out bitterly. "Indeed. My agony does not divert." And he followed her.

I couldn't hear them now. The hangar was lit by electric lights that glimmered very faintly through the brightness of the morning. But I saw them moving around, she working and he talking with grand gestures. Every once in a while I heard the sound of his voice, and I knew Mr. Penfield well enough to know he was in good form, eloquent in his self-dramatization. I hoped so, because he was talking for me.

The man who'd been helping came out, lit a cigarette and went off along the trail. I moved to the hangar itself, staying out of sight of the doorway. I leaned my back to the wall.

"You have a good nature," I heard Mrs. Bennett say.

"Oh my dear!"

"Would you like to go on a flight? Probably not. But a really long flight. Just the two of us. Would you consider it?"

"What? Where?"

"I don't know. The Far East. Shall we do that? Fly across the Pacific."

"The Far East?"

"Yes, pooh bear. A long flight. You and I. Oh, that's a *good* idea! Who knows what might happen." She burst out laughing. "Warren, if you could see the expression on your face! The dismay!"

"Lucinda, what—How is it possible? Am I misunderstood?"

"Oh, foolish thing—I don't mean that! Good God!" She was merry now. "It's a practice made too thoroughly disreputable by its devotees, don't you think?"

That evening the four of them met for dinner. I stood on the terrace just out of the light cast through the windows and I watched them at their drinks. A fire blazed in the huge fireplace. Mounted prey gazed down at them. Clara was wearing a gown of sequined silver. She looked cheap. She sat staring at the floor, cowed, maybe even stunned into silence, by the nuances of civilization in that room. The gentlemen wore black tie, in which Mr. Penfield managed to look as rumpled and ill-prepared for life as ever. With his characteristic expression of appeal for love and understanding he glanced habitually at the others, but especially Clara. Lucinda Bennett smiled faintly and kept up her end of the conversation. Only F. W. Bennett seemed to be enjoying himself. He became so animated he stood up to deliver his sentences. He went to a table behind the leather sofa and held up a large flat book opened, and resting on his arm, and he read from it and laughed and looked at the others for their reaction.

I went through the woods to Clara's cabin and found her luggage standing just inside the front door. There were three bags and a hatbox. I got all of them under my arms or hanging from my hands, and struggled up the hill to the garage on the far side of the tennis court. This was the old Loon Lake stable. It housed five cars. In the last stall was Mrs. Bennett's car, a rarely used gray two-door

Mercedes-Benz with a canvas top and spare tires in the front fender wells. I looked for the ignition key where Mr. Penfield had told me to—in the bud vase on the right-hand side in the back. Yes. I packed the bags in the trunk, which was not large, and put the hatbox in the back seat. I turned on the map light and by its glow learned the European-style shifting. There were four gears, and a diagram of their positions was imprinted on the mother-of-pearl knob of the floor shift. The dust on the seat cracked under me. I flicked at it with a chamois cloth. The odometer showed less than ten thousand miles. Then I saw it was not even miles, it was kilometers. Lucinda Bennett had told Mr. Penfield it was a 1933 model. Clearly, her interest in machines did not include cars. The license plate was up to date, however.

I swung open the doors as quietly as I could and got in and started the engine. I backed out. It was a noisy car—I later found it was only forty horsepower—and I drove it the few yards to the gas pump shushing it as if it were a baby. I filled it with Mr. Bennett's personal ethyl and then I gave each tire a shot of his air. I was wearing his knickers and argyle sweater and brown-and-white saddle shoes. I tried not to get them dirty.

I was ready to go. I waited behind the wheel. It was a snug little car. The seats were gray leather. The doors opened front to back. I went over some road maps. I sat there and got the feeling of the car and worried about driving it well, and wondered where to go and what I would say to Clara Lukács and what she would say to me. I worried that people seeing me behind the wheel would think I was rich. I didn't once reflect on the lately peculiar conforming of life to my desires. I didn't think of Lucinda Bennett's generosity or despair, or Mr. Penfield's, nor even reach the most obvious conclusion; that I was leaving Loon Lake in somewhat better condition than I had come. Calculating, heedless, and without gratitude, I accepted every circumstance that had put me there, only gunning my mind to the future, wanting more, expecting more, too intent on what was ahead to sit back and give thanks or to laugh or to feel bad.

I peered through the windshield. I watched the trees shaking in the night wind. I unlatched the canvas top and pushed it back a bit and looked at the stars, which seemed to shimmer and blur as if the wind were blowing through them.

Eventually she got there, hurrying along with Mr. Penfield holding her arm, while she held her gown off the ground to keep from tripping. She wore a fur jacket over the gown. He opened the door, but before she could slide in, he grabbed her and hugged her and started to gabble something. I saw all this with their heads cut off. I saw her push him away. "War-rin, please!" she said.

Then she was in the car beside me, in an atmosphere of fur and cold air, and she slammed the door. Penfield peered in, then ran around the front of the car to the driver's side. I started the engine and threw the toggle switch for the headlights. I adjusted the throttle. I rolled down my window and he thrust something in my hand, a wad of bills. "I wish it was more," he said. He gave us advice of many kinds, cheerful assurances, warnings about the road, the weather, appeals to keep in touch, phone numbers on bits of paper, promises, vows, thrown kisses—and to this fitful love song I put the car into first, and off we lurched down the road.

We were taking what was called the back road, away from the main house; there was a sudden bend, and Mr. Penfield, waving in the night in his black tie, veered out of my rear view.

I leaned forward, attentive to the clutching, and gradually, as we made our way bumping and sliding over this gravelly unpaved circuit through the Bennett preserve, I got the hang of it. We drove for quite a while. I glanced at her. In the glow of the dashboard I saw her young face.

I think now of that long drive down through the forest to the state road, dogs appearing from nowhere to gallop yelping alongside, their breath sounding metallic, like the engine; and disappearing just as suddenly, then again one or two of them, then for a mile a beating pack; and she saying nothing, only holding the leather strap by her window, looking out to the side, to the front, her eyes following them tracking them, the youth of her illuminated in the low light. Finally we outdistanced them all.

She sat back in her seat. She took a cigarette out of her purse and lit it.

"What do you think he'll do when he finds you gone?" I said.

"An interesting question," she said.

And so we descended from Loon Lake, Clara's clear eyes fixed on the farthest probe of the headlights, and I looking at her every other moment, in her composure of total attention, going with the ride.

Every morning she swept the dirt path outside the monastery wall. She always wore the same thing, a simple kimono and those wooden slippers, you know? She was fifteen or sixteen years old but her hair was cut in the bowl cut of young children. Hair as black as night. She never smiled, but when she glanced at me there was such a flash of recognition from my soul that I went weak with joy.

Oh, Warren.

I used to wake up before dawn and do my chores and manage always to be at the gate when the sun rose and she came to do hers. She was the daughter of some working family down the street. They sweep the streets there with straw brooms. The unpaved streets. They sweep the dirt, compose it. They compose everything, they pick the fallen leaves one at a time.

How did you get to her?

I wish you wouldn't phrase it that way, Lucinda. We knew each other on sight. We had to. My Japanese was less than rudimentary. Her English nonexistent. Only the upper classes studied English. It was a great social distinction to know English. A workman's daughter couldn't aspire to that.

Light me a cigarette, will you?

I have in my life just three times seen a face in dark light, at dusk or dawn or against a white pillow, in which there is a recognizably perfect perception of the world, some matched reflection of the world in her eye's light as terrifying and beautiful in equal measure. Am I coherent?

A moral light? Is that what you mean?

She lives through her fear to her curiosity, there is a stillness of apprehension, like an animal's stillness of perfect apprehension of its predator, and it is gallantry to break the heart.

I wish we had known each other when we were young.

Her father and several uncles made up a delegation to complain about my conduct to the monastery officials, who of course did not have to be told. I had broken every rule in the book. At the moment both sides gathered to come down on us we slipped away together and took the train to Tokyo. We found a room.

Is this when you became lovers?

I suppose so. I thought I could support us by teaching American customs and manners to Japanese businessmen. They wanted that. They were studying us intently. They listened to jazz and danced the Charleston. You're not crying, are you?

It makes me sad. I know what happened.

I left the house one morning. I had an appointment to see someone at the U.S. embassy. It was a Saturday, the first day in September, 1923. As I walked down the street, I lost my balance but suddenly people everywhere were screaming. The streets were cracking open. I ran back, the city was falling down everywhere, I climbed over rubble, I saw her coming after me with her arms raised, the cobblestones heaved, the street broke open, it filled with water, I reached her and grabbed her hand just as the earth sank away and she fell in, she fell from my hands and where the earth had been there was a steaming lake. What is that up ahead, Lucinda? It looks very dark.

It's nothing. A line squall.

The nights seemed to race by. The weather got colder. The freaks got nastier. We came one day to a town less promising than any I'd seen. It was shut down and boarded. One tavern and one store were open. I don't remember the name of this town, it was like a tree with just a branch or two still alive.

In a lot beside the boarded-up railroad depot Sim Hearn gave the signal and the carney put up for business. In the evening we turned on the lights and a few mountain people straggled in but most of the time the freaks talked to each other because nothing else was doing. The rides went around empty. I thought Sim Hearn had lost his marbles.

The next night the same thing, the wind blew through the booths and rattled the tent flaps, they sounded like over the mountains somewhere there was some gang war of Tommy guns going on.

I thought Sim Hearn was telling us the season was over by enacting the news. The cook built a fire on the ground and heated an ash can of water. He scrubbed his pots and pans with brown soap. Other people were packing. Mrs. Hearn grabbed my arm and we stepped behind a wagon.

"Hearn goes no farther," she said. "Look, a sweater I have for you so you wouldn't be cold."

She was a pain in the ass with her presents. She brought me cigarettes, oranges, she washed my clothes, all in secret of course. Nobody knew about it except the whole carney.

It chilled me to think Sim Hearn might know it. But his distance from me was unchanged and his peculiar authority maintained itself in my mind. It was as if no matter what I did to his wife I could never break through that supreme indifference. I decided no man was that godlike. I decided he didn't know. I wished he did know. Then I wouldn't be some nameless creature so low as to be beneath his line of vision.

The next morning we struck everything but the show tent. We raised the wood shutters on the wagons and nailed them shut. We pushed the wagons into an old car barn across the tracks from the depot. After lunch a few people left with their bags or bundles. Nobody said so long or even looked at anyone else. I think I was shocked. Despite all my other feelings about the carney, I could believe it was a privilege to be attached to it. It angered me that people would walk away as if Hearn Bros. had no more distinction than a mission flop.

On the other hand, why should it be different? Sim Hearn couldn't care less if any one of them lived or died and they knew that. He was going to take the trucks down to Florida for the winter and let them get down there on their own. If they showed up, he'd hire them; if they didn't, that was all right too.

Fanny the Fat Lady's wagon was in place and hadn't been moved. I saw Mrs. Hearn coming out of her trailer. "Fanny wheezes like calliope," she said.

"Well, why doesn't someone get a doctor?"

She put her hand on my cheek and looked in my eyes. "I worry to think someday if we are not together what will happen to you."

Several of the freaks were leaving in a group. I was told to take a truck and drive them about fifteen miles to a town called Chester, where there was a spur line to Albany. It was the afternoon, already getting dark. In the cab with me sat the woman who took care of Fanny. The whole ride she wept and blew her nose. She spoke to herself in Spanish as if her running stream of thoughts and sorrows came up over the banks every now and then. She thought I wasn't looking when she lifted her skirt and fingered the metal clip of her garter to make sure it was fastened properly. I saw tucked in the top of her stocking a wad of bills that looked like a lot of money.

I let off the truckload of freaks and their keepers in Chester, New York, and they hopped, climbed or were lowered from the tailgate. They went limping and scuttling into the waiting room carrying their bags like anyone. Why not? They were mostly immigrants, after all— the same people but with a twist who worked for pennies in the sawmills or stood on the bread lines. But I imagined the stationmaster seeing through his grill this company of freaks in ordinary streetclothes approaching him with questions of schedule and tickets.

Why didn't I get on the train with them? Did I really want to drive a truck to Florida? Did I want to bang Mrs. Magda Hearn in more states of the Union?

I thought of the freaks as pilgrims or revolutionaries of some angry religion nobody knew anything about yet.

When I got back it was already dark. I could tell something was wrong, there were lots of cars there and wagon teams. I cut the engine and stood on the running board. Beyond the lot was a hill that rose steeply, blacker than the sky, I could see its outline against the blue-black space of sky behind it. I thought I heard a scream. I listened—it was something else, a drumming of the earth or the sound of a rug being beaten. I walked toward the show tent, there was the dimmest light in there. A man stepped out of the shadow and put his hand on my arm. A flashlight shone in my eyes.

"Who's this?" a voice said.

And then I heard Magda Hearn. "It's all right. He's with the show."

My arm was still held and I could feel the consideration of this intelligence in the mind behind the light. The flashlight went off. I made out the figure of a state trooper, blocked hat and gun and Sam Browne belt. Then my arm was released, the marks of the fingers still on me, like the afterimage on the eye.

Magda Hearn was walking me toward the show tent. "Joe," she said, "I want you to see, to understand. And I wait for you in the car. Do you hear me?"

"What's going on?" I said. "What are the police doing here?"

"Joe, please to listen." She was whispering in my ear and in each cycle of her crippled gait, the sibilance rose and fell in waves of urgency.

Then I passed through the flaps.

The show tent had a few rows of wooden bleachers and a small ring where the ponies could run around and the bareback sisters, if they were so inclined, could do their turns. A cat act had been featured here for a while.

The bleachers were empty. One bulb burned from the tent pole. Eighty, maybe a hundred men stood in a circle in the dirt of the ring. I couldn't see over their backs but I heard the not unfamiliar night music, the grunts and gurgling moans and squeaks of Fanny the Fat Lady. As the rhythm got faster the crowd shouted encouragement. Then I heard that peculiar basso thumping as if the earth itself was being drummed. Then an abrupt silence and the hoarse male roar of expiration. Whistles and cheers came from the crowd, men turned outward, I saw them drinking from bottles, exchanging money. Staggering through the ring, buttoning his pants, was a grifter I recognized. He sank down on his knees beside me, removed a flask from his back pocket and took a long pull.

Some sort of hot shame rose from the roots of my sex into my stomach and chest: it felt like illness. I pushed forward and saw Fanny on her back, arms and legs flung outward. She was naked. She lay twitching, each spasm jerking her flesh into ripples. She wheezed and fought for breath. The sweated slathered flesh was caked in dirt, but with white crevasses in the folds of her and a red blotch in the middle. I was pushed aside and spun around. A moment later another lover had fallen on her. The crowd yelled and jammed up around me. She was quickly brought to pitch, her great back rising and thumping into the earth, but this one didn't last long, and to great merry raucous hoots and jeers he stumbled out of the ring.

Almost immediately another rube was moving forward for his turn. I jumped him just as he unbuckled his belt. I knocked him down and kicked him in the groin. He yowled, doubling up and clutching himself and I took his place crouching beside Fanny, facing them all, my fists clenched. I was screaming something, I don't remember what, it stunned them for a second, and then they were laughing and taunting me and shouting at me to wait my turn.

Fanny lay there trembling in her agony and her eyes were rolled into her head. Her mouth was open and giving off gasping animal wheezes. Maniacally, I felt betrayed by her, as by life itself, the human pretense. I became enraged with her! In my nostrils, mixed with the sharp fume of booze, was an organic stench, a bitter foul smell of burning nerves, and shit and scum.

Then something flew out at me, a pint bottle, or a rock, and caught me low on the forehead. I went down, dazed, clutching my eyes, bright lights in my brain. I had fallen on Fanny, she was like some soft rotten animal carcass. Her arms helplessly went around me. I was panicked and tried to get free. My struggles were mistaken—I was pulled out of her grasp by my feet and dragged through the dirt and kicked and rolled and yanked to my feet and given a clout on the side of the head.

I found myself on my knees, behind the crowd. I was wet. Blood streamed in my eye. But the ceremony continued. There were men drooling there. There were onanists. There were gamblers betting on the moment of death. Later there were men leaping on her, on each other, squatting on her head, crawling over her, falling on her, shoving bottles in her. There were gallants calling for order, for some law of decency if all pleasure was not to be lost. And Fanny giving up a human appearance by degrees, trumpeting her ecstasies to the killing passion of the rubes.

From one only was there absolute quiet in this mayhem. I looked at him. His face was hidden in the shadow of his hat brim. You wouldn't know his connection with these spermy rites except for the indolence of his stance as he leaned against the bleacher supports with his bony arms folded and his ankles crossed. And I could swear I heard, through the hoarse cries and shouts and shrieking and orgiastic death, the thoughtful and preoccupied sucking of Sim Hearn's tongue on his teeth.

Riding over the mountain in the Model A, Joe became aware of where he was. She accelerated, the headlights brightened; she braked, the headlights dimmed. The bones of his legs sounded the ground pitch of the engine. Mrs. Hearn's face luminous in the night, she urged the car forward with her chin, her furrowed brow, her shoulders putting english on the turns. At the bottom of a hill she gunned it, halfway up plunged with her left leg, shifted to second, she came over the tops of the hills with her horn blowing, headlights making a quick stab at the night sky.

"Of course they never live long, such creatures—the heart won't beat for them . . . All summer Sim Hearn watches—he watches and then he sees the signs—she doesn't take breath as she should—from the bed she cannot lift herself . . . The people know Hearn—he gives something special at end of summer, a grand finale . . . The word goes through the mountains . . . Look where we are—we make time better than I hoped."

In the early hours of the morning she judged us safely away and turned into a motor court and paid for a cabin in the pines farthest from the road. Wedged into the rumble seat was my broken-down valise with everything I possessed in the world. She had packed it for me. I carried it and her frayed black Gladstone into the room. She locked the car and locked the cabin door behind us and pulled the shades and then pulled the light cord.

The bed had a khaki blanket but no sheets. Two lumpy gray pillows. Magda Hearn rummaged in her bag for a white cotton face towel. She spread the towel on top of the bureau. The room had the shit smell of old untreated wood. She removed from her purse a manila envelope and from the envelope removed a stack of greenbacks which she placed on the cotton towel.

"Sim knows to get the money out before the fun starts," she said. "To Albany to the bank he thinks I am going."

She wet her thumb on her lower lip and stood at the bureau counting the money. I sat down on the bed and took off my shoes and socks. She wet her thumb on the inside of her lower lip, pulling it down so that for a moment her teeth showed her expression went slack. She was a while counting.

"Fifteen hundred and eighty-four dollars!"

She dug in her purse and extracted a wallet and from this withdrew another wad of bills.

"And plus salary which he never paid!" she said in a tone of vengeful triumph. The thumb applied to the red inside of her lip. She counted aloud this time. "Two hundred I squeeze from you, you bastard!"

She opened her Gladstone, interrupting herself to press her lips strongly on my mouth.

She pulled the string tie of a small canvas coin sack and spilled a stream of coins on the bed.

She lay on the bed making separate piles of nickels and dimes and quarters and halves, the little piles collapsed and came together because she was shaking the bed with her guttural glee. She started over, she was keen on pennies, too—if there had been coins of smaller denominations, she would have counted them, too. She was ready to count coins forever and to bitterly calculate the suffering she had done for each one.

"Joe Joe Joe! Tomorrow we trade his car and its license and buy new. We drive to California you and me.

We are in our new car on way to California before even
he thinks is something wrong!"

She gave up the count and lay on her back in the coins.
She lifted her arms. "Come to me, come to Magda. You
know what?" Kissing me, running hands on me, opening
one by one the buttons on my fly. "To Hollywood we are
going. I have read the magazines, I understand the movie
business. I sell my life story. A film of my life! Everyone
will know who Magda is." She unbuckled my belt, she
opened the buttons of my shirt. She kissed my chest and
pulled the shirt down off my shoulders. "And who knows
who knows, with your looks, my Joseph, with your body,
why you cannot be movie star? And we will love each
other and have great sooccess. Shall we?" Laughing,
going down on me. "Shall we?"

She had no idea I had actually caught evil as one
catches a fever, she didn't understand this, she thought
my passion matched hers. I wanted to do to her what had
been done to the Fat Lady, I wanted the force of a
hundred men in unholy fellowship, I went at her like a
murderous drunkard.

I fucked past her joy into her first alarm, I saw on her
face under the weak glare of the hanging bulb the dilated
eye. I was enraged by the flaws of her, the unnatural cleft
of her left hip, one buttock was actually atrophied, the
raised veins behind the knees, the hanging breasts like
deflated balloons, the yellowed face with loosened folds of
skin at the neck rising in parallel rows as she turned her
head from me this stinking Hungarian hag this thieving
crone bitch with the gall to think she had me for her toy
boy her lover chuffing now like a fucking steam engine I
brought the tears to her eyes she would acknowledge
nothing she resisted and then the voice did come, and
then the voice louder and more insistent, and finally she
seemed to be urging me along as if we were together, the
lying cunt in the Pine Grove Motor Court, our music
mingling with the night wind in the pines the tree trunks
creaking the million crickets. I ended and began again.
We wrestled. She begged me to stop. Tears of mourning
came from my eyes. I let her fall asleep. I woke her,

made her moan. At one point the coins sticking to the wet ass, the wet belly, I invented a use of Magda Hearn so unendurable to her that with the same cry that must have come from her the day she fell twisting from the trapeze, she flung herself off the bed—a moment's silence, then the sickening shaming sound of bone and flesh slamming into the floor, a grunt. I lay on my back on the bed not daring to look, I heard a small soprano cry, a deeper moan, a whispered curse. I lay still. After a while I realized I was listening to the snores of an exhausted human being.

I thought I saw the first crack of light under the window shade. I got off the bed and rolled my clothes and shoes into a bundle. I grabbed the stack of bills from the bureau. I unlatched the door quietly and closed it behind me. There were no other guests at the Pine Grove Motor Court. A thin frost lay on the windshield of the Model A. The wind blew.

With all my might I reared back and threw the bills into the wind. I thought of them as the Fat Lady's ashes.

I found a privy up the hill behind the cabins and next to it an outdoor shower. I stood in the shower of cold springwater and looked up at the swaying tops of the pine trees and watched the sky lighten and heard through the water and the toneless wind the sounds of the first birds waking.

I dried myself as best I could and put on my clothes in a tremble of stippled skin and turned my back on the cabins and struck off through the woods. I had no idea where I was going. It didn't particularly matter. I ran to get warm. I ran into the woods as to another world.

At Kamakura he climbed the spiral stairs inside the largest Buddha in the world. In the head of the largest Buddha, on the ledge of its chin, sat a tiny Buddha facing in the opposite direction. Simple idolatry held no interest for him, but a religion that joked held genuine interest. He felt all at once the immense power of a communication that used no words. I acknowledge Warren's lifelong commitment—cancel lifelong commitment—fatal attraction for any kind of communication whether from words, flags, pigeons or the touch of fingertips in hope of a common language, but we must remember how we are vulnerable to the repetition of our insights so that they tend to come to us not as confirmation of something we already know but as genuine discoveries each and every time. And so he descended, and by degrees over a period of several days, drifted south along the route of the old Tokaido. He saw thousands of Buddhas lined up in trays in the tourist shops or ranked in legions at the shrines, some in lead, some in wood, some carved in stone and dressed in little knitted caps and capes. He came to see in this ubiquitous phenomenon the Buddha's godlike propensity for self-division, the endless fractioning of himself into every perceivable aspect, an allegory made by the people of Japan from the cellular process of life. Thus enlightened, he turned his eyes on the people in the streets and the narrow shopping arcades, old women in black slapping along on their sandals, black-haired children of incredible beauty staring at him with their thumbs stuck in their plump cheeks, giggling pairs of young women in brightly colored kimonos, old shopkeepers with wispy goatees bowing as he passed, thoughtful peddlers, and young men who stopped in their tracks to glare at him and bear themselves with brazen umbrage—they were all the Buddha too in his infinite aspect. Traveling down this avenue of thought lit only by stone lanterns filled with small stones in lieu of flames, he saw the true dereliction of the planet and realized anew that convictions of friendship, love, the assumption of culture, the certainty of calendars were fragile constructs of the imagination, and there was no place to live that was truly home, neither for him nor for the multitudinous islanders of Japan.

In this he-took-for-appropriate state of mind, Warren arrived one day at road's end, Kyoto, the strange city whose chief industry was meditation. He wandered from one monastery to the next, there were whole neighborhoods of them, but where, where was the sign that one was for him? He was afflicted with a fluttering humility, not daring even to make inquiries, hovering at this gate or in that garden or touching down for just a moment of indecision before the small window with the visitor admission in yen painted in black calligraphy on white cardboard stuck into the grate as if he were looking for a movie to see. Late in the afternoon, weary and full of self-condemnation, he happened to stumble up the step of a wooden verandah overlooking one of these beautiful monastery gardens of raked gravel and moss and stone. Thus launched, his large Caucasian person hurtled through a rice-paper door, splintering its laths, and like an infant being born, he found himself with the back half of him still on the porch side of the door and the front half in a room, looking with wide, even horrified eyes at the benign polished wood Buddha sitting facing him with a little altar of flowers on either side and the sinuous smoke of incense appearing to squinch up its eyes. He had made a terrible thunderous racket but nobody came running, nobody came shouting, and after he crawled the rest of the way into the room he set about calmly picking up the pieces and preparing in his mind the self-demeaning speech by which he would beg the chance to make the most extended and profound restitution. As it happened, the monastery was empty; he was to learn it was the rare annual holiday of this particular establishment in which everyone was set free for twenty-four hours. Only after searching the grounds did Warren find an old caretaker willing to come look and see the awful thing he had done. This old caretaker was smoking a cigarette, which he held in his teeth. He took in smoke with each inhalation and with each exhalation smoke streamed out of his nostrils. He gazed at the carnage, the plumes of smoke from his nostrils indicating the depth and strength of each drawn breath, and it seemed to fascinate him that such a perfect and modest structure as a sliding paper door should have been turned into this. He was a very short, extremely bald old man, and he wore a torn ribbed undershirt and a pair of dirty white muslin knickers with flapping ties at the waist but the peculiar thing was that he was not unpleasant to look upon, it did not create feelings of pity or fear or other degrees of patronization to look upon him. He picked up a broken length of lath and looked at it and asked a question in unintelligible Japanese. I'll pay for it, Warren said and removed from his pocket a wad of yen. He unfolded the bills and looked at the old man squinting at the money through the cigarette smoke. Warren peeled off one bill and put it in the man's hand. Then another. Then another. He kept waiting for a sign that he'd met the cost. He hesitated. The old man looked at him and peremptorily slapped his arm with the lath. Warren was so astonished he dropped the whole wad of bills in the old man's hand. The caretaker put the bills into the pockets of his voluminous knickers, looked up at the Caucasian and swatted him again with the flat of the stick, this time across the side of his face. Then he laughed, and in so doing released his cigarette, which fell from his teeth and lay on the wooden floor glowing. Immediately Warren, thinking the whole place would go up, stepped on the tobacco ember with his large shoe, only realizing in that moment the defacement he had committed by stepping with street shoes on the monastery floors.

But the caretaker had turned and headed back to his garden shed with its straw brooms and clay pots and small pyramids of gravel. Warren experienced the uncanny sense of a sharply learned lesson. He slept that night at a Western hotel in the downtown section of Kyoto and found in the nightstand drawer a volume in English that seemed to be the Buddhist equivalent of the Bible. Gautama was an Indian prince kept at home by his father so as not to see life in any aspect but its most luxurious. But one day he went out and saw a beggar, an old crippled man, a monk and a corpse. He was thus able to conclude despite his own royal existence that life was suffering. Why couldn't he have figured that out without leaving the palace? Warren wondered. If death exists, life has to be suffering. Did his father hide death from Gautama? How was that done? The book said the cause of all suffering was desire, the desire to have the desire to be. Perhaps a prince would never experience the desire to have, but how could he avoid the desire to be? If desire by its nature is not gratified before it realizes itself, does it not exist in palaces too? Does it not exist especially in palaces? Nevertheless, he liked the story. He trusted Gautama Siddhartha and the simplicity of his reasoning. Not many people could get away with that sort of reasoning. He trusted the eightfold path for defeating desire and transcending suffering.

Early the next morning Warren went back to the monastery. The place was a shambles. Doors and shoji walls were splintered and torn everywhere. There were recumbent bodies on the verandah, and in the garden a monk lay in a pool of vomit. All the walls were torn and hanging, bodies lay about, as if dead. There was even a

body lying across the crest of the tile roof. The monastery
looked as if it had been bombed. But even as he gazed at
this dismal scene he heard the sound of small tinkling
bells coming from somewhere in the main monastery
building, and though the bells were soft and delicate they
had the astonishing effect of rousing the Zen Buddhists
from their drunken stupor. One by one they groaned, rose
to their feet and staggered off.

And then around the corner came a man in white
holding a staff of temple bells. His head was shaved, he
was stout, the folds of his neck were like ruffles of a
collar. He walked right up to Warren and inquired in
heavily accented English if he could be of help. I want to
discuss with someone the possibility of enrolling here for
Zen training, Warren said. Of course, the monk said. If
you don't mind waiting more than two moments but less
than six, I will approach the Master for you.

More than two but less than six, Warren thought as he
waited in an anteroom beside the front gate. That's a few.
Shortly thereafter he was escorted by the monk to a small
room with a beautiful Bodhisattva *pratima* and a vase of
flowers and straw mats and cushions, and without having
to be told, even by himself, he dropped to his knees and
bowed to the resident Master, who was seated and facing
him with a face of genial amusement. It was the old
caretaker. On the one day off of the year for all his
followers and monks, he, in perfect realization, had
stayed where he was. The Master was smoking a cigarette. Another monk came by and listened. He was laughing and telling the monk, in Japanese, about his first
meeting with Warren. Gusts of smoke came out of him.
As the story was elaborated, the Master rose and began
to act it out, and there to Warren's astonishment was a
perfect imitation of himself, the way he carried himself,
his walk, the tone of his voice, the shock on his face as
the lath slapped his cheek. The Japanese laughed till
there were tears in their eyes. Soon Warren began to smile
and then he too exploded into laughter. He would come
to understand in the months to follow that the Master so
perfectly realized whatever he chose to do, that a kind of

magnetic field was formed in which whoever was in his presence drew on its power. That is why interviews with the Master were so highly prized. His perfection was an impersonal force that you could feel and hope someday to manifest from yourself on a continuous basis. If he laughed, it was perfect laughter, and you had to laugh too. If he chose to cry, everyone around him would have to weep. But where did it come from, how did it happen? All Warren could work out was that the Master lived totally to the fullness of his being each and every moment of his existence. He was completely of the moment, then and there, in which you found him. Nothing of him was deadened by the suffering of his past life and there was no striving or fear in him for his future.

Would the Master feel a need to write poems?

No, because poems are the expression of longing and despair. Yes, because if the Master is one in every instant with what he sees and hears and feels, the poem is not the Master's written need but the world singing in the Master.

No, because the poem is a cry of the unborn heart. Yes, because the poem perfectly embodies the world, there is no world without poem.

Your register apologizes for rendering nonlinear thinking in linear language, the apperceptions of oneness in dualistic terminology. However, there is no difficulty representing the absolute physical torture of Warren Penfield's commitment to Zen meditation. He could not physically accomplish even the half lotus, his spine threatened to snap, his legs seemed to be in a vise; even the mudra—the bowl-shaped position of the hands, the thumbs lightly touching, a simple relaxed representation in the hand of the flow from right to left, from left to right, the rocking crescent continuity of the universe intimations of stars and ancient Eastern recognitions—became under the torment of his distracted physically weeping thought a spastic hand clench, a hardened manifestation of frozen fear and anguish, the exact opposite of the right practice, the body imprisoned, the mind entirely personal and self-involved and then God help you if you nod off every now and then as who could not, sitting like a damn beer pretzel twelve, sixteen hours a day he comes along and hits you with the damn slapstick the goddamn yellow-skinned bastard the next time he hits me with that stick I'm going to get up and wrap it around his goddamn yellow neck and break a goddamn Buddha doll over his goddamn shaven head this is not right thinking but tell me Gautama enlighten me if what you say is true why is it so difficult to attain wouldn't it all make a lot more sense if everyone could do it if everyone could be it without even thinking without being anything less before, without the death of my darling, and men drowning in the cold black coalwater of collapsed mines miles of coalstone sinking slowly upon their chests, or bullets perforating them like cutout coupons supposing I do attain it, supposing I find the right understanding what then what happens outside me how do I help Local 10110 of the Western Federation of Miners, Smelters, Sheepdippers and Zenpissers, and then there's the food, look what we wait for when at last the cute little tinkly bell rings and we may unpretzel ourself and try to regain the circulation in our swollen limbs, little bits of pickled leather, or some absolute excresence of the lowest sea life lightly salted or a congealed ball of rice dipped in some rank fermented fluid that smells to me like the stuff we dipped the pigeons in to kill the lice.

No, there is no problem expressing the inner record of Warren Penfield's quest for enlightenment: the whining despair, the uncharacteristic epithet, the rage, the backsliding giving up and consequent self-nauseation, the stubborn goings on, all of this silent, in a temple hall of inscrutable meditators, all of whom reminded him of the immigrant kids in the Ludlow Grade School around him totally serene and insulated in their lack of language the feeling what do they all know that I don't know why don't the storms of self taste fire and thunder across their brainbrow, why aren't they as sick and unsure of their dangerous selves as I am of mine, leading them to the false Zen-like casuistry as, for example, if we are to press ourselves on the world sticking to it like a decal, if I am

one with the rocks the trees the stars why is my memory
invalid and why then are the images of Clara on our beds
of slag in the cool mountain dusk of Colorado forbidden
me, I am my memory and the images of my past are me,
and if I am the rocks and stones and trees, Wordsworth,
rocked round in earth's diurnal course with rocks and
stones and trees, why are my phantoms less real why are
the ghostvoices of my mama and papa less real why is the
mud of the Marne less real why must I exclude exclude, if
everything is now and mind is matter is not everything
valid is not meditation the substance of the mind as well
as its practice?

Nor is it difficult to render the casually developed outer
circumstances of this monastic life, the old Master becoming at some times demonic in his teaching, a destroyer of ego, of humble ordinary lines of thought, an army of
right practice, right understanding overwhelming the frail
redoubts and trenches of Warren's Western mind. One
day they were in the temple and he came in screaming,
naked, climbed the Buddha like a bee alighting on a
flower and bending it with its own honeygravid weight
and they watched shocked and stunned as a beautiful
polished wood Buddha toppled to the floor under the
Master, an act of profound desecration with sexual impact, and the Buddha lay split like a log, a piece of wood
the aperture of an earthquake and nothing was ever said
of it again. He was a violent old man, one day Warren
was admitted for his counseling and the Master threw a
cup of cold green tea in his face and that was the lesson
of the day. One day he lectured them all, a particular
holy day and he shouted at them saying you were all
Masters when you first came through the gate and now
look at you, I have more respect for the horse that pulls
the shitwagon than I have for you—screaming and growling and trilling in the Japanese way of singsong, Warren
prostrate with all the rest. But everyone took it as material to be pondered and worked out, it was only a style of
pedagogy and only someone stupid enough to take emo-
tions seriously would be shocked threatened or angered
by the serene antics of the realized Buddha spirit of such

a great Master. Warren finally reached the preliminary kindergarten stage of getting his own koan, a paradoxical question to form the empty mind of meditation. Each devotee received his own koan like a rabbit's foot to stroke and treasure, an unanswerable question to torment him month after month, perhaps year after year, until enlightenment burst over and he was able to answer it when the Master gently asked it of him the hundred millionth time. Warren walked in bowed, kneeled on the straw mat. The Master was smoking and making each breath visible as a plume of cigarette smoke and Warren knew the standard koans, the famous ones, there were actually collections of them like college course outlines but the one given to him he had never heard before or read anywhere and it was delivered by the Master with a shake of his head, a sigh and a glance of helpless supplication at the ceiling: Penfield-san, said the Master, if this is a religion for warriors, what are *you* doing here? Warren thanked him, bowed and backed out of the room even though the Master looked as if he was going to say something more. Later in his first pondering of this infinitely resounding question he squatted by his favorite place, near the garden gate beyond the gravel garden, and saw through the slats as for the first time the beautiful little girl who swept the street.

I drove out of the mountains through the night and found the way to Utica, New York, coming into city streets in the rain at three o'clock, passing freight yards, warehouses. She was asleep, I didn't want to wake her, I bumped the car gently across the railroad tracks and headed south and west toward Pittsburgh.

I wanted to log as many miles as I could before Bennett got up in the morning.

By dawn I was clear-eyed exhausted, feeling my nerves finely strung, the weariness in the hinges of my jaws, you are never more alert. Red lights in the dawn at intersections between fields, I saw the light of dawn shoot clear down the telegraph wires like a surge of power, I passed milk trucks and heard train whistles the sun came up and flooded my left eye suddenly it was day commerce was on the roads we had survived Loon Lake and were cruising through the United States of America.

I woke her for breakfast, we walked into a diner— some town in Pennsylvania. Clara in her fur jacket and long dress and Junior in his knickers and sweater. Someone dropped a plate. Clara is not awake yet—a hard sleeper, a hard everything—she sits warming her hands on her coffee cup, studies the tabletop.

"This won't do," I said, steering her by the arm to the car.

"What?"

"It's asking for trouble."

I found an Army-Navy Surplus Store. I bought myself a regular pair of pants, work shirt, socks, a wool seaman's cap and khaki greatcoat. I bought Clara a black merchant marine pullover and a pea jacket. I made her change her clothes in the back of the store. Then I did.

Mr. Penfield had pressed upon me about eighty dollars in clean soft ones and fives, bills that looked as if they had spent years in a shoe box. I added to this the forty dollars or so of my own fortune. The clothes had come to twenty-eight, and another dollar and change for breakfast.

"What kind of money do you have?"

"Money?"

"I want to see what our cash assets are."

"I don't have any money."

"That's really swell."

"Look in my bag if you don't believe me."

"Well, how far did you think you could go without money?"

"I don't know. You tell me."

It was the best of conversations, all I could have wished for. I scowled. I drove hard.

We took the bumps in unison, we leaned at the same angle on the curves. I didn't know where we were going and she didn't ask. I drove to speed. I stopped wondering what she was feeling, what she was thinking. She was happy on the move, alert and at peace, all the inflamed spirit was lifted from her. She had various ways of arranging herself in the seat, legs tucked up or one under the other, or arms folded, head down, but in any position definitive, beautiful.

Come with me

Late that afternoon we were going up a steep hill along the Monongahela, Pittsburgh spreading out below us, stacks of smoke, black sky, crucible fire. By nightfall I was numb, I couldn't drive another mile. We were in some town in eastern Ohio, maybe it was Steubenville, I'm not sure. On a narrow street I found the Rutherford Hayes, a four-story hotel with fire escapes and a barber's pole at the entrance. I took a deep breath and pulled up to the curb.

In the empty lobby were the worn upholstered chairs and half-dead rubber plants that would have been elegance had I not been educated at Loon Lake. I had never stayed at a hotel but I knew what to do from the movies.

I got us upstairs without incident and tipped the bellboy fifty cents. "Yes, suh!" he said. I chain-locked the door behind him.

We had a corner room with large windows, each covered with a dark green pull shade and flimsy white curtains. Everything had a worn-out look, a great circle of wear in the middle of the rug. I liked that. I liked the idea of public accommodation, people passing through. Bennett could keep his Loon Lake. I looked out the window. We were on the top floor, we had a view of greater Steubenville. In the bathroom was a faucet for ice water.

Clara, who had been in hotels before, found the experience unexceptional. She opened her overnight bag and took over the bathroom. I smoked a cigarette and listened to the sounds of her bathing. I kept looking around the room as if I expected to see someone else. Who? We were alone, she was alone with me and nobody knew where we were. I was smiling. I was thinking of myself crouched in the weeds in the cold night while a train goes by and a naked girl holds a white dress before a mirror.

This was a double bed I had booked and she hadn't even blinked. That would seem reason to hope. But for Clara Lukács there was no necessary significance in sleeping beside somebody in the same bed. She came out of the bathroom without a stitch. I undressed and turned out the light as cool in my assumptions as I could be. A high whine of impatience, a kind of child's growl, and a poke of her elbow was what I got when I happened to move against her in the dark. Just testing.

She curled up with her back toward me, and those vertebrae which I had noticed and loved were all at once deployed like the Maginot Line.

In the morning she woke out of sorts, mean.

"What in hell am I doing here?" she muttered. "Jesus," she said, looking at me. "I must be out of my mind."

I was stunned. My first impulse was to appeal.

"Look at him, hunky king of the road there. Oh, this is great—this really is great." She snapped up the window shade and looked out. "God damn him," she said. "And his wives and his boats and choo-choo trains."

She began to dress. She held up blouses, skirts, looked at them, flung them down. She sat abruptly on the bed with her arms full of clothes and she stared at the floor.

"Hey," I said. "I told you I'd get you out of there and I did. Didn't I?"

She didn't answer.

"Hey, girlie," I said, "didn't I? You have a complaint? You think you're some hot-ass bargain?"

"You bet I am, hunky, I can promise you."

"Well then, go on," I said. "Go back to your fancy friends and see what they do for you. Look what they already done."

I got out of bed, pulled on my pants and socks, and stuck my feet in my shoes.

"Where are you going?" she said.

"Here," I said, taking out my wallet. I crumpled a couple of singles and threw them on the floor. "That and a twitch of your ass will get you back to the loons."

"You're not leaving," she said. "You're not leaving me here!"

"You can go back to your career fucking for old men," I said. I put on my shirt and combed my hair in the mirror over the dresser. "It's probably as good as you can do anyhow."

The mirror shattered. I didn't know what she had thrown. When I went for her she was reaching for the Gideon Bible to throw that. I grabbed her arm and we knocked the bedside lamp to the floor. I pinned her to the bed. She tried to bite me. I held her by the wrists and put my knees on each point of the pelvis.

"You're hurting me!" I moved back and let go of her. She lay still. A queer bitter smell came from her. It was anger that aroused her, confrontation was the secret.

But when I found her she was loving and soft and she shrank away softer and more innocent of her feelings than I had dreamed.

I held her, I loved the narrow shoulders, the small-boned frailness of her, the softness of her breasts against me. I was kissing her eyes, her cheeks, but she cried in the panic of the sensation, her legs couldn't find their place, she was like a swimmer kicking out or like someone trying to shinny up a pole.

I wanted her to know the sudden certainty declaring in me like God. I was where I belonged! I remembered this!

But she didn't seem to be aware of how I felt, there was this distracted spirit of her, her head shook from side to side with bursts of voice, like sobs, as if someone was mourned.

Our lovemaking was like song or like speech. "Don't you see," I asked again and again, "don't you understand?" And she shook her head from side to side in her distraction. I couldn't overcome this. I became insistent, I felt my time running out, I felt I had to break into her recognition. It's you, I wanted her to say, and she wouldn't she wouldn't say the words.

And then the tenderness was gone and I was pounding the breath from her, beating ugly grunts of sound from her, wanting her to form words but hearing savage stupid gusts of voiceless air coming from her.

In my moment of stunned paralytic grief I groan I go off bucking I think I hear her laugh.

For several days we made our life sleeping till mid-morning and getting on the road and driving again till the sun went down and we could find a bed. We drove through boarded-up towns, we ate blue-plate specials and we slept in rooming houses with linoleum on the floor and outhouses in back or in small motor-court cabins with the sound all night of the trucks rolling past. Night and morning we made love it was what we did our occupation our exercise. But always with great suspense in my mind. I never knew if it would happen again. I didn't have the feeling anything was established in her. She fucked in a kind of lonely self-intensification. She slept without touching me, she slept with no need to touch or hold me, she went off to sleep and it was as if I weren't there.

I would think about this lying in the dark while she slept. I was there for her, I was what she assumed, and I was willing to be that, to be the assumption she didn't even know she was making. And then one day she'd discover that she loved me.

Once in a while, usually in the numb exhaustion of daybreak, I'd look into her face and see an aspect there of the acknowledgment I wanted in the gold-washed green eyes. There would be humor in them. The lips slightly swollen and open, the small warm puff of breath. She'd giggle to see neither of us was dead and she'd give me a cracklipped kiss a soft dry kiss with the hot pulp of her lip against mine.

She liked to be inside her appetites and her feelings. Whatever they were. One day in a rainstorm I skidded off the road. I was frantically spinning the wheel, I couldn't see through the rain, it had turned white, opaque, but Clara was laughing and shrieking like a kid on a carnival ride. We thudded into a ditch. Water softened the canvas top and began to leak through and we sat at a tilt as if in a diving plane, in clouds. I thought we might drown. Then we felt the car rise, somehow the water floated us free, and when the storm passed over, we gently drifted a half mile or so in the flood like some stately barge down a stream. She loved it, she loved every second of it, her fingers gripping my arm, the nails digging into my skin.

Sometimes we went out at night walking some main street to a local movie. She liked to stop in a tavern and drink ten-cent beers, she liked the looks she got, the sexual alert that went off every time she walked into a bar or a diner. One time someone came over to the booth and started to talk to her as if I weren't even there. It seemed to me unavoidable what I had to do. He was an amiable fellow with a foolish grin, but with the strength in him of belonging in this bar, of being known in this bar, this town, he looked down and saw my knife, the tip making an indentation in the blue shirt and the sprung gut. He was genuinely astonished, they don't use knives in boondocks of the Midwest, he backed off with his palms up.

She had turned pale. "What's the idea, do you know what you're doing?" She spoke in a soft urgent whisper leaning toward me over the table.

"I do," I said, "and if you don't stand up and get your ass moving I'll do the same to you."

Outside I grabbed her arm. She was in a cold rage but I had the feeling, too, that I had done right, that I had shown her something she wanted to see.

"You know something?" she said as I hurried her along to our room. "You're crazy, you know that?"

I thought they were the first words of love I'd heard from her.

In Dayton, Ohio, I saw in the rear-view mirror the unmistakable professional interest of a traffic cop as we drove away from his intersection.

"I have not been smart," I said. "I suppose my mind has been on other things."

I made a sharp turn into a side street and started looking for the poor part of town.

"What's the matter?"

"A German convertible with bud vases and New York plates. You don't often see that in these here parts."

She thought awhile. "Is this a hot car?"

"In a manner of speaking."

Soon enough we were going through the dingy sections where the bums were standing on the sidewalks and the garbage spilled into the streets. The Buckeye State Used Cars enterprise looked grim and satisfactorily seedy, I turned in there and commenced a negotiation. The man with his fat dirty fingernails showed me there was not even a book on such a car. I said that was because it was so expensive they didn't figure anyone could afford it. He said maybe so, but how could he sell a car where you could not get the parts if they broke? I said nothing ever broke on a car like this. He said how could he take ownership on a car that had no papers? I said it was my family's car and since when did you walk around with papers of your own family's car? He said why did I want to sell my family's car? I said I was running away to get married and needed cash. "How are you going to run if you don't have no car anymore?" he said. "I'm going to buy a modest well-tuned vehicle from you," I said, looking with bright honest earnestness into his face.

He walked around the car several times. He glanced at Clara in the front seat, I had told her to put on her fur jacket. "That is my fiancée," I said to him softly, "of whom they don't approve." I could see him thinking: They wouldn't go after their own kid.

Come with me

Combust with me

"Someday," Clara said over the noise, "maybe you'll be able to buy it back, or one like it."

"What?"

"I said someday you could hope to get it back."

"I've got my car," I said, pounding the dashboard. "I've got papers for it. I've got a hundred fifty simoleons in my pocket. Is that bad? We can get to California if we're careful."

"California?"

"That's where we're going. Didn't you know?"

"I wasn't informed," she said, holding on to the leather strap over the door. She peered ahead, frowning. I had taken in partial trade a 1930 Chevrolet station wagon with wood-panel sides that shook and rattled, and floor-boards that jumped in the air every time we hit a bump. It had a high polish on its tan-and-brown body and admitted to fifty thousand miles.

I didn't know dead people were that unusual. I saw them all the time. I wandered around holding my bottle and seeing these dead hunkies lying on tables. I dragged my blanket around behind me. I wasn't frightened. My father would smile at me.

"When I was older I began to understand things a little more. I thought, for instance, that anyone who was dead had to have a hole in them. I didn't know people died without holes in them. Then I figured it out one day. Some old guy was being dressed who died of natural causes. He'd made it all the way. So I knew then about natural death.

"But it was just the business, you know, it was nothing special, we lived in an apartment right over the business I played after school outside in front of the stoop and there was my father driving up with his hearse, they'd back up into the garage and he and my brother took the body into the back. And that was the way things were on West Twenty-ninth Street.

"And then my mother died but my father didn't handle

it, someone else from another funeral parlor came and took her away. Just like doctors don't treat their own families. But maybe it was because she was religious. None of our church got buried with us. We were Greek Orthodox but the business was nondenominational. My father was not highly regarded in church. I saw more Romans and Jewish rabbis at Lukaćs' than I did priests. Anyway, my father moped around a long time. He didn't know what to do with me. He hired this black lady to take care of me. She was okay but she drank. She stood at the window whenever there was a funeral downstairs. She'd count the numbers of cars to see how important the dead guy was. She'd count the number of flower cars. Sometimes she called me to come look and I began to look too. You'd see all these flowers in the flower cars, sometimes in three, four cars of flowers, it was too much, like huge mounds of popcorn, I didn't like it. I hate cut flowers. All my life they made a stink coming up through the floor below, there was always somebody downstairs you could smell flowers through the dumbwaiter.

"But then if it was really a big affair it would be worth watching. My father and brother all dressed up in their shiny black suits. He'd hire on men on these days. People coming to pay their respects, filling the parlor, crowds standing out on the street. And then outside all the cars in a line, double-parked with their headlights on, all these black mourners' cars twice around the block. And the cops would be there checking on who showed up, standing across the street and watching. And the photographers with their big flash cameras taking pictures, and the next morning in the *News* or the *Mirror* there was a picture of somebody and in the background the canopy said Lukaćs' Funeral Parlor.

"But he didn't need the publicity and he didn't care. He was just some dumb hunky, he didn't care about anything, he didn't talk much, he just did this work. And he got this clientele over the years, he wasn't in the rackets himself, but he kept his mouth shut and didn't make judgments and he just got to be the one they used. He didn't care who he buried, why should he, the kind of work he did why get excited. After a while he had to expand. He bought the brownstone next door, and put a new streamlined face across both houses. And then there was a showroom and a reception desk.

"And I was pretty grown-up now. I wouldn't stay in school. I'd worked for a while at the five-and-ten just to have something to do. But he was getting fancy now and he needed someone for the reception desk and to answer the phone who could talk right. So he asked me. So I thought, Why not? I mean when I was a kid I used to get it at school. That's why I had no friends at St. Clare's. They came around at Halloween with sheets on and rang the front bell. Clara Cadaver, Clara Cadaver. Well, shit, I only had boyfriends, anyway. I mean as a kid my friends were boys. I played street hockey.

"But anyway, I didn't mind. I wore a black dress. I wore stockings and high-heeled shoes. I had an allowance for the beauty parlor. And that was my job. I got to meet some real people. It was an entrée, as they say. What's that sound? The engine doesn't sound right."

"No," I said, "it's okay. Maybe I need a little oil."

"It's getting dark, anyway—where do you suppose we are?"

"Are you hungry?"

"A little."

I had a terrible feeling, a chilled feeling because of her lineage, her criminal lineage, I thought of it as a caste, some kind of contamination she had been born into through no fault of her own and I thought it was mine now too; if I wanted her, what she was was mine too, what she brought with her we both had now.

But I was also happy that she had told me, that in the dreamlife of the road the hours sitting next to each other and facing in the same direction brought things out we might not have otherwise said. We told each other about our lives, we gave each other our lives while we looked at the road backward into ourselves. Even though afterward we didn't remember what we said, or were too proud to admit we remembered.

"We lived across the river from each other, you realize

that? We could have shouted at each other across the Hudson, two snot-nosed kids. Little did we know we were destined to meet! We saw the same Tom Mix movies. We ran along the sidewalks pointed to the sky at the same airships!"

"What?"

"No, really, playing hockey"—I wanted to make her smile—"don't you remember? Maybe our teams played each other. We made the puck from the end of the wooden cream-cheese box, right? We wrapped it in black tape, am I right?"

It seemed very important in this moment to make her smile.

"Don't you remember? Don't you remember the 'I cash clothes' man? On Twenty-ninth Street? The water wagon, running alongside it for the spray? Don't you remember how we went to the candy store for ice cream?"

"What are you talking about?"

"No, really, Clara. One hot afternoon we bought Dixie cups and stood on the sidewalk in the sun with our wooden spoons. You remember. Licking the ice cream off Joan Crawford's face?"

When Clara fell asleep I put on my coat, closed the door quietly and went out to look around. In addition to everything else snow had hit this burg, a heavy wet fall that stuck to your eyelashes and got into your shoes.

The rooming house was highway robbery—twelve dollars a week, paid in advance. Restaurants came to another two, three dollars a day. If I took her to the movies, another forty, fifty cents.

I had even bought her a gold wedding band—for her protection, I said.

I hadn't told her there was no money to get the valves reground. She thought we were in Jacksontown another day or two at the most. I could manage two day-coach fares to Chicago. But what would we do in Chicago—freeze our ass there?

And so, hunched in his khaki coat from the Great War, the big spender wandered through downtown Jacksontown, Indiana—Heart of the Hoosier Nation, as the sign said. Everything built of red brick, the bank, the library, the city hall, the armory. Stores occupied, the black cars parked at angles against the curbs, he notices the traffic, a heavy traffic rolling quietly through the snow, the sky gray, heavy flakes like soundproofing tamping down the horns, muffling the engines, even the streetcars grinding along hushed in the flanges, sparks flaring in the dark afternoon, the dark turrets of the armory the dark green cannon on the lawn with the mantle of white snow.

I saw everywhere on every street jalopies of every description, valises and boxes strapped to their fenders, children and grandparents high in the rear seats, scarfs wrapped around their heads. I saw furniture covered with blankets tied with rope on the beds of broken-down trucks. I saw out-of-state license plates: Kentucky Tennessee Georgia Arkansas Michigan Missouri.

I boarded the Railroad Street trolley to see what would happen. It banged its way sharply around corners and picked up speed. Soon it was out of the downtown area barreling between two endless rows of semi-attached bungalows, block after block. Eventually it veered into a dark street, a canyon of the sides of buildings, moving slowly now, many men walking in the street, the bell clanged, an unbroken chain-link fence blurred my eyes, if I opened the window I could touch it.

Last stop the doors hissed open at the main gate. Here a crowd of men stood waiting to get in, a quiet intense crowd not orderly but silent. The snow came down. Even as I watched, the crowd grew pulsing like something underwater.

Behind the locked gates uniformed men stood chatting as if nothing was going on.

I looked up at the block-long sign across the tops of two buildings. BENNETT AUTOBODY NUMBER SIX was what it said.

That evening I took Clara to dinner at the Jacksontown Inn, the best restaurant in town. It had tablecloths, candles, black busboys, and the roast beef au jus went for two dollars and a half.

"I see in the paper where every state is covered with snow from here to the Rockies," I said.

She eyed me warily. The true color of her hair beginning to come through, her hair was fluffier too, she had given up the beauty parlor she believed they would ruin her if she had her hair done in the Midwest.

"Anyway," I said, "I did a little exploring while you were having a nap. We could be in worse places. There are jobs here, people have money in their pockets, they're shopping in the stores and going to the movies. They have three movie houses downtown."

She cut her roast beef.

"And you want to hear something funny? The big employer and why everything is humming is your friend and mine Frankie W. Bennett. His Number Six plant."

She put down her knife and fork, dabbed at her mouth with her napkin and sat there.

"Oh, Clara," I said. "I'd be happy if I could just look at you across this table for the rest of my life."

"That would be a lot of roast beef," she said.

"You didn't wear your gold ring!"

"I forgot."

I ate and drank energetically. "Anyway," I said, "as long as we're stuck here—so long—as we're here awhile—I thought I'd tap into old Frank—build up our cash reserve for the run to California."

"What does that mean?"

"Well, they're hiring at the Number Six plant."

"So?"

A sip of water from my cut-glass goblet. "I caught on there this afternoon. Nothing to it. I just gave them my shining innocent face. I mean there were these guys standing around with their toolboxes and employment records all wanting the same dumb unskilled jobs I put in for. No contest."

"Why?"

"Because it was obvious I didn't have a union background. They don't want someone who's a wiseass. They want the ones who don't know any better."

"Why did you do it?" she said.

"I thought I explained," I said. "I thought I explained that."

She didn't say anything, we resumed dining. Occasionally she'd look up and smile sweetly at me, in the silence there at the Jacksontown Inn the unarguable terror of things was driven home to me.

"I don't see why you should get on your high horse," I said. "Is it any worse than sleeping in his bed? Is it any worse than stealing his car?"

"I think I've got to leave now." She stood.

"Do you mind if I pay the damn check?"

We walked through the snow back to the room. I grabbed her elbow, she shrugged me off. "Clara, for God's sake, what is it I've done, after all? I got a job! A job! Is it a fucking crime to get a job? There's no money! We're here in the real world now, don't you understand? There's no money!"

In the room she started to pack. I willed myself to be calm, there were other roomers on the same floor, I didn't need landlady trouble on top of everything else. "Clara, please don't be like this. Please listen. All right, this is the worst shithole town in the frozenest fucking country there is. It's so fucking cold I can't believe how cold it is. And there's no reason to stay here. Except that it's Bennett's! That's why, Clara. That is the true reason why. Because I'm gonna work his line without his knowing and walk away from his machine with my wages in my pocket and he's going to get us to California! That's why."

She was still.

"You hear me, Clara? Because it's living right under his nose. That's why. Because it's the riskiest thing! It's the toughest and most dangerous and the classiest thing. That's why."

She sat on the side of the bed. "And what am I supposed to do here all day while you work his line and make your classy wages? Huh, big boy? What am I supposed to do?"

My God, it was laughable, it was heartbreaking but at least she asked the question. Neither of us was twenty!

We were children—who were we, what chance did we have? In her question was one half of an instant's perceiving, dimly appreciated, of only the most obvious possibility of life comprising the history of mankind.

I sat on the side of the bed next to her, whispering in her ear, "You don't realize what you've done to me. Me, the carney kid! You're making an honest man of him, it's horrible. I have all these godawful longings to work to support you, to make a life with you, I want us to live together in one place, I don't care where, I don't care if it's the North Pole, I'll do any fucking thing to keep you in bonbons and French novels, Clara, and it's all your fault."

"Oh Jesus, he's crazy, this boy is crazy."

But I felt this weird tickle-behind-the-spine unprecedented truth of what I was saying. Before I said it I hadn't known I felt it: we could change, we could make our lives however we wanted! And the steps Clara had taken to molldom and to the high forest of Loon Lake were dainty steps, steps avoiding the muck of her reality and mine. And this was where we truly belonged, not on the road but stationary, in one place, working it all out in the hard life.

"You got anything better to do?" I said.

She sighed. "That's the crying shame of it."

Data comprising life F. W. Bennett undergoing review.
Shown in two instances twenty-five years apart of labor
relations lacking compassion or flexible policy understanding workers' needs.   His dramatization suggests life
devoted almost entirely to selfish accumulation of wealth
and ritual use thereof according to established patterns of
utmost class.   It is alleged he patronizes unsavory ele-
ments of society for his business gain.   It is alleged
that he is sexually exploitative.   It is suggested he is at
least unmoved by the violent death of another human
attributable to his calculated negligence.   Countervailing data re his apparent generosity to worthless poet
scrounge and likely drunkard Warren Penfield.   A hint
too of his pride in Lucinda Bailey Bennett's aviation
achievements.   A heart too for spunky derelict kids.
Your register respectfully advises the need for additional countervailing data.   History suggests of the
class of which Mr. F. W. Bennett is a member no unal-
loyed spirit of evil the dimes which John D. Rockefeller

senior gave away compulsively to people in the street became the multimillions of his sons' philanthropies.   Andrew Carnegie's beneficence well attested, as well as William Randolph Hearst's Milk Fund for Babies.   And
examination of the general practice of families of im-
measurable wealth in US suggests their generosity cannot
be explained entirely as self-serving public relations but
may be seen as manifesting anthropologically identified
principle of potlatch observed operating in primitive social
systems throughout the world from northern forest ab-
originals to unclad natives of tropical paradises.   The
principle regardless of currency of benefaction breadfruit
pigs palms fronds or dollars is that wealth is accumulated
so that it can be given away thus bringing honor to the
giver.   I refer to an American landscape from every
region of which rise hospitals universities libraries muse-
ums planetaria parks think-tanks and other institutions for
the public weal all of which are the benefactions of the
utmost class.   I cite achievements F. W. Bennett in his
lifetime the original endowments of the Western miners'
Black Lung Research Facility, Denver, Colorado.   The
Gymnasium of Miss Morris' School, Briarcliff Manor NY,
the Mexican Silver Workers' Church of the Holy St. Clare,
Popxacetl Mexico, The Bennett Library on the grounds
of Jordan College, Rhinebeck NY, the Bennett Engineering Institute, Albany NY, plus numerous ongoing benefactions of worthy charities and researches plus innumerable
acts of charity to individuals never publicized.
I attribute to F. W. Bennett in his death a last will and
testament of such public generosity as to receive acknowledgment on the front page of *The New York Times* data
available upon request.   Generally speaking a view
of the available economic systems that have been tested
historically must acknowledge the immense power of
capitalism to generate living standards food housing education the amenities to a degree unprecedented in human
civilization.   The benefits of such a system while occasionally random and unpredictable with periods of undeniable stress and misery depression starvation and deg-
radation are inevitably distributed to a greater and greater

percentage of the population.   The periods of economic
stability also ensure a greater degree of popular political
freedom and among the industrial Western democracies
today despite occasional suppression of free speech quash-
ing of dissent corruption of public officials and despite
the tendency of legislation to serve the interests of the
ruling business oligarchy the poisoning of the air water the
chemical adulteration of food the obscene development of
hideous weaponry the increased costs of simple survival
the waste of human resources the ruin of cities the servi-
tude of backward foreign populations, the standards of life
under capitalism by any criterion are far greater than under
state socialism in whatever forms it is found British Swed-
ish Cuban Soviet or Chinese.   Thus the good that fierce
advocacy of personal wealth accomplishes in the historical
run of things outweighs the bad.   And while we may not
admire always the personal motives of our business leaders
we can appreciate the inevitable percolation of the good
life as it comes down through our native American
soil.   You cannot observe the bounteous beauty of our
country nor take pleasure in its most ordinary institutions
in peace and safety without acknowledging the extraordinary achievement of American civilization.   There
are no Japanese bandits lying in wait on the Tokaidoways
after all.   Drive down the turnpike past the pretty
painted pipes of the oil refineries and no one will hurt you.
    No claim for the perfection of F. W. Bennett, only
that like all men he was of his generation and reflected
his times in his person.   We know that by the nineteen-
fifties at an advanced age he had come finally to see unions
as partners in enterprise and to cooperate fully on a first-
name basis with major labor leaders playing golf of course
at that age he only drove a ball twenty or thirty yards but
they called him Mr. Frank and with humor admired his
sportif outfits the beige-yellow slacks the brown-and-white
shoes with the tassels the Hawaiian shirt with his breasts
showing.   Note is made here too that this man had a
boyhood, after all, woke in the astonishment of a bedsheet
of sap suffered acne had feelings which frightened him and
he tried to suppress was cruelly motivated by unthinking

adults perhaps rebuffed or humiliated by a teacher these experiences are not the sole prerogative of the poor poverty is not a moral endowment and a man who has the strength to help himself can help others.   I cite too the ordinary fears of mortality the inspection of a fast-growing mole on the side of the nose blood in the stool a painful injury or the mournful witness of the slow death of a parent all this is given to all men as well as the starting awake in the nether hours of the night from such glutinous nightmare that one's self name relationships nationality place in life all data of specificity wipe out amnesiatically asiatically you don't even know the idea human it is such a low hour of the night and he shares that with all of us.   I therefore declare F. W. Bennett to embody the fullness of the perplexity of living, as they say.   I cite here his voice which people who knew him   only in his later years believed to be ridden and cracked with his age but in fact his voice had always been rather high reedy with a gravelly consistency around its edges and some people found this menacing but others thought it avuncular especially after his operation for cataracts when they wear those goggle glasses.   But it was one of those voices of such individual character that people who never heard it can imagine it just by the mention of his name and those standing in the great crush of honors at his funeral could believe themselves likely to hear it for many years afterward as if a man of this strong presence could not release his hold on life except very very slowly and, buried or not, manifest a half life, probably, of twenty-five thousand years.

was on headlights. First I attached with four screws two metal frames the screws lay in a bin the frames met at the convergence of two small belts the left frame from the left belt the right down the line. Sometimes the pieces didn't match, sometimes the wrong piece came down the wrong side and sometimes, the thread not being true, I had to hammer the screws in, everybody did.

Next I affixed the crossed pieces to the inside of a curl of tin shaped like a flowerpot. I then inserted through a hole in the pot about four feet of insulated wire that came to hand dangling from a big spool overhead. I snipped the wire with a pair of shears, knotted the wire so it wouldn't slip and put the whole thing back on the line for the next man, who did the electrical connections, slapped on the chrome and sent it on to the main line for mounting on a fender.

That was the operation it's what I did.

High above my head the windows of the great shed hung open like bins and the sun came through the meshed glass already broken down, each element of light attached to its own atom of dust and there was no light except on the dust and between was black space, like the night around stars. Mr. Autobody Bennett was a big man who could do that to light, make the universe punch in like the rest of us.

And all around me the noise of running machines, conveyor belts, the creaking of pulleys, screeching of worked metal, shouts, the great gongs of autobodies on the line, the blast of acetylene riveting, the rattling of moving treads, the cries of mistakes and mysterious intentions.

And then continuously multiplied the same sounds repeated compounded by echoes. An interesting philosophical problem: I didn't know at any moment what I heard was what was happening or what had already happened.

It was enough to make me think of my father. The man was a fucking hero.

Then they speed things up and I'm going too slow I drop one of the tin pots on the wrong side of the belt the guy there is throwing tires on wheel rims and giving the tubes a pump or two of air he ignores my shouts he can't take the time. And then the foreman is coming down the line to pay me a call I can't hear him but I don't have to—a red bulging neck of rage.

And then they stop coddling us and throw the throttle to full and this is how I handle it: I am Fred Astaire in top hat and tails tossing up the screws into the holes, bouncing the frames on the floor and catching them in my top hat of tin. I twirl the headlight kick it on the belt with a backward flip of my heel. I never stop moving and when the belt is too slow for me I jump up and stomp it along faster, my arms outstretched. Soon everyone in the plant has picked up on my routine—everyone is dancing! The foreman comes pirouetting along, putting stars next to each name on his clipboard. And descending from the steel rafter by insulated wire to dance backward on the moving parade of car bodies, Mr. Bennett himself in white tie and tails. He's singing with a smile, he's flinging money from his hands like stardust.

Shit, how many more hours of this ... I thought of Clara I thought of us driving to California in the spring. And then I thought, What if she just left, what if she met someone and said to him, *How do I get out of here?*

And then I resolved not to think at all, if I couldn't think well of Clara, I'd turn my mind from her knowing I was racked, knowing I couldn't physically feel hope in this hammering noise. But I didn't have to try not to think, by the middle of the afternoon my bones were vibrating like tuning forks. And so it had me, Bennett Autobody, just where it wanted me and I was screwed to the machines taking their form a mile away in the big shed, those black cars composed bit by bit from our life and the gift of opposition of thumb and forefinger, those precious vehicles, each one a hearse.

On the other hand everyone had the same problem I heard stories of people hauling off on a foreman, or pissing on the cars, or taking a sledge hammer to them, good stories, wonderful stories, probably not true. But the telling of them was important. I was the youngest on my line, jokes were made about that—what a woman could still hope for from someone my age. Jokes were important.

The line was a complex society with standards of conduct honor serious moral judgment. You did your work but didn't kiss ass, you stood up for yourself when you had to but didn't whine or complain, you kept your eyes open and your mouth shut, you didn't make outland-ish claims brag threaten.

Yet none of this was visible when we pressed through the gates in the evening, a nameless faceless surge of men in soft caps in full flight.

Clara and I lived on Railroad, the street of the endless two-family bungalows. I had my choice—to take the streetcar, which was faster, or walk and save the car-fare.

I ran.

I stopped only long enough to pick up a movie magazine or *True Confessions,* I liked to bring her small surprises keep her busy keep her occupied.

Sometimes I'd find her waiting at the window looking out the window—the dark industrial sky, the great bobbing crowd of men flowing down Railroad Street making a whispering sound on the cobblestones like some dry Midwestern sea—and she'd be holding her arms, the bleak mass life scared her as some elemental force she hadn't known, not even realized by the way she stood and watched that she gave it her deference.

We ate things heated from cans. We had two plates two cups two spoons two knives two forks. Our mansion was furnished army-camp fashion by the company. Behind the back porch was the outhouse.

We stayed in the kitchen till bedtime, I tossed pieces of coal in the stove, it never seemed to be enough. Clara sat reading, she wore her fur jacket she wore it all the time. She was fair and couldn't take the cold, the winter had done something to her face, coarsened it, rubbed the glamour from it. Five minutes out of doors her eyes watered, her cheeks flamed up. She didn't use make-up anymore.

All of it was all right with me. I still couldn't take my eyes off her. I tried to remember the insolent girl with the wineglass in her hand and the firelight in her eyes.

"I'm glad you're laughing," she said.

I had a scheme for getting us from kitchen to bed. I heated water in the black coffee pot and then ran the pot like a hot iron over the mattress. I undressed her under the covers.

I loved it cold, I loved the way she came to me when it was cold, as if she couldn't get close enough. But this particular evening I remember she stopped me in my lovemaking, she put her arm on my shoulder and said *Shhh.*

"You hear that?" she said.

"What?"

"Next door. They've got a radio."

I lay on my back and listened. I heard the wind

blowing the snow in gusts along Railroad Street. Sometimes the snow came in through the cracks and in the morning you'd find it lying like dust inside the front door.

"I don't hear anything," I said.

"Listen."

And then I heard it, very softly through the wall, it was dance music, the swing band of a warmer world, it made me think of men and women on a terrace under a full moon.

Their place—the mirror of our three rooms—astounds me. No trace of company domicile, it's all been washed from the walls and strained from the light coming in off the street. We sit on stuffed horsehair chairs, there is a matching sofa, behind the sofa a lamp with a square translucent shade of the deco design. A braided rug covers the parlor floor and glass curtains adorn the windows. Amazing. On the desk in the corner a private phone. Who would have thought people on Railroad Street had their own phones?

The subtle giving to the newcomers of their protection. Lyle James smiles sitting on the sofa with his hands on his overalled knees, he's one of those crackers, hair like steel wool, reddish going to gray, a face of freckles so that he appears to be behind them looking from his pink-lidded eyes through them as from some prison of his own innocence, buckteeth smiling.

What does he see? In Jacksontown, crossroads of the world, he thinks he'll see everything given enough time. These two are just getting their legs, the boy looking at her as if she's sick about to die, or have a fit, but it's his fit more likely, that's what's important to this boy, not how he feels but how she feels. And she, one spooked little old girl, she smokes her cigarettes, crosses her legs, stares at the floor, that's the way it is with folks from the East.

Mrs. James comes in from the kitchen holding a platter with chocolate cake and cups and saucers and napkins. Another freckled-face redhead, but a pretty one with light eyes, a plump mouth sullen in a child, provocative in a woman. Which is she? She is very shy, blushing when her husband boasts that she baked the cake herself. She wears an unbuttoned sweater over her dress, school shoes, ankle socks.

We're all Bennett people, neighbors, fellow workers, this is Clara, hello, this is Sandy, hi, Clara, this is Lyle, this is Joe.

They are Southerners, like so many of them here, but with my tenacity, I recognize it, they talk slower but feel the same. He must be thirty-five, a lot older than his wife, crow's-feet under the freckles, they act dumb but I don't believe it.

I detected the sly rube who liked to take city slickers.

Clara talks to the wife. Clara in this conversation is the older woman from New York, Mrs. James maybe sixteen years old stands in awe of that sophistication. And then a baby is brought out, the child wife has a baby!

The establishment of them sitting modestly for our admiration: people are strong, they prove themselves. You see, Clara? You can wrest life from a machine and walk away.

" 'A course," he was saying, "all this work ain't just the season. You wouldn't know but they was a wildcat strike last summer. Quite a to-do at the main gate. The company brought in strikebreakers. A feller was killed. They closed the plant down, fired everone. Everone!"

I nod, this is man talk.

The baby began to cry, the young mother unbuttoned and gave her breast right in the parlor, neither of them made anything of it. I glanced at Clara. She was intent. She watched the infant suck, she watched the mother and child. Expressed in Sandy James' face just that absorption in the task as the doll mother's in her solemn game.

"I started out in trim," Lyle says. "Now I hang doors. You get a few more cents a hour. Hands don't cut up so bad. Lemme see your hands," he said. I held them out, swollen paws, a thousand cuts. "Yeah," he says, "that's it."

After a while he went over to the radio we had heard, obviously his pride and joy, a Philco console of burled wood big as a jukebox. A circular dial lit up green when he turned it on, it had regular and shortwave broadcasts, and a magic tuning eye like a cat's green eye with a white pupil that grew narrow when he brought in a station.

He had turned it on as casual as he could be and while it warmed up consulted a newspaper. "How 'bout *Mr. First Nighter*," he said, "seein as you folks're from New York," he said to Clara.

Yes, they had culture!

We sat in dutiful appreciation and listened. Mrs. James had put her baby back to bed and sat now, a child herself, cross-legged on the floor right in front of the speaker, she wanted to get in there behind the cloth with those people.

In the casual grant of their warmth and circumstances we are so installed in the life as to have neighbors, we have started to live in their assumptions. I look at Clara she is way ahead of me, she is wearing her gold band.

As the drama crackled through the night the husband displayed enlightenment as to how the sound effects were made.

Someone kicked down a door. "They don't really wreck a door," he said. "At's just a ordinary vegetable crate they stomp on. Splinters real good."

A horse-drawn carriage. "Shucks, them's coconut shells rapped on the table."

"Hush, Loll," his wife said. "I cain't hear!"

After the program was over he lectured on how they made houses burn, typhoons blow, trees come down. He had us close our eyes and did these things up against our ears to get the effect of amplification. He was good, too, insane, I began to realize, once people got through their courtesy it was their madness they shared.

He had heard some *Arabian Nights* drama about a desert chieftain who skinned his victims alive.

"Ah don't wanna hear this, Loll," his wife said.

"Hold on, honey—see, Joe, I couldn't figger it out, Ah thought and thought, it was the damnedest thing! But I got it now, close your eyes a minute, this'll turn your hair white."

I hear a piteous wail, screams, sinister laughter and the unmistakable stripping off of human skin inch by inch. I have to look. Off my left ear he was tearing a piece of adhesive tape down the middle.

No, not exactly my type, I would not under ordinary circumstances choose to associate with Lyle Red James, but I knew when we walked off to work together in the morning Clara would have coffee with his wife, maybe during the day they'd go to the grocery store together I saw the child given from one pair of arms to the other—I would listen to a hundred nights of radio for that.

And at the front gates of the plant every morning a car or two of cops parked there, just happening to be there. Not that I thought they were looking for me but if they were I imagined Red James as my disguise. If the cops were looking at all, it was for a man walking by himself— that was my reasoning. And anyway, what they would have to accomplish to get to this point wasn't very likely. They would have first of all to locate Mrs. Lucinda Bennett's car in Dayton, the guy wasn't that stupid that he wouldn't paint it. But even if they did, they would know only that they were looking for a wooden station wagon registered to clever Joseph Bennett Jr. But even then, how did that get them to Jacksontown, Indiana? But supposing they were here, they wouldn't find it anyway, it was parked off the street behind a garage and under a ton of snow. I probably couldn't find it myself. But supposing they found it, they'd be on the lookout for a hobo boy, a loner walking by himself to work in the morning and not Mr. Joe Paterson loping along step for step with the world's biggest fucking hayseed.

It always proved out to my satisfaction if I thought about it but that didn't stop me from thinking about it again each morning going to the punch clocks under the thousand fists like rifle fire we are going into the trenches and over the top in the barrage of time clocks, I always checked my position before I went down there.

I sought disguise, every change in Clara and me a disguise, nobody who knew Clara Lukács and was in his right mind would look for her on Railroad Street. I liked us having neighbors, yes, and living to the life the same as everyone else, living married, looking like an automobile worker's family for life, appearing to these people next door as mirrors of themselves, shining in their eyes so they couldn't even describe us after we'd gone.

I remember the way Red James walked. He wasn't especially tall but he took long stiff-kneed strides, loping along there in the freezing morning while everyone else was hunched up, head bent in the wind, it was something you had to tear to get through, but here was Red, shoulders back, head up out of his collar, the long neck bobbing, and he chattered constantly, made jokes, told stories.

"A smart man'll put beans in his mule's feedbag. You know why?"

"Why?"

"Doubles the rate of progress."

"Come on."

" 'Strue! The fartin moves 'em along. Clocked a mule once sixty miles a hour on a handful of dry beans. Fastern' 'ese here cars."

That was the kind of thing. He held out his arms; the snow driving thick like white sheets flapping in your eyes, yelling "Toughen me up, God, usen me up to it!"

And he sang, too, always some damn hillbilly song in that adenoidal tenor of his kind as we went down toward the plant one point of raw color bobbing crowing

Hear the mighty eng-ine
Hear the lonesome hobos squall
. . . A-goin through the jungle
On the Warbash Cannonball!

And at work I found myself hearing his voice in the
machines, in the rhythm of the racket, without even
knowing it, doing headlight after headlight, I would sing
to myself in Red James' tenor: keeping time to the
pounding racket, I would hear the mighty eng-ine, hear
the lonesome hobos squall, a-goin through the jungle, on
the Warbash Cannonball.

One evening I came out of the gate and somebody tapped
me on the shoulder. I turned around, no one was there.
When I turned back, Red James was grinning at me.

"You comin to the meetin, ain't ya?"

"What meeting?"

"Union meetin."

"Well, I'm not a member, Red."

"I know you ain't. This is a recruitin meetin, anyone's
got the balls."

"Well, I don't know," I said. "I never told Clara I
wouldn't be home."

"Boy, the little woman sure has a holt a you. She's
with Sandy anyways, you come on with me, they'll figger
it out."

So I went along with him to this meeting in some
decrepit fraternal lodge a few blocks from the plant. It
was up a couple of flights, fifty or so men sitting on camp
chairs in a badly lighted room. I recognized a few faces
from the line, we smiled, catching each other out. I
thought, Look, if you're doing the life, do it. I took a seat
in the last row. Red had disappeared. The people running
the meeting sat at a table in front of the room. I couldn't
see all of them but they looked like Paterson toughs, they
wore buttons or had their union cards stuck in the bands
of their hats. I thought as Mr. Bennett was spread out
and made into a corporation he may have enlarged, but

so did the response, I couldn't see anyone in his personal service wearing his green putting a union button on their collar.

The meeting began with the pledge of allegiance and then the president rapped the gavel and called on the secretary to read the minutes.

Lyle Red James stood up and cleared his throat. "Herewith the o-fishul minutes a the last meetin," he said in a most formal manner. "As taken by yo Sec'tary Loll Jimes, Bennett Local Seventeen, union card number three six six oh eight?"

This called up a cheer and a burst of applause from the audience.

"Just read the damn minutes, James," the president said.

I hadn't known he was a union official, he had sprung it on me, it was queer, the faintest misgiving, I had thought the deception in our friendship was mine. I tried to think that whole meeting why I was bothered, I knew he was a damn clown I hadn't understood I was his audience.

I wanted to talk to Clara about it when I got home. Anyway, she'd be interested to know why I was late—but something else was on her mind entirely.

"Did you know," she said to me, "Sandy James is all of fifteen years old? Did you know that? She got married at thirteen. Can you beat that? And she does everything, she goes to the store she knows what's good and what isn't, she takes care of that kid like royalty, feeds that stupid hick better than he deserves, washes, shops, cleans, Jesus! The only thing I haven't seen her do is sew the American flag!"

What kind of time was this, a matter of a few weeks, a couple of days, minutes, and this other couple was in us, through us, I couldn't remember when we hadn't known them and lived next door.

In the second war we used to jam each other's radio signals, occupy the frequency, fill it with power.

Clara didn't think much of Red James but she never said no to one of their invitations, she had fixed on young Sandy, in that way she attached to people who interested her, locking on her with all her senses. I sometimes became jealous, actually jealous, I felt ashamed, stupid it was the diversion I had hoped for, it was just what I had counted on, I jammed myself when I saw the way Clara looked at Sandy, watched every move she made. Worrying about survival was something new to her and she was engaged by it, as by the little baby, the smell of milk and throwup, a bath in a galvanized-tin tub with water made hot on a coal stove, and all the ordinary outcomes of domestic life which presented themselves to her as adventure—how could I feel anything except gratitude! I thought every minute with Sandy James put Clara's old life further behind us, I felt each day working for my benefit I was a banker compounding his interest.

In the James kitchen Clara watches Sandy James dry the baby after her bath, the baby in towels on the kitchen table, two lovely heads together and laughing at the small outstretched arms, the gurgling infant, the women laughing with pleasure. I am noticed in the doorway, the heads conspire, the flushed faces, some not quite legible comment between them as they turn and look at me, smiling and giggling in what they know and what I don't.

I liked Sandy myself, I thought of her as my ally, the chaperone of my love, this child! I found her attractive especially in the occasional surprised look she gave me, as if she were an aspect of Clara and the current of attraction was stepped up by that.

"She was made to have babies," Clara said to me. "You can't see how strong she is because she doesn't know anything about clothes, all her things are too big for her, I don't know where she got them, but when she doesn't have anything on you can see how well built she is in the thighs and hips."

Clara's attentiveness to his wife did not go unnoticed by Red James, when we were all together he did what he could to affirm the universal order of things. One night he brought out his infant girl from their bedroom. Baby Sandy had no diaper or shirt. He held her up in his hand and said, "Looky here, Joe, you see this little darlin between her legs? You ever see them pitchers of gourami fish in the *National Geographical?* You know, them kissin fish? Ain't I right? Now I got two of em, two lovin women with poontangs just like that!"

This made Sandy James stare at the floor, her face reddening to the roots of her hair. "Lookit!" he said, laughing. "Colors up like the evenin sun!"

Clara sighed, stubbed out her cigarette and took Sandy and the baby into the other room.

He one night pours two shot glasses of Old Turkey I don't know what we're celebrating does he see Clara's hand touch Sandy's hair?

He says, "Hey, y'll see this here little girl, I kin make her do what I want, laugh, cry, anythang, watch." He begins to laugh, a silly high-pitched little laugh. Sandy ignores him, he jumps around to get in front of her puts his hand over his mouth, tries to keep from laughing, after a minute of his pyrotechnics she can't help herself, begins to laugh, protesting too of course, "Shh, shh, your gonna wake her Loll, shhh, you're wakin her up!," but he's really funny and she is laughing now, a child laughing, and in fact I'm laughing too at the mindlessness of the thing and suddenly he stops, face blank, staring at her puzzled his mouth turns down at the corners a sob comes out of him, he puts his arm up to his eyes, cries pitifully, we know what he is doing so does Sandy but she goes very quiet and asks him quietly to stop, he ignores her, keeps it up, crying to break your heart. "Oh Loll darlin'," she says, "you know I cain't tol'rate that," and then her eyes screw up, her lower lip protrudes, she is reduced, begins bawling, arm up, fist rubbing her eyes, she has a hole in the underarm of her dress, her red hair.

"What I tell you!" Red James says, laughing. "This li'l ole thang, look there she's a-just cryin her heart out!" and she is, she can't stop, he goes to her to comfort her maybe a bit sorry now that he's done this but she's furious. He tries to put his arms around her, she brings her leg up sharply, knees him in the groin, stalks off. Red James has to sit down, he takes a deep whistling breath.

And that's when Clara began to laugh.

In a great dramatic scrawl, full of flourishes:

To Joe—

Herein all my papers, copies of chapbooks, letters, *pensées*, journals, night thoughts—all that is left of me. Dear Libby is to keep them for your return. And you will return, I have no doubt about it. I have thought a good deal about you. You are what I would want my son to be. More's the pity. But who can tell, perhaps we all reappear, perhaps all our lives are impositions one on another.

W.P.
Loon Lake
Jan 6, 1937

hree little words. *Suree rittu waruz.* The girls had voices like cheap violins and they kept their wavery pitch as the car careened around abrupt corners, horns blasting, peddlers and old monks falling out of the way. It was three o'clock in the morning and the shopkeepers were already unrolling their mats heaving the flimsy boxes of fresh wet seagreens from the beds of trucks pitch-black the Tokyo sky above, Warren looked up as if to pray like a seasick sailor keeping his eye on a fixed point a light in the Oriental heavens channeled by tile roofs the heavens flowing in an orderly manner unlike the progress of the Cord, its headlights flashing the startled faces of the poor Japanese street class taking their morning fish soup hunkering beside small fires in metal drums. White-gowned attendants at the Shinto shrines sprinkled the cobblestoned courts with handfuls of water. *Suree rittu waruz.*

The car braked to a halt and Warren and the ladies pitched forward over each other hysteric laughter they all climbed down where are we he said and they led him triumphantly to the next bistro of the infinite night this

one a *mirikubawa*. A what? Warren kept saying as they
were led in through the smoke up on the platform three
black musicians were playing *jazzu* and a waitress got to
the little table almost before they sat down and they all
watched the expression on Warren's face as the drinks
were ordered and then the rollicking hysterico laughter as
he tasted the white substance in the sake cup *mirik* it was
milk this was a milk bar and their civilization had tri-
umphed again in producing for the American their friend
the one substance they never drank and were astonished
that anyone could, cow's milk, the very sort of thing that
made the Westerners smell that characteristic way from
their consumption from birth of the squirted churned
curded and boiled issue *issyouee* of the ridiculous cow.
They did not like the smell of course and only one *garu*
from whom he learned the *Chiara-stun* and what merriment that was that they had to teach him his dance, a
bold brown-eyed bow-legged thing with her bobbed hair
and low-waisted dress pleated to flare out above the knees
had the nerve in the intimacy of his room one dawn to
hold her fingers squeezing her own nostrils while he
fucked her looking down over the upraised knees upon
which he rested his bulk she was lying there holding her
nose and squeezing her eyes shut but making the sounds
of pleasure too how odd and later he said do I smell so
bad do I need to bathe no no she said with *moga*
merriment you can never washu away you it is *ura smerr,*
you *smerra butta* Penfield-san a *whore tubba butta*

They were his friends his introduction to the world of
flappers I had to come seven thousand miles from home
to meet a flapper he thought and all the things he had
read in the papers at home about the new people their
jazz their late nights their haircuts and merry step up
from provincialism he found there in Japan how odd they
were relentless and because he was American he was an
authority they came to him for authenticity and all the
protests he made were regarded with approval as ritual
modesty the kind of social grace they thought only they
had so he was an ideal teacher they thought he understood
the Japanese way so humble he fit right in and he learned

to make decisions simply because he was their authority. I'm from the working class he had announced when he first arrived with his introductions from his Seattle labor movement friends but something was misinterpreted here or there the upper class liberals the modern boys and girls rebels of the loins of the Meiji the *mobo* and the *moga* they took him up and he was forced to have cards printed in the Japanese way everywhere you went you presented your card or received someone's card on a salver a lacquered salver Mr. Warren Penfield Teacher of Western Customs ordinarily this consisted in not much more than appearing somewhere and allowing yourself to be observed your dark suit and rolled umbrella, one man to his embarrassment asked him to disrobe in front of the whole family to his boxer shorts so the women could see the undergarments and sock garters and make them on their own for the father the brother. Mr. Warren Penfield slowly learning the contact language by which he could communicate The Handshake lesson one The Tip of the Hat lesson two The Stroll with the Umbrella lesson three Helping Ladies Across the Street very *difficurr resson* four the deference shown to women the most genuinely unpleasant of the customs but they did it he looked at the *jazzu* pianist and the *jazzu* pianist looked at him and smiled and shook his head here they were together in service the smile said the frank and somewhat contemptuous self-awareness mirrored in the other doing the same thing what are we doing here man I mean I got an excuse what's yours that look of economically dependent expatriate we really down the ladder man to be stuck on this island making nigger faces for these little yellow men.

But one day Warren's reputation was made when a low-level official of the American embassy called and asked him to come by for a chat and it was to see if he would consent to offer his services to certain Japanese diplomats preparing themselves to sail to Washington, D.C., for an international naval conference cutaway striped coats gray trousers top hats I don't know anything Warren said my father mined coal I was a corporal in the Signal Corps what do I know but the embassy man said we have no choice you're up on the latest fashions everybody else has been here too long our faces are turning yellow yours is still pink and white like a cherry blossom he laughed and so Warren gave a lecture in recent cultural history in America about which he thought he knew nothing but which from having observed the Japanese he knew by refraction. There is a great liberalizing trend he said because of the Great War and internationalization of taste a sense the old ways must be overthrown and the old beliefs and restrictions are absurd. Young men and women marry because they fall in love and sometimes when they fall in love they don't even marry they live together in defiance of propriety half the point to the way they live is to insult propriety. People generally expect more, I think that is what you can say about us at this modern age of the 1920s, more love more money more freedom more dancing *Chiara-stun jazzu* men and women hold each other to dance in public and there is a music industry that produces their dance music for them and wickedness is a form of grace, transgression is seen as the liberation of the individual spirit but, he said, looking with alarm on the impassive frowns of his distinguished audience, you won't find any of that in Washington, D.C. Washington under Mr. Harding is the soul of propriety, he spoke slowly so the translators could keep up one word was equivalent to three or four sentences before the word, the word, after the word, the three little words blossomed like a bowl of chrysanthemums Mr. Harding himself is devoted to Bach and Boccherini especially the andantes, and the distinguished audience leaned back in its chairs and the look of impassive disapproval was replaced by the look of impassive approval. Afterward there was a reception and he found himself bowing it was easy quite easy and the embassy man said you missed your calling you should have come into State and he bowed to him too. A junior Japanese diplomat said he had studied at Harvard University. A blond young woman glanced at him. A Japanese publisher asked him if he did any writing. The same young woman glanced at him. She had a ring on her finger eventually they spoke she spoke of the entire Japanese nation as if they were all servants, making remarks about their character and reliability, she was married to one of the embassy staff. They became friends, Warren had now established within himself those women he was prone to love and those with whom he was most intimate in conversation two separate classes and always he recognized them when they appeared, this young woman was of the second class. Her husband was always busy but they were totally married in spirit in purpose in confidence so that all possibly naughty emanations from her were totally muffled in marriagehood, that was more than all right with Warren they became devoted friends she was a Midwesterner not that smart but in some blind instinctive way constantly putting him in touch with just the experiences that provoked his deepest response which then expressed what she might have felt had she been that articulate or generally sensitive to the meanings of things. She knew he was a poet. She was a prim neat young woman with a slender figure and the most appalling provincial drawbacks she had even found herself a Methodist congregation for Sunday mornings but she methodically introduced him to Japanese civilization. She knew the secret restaurants where you could get the best raw sea bream or salted baby eggplant or bean paste flavored with thrush liver or chrysanthemum petals dipped in lemon vinegar, they went to the shrines he sat in rooms perfectly furnished with no furniture slowly very slowly the authority on Western manners customs and English speech began to see things with a Japanese eye to cherish small things a lovely comb a lacquered bowl a shallow pond with fat orange carp the way some trees looked in their foliage as if tormented by wind or a madwoman having just extended her hair with the pads of her fingers. The young Midwestern wife became the audience for the drama of his life if she had not been there watching and finding it important he might never have changed but found his period with the irreverent flappers or lapsed into the paternal delusions of the foreign diplomatic community enjoying with a smirk the Japanese discovery of *besbol* the humor of Adolph Menjou Lillian Gish speaking in ideograms. Instead he began his withdrawal first from the Americans then from the Japanese trying to be like the Americans then from the wide streets of the city in which he shuddered to see men in derbies and rolled umbrellas riding in bicycle cabs, he grew thin and ate no meat he turned sallow and began to look actively for a style of expiation he could manage without self-consciousness but he couldn't have been that brave unless someone like the young wife from Minneapolis was there to pay attention.

The afternoon before he left on his pilgrimage she took him to the Bunraku puppet theater. Each large puppet was manipulated by three figures in black hoods one for the right arm and spine and face including the lifting of the eyebrows one for the left arm one for the feet, the puppets moved dipped bowed gesticulated raised arms to heaven walked ran, each movement was accompanied by the three black shadows behind to the side and underneath and to further disintegrate the human idea the voices of the puppets their growling thrilling anguish was delivered from the side of the stage by a reader whose chants were punctuated by the plunks of the samisen like drops of water falling on a rock and Warren Penfield after several hours of this thought yes it's exactly true, when I speak I hear someone else saying the words when I decide to do something someone else is propelling me when I look up at the sky or down at the ground I feel the talons on my neck how true what genius to make a public theater out of this why don't we all stand up and tear the place apart what brazen art to tell us this about ourselves knowing we'll sit here and not do a thing.

The puppet play told the story of two lovers who, faced with adversity, decided to commit suicide together and so at the intimate crucial moment there were eight presences onstage.

A cold bright sun glittering on the snow, dazzling the eyes, you couldn't tell where you were, in what desolate tundra of the world. But men got to work. The stamping of thousands of feet muffled by the deep snow.

Inside the Autobody the great clamoring noise seemed distant, a distant hum, as if the peculiar light reflecting the snow outside were a medium of shushing constraint.

It was an ominous day, I felt something was wrong, from down the line it came like a conveyed thing, going through my station like a hunk of shapeless metal with no definable function.

But I knew secrets, I was in on secrets.

At lunchtime the whistle blew, belts slowed down and stopped. I listened to one generator in particular, pitch whine dropping deeper and deeper to nothing. I went to my locker, men rubbed their hands on rags and looked at each other. Then someone came in who thought he knew where the trouble was, and holding our sandwiches and thermoses, we drifted toward it, we climbed over the car bodies and trod the motionless belts as if walking on tracks, and we came finally to an area flooded with bright daylight.

Two great corrugated sliding doors were open, I could see outside to a flatbed railroad car. Granulated snow gusting in. Sticking to spots of oil and grease. The cold sting of the day blowing in.

"Here, you men, you don't belong here!" A uniformed guard coming toward us with a scowl.

They were dismantling a whole section of machines, unbolting them from the floor and preparing to hoist them on pulleys. Someone said they were tool-and-die machines for the radiator grilles.

At quitting time I waited in front of the tavern across the street from the main gate. Red didn't show up. I walked quickly in the dark down Railroad Street.

"The train I ride on is a hundred coaches long, you can hear the whistle blow nine hundred miles. You see, Joe, when the New Year comes soon as everone's past the Xmas bonus, soon as everone begins to think a the spring layoffs as you cain't help but doin when the year swings round, that's when we're a-settin down. You understand the beauty o' that? The union's allotin considerable monies. You see what you don't know is that Number Six makes all the trim for the Bennett plants in three states. Do you take my meanin? Ever bumper. Ever hubcap. Ever runnin board. Ever light. When we set down come January, ever Bennett plant in Michigan, Ohio and Indiana is gonna feel it. 'Course I'm trustin you with this, you cain't tell no one, it's a powerful secret compris'n the fate of many. *Ohh-oh me, ohh-oh my, you can hear the whistle blow nine hundred miles."*

When I got home Clara wasn't there. I went next door. She was standing in the bedroom doorway holding Sandy's baby.

Two men were sitting in the parlor. They were dressed in work clothes. Sandy introduced me, they were members of the board of the local and I thought I recognized one of them from the meeting. He was a skinny little man and he didn't look at me as he talked. "Yeah, Paterson," he said, "I seen you around." His eyes darted to the phone on the desk.

The other man was younger, bulkier, he had a fixed smile on his face as if he had trained himself to it. "We're waitin fer Red," he said.

They sat back down. Sandy James didn't know what to do with them, she stood there rubbing her palms on her hips. The parlor was awfully crowded, I thought, with all of us and a Christmas tree too with the tip touching the ceiling the star awry.

"You and James buddies, Paterson?" the little man said.

"Yes."

He nodded, kept nodding as if unaware of the brevity of my answer.

And then the phone rang and he jumped up as if he had been waiting, and grabbed the receiver. "Yeah," he said, "yeah, that's it." He hung up.

"Well," he said looking at the other one, "I guess we'll be on our way," indicating the door with his chin. "Sorry to trouble you, Mrs. James."

"Red should be home right soon."

"No, no, that's okay," the little man said. "Just tell him we were in the neighborhood. Nothin important."

They left, she locked the door after them.

"Oh, it gives me the jitters," she said, "strangers comin round and askin questions."

"Like what?"

"Where we got our lovely furnishins? How long we had the radio?"

I went over to the desk, for the first time I noticed the phone had no number written on it the little white circle was blank.

"Where is Red?"

Sandy looked at me and down at the floor.

"Come on, Sandy, for God's sake," I said.

"To a meetin," she said. "A secret union meetin."

"A board meeting?"

"I guess."

I didn't argue with her. I motioned to Clara and we went back to our side. The house, banked with snow, was without draught, sealed, like a tomb. I didn't know why but I felt bad, I felt desolate, I didn't care about anything.

"Hey, big boy," Clara said. "Let me see you smile."

Later in our bed I was so huge with love for her it was a kind of mourning sound I made, plunged into my companion. The ceiling light was on. Her head was turned from me, her eyes were closed, her knuckles were in her teeth, high color spread up from her throat suffusing her face, her ears, this was not my alley cat of gasping contempt raking her nails down my back this was my wife connected to me by the bones of being, oh this clear ecstasy ravage on the skin, reluctance it was happening, lady's grief of coming.

I said to Red James, "Will you tell me what's going on?," my voice feeble and complaining. I already knew in this town of thirty thousand the crucial action was at my eyes, I was centered in it, it could not be less clear than something I would read in the newspaper. I was at the fulcrum where the smallest movement signified distant matters of great weight.

And he answered wonderfully not as if he had until this moment deceived me but as if I'd always known and admired him for what he was.

"See, Joe, I coulda stayed on, you know? Hell, I had it so finely made I mighta run for somethin someday in the national. But the client don't give a hoot fer that. He gets the intelligence and he spooks like a horse in a hurricane. I mean I'd laugh if I didn't feel like cryin."

We were walking home men everywhere talking in groups LAYOFFS! in the headlines flyers announcing a mass meeting trampled in the snow. Red suggested we stop in for a drink. We stood in front of a tavern I'd not been in before, the light in the window was gold and orange, it looked warm in there, I felt I'd better have something.

We sat in a booth in the back under a dip in the patterned ceiling. Behind us was the door to the toilet. We sat in this plywood booth drinking twenty-cent shots with water chasers I smelled the whiskey in my head odor of piss cigarette smoke the sweat of every man in the room.

" 'Course I ain't without choice, they's a little job at the Republic Steel in Chicago. Ain't no auto worker in Jacksontown gonna follow me to pull steel in Chicago. An' ifn there is, just in case, looky here."

He pulled a paper bag from his lunch pail, shook a small bottle uncapped it put a drop of liquid on his right index finger rubbed the liquid into the red hairs on the knuckles of his left hand. He spread the hand on the table: the red hairs were black.

"You like that?" he grinned, my stunned silence, he signaled the bartender for two more. "But hell, I'm thinkin to drop industrial work. You been to the city of Los Angeleez?"

I shook my head.

"Well, they's a need for operators there. They's so much messin around what with them movie stars and all, you see, ever good wife needs to make her case sooner or later, if you get my meanin. As does ever good husband. Yessir, they's opportunity in Los Angeleez."

He was nervous, talking with much careless confidence his glance kept flying up to the room behind me and coming back to me and flying off. It happened in the crowded bar that the lower register of his voice was lost in the babble of the room, so half of what he said I couldn't hear, I only saw the trouble he was in enacted on his face, in the animated appearance of him spiky unshaven red hair around the Adam's apple, the suddenly large teeth threatening to engulf his chin, pale white eyelashes pink-lidded eyes staring through their mask.

Joe was suspended, blasted. Gone was the wiseass street kid, gone in love, gone in aspiration, gone in the dazzlement of the whole man, the polished being.

"See, if the union was smart they wouldn't never let on they knowed. Take their losses this hand, play for the next, string me along without me knowin and use me against the company and tell me one thing and do another and trick Bennett right out of their shoes. An' shit, everyone woulda made out all around, the union 'cause they knowed 'bout me, the company still thinkin they had their inside op, and me still drawin my pay in good faith and doin my work."

He slumped against the back of the booth. "Hell, it's all the same anyways, the boys'll get their wages and grievance committees and such and it won't matter, the company'll just hike their prices, everthin'll be the same. But you see, they let me know they know and the company knows they know and I'm not good to anyone anymore leastwise to myself and now I gotta take that poor chile and move her out of her home."

"Red, it is so weird! You recruited me!"

"I surely did. I brought in numbers a good men an' true."

"Let me ask you, does Sandy know?"

"What, about me bein a detective? Aw, Joe," he said with a grin, "the poor chile has so much of a man in me already did I tell her the whole truth she'd go out of her natural mind with love!"

It now occurred to me to ask why I had been told. I was at the point of perceiving his peculiar genius, which was to make a lie even of the truth. He was waving his hand, calling someone, I turned just as two men arrived at the table.

"Set yourself down!" Red greeted them.

One slid in beside me, the other beside Red. I had never seen them before. They were heavy middle-aged men, one wore a suit and tie and coat with the collar turned up, the other had on a lumber jacket and a blue knit cap.

"See," Red said to them without any preamble, "I ain't sayin I didn't make a mistake. I don't want you to think that, whatever happens."

"That's all right, Mr. James," the one in the overcoat

said. He was sitting next to me. He pointed at me with his thumb. "And this is him?"

"My good friend and neighbor Mr. Paterson," Lyle Red James said.

"I see," the man in the overcoat said. He twisted in his seat and leaned back to look at me.

The fellow across from him pulled off his cap. He sat hunched over the table holding the cap in his fists. He was a white-haired man and his florid face was covered with gray stubble. He now spoke, his eyes lowered. "James," he said, "there is a particular place in hell, in fact its innermost heart, where reside for eternity the tormented souls of men of your sort. They freeze and burn at the same time, their skin is excoriated in sulfurous pools of their accumulated shit, the tentacles of foul slimy creatures drag them under to drink of it. This region is presided over by Judas Iscariot. You know the name, I trust."

Red began to laugh. "Aw, come on," he said, incredulous, "that ain't no kind of talk."

Then this man with the cap in his hands turned to Red and looked at him. I saw tears in his eyes. "On behalf of every workingman who has gone down under the club or been shot in the back, I consign you to that place. And may God have mercy on my soul, I will go to hell too, but it'll be a joyful thing if I can hear your screams and moans of useless contrition from now till the end of time."

"Hey, brother," Red James said, "come on now, you ain't even tried to see if I'm tellin the truth. That ain't exactly fair!"

Both men had risen. The man with the blue knit cap leaned over and spit in Red's face. The two of them made their way into the crowd and went out the door.

Red was impassive. He splashed some water from his glass onto his handkerchief and washed himself. He glanced at me. "Catholic fellers," he said.

A few minutes later we left the bar. My blood was lit with two whiskeys, and with the imagery of sin and death in my brain I wanted to ask him more questions—questions!—as if I didn't already know, like some fucking rube I beg your pardon would you spell it out for me please! Clara, I still had time, there was still time for me to get her and throw our things in a bag and get us the hell out of there. Instead I walked with Red James down Railroad Street in this peculiar identification I made with him, as if only he could guard me from what I had to fear from him, and on Railroad Street where it made a sharp turn there was a shortcut across an empty lot the moon was out and going across this terrain Red glanced at me as I tried to phrase my questions he looked at me with genuine curiosity, as if, with all his figuring he had not figured me to be, in this outcome, that stupid. And we went across the snow moon of the frigid night making our way to our joined homes and fates as if nothing had happened and two ordinary workers had only stopped for a drink in the time-honored way. He was singing now in his nasal tenor the ritual that comes on the excommunicated

The train I ride on is a hundred coaches long
You can hear the whistle blow nine hundred miles
Ohh-oh me, ohh-oh my
You can hear the whistle blow nine hundred miles.

At one point the police asked me if I knew who it was. I shook my head. "I never even saw them," I said. This technically was true. But I thought I knew them anyway. I recognized the sentiment. I heard in the furious contention the curses of my own kind. Swaying and tumbling all together, we were one being in the snow, one self-reproaching self-punishing being.

The police wore their blue tunics over sweaters. Their hips were made ponderous by all the belts and holsters and cuffs and sticks hanging from them. They were tough and stupid, there were four of them in the hospital emergency room, four cops writing their reports on pads wound with rubber bands. Then the reporter arrived from the local paper, a thin small man in a Mackinaw and fedora, and he asked them if they had found anything in the lot. I could tell it had not occurred to them to look.

When Clara got there with Sandy I was lying on a table in one of the treatment rooms and on the table next to me was the body. I think I'd been given something before they set my arm because I saw Sandy's stunned very white face but I didn't hear the sound she made. The attendant pulled away the sheet the lips were curled back from the teeth like he was grinning and Sandy passed out. Clara, who was holding the baby, grabbed Sandy's arm and kept her from falling while the attendant ran for the smelling salts. I thought it was still Red making her do whatever he wanted.

Sometime later I had a chance to talk to Clara for a minute.

"He was a company op," I said.

She shook her head. "The poor dumb galoot."

"None of this had anything to do with us," I said, "and I danced us right into it." I didn't want to talk this way. I looked in her eyes for the judgment and not finding it tried to put it there by talking this way.

She touched her fingers to my lips.

"He couldn't have been placed better," I said. "It was a secret strike plan, nobody knew except the officers. And then the company took out half the machines."

"Some men came to their house this afternoon," she said.

"What?"

"Just when it was getting dark. We happened to be on our side. At first Sandy thought it was the radio, that she left it on."

"Did you get a look at them?"

"I didn't want to. I heard what they were doing. They tore the place apart."

"Jesus."

"It's lousy that she got hit with all this," she said.

"Well, now I know why they didn't believe him."

"What? I don't think you should try to talk."

"No, it's all right, I'm doped up. I'm saying he was trying to pin it on me. I guess he couldn't think of anything better."

"What?"

"But they weren't buying it because they must have got into his files." I found myself panting in the effort to speak. I was having trouble catching my breath.

At this moment I saw in Clara's calm regard the disinterested understanding of a beat-up face—as if nothing I had to say was as expressive as the condition I was in.

"He tried to make me the fink," I said. I realized I was crying. "The son of a bitch. The goddamn hillbilly son of a bitch!"

She turned away.

I stayed that night in the hospital and once or twice I realized the moans on the ward were my own.

In the morning I caught a glimpse of myself in the metal mirror of the bathroom—arm in a sling, a swollen one-sided face, a beauty of a shiner. I found myself pissing blood.

I was released—I supposed on the grounds that I was still breathing. I walked a couple of blocks to the car line. A clear cold morning. I sat in the streetcar as it gradually was engulfed in the tide of men walking to work. I thought of trying to work the line with a broken arm. I was out of a job.

Men stepped aside to let the streetcar through. Faces looked up at me. I had pretended to be one of them. That was the detective's sin.

When I got home I found Clara and Sandy James and the baby asleep in my bed. The house was cold and there was a fetid smell, faintly redolent of throw-up or death, it was a very personal smell of mourning or despair. I got the fire going in the coal stove—I was learning with each passing moment the surprises of a one-armed life.

I went next door. The place was a shambles. Red's desk had been jimmied open, the sofa cushions and chair cushions were piled up, the braided rug was thrown back, his collection of pulp magazines was tossed everywhere. His secretarial ledgers were on the floor, one with the names and addresses of the membership, another with his meeting minutes. I found boxes of mimeographed form letters, a loose-leaf folder with directives of the National

Labor Relations Board, a scattered pack of blank union cards.

Inside the splintered front door, stuck in a crack, was the carbon copy of a handwritten memo dated some months before. It had been stepped on. It was addressed to someone with the initials C.I.S. It was signed not with a name but with a number. But I could tell who the writer was, Red wrote a very chatty espionage report, very folksy. He spelled grievance *greevins*.

The bedroom was no less worked over. I straightened the mattress and lay down and pulled a blanket over me. I knew that I should be thinking but I couldn't seem to make the effort. Eventually I fell asleep. A wind came along and worked at the broken front door, banging it open, banging it closed, and I kept waking or coming to with the intention of seeing who it was, who it was at the door who wanted to come into this pain and taste of blood.

In the parlor a man was picking up papers and tapping them into alignment on the floor. It was the tapping that woke me.

"Hey, pal," he said.

He wore a topcoat that was open and followed him like a train as he duckwalked from one item to another. His hat was pushed back on his head.

He stood up with an effort. "Oh boy," he said, "these old bones ain't what they used to be."

A lean face, pitted and scarred, very thick black eyebrows, and carbon-black eyes with deep grainy circles of black under them. A heavy five o'clock shadow. But the skin under all was pale and unhealthy-looking. He had collected Red's union records and was stuffing them now in a briefcase. He righted the armchairs and looked under the cushions. He felt around the desk drawers. He stacked Red's pulps, flipping through each one to see if there was anything in it. He was very thorough. And all the while he talked.

"Whatsamatter, the lady's husband come home early? Well, you tell me: was it worth it? I'll tell you: no. I know about ginch. It is seldom worth it. It is seldom worth what you have to go through to get it. I been married twice myself. I was happy in love for maybe five minutes each of those women."

It was speech intending to divert, patronizing speech, his eyes and hands busy all the while.

"Put that stuff back," I said. "It doesn't belong to you."

He smiled and shook his head. He came toward me. "Where's the widow?" he said.

"What?"

"His bereaved."

"I don't know."

He came over to me. "Hey, kid, look at you. Look at how they worked you over. How much can you take? What's the matter with you?"

I immediately recognized the professionalism of the threat.

"Listen," he said, "don't be a wiseass. I'm here with the money, her death benefit." He waved an envelope in front of my eyes. I could feel the breeze on my hot face.

"She's at my place. I'll get her."

"I would be grateful," he said.

The women were up, they were in the kitchen, Clara was drinking coffee, she was wearing the clothes she had slept in, she looked gaunt, grim.

Sandy James' eyes were large and glistening with the unassuageable hurt of someone betrayed. The corners of her mouth were turned down. She was trying to feed her baby and the baby was enraged, it was twisting and turning, and making dry smacking sounds. It pulled on her breast and waved its tiny arms.

I explained, but even as I did he appeared in the doorway behind me. Sandy stood and thrust the baby at me and pulled her dress closed and buttoned the buttons while I held the crying baby, wriggling and twisting against my cast.

Now we all stood there frozen in that way of those overtaken by ceremony. Even the baby quieted down.

"I'm sorry for your trouble, Mrs. James," the man said. He held a legal-looking paper in one hand, an uncapped fountain pen in the other. "Your husband, Mr. James, was a brave man. The company knows it has a responsibility to his family. It ain't something we have to do, you understand, but in these cases we like to. If you will sign this receipt and waiver, both copies, I have a death-benefit sum of two hundred and fifty dollars cash on the barrelhead."

Sandy James looked at Clara. Clara sat with her head lowered, the fall of her hair hiding her face.

Sandy James looked at me. I knew what the waiver meant. Two hundred and fifty dollars seemed to be the going rate. Sandy James age fifteen was in no position to sue anybody. I nodded and she signed the waiver.

The fellow tucked one copy in his pocket and put the other on the table. He glanced at Clara. He took out his wallet and counted the money and put it in Sandy's hand. He came over to me and stuck his finger in the baby's cheek. "Hey, beauty," he said. He looked at me and laughed. "Beauty and the beast," he said.

When he was gone Clara found a cigarette and lit it.

"Two one-hundred-dollar beels," Sandy James said. "And a fifty-dollar beel."

I sat on the kitchen table and read the waiver. The party of the first part was Mrs. Lyle James and all her heirs and assignees.

The party of the second part was Bennett Autobody Corporation and its agents, C.I.S., Inc.

I said to Sandy, "You know what C.I.S. stands for?"

She shook her head.

Clara cleared her throat. "It means Crapo Industrial Services," she said. She took the baby from me. She hugged her and began to pace the room, hugging the baby and saying soft things to her.

"Mah milk's dried up," Sandy said. "She'll have to get on that Carnation?"

"Red worked for Crapo Industrial Services," I said to Sandy. "Did you know that?"

"Nossir."

"Neither did I. Why should it surprise me?" I said. "Clara? Does it surprise you?"

Clara didn't answer.

"No? Then why should it surprise me?" I said. "After all, a corporation like Bennett Autobody needs its industrial services. Spying is an industrial service, isn't it? I suppose strikebreaking is an industrial service. Paying off cops, bringing in scabs. Let's see, have I left anything out?"

"Why don't you take it easy," Clara said.

"I'm trying to," I said. "I'm just one poor hobo boy. What else can I do?" I went out to the privy. The sky was clear but a wind was blowing dry snow in gusts along the ground. I was still pissing blood. When I spit, I spit blood. Someone who had business connections with F. W. Bennett was big-time. Tommy Crapo was big-time. Surely he did not even know the name Lyle Red James. It was a coincidence that the fucking hillbilly who lived next door to me was an operative of Crapo Industrial Services. That was all it was. It was not a plot against me. It was not the whole world ganging up on one poor hobo boy.

But in my mind I saw the death-benefit man stepping into a phone booth and placing a call.

I went back inside.

"Can you eat anything?" Clara said. She spoke in a hushed voice that irritated me. "Do you want some coffee?"

"Sit down," I said. I faced her across the kitchen table. "You knew that joker."

She folded her hands in her lap. She sighed.

"Well, who is he?"

"Just some guy. I used to see him around."

"A friend of yours?"

"Oh Christ, no. I don't think I ever spoke five words to him."

"What's his name?"

She shrugged.

"What's his name, Clara?"

"I don't remember. Buster. Yeah, I think they called him that."

"Buster. Well, did Buster say anything? Did he recognize you?"

She didn't answer.

"Clara, for Christ's sake—do you think he recognized you!"

Clara bowed her head. "He may have."

"Okay," I said. I stood up. "Fine. That's what I wanted to know. See, if we know what we're dealing with we know what to do. Am I right? We need to know what the situation is in order to know what to do. Now. Is Tommy Crapo in Jacksontown? You tell me."

"How should I know? I don't think so."

"Well, where would he be?"

She shrugged. "He could be anywhere. Chicago. He lives in Chicago."

"Good, fine. When Buster calls Mr. Tommy Crapo in Chicago to tell him he's found Miss Clara Lukács, what is Mr. Tommy Crapo likely to do?"

"I don't like this. I don't want to talk about this anymore."

I leaned over the table. "Hey, Clara? You want to talk about us? You want to tell me how you love me? What is Mr. Tommy Crapo likely to do?"

"I don't know."

"Is he going to hang up the phone and laugh and call in his manicurist? Or is he going to come get you?"

She wouldn't answer.

"I mean what happened at Loon Lake? Why did he leave you there? Did you do something to make him mad? Or was it just a business thing?"

She slumped against the back of the chair. Her mouth opened. But she didn't say anything.

"Well?"

"You fuckin' bastard," she said.

"Oh, swell," I said. "Let's hear it. Step a little closer folks. Sandy!" I shouted. "Come in here and listen to this. Hear the lady Clara speak!"

We heard the front door close.

"You're terrific, you know?" Clara said, her eyes brimming. "That kid has just lost her husband."

"Don't I know it. And what a terrific guy he was. They're coming at me right and left, all these terrific guys. They run in packs, all your terrific friends and colleagues."

I ran next door.

Sandy James had put the baby in her carriage and was standing in the middle of the room pushing the carriage to and fro very fast.

"Sandy," I said, "I'm very sorry for all this and when we have the time we'll talk about it if you want to. I'll tell you everything I can. Did Red ever give you instructions who to call or what to do in case something happened to him?"

"Nossir."

"Does he have family in Tennessee, anyone who should be notified? Anyone who could come help you?"

She shook her head.

"How about your family?"

Her lower lip was protruding. "They cain't do nothin."

"Well, did Red carry life insurance?"

She shook her head.

"Do you know what that is?"

She shook her head.

"Well, where does he keep the family papers? I mean like the kid's birth certificate. He must keep that somewhere."

That's when Sandy James began to cry. She tried not to. She kept rubbing her eyes with the heels of her hands as if she could press the tears back in.

I looked around the room. With Buster's tidying, the parlor was not too badly messed now. I began to go through it myself, opening the desk drawers, tossing things around. What was in my mind? I thought if Red James had not told his wife of an insurance policy, he would be likely to have one. I was looking with absolute conviction in the clarity of my thought for an insurance policy but why it seemed to me the first order of business I couldn't have said. I supposed it would lead to something. Different pieces of Lyle Red James had been lifted—his espionage self by the union avengers, his union self by the industrial-service hoods, surely there must be something left for me, something of value to me, something he owed me. Maybe there was a strongbox and maybe along with a birth certificate and an insurance policy there would be cash. He owed me something. He owed me a broken arm and a battered face and a considerable portion of my pride. He owed me my abused girl, he owed me the care and protection of his own wife and child. He owed me a lot. I ran into the bedroom and began to go through the closet. Every move I made was painful, but the more I searched—for what? where was it?—the more frenzied I became. My body had thought it out: I needed to get us all off Railroad Street. I needed to save Clara. I needed to get Sandy James and her baby home to Tennessee. I needed the money for all of this. I think I must have whimpered or moaned as I searched. I was in a cold sweat. At one point from the corner of my eyes I saw the two women standing in the door watching me. I took the sling off my arm so that I could move around more easily. Without the sling I felt the true weight of my cast. I thought of the weight as everything that had to be done before I could get out of Jacksontown. I wanted to shake this cement cast from my bones as I wanted to shake free of this weight of local life and disaster. None of it was mine, I thought, none of it was justly mine. I had stopped over. That was all. I wanted to be going again. I wanted to be back at my best, out of everyone's reach, in flight. But I had all this weight and I felt there was no time for condolence or ceremony or grief or shock or tears, there was hardly time for what I had to do in order to lift it from me so that we could get free.

E ventually it dawned on him, the fucking radio of course, he pushed it away from the wall.

It was a small radio in a big cabinet. Under the tubes and behind the black paper speaker was a cigar box. In the box a .32-caliber pistol. He had never handled a gun before. It was heavy, felt loaded smelled oiled and sufficient. He put it back closed the box.

Wedged in the space between the tube chassis and the cabinet one of those cardboard accordion files with a string tie. This he lifted out. He pushed the radio back against the wall.

"Sandy!"

He sat on the floor. She knelt next to him. He watched her hands, she withdrew a marriage license a white paper scroll, she unrolled it holding it with both hands to her face as if she were near-sighted. She withdrew newspaper cutout coupons, a pack of them, the kind people saved for premiums, she withdrew the baby's birth certificate, she withdrew a wedding photo of Mr. and Mrs. Lyle James all dressed up smiling on the steps of a clapboard church. He had to let her cry over that one in her silent way palming the tears as they flowed. She withdrew a leather drawstring purse, he thought the deliberation of her movements would drive him out of his mind, she untied the string widened the mouth of the purse and shook out several shiny bright medals with ribbons.

"Was Red in the war?"

"Nossir."

"Stupid of me to ask."

She withdrew a printed policy of the Tennessee Mutual Life Insurance Policy. Its face value was a thousand dollars. That would have to do.

"Aren't there people who cash these things right away? Wills, IOUs, stuff like that?"

"Factors," Clara said.

"Yeah, factors. I bet I could get sixty, seventy cents on the dollar. This is as good as cash."

"It's not yours," Clara said.

"I didn't say it was. Would you mind coming into the other room a minute?"

Clara followed him into the Jameses' bedroom. He closed the door.

"I don't know," he said, "maybe you want to see your old sweetheart again. Have a few laughs."

"Is that what you think?"

"I don't know what I think. But if we don't move our ass out of here we're finished."

"Maybe so, but that's our problem, not hers."

"If we are all tending to our own problems," he said, "we can walk out this minute. We'll let the fifteen-year-old widow shift for herself. Is that what you want?"

"You're hurting my arm!"

"Why do I have to explain these things!"

"Let go of me. It was your idea, big boy. I didn't tell you to move to this shithole."

He went back to the parlor.

"Sandy, I'm prepared to take you back to Tennessee. I mean we're all finished in Jacksontown, I assume you understand that. You will spend Christmas with your family at your ancestral home. I am proposing we join forces, you and Clara and me, pool what we have and help each other. And I give you my word I will make good on every penny of the whole thousand."

The kid was silent. He waited. He realized this meant yes. "Okay," he said, "it's settled. We have a lot to do. He has to be buried. What are we going to do about that?" He looked at Clara. "Hey, Sandy, I bet you didn't know we had an expert among us."

The briefest bewilderment on Clara's face, what had she done wrong, did he blame his broken arm on her, his stitches? His mind was functioning now, he had calmed down, he was the old Joe of Paterson working things out. But one nick of this gem of a mind flashed the spectral light of treachery.

She smiled appreciatively almost shyly, with a dip of her head, a curl at the corner of her lips, her eyes sparkled, she had it, she knew it before he did, the secret wish, the resolution.

"Ah want the best," Sandy James said.

"Why not?" said Clara. She knelt down next to Sandy and put her arm around her. She tilted her head till their heads touched. "You'll have the best," Clara murmured. She looked up at him. "In Jacksontown it won't cost that much."

While Clara was on the phone I asked Sandy James how she felt about her furniture.

"It's all paid," she said.

"So much the better. I could get it appraised and you'd make a clear profit."

She clutched her baby and looked around the parlor. Her eyes were large. "Wherever I live I'm gonna need a chair and table. I'm gonna need a bed to sleep in."

"Okay, okay, I'm just asking, is all. I'll figure something out."

An hour and a half later I had everyone packed. I called a Yellow Cab and by the time it pulled up I had both women and the baby and the bags out on the sidewalk.

Nobody was watching. No car followed us. I took us back to the rooming house Clara and I had stayed in when we first hit town. I rented two rooms adjoining. I got everyone settled.

"Do you mind telling me what you're doing?" Clara said.

"Not at all. I'm going to the factor. Then I'm going to pick up my back pay. Then I'm going to see what I can do about a truck for all that shit of theirs."

"You better slow down. You don't look so good."

"I can imagine."

"You can't leave town before the funeral."

"I understand that. But we'll get a good night's sleep. You don't object to a good night's sleep, do you?"

"She doesn't know what hit her yet. You're not giving her the chance."

"I'll leave that to you."

We stand on either side of Sandy James, who holds her baby. I hunch into my khaki greatcoat. It is buttoned over my cast and I have pinned the sleeve. The grave has been dug through the snow and through the ice and, with scalloped shovel marks, into the frozen earth. I study the crystal formations of the grave walls. I imagine lying there forever, as he is about to do.

The stones around us lean at all angles as if bent to the weight of the snow banked against them. The graveyard is in a desolate outlying section of town. It is on a rise that commands a view of the adjoining streets, one filled with the blank wall of a warehouse, the other fronting a lumberyard. A traffic light at the intersection. Over the racks and open sheds of the lumberyard I can see to the tracks and signals and swing gates of the Indiana Central.

The Baptist preacher is garrulous, Southern, like the fellow in the coffin. He speaks of God's peppers. An image comes into my mind of a green field of pepper plants and I wonder at the eccentricity of all the glories of God's fecund earth to speak of peppers.

I look from the corner of my eye at Sandy James. She stares into the grave. I see the tracks of her tears on her cheeks. I see the corneal profile of her green eyes. The baby comes into view, leaning forward in curiosity, her arms wave over the grave, cheeks puffing their steam of baby breath.

I cannot see Clara, the mother and baby block my view of Clara.

I shift my weight from one leg to the other. A dozen or so union men are standing behind us. They hold their caps. There are others too. The reporter who questioned me in the hospital, his ferret face under a brim hat, his plaid Mackinaw.

Two green-and-white police sedans and a police motorcycle and sidecar are parked in front of the warehouse across the street from the entrance to the graveyard. The cops sit on their fenders and smoke cigarettes.

A cream-colored La Salle with whitewall tires turns the corner and slowly cruises past the cops and out of my line of vision. I hear a motor cut off, the wrench of a handbrake.

"Do not question God's peppers," says the preacher.

I'm trying to think. What are all these people doing here? All night I sat in a chair by the door with a heavy pistol in my lap and I tried to think. I tried to lift my head and open my eyes, shake off the exhaustion of my bones to think.

Now I do have a thought. It is really very foolish. It is that these people—the union men, the cops, the reporter—they're all staying. I mean this is where they live, Jacksontown, Hoosier Heart of the Nation, it's their home, it's where they make their lives. The reason this preacher twangs on and on is because he too lives here. He's in no hurry, why should he be?

All of them, it's a big thing this funeral, an event. I look at the landscape, nothing is moving, even the sky looks fixed, residential.

I shiver, a chill ripples through me. I feel their entirety

of interest and attention as some kind of muscling force. Some large proprietary claim in the presence of these people displaces me.

I am dispossessed.

I square my shoulders and stare straight ahead. It seems important not to reveal from my expression or my posture that I understand this. I know what it is now. It is the whispering return to my body of my derelict soul. Oh, my derelict soul of the great depression! What's happening to me—I feel guilty! Guilty of what? I don't know, I can't even imagine!

Finally the twanging ends and with great satisfaction in the holiness of his calling, he closes his Bible, turns his face upon me and I nod and shake his hand. The ten-dollar bill folded in my palm passes to his. He murmurs something to the widow and for no additional charge grazes the baby's cheek with the tips of his theistic fingers. Then he's gone. Clara moves around in front of Sandy and hugs her and turns her away from the gravedigger, who with his shovel propped against his hip is spitting on his hands getting ready to go to work.

We walk slowly to the gate, a hand taps me on the shoulder. "Paterson?"

I turn. The heavyset man with the blue knit cap the expert on hell. Behind him three or four others.

"We don't want to disturb Mrs. James at this time. We have made up a pot." He puts a folded wad of bills into my hand. "The boys from the local."

I must have looked shocked. He moves close to me.

"Do you think, Paterson," he says in my ear, "that we would be so stupid as to permit ourselves to be overheard threatening a man in public not ten minutes before we meant to jump him in a dark alley?"

"What?"

"Use your brains, lad. I'm sorry for the beating you took, but if it was us you'd be in the grave beside him."

He moves off, I find Sandy and Clara, I hold Sandy's arm, I feel her bewilderment of sorrow. Faces appear, condolences drift in the cold air flutter for a moment fall.

They knew my name.

They thought it matters to me who killed him.

Clara catches sight of the cream-colored La Salle. She frowns and turns away with an involuntary glance back uphill to the grave. The color in her cheeks, the thin skin she has for the cold, the blue translucence of the eyelids, the tears in the corners of her eyes.

We are through the gate, walking on pavement. I'm between the two women. I hold their arms. It is becoming more difficult to move forward. Several bulky policemen, awkward, they don't seem to know what to do with themselves.

"Pardon me." A man tips his hat to Sandy. "Mr. Paterson, I wonder if you'd mind." I can't hear him.

"What?" There seems to be some problem. It is some misunderstanding, it's becoming difficult to move forward, we're in a crowd, it banks higher and higher against our progress.

"What?" I hear my own voice. "What questions? I already answered questions."

"We just want to talk to you a few minutes, clear up some things."

I look behind me—we're completely hemmed in now, cops in front, the working stiffs behind us, the reporter at the edge of things his chin upraised. Everyone is terribly interested.

"I'm sorry," I say truthfully, "there's no time."

I hear laughter.

"I'm responsible for these ladies, I can't leave them alone here."

It is explained that they will come down to the station house with me. They can wait for me where it's warm. I am reasoned with. Just a few minutes. Sorry for the inconvenience. Clara and Sandy are being led to one police car, I to another. Just as the door opens for me I balk. "Clara!" I try to turn around, call her. I have changed my mind. I want to put her and Sandy in a cab. I want them to wait at the rooming house.

"Don't make it hard," a cop says.

My good arm is twisted behind my back I am bent

forward at the waist the muffling of blue bulk a stick is brought up smartly between my legs I'm pushed into the car. I have the terrible sickness. I'm aware of people scattering as the police car makes a careening U-turn and picks up speed. A siren. I'm thrown against the back seat against the door we veer around the corner the cop next to me pushes me away with the tips of his fingers. "Relax, sonny," he says. "Enjoy the ride."

At a certain point Railroad Street made a ninety-degree curve and you could leave it, cut across an empty lot, and reach it again a block closer to home. The lot was filled with rubble, bricks, rusted sled runners, pieces of baby carriage, garbage a feast for Saint Garbage remnants of chimneys and basement foundations and all of it covered with snow. I was thinking it was the place to be, the place to be, I stumbled along drunk, to tell the truth, drunk on two glasses of rye through this moonscape of white shit. I heard the distant bell of the trolley and saw over a tenement roof the flash of its power line like the explosion of a star. I fell and fell again, cutting my knee on something sharp, getting a sockful of snow, but Red James jaunted along smoothly he even sang one of his songs the funeral dirge of the Southern mountains, hearing the whistle blow nine hundred miles, the condemned man in prison the betrayed lover the orphaned child everyone across the night suffering loss and failed love and time run out raising his head to hear the whistle blow through the valleys of the cold mountains. And then I was down again, hard this time and I shook my head to find myself on all fours I hadn't fallen. I heard something terrible, a grunt of punched-out breath, snapped bone, a man retching. I tried to stand I was flattened by a great weight, a violent steam-rolling weight pressing my face in the snow my forehead slashes on something sharp at my eye the snow turning wet and black the weight is gone, I scramble to my knees, breathing that is tearful, a desperate exertion, a mass of bodies tumbled past me I heard Red scream and hurtled myself against this mass of black movement butting it with my head taking purchase like a wrestler grabbing a leg a sleeve a back. Everything fell on me and I felt going down my arm twisted the wrong way I heard it break. This seemed to me worth a moment's contemplation. I lay still and even found a small space in the snow to spit out blood. I lay there under the murder. The intimacy of the shifting weights, the texture of their coats on my face, sobbing rages, one vehement crunch and I heard, we all heard, the unmistakable wail of a dead man. Then a hissing gurgling sound. Then no sound. After which, silence from us all and the night coming back in this silence, the weight lifted from me by degrees I look up portions of the night sky reappear suffused in the milk light of the moon I hear something sibilant, hoarse, it is my own breath, the wind brushing past my ears, I hear hitting hitting but it is the heart pounding in my chest.

He was heavier than he looked, I dragged him one-handed by the collar he kept snagging on things at the edge of the lot I found the right terrain, pulled him to the top of a flat rock and then sitting on the incline below it and easing him over my shoulder and sliding down in a sitting position to the sidewalk and standing up with the full heft of him in a fireman's carry on my good side, I took us to the curb under the streetlight to wait for someone passing by.

The police chief nods. It's cold in this room. I sit shivering in my coat. There's a clock on the wall, like the clocks in grade school. The minute hand leaps forward from one line to the next.

The chief is not cold. He sits at his desk in a short-sleeved shirt. Arms like trees. His wrist watch appears to be imbedded in the flesh. His badge, pinned to his shirt pocket, pulls the material to a point. He's enormous but with an oddly handsome unlined face prominent jawline straight nose. He is a freak who has managed to make himself a full life out of being born and raised in Jacksontown. I try to look as if this is not my opinion. He goes back to reading his file.

I have been very cooperative. Even though they did that to me I have told my story as completely and accurately as I can.

I hear the minute hand move on the clock.

We're in some room on the ground floor that looks into the courtyard. A couple of cops are standing around out there. The window has bars.

I don't even ask to smoke. I show no impatience. I don't want to give them anything to work on, if I don't seem to be in a hurry they'll be quicker to let me go.

A cream-white La Salle with whitewall tires pulls up in the courtyard just outside the window. The driver holds open the rear door and the man who gets out immediately has the attention of the cops. He wears a dark overcoat with a fur collar. A pearl-gray fedora. They seem to know him, they come over, they seem eager to shake his hand. He says something and one of the cops moves out of my view.

"Are you deaf, son?"

"What?"

"I said where are you from?"

"I'm from Paterson. Paterson, New Jersey."

"Like your name."

"Yeah."

He nods. "I see. What was your last job?"

"What? I rousted for a carnival."

"Whereabouts."

"Uh, upstate New York. New England."

"What carnival?"

"What?"

"What was the name of it?"

"I don't remember."

"You don't remember the name?"

"No."

"Well, how long did you work for them?"

"I don't know. Listen, is this going to take much longer?"

"It's up to you. You worked at this carnival?"

"Yeah. A couple of months. It was a summer job. Some lousy carnival."

"And before that?"

The man in the courtyard sees something. He removes one gray kidskin glove, takes off his hat. He's a short man, dark-complected, his black hair shines, shows the tracks of the comb. He is shaking his head, he seems genuinely relieved, he raises his arm, lets it fall. His eyes are large, dark, glistening, with long black lashes, they are shockingly feminine eyes.

There is Clara.

They look at each other, a wave of emotion overcomes them both and they hug. He holds her at arm's length and he laughs. He is charmed by her. He shakes his head as if to say, Oh what am I going to do with you!

"Sit down, son."

Side by side they lean against the cream-colored car and they talk. Clara's wearing her fur jacket. He says something to her, he smiles and holds her arm, whispers in her ear, it is as if he is in some night club somewhere at a dark table, and the intimate things he has to say are covered by the music of the swing band.

I am at the window.

"Son of a bitch, what does he see out there?"

"Clara!"

She has pulled her arm away, I hear something, I hear the high wordless whine of impatience with which she sometimes fends off the male approach.

"Clara!" I pound the window. He seems undismayed by her response, as if he knows too well it is a ritual, that it is in fact a form of encouragement.

"CLARA!" My arm, I am jerked back, a cop is pulling down the dark shade, is this my last sight of her head half turned as if she's heard something hair blowing back from her face eyes shining the winter courtyard as if she's heard something in her past, someone, just losing hold in her consciousness?

"Boy, don't you know you're being interrogated? Don't you understand that?"

I am slammed back in the chair.

"I gotta talk to Clara Lukács. She's out there."

"All in good time."

"It's important! Look, I'll answer anything any goddamn questions you can think of just let me talk to her a minute."

The cop is still behind me I have risen from my chair he presses me back down.

Another cop has come in and places Red James' gun on the desk. He takes up position with his back to the door, his arms folded.

The chief examines the gun. "A very serious piece of equipment. This is what the department should be carrying," he says to the cop. "Not the shit we got."

"Never been fired," the cop says.

Do I hear a car door slam? If I am to remain sane I must believe she is not leaving. I must believe she is handling things in her own way. I must believe that she is capable of dealing with Tommy Crapo as she knows he must be dealt with to get him off our backs. I will believe these things, and take heart and deal for my part with the situation in this room. An hour from now we'll be on our way. We'll make a slight detour down to Tennessee and then head for California. We'll be laughing about all of this. We'll be talking about the adventure we had.

"Where'd you get this, son?"

"It's his. Red James'."

He shakes his head and smiles. "Didn't do him much good, did it? You take it off him?"

"No, it was in his house. It was hidden behind the radio."

"Yesterday you went down to Mallory the pawnbroker's. You collected six hundred dollars on the deceased's insurance policy."

"That's right. The money belongs to Mrs. James. I'm holding it for her. She's fifteen years old and we're taking her home to her folks."

He nods, not to indicate he believes me, but as if to maintain the rhythm of the questioning. I look at the clear-eyed, steadfast face of the police chief, the lean face carved from his mountainous self. I've underestimated him.

"You expect them to give you trouble?" he says.

"Who?"

"Her folks you're taking her home to. That you were packing this thing."

"It wasn't for that."

"What was it for, then?"

"I was glad to find it. I sat up all night guarding the door with it."

"Why?"

"Until we got out of town, in case someone came after me."

He gives me his full attention. "Who?"

"I don't know who. Whoever killed Red."

"Why would they do that?"

"I don't know. If they thought I saw them? If they thought I could pin it on them?"

"Could you?"

"I told you. I didn't see anything. I got hit from behind and went down and it all fell on top of me. Could I see my girl, please?"

"Well, if you were afraid, why didn't you call the police? You think this is the Wild West?"

The policemen guffaw.

"Why would anyone want to kill him, anyway?" the chief says.

"I don't know."

"You're in the union, ain't you?"

"You have my billfold!"

"Maybe you killed him," he says.

"What? Jesus H. Christ!"

"Sit down, son. And watch your language."

"Oh, this is swell. This is really swell. No, I didn't kill

him, he was my friend, we lived next door to each other!"

"Did you fool with his wife?"

I hear the ticking of the school clock. From far away comes the metallic screech and thunder of the car couplings as they make up the trains at the freight yards.

"Answer, please. Did you fool with his wife?"

The way is open for my full perception of official state-empowered rectitude. I am suddenly so terrified I cannot talk.

"Did you?"

I shake my head. A weakness, a palpable sense of my insufficiency drifts through my blood and bones.

"Okay," he says, "we could hold you for possession. But I think we have enough to hold you as material witness. You know what that is?"

I shake my head.

"You're all we have to go on. You were there when it happened. It means we hold you while we work up the case. I make it you diddled the wife and decided you liked it too much. The insurance didn't hurt neither."

And now I find my voice. I'm swallowing on tears, I'm producing tears and swallowing them so that they don't appear in my eyes. "Hey, mister," I say, "look at me, I don't look like much, do I? My arm's been broke, one side of my face is stitched up, I've been pissing blood . . . Jesus, since I came to this town I've been short-paid, tricked, threatened, doublecrossed, and your Jacktown finest felt they had to work me over to get me here. I probably don't smell so good either. But I tell you something. You wouldn't hear from my mouth the filth that has just come from yours. I mean that is so rotten and filthy, I'd get down on my knees and beg that little girl's forgiveness if I was you."

"You oughtn't to tell me to do anything, son."

"Or else you're being funny. Is that it, are you being funny? I mean what's the idea—that I killed him before he broke my arm or did I kill him after he broke my arm? After? Oh yes. It makes great sense, it really does: with my one arm I was able to get him to hold still so as I could bash his head in. And then just to make sure everyone would know it I lifted him on my back and took him out to the street to get a ride to the hospital. Smart!"

"He's pretty stupid," the police chief says to the cop, "if he thinks we have to be smart."

The policeman laughs. The chief looks at me with the barest hint of a smile on his face. "You don't like my story, maybe you have a better one."

You don't like my story, maybe you have a better one.

Do you think, Paterson, we'd threaten a man in public a few minutes before we meant to jump him in a dark alley use your brains lad.

My brains.

Clara asked me about my work one day I told her she was furious. What's the matter? Don't move, look at how you're standing: it was so, my hands were in the air as if I were tying the cable, my feet were spread as if I were standing on the vibrating cement floor, I had not only told her, I had acted it out and I hadn't known I was doing that. I understood then the abhorrence of men on the line for bravado. The failure of perception is what did you in.

A murder is valuable property it gives dividends how much and to whom depends on how it's adjudicated.

I thought this was about Clara it is not it is about my life.

Tommy Crapo didn't think this up, he didn't do this to me, he didn't have to. You don't have to buy the police chief in a company town—he's in place! This dolmen stone skull has been here since the beginning of time.

I held up my hands. "Look," I say softly, new tone of voice, "you're making it wrong, it wasn't like that. We were family friends, Red and me. My fiancée Clara and his wife Sandy. We took care of their baby for them when they went to the movies."

"Your fiancée!"

"Yes, sir," I say, "that's what I'm trying to tell you. Clara and I are engaged to be married. You don't know my Clara or you wouldn't think I had an eye for another woman."

"She's something, eh?"

"Well"—I sit back in my chair and smile in reflection—"only the best, most beautiful girl in the world!"

The chief folds his arms. One of the cops leans over, whispers something to him. He listens while he stares at me. "Maybe we ought to see the little lady," he says.

The cop leaves, closing the door behind him. We all sit there waiting. It might be night the dark shade a globe light hangs from the middle of the ceiling the wood floor the oak furniture my chair creaks. The walls are painted dark green from the floor to halfway up, light green to the ceiling. I hear footsteps. I stand. The door opens the cop holds it open for Sandy James with her baby. From the empty hall behind her a cold wind sweeps into the room.

"Sandy, where's Clara?"

She stares at me unable to speak. But from her eyes gleams a sorrow not her own and a small light of courage or hope of possession. I see the decisive functioning matriarchy I have not before seen in her. It comes to them regardless of their age or intelligence when they have settled their claims.

In the winter of 1919 Penfield is in Seattle, walking the streets down by the docks, the rain green-gray, the escalloped seascape etched by rain. Life is a mist shining on his young face soothing his eyes, what his eyes have seen. He is wet and cold but not uncomfortable, there seems in this section of the world at this moment of his life a letting up of insistent death, no one he loves had died lately, he is all out, no mother father lover or signalman the bombs are still, the machine guns silent, the awful murderous insolence of mankind for the moment distracted. But the peace is killing him. Why is he here? He knows no one in Seattle, he knows no one in the whole country, he is one hundred percent bereft, he has come across the continent because it made the longest journey, there had been in his mind some expectation, the importance given to the being from the presumption of travel, but he has a room in a boarding house in West Seattle like the room they gave him in Nutley, New Jersey, in return for his medal and he walks down the hills to the docks. Why? He stands on pilings and looks at the water sloshing into itself infinitely accommodating to all blows objects hammers rainpocks taking it all, pour beaches in drop mountains in break off continental shelves the water gulps the water caresses it is the nature of the water to leave nothing untouched unloved even me thinks Warren Penfield. It is not that he has the urge to jump in but only that he lacks arguments why he should not. It is a rather thoughtful unemotional contemplation. This dark drizzly afternoon he throws his book in, one of the precious copies of his volume of verse, *Sangre de Cristo,* it blots, spreads, wafts, and solemnly raising its binding like wings dives into the great Sound. He leaves the pier and goes down a cobblestone alley and finds a bar a space for his own broad back collar up between the other broad-backed collars up a whiskey the bar dark wood honorably scarred a whiskey the damp air hung with smoke making the smoke of cigarettes a cloudmist he notices how crowded the bar is on a working afternoon he leaves the mist now inside the brain drifting over the lobes of the brain like clouds over the stone mountains the city is still. A block or two from the waterfront it looks better to him at the end of streets the bows of steamships loom over the clapboard buildings, he finds the conjunction of the sea and the street exciting, bowsprits and lines of the old coal-fired riggers gently bobbing over the cobblestones, the creak in the green-gray rain the gulls in glistening drift through the rain there is another country, of course! the sea is to connect waterfront streets at the far ends of the earth. Such moments of elation keep him gliding over his despair he goes now for the solace that never fails up the hill toward the center of town to the public library. What goes on here the library is packed with men reading the newspapers riffling the card boxes roaming the stacks making the shapes of the words with their lips the librarians flustered by the sudden accession to learning of the working world flush-faced, glasses slipping down their noses they are reduced to whispering among themselves and feeling hurt. But Warren likes this! He unbuttons his jacket pulls off his cap sits at an oak table and feels the . strength of these men reading the papers on sticks quiet

respectful as can be of this repository of words he starts
to ask a question quailed by the frown of the man next to
him who *knows* you're not supposed to talk in a library
Warren goes to the granite front steps the men clustered
here smoking hunched in their collars in the sweet rain he
is too shy as usual but something is happening that is very
strange his landlady said nothing he will get a newspaper
but block after block no newsboys on the corners alarmed
now it is February getting dark in the afternoon the green
is leaving the sky the street lamps beginning to glow
weakly the rained emptiness of the city he hears something missing, no streetcars! the overhead wires gather the
last light in silver lines an inadequately populated city in
the bakery window there is no bread in the grocery no
milk everyone knows something he does not know he
waves at a passing car black ignoring him he begins to
run stores closed where has he been follows men walking
following other men walking stays close stays in step
hears now a human sound of population turns a corner a
suddenly illuminated warehouse great golden light pouring through the doors they are all going here and suddenly he is inside the clatter of plates and flatware, the steam
of soup and the skyline of sliced bread he knows what to do
it is twenty-five cents, a bowl of soup two slices of bread
gobs of tub butter stew mashed potatoes an apple coffee
in a tin cup twenty-five cents rows of sawhorse tables in
endless lines refectory benches under the warehouse lights
animation conversation all men thousands of men eating
dinner and down at the end of one table at the far end in
front of his tray in wonder Warren Penfield poet coat
open the sound is of raucous life chopped fine in silver
flutes and strings and drumfeet and shimmering lifesong
the men eat hot food drink strong coffee it is not Ludlow
it is not billets it is not distant thunder it is not the
whingwhir of machine guns it is the General Strike of
Seattle February 6, 1919, the first of its kind in the whole
history of the United States of America.

Everyone is out the printers and milk-wagon drivers
butchers and laundry workers hotel porters store clerks
and seamstresses newsboys and electricians and bakers

and cooks steam fitters and barbers all under the management of the central labor council and it is a very well organized show Warren stands in the streets some trucks are running with signs under the authority of the strike committee and the milk gets to the babies and the lights stay on in the hospitals and the linen is picked up the food cold storage continues to hum and the water from the waterworks and the garbage trucks exempt by the strike committee continue to pick up the wet garbage but not the ashes and the watchmen continue to guard the fences and the mayor confers with the strike committee and not a shot is fired not a fist flies not a harsh word they even have their own cops war veterans big men standing with armbands the Labor War Veteran Guard to keep the strike out of the streets, to break up crowds, keep the soldiers and cops from finding excuses to make trouble they can't machine-gun air they tell Warren move on brother keep your temper enjoy your vacation and by the third day the provision trades are feeding thirty thousand men in their neighborhood kitchen and the nonprofit stores are springing up everywhere not even the union newspaper is allowed to print for fear of unfair competition to the struck big papers Warren is thrilled the city is being run by workingpeople it is that simple they are learning the management techniques it started with the shipyard strike and now it is Revolution pure and simple says Warren's landlady big woman large jaw blue eyes taller than he wiping red hands on her apron the Bolsheviks are in Seattle they're here just like in Russia, they are a plague like the flu it spreads like the flu they ought to be taken out and shot I've worked hard all my life and never asked favors nor expected them and that's why I'm free and beholden to no one Warren tries to explain that's the same thing he's seen the feeling beholden to no one independent men of their own fate and also the incredible tangible emotion of solidarity key word no abstract idealization but an actual feeling I had it too in the signal battalion the way we looked after each other and were in it together an outfit many men one outfit and I swear Mrs. Farmer that has got to be a good thing when you feel it not necessarily the woman said the Huns felt the same feelings I'll bet and took care of each other in their trenches and that don't make me love them anymore they sank ships with babies in them she is in her way a well-entrenched opponent and as always Warren thinks about this point of view to which he is opposed to find the merit in it and test it against his deepest suppositions they are having a good time at the kitchen table she likes him he talks well and is a gentleman and a veteran and pays in advance every two weeks look Mr. Penfield supposing they came in here and told me how to run my house and when to clean the stairs and when to change the sheets and what church to go to and how to teach my children at this moment one of them runs in a remarkable five-year-old little girl broad smooth brow wideset huge light eyes thick hair natural grace dirty knees little socks drooping wild little thing stands between the great-legged mother stares at the boarder with head tilted light in eye clear recognition of his total flawed being what's that Mr. Penfield the great granite mother how could she produce this wisp this unmistakable deity she is scratching the inside of her thigh now with the heel of her shoe a ballet dirty white underdrawers he says inspired well Mrs. Farmer I'll tell you now not hesitant confident fearless of opposing opinion nobody knows what human nature is in the raw it's never been seen on this earth even Robinson Crusoe came from something even Friday and so it seems to me the Huns like us shoot if you give them guns and enemies but love if you will give them friendship and a common goal come down with me and walk among these men and see their spirits change because they're not under someone's heel you take away men's fear and be surprised how decent they can be you don't make them climb over each other for their sustenance give them their dignity and the right to run their lives you release the genius of the race in the forms of art and love and Christian brotherhood. Oh Mr. Penfield you're a good gentle man I'm afraid you don't know the ways of the world very well I have some leftover pie here let me make a pot of tea go along and play honey the child doesn't

move she is cleaning her lips with her tongue like a cat
arms resting indolently on her mother's skirted thighs outside the kitchen curtain the green rain makes its soft hiss
it is Warren who runs along in a flurry of stumbling
knocking over the kitchen chair proving his lack of ease
in the ways of the world she looks after him shaking her
great jawed head sweet dupe he goes to his room grabs
books passport razor the child runs upstairs to the hall-
landing window looks out at Warren Penfield hurrying
downhill he sees turns his head back sees her the power
of her eyes like a jolt to his heart his face is wet the rain
like her tonguelicks it is this more than anything which
sends him back to the docks in torment in scorn the
woman is right I am a fool if this strike goes on the
committee who runs things will be as bad as dictators
everything'll be the same only with different names do
these men on strike absolve themselves of personal private insensitivity in bed in kitchen do they know how to
deal with their own children or parents refrain from
gossip and all the heavy baggage of personal private evils
vanity lust self-abuse the things in Latin the dreams it
was she God what are you doing she is come back in
impossible form God what are you doing I am haunted
hounded you torment me with the little I have to live for
God what are you doing a basso horn from the sound
another from the harbor white smoke like Morse code
from the stacks of the ships berthed along the streets
what is going on pardon me a small Japanese turns what
is all the horn-blowing he scintillating merry-unsmiling we
go now he says *stoorock ober* What? Impatient Japanese shouts to clarify to this white fool *stoorock ober!*
stoorock ober! runs off from the hills of the city church
bells car toots the distant shouts of men who have been
men sounding like the gentle rain the Japanese runs up a
gangplank one bulb hung from the prow throwing a
dazzling green halo of rain over Warren's eyes the *stoorock* is *ober* Warren goes aboard the *Yokahama Trader*
books passage God what are you doing

"**Y**ou've got the wrong man," I said. The chief smiled. He wore his hexagonal blue cap now with the raised gold embroidery on the peak. He wore his tunic. He was sitting here for revelation, he had brought in a stenographer, more cops, and an older man in plain clothes.

I said, "The F. W. Bennett Company employs an industrial espionage agency to find out what's going on in their plants. The name of the agency is Crapo Industrial Services. Maybe you don't know this but I think you do. They put spies on the line and if possible in the unions themselves."

"Let's not waste time," the chief said.

"Red James was one of these spies. He came here two, three years ago just as the union began to organize the men. He got to be an officer of the local. He was secretary, he took minutes, he kept records, he made reports to his employer Crapo Industrial Services."

The chief turned to the stenographer, a gray-haired woman with a mole on her chin. She closed her book. I might be setting up to finger the union but I was talking funny. True! I had found a voice to give authority to the claim I was making—without knowing what that claim would be, I had found the voice for it, I listened myself to the performance as it went on. These fucking rubes!

"The union scheduled a strike just after the new year," I said. "The idea, see, was that if the trim line was shut down, eventually every other Bennett plant would have to shut down too because Number Six makes all the trim. So it was a big strategy of theirs and Red reported this. Right away there are layoffs, half the machines are dismantled and shipped to another plant, and the strike is up the creek."

"And that's why the union goons killed him," the chief said, looking at the plain-clothes man.

"But it wasn't them," I said. "It *looked* like it should be, I myself thought for a moment it was, let me tell you, Chief, you don't look for complications when your head's getting beat in. Does anyone have a Lucky?"

Where was this coming from? I had learned the basics from my dead friend Lyle James. But the art of it from Mr. Penfield, yes, the hero of his own narration with life and sun and stars and universe concentrically disposed on the locus of his tongue—pure Penfield.

"I'll try to make this as clear as I can," I said, taking a deep drag on my cigarette and nodding thanks to the cop with a match. "I know by sight every officeholder in the local, and every national big shot who's been in town since October. I know by sight most of the members—and this will surprise you but there aren't that many, considering the size of the work force at Number Six. But there are people who wear the same clothes and talk the same talk who don't work on the line and never will. And they are the ones who jumped us."

The police chief had risen. "You better know what you're doing, son."

"I made them for a traveling band, one of Crapo's industrial services," I said. "And that's who they were. If you really want Red James's killers, it's very simple. Speak to Mr. Thomas Crapo, president. You can reach him in the phone book—unless he's on his honeymoon."

The man in plain clothes stepped foward. It was clear to me now he was not in the department at all. He was dressed in a pin-stripe suit with a vest and a high collar and a stickpin in his tie. He had thin graying hair, and had the prim mouth of a town elder or business executive. To this day I don't know who he was—a manager of Number Six, a town councilman, but anyway, not a cop. I knew I could work him.

"What is it you're trying to say, young man?"

"I'll spell it out for you, sir. The agency murdered its own operative."

"That's a most serious charge."

"Yes, sir," I said. "It certainly is. But we're in a war, we're talking about a war here, and anything's possible. Once the company moved the machines, Red's days were numbered. The union found him out. That made him no longer of any use to Crapo, in fact he was worse than no use, he was a real danger."

"What?"

"He was an angry man. They'd left him to the dogs. He knew probably as much about Crapo as he knew about the local. He wasn't just your average fink who's been hooked for a few dollars and doesn't even know what he's doing. Red was a professional, an industrial detective, and he worked for Crapo in steel, he worked in coal, he'd done a lot of jobs and this particular assignment was very crucial and only the most experienced man could be trusted with it."

The police chief shook his head. He motioned to the stenographer to leave the room. He stood quite still and watched her close the door behind her. He turned to me he understood the reckless suicidal thing I was doing.

"But as I say, if you read your history of the trenches, the front lines at Belleau Wood, the Argonne, and so on, you find more than once the practice of sending out the patrol either to rescue or to kill their own man who has been captured—so that he doesn't give them away. War is war, other lives are at stake and war is war."

"I was with the Marines at Belleau Wood," the man in the business suit said. "I know of no such story."

"It was the British who did it," I said quickly. "I disremember the place and time, but it wasn't the Americans, it was the British and the French, and of course the Huns they did that all the time. But you don't have to believe it. Look at the chief here. First thing he thinks, a Crapo man is killed, it's the union who killed him. Why not, who would think different! And if he can make that case, if Crapo can trick him into making it, look what he's accomplished. He's set the union back twenty years. They're no union anymore, they're hoods and killers, nobody wants them, no working stiff wants comrades like that, not even Roosevelt wants that. Why, that in itself is enough to make it worthwhile—just to get the union defending itself from charges, just putting suspicion in people's minds—that's worth one op's life, I can tell you."

"All right, son," the chief said, coming around to the front of the desk.

"I know my rights," I said. "You are all witnesses. I'm telling you the truth as I know it, it's out now, it's out in this room and will be on every wire service in the country if you got any ideas of changing my testimony."

"I don't understand what's going on here," said the man in the business suit.

"This boy lies," the chief said. "He lied before and he's lying now. He's a punk from New Jersey who we found with a gun and the widow's insurance money in his kick. He's making this all up."

"That's right," I said. "I made up Tommy Crapo and I made up Crapo Industrial Services, didn't I? Or did I get it from the newspaper? That must be it, they must advertise in the newspaper. I can give you Red James' op number, the one he put on his reports, but that'll be made up too. I can give you the Illinois plate number of a cream-colored La Salle coupe with white sidewalls, but that's made up too. It's all made up. Buster is made up too, he doesn't exist."

"Who is Buster?"

"Buster who got Mrs. James to waive her rights for two hundred and fifty Industrial Services' dollars. Oh listen, mister, why doesn't anyone ask the right questions around here? Look at this, a roomful of ace detectives and not one of them thinks to ask how I know so much, how I knew Lyle James, how I got to be his friend, what I'm doing in this lousy town. Is it an accident? Do you think I like going around getting my arm broken and stitches taken in my face? Do you think I do this for laughs?"

An amazing current, a manic surge, I couldn't stop talking, listen Clara, listen! "I wonder at the human IQ when professionals cannot see through disguises. But if I was wearing a regular suit like this gentleman, if I was wearing my own suit and tie and my face was washed and my hair combed, then you would listen, oh yes. And if I told you Lyle Red James was not just an operative for Crapo but a double operative, that he really worked for the union, that they made him not two weeks after he came to this town, because you know, don't you, he was not much good, he was a fool, a hillbilly, a rube, I mean they saw him coming! And they made him, and showed him how if he kept working and nobody the wiser, he'd get not only his pay envelope from Bennett and not only his salary from Crapo but his payoff from the union's cash box! Why, this strike at Number Six was a decoy! They never intended to strike Jacksontown, that was to send the company on a wild-goose chase shipping its damn machines every which way. Oh yes, gentlemen, when that strike comes, and it is coming, the birds will be singing in Jacksontown, it will be a peaceful day at Number Six and you won't know a thing till you hear it on the radio."

"What's this?" the businessman said. "What strike? Where?"

"Or maybe that isn't a good enough reason for taking care of Lyle Red James, that he was a dirty double-crossing Benedict Arnold."

It was an amazing discovery, the uses of my ignorance, a kind of industrial manufacture of my own. And the more it went on, the more I believed it, taking this fact and that possibility and assembling them, then sending the results down the line a bit and adding another fact and dropping an idea on the whole thing and sending it on a bit for another operation, another bolt to the construction, my own factory of lies, driven by rage, Paterson Autobody doing its day's work. I was going to make it! This was survival at its secret source, and no amount of time on the road or sentimental education could have brought me to it if the suicidal boom of my stunned heart didn't threaten my extinction.

"What strike, how do you know these things!" The businessman was beside himself. "Who is this fellow?" he said. "Damn it all, I want the truth. I want it now."

The police chief went back behind his desk and sat down. He looked at me, fingered the corners of his mouth. He lifted his hat and ran his fingers through his hair and put his hat back on.

"You don't like Crapo very much, do you?"

"We fancy the same girl," I said.

"And that's why you're fingering him—or trying to?"

"No more than he's done to me, Chief," I said. "But I got a better reason: I don't condone killing and neither does Mr. Bennett."

"Mr. who Bennett?" he said, frowning terribly.

"Mr. F. W. Bennett of Bennett Autobody. Is there any other?"

Here the man in the suit found a chair near the wall and sat down and glared at me.

"I'm a special confidential operative," I said. "I was sent here by Mr. F. W. Bennett personally to check on the Crapo organization. Their work has been falling off lately. Mr. Bennett takes nothing for granted, especially not the loyalty of gangsters. I worked into the confidence of Crapo's chief man in Number Six, Lyle James. Mr. Bennett himself arranged for the next door to be available. He thought I had a better disguise to be married and so I brought with me a lady"—here I faltered—"I happened to be serious about. This is the unofficial part, Chief, and I expect every man in this room to keep quiet about this part. I met this lady when she was with Mr. Crapo and we took to each other. We couldn't help it. And, well, he is not a man to forgive, as you can see by my condition and the circumstance of my being here before you."

And now there was silence in the room.

"You are awful young to be what you say," said the police chief. He turned to the others. "It's too crazy. Jacksontown don't need stuff like this. There are so many holes in this story it's like a punchboard. Why should Mr. Bennett need to do these things, you tell me? And if he did them, why would he find some kid like this not old enough to wipe the snot from his nose? No, I'm sorry, Mr. Paterson," he said, "you're smart enough to throw the names around, but you were a punk when we pulled you in and as far as I'm concerned you're still a punk."

"My name isn't Paterson," I said. I smiled and looked at the man in the suit and vest. "It's easy enough to check," I said. "In my billfold on a piece of paper is the phone number of Mr. Bennett's residence at Loon Lake in the Adirondack Mountains of New York. You may not know about that place, it's his hideaway. Call him for me. I get a phone call of my choosing anyway, isn't that the law? That's who I choose to call. Tell him also I'm sorry about the Mercedes. It may be on the lot of Buckeye State Used Cars in Dayton, Ohio. But it may not. Tell him I'm very sorry."

I thought in the silence that ensued they could hear my heart beating its way back to survival.

"Yes, sir," the chief said, "and who should we say is calling?"

One of the men laughed. I was livid with rage. Oh Penfield. Oh my soul. I could barely get the words out. "You stupid son of a bitch," I said to the chief. "Tell Mr. Bennett it's his son calling. Tell him it's his son, Joe."

I don't remember the names of towns I remember the route, southwest through Kentucky and Arkansas, across northern Oklahoma and the top of the Texas Panhandle and then into New Mexico, a spooncurve that I thought would drop us gently into the great honeypot of lower California.

We drove through small boarded-up towns, we drove down dirt rut roads and through hollows where shacks were terraced on the hill beside the coal tipple. We drove through canyons of slag and stopped to pick up chunks of coal to burn in the stoves of our rented cabins. The road went along railroad tracks, alongside endlessly linked coalcars loaded and still.

We drove over wood-paved iron bridges I remember rivers frozen with swirls of yellow scum I remember whole forests of evergreen glazed in clear ice, shattered sunlight, I had to strap a slitted piece of cardboard over my eyes to see the road.

In January the thaw and false spring in the Southwestern air and when we were stopped at a roadside picnic grove for our lunch we could hear the thunderous cracks and groans of rivers we couldn't see. But then it froze again, cold and snowless and I remember stretches of brown land treeless swells of hardscrabble imbedded with rotted-out car frames and broken farm tools.

We had problems with the truck blown tires batteries fan belts oilsmoking flipping up the vented hood hot to the touch it was a journey fraught with peril. But you didn't have to think. It was simple, life was staying warm keeping on the move finding food beds being thrifty. We met people in trucks loaded like ours with furniture and we talked with them and gave the appraising looks of peers, the few chilled humans in motion. But most of the time we had the road to ourselves.

I bought the newspaper wherever we were. In Arkansas and Oklahoma lots of people were robbing banks, it seemed to me important to come into a town looking respectable. People on the go did not have social standing. The eyes of the waitresses in the cafés or the grudging grim men and women who rented rooms. I held the baby like a badge. Cleanliness, propriety, the cheerful honest face, mediation in a cold suspicious land. I made a point of tipping well and flashing my roll, I didn't like that moment of hesitation before the man cranked up the gas tank or the landlady took the key off the board.

In every state Sandy noticed the Justice of the Peace signs in front of clapboard houses. I told her they were legalized highway robbers who lifted travelers of five- and ten-dollar bills I said they handed out jail sentences to hobos but she knew them from the movies as kindly old men who would open their doors late at night to marry people they had wives in hair curlers and ratty bathrobes who smiled and clasped their hands Sandy and I were not mental intimates.

I don't mean she was stupid she was not, only that she asked no questions, she was already persuaded, like Libby at Loon Lake. She took instruction from the newspapers and radio she marveled at the Dionne quintuplets. But I was very kind to her and patient. We had shared sorrows, we knew something together, and this made me tender

toward her. I liked the smell of her after a night in bed,
the heat of her under the covers. I took a sweet pleasure
in our lovemaking even though she was shockingly ignorant of what she could get from it. The first time as I sat
on the edge of the bed she hiked up her flannel nightgown
lay herself across my lap. "Not too hard?" she said over
her shoulder and buried her face in a pillow. I caressed
her ample buttocks and backs of the thighs I felt a film of
clammy sweat in the small of her back I thought I had
learned more of her late husband's tastes than I needed to
know. She seemed relieved that I wanted no preliminaries
and arranged herself on all fours on the bed presenting
herself to me dog fashion here I did not demur. One had
limits. She braced her arms and set her haunches and
even gave them a little twirl now and then. I came quickly
for which she afterward rewarded me with a quick kiss on
the mouth before she went off to the bathroom.

She thought of it like cooking or changing the baby, a
responsibility of domestic life. I wanted to awaken her
surprise her but I was in no hurry. I enjoyed her the way
she was. One morning with the light showing the streaks
in the window shade I studied her face as she lay in my
arms and suddenly her eyes flew open and she stared at
me fearfully but not moving in that second or two before
she remembered where she was who she was who I was.
She drew a sharp breath and her green eyes swam with
life. I hugged her and decided I loved her. I put her on
her back and made love to her and took my time about it
and detected a degree of thought or contemplation in her
before the thing was done and she jumped out of bed to
see to her baby.

Ahead of us on the road each morning a lowering sky,
I felt under it as under a billowing tent as far as the eye
could see. The roads became straighter, the land flattened
out. No snow now, what blew across the land was a gritty
red dust that shimmered on the road in the sun in rain-
bows of iridescence. Also accreting spindly balls of desert
rubbish bouncing over the rocks and blowing up against
the fences like creatures watching us go by. We went
through one-street towns with red brick feed stores and

tractors parked in the unpaved streets. We passed fore-
closed farms with notices slapped on the fenceposts like
circus bills. The towns were less frequent. There were no
rivers creeks mountains trees, just this rocky flatland. But
one day Sandy yelled to stop the truck. I pulled over. She
thrust the baby in my hands and jumped down from the
cab and ran back along the ditch. I watched her in the
mirror. She came back with a sprig of tiny blue flowers,
she was so happy, she tied them with a string and hung
them from the sun visor.

The desert didn't alarm her. She had grown up in the
mountains but country was country and she knew its rules
and regulations. She knew the names of snakes and birds
and pointed out the dry beds of creeks. One day the truck
broke down in the middle of nowhere and she turned all
around with her hand shading her eyes wise Indian maid
and figured where to get help by the way the land was
fenced. I remember that. We found a ranch about three
miles down a dirt road intersecting the road we were on,
just as she predicted.

But it was slow going, I began to think we were strung
between outposts of civilization, the shadow range of
mountains that cheered me when I first saw it one late
afternoon seemed each new day as far away on the
windshield. I didn't know what we would do in California
but I knew it would take as much money as we could
save to do it with. I came awake at night and wondered
what I had in mind. The truth was I had no ambition, no
ideas, no true desire or hope for anything. I was aware in
the darkness of the forced character of my affections. I'd
find myself angry at Sandy. I liked to surprise her in her
sleep and be in her before her body could respond to
make it easier. She would come awake gasping but throw
her arms around me and hold on for dear life.

One evening, trying to do something about the way I
felt, I found a reasonably good roadside café and we had
steaks and beans and red wine. There were candles in
little red glasses on the table.

"Clara told me about you," Sandy said.

"What?"

"Oh, long before I dreamed anything like this."

"What did she say?"

"Just that she was sweet on you. You know. The way girls talk."

"Yeah, well, I was sweet on her too."

"I thought you was married. I thought she was your wife!"

"Yeah, well, she'd be anything you wanted if you wanted it badly enough."

A particularly cold day, with the enormous blue sky turned almost white, we saw a man and a woman and a boy at the side of the road beside their old Packard touring car. I pulled up. Their gears were locked. A decision was made that the man would remain with the car and its heavy freight of steamer trunks and crates. He wrapped a scarf around his head and folded his arms and sat down on his running board and his family got up in the truck with us to ride to the next town. The woman must have been in her forties. She wore a dusty black coat with a fur collar half rubbed away and a tired felt hat that was nevertheless set off at a smart angle. She said her husband was a pharmacist. He had had his own store back in Wilmington, Delaware. Now they were on their way to San Diego, where they hoped to make a new start. "A new start!" Sandy said. "Why, that's what *we're* doing!"

When we had dropped them I said, "What do you mean we're making a new start?"

"What?"

"All they want is to open another drugstore. They want to do what they've always done. That's what a new start means."

"Well, I was just chattin with that lady."

"You think I want a job in an automobile factory? Or is it *your* new start you're talking about? I mean this furniture of yours we're dragging three thousand miles: Is *that* your new start? So you can find some rooms and put the furniture in them just the way you had it in Jacktown? That kind of new start?"

"I don't know why you're so put out with me."

"Because if that's what you mean, say so. Let's settle it

here and now. I'm not your husband and even if I was I wouldn't make my living as a stoolpigeon."

She looked at me now in bewilderment, and holding her baby to her, sat as far from me as she could get. She stared out the windshield with her chin on the baby's head. God knows her remark was innocent enough. But the confidence behind it I found irritating—as if living and traveling with her I must fit her preconceptions. I suppose what really bothered me was the strength of character behind this. I felt if she didn't even know what she was doing as she did it, I couldn't hope to change her.

Then of course in a few miles Joe was sorry, he apologized, which encouraged her to sulk and afterward to regain her good cheer.

Sandy could have said he was traveling on her money. But it never occurred to her. It occurred to him, however—he was not unaware of his talent for using other people's money, he was not unaware of his attraction to other men's wives, he was not unmindful that his life since leaving Paterson had been a picaresque of other men's money and other men's women, who in hell was he to get righteously independent with anyone? This kid was giving him her life everything she owned and all he could do was kick her in the ass for it.

He wondered seriously if love wasn't a feeling at all but a simple characterless state of shared isolation. If you were alone with a woman your feelings might change from moment to moment but the circumstance of your shared fate did not change. Maybe that's where the love was, in the combined circumstance. This was not the Penfield view but it could be argued. Joe looked at other couples old and young and wondered what they saw in each other, working their little businesses, or pushing their jalopies west, or eating their meals together or holding the hands of a child between them. Maybe all the world's pairs, dreary and toothless and stumbling drunk, or picking at garbage pails or waiting on the street for a flop knew about love as, say, he and Clara Lukaćs never had. They knew it could incorporate passion or prim distaste, it might be joyous or full of rage, it might carry extreme concern of any kind, or unconcern, but it was presumed to survive challenge. All it was, was a kind of neutral constancy. Sandy knew it! You just made the decision, all you needed to do was decide to have it and love was yours. Nothing grand, nothing monumental, and not a prison either, but a sort of sturdy structure of outlook, one that wouldn't break under the weight of ideas and longing feelings terrors visions and the world's awful mordant surprises.

"Sandy," he said, "let's get married."

She hugged him until he thought the truck would go off the road.

"We don't want a new start, Sandy, we want a new life. A whole new life. When we get to California. Okay? That's the place."

She was more than amenable. "Oh my, oh my," she said, hugging the baby. "You hear that, darlin? We're gonna have a proper daddy. Yes we are! Oh my!"

There followed a period of solemn discussion. I explained that to make a true marriage we both had to shuck the ways of our old lives, its attitudes, its assumptions. "I know I won't be able to live a road life anymore," I said. "I know I have to plan to make something of myself. And I have ideas, Sandy, a man can do a lot starting from a small investment. More than one fortune has been made that way, I can tell you."

She nodded.

"So I know I've got to give up my past life and I want you to think about giving up yours. Do you ask in what way?"

"Yes sir."

"In the way of style, Sandy honey. In the way of more ambition of style. Now, take this truck for instance. They stop trucks like this by the hundreds at the California state line. They don't want people coming in looking like Okies, you know? In fact I've read if you can't prove you have a job waiting they won't even let you in."

"This truck is bad?"

"Very bad."

"But how else we gonna move the furniture and all?"

"Ah, well, the furniture, that's the next thing I want to talk to you about."

An hour later we were in a fair-sized town east of Albuquerque, New Mexico. There was a big junk store at the edge of town. Sandy and I stood with our luggage in the dusty street while the furniture was unloaded. A man scrawled a big number in chalk on each piece or tied a tag to its leg. Sandy watched her chair and sofa, her big Philco radio disappear into the darkness of the store. I patted her shoulder.

It was cold and very sunny. The man counted out sixty dollars into my hand.

"Where's there a used-car lot?" I said to him. He walked around the truck, looking it up and down. He leaned his weight on the lowered tailgate. "I'll take it off your hands," he said. "Not worth much, though."

I got seventy-five dollars for the truck, for which I had paid a hundred in Jacksontown. Twenty-five dollars to transport us across six states didn't seem at all bad.

I tied two of Sandy's bags with rope and slung them over my good shoulder. I held another valise under my good arm and a fourth in my good hand. Sandy carried the baby and the remaining bag and, slowly, and with many halts, we shuffled several blocks to the railroad depot. It was a small station on the Santa Fe line and in a couple of hours a train was coming through to Los Angeles.

I checked the bags and took my wife-and-baby-to-be across the street to a diner and left them there. I found a barbershop a few blocks away. The barber removed my bandages and pulled out the stitches. He shaved me and gave me a haircut. He gave me a hot towel.

Then I had an idea. I stopped in a drugstore. My cast was supposed to be on for six weeks, but it was a torment. The druggist did the job as several customers looked on.

I was shocked by my pale thin arm. The break had been down toward the wrist. My fingers ached when I tried to move them. But it was good to be rid of the weight of all that plaster and to sport instead a couple of splints and adhesive tape.

To celebrate I stopped in a haberdasher's and bought a dark suit with a vest and two pairs of pants. Eighteen dollars. The tailor did up the cuffs for me on the spot. I bought a white shirt and a blue tie for three-fifty. Even my old khaki greatcoat looked good after the man brushed it and put the collar down. "Wear it open," he said, "so the suit shows."

Sandy didn't recognize me when I walked back into the diner.

"Is that you?"

"It's either me or George Raft," I said.

The idea was coming clear to her. We still had an hour before the train arrived. She took one of her bags from the check-in and repaired to the ladies' room.

I remember that depot: it had wooden strip wainscoting and a stove and arched windows caked with chalk dust. I sat on the bench with Baby Sandy and held her on my lap. I felt her life as she squirmed to look at this or that. She wore a wool cap from which hair of the lightest color peeked through. I untied the string under her chin and pushed back the hat and it seemed to me now the hair was more red than I remembered. It seemed to me too as we regarded each other that her facial structure was changing and the father was beginning to show. "Oh, that would be a shame," I said aloud. She grabbed my tie in her fist.

And then I looked up and standing there Sandy James in a dress of Clara's and hose and Clara's high-heeled shoes. She was looking at the floor and holding her arms out as if she were on a high wire. Her face was flushed, she dropped her bag and grabbed hold of the bench.

"I'm fallin!" she said with a shriek.

"You're not falling," I said.

She had combed her hair back and put on lipstick a little bit crooked. She wore a coat open over the dress I hadn't seen it before it was creased but it was fine a dark creased coat not originally hers any more than the dress or the shoes, but it looked fine, it all looked fine.

She was awaiting judgment with mouth slightly open eyes wide.

"Aw, Sandy," I said, "you look swell. Oh honey, oh my, yes." And she broke into smiles, glowing through her freckles, her pale eyes crescented behind her cheekbones in a great face of pleasure, and there was our life to come in the sun of California—all in the beaming presence she made.

And so we sat waiting for our train, this young family, who would know what we had come from and through what struggle? We were an establishment with not a little pride in ourselves and the effect we made in the world. I thought of a bungalow under palm trees, something made of stucco with a red tile roof. I thought of the warm sun. I imagined myself driving up to my bungalow in the palm trees, driving up in an open roadster and tooting the horn as I pulled up to the curb.

A while later an interesting thing happened. The stationmaster told us through the gate that the famous Super Chief was coming through from Los Angeles. We went out on the platform to watch it go by on the far track. And after a minute it thundered by, two streamlined diesel engines back to back, and cars of ridged shiny silver with big windows. It shook the station windows with its basso horn, and a great swirl of dirt flew into our eyes. It was going fast but we could see flashes of people in their compartments.

Sandy grabbed my arm: "You see her! It's her, omigod, oh, she looked right at me!"

A moment later the train was gone and I stood watching it get smaller and smaller down the track. "Didn't you see her?" Sandy asked. "Oh, what's her name! Oh, you know that movie star, you know who I mean! Oh, she's so beautiful?"

It was true, the stationmaster said a few minutes later, you could get a glimpse of Hollywood stars every day, east and west, as the Super Chief and the Chief went by. But he wouldn't know in particular which one we had seen. "Oh, you know," Sandy kept saying to me. "You know who it is!" She stamped her foot trying to remember.

I had thought it was Clara. I laughed at myself and lit a cigarette, but long afterward something remained of the moment and located itself in my chest, some widening sense of loss, some heartsunk awareness of the value I once placed on myself.

The cars were crowded, valises and trunks piled near the doors at each end, bags and bundles stuffed in the overhead racks. We found a place toward the rear of one overheated car and we settled ourselves. We sat stiffly in recognition of the established residence of the other passengers. The car gave off the smell of orange peel and egg salad. People wore slippers instead of shoes, they slept covered with their own blankets and they chatted with each other like neighbors. Children ran up and down the aisle.

Passers-by stopped to admire the baby. We could not resist the social demands of the situation. Sandy was soon talking away, introducing us in our prematurely married state. Everyone else in the car, and in the car ahead of it and the car behind, was from the same town in Illinois. They were members of a Pentecostal church. A man told us they were moving to California to set up a new community on donated land south of Los Angeles. "Yes, thank Jesus Christ our Lord," he said. "We shall take ourselves into the Pacific and be baptized in the waters of His ocean." The idea so overwhelmed him that he broke into song. Soon everyone in the car was singing and clapping hands. Sandy smiled at me in the excitement of the moment, she was thrilled.

By evening I believed I had heard every number in the repertoire. They were good generous people if you didn't mind their conviction. After Sandy fell asleep across our seat they covered her with their blankets. An older woman happily shushed Baby Sandy to sleep in her arms.

I stood between the cars and smoked my cigarettes.

This train was no Chief, it made frequent stops, and each time I got off to look around. As the night wore on, the train lingered at each stop although no one got on or off and only a sack or two was flung aboard the mail car. At one station, a small town in the desert, I thought I smelled something different in the air, like a warmer breeze or another land. It was very late. All the pilgrims on the train were asleep. Steam drifted back from the engine. I felt strange, as if coming out of shock. I felt as if I knew no one on earth.

I wondered if this wasn't really the last stop, if California was like heaven, unproven. In this flatland of grit and rubble, you might sense the barest whiff of it in the air or intimation in the light of the sky—but this was as far as you got.

I wandered to the rear to the end of the platform. I picked up a folded newspaper from a Railway Express baggage cart—the rotogravure section of a Sunday paper a week or two old. I looked at the pictures. I was looking at Lucinda Bailey Bennett the famous aviatrix, two whole pages of her at various times of her life. She stood beside different airplanes or sat in their cockpits. A separate ruled column listed her speed and endurance records by date. At the bottom right-hand page of the story she was shown under the wing of a big two-engine seaplane. She was waving at the camera. The caption said: HER LAST FLIGHT. Behind her, climbing into the cabin, was a large man, broad of beam, unidentified.

I turned back and found the beginning of the feature: Lucinda Bennett's plane *The Loon* had been given up for lost over the Pacific somewhere between Hawaii and Japan. F. W. Bennett was quoted as saying that if his wife had to die, surely this was the way she would prefer, at the controls of her machine, flying toward some great personal ideal.

Images of falling through space through sky through dreams through floor downstairs down well down hole downpour.   Birds that fall into the sea as a matter of lifestyle include kingfishers canvasbacks gulls heron osprey pipers tweaks.   Birds that fall most prominently into fresh water are loons a type of grebe. Sixteen lakes in the Adirondack Mountains named Loon Lake.   The cry of loons once heard is not forgotten.

Clara has time to think, the space to realize her thinking mind. Never in her life has her life been so uncrowded, something she never before realized consciously how crowded her life was how people from her infancy had always been in her eyes, how the sounds of them had always been in her ears, how their presence moved in her their wills directed her even insofar as she created opposition she had been crowded by them their wills their voices their appearance directing her their cars and trucks the rumble of the elated horns horses pulling wagons splatting dung in the street, peddlers pushing their carts the stone blasting out of the rock of Manhattan tying in the girders with rivets, slapping in the stone, every manner of machine whining growling rumbling roaring in its own pitch, and all the gangsters of menace all the pain, others and her own, and the sound of fear in her, her own fear which she hated most of all because it was the loudest noise in the universe, the nuns at their prayers, kids shouting down the street, the muttering of murderous intention, and every square inch of space in her eyes blocked out by stone and tar and moving metal, by dark stairs and painted apartment walls, by overstuffed furniture by cots and pots and sinks and roaches and tin plates and later by phony butlers and the pretensions of the earth's scum, there was nothing left in her eyes for a bee gravid with being bending a flower to the earth, or for simple blue skycolor unpenetrated by the spires of skyscrapers, or for something small and lovely to be contemplated for its own seriousness, like a comb or a hand mirror or a goldfish in a bowl, there was no chance, nothing reflected, nothing gave back from the contemplation of it, even her dreams were pure shit they did nothing for her, they were her days all over again, filled with the same people the same things in different arrangements or proportions but the same the same. So she stands quietly after some days molecularly reassembled widely spaced in her own density and watches through some branches and some leaves which have interest in themselves and pay her for the most marginal attention as she watches between them the lake water flung like a cast of silver grain in the gray day, two wakes widening behind the pontoons of the airplane finally losing the chase like porpoises turning back underwater as the green-and-white plane exchanges one environment for another and rising slowly turns, twists in the air rising turning its wings concentrating to a point then flaring out the plane falling swiftly away into the sky losing its color finally its shape and becoming possibly a speck of dust in her eye and when she blinks it is gone altogether, made of cloud made of sky gone even the sound of it gone, and she stares at the silver-scattered lake, the green leaves at her eyes, the branches and the big important journey of the ant along the twig.

So she's alone with him at Loon Lake and finds that still there is no intimacy and the mysteriousness of this fact begins to interest her. This is the way the rich do things. Getting herself dressed, she marches downstairs defiantly accepting it all and sits down for breakfast on the terrace overlooking the lake and waiting till they came out to see what she wants and eating a half grapefruit sitting in its silver shell in ice and daring anyone Bennett included to look at her the wrong way.

But nothing has happened, the schedule is unaltered, the drinks at certain hours, the meals at certain hours, the morning a certain time in a certain place, the afternoon and evenings all timed, the past between them unacknowledged, the past ignored, personal reactions forsworn, you-naughty-girl forborne, every breath in its good time and Bennett keeps his distance with the utmost courtesy and only sees her at the times planned for seeing, at table, or on the tennis court her lesson or riding on the trail and she is left alone at her wish and settled into the timed ordered planned encounters of the rich in their family life who dole out time in carefully measured amounts to each other, they even sleep in separate rooms so as not to wear out their lives on each other, so as to avoid anything like the fluid mess of most people's lives, and those who are closest to each other are as timed to be apart as anyone else. So at last she understands what wealth is, the desire for isolation, its greatest achievement is isolation, its godliness is in its isolation and that's why never in her life before, her days and nights of time, has she enlarged this way, has her mind enlarged to the space this way, and has this voice been heard this way in reflection of herself. And the point is that she is growing to the environment, beginning to match it, and it is all beginning to make proportional sense, the timed encounters, the ceremony of courteous meetings, the space between people sharing space, the great distance to be traveled even in an obvious situation like this, so crudely obvious as to outcome, the aloneness of the two of them now, not the ironic wife not the fat poet sharing the fifty thousand acres, even now the isolated distance will have to be traveled before he can allow himself to put his hands on her. And that makes her smile. Because now she will know when that time is too, it will match her awareness and nothing will shock her or surprise her because the distance he must travel is the function of his wealth, as separative as it is powerful, and she waits in grim amusement knowing that by the time something happens he will have become recognizable to her, her familiar, and their intimacy will be all that's possible for her, so natural she will wonder what it ever was that enraged her when her gangster left her sleeping and took the private train.

But it was all in my mind, it was the furthest thing from everyone's mind except mine. She had not come back, he had not thought of bringing her back, the world had gone on and only I, like Warren Penfield, mourned its going. The ant on the twig was at my eye and I saw no plane and in fact knew I wouldn't, in fact felt the wolfish smile of secret satisfaction on my face, a simple mindless excitement just being back at this place, redballed home in comprehensive correction of my life, more comprehensive than the wild hope of seeing Clara again or the desire to take revenge. No simple motive could fill the totality of my return.

Following job description fall into sea: fighter pilot naval   bomber pilot naval, navigator bombardier gunner naval   carrier-based Pacific Fleet World War Two   with or without parachute drowned strafed dead of exposure or rescued one thousand and eight six.   This is apart from individuals going down in their aircraft   shot down or deprived of carrier landing   from attack of Divine Wind or heavy seas collapsing their landing gear or snapping constraint cable   or sailing into lower deck amidships   or otherwise stippling the sea like rain like the hammers of sculptors.

I thought oddly of eviction, a city street miniaturized in one cell of the remembering brain, a cityscape of old cheap furniture piled on the sidewalk and an old woman sitting on one of the chairs looking at old photographs of Paterson in an album. The chair arm had a doily. She showed me the picture she was looking at, herself as a girl, and she smiled. She smelled of urine, her hands were frighteningly swollen and twisted, she was totally unashamedly in residence on the sidewalk with her furniture, in some state of dreamy peace, careless of the cold, the first snowflakes came down toward evening and there was no derision from the tough kids on the street because she didn't weep or bow her head or display grief or fear in her misfortune and so not misfortune itself, but sat and thought her chin in her hand, her elbow propped on the armchair doily, while the snow turned her hair white. What frightened them off was the triumph of her senescence, only a stickler for custom would demand that such a lady of property be required to have four walls around her a ceiling above her a light in the lamp and tea in her cup.

I had this same mind, unhoused but triumphant coming off the streets through the dogs up the mountain to Loon Lake. And I greeted him like a complicitor while he stared at me quite astonished and then turned nodding as if he understood and continued to make his lunch in the spring sun. I was given Penfield's old room. That night I heard the sound of surging power, some transformed connection, an electric pungency and pop, and everywhere around all the houses of the compound great floodlights came on, over every bit of space, the courts, the boathouse, the staff house, the stables. And a while later I heard the dogs but they came this time on leashes pulling three men with shotguns broken in one hand and leash straps in the other woven like reins, a dozen yelping matched hounds and uniformed guards with Sam Browne belts and boots.

I read the Penfield papers at his window from this outside light a peculiar bright amber night, and I heard the Poet's voice and saw his large debauched pleading eyes and tried to understand his death, what it was, what was terminated, if the voice and the face remained, if the presence lay in the rooms, and the faint winy redolence of his being was sniffed on my every breath. A wineglass still sat on the mantel, the dregs evaporated to a glazed scab in the bottom of the petal.

I mourn all change even for the better and in the days of my return I measured what I had known as the injured intruder against what I saw now as the sole guest. I mourned the absence of terror, the absence of hopeless desire, the absence of betrayals still to come.

I thought of Sandy James asleep in the train coach, curled on the seat and from the wrist under her cheek the trembling droop of her five-and-ten charm bracelet, a tiny tarnished lady's shoe, a tiny tarnished bottle, a tiny tarnished steam engine.

Bennett had changed too, he was in an interesting derelict state of mourning. A gray stubble grew on his face and he wore the same plaid flannel shirt day after day. The white hair of the careful shining pompadour was uncombed, shocked forward over his forehead and suggesting from a flash of boyishness what he might have been had he not been a Bennett—a farmer perhaps, a logger, or heavy-chested stevedore of some honest life. We took our meals together, the two of us alone, with a manservant serving heated canned food. All the women of the light green were gone, as if having lost Lucinda Bailey Bennett he wanted the race expunged. A couple of the outside men were now doing the household work and the cooking. In the kitchen the dishes were piled unwashed. I saw roaches going along the floor. It was as if the establishment was in some accelerating state of decrepitude, beginning with Bennett's heart and working outward. The grounds were immaculate as ever, Loon Lake was groomed for its spring. The stables were clean and horses shining and fit. But if he went on like this, the men of dark green too would be sent away and the boats would sink in their berths, the earth around the dolmen would grow back and the fence around the tennis court would fall and the clay court would crack like the surface of a blasted planet. Mourning had illuminated the natural drift of his life to isolation, and if it was not corrected it would

go on, outward in all directions, spreading out over the
universe in some infinite looming reclusiveness.

But his eyes were curious when they lit on me for a
moment or two at each measured meal. And the days
were, after all, timed just as they had been, the hours
appointed for drinking and eating, and naps, and exercise.
He looked at me as if he were waiting. I met him each
day in a renewed wonder of my own. I had seen his
kingdom and I appreciated him almost more for the
distracted humanity he displayed, broken as easily as
anyone by simple events. For men all over the country he
was, finally, a condition of their life. Yet he wandered
about here in his grief, caring for nothing, barely raising
his head when the phone rang. He moved slowly, almost
listlessly, which brought out the natural lurch of the
short-legged top-heaviness of him.

In the mornings I heard the horses stomping in the
stable, and looking out the window, saw Bennett come
out galloping, having spurred his horse from the very
portal.

At noon we took lunch on the terrace if the day was
fair and he'd glance at the sky over the lake as if expecting a plane to appear.

At night while the guards in their belted uniforms
walked the floodlit grounds with their dogs I heard him
playing his phonograph records, his favorites, I heard the
song of the night of my arrival.

> I know why I've waited
> Know why I've been blue
> Prayed each night for someone
> Exactly like you.

He began to talk of Lucinda Bennett, imparting confidences that at first excited me inasmuch as I was there on
the terrace in the sun at Loon Lake, in all the world the
only one privileged to receive them. His voice lacked
regret, his delivery was thoughtful, he chose his words as
someone does who wants in as orderly a way as possible
to impart information. So I hoped he was giving these

thoughts to *me,* as instruction, and I trusted that his reasons would be forthcoming, that he had some plan, and that by being patient and attentive I would eventually learn what it was. Then I wondered if the confession itself was the gracious means by which I would pass through some subtle imperceptible moment of assumption from being something to being something else. But he went on, and the obsession of the subject became so apparent to me, and the confidences so intimate, I couldn't believe he was aware that I listened or that he would seriously divulge them if I did not lack all importance to him. Day after day I listened. I watched the white clouds disembowel themselves in the high pines across the lake. His man served canned soup, canned spaghetti, canned peaches. Bennett grew shaggier and smellier, looking more like a troll every day. I watched his beard grow. While I waited for a place in his mind I tested my status with the staff. I rode a horse one day with the stableman beside me showing me the elementals. I went upstairs to the storerooms that the maid Libby had shown me so long ago and took several outfits for myself, white ducks already cuffed, argyle sweaters, saddle shoes, shirts, ties, a pair of boots. I had the man in the boathouse bring out the mahogany speedboat and hold the line while I boarded her. I got the hang of it soon enough. I cruised around looking at the beaver lodges, the islands where the loons made their nests, and saw from the water the concrete ramp and hangar where Mr. Penfield and Mrs. Bennett began their round-the-world flight.

"She was a student when I met her. She was then, and remained, the most handsome woman I had ever seen. I secured a divorce to marry Lucinda. And in the years as they went by, no matter what passed between us, whenever she saw fit to spend time with me I was pleased to see her, I mean that no matter what the state of our affections I was always pleased when she came into a room. If she came into a room I had to look at her. I could not not look at her.

"I respect character in a man but I revere it in a

woman. I am done in when I find it in a woman. That little doxie had it in a cheap sort of way. But in Lucinda it tested like the best ore, through and through, in the bones and in the beam of the eye.

"Long ago she lost the pleasure of—what?—the engagement. And I was able to appreciate her character in the depth of her withdrawal from me. And then how I wished she had less of it! Less pride, less distaste for— surprises. Less neatness of soul. I told her she liked the sky because it was clean. She liked to go up in rain. I never flew with her because I sensed that it was her realm. But everyone told me what a wonderful pilot she was. How cool. How capable. And then she began to pull down the prizes and I knew it was so.

"I was very proud of her. I bought her whatever she needed. She may have fallen in love with a fellow, some mail-service pilot, one of those adventurer types, and I was going to have it looked into. But when I thought about it I knew Lucinda would never permit herself an affair. It was not something to which she would give rein. And gradually she ceased to mention him. If it were possible for Lucinda to exist without a body she would have chosen to. Her body was of no interest to her. She did not like it . . . handled. She was a very orderly woman, Lucinda. If you look upstairs in her apartment you will see the order of her mind. She did everything with precision, and so was she affectionate with precision.

"She flew planes but her tastes were very delicate and refined. She knew art, she knew music. She had small bones as befitting a fine mugwump family. They none of them liked me. I took great relish in that. It was one of those things. I have no taste of my own but I could recognize the quality of hers. She could look at something for a long time, a painting, a piece of porcelain. Then I knew it was fine. I envied her vulnerability—that she could be transfixed by something that was beautiful. She became pregnant just once and immediately took measures to have it rescinded. We had no children. I have one child by my first marriage but he is an incompetent, I mean legally, a macrocephalic, he has water in the head, and he lives in a home in Sweden. They take too good care of him. By all rights he should have been dead years ago.

"Lucinda went once to see him. Thereafter she sent him thoughtfully chosen gifts, toys, tins of cookies, picture books appropriate to his mental age. She always sent him things. She liked helpless beings. I don't mean that the way it sounds. I mean she had a heart for people. It was she who saved Penfield a jail sentence. Penfield was from the working class and he decided to come here in the late twenties to assassinate me. You knew that of course. Well, the fellow was pathetic but she kept him on as a sort of a cause in personal rehabilitation. A sort of one-woman Salvation Army, except without the prayer. Lucinda was not religious except perhaps in some vague pantheistic way. She decided the poor man was a poet. I got to like him myself. He read aloud very well, he probably should have been an actor. He read Wordsworth and Keats, all that kind of thing. He was a sort of house pet she kept on and I indulged her. But then of course I did something I shouldn't have. I took Penfield's own verses to the president of the New York Public Library and asked him his opinion. In turn he called on a professor who was an expert in the field of literature. Oh my. And I showed Lucinda this fellow's letter. She perceived, accurately, that the opinion didn't matter so much as my malice in having asked for it. She threw the letter in the fire. She was a wonderful woman. She was not a prey to fashion, didn't give a damn for it. She always looked smart by looking herself. She always wore her hair the same way, cut short and brushed back from her temples. I thought it was most seemly. She had a thin, fit body. Thin waist. Ribs showed. She had good hands, small and squarish, nails trim, cut close. She would not paint her nails or wear make-up. I liked her mouth, a generous mouth. Sweet smile. A light came into her eyes when she smiled. She had almost no bosom. Just a slight rise there with good thick nipples. She told me once if I liked her body I must really like boys."

He paused. "You've come here to kill me too, I suppose."

"What?"

"But you don't have the guts for it—anymore than he."

"What?"

"See? I'm not even carrying my gun."

He pushed his chair back from the table and held out his arms.

The room empties. They have gone to make the call. I walk back and forth shaking a fist in the air. The fuckers! By my wits I have done this thing and the stupid sons of bitches have gone for it. But why not? They will hear him laugh, they'll hear him say, *Yes, let him go.* My heart fills with a passionate conviction. He and I are complicitors. We're both against them. As if, having made this up, I cannot make it work unless I believe it myself.

And I am released. And I strut out of that room bone-cracked, skin-stitched and betrayed and I glare at them all as I lead her by the arm out the door. I take my time. I think the illusion will endure only if I do not break and run. I sleep in Sandy James' parlor. I sleep eighteen hours. I take her money, buy a truck. I hire two men to load it. In the rear-view mirror I see only a black industrial cloud where Jacktown was. I press the accelerator. Cars turn on their lights, the red lights of moving cars ahead of me. The furniture shifts and bangs against the tailgate. The heavy furniture rises in the air on the bumps. I am in transit on the road, the child bride beside me, bracing herself with her knee against the dashboard and holding her baby tightly. I open the window for the cold air. I want the wind to blow these feelings out of my eyes, blow them away, leave me without memory or love, leave me to myself.

"If you thought I would want to kill you," I said, "why did you tell them to let me go?"

"What?"

"When the police called from Jacksontown," I said to him. "With that message." I was smiling like a fatuous idiot.

"What message? I don't know what you're talking about. From whom?"

I choked on the answer. Bennett got up and stood at the parapet. He stood looking over the lake with his hands in his pockets.

That night we steal upon a station of the Tokaido and purchase disguises. We are a country lord and his serving boy. She wears bloused trousers. We travel in this humble manner because my mission is clandestine. Soldiers of the daimyo eye us warily. We book rooms in a modest inn where, to avoid suspicion, I call for a woman. She is a tired fat *artiste* who responds to the humor of the situation. The two of us climb all over her, I with ordinary lasciviousness, my young ward with the affection of a child for her mother. Of course the old whore is terribly moved. She reaches into the child's pantaloons, and my hand, like a band of steel, clamps around her wrist. If she discovers my serving boy is a girl, all is lost. Even so the situation is difficult. I use all the sexual arts of which I am capable to divert the old bag. But in the midst of passion I intuit that the more undone she becomes, the more shrewd. It is actually interesting. At the moment of her release she is totally withdrawn and quietly aware that we are not what we appear to be. But her tongue is extended. I grab the tongue and impale it to the polished floor with an awl. I shout and stamp about and raise an uproar. The innkeeper comes to the door. Other travelers come running. I berate the innkeeper for the poor quality of his house. He is abject. The woman moans, rump up, head on the floor, eyes glazed like a pig to be served. I put my foot on her back and behead her. The innkeeper begs my pardon.

At dawn we continue our journey. The sky is pink. We climb the trail alongside an amazing stream, so rock-strewn that the water, broken into millions of drops, falls like the sound of hail and bounces like steel pellets. I scrape the bark from a small pine tree tortured by the wind to grow like sunrays toward the earth. This lime-green powdery moss I allow to dry for four minutes in the palm of my hand. I then lick this powder from my palm

and immediately my young love becomes a giantess looking down at me with amazement. I trip her and she falls
backward, quaking the earth, I run into her vulva and by
that means continue my lifelong search for the godhead.
It is some sort of gland somewhere. The way becomes
slippery. In this viscous darkness I use my knees and my
hands like a water spider. The way becomes narrower.
Soon I am flattened, drawn like a mote toward some
powerful brilliantly lit eye. I feel myself enlarging. The
light is blinding. I become my own size and break her
open like an egg.

You are thinking it is a dream. It is no dream. It is
the account in helpless linear translation of the unending
love of our simultaneous but disynchrous lives.

Data linkage escape this is not emergency
Come with me compute with me
Coupling with me she becomes a couplet
Lovers leap in the sea
A drop of sunlit pee between two lips
Substitute a priapic navigator
I see inappropriate behavior
I recall Father Damien seeing his own pale blue eyes
Regarding him from a face resembling his own
enlarged redblue heart.   It is a woman, a leperess,
expressing his sentiments.   I refer to the paired animals going up the ramp of the ark   leopard leopard
aardvark aardvark porpoise porpoise inchworm inchworm.   The story of Noah is the religious vision of
cloning.   Scientists tweeze pollen eyedrop sperma-
tozoa   dispatch flights of sexy sterile white moths
to eliminate specie.   They notice human lovers com-
monly resemble each other   test it at home looking
at their wives friends friends wives   or if not each
other then each other's brother or sister   but in any
event that love conducts a shock of recognition.   Question haven't I seen you somewhere before
answer yes in the mirror.   Given wars before wars
after wars genocides   and competition for markets
cloning will eliminate all chance   and love will be
one hundred percent efficient.   No *Sturm und Drang*

German phrase no disynchronicity   but everyone
having seen everyone else somewhere before   we
will have realized serenity of perfect universal
love   univerself love uniself love unilove   until
the race withers and blows away like the dried
husks of moths but who's complaining.

They had either believed me or not believed me. If they
had believed me I had been so effective, so frighteningly
effective that they did not want to confirm what I told
them, they were afraid to. If they called, he would want
their names. So they had let me go.

If they had not believed me, then my desperation was
so patent or my cravenness so truly loathsome that they
didn't have the heart to go on with it. Perhaps there were
moral operations in this world that transcended the individual responsible for them and threatened to ruin
everyone. Was that it? Was I perceived as a leper who
threatened to contaminate them?

In either case the result was the same, wasn't that so? I
had been released thinking I'd made contact with Bennett
and I had not.

That night I lay in Penfield's bed and stared at the
amber windowpanes and listened to the watchdogs baying. I tried to compose my terrible shame into something
I could deal with, I tried to comprehend the weird sick
brokenness I felt, the sense of irreparable damage I had
done to myself the catastrophic discomposure of everything but the small light in my mind. It was most difficult.

Sandy James asleep forever on the coach seat amid the
pilgrims: I take a few dollars out of my wallet and tuck
the fat wallet with her death benefits under her chin she
does not wake the train begins to move the small flaked
tarnished charms of her charm bracelet swing in their arc
the train picks up speed I jump hit the embankment the
cinders imbedding themselves in my knees.

Compare the private railroad car of the Meiji emperor
the imperial beloved, as it makes its way through the
sunlit valley of the Bunraku province. It moves slowly
and from the populated fields no closer than a mile
thousands of little children wave paper flags in time to the

small white puffs of smoke rising from the engine. The children are well behaved. Their parents kneel beside them and hold their shoulders. Their grandparents lie prostrate on the ground not even daring to glance toward the distant train where the line of mounted imperial guardsmen cantering at the base of the embankment alongside the dark green imperial car give it the look of a lampshade with a rippling fringe.

The man resisted all approaches he was stone he was steel I hated his grief his luxurious dereliction I hated his thoughts the quality of his voice his walk the way he spent his life proving his importance ritualizing his superiority his exercises of freedom his arrogant knowledge of the human heart I hated the back of his neck he was a killer of poets and explorers, a killer of boys and girls and he killed with as little thought as he gave to breathing, he killed by breathing he killed by existing he was an emperor, a maniac force in pantaloons and silk slippers and lacquered headdress dispensing like treasure pieces of his stool, making us throw ourselves on our faces to be beheaded one by one with gratitude, the outrageous absurdity of him was his power, his clucking crowing mewing shouting whistling ridiculousness is what stunned us into submission but not this boy, I know what to do about this pompous little self-idolator, I'm going to put the fucker where he belongs I swear oh my Clara I swear Mr. Penfield I swear by the memory of the Fat Lady I know how to do it, I know how to do it and I have the courage to do it and it will be a beautiful monumental thing I do I will testify to God that he is a human being, that is how, I will save him from wasting away, I will save him from crumbling into a piece of dried shit, into a foul eccentric, you see, I will give him hope, I will extend his reign, I will raise him and do it all so well with such style that he will thank me, thank me for growing in his heart his heart bursting his son.

And in the morning the whole spring of the earth has come forth and Loon Lake is a bowl of light. A sweet blue haze hangs in the trees. The sun is shining, a filigree of pale green leaf laces through the evergreens across the

water. I run down the hill to the lake side pulling off my
clothes as I go. I stop to remove my shoes. My feet
thump along the boathouse deck. I stand poised on the
edge and dive into the water. With powerful strokes
learned in the filth of industrial rivers Joe swims a great
circle crawl in the sweet clear cold mountain lake. He
pulls himself up on the float and stands panting in the sun,
his glistening white young body inhaling the light, the sun
healing my scars my cracked bones my lacerated soul, the
sun powering my loins warming them to a stir. I toss my
hair back, smooth it back, shake the water from my arms,
open my eyes. Up on the hill Bennett stands on his
terrace, a tiny man totally attentive. He has seen the
whole thing, as I knew he would. He waves at me. I smile
my white teeth. I wave back.

Herewith bio Joseph Korzeniowski.

Born to a working-class family Paterson New Jersey
August 2 1918.   Graduated Paterson Latin Grade
School 1930.   Graduated Paterson Latin High School
1936.   Voted by classmates Best Shape of the
Head.   Hobbies Street hockey, petit larceny.   Roust-
about Hearn Bros. Carnival, summer 1936.   Aka Joe
of Paterson, Loon Lake NY autumn 1936.   Employed
Bennett Autobody Number Six, headlight man, winter
1936.   Enrolled Williams College September 1937.
Letters in lacrosse swimming.   Graduated *cum laude*,
honors in Political Science, 1941.   Voted by classmates
Captain ROTC and Most Likely to Succeed.   Commis-
sioned Second Lieutenant U.S. Air Corps.   Legal name
change Joseph Paterson Bennett, June 1941.   Assigned
newly formed Office of Strategic Services 1942 parachut-
ing into France in black sweater flight jacket trousers black
boots false passport black wool cap black parachute pockets of francs four thousand feet into windy void face blackened teeth blackened, heart blackened dropping into
blackness.   Awarded Bronze Star with oak leaf cluster
1943.   Awarded Silver Star with oak leaf cluster
1944.   Decommissioned 1945 rank of Major, Office of
Strategic Services.   Appointed organization staff Central Intelligence Agency 1947.   Married Dru Channing

Smith 1947, divorced 1950; no issue.   Married Kimberly Andrea Kennedy 1951, divorced 1954; no issue.   Continuous service Central Intelligence Agency to resignation 1974.   Retiring rank Deputy Assistant Director.   Retired US State Department rank of Ambassador 1975.   Chairman and Chief Operating Officer Bennett Foundation.   Board of Directors James-Pennsylvania Steel Corporation.   Board of Directors Chilean-American Copper Corporation.   Trustee Jordan and Naismith colleges, Rhinebeck NY.   Trustee Miss Morris' School for Young Women, Briarcliff Manor NY.   Member Knickerbocker, Acropolis, New York; Silks, Saratoga Springs; Rhode Island Keel, Newport. Master of Loon Lake.

ABOUT THE AUTHOR

E. L. Doctorow was born in New York City. He attended Kenyon College and Columbia University. His previous novels include *Welcome to Hard Times* (1960), *The Book of Daniel*, a National Book Award nominee (1971), and *Ragtime*, winner of the National Book Critics Circle Award (1975). A play, *Drinks Before Dinner*, was given its first production at the New York Shakespeare Festival's Public Theater and published in 1979.

W9-CZR-299

"CORNWELL IS A GIFTED STORYTELLER AND
ORCHESTRATOR OF SUSPENSE WITH A FLAIR FOR
PUTTING YOU IN THE THICK OF BATTLE ACTION."
Philadelphia Inquirer

*In a time of treachery and brutality,
a courageous warrior will face
the fires of battle as he journeys
on the ultimate quest:
the search for the Holy Grail*

1347. Five years have passed since Thomas of Hookton began his quest for justice . . . and the Holy Grail. Now, as England's army fights in France, her Scottish foes plan a bloody invasion that will embroil the young archer. Yet nothing will stop him from his mission. Not the mysterious black-clad knight who murdered his father, nor even his new nemesis, a sinister Dominican Inquisitor. Escaping across the sea, Thomas will soon be caught in one of the bloodiest fights of the Hundred Years' War: a battle of blood, flames, and butchery that will bring him face-to-face with his enemies . . . and test him as never before.

"Spectacular, rattling good stuff."
The Times (London)

"Cornwell is a gifted storyteller and
orchestrator of suspense with a flair for putting
you in the thick of battle action."
Philadelphia Inquirer

"Another superb adventure . . . As a chronicler of
battles, Bernard Cornwell has few equals.
In his turbulent adventure stories you can hear
the ear-shattering crack of the cannons,
smell the fires from burning villages, detect the
dying screams of horses caught up in the
awesome delivery of arrows or shot,
and slither in the blood of foot soldiers with
wounds so ghastly they have become
unrecognisable as human beings."
Birmingham Post

"One of the undisputed masters
of historical fiction."
Booklist

"The direct heir to Patrick O'Brian."
The Economist

"Brings an intriguing period to life."
Publishers Weekly

Books by Bernard Cornwell

The Sharpe Novels
(in chronological order)

The Nathaniel Starbuck Chronicles

The Grail Quest Series

Other Novels

*Published by HarperCollins*Publishers*

Vagabond

BERNARD CORNWELL

HarperTorch
An Imprint of HarperCollinsPublishers

HARPERTORCH
An Imprint of HarperCollins*Publishers*
10 East 53rd Street
New York, New York 10022-5299

Copyright © 2002 by Bernard Cornwell
Excerpt from *Heretic* copyright © 2003 by Bernard Cornwell
ISBN: 0-06-053268-8

Originally published in Great Britain in 2002 by HarperCollins Publishers.

First HarperTorch paperback printing: October 2003
First HarperCollins hardcover printing: December 2002

Printed in the United States of America

Visit HarperTorch on the World Wide Web at www.harpercollins.com

10 9 8 7 6 5 4 3 2 1

Vagabond
is for
June and Eddie Bell
in friendship and gratitude

Contents

✿

Vagabond

PART ONE

England, October 1346

Arrows on the Hill

I T WAS OCTOBER, the time of the year's dying when cattle were being slaughtered before winter and when the northern winds brought a promise of ice. The chestnut leaves had turned golden, the beeches were trees of flame and the oaks were made from bronze. Thomas of Hookton, with his woman, Eleanor, and his friend, Father Hobbe, came to the upland farm at dusk and the farmer refused to open his door, but shouted through the wood that the travelers could sleep in the byre. Rain rattled on the moldering thatch. Thomas led their one horse under the roof that they shared with a woodpile, six pigs in a stout timber pen and a scattering of feathers where a hen had been plucked. The feathers reminded Father Hobbe that it was St. Gallus's day and he told Eleanor how the blessed saint, coming home in a winter's night, had found a bear stealing his dinner. "He told the animal off!" Father Hobbe said. "He gave it a right talking-to, he did, and then he made it fetch his firewood."

"I've seen a picture of that," Eleanor said. "Didn't the bear become his servant?"

"That's because Gallus was a holy man," Father Hobbe explained. "Bears wouldn't fetch firewood for just anyone! Only for a holy man."

"A holy man," Thomas put in, "who is the patron saint of hens." Thomas knew all about the saints, more indeed than

Father Hobbe. "Why would a chicken want a saint?" he inquired sarcastically.

"Gallus is the patron of hens?" Eleanor asked, confused by Thomas's tone. "Not bears?"

"Of hens," Father Hobbe confirmed. "Indeed of all poultry."

"But why?" Eleanor wanted to know.

"Because he once expelled a wicked demon from a young girl." Father Hobbe, broad-faced, hair like a stickleback's spines, peasant-born, stocky, young and eager, liked to tell stories of the blessed saints. "A whole bundle of bishops had tried to drive the demon out," he went on, "and they had all failed, but the blessed Gallus came along and he cursed the demon. He cursed it! And it screeched in terror"—Father Hobbe waved his hands in the air to imitate the evil spirit's panic—"and then it fled from her body, it did, and it looked just like a black hen—a pullet. A black pullet."

"I've never seen a picture of that," Eleanor remarked in her accented English, then, gazing out through the byre door, "but I'd like to see a real bear carrying firewood," she added wistfully.

Thomas sat beside her and stared into the wet dusk, which was hazed by a small mist. He was not sure it really was St. Gallus's day for he had lost his reckoning while they traveled. Perhaps it was already St. Audrey's day? It was October, he knew that, and he knew that one thousand, three hundred and forty-six years had passed since Christ had been born, but he was not sure which day it was. It was easy to lose count. His father had once recited all the Sunday services on a Saturday and he had had to do them again the next day. Thomas surreptitiously made the sign of the cross. He was a priest's bastard and that was said to bring bad luck. He shivered. There was a heaviness in the air that owed nothing to the setting sun nor to the rain clouds nor to the mist. God help us, he thought, but there was an evil in this dusk and he made the sign of the cross again and said a silent prayer to

St. Gallus and his obedient bear. There had been a dancing bear in London, its teeth nothing but rotted yellow stumps and its brown flanks matted with blood from its owner's goad. The street dogs had snarled at it, slunk about it and shrank back when the bear swung on them.

"How far to Durham?" Eleanor asked, this time speaking French, her native language.

"Tomorrow, I think," Thomas answered, still gazing north to where the heavy dark was shrouding the land. "She asked," he explained in English to Father Hobbe, "when we would reach Durham."

"Tomorrow, pray God," the priest said.

"Tomorrow you can rest," Thomas promised Eleanor in French. She was pregnant with a child that, God willing, would be born in the springtime. Thomas was not sure how he felt about being a father. It seemed too early for him to become responsible, but Eleanor was happy and he liked to please her and so he told her he was happy as well. Some of the time, that was even true.

"And tomorrow," Father Hobbe said, "we shall fetch our answers."

"Tomorrow," Thomas corrected him, "we shall ask our questions."

"God will not let us come this far to be disappointed," Father Hobbe said, and then, to keep Thomas from arguing, he laid out their meager supper. "That's all that's left of the bread," he said, "and we should save some of the cheese and an apple for breakfast." He made the sign of the cross over the food, blessing it, then broke the hard bread into three pieces. "We should eat before nightfall."

Darkness brought a brittle cold. A brief shower passed and after it the wind dropped. Thomas slept closest to the byre door and sometime after the wind died he woke because there was a light in the northern sky.

He rolled over, sat up and he forgot that he was cold, forgot his hunger, forgot all the small nagging discomforts of life, for he could see the Grail. The Holy Grail, the most precious of all Christ's bequests to man, lost these thousand years and more, and he could see it glowing in the sky like shining blood and about it, bright as the glittering crown of a saint, rays of dazzling shimmer filled the heaven.

Thomas wanted to believe. He wanted the Grail to exist. He thought that if the Grail were to be found then all the world's evil would be drained into its depths. He so wanted to believe and that October night he saw the Grail like a great burning cup in the north and his eyes filled with tears so that the image blurred, yet he could see it still, and it seemed to him that a vapor boiled from the holy vessel. Beyond it, in ranks rising to the heights of the air, were rows of angels, their wings touched by fire. All the northern sky was smoke and gold and scarlet, glowing in the night as a sign to doubting Thomas. "Oh, Lord," he said aloud and he threw off his blanket and knelt in the byre's cold doorway, "oh, Lord."

"Thomas?" Eleanor, beside him, had awoken. She sat up and stared into the night. "Fire," she said in French, *"c'est un grand incendie."* Her voice was awed.

"C'est un incendie?" Thomas asked, then came fully awake and saw there was indeed a great fire on the horizon from where the flames boiled up to light a cup-shaped chasm in the clouds.

"There is an army there," Eleanor whispered in French. "Look!" She pointed to another glow, farther off. They had seen such lights in the sky in France, flamelight reflected from cloud where England's army blazed its way across Normandy and Picardy.

Thomas still gazed north, but now in disappointment. It was an army? Not the Grail?

"Thomas?" Eleanor was worried.

"It's just rumor," he said. He was a priest's bastard and he had been raised on the sacred scriptures and in Matthew's Gospel it had been promised that at the end of time there would be battles and rumors of battles. The scriptures promised that the world would come to its finish in a welter of war and blood, and in the last village, where the folk had watched them suspiciously, a sullen priest had accused them of being Scottish spies. Father Hobbe had bridled at that, threatening to box his fellow priest's ears, but Thomas had calmed both men down, and then spoken with a shepherd who said he had seen smoke in the northern hills. The Scots, the shepherd said, were marching south, though the priest's woman scoffed at the tale, claiming that the Scottish troops were nothing but cattle raiders. "Bar your door at night," she advised, "and they'll leave you alone."

The far light subsided. It was not the Grail.

"Thomas?" Eleanor frowned at him.

"I had a dream," he said, "just a dream."

"I felt the child move," she said, and she touched his shoulder. "Will you and I be married?"

"In Durham," he promised her. He was a bastard and he wanted no child of his to carry the same taint. "We shall reach the city tomorrow," he reassured Eleanor, "and you and I will marry in a church and then we shall ask our questions." And, he prayed, let one of the answers be that the Grail did not exist. Let it be a dream, a mere trick of fire and cloud in a night sky, for else Thomas feared it would lead to madness. He wanted to abandon this search; he wanted to give up the Grail and return to being what he was and what he wanted to be: an archer of England.

Bernard de Taillebourg, Frenchman, Dominican friar and Inquisitor, spent the autumn night in a pig pen and when dawn came thick and white with fog, he went to his

knees and thanked God for the privilege of sleeping in
fouled straw. Then, mindful of his high task, he said a prayer
to St. Dominic, begging the saint to intercede with God to
make this day's work good. "As the flame in thy mouth
lights us to truth"—he spoke aloud—"so let it light our path
to success." He rocked forward in the intensity of his emotion and his head struck against a rough stone pillar that supported one corner of the pen. Pain jabbed through his skull
and he invited more by forcing his forehead back against the
stone, grinding the skin until he felt the blood trickle down
to his nose. "Blessed Dominic," he cried, "blessed Dominic!
God be thanked for thy glory! Light our way!" The blood
was on his lips now and he licked it and reflected on all the
pain that the saints and martyrs had endured for the Church.
His hands were clasped and there was a smile on his haggard
face.

Soldiers who, the night before, had burned much of the
village to ash and raped the women who failed to escape and
killed the men who tried to protect the women, now watched
the priest drive his head repeatedly against the blood-
spattered stone. "Dominic," Bernard de Taillebourg gasped,
"oh, Dominic!" Some of the soldiers made the sign of the
cross for they recognized a holy man when they saw one.
One or two even knelt, though it was awkward in their mail
coats, but most just watched the priest warily, or else
watched his servant who, sitting outside the sty, returned
their gaze.

The servant, like Bernard de Taillebourg, was a Frenchman, but something in the younger man's appearance suggested a more exotic birth. His skin was sallow, almost as
dark as a Moor's, and his long hair was sleekly black which,
with his narrow face, gave him a feral look. He wore mail
and a sword and, though he was nothing but a priest's servant, he carried himself with confidence and dignity. His
dress was elegant, something strange in this ragged army. No

one knew his name. No one even wanted to ask, just as no one wanted to ask why he never ate or chatted with the other servants, but kept himself fastidiously apart. Now the mysterious servant watched the soldiers and in his left hand he held a knife with a very long and thin blade, and once he knew enough men were looking at him, he balanced the knife on an outstretched finger. The knife was poised on its sharp tip, which was prevented from piercing the servant's skin by the cut-off finger of a mail glove that he wore like a sheath. Then he jerked the finger and the knife span in the air, blade glittering, to come down, tip first, to balance on his finger again. The servant had not looked at the knife once, but kept his dark-eyed gaze fixed on the soldiers. The priest, oblivious to the display, was howling prayers, his thin cheeks laced with blood. "Dominic! Dominic! Light our path!" The knife span again, its wicked blade catching the foggy morning's small light. "Dominic! Guide us! Guide us!"

"On your horses! Mount up! Move yourselves!" A gray-haired man, a big shield slung from his left shoulder, pushed through the onlookers. "We've not got all day! What in the name of the devil are you all gawking at? Jesus Christ on His goddamn cross, what is this, Eskdale bloody fair? For Christ's sake, move! Move!" The shield on his shoulder was blazoned with the badge of a red heart, but the paint was so faded and the shield's leather cover so scarred that the badge was hard to distinguish. "Oh, suffering Christ!" The man had spotted the Dominican and his servant. "Father! We're going now. Right now! And I don't wait for prayers." He turned back to his men. "Mount up! Move your bones! There's devil's work to be done!"

"Douglas!" the Dominican snapped.

The gray-haired man turned back fast. "My name, priest, is Sir William, and you'll do well to remember it."

The priest blinked. He seemed to be suffering a momentary confusion, still caught up in the ecstasy of his pain-

driven prayer, then he gave a perfunctory bow as if acknowledging his fault in using Sir William's surname. "I was talking to the blessed Dominic," he explained.

"Aye, well, I hope you asked him to shift this damn fog?"

"And he will lead us today! He will guide us!"

"Then he'd best get his damn boots on," Sir William Douglas, Knight of Liddesdale, growled at the priest, "for we're
leaving whether your saint is ready or not." Sir William's
chain mail was battle-torn and patched with newer rings.
Rust showed at the hem and at the elbows. His faded shield,
like his weather-beaten face, was scarred. He was forty-six
now and he reckoned he had a sword, arrow or spear scar for
each of those years that had turned his hair and short beard
white. Now he pulled open the sty's heavy gate. "On your
trotters, father. I've a horse for you."

"I shall walk," Bernard de Taillebourg said, picking up a
stout staff with a leather thong threaded through its tip, "as
our Lord walked."

"Then you'll not get wet crossing the streams, eh, is that
it?" Sir William chuckled. "You'll walk on water will you,
father? You and your servant?" Alone among his men he did
not seem impressed by the French priest or wary of the
priest's well-armed servant, but Sir William Douglas was fa-
mously unafraid of any man. He was a border chieftain who
employed murder, fire, sword and lance to protect his land
and some fierce priest from Paris was hardly likely to impress him. Sir William, indeed, was not overfond of priests,
but his King had ordered him to take Bernard de Taillebourg
on this morning's raid and Sir William had grudgingly con-
sented.

All around him soldiers pulled themselves into their saddles. They were lightly armed for they expected to meet no
enemies. A few, like Sir William, carried shields, but most
were content with just a sword. Bernard de Taillebourg, his

friar's robes mud-spattered and damp, hurried alongside Sir William. "Will you go into the city?"

"Of course I'll not go into the bloody city. There's a truce, remember?"

"But if there's a truce . . ."

"If there's a bloody truce then we leave them be."

The French priest's English was good, but it took him a few moments to work out what Sir William's last three words had meant. "There'll be no fighting?"

"Not between us and the city, no. And there's no god-damned English army within a hundred miles so there'll be no fighting. All we're doing is looking for food and forage, father, food and forage. Feed your men and feed your animals and that's the way to win your wars." Sir William, as he spoke, climbed onto his horse, which was held by a squire. He pushed his boots into the stirrups, plucked the skirts of his mail coat from under his thighs and gathered the reins. "I'll get you close to the city, father, but after that you'll have to shift for yourself."

"Shift?" Bernard de Taillebourg asked, but Sir William had already turned away and spurred his horse down a muddy lane that ran between low stone walls. Two hundred mounted men-at-arms, grim and gray on this foggy morning, streamed after him and the priest, buffeted by their big dirty horses, struggled to keep up. The servant followed with apparent unconcern. He was evidently accustomed to being among soldiers and showed no apprehension, indeed his demeanor suggested he might be better with his weapons than most of the men who rode behind Sir William.

The Dominican and his servant had traveled to Scotland with a dozen other messengers sent to King David II by Philip of Valois, King of France. The embassy had been a cry for help. The English had burned their way across Normandy and Picardy, they had slaughtered the French King's army near a village called Crécy and their archers now held a dozen fastnesses in Brittany while their savage horsemen rode from Edward of England's ancestral possessions in Gascony. All that was bad, but even worse, and as if to show all Europe that France could be dismembered with impunity, the English King was now laying siege to the great fortress harbor of Calais. Philip of Valois was doing his best to raise the siege, but winter was coming, his nobles grumbled that their King was no warrior, and so he had appealed for aid to Scotland's King David, son of Robert the Bruce. Invade England, the French King had pleaded, and thus force Edward to abandon the siege of Calais to protect his homeland. The Scots had pondered the invitation, then were persuaded by the French King's embassy that England lay defenseless. How could it be otherwise? Edward of England's army was all at Calais or else in Brittany or Gascony, and there was no one left to defend England, and that meant the old enemy was helpless, it was asking to be raped and all the riches of England were just waiting to fall into Scottish hands.

And so the Scots had come south.

It was the largest army that Scotland had ever sent across the border. The great lords were all there, the sons and grandsons of the warriors who had humbled England in the bloody slaughter about the Bannockburn, and those lords had brought their men-at-arms who had grown hard with incessant frontier battles, but this time, smelling plunder, they were accompanied by the clan chiefs from the mountains and islands: chiefs leading wild tribesmen who spoke a language of their own and fought like devils unleashed. They had come in their thousands to make themselves rich and the French messengers, their duty done, had sailed home to tell Philip of Valois that Edward of England would surely raise his siege of Calais when he learned that the Scots were ravaging his northern lands.

The French embassy had sailed for home, but Bernard de

Taillebourg had stayed. He had business in northern England, but in the first days of the invasion he had experienced nothing except frustration. The Scottish army was twelve thousand strong, larger than the army with which Edward of England had defeated the French at Crécy, yet once across the frontier the great army had stopped to besiege a lonely fortress garrisoned by a mere thirty-eight men, and though the thirty-eight had all died, it had wasted four days. More time was spent negotiating with the citizens of Carlisle who had paid gold to have their city spared, and then the young Scottish King frittered away three more days pillaging the great priory of the Black Canons at Hexham. Now, ten days after they had crossed the frontier, and after wandering across the northern English moors, the Scottish army had at last reached Durham. The city had offered a thousand golden pounds if they could be spared and King David had given them two days to raise the money. Which meant that Bernard de Taillebourg had two days to find a way to enter the city, to which end, slipping in the mud and half blinded by the fog, he followed Sir William Douglas into a valley, across a stream and up a steep hill. "Which way is the city?" he demanded of Sir William.

"When the fog lifts, father, I'll tell you."

"They'll respect the truce?"

"They're holy men in Durham, father," Sir William answered wryly, "but better still, they're frightened men." It had been the monks of the city who had negotiated the ransom and Sir William had advised against acceptance. If monks offered a thousand pounds, he reckoned, then it would have been better to have killed the monks and taken two thousand, but King David had overruled him. David the Bruce had spent much of his youth in France and so considered himself cultured, but Sir William was not thus hampered by scruples. "You'll be safe if you can talk your way into the city," Sir William reassured the priest.

The horsemen had reached the hilltop and Sir William turned south along the ridge, still following a track that was edged with stone walls and which led, after a mile or so, to a deserted hamlet where four cottages, so low that their shaggy thatched roofs seemed to swell out of the straggling turf, clustered by a crossroads. In the center of the crossroads, where the muddy ruts surrounded a patch of nettles and grass, a stone cross leaned southward. Sir William curbed his horse beside the monument and stared at the carved dragon encircling the shaft. The cross was missing one arm. A dozen of his men dismounted and ducked into the low cottages, but they found no one and nothing, though in one cottage the embers of a fire still glowed and so they used the smoldering wood to fire the four thatched roofs. The thatch was reluctant to catch the fire for it was so damp that mushrooms grew on the mossy straw.

Sir William took his foot from the stirrup and tried to kick the broken cross over, but it would not shift. He grunted with the effort, saw Bernard de Taillebourg's disapproving expression and scowled. "It's not holy ground, father. It's only bloody England." He peered at the carved dragon, its mouth agape as it stretched up the stone shaft. "Ugly bastard thing, isn't it?"

"Dragons are creatures of sin, things of the devil," Bernard de Taillebourg said, "so of course it is ugly."

"A thing of the devil, eh?" Sir William kicked the cross again. "My mother," he explained as he gave the cross a third futile kick, "always told me that the bloody English buried their stolen gold beneath dragons' crosses."

Two minutes later the cross had been heaved aside and a half-dozen men were peering disappointedly into the hole it had left. Smoke from the burning roofs thickened the fog, swirled over the road and vanished into the grayness of the morning air. "No gold," Sir William grunted, then he summoned his men and led them southward out of the choking smoke. He was looking for any livestock that could be driven back to the Scottish army, but the fields were empty. The fire of the burning cottages was a hazed gold and red in the fog behind the raiders, a glow that slowly faded until only the smell of the fire was left and then, suddenly, hugely, filling the whole world with the alarm of its noise, a peal of bells clanged about the sky. Sir William, presuming the sound came from the east, turned through a gap in the wall into a pasture where he checked his horse and stood in the stirrups. He was listening to the sound, but in the fog it was impossible to tell where the bells were or how far away they were being tolled and then the sound stopped as suddenly as it had begun. The fog was thinning now, shredding away through the orange leaves of a stand of elms. White mushrooms dotted the empty pasture where Bernard de Taillebourg dropped to his knees and began to pray aloud. "Quiet, father!" Sir William snapped.

The priest made the sign of the cross as though imploring heaven to forgive Sir William's impiety in interrupting a prayer. "You said there was no enemy," he complained.

"I'm not listening for any bloody enemy," Sir William said, "but for animals. I'm listening for cattle bells or sheep bells." Yet Sir William seemed strangely nervous for a man who sought only livestock. He kept twisting in his saddle, peering into the fog and scowling at the small noises of curb chains or hooves stamping on damp earth. He snarled at the men-at-arms closest to him to be silent. He had been a soldier before some of these men had even been born and he had not stayed alive by ignoring his instincts and now, in this damp fog, he smelled danger. Sense told him there was nothing to fear, that the English army was far away across the sea, but he smelled death all the same and, quite unaware of what he was doing, he pulled the shield off his shoulder and pushed his left arm through its carrying loops. It was a big shield, one made before men began adding plates of armor to their mail, a shield wide enough to screen a man's whole body.

A soldier called out from the pasture's edge and Sir William grasped his sword's hilt, then he saw that the man had only exclaimed at the sudden appearance of towers in the fog which was now little more than a mist on the ridge's top, though in the deep valleys either side the fog flowed like a white river. And across the eastern river, way off to the north where they emerged from the spectral whiteness of another hill crest, was a great cathedral and a castle. They towered through the mist, vast and dark, like buildings from some doom-laden wizard's imagination, and Bernard de Taillebourg's servant, who felt he had not seen civilization in weeks, stared entranced at the two buildings. Black-robed monks crowded the tallest of the cathedral's two towers and the servant saw them pointing at the Scottish horsemen.

"Durham," Sir William grunted. The bells, he reckoned, must have been summoning the faithful to their morning prayers.

"I have to go there!" The Dominican climbed from his knees and, seizing his staff, set off toward the mist-shrouded city.

Sir William spurred his horse in front of the Frenchman. "What's your hurry, father?" he demanded, and de Taillebourg tried to dodge past the Scotsman, but there was a scraping sound and suddenly a blade, cold and heavy and gray, was in the Dominican's face. "I asked you, father, what the hurry was." Sir William's voice was as cold as his sword; then, alerted by one of his men, he glanced over and saw that the priest's servant had half drawn his own weapon. "If your bastard man doesn't sheathe his blade, father"—Sir William spoke softly, but there was a terrible menace in his voice—"I'll have his collops for my supper."

De Taillebourg said something in French and the servant reluctantly pushed the blade fully home. The priest looked up at Sir William. "Have you no fear for your mortal soul?" he asked.

Sir William smiled, paused and looked about the hilltop, but he saw nothing untoward in the shredding fog and decided his earlier nervousness had been the result of imagination. The result, perhaps, of too much beef, pork and wine the previous night. The Scots had feasted in the captured home of Durham's prior and the prior lived well, judging by his larder and cellar, but rich suppers gave men premonitions. "I keep my own priest to worry about my soul," Sir William said, then raised the tip of his sword to force de Taillebourg's face upward. "Why does a Frenchman have business with our enemies in Durham?" he demanded.

"It is Church business," de Taillebourg said firmly.

"I don't give a damn whose business it is," Sir William said, "I still wish to know."

"Obstruct me," de Taillebourg said, pushing the sword blade away, "and I shall have the King punish you and the Church condemn you and the Holy Father send your soul to eternal perdition. I shall summon—"

"Shut your goddamned bloody face!" Sir William said. "Do you think, priest, that you can frighten me? Our King is a puppy and the Church does what its paymasters tell it to do." He moved the blade back, this time resting it against the Dominican's neck. "Now tell me your business. Tell me why a Frenchman stays with us instead of going home with his countrymen. Tell me what you want in Durham."

Bernard de Taillebourg clutched the crucifix that hung about his neck and held it toward Sir William. In another man the gesture might have been taken as a display of fear, but in the Dominican it looked rather as though he threatened Sir William's soul with the powers of heaven. Sir William merely gave the crucifix a hungry glance as if appraising its value, but the cross was of plain wood while the little figure of Christ, twisted in death's agony, was only made of yellowed bone. If the figure had been made of gold then Sir William might have taken the bauble, but instead he spat in derision. A few of his men, fearing God more than their master, made the sign of the cross, but most did not care. They watched the servant closely, for he looked dangerous, but a middle-aged cleric from Paris, however fierce and gaunt he might be, did not scare them. "So what will you do?" de Taillebourg asked Sir William scornfully. "Kill me?"

"If I must," Sir William said implacably. The presence of the priest with the French embassy had been a puzzle, and his staying on when the others left only compounded the mystery, but a garrulous man-at-arms, one of the Frenchmen who had brought two hundred suits of plate armor as a gift to the Scots, had told Sir William that the priest was pursuing a great treasure and if that treasure was in Durham then Sir William wanted to know. He wanted a share. "I've killed priests before," he told de Taillebourg, "and another priest sold me an indulgence for the killings, so don't think I fear you or your Church. There's no sin that can't be bought off, no pardon that can't be purchased."

The Dominican shrugged. Two of Sir William's men were behind him, their swords drawn, and he understood that these Scotsmen would indeed kill him and his servant. These men who followed the red heart of Douglas were border ruffians, bred to battle as a hound was raised to the chase and the Dominican knew there was no point in continuing to threaten their souls for they gave no thought to such things. "I am going into Durham," de Taillebourg said, "to find a man."

"What man?" Sir William asked, his sword still at the priest's neck.

"He is a monk," de Taillebourg explained patiently, "and an old man now, so old that he may not even be alive. He is a Frenchman, a Benedictine, and he fled Paris many years ago."

"Why did he run?"

"Because the King wanted his head."

"A monk's head?" Sir William sounded skeptical.

"He was not always a Benedictine," de Taillebourg said, "but was once a Templar."

"Ah." Sir William began to understand.

"And he knows," de Taillebourg continued, "where a great treasure is hidden."

"The Templar treasure?"

"It is said to be hidden in Paris," de Taillebourg said, "hidden for all these years, but it was only last year that we discovered the Frenchman was alive and in England. The Benedictine, you see, was once the sacrist of the Templars. You know what that is?"

"Don't patronize me, father," Sir William said coldly.

De Taillebourg inclined his head to acknowledge the justice of the reproof. "If any man knows where the Templar treasure is," he went on humbly, "it is the man who was their sacrist, and now, we hear, that man lives in Durham."

Sir William took the sword away. Everything the priest said made sense. The Knights Templar, an order of monkish soldiers who were sworn to protect the pilgrims' roads between Christendom and Jerusalem, had become rich beyond the dreams of kings, and that was foolish for it made kings jealous and jealous kings make bad enemies. The King of France was just such an enemy and he had ordered the Templars destroyed: to which end a heresy had been cooked up, lawyers had effortlessly distorted truths and the Templars had been suppressed. Their leaders had been burned and their lands confiscated, but their treasures, the fabled treasures of the Templars, had never been found and the order's sacrist, the man responsible for keeping those treasures safe, would surely know their fate, "When were the Templars disbanded?" Sir William asked.

"Twenty-nine years ago," de Taillebourg answered.

So the sacrist could yet be alive, Sir William thought. He

would be an old man, but alive. Sir William sheathed his
sword, utterly convinced by de Taillebourg's tale, yet none
of it was true except that there was an old monk in Durham,
but he was not French and he had never been a Templar and,
in all probability, knew nothing of any Templar treasure. But
Bernard de Taillebourg had spoken persuasively, and the
story of the missing hoard was one that echoed through Europe, spoken of whenever men gathered to exchange tales of
marvels. Sir William wanted the story to be true and that,
more than anything, persuaded him it was. "If you find this
man," he said to de Taillebourg, "and if he lives, and if you
then find the treasure, then it will be because we made it
possible. It will be because we brought you here, and because we protected you on your journey to Durham."

"True, Sir William," de Taillebourg said.

Sir William was surprised by the priest's ready agreement. He frowned, shifted in his saddle and stared down at
the Dominican as if gauging the priest's trustworthiness. "So
we must share in the treasure," he demanded.

"Of course," de Taillebourg said instantly.

Sir William was no fool. Let the priest go into Durham
and he would never see the man again. Sir William twisted
in his saddle and stared north toward the cathedral. The
Templar treasure was said to be the gold from Jerusalem,
more gold than men could dream of, and Sir William was
honest enough to know that he did not possess the resources
to divert some of that golden trove to Liddesdale. The King
must be used. David II might be a weak lad, scarce breeched
and too softened by having lived in France, but kings had resources denied to knights and David of Scotland could talk
to Philip of France as a near equal, while any message from
William Douglas would be ignored in Paris. "Jamie!" he
snapped at his nephew who was one of the two men guarding de Taillebourg. "You and Dougal will take this priest
back to the King."

"You must let me go!" Bernard de Taillebourg protested.

Sir William leaned from his saddle. "You want me to cut off your priestly balls to make myself a purse?" He smiled at the Dominican, then looked back to his nephew. "Tell the King this French priest has news that concerns us and tell him to hold him safe till I return." Sir William had decided that if there was an ancient French monk in Durham then he should be questioned by the King of Scotland's servants and the monk's information, if he had any, could then be sold to the French King. "Take him, Jamie," he commanded, "and watch that damned servant! Take his sword."

James Douglas grinned at the thought of a mere priest and his servant giving him trouble, but he still obeyed his uncle. He demanded that the servant yield his sword and, when the man bridled at the order, Jamie half drew his own blade. De Taillebourg sharply instructed his servant to obey and the sword was sullenly handed over. Jamie Douglas grinned as he hung the sword from his own belt. "They'll not bother me, uncle."

"Away with you," Sir William said and watched as his nephew and his companion, both well mounted on fine stallions captured from the Percy lands in Northumberland, escorted the priest and his servant back toward the King's encampment. Doubtless the priest would complain to the King and David, so much weaker than his great father, would worry about the displeasure of God and the French, but David would worry a great deal more about Sir William's displeasure. Sir William smiled at that thought, then saw that some of his men on the far side of the field had dismounted. "Who the devil told you to unhorse?" he shouted angrily, then he saw they were not his men at all, but strangers revealed by the shredding mist, and he remembered his instincts and cursed himself for wasting time on the priest.

And as he cursed so the first arrow flickered from the

south. The sound it made was a hiss, feather in air, then it struck home and the noise was like a pole-axe cleaving flesh. It was a heavy thump edged with the tearing of steel in muscle and ending with the harsh scrape of blade on bone, and then a grunt from the victim and a heartbeat of silence.

And after that the scream.

THOMAS OF HOOKTON heard the bells, deep-toned and sonorous, not the sound of bells hung in some village church, but bells of thunderous power. Durham, he thought, and he felt a great weariness for the journey had been so long.

It had begun in Picardy, on a field stinking of dead men and horses, a place of fallen banners, broken weapons and spent arrows. It had been a great victory and Thomas had wondered why it left him dulled and nervous. The English had marched north to besiege Calais, but Thomas, duty bound to serve the Earl of Northampton, had received the Earl's permission to take a wounded comrade to Caen where there was a doctor of extraordinary skill. Then, however, it was decreed that no man could leave the army without the King's permission and so the Earl approached the King and thus Edward Plantagenet heard of Thomas of Hookton and how his father had been a priest who had been born to a family of French exiles called Vexille, and how it was rumored that the Vexille family had once possessed the Grail. It was only a rumor, of course, a wisp of a story in a hard world, yet the story was of the Holy Grail and that was the most precious thing that had ever existed, if indeed it had existed; and the King had questioned Thomas of Hookton and Thomas had tried to scorn the truth of the Grail story, but then the Bishop of Durham, who had fought in the shield wall that broke the French assaults, told how Thomas's father had once been imprisoned in Durham. "He was mad," the bishop explained to the King, "wits flown to the winds! So they locked him up for his own good."

"Did he talk of the Grail?" the King asked, and the Bishop of Durham had answered that there was one man left in his diocese who might know, an old monk called Hugh Collimore who had nursed the mad Ralph Vexille, Thomas's father. The King might have dismissed the tales as so much churchly gossip had not Thomas recovered his father's heritage, the lance of St. George, in the battle that had left so many dead on the green slope above the village of Crécy. The battle had also left Thomas's friend and commander Sir William Skeat wounded and he wanted to take Skeat to the doctor in Normandy, but the King had insisted that Thomas go to Durham and speak with Brother Collimore. So Eleanor's father had taken Sir William Skeat to Caen and Thomas, Eleanor and Father Hobbe had accompanied a royal chaplain and a knight of King Edward's household to England, but in London the chaplain and the knight had both fallen sick with an early winter fever and so Thomas and his companions had traveled north alone and now they were close to Durham, on a foggy morning, listening to the cathedral's bells. Eleanor, like Father Hobbe, was excited for she believed that discovering the Grail would bring peace and justice to a world that stank of burned cottages. There would be no more sorrow, Eleanor thought, and no more war, and perhaps even no more sickness.

Thomas wanted to believe it. He wanted his night vision to be real, not flame and smoke, yet if the Grail existed at all he thought that it would be in some great cathedral, guarded by angels. Or else it was gone from this world, and if there was no Grail on earth then Thomas's faith was in a war bow made of Italian yew, painted black, strung with hemp, that drove an arrow made of ash, fledged with goose feathers and tipped with steel. On the bow's belly, where his left hand gripped the yew, there was a silver plate engraved with a yale, a fabulous beast of claws and horns and tusks and scales that was the badge of his father's family, the Vexilles. The yale held a cup and Thomas had been told it was the Grail. Always the Grail. It beckoned him, mocked him, bent his life, changed all, yet never appeared except in a dream of fire. It was mystery, just as Thomas's family was a mystery, but perhaps Brother Collimore could cast light on that mystery and so Thomas had come north. He might not learn of the Grail, but he expected to discover more about his family and that, at least, made the journey worthwhile.

"Which way?" Father Hobbe asked.

"God knows," Thomas said. Fog shrouded the land.

"The bells sounded that way." Father Hobbe pointed north and east. He was energetic, full of enthusiasm, and naïvely trusting in Thomas's sense of direction, though in truth Thomas did not know where he was. Earlier they had come to a fork in the road and he had randomly taken the left-hand track that now faded to a mere scar on the grass as it climbed. Mushrooms grew in the pasture, which was wet and heavy with dew so that their horse slipped as it climbed. The horse was Thomas's mare and it was carrying their small baggage and in one of the sacks hanging from the saddle's pommel was a letter from the Bishop of Durham to John Fossor, the Prior of Durham. "Most beloved brother in Christ," the letter began, and went on to instruct Fossor to allow Thomas of Hookton and his companions to question Brother Collimore concerning Father Ralph Vexille, "whom you will not remember for he was kept closed up in your house before you came to Durham, indeed before I came to the See, but there will be some who know of him and Brother Collimore, if it pleases God that he yet lives, will have certain knowledge of him and of the great treasure that he concealed. We request this in the name of the King and in the service of Almighty God who has blessed our arms in this present endeavor."

"*Qu'est-ce que c'est?*" Eleanor asked, pointing up the hill where a dull reddish glow discolored the fog.

"What?" Father Hobbe, the only one who did not speak French, asked.

"Quiet," Thomas warned him, holding up his hand. He could smell burning and see the flicker of flames, but there were no voices. He took his bow from where it hung from the saddle and he strung it, bending the huge stave to loop the hemp string over the piece of nocked horn. He pulled an arrow from the bag and then, motioning Eleanor and Father Hobbe to stay where they were, he edged up the track to the shelter of a deep hedge where larks and finches flitted through the dying leaves. The fires were roaring, suggesting they were newly set. He crept closer, the bow half drawn, until he could see there had been three or four cottages about a crossroads and their rafters and thatch were well ablaze and sending sparks whirling up into the damp gray. The fires looked recent, but there was no one in sight: no enemy, no men in mail, so he beckoned Eleanor and Father Hobbe forward and then, over the sound of the fire, he heard a scream. It was far off, or perhaps it was close but muffled by fog, and Thomas stared through the smoke and the fog and past the seething flames and suddenly two men in mail, both mounted on black stallions, cantered into view. The horsemen had black hats, black boots and black scabbarded swords and they were escorting two other men who were on foot. One was a priest, a Dominican judging by his black and white garb, and he had a bloodied face, while the other man was tall, dressed in mail, and had long black hair and a narrow, intelligent face. The two followed the horsemen through the smoky fog, then paused at the crossroads where the priest dropped to his knees and made the sign of the cross.

The leading horseman seemed irritated by the priest's prayer for he turned his horse back and, drawing his sword, prodded the blade at the kneeling man. The priest looked up and, to Thomas's astonishment, suddenly rammed his staff up into the stallion's throat. The beast twitched away and the priest slammed the staff hard at the rider's sword arm. The horseman, unbalanced by his stallion's jerking motion, tried to cut down across his body with his long blade. The second horseman was already unsaddled, though Thomas had not seen him fall, and the black-haired man in mail was astride his body with a long knife drawn. Thomas just stared in puzzlement for he was convinced that neither the two horsemen nor the priest nor the black-haired man had uttered the scream, yet no other folk were in sight. One of the two horsemen was already dead and the other now fought the priest in silence and Thomas had a sense that the conflict was unreal, that he was dreaming, that in truth this was a morality play in dumb show: the black-clad horseman was the devil and the priest was God's will and Thomas's doubts about the Grail were about to be resolved by whoever won and then Father Hobbe seized the great bow from Thomas. "We must help!"

Yet the priest hardly needed help. He used the staff like a sword, parrying his opponent's cut, lunging hard to bruise the rider's ribs, then the man with the long black hair rammed a sword up into the horseman's back and the man arched, shivered, and his own sword dropped. He stared down at the priest for a moment, then he fell backward from his saddle. His feet were momentarily trapped in the stirrups and the horse, panicking, galloped uphill. The killer wiped the blade of his sword, then took a scabbard from one of the dead men.

The priest had run to secure the other horse and now, sensing he was being watched, he turned to see two men and a woman in the fog. One of the men was a priest who had an arrow on a bowstring. "They were going to kill me!" Bernard de Taillebourg protested in French. The black-haired man turned fast, the sword rising in threat.

"It's all right," Thomas said to Father Hobbe and he took the black bow away from his friend and hung it on his shoulder. God had spoken, the priest had won the fight and Thomas was reminded of his night vision when the Grail had loomed in the clouds like a cup of fire. Then he saw that under the bruises and blood the strange priest's face was hard and lean, a martyr's face, with the look of a man who had hungered for God and achieved an evident saintliness and Thomas almost fell to his knees. "Who are you?" he called to the Dominican.

"I am a messenger." Bernard de Taillebourg snatched at any explanation to cover his confusion. He had escaped from his Scottish escort and now he wondered how he was to escape from the tall young man with the long black bow, but then a flight of arrows hissed from the south and one thumped into a nearby elm trunk while a second skidded along the wet grass, and a horse shrieked nearby and men were shouting in disorder. Father de Taillebourg called to his servant to catch the second horse, which was trotting uphill and, by the time it was caught, de Taillebourg saw that the stranger with the bow had forgotten him and was staring south to where the arrows flew.

So he turned toward the city, called his servant to follow him and kicked back his heels.

For God, for France, for St. Denis and for the Grail.

SIR WILLIAM DOUGLAS cursed. Arrows were hissing all about him. Horses were screaming and men were lying dead or injured on the grass. For a heartbeat he felt bewildered, then he realized that his forage party had blundered into an English force, but what kind of force? There was no English army nearby! The whole English army was in France, not here! Which meant, surely, that the citizens of Durham had broken their truce and that thought filled Sir William with a terrible anger. Christ, he thought, but there would not be one stone left on another when he had finished with the city, and he tugged the big shield to cover his body and spurred south toward the bowmen who were lining a low hedge. He reckoned there were not so many of them, maybe only fifty, and he still had nearly two hundred men mounted and so he roared the order to charge. Swords scraped from scabbards. "Kill the bastards!" Sir William shouted. "Kill them!" He was savaging his horse with his spurs and thrusting other confused horsemen aside in his eagerness to reach the hedge. He knew the charge would be ragged, knew some of his men must die, but once they were over the blackthorn and in among the bastards they would kill them all.

Bloody archers, he thought. He hated archers. He especially hated English archers and he detested traitorous, truce-breaking Durham archers above all others. "On! On!" he shouted. "Douglas! Douglas!" He liked to let his enemies know who was killing them, and who would be raping their wives when they were dead. If the city had broken the truce, then God help that city for he would sack, rape and burn the whole of it. He would fire the houses, plough the ashes and leave the bones of its citizens to the winter blight, and for years men would see the bare stones of the ruined cathedral and watch the birds nesting in the castle's empty towers and they would know that the Knight of Liddesdale had worked his revenge.

"Douglas!" he shouted, "Douglas!" and he felt the thump of arrows smacking into his shield and then his horse screamed and he knew more arrows must have driven deep into its chest for he could feel the beast stumbling. He

kicked his feet from the stirrups as the horse slewed sideways. Men charged past him, screaming defiance, then Sir
William threw himself out of the saddle and onto his shield
that slid along the wet grass like a sledge, and he heard his
horse screaming in pain, but he himself was unhurt, hardly
even bruised and he pushed himself up, found his sword that
he had dropped when he fell and ran on with his horsemen.
A rider had an arrow sticking from his knee. A horse went
down, eyes white, teeth bared, blood flecking from the arrow
wounds. The first horsemen were at the hedge and some had
found a gap and were spurring through and Sir William saw
that the damned English bowmen were running away. Bastards, he thought, cowardly bloody English rotten whoreson
bastards, then more bows sounded harsh to his left and he
saw a man fall from a horse with an arrow through his head
and the fog lifted enough to show that the enemy archers had
not run away, but had merely joined a solid mass of dismounted men-at-arms. The bowstrings sounded again. A
horse reared in pain and an arrow sliced into its belly. A man
staggered, was struck again and fell back with a crash of
mail.

Sweet Christ, Sir William thought, but there was a
damned army here! A whole damned army! "Back! Back!"
he bellowed. "Haul off! Back!" He yelled till he was hoarse.
Another arrow drove into his shield, its point whipping
through the leather-covered willow and, in his rage, he
slapped at it, breaking the ash shaft.

"Uncle! Uncle!" a man shouted and Sir William saw it
was Robbie Douglas, one of his eight nephews who rode
with the Scottish army, bringing him a horse, but a pair of
English arrows struck the beast's quarter and, enraged by
pain, it broke away from Robbie's grasp.

"Go north!" Sir William shouted at his nephew. "Go on,
Robbie!"

Instead Robbie rode to his uncle. An arrow struck his saddle, another glanced off his helmet, but he leaned down, took Sir William's hand and dragged him northward. Arrows followed them, but the fog swirled thick and hid them. Sir William shook off his nephew's grip and stumbled north, made clumsy by his shield stuck with arrows and by his heavy mail. God damn it, God damn it!

"Mind left! Mind left!" a Scottish voice cried and Sir William saw some English horsemen coming from the hedgerow. One saw Sir William and thought he would be easy pickings. The English had been no more ready for battle than the Scotsmen. A few wore mail, but none was properly armored and none had lances. But Sir William reckoned they must have detected his presence long before they loosed their first arrows, and the anger at being so ambushed made him step toward the horseman who was holding his sword out like a spear. Sir William did not even bother to try and parry. He just thrust his heavy shield up, punching it into the horse's mouth, and he heard the animal whinny in pain as he swept his sword at its legs and the beast twisted away and the rider was flailing for balance and was still trying to calm his horse when Sir William's sword tore up under his mail and into his guts. "Bastard," Sir William snarled and the man was whimpering as Sir William twisted the blade, and then Robbie rode up on the man's far side and chopped his sword down onto his neck so that the Englishman's head was all but severed as he fell from the saddle. The other horsemen had mysteriously shied away, but then arrows flew again and Sir William knew the fickle fog was thinning. He dragged his sword free of the corpse, scabbarded the wet blade and hauled himself into the dead man's saddle. "Away!" he shouted at Robbie, who seemed inclined to take on the whole English force single-handedly. "Away, boy! Come on!"

By God, he thought, but it hurt to run from an enemy, yet

there was no shame in two hundred men fleeing six or seven hundred. And when the fog lifted there could be a proper battle, a murderous clash of men and steel, and Sir William would teach these bastard English how to fight. He kicked his borrowed horse on, intent on carrying news of the English to the rest of the Scottish army, but then saw an archer lurking in a hedge. A woman and a priest were with the man and Sir William put a hand to his sword hilt and thought about swerving aside to take some revenge for the arrows that had ripped into his forage party, but behind him the other Englishmen were shouting their war cry: "St. George! St. George!" and so Sir William left the isolated archer alone. He rode on, leaving good men on the autumn grass. They were dead and dying, wounded and frightened. But he was a Douglas. He would come back and he would have his revenge.

A RUSH OF PANICKED HORSEMEN galloped past the hedge where Thomas, Eleanor and Father Hobbe crouched. Half a dozen horses were riderless while at least a score of others were bleeding from wounds out of which the arrows jutted with their white goose feathers spattered red. The riders were followed by thirty or forty men on foot, some limping, some with arrows stuck in their clothes and a few carrying saddles. They hurried past the burning cottages as a new volley of arrows hastened their retreat, then the thump of hooves made them look back in panic and some of the fugitives broke into a clumsy run as a score of mail-clad horsemen thundered from the mist. Great clods of wet earth spewed up from the horses' hooves. The stallions were being curbed, forced to take brief steps as their riders took aim at their victims, then the spurs went back as the horses were released to the kill and Eleanor cried aloud in anticipation of the carnage. The heavy swords chopped down. One or two of the fugitives dropped to their knees and held their hands up in surrender, but most tried to escape. One dodged behind a galloping horseman and fled toward the hedge, saw Thomas and his bow and turned straight back into the path of another rider who drove the edge of his heavy sword into the man's face. The Scotsman went onto his knees, mouth open as though he would scream, but no sound came, only blood seeping between the fingers that were clasped over his nose and eyes. The horseman, who had no shield or helmet, turned his stallion and then leaned out of the saddle to chop his sword into his victim's neck, killing the man as if he were a cow being pole-axed and that was oddly appropriate because Thomas saw that the mounted killer was wearing the badge of a brown cow on his jupon, which was a short jerkin-like coat half covering his mail hauberk. The jupon was torn, bloodstained and the cow badge had faded so that at first Thomas thought it was a bull. Then the horseman swerved toward Thomas, raised his bloody sword in threat and then noticed the bow and checked his horse. "English?"

"And proud of it!" Father Hobbe answered for Thomas.

A second horseman, this one with three black ravens embroidered on his white jupon, reined in beside the first. Three prisoners were being pushed toward the two horsemen. "How the devil did you get this far in front?" the newly arrived man asked Thomas.

"In front?" Thomas asked.

"Of the rest of us."

"We walked," Thomas said, "from France. Or at least from London."

"From Southampton!" Father Hobbe corrected Thomas with a pedantry that was utterly out of place on this smoke-stinking hilltop where a Scotsman writhed in his death agonies.

"France?" The first man, tangle-haired, brown-faced, and with a northern accent so thick that Thomas found it hard to understand, sounded as if he had never heard of France. "You were in France?" he asked.

"With the King."

"You're with us now," the second man said threateningly, then looked Eleanor up and down. "Did you bring the doxie back from France?"

"Yes," Thomas replied curtly.

"He lies, he lies," a new voice said and a third horseman pushed himself forward. He was a lanky man, maybe thirty years old, with a face so red and raw that it looked as though he had scraped his skin off with the bristles when he shaved his sunken cheeks and long jaw. His dark hair was worn long and tied at the nape of his neck with a leather lace. His horse, a scarred roan, was as thin as the rider and had white nervous eyes. "I hate goddamn liars," the man said, staring at Thomas, then he turned and gave a baleful glance at the prisoners, one of whom wore the red heart badge of the Knight of Liddesdale on his jupon. "Almost as much as I hate goddamn Douglases."

The newcomer wore a padded gambeson in place of a hauberk or habergeon. It was the kind of protection an archer might wear if he could afford nothing better, yet this man plainly outranked archers for he wore a gold chain about his neck, a mark of distinction reserved for the gentry and above. A battered pig-snouted helmet, as scarred as the horse, hung from his saddle's pommel, a sword, plainly scabbarded in leather was at his hip, while a shield, painted white with a black axe, hung from his left shoulder. He also had a coiled whip hanging at his belt. "The Scots have archers," the man said, looking at Thomas, then his unfriendly gaze moved on to Eleanor, "and they have women."

"I'm English," Thomas insisted.

"We're all English," Father Hobbe said firmly, forgetting that Eleanor was a Norman.

"A Scotsman would say he was English if it stopped him from being gutted," the raw-faced man said caustically. The other two horsemen had fallen back, evidently wary of the thin man who now uncoiled the leather whip and, with a casual skill, flicked it so that the tip snaked out and cracked the air an inch or so from Eleanor's face. "Is she English?"

"She's French," Thomas said.

The horseman did not answer straightaway, but just stared

at Eleanor. The whip rippled as his hand trembled. He saw a fair, slight girl with golden hair and large, frightened eyes. Her pregnancy did not show yet and there was a delicacy to her that spoke of luxury and rare delight. "Scot, Welsh, French, what does it matter?" the man asked. "She's a woman. Do you care where a horse was born before you ride it?" His own scarred and thin horse became frightened just then because the veering wind blew a sour gust of smoke to its nostrils. It stepped sideways in a series of small, nervous steps until the man drove his spurs back so savagely that he pierced the padded trapper and made the destrier stand shivering in fear. "What she is"—the man spoke to Thomas and pointed his whip handle at Eleanor—"don't matter, but you're a Scot."

"I'm English," Thomas said again. A dozen other men wearing the badge of the black axe had come to gaze at Thomas and his companions. The men surrounded the three Scottish prisoners who seemed to know who the horseman with the whip was and did not like the knowledge. More bowmen and men-at-arms watched the cottages burning and laughed at the panicked rats that scrambled from what was left of the collapsed mossy thatch.

Thomas took an arrow from his bag and immediately four or five archers wearing the black-axe livery put arrows on their own strings. The other men in the axe livery grinned expectantly as if they knew this game and enjoyed it, but before it could be played out the horseman was distracted by one of the Scottish prisoners, the man wearing Sir William Douglas's badge who, taking advantage of his captors' interest in Thomas and Eleanor, had broken free and run northward. He had not gone twenty paces before he was ridden down by one of the English men-at-arms and the thin man, amused by the Scotsman's desperate bid for freedom, pointed at one of the burning cottages. "Warm the bastard up," he ordered. "Dickon! Beggar!" He spoke to two dismounted men-at-arms. "Look after those three." He nodded toward Thomas. "Watch 'em close!"

Dickon, the younger of the two, was round-faced and grinning, but Beggar was an enormous man, a shambling giant with a face so bearded that his nose and eyes alone could be seen through the tangled, crusted hair beneath the brim of the rusted iron cap that served as a helmet. Thomas was six feet in height, the length of a bow, but he was dwarfed by Beggar whose vast chest strained at a leather jerkin studded with metal plates. At the giant's waist, suspended by two lengths of rope, were a sword and a morningstar. The sword had no scabbard and its edge was chipped, while one of the spikes on the big metal ball of the morningstar was bent and smeared with blood and hair. The weapon's three-foot haft banged against the giant's bare legs as he lurched toward Eleanor. "Pretty," he said, "pretty."

"Beggar! Down, boy! Down!" Dickon ordered cheerfully and Beggar dutifully twitched away from Eleanor, though he still gazed at her and made a low growling noise in his throat. Then a scream made him look toward the nearest burning cottage where the Scotsman, stripped naked now, had been thrust in and out of the fire. The prisoner's long hair was alight and he frantically beat at the flames as he ran in panicked circles to the amusement of his English captors. Two other Scottish prisoners were squatting nearby, held on the ground by drawn swords.

The thin horseman watched as an archer swathed the prisoner's hair in a piece of sacking to extinguish the flames. "How many of you are there?" the thin man asked.

"Thousands!" the Scotsman answered defiantly.

The horseman leaned on his saddle's pommel. "How many thousands, cully?"

The Scotsman, his beard and hair smoking and his naked

skin blackened by embers and lacerated by cuts, did his best to look defiant. "More than enough to take you back home in a cage."

"He shouldn't say that to Scarecrow!" Dickon said, amused. "He shouldn't say that!"

"Scarecrow?" Thomas asked. It seemed an appropriate nickname for the horseman with the black-axe badge was lean, poor and frightening.

"He be Sir Geoffrey Carr to you, cully," Dickon said, watching the Scarecrow admiringly.

"And who is Sir Geoffrey Carr?" Thomas asked.

"He be Scarecrow and he be Lord of Lackby," Dickon said in a tone which suggested everyone knew who Sir Geoffrey Carr was, "and he be having his Scarecrow games now!" Dickon grinned because Sir Geoffrey, the whip coiled at his waist again, had dropped down from his horse and with a drawn knife, approached the Scottish prisoner.

"Hold him down," Sir Geoffrey ordered the archers, "hold him down and spread his legs."

"*Non!*" Eleanor cried in protest.

"Pretty," Beggar said in his voice that rumbled deep inside his huge chest.

The Scotsman screamed and tried to pull himself away, but he was tripped, then held down by three archers while the man evidently known throughout the north as the Scarecrow knelt between his legs. Somewhere in the clearing fog a raven cawed. A handful of archers was staring north in case the Scots returned, but most were watching the Scarecrow and his knife. "You want to keep your shriveled collops?" Sir Geoffrey asked the Scotsman. "Then tell me how many there are of you."

"Fifteen thousand? Sixteen?" The Scotsman was suddenly eager to talk.

"He means ten or eleven thousand," Sir Geoffrey announced to the listening archers, "which is more than enough for our few arrows. And is your bastard King here?"

The Scotsman bridled at that, but a touch of the knife blade to his groin reminded him of his predicament. "David Bruce is here, aye."

"Who else?"

The desperate Scotsman named his army's other leaders. The King's half-brother and heir to his throne, Lord Robert Stewart, was with the invading army, as were the Earls of Moray, of March, of Wigtown, Fife and Menteith. He named others, clan chiefs and wild men from the wastelands of the far north, but Carr was more interested in two of the earls. "Fife and Menteith?" he asked. "They're here?"

"Aye, sir, they are."

"But they swore fealty to King Edward," Sir Geoffrey said, evidently disbelieving the man.

"They march with us now," the Scotsman insisted, "as does Douglas of Liddesdale."

"That ripe bastard," Sir Geoffrey said, "that shit of hell." He stared northward through the fog shredding from the ridge, which was being revealed as a narrow and rocky plateau running north and south. The pasture on the plateau was thin and the ridge's weathered stone protruded through the grass like the ribs of a starving man. Off to the northeast, beyond the valley of mist, the cathedral and castle of Durham reared up on their river-lapped crag, while to the west were hills and woods and stone-walled fields cut with small streams. Two buzzards sailed above the ridge, going toward the Scottish army that was still concealed by the fog which lingered to the north, but Thomas was thinking that it would not be long before troops came to find the men who had run their fellow Scots away from the crossroads.

Sir Geoffrey leaned back and went to return his knife to its scabbard, then seemed to remember something and grinned at the prisoner. "You were going to take me back to Scotland in a cage, is that right?"

"No!"

"But you were! And why would I want to see Scotland? I can peer down a jakes whenever I want." He spat at the prisoner then nodded at the archers. "Hold him."

"No!" the Scotsman shouted, then the shout turned to a terrible scream as Sir Geoffrey leaned forward with the knife again. The prisoner twitched and heaved as the Scarecrow, the front of his padded gambeson now sheeted with blood, stood up. The prisoner was still screaming, hands clutched to his bloody groin, and the sight brought a smile to the Scarecrow's lips. "Throw the rest of him into the fire," he said, then turned to look at the other two Scottish prisoners. "Who is your master?" he demanded of them.

They hesitated, then one licked his lips. "We serve Douglas," he said proudly.

"I hate Douglas. I hate every Douglas that ever dropped out of the devil's backside." Sir Geoffrey shuddered, then turned to his horse. "Burn them both," he ordered.

Thomas, looking away from the sudden blood, had seen a stone cross fallen at the crossroad's center. He stared at it, not seeing the carved dragon, but hearing the echoes of the noise and then the new screams as the prisoners were hurled into the flames. Eleanor ran to him and held his arm tight.

"Pretty," Beggar said.

"Here, Beggar, here!" Sir Geoffrey called. "Hoist me!" The giant made a step with his hands and Sir Geoffrey used it to climb into his saddle, then he kicked the horse toward Thomas and Eleanor. "I'm always hungry," Sir Geoffrey said, "after a gelding." He turned to watch the fire where one of the Scotsmen, hair flaming, tried to escape, but was prodded back into the inferno by a dozen bowstaves. The man's howl was abruptly cut short as he collapsed. "I'm in the mood to geld and burn Scotsmen today," Sir Geoffrey said, "and you look like a Scot to me, boy."

"I'm not a boy," Thomas said, the anger rising in him.

"You look like a bloody boy to me, boy. A Scots boy, maybe?" Sir Geoffrey, plainly amused by Thomas's temper, grinned at his newest victim who did indeed look young, though Thomas was twenty-two summers old and had fought for the last four of them in Brittany, Normandy and Picardy. "You look Scots, boy," the Scarecrow said, daring Thomas to defy him again. "All the Scots are black!" he appealed to the crowd to judge Thomas's complexion, and it was true that Thomas had a sun-darkened skin and black hair, but so did a score or more of the Scarecrow's own archers. And though Thomas looked young he also looked hard. His hair was cropped close to his skull and four years of war had hollowed his cheeks, but there was still something distinctive in his looks, a handsomeness that attracted the eye and served to spur Sir Geoffrey Carr's jealousy. "What's on your horse?" Sir Geoffrey jerked his head toward Thomas's mare.

"Nothing of yours," Thomas said.

"What's mine is mine, boy, and what's yours is mine if I want it. Mine to take or mine to give. Beggar! You want that girl?"

Beggar grinned behind his beard and jerked his head up and down. "Pretty," he said. He scratched at the lice in his beard. "Beggar likes pretty."

"I reckon you can have the pretty when I'm through with her," Sir Geoffrey said with a grin and he took the whip from where it hung at his waist and cracked it in the air. Thomas saw that the long leather thong had a small iron claw at its end. Sir Geoffrey grinned at Thomas again, then drew back the whip as a threat. "Strip her, Beggar," he said, "let's give the boys a bit of pleasure," and he was still grinning as Thomas swung his heavy bowstave hard into the teeth of Sir Geoffrey's horse and the animal reared up, screaming, as Thomas knew it would, and the Scarecrow, unready for the motion, fell backward, flailing for balance, and his men, who should have protected him, were so intent on the burning Scottish prisoners that not one drew a bow or a blade before Thomas had dragged Sir Geoffrey down from the saddle and had him on the ground with a knife at his throat.

"I've been killing men for four years," Thomas said, "and not all of them were Frenchmen."

"Thomas!" Eleanor screamed.

"Take her, Beggar! Take her!" Sir Geoffrey shouted. He heaved up, but Thomas was an archer and years of drawing his big black bow had given him extraordinary strength in the arms and chest and Sir Geoffrey could not budge him, so he spat at Thomas instead. "Take her, Beggar!" he yelled again.

The Scarecrow's men ran toward their master, but checked when they saw that Thomas had a knife at his captive's throat.

"Strip her, Beggar! Strip the pretty! We'll all have her!" Sir Geoffrey bawled, apparently oblivious of the blade at his gullet.

"Who reads here? Who reads?" Father Hobbe bellowed. The odd question checked everyone, even Beggar who had already snatched off Eleanor's hat and now had his huge left arm around her neck while his right hand gripped the neckline of her frock. "Who in this company can read?" Father Hobbe demanded again as he brandished the parchment he had taken from one of the sacks on the back of Thomas's horse. "This is a letter from my lord the Bishop of Durham who is with our lord the King in France and it is sent to John Fossor, Prior of Durham, and only Englishmen who have fought with our King would carry such a letter. We have brought it from France."

"It proves nothing!" Sir Geoffrey shouted, then spat at Thomas again as the blade was pressed hard into his throat.

"And in what language is this letter written?" A new horseman had spurred through the Scarecrow's men. He wore no surcoat or jupon, but the badge on his battered shield was a scallop shell on a cross and it proclaimed that he was not one of Sir Geoffrey's followers. "What language?" he asked once more.

"Latin," Thomas said, his knife still pressing hard into Sir Geoffrey's neck.

"Let Sir Geoffrey up," the newcomer commanded Thomas, "and I shall read the letter."

"Tell him to let my woman go," Thomas snarled.

The horseman looked surprised at being given an order by a mere archer, but he did not protest. Instead he urged his horse toward Beggar. "Let her go," he said and, when the big man did not obey, he half drew his sword. "You want me to crop your ears, Beggar? Is that it? Two ears gone? Then your nose, then your cock, is that what you want, Beggar? You want to be shorn like a summer ewe? Trimmed down like an elf?"

"Let her go, Beggar," Sir Geoffrey said sullenly.

Beggar obeyed and stepped back and the horseman leaned down from his saddle to take the letter from Father Hobbe. "Let Sir Geoffrey go," the newcomer ordered Thomas, "for we shall have peace between Englishmen today, at least for a day."

The horseman was an old man, at least fifty years old, with a great shock of white hair that looked as though it had never been close to a brush or comb. He was a large man, tall and big-bellied, on a sturdy horse that had no trapper, but only a tattered saddle cloth. The man's full-length mail coat was sadly rusted in places and torn in others, while over the coat he had a breastplate that had lost two of its straps. A long sword hung at his right thigh. He looked to Thomas like a yeoman farmer who had ridden to war with whatever equipment his neighbors could lend him, but he had been recognized by Sir Geoffrey's archers who had snatched off their hats and helmets when he appeared and who now treated him with deference. Even Sir Geoffrey seemed cowed by the white-haired man who frowned as he read the letter. "*Thesaurus*, eh?" He was speaking to himself. "And a fine kettle of fish that is! A *thesaurus* indeed!" *Thesaurus* was Latin, but the rest of his words were spoken in Norman French and he was evidently confident that no archer would understand him.

"Mention of treasure"—Thomas used the same language, which had been taught to him by his father—"makes men excited. Overexcited."

"Good Lord above, good Lord indeed, you speak French! Miracles never cease. *Thesaurus*, it does mean treasure, doesn't it? My Latin is not what it was when I was young. I had it flogged into me by a priest and it seems to have mostly leaked out since. A treasure, eh? And you speak French!" The horseman showed genial surprise that Thomas spoke the language of aristocrats, though Sir Geoffrey, who did not speak French, looked alarmed for it suggested Thomas might be a good deal better born than he had thought. The horseman gave the letter back to Father Hobbe, then spurred to Sir Geoffrey. "You were picking a squabble with an Englishman, Sir Geoffrey, a messenger, no less, from our lord the King. How do you explain that?"

"I don't have to explain anything," Sir Geoffrey said, "my lord." The last two words were added reluctantly.

"I should fillet you now," his lordship said mildly, "then have you stuffed and mounted on a pole to scare the crows away from my newly born lambs. I could show you at Skipton Fair, Sir Geoffrey, as an example to other sinners." He seemed to consider that idea for a few heartbeats, then shook his head. "Just get on your horse," he said, "and fight the Scots today instead of quarrelling with your fellow Englishman." He turned in his saddle and raised his voice so all the archers and men-at-arms could hear him. "All of you, back down the ridge! And quick, before the Scots come and drive you off! You want to join those rascals in the fire?" He pointed to the three Scottish prisoners who were now nothing but dark shriveled shapes in the bright flames, then he beckoned Thomas and changed his language to French. "You've really come from France?"

"Yes, my lord."

"Then do me the courtesy, my dear fellow, of speaking with me."

They went south, leaving a broken stone cross, burned men and arrow-struck corpses in a thinning mist, where the army of Scotland had come to Durham.

BERNARD DE TAILLEBOURG took the crucifix from about his neck and kissed the writhing figure of Christ that was pinned to the small wooden cross. "God be with you, my brother," he murmured to the old man lying on the stone bench cushioned by a palliasse of straw and a folded blanket. A second blanket, just as thin, covered the old man whose hair was white and wispy.

"It is cold," Brother Hugh Collimore said feebly, "so cold." He spoke in French, though to de Taillebourg the old monk's accent was barbarous for it was the French of Normandy and of England's Norman rulers.

"Winter comes," de Taillebourg said. "You can smell it on the wind."

"I am dying"—Brother Collimore turned his red-rimmed eyes on his visitor—"and can smell nothing. Who are you?"

"Take this," de Taillebourg said and gave his crucifix to the old monk, then he stoked up the wood fire, put two more logs on the revived blaze and sniffed a jug of mulled wine that sat in the hearth. It was not too rank and so he poured some into a horn cup. "At least you have a fire," he said, stooping to peer through the small window, no bigger than an arrow slit, that faced west across the encircling Wear. The monk's hospital was on the slope of Durham's hill, beneath the cathedral, and de Taillebourg could see the Scottish men-at-arms carrying their lances through the straggling remnants of mist on the skyline. Few of the mail-clad men had horses, he noticed, suggesting that the Scots planned to fight on foot.

Brother Collimore, his face pale and his voice frail, gripped the small cross. "The dying are allowed a fire," he said, as though he had been accused of indulging himself in luxury. "Who are you?"

"I come from Cardinal Bessières," de Taillebourg said, "in Paris, and he sends you his greetings. Drink this, it will warm you." He held the mulled wine toward the old man.

Collimore refused the wine. His eyes were cautious. "Cardinal Bessières?" he asked, his tone implying that the name was new to him.

"The Pope's legate in France." De Taillebourg was surprised that the monk did not recognize the name, but thought perhaps the dying man's ignorance would be useful. "And the Cardinal is a man," the Dominican went on, "who loves the Church as fiercely as he loves God."

"If he loves the Church," Collimore said with a surprising force, "then he will use his influence to persuade the Holy Father to take the papacy back to Rome." The statement exhausted him and he closed his eyes. He had never been a big man, but now, beneath his lice-ridden blanket, he seemed to have shrunk to the size of a ten-year-old and his white hair was thin and fine like a small infant's. "Let him move the papacy to Rome," he said again, though feebly, "for all our troubles have worsened since it was moved to Avignon."

"Cardinal Bessières wants nothing more than to move the Holy Father back to Rome," de Taillebourg lied, "and perhaps you, brother, can help us achieve that."

Brother Collimore appeared not to hear the words. He had opened his eyes again, but just lay gazing up at the whitewashed stones of the arched ceiling. The room was low, chill and white. Sometimes, when the summer sun was high, he could see the flicker of reflected water on the white stones. In heaven, he thought, he would be forever within sight of crystal rivers and under a warm sun. "I was in Rome once," he said wistfully. "I remember going down some steps into a church where a choir sang. So beautiful."

"The Cardinal wants your help," de Taillebourg said.

"There was a saint there." Collimore was frowning, trying to remember. "Her bones were yellow."

"So the Cardinal sent me to see you, brother," de Taillebourg said softly. His servant, dark-eyed and elegant, watched from the door.

"Cardinal Bessières," Brother Collimore said in a whisper.

"He sends you his greetings in Christ, brother."

"What Bessières wants," Collimore said, still in a whisper, "he takes with whips and scorpions."

De Taillebourg half smiled. So Collimore did know of Cardinal Bessières after all, and no wonder, but perhaps fear of Bessières would be sufficient to elicit the truth. The monk had closed his eyes again and his lips were moving silently, suggesting he was praying. De Taillebourg did not disturb the prayers, but just gazed through the small window to where the Scots were making their battle line on the far hill. The invaders faced southward so that the left end of their line was nearest to the city and de Taillebourg could see men jostling for position as they tried to take the places of honor closest to their lords. The Scots had evidently decided to fight on foot so that the English archers could not destroy

their men-at-arms by cutting down their horses. There was
no sign of those English yet, though from all de Taillebourg
had heard they could not have assembled a great force. Their
army was in France, outside Calais, not here, so perhaps it
was merely a local lord leading his retainers? Yet plainly
there were enough men to persuade the Scots to form a battle line, and de Taillebourg did not expect David's army to
be delayed for long. Which meant that if he wanted to hear
the old man's story and be away from Durham before the
Scots entered the city then he had best make haste. He
looked back at the monk, "Cardinal Bessières wants only the
glory of the Church and of God. And he wants to know
about Father Ralph Vexille."

"Dear God," Collimore said, and his fingers traced the
bone figure on the small crucifix as he opened his eyes and
turned his head to stare at the priest. The monk's expression
suggested it was the first time he had really noticed de
Taillebourg and he shuddered, recognizing in his visitor a
man who believed suffering gave merit. A man, Collimore
reflected, who would be as implacable as his master in Paris.
"Vexille!" Collimore said, as though he had almost forgotten
the name, and then he sighed. "It is a long tale," he said
tiredly.

"Then I will tell you what I know of it," de Taillebourg
said. The gaunt Dominican was pacing the room now, turning and turning again in the small space under the highest
part of the arched ceiling. "You have heard," he demanded,
"that a battle was fought in Picardy in the summer? Edward
of England fought his cousin of France and a man came
from the south to fight for France and on his banner was the
device of a yale holding a cup." Collimore blinked, but said
nothing. His eyes were fixed on de Taillebourg who, in turn,
stopped his pacing to look at the priest. "A yale holding a
cup," he repeated.

"I know the beast," Collimore said sadly. A yale was an heraldic animal, unknown in nature, clawed like a lion, horned like a goat and scaled like a dragon.

"He came from the south," de Taillebourg said, "and he thought that by fighting for France he would wash from his family's crest the ancient stains of heresy and of treason." Brother Collimore was far too sick to see that the priest's servant was now listening intently, almost fiercely, or to notice that the Dominican had raised his voice slightly to make it easier for the servant, who still stood in the doorway, to overhear. "This man came from the south, riding in pride, believing his soul to be beyond reproof, but no man is beyond God's reach. He thought he would ride in victory into the King's affections, but instead he shared France's defeat. God will sometimes humble us, brother, before raising us to glory." De Taillebourg spoke to the old monk, but his words were for his servant's ears. "And after the battle, brother, when France wept, I found this man and he talked of you."

Brother Collimore looked startled, but said nothing.

"He talked of you," Father de Taillebourg said, "to me. And I am an Inquisitor."

Brother Collimore's fingers fluttered in an attempt to make the sign of the cross. "The Inquisition," he said feebly, "has no authority in England."

"The Inquisition has authority in heaven and in hell, and you think little England can stand against us?" The fury in de Taillebourg's voice echoed in the hospital cell. "To root out heresy, brother, we will ride to the ends of the earth."

The Inquisition, like the Dominican order of friars, was dedicated to the eradication of heresy, and to do it they employed fire and pain. They could not shed blood, for that was against the law of the Church, but any pain inflicted without blood-letting was permitted, and the Inquisition knew well that fire cauterized bleeding and that the rack did not pierce a heretic's skin and that great weights pressed on a man's chest burst no veins. In cellars reeking of fire, fear, urine and smoke, in a darkness shot through with flamelight and the screams of heretics, the Inquisition hunted down the enemies of God and, by the application of bloodless pain, brought their souls into a blessed unity with Christ.

"A man came from the south," de Taillebourg said to Collimore again, "and the crest on his shield was a yale holding a cup."

"A Vexille," Collimore said.

"A Vexille," de Taillebourg said, "who knew your name. Now why, brother, would a heretic from the southern lands know the name of an English monk in Durham?"

Brother Collimore sighed. "They all knew," he said tiredly, "the whole family knew. They knew because Ralph Vexille was sent to me. The bishop thought I could cure him of madness, but his family feared he would tell me secrets instead. They wanted him dead, but we locked him away in a cell where no one but I could reach him."

"And what secrets did he tell you?" de Taillebourg asked.

"Madness," Brother Collimore said, "just madness." The servant stood in the doorway and watched him.

"Tell me of the madness," the Dominican ordered.

"The mad speak of a thousand things," Brother Collimore said, "they speak of spirits and phantoms, of snow in summer and darkness in the daylight."

"But Father Ralph spoke to you of the Grail," de Taillebourg said flatly.

"He spoke of the Grail," Brother Collimore confirmed.

The Dominican let out a sigh of relief. "What did he tell you of the Grail?"

Hugh Collimore said nothing for a while. His chest rose and fell so feebly that the motion was scarcely visible, then he shook his head. "He told me that his family had owned the Grail and that he had stolen and hidden it! But he spoke of a hundred such things. A hundred such things."

"Where would he have hidden it?" de Taillebourg inquired.

"He was mad. Mad. It was my job, you know, to look after the mad? We starved or beat them to drive the devils out, but it did not always work. In winter we would plunge them into the river, through the ice, and that worked. Devils hate the cold. It worked with Ralph Vexille, or mostly it worked. We released him after a while. The demons were gone, you see."

"Where did he hide the Grail?" De Taillebourg's voice was harder and louder.

Brother Collimore stared at the flicker of reflected water light on the ceiling. "He was mad," he whispered, "but he was harmless. Harmless. And when he left here he was sent to a parish in the south. In the far south."

"At Hookton in Dorset?"

"At Hookton in Dorset," Brother Collimore agreed, "where he had a son. He was a great sinner, you see, even though he was a priest. He had a son."

Father de Taillebourg stared at the monk who had, at last, given him some news. A son? "What do you know of the son?"

"Nothing." Brother Collimore sounded surprised that he should be asked.

"And what do you know of the Grail?" de Taillebourg probed.

"I know that Ralph Vexille was mad," Collimore said in a whisper.

De Taillebourg sat on the hard bed. "How mad?"

Collimore's voice became even softer. "He said that even if you found the Grail then you would not know it, not unless you were worthy." He paused and a look of puzzlement, almost amazement, showed briefly on his face. "You had to be worthy, he said, to know what the Grail was, but if you were worthy then it would shine like the very sun. It would dazzle you."

De Taillebourg leaned close to the monk. "You believed him?"

"I believe Ralph Vexille was mad," Brother Collimore said.

"The mad sometimes speak truth," de Taillebourg said.

"I think," Brother Collimore went on as though the Inquisitor had not spoken, "that God gave Ralph Vexille a burden too great for him to bear."

"The Grail?" de Taillebourg asked.

"Could you bear it? I could not."

"So where is it?" de Taillebourg persisted. "Where is it?"

Brother Collimore looked puzzled again. "How would I know?"

"It was not at Hookton," de Taillebourg said, "Guy Vexille searched for it."

"Guy Vexille?" Brother Collimore asked.

"The man who came from the south, brother, to fight for France and ended in my custody."

"Poor man," the monk said.

Father de Taillebourg shook his head. "I merely showed him the rack, let him feel the pincers and smell the smoke. Then I offered him life and he told me all he knew and he told me the Grail was not at Hookton."

The old monk's face twitched in a smile. "You did not hear me, father. If a man is unworthy then the Grail would not reveal itself. Guy Vexille could not have been worthy."

"But Father Ralph did possess it?" De Taillebourg sought reassurance. "You think he really possessed it?"

"I did not say as much," the monk said.

"But you believe he did?" de Taillebourg asked and, when Brother Collimore said nothing, he nodded to himself. "You do believe he did." He slipped off the bed, going to his knees and a look of awe came to his face as his linked hands clawed at each other. "The Grail," he said in a tone of utter wonder.

"He was mad," Brother Collimore warned him.

De Taillebourg was not listening. "The grail," he said again, "*le Graal!*" He was clutching himself now, rocking back and forth in ecstasy. "*Le Graal!*"

"The mad say things," Brother Collimore said, "and they do not know what they say."

"Or God speaks through them," de Taillebourg said fiercely.

"Then God sometimes has a terrible tongue," the old monk replied.

"You must tell me," de Taillebourg insisted, "all that Father Ralph told you."

"But it was so long ago!"

"It is *le Graal!*" de Taillebourg shouted and, in his frustration, he shook the old man. "It is *le Graal!* Don't tell me you have forgotten." He glanced through the window and saw, raised on the far ridge, the red saltire on the yellow banner of the Scottish King and beneath it a mass of gray-mailed men with their thicket of lances, pikes and spears. No English foe was in sight, but de Taillebourg would not have cared if all the armies of Christendom were come to Durham for he had found his vision, it was the Grail, and though the world should tremble with armies all about him, he would pursue it.

And an old monk talked.

THE HORSEMAN with the rusted mail, broken-strapped breastplate and scallop-decorated shield named himself as Lord Outhwaite of Witcar. "Do you know the place?" he asked Thomas.

"Witcar, my lord? I've not heard of it."

"Not heard of Witcar! Dear me. And it's such a pleasant place, very pleasant. Good soil, sweet water, fine hunting. Ah, there you are!" This last was to a small boy mounted on a large horse and leading a second destrier by the reins. The boy wore a jupon that had the scalloped cross emblazoned in yellow and red and, tugging the warhorse behind him, he spurred toward his master.

"Sorry, my lord," the boy said, "but Hereward do haul away, he do." Hereward was evidently the destrier he led. "And he hauled me clean away from you!"

"Give him to this young man here," Lord Outhwaite said. "You can ride?" he added earnestly to Thomas.

"Yes, my lord."

"Hereward is a handful though, a rare handful. Kick him hard to let him know who's master."

A score of men appeared in Lord Outhwaite's livery, all mounted and all with armor in better repair than their master's. Lord Outhwaite turned them back south. "We were marching on Durham," he told Thomas, "just minding our own affairs as good Christians should, and the wretched Scots appeared! We won't make Durham now. I was married there, you know? In the cathedral. Thirty-two years ago, can you credit it?" He beamed happily at Thomas. "And my dear Margaret still lives, God be praised. She'd like to hear your tale. You really were at Wadicourt?"

"I was, my lord."

"Fortunate you, fortunate you!" Lord Outhwaite said, then hailed yet more of his men to turn them about before they blundered into the Scots. Thomas was rapidly coming to realize that Lord Outhwaite, despite his ragged mail and disheveled appearance, was a great lord, one of the magnates of the north country, and his lordship confirmed this opinion by grumbling that he had been forbidden by the King to fight in France because he and his men might be needed to fend off an invasion by the Scots. "And he was quite right!" Lord Outhwaite sounded surprised. "The wretches have come south! Did I tell you my eldest boy was in Picardy? That's why I'm wearing this." He plucked at a rent in the old mail coat. "I gave him the best armor we had because I thought we wouldn't need it here! Young David of Scotland always seemed peaceable enough to me, but now England's overrun by his fellows. Is it true that the slaughter at Wadicourt was vast?"

"It was a field of dead, my lord."

"Theirs, not ours, God and His saints be thanked." His lordship looked across at some archers straggling southward. "Don't dawdle!" he called in English. "The Scots will be looking for you soon enough." He looked back to Thomas and grinned. "So what would you have done if I hadn't come along?" he asked, still using English. "Cut the Scarecrow's throat?"

"If I had to."

"And had your own slit by his men," Lord Outhwaite observed cheerfully. "He's a poisonous tosspot. God only knows why his mother didn't drown him at birth, but then she was a goddamned turd-hearted witch if ever there was one." Like many lords who had grown up speaking French, Lord Outhwaite had learned his English from his parents' servants and so spoke it coarsely. "He deserves a slit throat, the Scarecrow does, but he's a bad enemy to have. He holds a grudge better than any man alive, but he has so many grudges that maybe he don't have room for one more. He hates Sir William Douglas most of all."

"Why?"

"Because Willie had him prisoner. Mind you, Willie Douglas has held most of us prisoner at one time or another and one or two of us have even held him in return, but the ransom near killed Sir Geoffrey. He's down to his last score of retainers and I'd be surprised if he's got more than three halfpennies in a pot. The Scarecrow's a poor man, very poor, but he's proud, and that makes him a bad enemy to have." Lord Outhwaite paused to raise a genial hand to a group of archers wearing his livery. "Wonderful fellows, wonderful. So tell me about the battle at Wadicourt. Is it true that the French rode down their own archers?"

"They did, my lord. Genoese crossbowmen."

"So tell me all that happened."

Lord Outhwaite had received a letter from his eldest son that told of the battle in Picardy, but he was desperate to hear of the fight from someone who had stood on that long green slope between the villages of Wadicourt and Crécy, and Thomas now told how the enemy had attacked late in the afternoon and how the arrows had flown down the hill to cut the King of France's great army into heaps of screaming men and horses, and how some of the enemy had still come through the line of newly dug pits and past the arrows to hack at the English men-at-arms, and how, by the battle's end, there were no arrows left, just archers with bleeding fingers and a long hill of dying men and animals. The very sky had seemed rinsed with blood.

The telling of the tale took Thomas down off the ridge and out of sight of Durham. Eleanor and Father Hobbe walked behind, leading the mare and sometimes interjecting with their own comments, while a score of Lord Outhwaite's retainers rode on either side to listen to the battle's tale. Thomas told it well and it was plain Lord Outhwaite liked him; Thomas of Hookton had always possessed a charm that had protected and recommended him, even though it sometimes made men like Sir Geoffrey Carr jealous. Sir Geoffrey had ridden ahead and, when Thomas reached the water meadows where the English force gathered, the knight pointed at him as if he were launching a curse and Thomas countered by making the sign of the cross. Sir Geoffrey spat. Lord Outhwaite scowled at the Scarecrow. "I have not forgotten the letter your priest showed me"—he spoke to Thomas in French now—"but I trust you will not leave us to deliver it to Durham yourself? Not while we have enemies to fight?"

"Can I stand with your lordship's archers?" Thomas asked.

Eleanor hissed her disapproval, but both men ignored her. Lord Outhwaite nodded his acceptance of Thomas's offer, then gestured that the younger man should climb down from the horse. "One thing does puzzle me, though," he went on, "and that is why our lord the King should entrust such an errand to one so young."

"And so base born?" Thomas asked with a smile, knowing that was the real question Lord Outhwaite had been too fastidious to ask.

His lordship laughed to be found out. "You speak French, young man, but carry a bow. What are you? Base or well born?"

"Well enough, my lord, but out of wedlock."

"Ah!"

"And the answer to your question, my lord, is that our lord the King sent me with one of his chaplains and a household knight, but both caught a sickness in London and that is where they remain. I came on with my companions."

"Because you were eager to speak with this old monk?"

"If he lives, yes, because he can tell me about my father's family. My family."

"And he can tell you about this treasure, this *thesaurus*. You know of it?"

"I know something of it, my lord," Thomas said cautiously.

"Which is why the King sent you, eh?" Lord Outhwaite queried, but did not give Thomas time to answer the question. He gathered his reins. "Fight with my archers, young man, but take care to stay alive, eh? I would like to know more of your *thesaurus*. Is the treasure really as great as the letter says?"

Thomas turned away from the ragged-haired Lord Outhwaite and stared up the ridge where there was nothing to be seen now except the bright-leaved trees and a thinning plume of smoke from the burned-out hovels. "If it exists, my lord"—he spoke in French—"then it is the kind of treasure that is guarded by angels and sought by demons."

"And you seek it?" Lord Outhwaite asked with a smile.

Thomas returned the smile. "I merely seek the Prior of Durham, my lord, to give him the bishop's letter."

"You want Prior Fossor, eh?" Lord Outhwaite nodded toward a group of monks. "That's him over there. The one in the saddle." He had indicated a tall, white-haired monk who was astride a gray mare and surrounded by a score of other monks, all on foot, one of whom carried a strange banner that was nothing but a white scrap of cloth hanging from a painted pole. "Talk to him," Lord Outhwaite said, "then seek my flag. God be with you!" He said the last four words in English.

"And with your lordship," Thomas and Father Hobbe answered together.

Thomas walked toward the Prior, threading his way through archers who clustered about three wagons to receive spare sheaves of arrows. The small English army had been marching toward Durham on two separate roads and now the men straggled across fields to come together in case the Scots descended from the high ground. Men-at-arms hauled mail coats over their heads and the richer among them buckled on whatever pieces of plate armor they owned. The army's leaders must have had a swift conference for the first standards were being carried northward, showing that the English wanted to confront the Scots on the higher ground of the ridge rather than be attacked in the water meadows or try to reach Durham by a circuitous route. Thomas had become accustomed to the English banners in Brittany, Normandy and Picardy, but these flags were all strange to him: a silver crescent, a brown cow, a blue lion, the Scarecrow's black axe, a red boar's head, Lord Outhwaite's scallop-emblazoned cross and, gaudiest of all, a great scarlet flag showing a pair of crossed keys thickly embroidered in gold and silver threads. The prior's flag looked shabby and cheap compared to all those other banners for it was nothing but a small square of frayed cloth beneath which the prior was working himself into a frenzy. "Go and do God's work," he shouted at some nearby archers, "for the Scots are animals! Animals! Cut them down! Kill them all! God will reward each death! Go and smite them! Kill them!" He saw Thomas approaching. "You want a blessing, my son? Then God give strength to your bow and add bite to your arrows! May your arm never tire and your eye never dim. God and the saints bless you while you kill!"

Thomas crossed himself then held out the letter. "I came to give you this, sir," he said.

The prior seemed astonished that an archer should address him so familiarly, let alone have a letter for him and at first he did not take the parchment, but one of his monks snatched it from Thomas and, seeing the broken seal, raised his eyebrows. "My lord the bishop writes to you," he said.

"They are animals!" the prior repeated, still caught up in his peroration, then he realized what the monk had said. "My lord bishop writes?"

"To you, brother," the monk said.

The prior seized the painted pole and dragged the makeshift banner down so it hung near to Thomas's face. "You may kiss it," he said grandly.

"Kiss it?" Thomas was quite taken aback. The ragged cloth, now it was close by his nose, smelled musty.

"It is St. Cuthbert's corporax cloth," the prior said excitedly, "taken from his tomb, my son! The blessed St. Cuth-

bert will fight for us! The very angels of heaven will follow
him into the battle."

Thomas, faced with the saint's relic, went to his knees and
drew the cloth to his lips. It was linen, he thought, and now
he could see it was embroidered about its edge with an intri-
cate pattern in faded blue thread. In the center of the cloth,
which was used during Mass to hold the wafers, was an
elaborate cross, embroidered in silver threads that scarcely
showed against the frayed white linen. "It is really St. Cuthbert's cloth?" he asked.

"His alone!" the prior exclaimed. "We opened his tomb in
the cathedral this very morning, and we prayed to him and
he will fight for us today!" The prior jerked the flag up and
waved it toward some men-at-arms who spurred their horses
northward. "Perform God's work! Kill them all! Dung the
fields with their noxious flesh, water it with their treacherous
blood!"

"The bishop wants this young man to speak with Brother
Hugh Collimore," the monk who had read the letter now told
the prior, "and the King wishes it too. His lordship says
there is a treasure to be found."

"The King wishes it?" the prior looked in astonishment at
Thomas. "The King wishes it?" he asked again and then he
came to his senses and realized there was great advantage in
royal patronage and so he snatched the letter and read it himself, only to find even more advantage than he had anticipated. "You come in search of a great *thesaurus*?" he asked
Thomas suspiciously.

"So the bishop believes, sir," Thomas responded.

"What treasure?" the prior snapped and all the monks
gaped at him as the notion of a treasure momentarily made
them forget the proximity of the Scottish army.

"The treasure, sir"—Thomas avoided giving a truthful answer—"is known to Brother Collimore."

"But why send you?" the prior asked, and it was a fair

question for Thomas looked young and possessed no apparent rank.

"Because I have some knowledge of the matter too," Thomas said, wondering if he had said too much.

The prior folded the letter, inadvertently tearing off the seal as he did so, and thrust it into a pouch that hung from his knotted belt. "We shall talk after the battle," he said, "and then, and only then, I shall decide whether you may see Brother Collimore. He is sick, you know? Ailing, poor soul. Maybe he is dying. It may not be seemly for you to disturb him. We shall see, we shall see." He plainly wanted to talk to the old monk himself and so be the sole possessor of whatever knowledge Collimore might have. "God bless you, my son," the prior dismissed Thomas, then hoisted his sacred banner and hurried north. Most of the English army was already climbing the ridge, leaving only their wagons and a crowd of women, children and those men too sick to walk. The monks, making a procession behind their corporax cloth, began to sing as they followed the soldiers.

Thomas ran to a cart and took a sheaf of arrows, which he thrust into his belt. He could see that Lord Outhwaite's men-at-arms were riding toward the ridge, followed by a large group of archers. "Maybe the two of you should stay here," he said to Father Hobbe.

"No!" Eleanor said. "And you should not be fighting."

"Not fight?" Thomas asked.

"It is not your battle!" Eleanor insisted. "We should go to the city! We should find the monk."

Thomas paused. He was thinking of the priest who, in the swirl of fog and smoke, had killed the Scotsman and then spoken to him in French. I am a messenger, the priest had said. "*Je suis un avant-coureur,*" had been his exact words and an *avant-coureur* was more than a mere messenger. A herald, perhaps? An angel even? Thomas could not drive away the image of that silent fight, the men so ill matched, a soldier against a priest, yet the priest had won and then had turned his gaunt, bloodied face on Thomas and announced himself: "*Je suis un avant-coureur.*" It was a sign, Thomas thought, and he did not want to believe in signs and visions, he wanted to believe in his bow. He thought perhaps Eleanor was right and that the conflict with its unexpected victor was a sign from heaven that he should follow the *avant-coureur* into the city, but there were also enemies up on the hill and he was an archer and archers did not walk away from a battle. "We'll go to the city," he said, "after the fight."

"Why?" she demanded fiercely.

But Thomas would not explain. He just started walking, climbing a hill where larks and finches flitted through the hedges and fieldfares, brown and gray, called from the empty pastures. The fog was all gone and a drying wind blew across the Wear.

And then, from where the Scots waited on the higher ground, the drums began to beat.

SIR WILLIAM DOUGLAS, Knight of Liddesdale, prepared himself for battle. He pulled on leather breeches thick enough to thwart a sword cut and over his linen shirt he hung a crucifix that had been blessed by a priest in Santiago de Compostela where St. James was buried. Sir William Douglas was not a particularly religious man, but he paid a priest to look after his soul and the priest had assured Sir William that wearing the crucifix of St. James, the son of thunder, would ensure he received the last rites safe in his own bed. About his waist he tied a strip of red silk that had been torn from one of the banners captured from the English at Bannockburn. The silk had been dipped in the holy water of the font in the chapel of Sir William's castle at Hermitage and Sir William had been persuaded that the scrap of silk would ensure victory over the old and much hated enemy.

He wore a habergeon taken from an Englishman killed in

one of Sir William's many raids south of the border. Sir
William remembered that killing well. He had seen the quality of the Englishman's habergeon at the very beginning of
the fight and he had bellowed at his men to leave the fellow
alone, then he had cut the man down by striking at his ankles
and the Englishman, on his knees, had made a mewing
sound that had made Sir William's men laugh. The man had
surrendered, but Sir William had cut his throat anyway because he thought any man who made a mewing sound was
not a real warrior. It had taken the servants at Hermitage two
weeks to wash the blood out of the fine mesh of the mail.
Most of the Scottish leaders were dressed in hauberks,
which covered a man's body from neck to calves, while the
habergeon was much shorter and left the legs unprotected,
but Sir William intended to fight on foot and he knew that a
hauberk's weight wearied a man quickly and tired men were
easily killed. Over the habergeon he wore a full-length surcoat that showed his badge of the red heart. His helmet was
a sallet, lacking any visor or face protection, but in battle Sir
William liked to see what his enemies to the left and right
were doing. A man in a full helm or in one of the fashionable
pig-snouted visors could see nothing except what the slit
right in front of his eyes let him see, which was why men in
visored helmets spent the battle jerking their heads left and
right, left and right, like a chicken among foxes, and they
twitched until their necks were sore and even then they
rarely saw the blow that crushed their skulls. Sir William, in
battle, looked for men whose heads were jerking like hens,
back and forth, for he knew they were nervous men who
could afford a fine helmet and thus pay a finer ransom. He
carried his big shield. It was really too heavy for a man on
foot, but he expected the English to loose their archery storm
and the shield was thick enough to absorb the crashing impact of yard-long, steel-pointed arrows. He could rest the
foot of the shield on the ground and crouch safe behind it

and, when the English ran out of arrows, he could always discard it. He carried a spear in case the English horsemen charged, and a sword, which was his favorite killing weapon. The sword's hilt encased a scrap of hair cut from the corpse of St. Andrew, or at least that was what the pardoner who had sold Sir William the scrap had claimed.

Robbie Douglas, Sir William's nephew, wore mail and a sallet, and carried a sword and shield. It had been Robbie who had brought Sir William the news that Jamie Douglas, Robbie's older brother, had been killed, presumably by the Dominican priest's servant. Or perhaps Father de Taillebourg had done the killing? Certainly he must have ordered it. Robbie Douglas, twenty years old, had wept for his brother. "How could a priest do it?" Robbie had demanded of his uncle.

"You have a strange idea of priests, Robbie," Sir William had said. "Most priests are weak men given God's authority and that makes them dangerous. I thank God no Douglas has ever put on a priest's robe. We're all too honest."

"When this day's done, uncle," Robbie Douglas said, "you'll let me go after that priest."

Sir William smiled. He might not be an overtly religious man, but he did hold one creed sacred and that was that any family member's murder must be avenged and Robbie, he reckoned, would do vengeance well. He was a good young man, hard and handsome, tall and straightforward, and Sir William was proud of his youngest sister's son. "We'll talk at day's end," Sir William promised him, "but till then, Robbie, stay close to me."

"I will, uncle."

"We'll kill a good few Englishmen, God willing," Sir William said, then led his nephew to meet the King and to receive the blessing of the royal chaplains.

Sir William, like most of the Scottish knights and chieftains, was in mail, but the King wore French-made plate, a

thing so rare north of the border that men from the wild
tribes came to stare at this sun-reflecting creature made of
moving metal. The young King seemed just as impressed for
he took off his surcoat and walked up and down admiring
himself and being admired as his lords came for a blessing
and to offer advice. The Earl of Moray, whom Sir William
believed was a fool, wanted to fight on horseback and the
King was tempted to agree. His father, the great Robert the
Bruce, had beaten the English at the Bannockburn on horseback, and not just beaten them, but humiliated them. The
flower of Scotland had ridden down the nobility of England
and David, King now of his father's country, wanted to do
the same. He wanted blood beneath his hooves and glory attached to his name; he wanted his reputation to spread
through Christendom and so he turned and gazed longingly
at his red and yellow painted lance propped against the
bough of an elm.

Sir William Douglas saw where the King was looking.
"Archers," he said laconically.

"There were archers at the Bannockburn," the Earl of
Moray insisted.

"Aye, and the fools didn't know how to use them," Sir
William said, "but you can't depend on the English being
fools for ever."

"And how many archers can they have?" the Earl asked.
"There are said to be thousands of bowmen in France, hundreds more in Brittany and as many again in Gascony, so
how many can they have here?"

"They have enough," Sir William growled curtly, not
bothering to hide the contempt he felt for John Randolph,
third Earl of Moray. The Earl was just as experienced in war
as Sir William, but he had spent too long as a prisoner of the
English and the consequent hatred made him impetuous.

The King, young and inexperienced, wanted to side with
the Earl whose friend he was, but he saw that his other lords

were agreeing with Sir William who, though he held no great title nor position of state, was more battle-hardened than any man in Scotland. The Earl of Moray sensed that he was losing the argument and he urged haste. "Charge now, sir," he suggested, "before they can make a battle line." He pointed southward to where the first English troops were appearing in the pastures. "Cut the bastards down before they're ready."

"That," the Earl of Menteith put in quietly, "was the advice given to Philip of Valois in Picardy. It didn't serve there and it won't serve here."

"Besides which," Sir William Douglas remarked caustically, "we have to contend with stone walls." He pointed to the walls which bounded the pastures where the English were beginning to form their line. "Maybe Moray can tell us how armored knights get past stone walls?" he suggested.

The Earl of Moray bridled. "You take me for a fool, Douglas?"

"I take you as you show yourself, John Randolph," Sir William answered.

"Gentlemen!" the King snapped. He had not noticed the stone walls when he formed his battle line beside the burning cottages and the fallen cross. He had only seen the empty green pastures and the wide road and his even wider dream of glory. Now he watched the enemy straggle from the far trees. There were plenty of archers coming, and he had heard how those bowmen could fill the sky with their arrows and how their steel arrow heads drove deep into horses and how the horses then went mad with pain. And he dared not lose this battle. He had promised his nobles that they would celebrate the feast of Christmas in the hall of the English King in London and if he lost then he would lose their respect and encourage some to rebellion. He had to win and, being impatient, he wanted to win quickly. "If we charge fast enough," he suggested tentatively, "before they all reach their lines—"

"Then, you'll break your horse's legs on the stone walls," Sir William said with scant respect for his royal master. "If your majesty's horse even gets that far. You can't protect a horse from arrows, sir, but you can weather the storm on foot. Put your pikes up front, but mix them with men-at-arms who can use their shields to protect the pike-holders. Shields up, heads down and hold hard, that's how we win this."

The King tugged at the espalier which covered his right shoulder and had an annoying habit of riding up on the top edge of the breastplate. Traditionally the defense of Scottish armies was in the hands of pikemen who used their monstrously long weapons to hold off the enemy knights, but pikemen needed both hands to hold their unwieldy blades and so became easy targets for English bowmen who liked to boast that they carried the lives of Scottish pikemen in their arrow bags. So protect the pikemen with the shields of the men-at-arms and let the enemy waste their arrows. It made sense, but it still irked David Bruce that he could not lead his horsemen in an earth-shaking assault while the trumpets screamed at the heavens.

Sir William saw his King's hesitation and pressed his argument. "We have to stand, sir, and we have to wait, and we have to let our shields take the arrows, but in the end, sir, they'll tire of wasting shafts and they'll come to the attack and that's when we'll chop them down like dogs."

A growl of assent greeted this. The Scottish lords, hard men all, armed and armored, bearded and grim, were confident that they could win this fight because they so outnumbered the enemy, but they also knew there was no shortcut to victory, not when archers opposed them, and so they would have to do what Sir William said: endure the arrows, goad the enemy, then give them slaughter.

The King heard his lords agree with Sir William and so,

reluctantly, he abandoned his dream of breaking the enemy with mounted knights. That was a disappointment, but he looked about his lords and thought that with such men beside him he could not possibly lose. "We shall fight on foot," he decreed, "and chop them down like dogs. We shall slaughter them like whipped puppies!" And afterward, he thought, when the survivors were fleeing southward, the Scottish cavalry could finish the slaughter.

But for now it would be footman against footman and so the war banners of Scotland were carried forward and planted across the ridge. The burning cottages were mere embers now that cradled three shrunken bodies, black and small as children, and the King planted his flags close to those dead. He had his own standard, red saltire on yellow field, and the banner of Scotland's saint, white saltire on blue, in the line's center and to left and right the flags of the lesser lords flew. The lion of Stewart brandished its blade, the Randolph falcon spread its wings while to east and west the stars and axes and crosses snapped in the wind. The army was arrayed in three divisions, called sheltrons, and the three sheltrons were so large that the men on the far flanks jostled in toward the center to keep themselves on the flatter ground of the ridge's summit.

The rearmost ranks of the sheltrons were composed of the tribesmen from the islands and the north, men who fought bare-legged, without metal armor, wielding vast swords that could club a man to death as easily as cut him down. They were fearsome fighters, but their lack of armor made them horribly vulnerable to arrows and so they were placed at the rear and the leading ranks of the three sheltrons were filled by men-at-arms and pikemen. The men-at-arms carried swords, axes, maces or war-hammers and, most important, the shields that could protect the pikemen whose weapons were tipped with a spike, a hook and an axehead. The spike could hold an enemy at bay, the hook could haul an armored man out of the saddle or off his feet, and the axe could smash through his mail or plate. The line bristled with the pikes that made a steel hedge to greet the English and priests walked along the hedge consecrating the weapons and the men who held them. Soldiers knelt to receive their blessings. A few of the lords, like the King himself, were mounted, but only so that they could see over the heads of their army, and those men stared south to see the last of the English troops come into view. So few of them! Such a small army to beat! To the left of the Scots was Durham, its towers and ramparts thick with folk watching the battle, and in front was this small army of Englishmen who did not possess the sense to retreat south toward York. They would fight on the ridge instead and the Scots had the advantage of position and numbers. "If you hate them!" Sir William Douglas shouted at his men on the right of the Scottish battle line, "then let them hear you!"

The Scots bellowed their hatred. They clashed swords and spears against their shields, they shrieked to the sky and, in the line's center, where the King's sheltron waited under the banners of the cross, a troop of drummers began to beat huge goatskin drums. Each drum was a big ring of oak over which was stretched two goat skins that were tightened with ropes until an acorn, dropped onto a skin, would bounce as high as the hand that had let it go and the drums, beaten with withies, made a sharp, almost metallic sound that filled the sky. They made an assault of pure noise.

"If you hate the English, let them know!" the Earl of March shouted from the left of the Scottish line that lay closest to the city. "If you hate the English, let them know!" and the roar became louder, the clash of spear stave on shield was stronger, and the noise of Scotland's hate spread across the ridge so that nine thousand men were howling at the three thousand who were foolish enough to confront them.

"We shall cut them down like stalks of barley," a priest

promised, "we shall soak the fields with their stinking blood and fill all hell with their English souls."

"Their women are yours!" Sir William told his men. "Their wives and their daughters will be your toys tonight!" He grinned at his nephew Robbie. "You'll have your pick of Durham's women, Robbie."

"And London's women," Robbie said, "before Christmas."

"Aye, them too," Sir William promised.

"In the name of the Father, and of the Son, and of the Holy Ghost," the King's senior chaplain shouted, "send them all to hell! Each and every foul one of them to hell! For every Englishman you kill today means a thousand less weeks in purgatory!"

"If you hate the English," Lord Robert Stewart, Steward of Scotland and heir to the throne, called, "let them hear!" And the noise of that hate was like a thunder that filled the deep valley of the Wear, and the thunder reverberated from the crag where Durham stood and still the noise swelled to tell the whole north country that the Scots had come south.

And David, King of those Scots, was glad that he had come to this place where the dragon cross had fallen and the burning houses smoked and the English waited to be killed. For this day he would bring glory to St. Andrew, to the great house of Bruce, and to Scotland.

THOMAS, Father Hobbe and Eleanor followed the prior and his monks who were still chanting, though the brothers' voices were now ragged for they were breathless from hurrying. St. Cuthbert's corporax cloth swayed to and fro and the banner attracted a straggling procession of women and children who, not wanting to wait out of sight of their men, carried spare sheaves of arrows up the hill. Thomas wanted to go faster, to get past the monks and find Lord Outhwaite's men, but Eleanor deliberately hung back until he turned on her angrily. "You can walk faster," he protested in French.

"I can walk faster," she said, "and you can ignore a battle!" Father Hobbe, leading the horse, understood the tone even though he did not comprehend the words. He sighed, thus earning himself a savage look from Eleanor. "You do not need to fight!" she went on.

"I'm an archer," Thomas said stubbornly, "and there's an enemy up there."

"Your King sent you to find the Grail!" Eleanor insisted. "Not to die! Not to leave me alone! Me and a baby!" She had stopped now, hands clutching her belly and with tears in her eyes. "I am to be alone here? In England?"

"I won't die here," Thomas said scathingly.

"You know that?" Eleanor was even more scathing. "God

spoke to you, perhaps? You know what other men do not? You know the day of your dying?"

Thomas was taken aback by the outburst. Eleanor was a strong girl, not given to tantrums, but she was distraught and weeping now. "Those men," Thomas said, "the Scarecrow and Beggar, they won't touch you. I'll be here."

"It isn't them!" Eleanor wailed. "I had a dream last night. A dream."

Thomas put his hands on her shoulders. His hands were huge and strengthened by hauling on the hempen string of the big bow. "I dreamed of the Grail last night," he said, knowing that was not quite true. He had not dreamed of the Grail, rather he had woken to a vision which had turned out to be a deception, but he could not tell Eleanor that. "It was golden and beautiful," he said, "like a cup of fire."

"In my dream," Eleanor said, gazing up at him, "you were dead and your body was all black and swollen."

"What is she saying?" Father Hobbe asked.

"She had a bad dream," Thomas said in English, "a nightmare."

"The devil sends us nightmares," the priest asserted. "It is well known. Tell her that."

Thomas translated that for her, then he stroked a wisp of golden hair away from her forehead and tucked it under her knitted cap. He loved her face, so earnest and narrow, so cat-like, but with big eyes and an expressive mouth. "It was just a nightmare," he reassured her, "*un cauchemar.*"

"The Scarecrow," Eleanor said with a shudder, "he is the *cauchemar.*"

Thomas drew her into an embrace. "He won't come near you," he promised her. He could hear a distant chanting, but nothing like the monks' solemn prayers. This was a jeering, insistent chant, heavy as the drumbeat that gave it rhythm. He could not hear the words, but he did not need to. "The enemy," he said to Eleanor, "are waiting for us."

"They are not my enemy," she said fiercely.

"If they get into Durham," Thomas retorted, "then they will not know that. They will take you anyway."

"Everyone hates the English. Do you know that? The French hate you, the Bretons hate you, the Scots hate you, every man in Christendom hates you! And why? Because you love fighting! You do! Everyone knows that about the English. And you? You have no need to fight today, it is not your quarrel, but you can't wait to be there, to kill again!"

Thomas did not know what to say, for there was truth in what Eleanor had said. He shrugged and picked up his heavy bow. "I fight for my King, and there's an army of enemies on the hill here. They outnumber us. Do you know what will happen if they get into Durham?"

"I know," Eleanor said firmly, and she did know for she had been in Caen when the English archers, disobeying their King, had swarmed across the bridge and laid the town waste.

"If we don't fight them and stop them here," Thomas said, "then their horsemen will hunt us all down. One after the other."

"You said you would marry me," Eleanor declared, crying again. "I don't want my baby to be fatherless, I don't want it to be like me." She meant illegitimate.

"I will marry you, I promise. When the battle is done we shall be married in Durham. In the cathedral, yes?" He smiled at her. "We can be married in the cathedral."

Eleanor was pleased with the promise, but too furious to show her pleasure. "We should go to the cathedral now," she snapped. "We would be safe there. We should pray at the high altar."

"You can go to the city," Thomas said. "Let me fight my King's enemies and you go to the city, you and Father Hobbe, and you find the old monk and you can both talk to him, and afterward you can go to the cathedral and wait for me there." He unstrapped one of the big sacks on the mare's back and took out his habergeon, which he hauled over his head. The leather lining felt stiff and cold, and smelled of mold. He forced his hands down the sleeves, then strapped the sword belt about his waist and hung the weapon on his right side. "Go to the city," he told Eleanor, "and talk to the monk."

Eleanor was crying. "You are going to die," she said, "I dreamed it."

"I can't go to the city," Father Hobbe protested.

"You're a priest," Thomas barked, "not a soldier! Take Eleanor to Durham. Find Brother Collimore and talk to him." The prior had insisted that Thomas wait and suddenly it seemed very sensible to send Father Hobbe to talk to the old monk before the prior poisoned his memories. "Both of you," Thomas insisted, "talk to Brother Collimore. You know what to ask him. And I shall see you there this evening, in the cathedral." He took his sallet, with its broad rim to deflect the downward stroke of a blade, and tied it onto his head. He was angry with Eleanor because he sensed she was right. The imminent battle was not his concern except that fighting was his trade and England his country. "I will not die," he told Eleanor with an obstinate irrationality, "and you will see me tonight." He tossed the horse's reins to Father Hobbe. "Keep Eleanor safe," he told the priest. "The Scarecrow won't risk anything inside the monastery or in the cathedral."

He wanted to kiss Eleanor goodbye, but she was angry with him and he was angry with her and so he took his bow and his arrow bag and walked away. She said nothing for, like Thomas, she was too proud to back away from the quarrel. Besides, she knew she was right. This clash with the Scots was not Thomas's fight, whereas the Grail was his duty. Father Hobbe, caught between their obstinacy, walked in silence, but did note that Eleanor turned more than once, evidently hoping to catch Thomas looking back, but all she saw was her lover climbing the path with the great bow across his shoulder.

It was a huge bow, taller than most men and as thick about its belly as an archer's wrist. It was made from yew; Thomas was fairly sure it was Italian yew though he could never be certain because the raw stave had drifted ashore from a wrecked ship. He had shaped the stave, leaving the center thick, and he had steamed the tips to curve them against the way the bow would bend when it was drawn. He had painted the bow black, using wax, oil and soot, then tipped the two ends of the stave with pieces of nocked antler horn to hold the cord. The stave had been cut so that at the belly of the bow, where it faced Thomas when he drew the hempen string, there was hard heartwood which was compressed when the arrow was hauled back while the outer belly was springy sapwood, and when he released the cord the heartwood snapped out of its compression and the sapwood pulled it back into shape and between them they sent the arrow hissing with savage force. The belly of the bow, where his left hand gripped the yew, was whipped with hemp and above the hemp, which had been stiffened with hoof glue, he had nailed a scrap of silver cut from a crushed Mass vessel that his father had used in Hookton church, and the piece of silver cup showed the yale with the Grail in its clawed grip. The yale came from Thomas's family's coat of arms, though he had not known that when he grew up for his father had never told him the tale. He had never told Thomas he was a Vexille from a family that had been lords of the Cathar heretics, a family that had been burned out of their home in southern France and which had fled to hide themselves in the darkest corners of Christendom.

Thomas knew little of the Cathar heresy. He knew his bow and he knew how to select an arrow of slender ash or birch or hornbeam, and he knew how to fledge the shaft with goose feathers and how to tip it with steel. He knew all that, yet he did not know how to drive that arrow through shield, mail and flesh. That was instinct, something he had practiced since childhood; practiced till his string fingers were bleeding; practiced until he no longer thought when he drew the string back to his ear; practiced until, like all archers, he was broad across the chest and hugely muscled in his arms. He did not need to know how to use a bow, it was just an instinct like breathing or waking or fighting.

He turned when he reached a stand of hornbeams that guarded the upper path like a rampart. Eleanor was walking stubbornly away and Thomas had an urge to shout to her, but knew she was already too far off and would not hear him. He had quarreled with her before; men and women, it seemed to Thomas, spent half their lives fighting and half loving and the intensity of the first fed the passion of the second, and he almost smiled for he recognized Eleanor's stubbornness and he even liked it; and then he turned and walked through the trampled drifts of fallen hornbeam leaves along the path between stone-walled pastures where hundreds of saddled stallions were grazing. These were the warhorses of the English knights and men-at-arms and their presence in the pastures told Thomas that the English expected the Scots to attack because a knight was far better able to defend himself on foot. The horses were kept saddled so that the mailed men-at-arms could either retreat swiftly or else mount up and pursue a beaten enemy.

Thomas could still not see the Scottish army, but he could hear their chanting, which was given force by the hellish beat of the big drums. The sound was making some of the pastured stallions nervous and three of them, pursued by pageboys, galloped beside the stone wall with their eyes showing white. More pages were exercising destriers just behind the English line, which was divided into three battles. Each battle had a knot of horsemen at the center of its rear rank, the mounted men being the commanders beneath their bright banners, while in front of them were four or five rows of men-at-arms carrying swords, axes, spears and shields, and ahead of the men-at-arms, and crowded thick in the spaces between the three battles, were the archers.

The Scots, two arrow shots away from the English, were on slightly higher ground and also divided into three divisions which, like the English battles, were arrayed beneath their clusters of commanders' banners. The tallest flag, the red and yellow royal standard, was in the center. The Scottish knights and men-at-arms, like the English, were on foot, but each of their sheltrons was much larger than its opposing English battle, three or four times larger, but Thomas, tall enough to look over the English line, could see there were not many archers in the enemy ranks. Here and there along the Scottish line he could see some long bowstaves and there were a few crossbows visible among the thicket of pikes, but there were not nearly so many bowmen as were in the English array, though the English, in turn, were hugely outnumbered by the Scottish army. So the battle, if it ever started, would be between arrows and Scottish pikes and men-at-arms, and if there were not enough arrows then the ridge must become an English graveyard.

Lord Outhwaite's banner of the cross and scallop shell was in the left-hand battle and Thomas crossed to it. The prior, dismounted now, was in the space between the left and center divisions where one of his monks swung a censer and another brandished the Mass cloth on its painted pole. The prior himself was shouting, though Thomas could not tell whether he called insults at the enemy or prayers to God for the Scottish chanting was so loud. Thomas could not distinguish the enemy's words either, but the sentiment was plain enough and it was sped on its way by the massive drums.

Thomas could see the huge drums now and observe the

passion with which the drummers beat the great skins to make a noise as sharp as snapping bone. Loud, rhythmic and reverberating, an assault of ear-piercing thunder, and in front of the drums at the center of the enemy line some bearded men whirled in a wild dance. They came darting from the rear of the Scottish line and they wore no mail or iron, but were draped in thick folds of cloth and brandished long-bladed swords about their heads and had small round leather shields, scarce larger than serving platters, strapped to their left forearms. Behind them the Scottish men-at-arms beat the flats of their sword blades against their shields while the pikemen thumped the ground with the butts of their long weapons to add to the noise of the huge drums. The sound was so great that the prior's monks had abandoned their chanting and now just gazed at the enemy.

"What they do"—Lord Outhwaite, on foot like his men, had to raise his voice to make himself heard—"is try to scare us with noise before they kill us." His lordship limped, whether through age or some old wound, Thomas did not like to ask; it was plain he wanted somewhere he could pace about and kick the turf and so he had come to talk with the monks, though now he turned his friendly face on Thomas. "And you want to be most careful of those scoundrels," he said, pointing at the dancing men, "because they're wilder than scalded cats. It's said they skin their captives alive." Lord Outhwaite made the sign of the cross. "You don't often see them this far south."

"Them?" Thomas asked.

"They're tribesmen from the farthest north," one of the monks explained. He was a tall man with a fringe of gray hair, a scarred face and only one eye. "Scoundrels, they are," the monk went on, "scoundrels! They bow down to idols!" He shook his head sadly. "I've never journeyed that far north, but I hear their land is shrouded in perpetual fog and that if a man dies with a wound to his back then his woman eats her own young and throws herself off the cliffs for the shame of it."

"Truly?" Thomas asked.

"It's what I've heard," the monk said, making the sign of the cross.

"They live on birds' nests, seaweed and raw fish." Lord Outhwaite took up the tale, then smiled. "Mind you, some of my people in Witcar do that, but at least they pray to God as well. At least I think they do."

"But your folk don't have cloven hooves," the monk said, staring at the enemy.

"The Scots do?" a much younger monk with a face left horribly scarred by smallpox asked anxiously.

"The clansmen do," Lord Outhwaite said. "They're scarcely human!" He shook his head then held out a hand to the older monk. "It's Brother Michael, isn't it?"

"Your lordship flatters to remember me," the monk answered, pleased.

"He was once a man-at-arms to my Lord Percy," Lord Outhwaite explained to Thomas, "and a good one!"

"Before I lost this to the Scots," Brother Michael said, raising his right arm so that the sleeve of his robe fell to reveal a stump at his wrist, "and this," he pointed to his empty eye socket, "so now I pray instead of fight." He turned and gazed at the Scottish line. "They are noisy today," he grumbled.

"They're confident," Lord Outhwaite said placidly, "and so they should be. When was the last time a Scottish army outnumbered us?"

"They might outnumber us," Brother Michael said, "but they've picked a strange place to do it. They should have gone to the southern end of the ridge."

"And so they should, brother," Lord Outhwaite agreed, "but let us be grateful for small mercies." What Brother

Michael meant was the Scots were sacrificing their advantage of numbers by fighting on the narrow ridge top where the English line, though thinner and with far fewer men, could not be overlapped. If the Scots had gone farther south, where the ridge widened as it fell away to the water meadows, they could have outflanked their enemy. Their choice of ground might have been a mistake that helped the English, but that was small consolation when Thomas tried to estimate the size of the enemy army. Other men were doing the same and their guesses ranged from six to sixteen thousand, though Lord Outhwaite reckoned there were no more than eight thousand Scots. "Which is only three or four times our number," he said cheerfully, "and not enough of them are archers. God be thanked for English archers."

"Amen," Brother Michael said.

The smallpox-scarred younger monk was staring in fascination at the thick Scottish line. "I've heard that the Scots paint their faces blue. I can't see any though."

Lord Outhwaite looked astonished. "You heard what?"

"That they paint their faces blue, my lord," the monk said, embarrassed now, "or maybe they only paint half the face. To scare us."

"To scare us?" His lordship was amused. "To make us laugh, more like. I've never seen it."

"Nor I," Brother Michael put in.

"It's just what I've heard," the young monk said.

"They're frightening enough without paint." Lord Outhwaite pointed to a banner opposite his own part of the line. "I see Sir William's here."

"Sir William?" Thomas asked.

"Willie Douglas," Lord Outhwaite said. "I was a prisoner of his for two years and I'm still paying the bankers because of it." He meant that his family had borrowed money to pay the ransom. "I liked him, though. He's a rogue. And he's fighting with Moray?"

"Moray?" Brother Michael asked.

"John Randolph, Earl of Moray." Lord Outhwaite nodded at another banner close to the red-heart flag of Douglas. "They hate each other. God knows why they're together in the line." He stared again at the Scottish drummers who leaned far back to balance the big instruments against their bellies. "I hate those drums," he said mildly. "Paint their faces blue! I never heard such nonsense!" he chuckled.

The prior was haranguing the nearest troops now, telling them that the Scots had destroyed the great religious house at Hexham. "They defiled God's holy church! They killed the brethren! They have stolen from Christ Himself and put tears onto the cheeks of God! Wreak His vengeance! Show no mercy!" The nearest archers flexed their fingers, licked lips and stared at the enemy who were showing no sign of advancing. "You will kill them," the prior shrieked, "and God will bless you for it! He will shower blessings on you!"

"They want us to attack them," Brother Michael remarked dryly. He seemed embarrassed by his prior's passion.

"Aye," Lord Outhwaite said, "and they think we'll attack on horseback. See the pikes?"

"They're good against men on foot too, my lord," Brother Michael said.

"That they are, that they are," Lord Outhwaite agreed. "Nasty things, pikes." He fidgeted with some of the loose rings of his mail coat and looked surprised when one of them came away in his fingers. "I do like Willie Douglas," he said. "We used to hunt together when I was his prisoner. We caught some very fine boar in Liddesdale, I remember." He frowned. "Such noisy drums."

"Will we attack them?" the young monk summoned up the courage to inquire.

"Dear me no, I do hope not," Lord Outhwaite said. "We're outnumbered! Much better to hold our ground and let them come to us."

"And if they don't come?" Thomas asked.

"Then they'll slink off home with empty pockets," Lord Outhwaite said, "and they won't like that, they won't like it at all. They're only here for plunder! That's why they dislike us so much."

"Dislike us? Because they're here for plunder?" Thomas had not understood his lordship's thinking.

"They're envious, young man! Plain envious. We have riches, they don't, and there are few things more calculated to provoke hatred than such an imbalance. I had a neighbor in Witcar who seemed a reasonable fellow, but then he and his men tried to take advantage of my absence when I was Douglas's prisoner. They tried to ambush the coin for my ransom, if you can believe it! It was just envy, it seems, for he was poor."

"And now he's dead, my lord?" Thomas asked, amused.

"Dear me, no," his lordship said reprovingly, "he's in a very deep hole in the bottom of my keep. Deep down with the rats. I throw him coins every now and then to remind him why he's there." He stood on tiptoe and gazed westward where the hills were higher. He was looking for Scottish men-at-arms riding to make an assault from the south, but he saw none. "His father," he said, meaning Robert the Bruce, "wouldn't be waiting there. He'd have men riding around our flanks to put the fear of God up our arses, but this young pup doesn't know his trade, does he? He's in the wrong place altogether!"

"He's put his faith in numbers," Brother Michael said.

"And perhaps their numbers will suffice," Lord Outhwaite replied gloomily and made the sign of the cross.

Thomas, now that he had a chance to see the ground between the armies, could understand why Lord Outhwaite was so scornful of the Scottish King who had drawn up his army just south of the burned cottages where the dragon cross had fallen. It was not just that the narrowness of the

ridge confined the Scots, denying them a chance to outflank
the numerically inferior English, but that the ill-chosen battlefield was obstructed by thick blackthorn hedges and at
least one stone wall. No army could advance across those
obstacles and hope to hold its line intact, but the Scottish
King seemed confident that the English would attack him
for he did not move. His men shouted insults in the hope of
provoking an attack, but the English stayed stubbornly in
their ranks.

The Scots jeered even louder when a tall man on a great
horse rode out from the center of the English line. His stallion had purple ribbons twisted into its black mane and a
purple trapper embroidered with golden keys that was so
long that it swept the ground behind the horse's rear hooves.
The stallion's head was protected by a leather face plate on
which was mounted a silver horn, twisted like a unicorn's
weapon. The rider wore plate armor that was polished bright
and had a sleeveless surcoat of purple and gold, the same
colors displayed by his page, standard-bearer and the dozen
knights who followed him. The tall rider had no sword, but
instead was armed with a great spiked morningstar like the
one Beggar carried. The Scottish drummers redoubled their
efforts, the Scots soldiers shouted insults and the English
cheered until the tall man raised a mailed hand for silence.

"We're to get a homily from his grace," Lord Outhwaite
said gloomily. "Very fond of the sound of his own voice is
his grace."

The tall man was evidently the Archbishop of York and,
when the English ranks were silent, he again raised his
mailed right hand high above his purple plumed helmet and
made an extravagant sign of the cross. "*Dominus vobiscum*,"
he called. "*Dominus vobiscum*." He rode down the line, re-
peating the invocation. "You will kill God's enemy today,"
he called after each promise that God would be with the English. He had to shout to make himself heard over the din of

the enemy. "God is with you, and you will do His work by making many widows and orphans. You will fill Scotland with grief as a just punishment for their godless impiety. The Lord of Hosts is with you; God's vengeance is your task!" The Archbishop's horse stepped high, its head tossing up and down as his grace carried his encouragement out to the flanks of his army. The last wisps of mist had long burned away and, though there was still a chill in the air, the sun had warmth and its light glinted off thousands of Scottish blades. A pair of one-horse wagons had come from the city and a dozen women were distributing dried herrings, bread and skins of ale.

Lord Outhwaite's squire brought an empty herring barrel so his lordship could sit. A man played a reed pipe nearby and Brother Michael sang an old country song about the badger and the pardoner and Lord Outhwaite laughed at the words, then nodded his head toward the ground between the armies where two horsemen, one from each army, were meeting. "I see we're being courteous today," he remarked. An English herald in a gaudy tabard had ridden toward the Scots and a priest, hastily appointed as Scotland's herald, had come to greet him. The two men bowed from their saddles, talked a while, then returned to their respective armies. The Englishman, coming near the line, spread his hands in a gesture that said the Scots were being stubborn.

"They come this far south and won't fight?" the prior demanded angrily.

"They want us to start the battle," Lord Outhwaite said mildly, "and we want them to do the same." The heralds had met to discuss how the battle should be fought and each had plainly demanded that the other side begin by making an assault, and both sides had refused the invitation, so now the Scots tried again to provoke the English by insult. Some of the enemy advanced to within bowshot and shouted that the English were pigs and their mothers were sows, and when an archer raised his bow to reward the insults an English captain shouted at him. "Don't waste arrows on words," he called.

"Cowards!" A Scotsman dared to come even closer to the English line, well within half a bowshot. "You bastard cowards! Your mothers are whores who suckled you on goat piss! Your wives are sows! Whores and sows! You hear me? You bastards! English bastards! You're the devil's turds!" The fury of his hatred made him shake. He had a bristling beard, a ragged jupon and a coat of mail with a great rent in its backside so that when he turned round and bent over he presented his naked arse to the English. It was meant as an insult, but was greeted by a roar of laughter.

"They'll have to attack us sooner or later," Lord Outhwaite stated calmly. "Either that or go home with nothing, and I can't see them doing that. You don't raise an army of that size without hope of profit."

"They sacked Hexham," the prior observed gloomily.

"And got nothing but baubles," Lord Outhwaite said dismissively. "The real treasures of Hexham were taken away for safekeeping long ago. I hear Carlisle paid them well enough to be left alone, but well enough to make eight or nine thousand men rich?" He shook his head. "Those soldiers don't get paid," he told Thomas, "they're not like our men. The King of Scotland doesn't have the cash to pay his soldiers. No, they want to take some rich prisoners today, then sack Durham and York, and if they're not to go home poor and empty-handed then they'd best hitch up their shields and come at us."

But still the Scots would not move and the English were too few to make an attack, though a straggle of men were constantly arriving to reinforce the Archbishop's army. They were mostly local men and few had any armor or any weapons other than farm implements like axes and mattocks. It was close to midday now and the sun had chased the chill off the land so that Thomas was sweating under his leather and mail. Two of the prior's lay servants had arrived with a horse-drawn cart loaded with casks of small beer, sacks of bread, a box of apples and a great cheese, and a dozen of the younger monks carried the provisions along the English line. Most of the army was sitting now, some were even sleeping and many of the Scots were doing the same. Even their drummers had given up, laying their great instruments on the pasture. A dozen ravens circled overhead and Thomas, thinking their presence presaged death, made the sign of the cross, then was relieved when the dark birds flew north across the Scottish troops.

A group of archers had come from the city and were cramming arrows into their quivers, a sure sign that they had never fought with the bow for a quiver was a poor instrument in battle. Quivers were likely to spill arrows when a man ran, and few held more than a score of points. Archers like Thomas preferred a big bag made of linen stretched about a withy frame in which the arrows stood upright, their feathers kept from being crushed by the frame and their steel heads projecting through the bag's neck, which was secured by a lace. Thomas had selected his arrows carefully, rejecting any with warped shafts or kinked feathers. In France, where many of the enemy knights possessed expensive plate armor, the English would use bodkin arrows with long, narrow and heavy heads that lacked barbs and so were more likely to pierce breastplates or helmets, but here they were still using the hunting arrows with their wicked barbs that made them impossible to pull out of a wound. They were called flesh arrows, but even a flesh arrow could pierce mail at two hundred paces.

Thomas slept for a time in the early afternoon, only waking when Lord Outhwaite's horse almost stepped on him. His lordship, along with the other English commanders, had been summoned to the Archbishop and so he had called for

his horse and, accompanied by his squire, rode to the army's
center. One of the Archbishop's chaplains carried a silver
crucifix along the line. The crucifix had a leather bag hanging just below the feet of Christ and in the bag, the chaplain
claimed, were the knuckle bones of the martyred St. Os-
wald. "Kiss the bag and God will preserve you," the chaplain promised, and archers and men-at-arms jostled for a
chance to obey. Thomas could not get close enough to kiss
the bag, but he did manage to reach out and touch it. Many
men had amulets or strips of cloth given them by their
wives, lovers or daughters when they left their farms or
houses to march against the invaders. They touched those
talismans now as the Scots, sensing that something was
about to happen at last, climbed to their feet. One of their
great drums began its awful noise.

Thomas glanced to his right where he could just see the
tops of the cathedral's twin towers and the banner flying
from the castle's ramparts. Eleanor and Father Hobbe should
be in the city by now and Thomas felt a pang of regret that
he had parted from his woman in such anger, then he
gripped his bow so that the touch of its wood might keep her
from evil. He consoled himself with the knowledge that
Eleanor would be safe in the city and tonight, when the battle was won, they could make up their quarrel. Then, he supposed, they would marry. He was not sure he really wanted
to marry, it seemed too early in his life to have a wife even if
it was Eleanor, whom he was sure he loved, but he was
equally sure she would want him to abandon the yew bow
and settle in a house and that was the very last thing Thomas
wanted. What he wanted was to be a leader of archers, to be
a man like Will Skeat. He wanted to have his own band of
bowmen that he could hire out to great lords. There was no
shortage of opportunity. Rumor said that the Italian states
would pay a fortune for English archers and Thomas wanted
a part of it, but Eleanor must be looked after and he did not

want their child to be a bastard. There were enough bastards in the world without adding another.

The English lords talked for a while. There were a dozen of them and they glanced constantly at the enemy and Thomas was close enough to see the anxiety on their faces. Was it worry that the enemy was too many? Or that the Scots were refusing battle and, in the next morning's mist, might vanish northward?

Brother Michael came and rested his old bones on the herring barrel that had served Lord Outhwaite as a seat. "They'll send you archers forward. That's what I'd do. Send you archers forward to provoke the bastards. Either that or drive them off, but you don't drive Scotsmen off that easily. They're brave bastards."

"Brave? Then why aren't they attacking?"

"Because they're not fools. They can see these." Brother Michael touched the black stave of Thomas's bow. "They've learned what archers can do. You've heard of Halidon Hill?" He raised his eyebrows in surprise when Thomas shook his head. "Of course, you're from the south. Christ could come again in the north and you southerners would never hear about it, or believe it if you did. But it was thirteen years ago now and they attacked us by Berwick and we cut them down in droves. Or our archers did, and they won't be enthusiastic about suffering the same fate here." Brother Michael frowned as a small click sounded. "What was that?"

Something had touched Thomas's helmet and he turned to see the Scarecrow, Sir Geoffrey Carr, who had cracked his whip, just glancing the metal claw at its tip off the crest of Thomas's sallet. Sir Geoffrey coiled his whip as he jeered at Thomas. "Sheltering behind monks' skirts, are we?"

Brother Michael restrained Thomas. "Go, Sir Geoffrey," the monk ordered, "before I call down a curse onto your black soul."

Sir Geoffrey put a finger into a nostril and pulled out

something slimy that he flicked toward the monk. "You think you frighten me, you one-eyed bastard? You who lost your balls when your hand was chopped off?" He laughed, then looked back to Thomas. "You picked a fight with me, boy, and you didn't give me a chance to finish it."

"Not now!" Brother Michael snapped.

Sir Geoffrey ignored the monk. "Fighting your betters, boy? You can hang for that. No"—he shuddered, then pointed a long bony finger at Thomas—"you *will* hang for that! You hear me? You will hang for it." He spat at Thomas, then turned his roan horse and spurred it back down the line.

"How come you know the Scarecrow?" Brother Michael asked.

"We just met."

"An evil creature," Brother Michael said, making the sign of the cross, "born under a waning moon when a storm was blowing." He was still watching the Scarecrow. "Men say that Sir Geoffrey owes money to the devil himself. He had to pay a ransom to Douglas of Liddesdale and he borrowed deep from the bankers to do it. His manor, his fields, everything he owns is in danger if he can't pay, and even if he makes a fortune today he'll just throw it away at dice. The Scarecrow's a fool, but a dangerous one." He turned his one eye on Thomas. "Did you really pick a fight with him?"

"He wanted to rape my woman."

"Aye, that's our Scarecrow. So be careful, young man, because he doesn't forget slights and he never forgives them."

The English lords must have come to some agreement for they reached out their mailed fists and touched metal knuckle on metal knuckle, then Lord Outhwaite turned his horse back toward his men. "John! John!" he called to the captain of his archers. "We'll not wait for them to make up their minds," he said as he dismounted, "but be provocative." It seemed Brother Michael's prognostication was right; the archers would be sent forward to annoy the Scots. The plan was to enrage them with arrows and so spur them into a hasty attack.

A squire rode Lord Outhwaite's horse back to the walled pasture as the Archbishop of York rode his destrier out in front of the army. "God will help you!" he called to the men of the central division that he commanded. "The Scots fear us!" he shouted. "They know that with God's help we will make many children fatherless in their blighted land! They stand and watch us because they fear us. So we must go to them." That sentiment brought a cheer. The Archbishop raised a hand to silence his men. "I want the archers to go forward," he called, "only the archers! Sting them! Kill them! And God bless you all. God bless you mightily!"

So the archers would begin the battle. The Scots were stubbornly refusing to move in hope that the English would make the attack, for it was much easier to defend ground than assault a formed enemy, but now the English archers would go forward to goad, sting and harass the enemy until they either ran away or, more likely, advanced to take revenge.

Thomas had already selected his best arrow. It was new, so new that the green-tinted glue that was pasted about the thread holding the feathers in place was still tacky, but it had a breasted shaft, one that was slightly wider behind the head and then tapered away toward the feathers. Such a shaft would hit hard and it was a lovely straight piece of ash, a third as long again as Thomas's arm, and Thomas would not waste it even though his opening shot would be at very long range.

It would be a long shot for the Scottish King was at the rear of the big central sheltron of his army, but it would not be an impossible shot for the black bow was huge and Thomas was young, strong and accurate.

"God be with you," Brother Michael said.

"Aim true!" Lord Outhwaite called.

"God speed your arrows!" the Archbishop of York shouted.

The drummers beat louder, the Scots jeered and the archers of England advanced.

BERNARD DE TAILLEBOURG already knew much of what the old monk told him, but now that the story was flowing he did not interrupt. It was the tale of a family that had been lords of an obscure county in southern France. The county was called Astarac and it lay close to the Cathar lands and, in time, became infected with the heresy. "The false teaching spread," Brother Collimore had said, "like a murrain. From the inland sea to the ocean, and northward into Burgundy." Father de Taillebourg knew all this, but he had said nothing, just let the old man go on describing how, when the Cathars were burned out of the land and the fires of their deaths had sent the smoke pouring to heaven to tell God and His angels that the true religion had been restored to the lands between France and Aragon, the Vexilles, among the last of the nobility to be contaminated by the Cathar evil, had fled to the farthest corners of Christendom. "But before they left," Brother Collimore said, gazing up at the white painted arch of the ceiling, "they took the treasures of the heretics for safekeeping."

"And the Grail was among them?"

"So they said, but who knows?" Brother Collimore turned his head and frowned at the Dominican. "If they possessed the Grail, why did it not help them? I have never understood that." He closed his eyes. Sometimes, when the old man was pausing to draw breath and almost seemed asleep, de Taillebourg would look through the window to see the two armies on the far hill. They did not move, though the noise they made was like the crackling and roaring of a great fire. The roaring was the noise of men's voices and the crackling was the drums and the twin sounds rose and fell with the vagaries of the wind gusting in the rocky defile above the River Wear. Father de Taillebourg's servant still stood in the doorway where he was half hidden by one of many piles of undressed stone that were stacked in the open space between the castle and the cathedral. Scaffolding hid the cathedral's nearest tower and small boys, eager to get a glimpse of the fighting, were scrambling up the web of lashed poles. The masons had abandoned their work to watch the two armies.

Now, after questioning why the Grail had not helped the Vexilles, Brother Collimore did fall into a brief sleep and de Taillebourg crossed to his black-dressed servant. "Do you believe him?"

The servant shrugged and said nothing.

"Has anything surprised you?" de Taillebourg asked.

"That Father Ralph has a son," the servant answered. "That was new to me."

"We must speak with that son," the Dominican said grimly, then turned back because the old monk had woken.

"Where was I?" Brother Collimore asked. A small trickle of spittle ran from a corner of his lips.

"You were wondering why the Grail did not help the Vexilles," Bernard de Taillebourg reminded him.

"It should have done," the old monk said. "If they possessed the Grail why did they not become powerful?"

Father de Taillebourg smiled. "Suppose," he said to the old monk, "that the infidel Muslims were to gain possession of the Grail, do you think God would grant them its power? The Grail is a great treasure, brother, the greatest of all the treasures upon the earth, but it is not greater than God."

"No," Brother Collimore agreed.

"And if God does not approve of the Grail-keeper then the Grail will be powerless."

"Yes," Brother Collimore acknowledged.

"You say the Vexilles fled?"

"They fled the Inquisitors," Brother Collimore said with a

sly glance at de Taillebourg, "and one branch of the family came here to England where they did some service to the King. Not our present King, of course," the old monk made clear, "but his great-grandfather, the last Henry."

"What service?" de Taillebourg asked.

"They gave the King a hoof from St. George's horse." The monk spoke as though such things were commonplace. "A hoof set in gold and capable of working miracles. At least the King believed it did for his son was cured of a fever by being touched with the hoof. I am told the hoof is still in Westminster Abbey."

The family had been rewarded with land in Cheshire, Collimore went on, and if they were heretics they did not show it, but lived like any other noble family. Their downfall, he said, had come at the beginning of the present reign when the young King's mother, aided by the Mortimer family, had tried to keep her son from taking power. The Vexilles had sided with the Queen and when she lost they had fled back to the continent. "All of them except one son," Brother Collimore said, "the eldest son, and that was Ralph, of course. Poor Ralph."

"But if his family had fled back to France, why did you treat him?" de Taillebourg asked, puzzlement marring the face that had blood scabs on the abrasions where he had beaten himself against the stone that morning. "Why not just execute him as a traitor?"

"He had taken holy orders," Collimore protested, "he could not be executed! Besides, it was known he hated his father and he had declared himself for the King."

"So he was not all mad," de Taillebourg put in dryly.

"He also possessed money," Collimore went on, "he was noble and he claimed to know the secret of the Vexilles."

"The Cathar treasures?"

"But the demon was in him even then! He declared himself a bishop and preached wild sermons in the London streets. He said he would lead a new crusade to drive the infidel from Jerusalem and promised that the Grail would ensure success."

"So you locked him up?"

"He was sent to me," Brother Collimore said reprovingly, "because it was known that I could defeat the demons." He paused, remembering. "In my time I scourged hundreds of them! Hundreds!"

"But you did not fully cure Ralph Vexille?"

The monk shook his head. "He was like a man spurred and whipped by God so that he wept and screamed and beat himself till the blood ran." Brother Collimore, unaware that he could have been describing de Taillebourg, shuddered. "And he was haunted by women too. I think we never cured him of that, but if we did not drive the demons clean out of him we did manage to make them hide so deep that they rarely dared show themselves."

"Was the Grail a dream given to him by demons?" the Dominican asked.

"That was what we wanted to know," Brother Collimore replied.

"And what answer did you find?"

"I told my masters that Father Ralph lied. That he had invented the Grail. That there was no truth in his madness. And then, when his demons no longer made him a nuisance, he was sent to a parish in the far south where he could preach to the gulls and to the seals. He no longer called himself a lord, he was simply Father Ralph, and we sent him away to be forgotten."

"To be forgotten?" de Taillebourg repeated. "Yet you had news of him. You discovered he had a son."

The old monk nodded. "We had a brother house near Dorchester and they sent me news. They told me that Father

Ralph had found himself a woman, a housekeeper, but what country priest doesn't? And he had a son and he hung an old spear in his church and said it was St. George's lance."

De Taillebourg peered at the western hill for the noise had become much louder. It looked as though the English, who were by far the smaller army, were advancing and that meant they would lose the battle and that meant Father de Taillebourg had to be out of this monastery, indeed out of this city, before Sir William Douglas arrived seeking vengeance. "You told your masters that Father Ralph lied. Did he?"

The old monk paused and to de Taillebourg it seemed as if the firmament itself held its breath. "I don't think he lied," Collimore whispered.

"So why did you tell them he did?"

"Because I liked him," Brother Collimore said, "and I did not think we could whip the truth out of him, or starve it from him, or pull it out by trying to drown him in cold water. I thought he was harmless and should be left to God."

De Taillebourg gazed through the window. The Grail, he thought, the Grail. The hounds of God were on the scent. He would find it! "One of the family came back from France," the Dominican said, "and stole the lance and killed Father Ralph."

"I heard."

"But they did not find the Grail."

"God be thanked for that," Brother Collimore said faintly.

De Taillebourg heard a movement and saw that his servant, who had been listening intently, was now watching the courtyard. The servant must have heard someone approaching and de Taillebourg, leaning closer to Brother Collimore, lowered his voice so he would not be overheard. "How many people know of Father Ralph and the Grail?"

Brother Collimore thought for a few heartbeats. "No one has spoken of it for years," he said, "until the new bishop

came. He must have heard rumors for he asked me about it.
I told him that Ralph Vexille was mad."

"He believed you?"

"He was disappointed. He wanted the Grail for the cathedral."

Of course he did, de Taillebourg thought, for any cathedral that possessed the Grail would become the richest church in Christendom. Even Genoa, which had its gaudy piece of green glass that they claimed was the Grail, took money from thousands of pilgrims. But put the real Grail in a church and folk would come to it in their hundreds of thousands and they would bring coins and jewels by the wagonload. Kings, queens, princes and dukes would throng the aisle and compete to offer their wealth.

The servant had vanished, slipping soundlessly behind one of the piles of building stone, and de Taillebourg waited, watching the door and wondering what trouble would show there. Then, instead of trouble, a young priest appeared. He wore a rough cloth gown, had unruly hair and a broad, guileless, sunburned face. A young woman, pale and frail, was with him. She seemed nervous, but the priest greeted de Taillebourg cheerfully. "A good day to you, father."

"And to you, father," de Taillebourg responded politely. His servant had reappeared behind the strangers, preventing them from leaving unless de Taillebourg gave his permission. "I am taking Brother Collimore's confession," de Taillebourg said.

"A good one, I hope," Father Hobbe said, then smiled. "You don't sound English, father?"

"I am French," de Taillebourg said.

"As am I," Eleanor said in that language, "and we have come to talk with Brother Collimore."

"Talk with him?" de Taillebourg asked pleasantly.

"The bishop sent us," Eleanor said proudly, "and the King did too."

"Which King, child?"

"*Edouard d'Angleterre*," Eleanor boasted. Father Hobbe, who spoke no French, was looking from Eleanor to the Dominican.

"Why would Edward send you?" de Taillebourg asked and, when Eleanor looked flustered, he repeated the question. "Why would Edward send you?"

"I don't know, father," Eleanor said.

"I think you do, my child, I think you do." He stood and Father Hobbe, sensing trouble, took Eleanor's wrist and tried to pull her from the room, but de Taillebourg nodded at his servant and gestured toward Father Hobbe and the English priest was still trying to understand why he was suspicious of the Dominican when the knife slid between his ribs. He made a choking noise, then coughed and the breath rattled in his throat as he slid down to the flagstones. Eleanor tried to run, but she was not nearly fast enough and de Taillebourg caught her by the wrist and jerked her roughly back. She screamed and the Dominican silenced her by clapping a hand over her mouth.

"What's happening?" Brother Collimore asked.

"We are doing God's work," de Taillebourg said soothingly, "God's work."

And on the ridge the arrows flew.

THOMAS ADVANCED with the archers of the left-hand battle and they had not gone more than twenty yards when, just beyond a ditch, a bank and some newly planted blackthorn saplings, they were forced to their right because a great scoop had been taken out of the ridge's flank to leave a hollow of ground with sides too steep for the plough. The hollow was filled with bracken that had turned yellow and at its far side was a lichen-covered stone wall and Thomas's arrow bag caught and tore on a rough piece of the coping as he clambered across. Only one arrow fell out, but it dropped into a mushroom fairy ring and he tried to work out whether that was a good or a bad omen, but the noise of the Scottish drums distracted him. He picked up the arrow and hurried on. All the enemy drummers were working now, rattling their skins in a frenzy so that the air itself seemed to vibrate. The Scottish men-at-arms were hefting their shields, making sure they protected the pikemen, and a crossbowman was working the ratchet that dragged back his cord and lodged it on the trigger's hook. The man glanced up anxiously at the advancing English bowmen, then discarded the ratchet handles and laid a metal quarrel in the crossbow's firing trough. The enemy had begun to shout and Thomas could distinguish some words now. "If you hate the English," he heard, then a crossbow bolt hummed past him and he forgot about the enemy chant. Hundreds of English archers were advancing through the fields, most of them running. The Scots only had a few crossbows, but those weapons outranged the longer war bows of the English who were hurrying to close that range. An arrow slithered across the grass in front of Thomas. Not a crossbow bolt, but an arrow from one of the few Scottish yew bows and the sight of the arrow told him he was almost in range. The first of the English archers had stopped and drawn back their cords and then their arrows flickered into the sky. A bowman in a padded leather jerkin fell backward with a crossbow bolt embedded in his forehead. Blood spurted skyward where his last arrow, shot almost vertically, soared uselessly.

"Aim at the archers!" a man in a rusted breastplate bellowed. "Kill their archers first!"

Thomas stopped and looked for the royal standard. It was off to his right, a long way off, but he had shot at farther targets in his time and so he turned and braced himself and then, in the name of God and St. George, he put his chosen

arrow onto the string and drew the white goose feathers back
to his ear. He was staring at King David II of Scotland, saw
the sun glint gold off the royal helmet, saw too that the
King's visor was open and he aimed for the chest, nudged
the bow right to compensate for the wind, and loosed. The
arrow went true, not vibrating as a badly made arrow would,
and Thomas watched it climb and saw it fall and saw the
King jerk backward and then the courtiers closed about him
and Thomas laid his second arrow across his left hand and
sought another target. A Scottish archer was limping from
the line, an arrow in his leg. The men-at-arms closed about
the wounded man, sealing their line with heavy shields.
Thomas could hear hounds baying deep among the enemy
formation, or perhaps he was hearing the war howl of the
tribesmen. The King had turned away and men were leaning
toward him. The sky was filled with the whisper of flying arrows and the noise of the bows was a steady, deep music.
The French called it the devil's harp music. There were no
Scottish archers left that Thomas could see. They had all
been made targets by the English bowmen and the arrows
had ripped the enemy archers into bloody misery, so now the
English turned their missiles on the men with pikes, swords,
axes and spears. The tribesmen, all hair and beard and fury,
were beyond the men-at-arms who were arrayed six or
eight men deep, so the arrows rattled and clanged on armor
and shields. The Scottish knights and men-at-arms and
pike-carriers were sheltering as best they could, crouching
under the bitter steel rain, but some arrows always found
the gaps between the shields while others drove clean
through the leather-covered willow boards. The thudding
sound of the arrows hitting shields was rivaling the sharper
noise of the drums.

"Forward, boys! Forward!" One of the archers' leaders
encouraged his men to go twenty paces nearer the enemy so
that their arrows could bite harder into the Scottish ranks.

"Kill them, lads!" Two of his men were lying on the grass, proof that the Scottish archers had done some damage before they were overwhelmed with English arrows. Another Englishman was staggering as though he were drunk, weaving back toward his own side and clutching his belly from which blood trickled down his leggings. A bow's cord broke, squirting the arrow sideways as the archer swore and reached under his tunic to find a spare.

The Scots could do nothing now. They had no archers left and the English edged closer and closer until they were driving their arrows in a flat trajectory that whipped the steel heads through shields, mail and even the rare suit of plate armor. Thomas was scarce seventy yards from the enemy line and choosing his targets with cold deliberation. He could see a man's leg showing under a shield and he put an arrow through the thigh. The drummers had fled and two of their instruments, their skins split like rotten fruit, lay discarded on the turf. A nobleman's horse was close behind the dismounted ranks and Thomas put a missile deep into the destrier's chest and, when he next looked, the animal was down and there was a flurry of panicking men trying to escape its thrashing hooves and all of those men, exposing themselves by letting their shields waver, went down under the sting of the arrows and then a moment later a pack of a dozen hunting dogs, long-haired, yellow-fanged and howling, burst out of the cowering ranks and were tumbled down by the slicing arrows.

"Is it always this easy?" a boy, evidently at his first battle, asked a nearby archer.

"If the other side don't have archers," the older man answered, "and so long as our arrows last, then it's easy. After that it's shit hard."

Thomas drew and released, shooting at an angle across the Scottish front to whip a long shaft behind a shield and into a bearded man's face. The Scottish King was still on his horse, but protected now by four shields that were all bristling with arrows and Thomas remembered the French horses laboring up the Picardy slope with the feather-tipped shafts sticking from their necks, legs and bodies. He rummaged in his torn arrow bag, found another missile and shot it at the King's horse. The enemy was under the flail now and they would either run from the arrow storm or else, enraged, charge the smaller English army and, judging by the shouts coming from the men behind the arrow-stuck shields, Thomas suspected they would attack.

He was right. He had time to shoot one last arrow and then there was a sudden terrifying roar and the whole Scottish line, seemingly without anyone giving an order, charged. They ran howling and screaming, stung into the attack by the arrows, and the English archers fled. Thousands of enraged Scotsmen were charging and the archers, even if they shot every arrow they possessed into the advancing horde, would be overwhelmed in a heartbeat and so they ran to find shelter behind their own men-at-arms. Thomas tripped as he climbed the stone wall, but he picked himself up and ran on, then saw that other archers had stopped and were shooting at their pursuers. The stone wall was holding up the Scots and he turned round himself and put two arrows into defenseless men before the enemy surged across the barrier and forced him back again. He was running toward the small gap in the English line where St. Cuthbert's Mass cloth waved, but the space was choked with archers trying to get behind the armored line and so Thomas went to his right, aiming for the sliver of open ground that lay between the army's flank and the ridge's steep side.

"Shields forward!" a grizzled warrior, his helmet visor pushed up, shouted at the English men-at-arms. "Brace hard! Brace hard!" The English line, only four or five ranks deep, steadied to meet the wild attack with their shields thrust forward and right legs braced back. "St. George! St.

George!" a man called. "Hold hard now! Thrust hard and hold hard!"

Thomas was on the flank of the army now and he turned to see that the Scots, in their precipitate charge, had widened their line. They had been arrayed shoulder to shoulder in their first position, but now, running, they had spread out and that meant their westernmost sheltron had been pushed down the ridge's slope and into the deep hollow that so unexpectedly narrowed the battle ground. They were down in the hollow's bottom, staring up at the skyline, doomed.

"Archers!" Thomas shouted, thinking himself back in France and responsible for a troop of Will Skeat's bowmen. "Archers!" he bellowed, advancing to the hollow's lip. "Now kill them!" Men came to his side, yelped in triumph and drew back their cords.

Now was the killing time, the archers' time. The Scottish right wing was down in the sunken ground and the archers were above them and could not miss. Two monks were bringing spare sheaves of arrows, each sheaf holding twenty-four shafts evenly spaced about two leather discs that kept the arrows apart and so protected their feathers from being crushed. The monks cut the twine holding the arrows and spilled the missiles on the ground beside the archers who drew again and again and killed again and again as they shot down into the pit of death. Thomas heard the deafening crash as the men-at-arms collided in the field's center, but here, on the English left, the Scots would never come to their enemy's shields because they had spilled into the low yellow bracken of death's kingdom.

Thomas's childhood had been spent in Hookton, a village on England's south coast where a stream, coming to the sea, had carved a deep channel in the shingle beach. The channel curved to leave a hook of land that protected the fishing boats and once a year, when the rats became too thick in the holds and bilges of the boats, the fishermen would strand their craft at the bottom of the stream, fill their bilges with stones and let the incoming tide flood the stinking hulls. It was a holiday for the village children who, standing on the top of the Hook, waited for the rats to flee the boats and then, with cheers and screams of delight, they would stone the animals. The rats would panic and that would only increase the children's glee as the adults stood around and laughed, applauded and encouraged.

It was like that now. The Scots were in the low ground, the archers were on the lip of the hill and death was their dominion. The arrows were flashing straight down the slope, scarce any arc in their flight, and striking home with the sound of cleavers hitting flesh. The Scots writhed and died in the hollow and the yellow autumn bracken turned red. Some of the enemy tried to climb toward their tormentors, but they became the easiest targets. Some attempted to escape up the far side and were struck in the back, while some fled down the hill in ragged disarray. Sir Thomas Rokeby, Sheriff of Yorkshire and commander of the English left, saw their escape and ordered two score of his men to mount their horses and scour the valley. The mailed riders swung their swords and morningstars to finish the archers' bloody work.

The base of the hollow was a writhing, bloody mass. A man in plate armor, a plumed helmet on his head, tried to climb out of the carnage and two arrows whipped through his breastplate and a third found a slit in his visor and he fell back, twitching. A thicket of arrows jutted from the falcon on his shield. The arrows became fewer now, for there were not many Scotsmen left to kill and then the first archers scrambled down the slope with drawn knives to pillage the dead and kill the wounded.

"Who hates the English now?" one of the archers jeered. "Come on, you bastards, let's hear you? Who hates the English now?"

Then a shout sounded from the center. "Archers! To the

right! To the right!" The voice had a note of sheer panic. "To the right! For God's sake, now!"

THE MEN-AT-ARMS of the English left were scarcely engaged in the fight because the archers were slaughtering the Scots in the low bracken. The English center was holding firm for the Archbishop's men were arrayed behind a stone wall which, though only waist high, was a more than adequate barrier against the Scottish assault. The invaders could stab, lunge and hack over the wall's coping, and they could try to climb it and they could even try to pull it down stone by stone, but they could not push it over and so they were checked by it and the English, though far fewer, were able to hold even though the Scots were lunging at them with their heavy pikes. Some English knights called for their horses and, once mounted and armed with lances, pressed up close behind their beleaguered comrades and rammed the lances at Scottish eyes. Other men-at-arms ducked under the unwieldy pikes and hacked with swords and axes at the enemy and all the while the long arrows drove in from the left. The noise in the center was the shouting of men in the rearward ranks, the screaming of the wounded, the clangor of blade on blade, the crack of blade on shield and the clatter of lance on pike, but the wall meant that neither side could press the other back and so, crammed against the stones and encumbered by the dead, they just lunged, hacked, suffered, bled and died.

But on the English right, where Lord Neville and Lord Percy commanded, the wall was unfinished, nothing more than a pile of stones that offered no obstacle to the assault of the Scottish left wing that was commanded by the Earl of March and by the King's nephew, Lord Robert Stewart. Their sheltron, closest to the city, was the largest of the three Scottish divisions and it came at the English like a pack of wolves who had not fed in a month. The attackers wanted blood and the archers fled from their howling charge like sheep scattering before fangs and then the Scots struck the English right and the sheer momentum of their assault drove the defenders back twenty paces before, somehow, the men-at-arms managed to hold the Scots who were now stumbling over the bodies of the men they had wounded or killed. The English, cramming themselves shoulder to shoulder, crouched behind their shields and shoved back, stabbing swords at ankles and faces, and grunting with the effort of holding the vast pressure of the Scottish horde.

It was hard to fight in the front ranks. Men shoved from behind so that Englishmen and Scotsmen were close as lovers, too close to wield a sword in anything except a rudimentary stab. The ranks behind had more room and a Scots-man chopped down with a pike that he wielded like a giant axe, its blade crunching down into an enemy's head to split helmet, leather liner, scalp and skull as easily as an unboiled egg. Blood fountained across a dozen men as the dead soldier fell and other Scots pushed into the gap his death had caused, and a clansman tripped on the body and screamed as an Englishman sawed at his exposed neck with a blunt knife. The pike dropped again, killing a second man, and this time, when it was lifted up, the dead man's crumpled visor was caught on the pike's bloody spike.

The drums, those that were still whole, had begun their noise again, and the Scots heaved to their rhythm. "The Bruce! The Bruce!" some chanted while others called on their patron, "St. Andrew! St. Andrew!" Lord Robert Stewart, gaudy in his blue and yellow colors and with a thin fillet of gold about the brow of his helmet, used a two-handed sword to chop at the English men-at-arms who cowered from the rampant Scots. Lord Robert, safe from arrows at last, had lifted his visor so he could see the enemy. "Come on!" he screamed at his men. "Come on! Hard into them!

Kill them! Kill them!" The King had promised that the Christmas feast would be in London and there seemed only a small screen of frightened men to break before that promise could come true. The riches of Durham, York and London were just a few sword strokes away; all the wealth of Norwich and Oxford, of Bristol and Southampton was only a handful of deaths from Scottish purses. "Scotland! Scotland! Scotland!" Lord Robert called. "Scotland!" And the pikeman, because the trapped visor was obstructing his blade, was beating on a man's helmet with the hook side of his weapon's head, not chopping through the metal, but smashing it, hammering the broken helmet into the dying man's brain so that blood and jelly oozed from the visor's slits. An Englishman screamed as a Scottish pike struck through his mail into his groin. A boy, perhaps a page, reeled back with his eyes bloodied from a sword slash. "Scotland!" Lord Robert could smell the victory now. So close! He shoved on, felt the English line jar and move back, saw how thin it was, fended off a lunge with his shield, stabbed with his sword to kill a fallen and wounded enemy, shouted at his squires to keep a watch for any rich English nobleman whose ransom could enrich the house of Stewart. Men grunted as they stabbed and hacked. A tribesman reeled from the fight, gasping for breath, trying to hold his guts inside his slashed belly. A drummer was beating the Scots on. "Bring my horse!" Lord Robert called to a squire. He knew that the beaten English line had to break in a moment and then he would mount, take his lance, and pursue the beaten enemy. "On! On!" he shouted. "On!" And the man wielding the long-hafted pike, the huge Scotsman who had driven a gap into the English front rank and who seemed to be carving a bloody path south all by himself, suddenly made a mewing noise. His pike, high in the air where it was still fouled with the bent visor, faltered. The man jerked and his mouth opened and closed, opened and closed again, but he could not speak because an arrow, its white feathers bloodied, jutted from his head.

An arrow, Lord Robert saw, and suddenly the air was thick with them and he pulled down the visor of his helmet so that the day went dark.

The damned English archers were back.

S IR WILLIAM DOUGLAS had not realized how deep and steep-sided was the bracken-covered saddle in the ridge's flank until he reached its base and there, under the flail of the archers, found he could neither go forward nor back. The front two ranks of Scottish men-at-arms were all either dead or wounded and their bodies made a heap over which he could not climb in his heavy mail. Robbie was screaming defiance and trying to scramble over that heap, but Sir William unceremoniously dragged his nephew back and thrust him down into the bracken. "This isn't a place to die, Robbie!"

"Bastards!"

"They may be bastards, but we're the fools!" Sir William crouched beside his nephew, covering them both with his huge shield. To go back was unthinkable, for that would be running from the enemy, yet he could not advance and so he just marveled at the force of the arrows as they thumped into the shield's face. A rush of bearded tribesmen, more nimble than the men-at-arms because they refused to wear metal armor, seethed past him, howling their wild defiance as they scrambled bare-legged across the heap of dying Scots, but then the English arrows began to strike and hurl the clansmen back. The arrows made sounds like bladders rupturing as they struck and the clansmen mewed and groaned, twitching as more arrows thumped home. Each missile provoked a spurt of blood so that Sir William and Robbie Douglas, unscathed beneath their heavy shield, were spattered with gore.

A sudden tumult among the nearby men-at-arms provoked more arrows and Sir William bellowed angrily at the soldiers to lie down, hoping that stillness would persuade the English archers that no Scotsmen lived, but the men-at-arms called back that the Earl of Moray had been hit. "Not before time," Sir William growled to Robbie. He hated the Earl more than he hated the English, and he grinned when a man shouted that his lordship was not just hit, but dead, and then another hail of arrows silenced the Earl's retainers and Sir William heard the missiles clanging on metal, thumping into flesh and striking the willow boards of shields, and when the rattle of arrows was done there was just the moaning and weeping, the hissing of breath, and the creak of leather as men died or tried to extricate themselves from under the piles of dying.

"What happened?" Robbie asked.

"We didn't scout the land properly," Sir William answered. "We outnumber the bastards and that made us confident." Ominously, in the arrowless quiet, he heard laughter and the thump of boots. A scream sounded and Sir William, who was old in war, knew that the English troops were coming down into the bowl to finish off the injured. "We're going to run back soon," he told Robbie, "there's no choice in it. Cover your arse with your shield and run like the devil."

"We're running away?" Robbie asked, appalled.

Sir William sighed. "Robbie, you damned fool, you can run forward and you can die and I'll tell your mother you died like a brave man and a halfwit, or you can get the hell back up the hill with me and try to win this battle."

Robbie did not argue, but just looked back up the Scottish

side of the hollow where the bracken was flecked with white-feathered arrows. "Tell me when to run," he said.

A dozen archers and as many English men-at-arms were using knives to cut Scottish throats. They would pause before finishing off a man-at-arms to discover whether he had any value as a source of ransom, but few men had such value and the clansmen had none. The latter, hated above all the Scots because they were so different, were treated as vermin. Sir William cautiously raised his head and decided this was the moment to retreat. It was better to scramble out of this bloody trap than be captured and so, ignoring the indignant shouts of the English, he and his nephew scrambled back up the slope. To Sir William's surprise no arrows came. He had expected the grass and bracken to be thrashed with arrows as he clambered out of the hollow, but he and Robbie were left alone. He turned halfway up the slope and saw that the English bowmen had vanished, leaving only men-at-arms on this flank of the field. At their head, watching him from the hollow's farther lip, was Lord Outhwaite, who had once been Sir William's prisoner. Outhwaite, who was lame, was using a spear as a stave and, seeing Sir William, he raised the weapon in greeting.

"Get yourself some proper armor, Willie!" Sir William shouted. Lord Outhwaite, like the Knight of Liddesdale, had been christened William. "We're not done with you yet."

"I fear not, Sir William, I do indeed fear not," Lord Outhwaite called back. He steadied himself with his spear. "I trust you're well?"

"Of course I'm not well, you bloody fool! Half my men are down there."

"My dear fellow," Outhwaite said with a grimace, and then waved genially as Sir William pushed Robbie on up the hill and followed him to safety.

Sir William, once back on the high ground, took stock. He could see that the Scots had been beaten here on their right, but that had been their own fault for charging headlong into the low ground where the archers had been able to kill with impunity. Those archers had mysteriously vanished, but Sir William guessed they had been pulled clear across the field to the Scottish left flank that had advanced a long way ahead of the center. He could tell that because Lord Robert Stewart's blue and yellow banner of the lion was so far ahead of the King's red and yellow flag. So the battle was going well on the left, but Sir William could see it was going nowhere in the center because of the stone wall that obstructed the Scottish advance.

"We'll achieve nothing here," he told Robbie, "so let's be useful." He turned and raised his bloody sword. "Douglas!" he shouted. "Douglas!" His standard-bearer had disappeared and Sir William supposed that the man, with his red-hearted flag, was dead in the low ground. "Douglas!" he called again and, when sufficient of his men had come to him, he led them to the embattled central sheltron. "We fight here," he told them, then pushed his way to the King who was on horseback in the second or third rank, fighting beneath his banner that was thick stuck with arrows. He was also fighting with his visor raised and Sir William saw that the King's face was half obscured with blood. "Put your visor down!" he roared.

The King was trying to stab a long lance across the stone wall, but the press of men made his efforts futile. His blue and yellow surcoat had been torn to reveal the bright plate metal beneath. An arrow thudded into his right espalier that had again ridden up on the breastplate and he tugged it down just as another arrow ripped open the left ear of his stallion. He saw Sir William and grinned as though this was fine sport. "Pull your visor down!" Sir William bellowed and he

saw that the King was not grinning, but rather a whole flap
of his cheek had been torn away and the blood was still
welling from the wound and spilling from the helmet's
lower rim to soak the torn surcoat. "Have your cheek bandaged!" Sir William shouted over the din of fighting.

The King let his frightened horse back away from the
wall. "What happened on the right?" His voice was made indistinct by his wound.

"They killed us," Sir William said curtly, inadvertently
jerking his long sword so that drops of blood sprayed from
its tip. "No, they murdered us," he growled. "There was a
break in the ground and it snared us."

"Our left is winning! We'll break them there!" The King's
mouth kept filling with blood, which he spat out, but despite
the copious bleeding he did not seem over-concerned with
the wound. It had been inflicted at the very beginning of the
battle when an arrow had hissed over the heads of his army
to rip a gouge in his cheek before spending itself in his helmet's liner. "We'll hold them here," he told Sir William.

"John Randolph's dead," Sir William told him. "The Earl
of Moray," he added when he saw that the King had not understood his first words.

"Dead?" King David blinked, then spat more blood. "He's
dead? Not a prisoner?" Another arrow slapped at his flag,
but the King was oblivious of the danger. He turned and
stared at his enemy's flags. "We'll have the Archbishop say a
prayer over his grave, then the bastard can say grace over
our supper." He saw a gap in the front Scottish rank and
spurred his horse to fill it, then lunged with his lance at an
English defender. The King's blow broke the man's shoulder, mangling the bloody wound with the debris of torn
mail. "Bastards!" the King spat. "We're winning!" he called
to his men, then a rush of Douglas's followers pushed between him and the wall. The newcomers struck the stone

wall like a great wave, but the wall proved stronger and the wave broke on its stones. Swords and axes clashed over the coping and men from both sides dragged the dead out of their paths to clear a passage to the slaughter. "We'll hold the bastards here," the King assured Sir William, "and turn their right."

But Sir William, his ears ever attuned to the noise of battle, had heard something new. For the last few minutes he had been listening to shouts, clangor, screams and drums, but one sound had been missing and that was the devil's harp music, the deep-toned pluck of bowstrings, but he heard it again now and he knew that though scores of the enemy might have been killed, few of those dead were archers. And now the bows of England had begun their awful work again. "You want advice, sire?"

"Of course." The King looked bright-eyed. His destrier, wounded by several arrows, took small nervous steps away from the thickest fighting that raged just paces away.

"Put your visor down," Sir William said, "and then pull back."

"Pull back?" The King wondered if he had misheard.

"Pull back!" Sir William said again, and he sounded hard and sure, yet he was not certain why he had given the advice. It was another damn premonition like the one he had experienced in the fog at dawn, yet he knew the advice was good. Pull back now, pull all the way back to Scotland where there were great castles that could withstand a storm of arrows, yet he knew he could not explain the advice. He could find no reason for it. A dread had seized his heart and filled him with foreboding. From any other man the advice would have been reckoned cowardice, but no one would ever accuse Sir William Douglas, the Knight of Liddesdale, of cowardice.

The King thought the advice was a bad jest and he gave a snorting laugh. "We're winning!" he told Sir William as more blood spilled from his helmet and slopped down to his saddle. "Is there any danger on the right?" he asked.

"None," Sir William said. The hollow in the ground would be as effective at stopping an English advance as it had been at foiling the Scottish attack.

"Then we'll win this battle on our left," the King declared, then hauled on his reins to turn away. "Pull back indeed!" The King laughed, then took a piece of linen from one of his chaplains and pushed it between his cheek and his helmet. "We're winning!" he said to Sir William again, then spurred to the east. He was riding to bring Scotland victory and to show that he was a worthy son of the great Bruce. "St. Andrew!" he shouted through thick blood. "St. Andrew!"

"You think we should pull back, uncle?" Robbie Douglas asked. He was as confused as the King. "But we're winning!"

"Are we?" Sir William listened to the music of the bows. "Best say your prayers, Robbie," he said, "best say your bloody prayers and ask God to let the devil take the bloody archers."

And pray that God or the devil was listening.

SIR GEOFFREY CARR was stationed on the English left where the Scots had been so decisively rebuffed by the terrain and his few men-at-arms were now down in the blood-reeking hollow in search of prisoners. The Scarecrow had watched the Scots trapped in the low ground and he had grinned with feral delight as the arrows had slashed down into the attackers. One enraged tribesman, his thick folds of swathing plaid stuck with arrows as thick as a hedgehog's spines, had tried to fight up the slope. He had been swearing and cursing, repeatedly struck by arrows, one was even sticking from his skull, which was smothered in tangled hair, and another was caught in the thicket of his beard, yet still he had come, bleeding and ranting, so filled with hate that he did not even know he should be dead, and he managed to struggle within five paces of the bowmen before Sir Geoffrey had flicked his whip to take the man's left eye from its socket clean as a hazel from its shell and then an archer had stepped forward and casually split the man's arrow-spitted skull with an axe. The Scarecrow coiled the whip and fingered the damp on the tip's iron claw. "I do enjoy a battle," he had said to no one in particular. Once the attack was stalled he had seen that one of the Scottish lords, all gaudy in blue and silver, was lying dead among the heap of corpses and that was a pity. That was a real pity. There was a fortune gone with that death and Sir Geoffrey, remembering his debts, had ordered his men down into the pit to cut throats, pillage corpses and find any prisoner worth a half-decent ransom. His archers had been taken off to the other side of the field, but his men-at-arms were left to find some cash. "Hurry, Beggar!" Sir Geoffrey shouted, "Hurry! Prisoners and plunder! Look for gentlemen and lords! Not that there are any gentlemen in Scotland!" This last observation, made only to himself, amused the Scarecrow so that he laughed aloud. The joke seemed to improve as he thought about it and he almost doubled over in merriment. "Gentlemen in Scotland!" he repeated and then he saw a young monk staring worriedly at him.

The monk was one of the prior's men, distributing food and ale to the troops, but he had been alarmed by Sir Geoffrey's wild cackle. The Scarecrow, going abruptly silent, stared wide-eyed at the monk and then, silently, let the coils of the whip fall from his hand. The soft leather made no sound as it rippled down, then Sir Geoffrey moved his right arm at lightning speed and the whip struck to loop itself about the young monk's neck. Sir Geoffrey jerked the lash. "Come here, boy," he ordered.

The jerk made the monk stumble so that he dropped the bread and apples he had been carrying, then he was standing close beside Sir Geoffrey's horse and the Scarecrow was leaning down from the saddle so that the monk could smell his fetid breath. "Listen, you pious little turd," Sir Geoffrey hissed, "if you don't tell me the truth I'll cut off what you don't need and what you don't use except to piss through and feed it to my swine, do you understand me, boy?"

The monk, terrified, just nodded.

Sir Geoffrey looped the whip one more time round the young man's neck and gave it a good tug just to let the monk know who was in charge. "An archer, fellow with a black bow, had a letter for your prior."

"He did, sir, yes, sir."

"And did the prior read it?"

"Yes, sir, he did, sir."

"And did he tell you what was in it?"

The monk instinctively shook his head, then saw the rage in the Scarecrow's eye and in his panic he blurted out the word he had first overheard when the letter was opened. "*Thesaurus*, sir, that's what's in it, *thesaurus*."

"*Thesaurus*?" Sir Geoffrey said, stumbling over the foreign word. "And what, you gelded piece of weasel shit, what, in the name of a thousand virgins, is a *thesaurus*?"

"Treasure, sir, treasure. Latin, sir. *Thesaurus*, sir, is Latin for . . ." the monk's voice trailed away. ". . . treasure," he finished lamely.

"Treasure." Sir Geoffrey repeated the word flatly.

The monk, half choking, was suddenly eager to repeat the gossip that had circulated amongst the brethren since Thomas of Hookton had encountered the prior. "The King sent him, sir, his majesty himself, and my lord the bishop too, sir, from France, and they're looking for a treasure, sir, but no one knows what it is."

"The King?"

"Or where it is, sir, yes, sir, the King himself, sir. He sent him, sir."

Sir Geoffrey looked into the monk's eyes, saw no guile and so unlooped the whip. "You dropped some apples, boy."

"I did, sir, I did, sir, yes."

"Feed one to my horse." He watched the monk retrieve an apple, then his face suddenly contorted with anger. "Wipe the mud off it first, you toadspawn! Clean it!" He shuddered, then stared northward, but he was not seeing the surviving Scots of the enemy's right wing scramble out of the low ground and he did not even notice the escape of his hated enemy, Sir William Douglas, who had impoverished him. He saw none of these things because the Scarecrow was thinking of treasure. Of gold. Of heaps of gold. Of his heart's desire. Of money and jewels and coins and plate and women and everything a heart could ever want.

THE SHELTRON on the Scottish left, rampant and savage, forced the English right so far back that a great gap appeared between the English center, behind its stone wall, and the retreating division on its right. That retreat meant that the right flank of the central division was now exposed to Scottish attack, indeed the rear of the Archbishop's battle was exposed to the Scots, but then, from all across the ridge, the archers came to the rescue.

They came to make a new line that protected the Archbishop's flank, a line that faced sideways onto the triumphant Scottish assault and the swarm of archers drove their arrows into Lord Robert Stewart's sheltron. They could not miss. These were bowmen who started their archery practice at a hundred paces and finished over two hundred paces from the straw-filled targets, and now they were shooting at twenty paces and the arrows flew with such force that some pierced through mail, body and mail again. Men in armor were being spitted by the arrows and the left-hand side of the Scottish advance crumpled in blood and pain, and every man who fell exposed another victim to the bowmen who were shooting as fast as they could lay their arrows on the cords. The Scots were dying by the score. They were dying and they were screaming. Some men instinctively tried to charge the archers, but were immediately cut down; no troops could stand that assault of feathered steel and suddenly the Scots were pulling back, tripping over the dead left by their charge, stumbling back across the pasture to where they had begun their charge and they were pursued every step of the way by the hissing arrows until, at last, an English voice ordered the archers to rest their bows. "But stay here!" the man ordered, wanting the archers who had come from the left wing to stay on the beleaguered right.

Thomas was among the archers. He counted his arrows, finding only seven left in his bag and so he began hunting in the grass for shot arrows that were not badly damaged, but then a man nudged him and pointed to a cart that was trundling across the field with spare sheaves. Thomas was astonished. "In France we were ever running out of arrows."

"Not here." The man had a hare lip, which made him hard to understand. "They keep 'em in Durham. In the castle. Three counties send 'em here." He scooped up two new sheaves.

The arrows were made all across England and Wales. Some folk cut and trimmed the shafts, others collected the feathers, women span the cords and men boiled the hide, hoof and verdigris glue while smiths forged the heads, and then the separate parts were carried to towns where the arrows were assembled, bundled and sent on to London, York, Chester or Durham where they awaited an emergency. Thomas broke the twine on two sheaves and put the new arrows in a bag he had taken from a dead archer. He had found the man lying behind the Archbishop's troops and Thomas had left his old torn bag beside the man's body and now had a new bag filled with fresh arrows. He flexed the fingers of his right hand. They were sore, proof he had not shot enough arrows since the battle in Picardy. His back ached as it always did after he had shot the bow twenty or more times. Each draw was the equivalent of lifting a man one-handed and the effort of it dug the ache deep into his spine, but the arrows had driven the Scottish left wing clean back to where it had started and where, like their English enemies, they now drew breath. The ground between the two armies was littered with spent arrows, dead men and wounded, some of whom moved slowly as they tried to drag themselves back to their comrades. Two dogs sniffed at a corpse, but skittered away when a monk shied a stone at them.

Thomas unlooped the string of his bow so that the stave straightened. Some archers liked to leave their weapons permanently strung until the stave had taken on the curve of a tensioned bow, and were said to have followed the string; the curve was supposed to show that the bow was well used and thus that its owner was an experienced soldier, but Thomas reckoned a bow that had followed the string was weakened and so he unstrung his as often as he could. That also helped to preserve the cord. It was difficult to fashion a cord of exactly the right length, and inevitably it stretched, but a good hempen string, soaked with glue, could last the best part of a year if it was kept dry and not subjected to constant tension. Like many archers, Thomas liked to reinforce his bowcords with women's hair because that was meant to protect the strings from snapping in a fight. That and praying to St. Sebastian. Thomas let the string hang from the top of the bow, then squatted in the grass where he took the arrows from his bag one by one and span them between his fingers to detect any warping in their shafts.

"The bastards will be back!" A man with a silver crescent on his surcoat strode down the line. "They'll be back for more! But you've done well!" The silver crescent was half obscured by blood. An archer spat and another impulsively stroked his unstrung bow. Thomas thought that if he lay down he would probably sleep, but he was assailed by the ridiculous fear that the other archers would retreat and leave him there, sleeping, and the Scots would find and kill him. The Scots, though, were resting like the English. Some men were bent over as if they caught their breath, others were sitting on the grass while a few clustered round a barrel of water or ale. The big drums were silent, but Thomas could hear the scrape of stone on steel as men sharpened blades blunted by the battle's first clash. No insults were being shouted on either side now, men just eyed each other warily. Priests knelt beside dying men, praying their souls into heaven, while women shrieked because their husbands, lovers or sons were dead. The English right wing, its numbers thinned by the ferocity of the Scottish attack, had moved back to its original place and behind them were scores of dead and dying men. The Scottish casualties left behind by the precipitate retreat were being stripped and searched and a fight broke out between two men squabbling over a handful of tarnished coins. Two monks carried water to the wounded. A small child played with broken rings from a mail coat while his mother attempted to prize a broken visor off a pike that she reckoned would make a good axe. A Scotsman, thought dead, suddenly groaned and turned over and a man-at-arms stepped to him and stabbed down with his sword. The enemy stiffened, relaxed and did not move again. "Ain't resurrection day yet, you bastard," the man-at-arms said as he dragged his sword free. "Goddamn son of a whore," he grumbled, wiping his sword on the dead man's ragged surcoat, "waking up like that! Gave me a turn!" He was not speaking to anyone in particular, but just crouched beside the man he had killed and began searching his clothes.

The cathedral towers and castle walls were thick with

spectators. A heron flew beneath the ramparts, following the looping river that sparkled prettily under the autumn sun. Thomas could hear corncrakes down the slope. Butterflies, surely the last of the year, flew above the blood-slicked grass. The Scots were standing, stretching, pulling on helmets, pushing their forearms into their shield loops and hefting newly sharpened swords, pikes and spears. Some glanced over to the city and imagined the treasures stored in the cathedral crypt and castle cellars. They dreamed of chests crammed with gold, vats overflowing with coin, rooms heaped with silver, taverns running with ale and streets filled with women. "In the name of the Father and of the Son," a priest called, "and of the Holy Ghost. St. Andrew is with you. You fight for your King! The enemy are godless imps of Satan! God is with us!"

"Up, boys, up!" an archer called on the English side. Men stood, strung their bows and took the first arrow from the bag. Some crossed themselves, oblivious that the Scots did the same.

Lord Robert Stewart, mounted on a fresh gray stallion, pushed his way toward the front of the Scottish left wing. "They'll have few arrows left," he promised his men, "few arrows. We can break them!" His men had so nearly broken the damned English last time. So nearly, and surely another howling rush would obliterate the small defiant army and open the road to the opulent riches of the south.

"For St. Andrew!" Lord Robert called and the drummers began their beating, "for our King! For Scotland!"

And the howling began again.

BERNARD DE TAILLEBOURG went to the cathedral when his business in the monastery's small hospital was finished. His servant was readying the horses as the Dominican strode down the great nave between the vast pillars painted in jagged stripes of red, yellow, green and blue. He went to

the tomb of St. Cuthbert to say a prayer. He was not certain
that Cuthbert was an important saint—he was certainly not
one of the blessed souls who commanded the ear of God in
heaven—but he was much revered locally, and his tomb,
thickly decorated with jewels, gold and silver, testified to
that devotion.

At least a hundred women were gathered about the grave,
most of them crying, and de Taillebourg pushed some out of
his way so he could get close enough to touch the embroidered pall that shrouded the tomb. One woman snarled at
him, then realized he was a priest and, seeing his bloodied,
bruised face, begged his forgiveness. Bernard de Taillebourg
ignored her, stooping instead to the tomb. The pall was tas-
seled and the women had tied little shreds of cloth to the tassels, each scrap a prayer. Most prayers were for health, for
the restoration of a limb, for the gift of sight, or to save a
child's life, but today they were begging Cuthbert to bring
their menfolk safely down from the hill.

Bernard de Taillebourg added his own prayer. Go to St.
Denis, he beseeched Cuthbert, and ask him to speak to God.
Cuthbert, even if he could not hold God's attention, could
certainly find St. Denis who, being French, was bound to be
closer to God than Cuthbert. Beg Denis to pray that God's
speed attend my errand and that God's blessing be upon the
search and that God's grace give it success. And pray God to
forgive us our sins, but know that our sins, grievous though
they be, are committed only in God's service. He moaned at
the thought of this day's sins, then he kissed the pall and
took a coin from the purse under his robe. He dropped the
coin in the great metal jar where pilgrims gave what they
could to the shrine and then he hurried back down the cathedral's nave. A crude building, he thought, its colored pillars
so fat and gross and its carvings as clumsy as a child's
scratchings, so unlike the new and graceful abbeys and
churches that were rising in France. He dipped his fingers in

the holy water, made the sign of the cross and went out into the sunlight where his servant was waiting with their mounts.

"You could have left without me," he said to the servant.

"It would be easier," the servant said, "to kill you on the road and then go on without you."

"But you won't do that," de Taillebourg said, "because the grace of God has come into your soul."

"Thanks be to God," the servant said.

The man was not a servant by birth, but a knight and gently born. Now, at de Taillebourg's pleasure, he was being punished for his sins and for the sins of his family. There were those, and Cardinal Bessières was among them, who thought the man should have been stretched on the rack, that he should have been pressed by great weights, that the burning irons should have seared into his flesh so that his back arched as he screamed repentance at the ceiling, but de Taillebourg had persuaded the Cardinal to do nothing except show this man the instruments of the Inquisition's torture. "Then give him to me," de Taillebourg had said, "and let him lead me to the Grail."

"Kill him afterward," the Cardinal had instructed the Inquisitor.

"All will be different when we have the Grail," de Taillebourg had said evasively. He still did not know whether he would have to kill this thin young man with the sun-dark skin and the black eyes and the narrow face who had once called himself the Harlequin. He had adopted the name out of pride because harlequins were lost souls, but de Taillebourg believed he might well have saved this harlequin's soul. The Harlequin's real name was Guy Vexille, Count of Astarac, and it had been Guy Vexille whom de Taillebourg had been describing when he spoke to Brother Collimore about the man who had come from the south to fight for France in Picardy. Vexille had been seized after the battle when the French King had been looking for scapegoats and a man who dared display the crest of a family declared heretic and rebel had made a good scapegoat.

Vexille had been given to the Inquisition in the expectation that they would torture the heresy out of him, but de Taille-bourg had liked the Harlequin. He had recognized a fellow soul, a hard man, a dedicated man, a man who knew that this life meant nothing because all that counted was the next, and so de Taillebourg had spared Vexille the agonies. He had merely shown him the chamber where men and women screamed their apologies to God, and then he had questioned him gently and Vexille had revealed how he had once sailed to England to find the Grail and, though he had killed his uncle, Thomas's father, he had not found it. Now, with de Taillebourg, he had listened to Eleanor tell Thomas's story. "Did you believe her?" the Dominican now asked.

"I believed her," Vexille said.

"But was she deceived?" The Inquisitor wondered. Eleanor had told them that Thomas had been charged to seek the Grail, but that his faith was weak and his search half-hearted. "We shall still have to kill him," de Taillebourg added.

"Of course."

De Taillebourg frowned. "You do not mind?"

"Killing?" Guy Vexille sounded surprised that de Taille-bourg should even ask. "Killing is my job, father," the Harlequin said. Cardinal Bessières had decreed that everyone who sought the Grail should be killed, all except those who sought it on the Cardinal's own behalf, and Guy Vexille had willingly become God's murderer. He certainly had no qualms about slitting his cousin Thomas's throat. "You want to wait here for him?" he asked the Inquisitor. "The girl said he would be in the cathedral after the battle."

De Taillebourg looked across to the hill. The Scots would win, he was sure, and that made it doubtful that Thomas of

Hookton would come to the city. More likely he would flee southward in panic. "We shall go to Hookton."

"I searched Hookton once," Guy Vexille said.

"Then you will search it again," de Taillebourg snapped.

"Yes, father." Guy Vexille humbly lowered his head. He was a sinner; it was required of him that he show penitence and so he did not argue. He just did de Taillebourg's bidding and his reward, he had been promised, would be reinstatement. He would be given back his pride, allowed to lead men to war again and forgiven by the Church.

"We shall leave now," de Taillebourg said. He wanted to go before William Douglas came in search of them and, even more urgently, before anyone discovered the three bodies in the hospital cell. The Dominican had closed the door on the corpses and doubtless the monks would believe Collimore was sleeping and so would not disturb him, but de Taillebourg still wanted to be free of the city when the bodies were found and so he pulled himself into the saddle of one of the horses they had stolen from Jamie Douglas that morning. It seemed a long time ago now. He pushed his shoes into the stirrups, then kicked a beggar away. The man had been clawing at de Taillebourg's leg, whining that he was hungry, but now reeled away from the priest's savage thrust.

The noise of battle swelled. The Dominican looked at the ridge again, but the fight was none of his business. If the English and the Scots wished to maul each other then let them. He had greater matters on his mind, matters of God and the Grail and of heaven and hell. He had sins on his conscience too, but they would be shriven by the Holy Father and even heaven would understand those sins once he had found the Grail.

The gates of the city, though strongly guarded, were open so that the wounded could be brought inside and food and drink carried to the ridge. The guards were older men and had been ordered to make certain that no Scottish raiders tried to enter the city, but they had not been charged to stop anyone leaving and so they took no notice of the haggard priest with the bruised face mounted on a warhorse, nor of his elegant servant. So de Taillebourg and the Harlequin rode out of Durham, turned toward the York road, put back their heels and, as the sound of battle echoed from the city's crag, rode away southward.

IT WAS MID-AFTERNOON when the Scots attacked a second time, but this assault, unlike the first, did not come hard on the heels of fleeing archers. Instead the archers were drawn up ready to receive the charge and this time the arrows flew thick as starlings. Those on the Scottish left who had so nearly broken the English line were now faced by twice as many archers, and their charge, which had begun so confidently, slowed to a crawl and then stopped altogether as men crouched behind shields. The Scottish right never advanced at all, while the King's central sheltron was checked fifty paces from the stone wall behind which a crowd of archers sent an incessant shower of arrows. The Scots would not retreat, they could not advance, and for a time the long-shafted arrows thumped onto shields and into carelessly exposed bodies, then Lord Robert Stewart's men edged back out of range and the King's sheltron followed and so another pause came over the red-earthed battlefield. The drums were silent and no more insults were being shouted across the littered pastureland. The Scottish lords, those who still lived, gathered under their King's saltire banner and the Archbishop of York, seeing his enemies in council, called his own lords together. The Englishmen were gloomy. The enemy, they reasoned, would never expose themselves to what the Archbishop described as a third baptism of arrows. "The bastards will slink off northward," the Archbishop predicted, "God damn their bloody souls."

"Then we follow them," Lord Percy said.

"They move faster than us," the Archbishop said. He had taken off his helmet and its leather liner had left an indentation in his hair, circling his skull.

"We'll slaughter their foot," another lord said wolfishly.

"Damn their infantry," the Archbishop snapped, impatient with such foolery. He wanted to capture the Scottish lords, the men mounted on the swiftest and most expensive horses, for it was their ransoms that would make him rich, and he especially wanted to capture those Scottish nobles like the Earl of Menteith who had sworn fealty to Edward of England and whose presence in the enemy army proved their treachery. Such men would not be ransomed, but would be executed as an example to other men who broke their oaths, but if the Archbishop was victorious today then he could lead this small army into Scotland and take the traitors' estates. He would take everything from them: the timber from their parks, the sheets from their beds, the beds themselves, the slates off their roofs, their pots, their pans, their cattle, even the rushes from their streambeds. "But they won't attack again," the Archbishop said.

"Then we shall have to be clever," Lord Outhwaite put in cheerfully.

The other lords looked suspiciously at Outhwaite. Cleverness was not a quality they prized for it hunted no boars, killed no stags, enjoyed no women and took no prisoners. Churchmen could be clever, and doubtless there were clever fools at Oxford, and even women could be clever so long as they did not flaunt it, but on a battlefield? Cleverness?

"Clever?" Lord Neville asked pointedly.

"They fear our archers," Lord Outhwaite said, "but if our archers are seen to have few arrows, then that fear will go and they might well attack again."

"Indeed, indeed . . ." the Archbishop began and then stopped, for he was quite as clever as Lord Outhwaite, clever enough, indeed, to hide how clever he was. "But how would we convince them?" he asked.

Lord Outhwaite obliged the Archbishop by explaining what he suspected the Archbishop had already grasped. "I think, your grace, that if our archers are seen scavenging the field for arrows then the enemy will draw the correct conclusion."

"Or, in this case," the Archbishop laid it on broadly for the benefit of the other lords, "the incorrect conclusion."

"Oh, that's good," one of those other lords said warmly.

"It could be made even better, your grace," Lord Outhwaite suggested diffidently, "if our horses were brought forward? The enemy might then assume we were readying ourselves to flee?"

The Archbishop did not hesitate. "Bring all the horses up," he said.

"But . . ." A lord was frowning.

"Archers to scavenge for arrows, squires and pages to bring up the horses for the men-at-arms," the Archbishop snapped, understanding completely what Lord Outhwaite had in mind and eager to put it into effect before the enemy decided to withdraw northward.

Lord Outhwaite gave the orders to the bowmen himself and, within a few moments, scores of archers were out in the space between the armies where they gathered spent arrows. Some of the archers grumbled, calling it tomfoolery because they felt exposed to the Scottish troops who once again began to jeer them. One archer, farther forward than most, was struck in the chest by a crossbow quarrel and he fell to his knees, a look of astonishment on his face, and choked up blood into his cupped palm. Then he began weeping and that only made the choking worse and then a second man, going to help the first, was hit in the thigh by the same crossbow.

The Scots were howling their derision at the wounded men, then cowered as a dozen English archers loosed arrows at the lone crossbowman. "Save your arrows! Save your arrows!" Lord Outhwaite, mounted on his horse, roared at the bowmen. He galloped closer to them. "Save your arrows! For God's sake! Save them!" He was bellowing loud enough for the enemy to hear him, then a group of Scotsmen, tired of sheltering from the archers, ran forward in an evident attempt to cut off Lord Outhwaite's retreat and all the English scampered for their own line. Lord Outhwaite put back his spurs and easily evaded the rush of men who contented themselves with butchering the two wounded archers. The rest of the Scots, seeing the English run, laughed and jeered. Lord Outhwaite turned and gazed at the two dead bowmen. "We should have brought those lads in," he chided himself.

No one answered. Some of the archers were looking resentfully at the men-at-arms, supposing that their horses had been brought up to aid their flight, but then Lord Outhwaite barked at groups of archers to get behind the men-at-arms. "Line up at the back! Not all of you. We're trying to make them believe we're short of arrows and if you didn't have arrows you wouldn't be standing out in front, now would you? Hold the horses where they are!" He shouted this last order to the squires, pages and servants who had brought up the destriers. The men-at-arms were not to mount yet, the horses were simply being held at the back of the line, just behind the place where half the archers now formed. The enemy, seeing the horses, must conclude that the English, short of arrows, were contemplating flight.

And so the simple trap was baited.

A silence fell on the battlefield, except that the wounded were moaning, ravens calling and some women crying. The monks began to chant again, but they were still on the English left and to Thomas, now on the right, the sound was faint. A bell rang in the city. "I do fear we're being too clever," Outhwaite remarked to Thomas. His lordship was not a man who could keep silent and there was no one else in the right-hand division convenient for conversation and so he selected Thomas. He sighed. "It doesn't always work, being clever."

"It worked for us in Brittany, my lord."

"You were in Brittany as well as Picardy?" Lord Outhwaite asked. He was still mounted and was gazing over the men-at-arms toward the Scots.

"I served a clever man there, my lord."

"And who was that?" Lord Outhwaite was pretending to be interested, perhaps regretting that he had even begun the conversation.

"Will Skeat, my lord, only he's Sir William now. The King knighted him at the battle."

"Will Skeat?" Lord Outhwaite was engaged now. "You served Will? By the good Lord, you did? Dear William. I haven't heard that name in many a year. How is he?"

"Not well, my lord," Thomas said, and he told how Will Skeat, a commoner who had become the leader of a band of archers and men-at-arms who were feared wherever men spoke French, had been grievously wounded at the battle in Picardy. "He was taken to Caen, my lord."

Lord Outhwaite frowned. "That's back in French hands, surely?"

"A Frenchman took him there, my lord," Thomas explained, "a friend, because there's a doctor in the city who can work miracles." At the end of the battle, when men could at last think they had lived through the horror, Skeat's skull had been opened to the sky and when Thomas had last seen him Skeat had been dumb, blind and powerless.

"I don't know why the French make better physicians," Lord Outhwaite said in mild annoyance, "but it seems they do. My father always said they did, and he had much trouble with his phlegm."

"This man's Jewish, my lord."

"And with his shoulders. Jewish! Did you say Jewish?" Lord Outhwaite sounded alarmed. "I have nothing against Jews," he went on, though without conviction, "but I can think of a dozen good reasons why one should never resort to a Jewish physician."

"Truly, my lord?"

"My dear fellow, how can they harness the power of the saints? Or the healing properties of relics? Or the efficacy of holy water? Even prayer is a mystery to them. My mother, rest her soul, had great pain in her knees. Too much praying, I always thought, but her physician ordered her to wrap her legs in cloths that had been placed on the grave of St. Cuthbert and to pray thrice a day to St. Gregory of Nazianzus and it worked! It worked! But no Jew could prescribe such a cure, could he? And if he did it would be blasphemous and bound to fail. I must say I think it most ill advised to have placed poor Will into a Jew's hands. He deserves better, indeed he does." He shook his head reprovingly. "Will served my father for a time, but was too smart a fellow to stay cooped up on the Scottish border. Not enough plunder, you see? Went off on his own, he did. Poor Will."

"The Jewish doctor," Thomas said stubbornly, "cured me."

"We can only pray." Lord Outhwaite ignored Thomas's claim and spoke in a tone which suggested that prayer, though needful, would almost certainly prove useless. Then he cheered up suddenly. "Ah! I think our friends are stirring!" The Scottish drums had begun to beat and all along the enemy's line men were hitching up shields, dropping visors or hefting swords. They could see that the English had brought their horses closer, presumably to aid their retreat, and that the enemy line was apparently stripped of half its archers, so they must have believed that those bowmen were perilously short of missiles, yet the Scots still chose to advance on foot, knowing that even a handful of arrows could

madden their horses and throw a mounted charge into chaos.
They shouted as they advanced, as much to hearten themselves as put fear in the English, but they became more confident when they reached the place where the bodies lay
from their last charge and still no arrows flew.

"Not yet, lads, not yet." Lord Outhwaite had taken command of the archers on the right wing. The Lords Percy and
Neville commanded here, yet both were content to allow the
older man to give orders to the bowmen while they waited
with their men-at-arms. Lord Outhwaite glanced constantly
across the field to where the Scots advanced on the English
left wing, where his own men were, but he was satisfied that
the hollow of ground would go on protecting them just
as the stone wall shielded the center. It was here on the side
of the ridge closest to Durham where the Scots were
strongest and the English most vulnerable. "Let them get
closer," he warned the archers. "We want to finish them off
once and for all, poor fellows." He began tapping his fingers
on his saddle's pommel, keeping time with the few remaining big Scottish drums and waiting until the front rank of
Scots was only a hundred paces away. "Foremost archers,"
he called when he judged the enemy was close enough,
"that's you fellows in front of the line! Start shooting!"

About half the archers were in plain sight in the army's
front and they now drew their bows, cocked the arrows up
into the air and loosed. The Scots, seeing the volley coming,
began to run, hoping to close the range quickly so that only
a handful of the arrows would hurt.

"All archers!" Lord Outhwaite boomed, fearing he had
waited too long, and the archers who had been concealed behind the men-at-arms began to shoot over the heads of the
troops in front. The Scots were close now, close enough so
that even the worst archer could not fail to hit his mark, so
close that the arrows were again piercing through mail and
bodies, and strewing the ground with more wounded and dy-

ing men. Thomas could hear the arrows striking home. Some clanged off armor, some thumped into shields, but many made a sound like a butcher's axe when it slaughtered cattle at winter's coming. He aimed at a big man whose visor was raised and sent an arrow down his throat. Another arrow into a tribesman whose face was contorted with hate. Then an arrow's nock split on him, spinning the broken missile away when he released the string. He plucked the feathered scraps from the string, took a new arrow and drove it into another bearded tribesman who was all fury and hair. A mounted Scotsman was encouraging his men forward and then he was flailing in the saddle, struck by three arrows and Thomas loosed another shaft, striking a man-at-arms clean in the chest so that the point ripped through mail, leather, bone and flesh. His next arrow sank into a shield. The Scots were floundering, trying to force themselves into the rain of death. "Steady, boys, steady!" an archer called to his fellows, fearing they were snatching at the strings and thus not using the full force of their bows.

"Keep shooting!" Lord Outhwaite called. His fingers still tapped the pommel of his saddle, though the Scottish drums were faltering. "Lovely work! Lovely work!"

"Horses!" Lord Percy ordered. He could see that the Scots were on the edge of despair for the English archers were not after all short of arrows. "Horses!" he bellowed again, and his men-at-arms ran back to haul themselves into saddles. Pages and squires handed up the big heavy lances as men fiddled armored feet into stirrups, glanced at the suffering enemy and then snapped down their visors.

"Shoot! Shoot!" Lord Outhwaite called. "That's the way, lads!" The arrows were pitiless. The Scottish wounded cried to God, called for their mothers and still the feathered death hammered home. One man, wearing the lion of Stewart, spewed a pink mist of blood and spittle. He was on his knees, but managed to stand, took a step, fell to his knees again, shuffled forward, blew more blood-stained bubbles and then an arrow buried itself in his eye and went through his brain to scrape against the back of his skull and he went backward as though hit by a thunderbolt.

Then the great horses came.

"For England, Edward and St. George!" Lord Percy called and a trumpeter took up the challenge as the great destriers charged. They unceremoniously thrust the archers aside as the lances dropped.

The turf shook. Only a few horsemen were attacking, but the shock of their charge struck the enemy with stunning force and the Scots reeled back. Lances were relinquished in men's bodies as the knights drew swords and hacked down at frightened, cowering men who could not run because the press of bodies was too great. More horsemen were mounting up and those men-at-arms who did not want to wait for their stallions were running forward to join the carnage. The archers joined them, drawing swords or swinging axes. The drums were at last silent and the slaughter had begun.

Thomas had seen it happen before. He had seen how, in an eyeblink, a battle could change. The Scots had been pressing all day, they had so nearly shattered the English, they were rampant and winning, yet now they were beaten and the men of the Scottish left, who had come so close to giving their King his victory, were the ones who broke. The English warhorses galloped into their ranks to make bloody lanes and the riders swung swords, axes, clubs and morningstars at panicked men. The English archers joined in, mobbing the slower Scots like packs of hounds leaping onto deer. "Prisoners!" Lord Percy shouted at his retainers. "I want prisoners!" A Scotsman swung an axe at his horse, missed and was chopped down by his lordship's sword; an archer finished the job with a knife and then slit the man's padded jerkin to search for coins. Two carpenters from Durham hacked with woodworker's adzes at a struggling

man-at-arms, bludgeoning his skull, killing him slowly. An
archer reeled back, gasping, his belly cut open and a Scot
followed him, screaming in rage, but then was tripped by a
bowstave and went down under a swarm of men. The trap-
pers of the English horses were dripping with blood as their
riders turned to cut their way back through the Scottish host.
They had ridden clean through and now spurred back to
meet the next wave of English men-at-arms who fought with
visors open for the panicking enemy was not offering any
real resistance.

Yet the Scottish right and center were intact.

The right had again been pushed into the low ground, but
now, instead of archers fighting them from the rim, they
faced the English men-at-arms who were foolish enough to
go down into the hollow to meet the Scottish charge. Mailed
men clashed over the bodies of the Scottish dead, clambering awkwardly in their metal suits to swing swords and axes
against shields and skulls. Men grunted as they killed. They
snarled, attacked and died in the muddy bracken, yet the
fight was futile for if either side gained an advantage they
only pressed their enemy back up the slope and immediately
the losing side had the ground as their ally and they would
press back downhill and more dead joined the corpses in the
hollow's bottom and so the fight surged forward and back,
each great swing leaving men weeping and dying, calling on
Jesus, cursing their enemy, bleeding.

Beggar was there, a great rock of a man who stood astride
the corpse of the Earl of Moray, mocking the Scots and
inviting them to fight, and half a dozen came and were killed
before a pack of Highland clansmen came screaming to kill
him and he roared at them, swinging his huge spiked mace,
and to the Scarecrow, watching from above, he looked like a
great shaggy bear assailed by mastiffs. Sir William Douglas,
too canny to be caught a second time in the low ground, also
watched from the opposing rim and was amazed that men

would go willingly down to the slaughter. Then, knowing that the battle would neither be won nor lost in that pit of death, he turned back to the center where the King's sheltron still had a chance of gaining a great victory despite the disaster on the Scottish left.

For the King's men had got past the stone wall. In places they had pulled it down and in others it had at last collapsed before the press of men, and though the fallen stones still presented a formidable obstacle to soldiers cumbered by heavy shields and coats of mail they were clambering across and thrusting back the English center. The Scots had charged into the arrows, endured them and even trapped a score of archers whom they slaughtered gleefully and now they hacked and stabbed their way toward the Archbishop's great banner. The King, his visor sticky with blood from his wounded cheek, was in the forefront of the sheltron. The King's chaplain was beside his master, wielding a spiked club, and Sir William and his nephew joined the attack. Sir William was suddenly ashamed of the premonition that had made him advise a retreat. This was how Scotsmen fought! With passion and savagery. The English center was reeling back, scarce holding its ranks. Sir William saw that the enemy had fetched their horses close up to the battle line and he surmised they were readying themselves to flee and so he redoubled his efforts. "Kill them!" he roared. If the Scots could break the line then the English would be in chaos, unable to reach their horses, and mere meat for the butchers.

"Kill! Kill!" the King, conspicuous on horseback, shouted at his men.

"Prisoners!" the Earl of Menteith, more sensible, called. "Take prisoners!"

"Break them! Break them now!" Sir William roared. He slammed his shield forward to receive a sword stroke, stabbed beneath it and felt his blade pierce a mail coat. He turned the sword and jerked it free before the flesh could grip the steel. He pushed with his shield, unable to see over its top rim, felt the enemy stagger back, lowered the shield in anticipation of a lunge underneath, then rammed it forward again, throwing the enemy back. He stumbled forward, almost losing his footing by tripping on the man he had wounded, but he caught his weight by dropping the bottom edge of the shield on the ground, pushed himself upright and thrust the sword into a bearded face. The blade glanced off the cheekbone, taking an eye, and that man fell backward, mouth agape, abandoning the fight. Sir William half ducked to avoid an axe blow, caught another sword on his shield and stabbed wildly toward the two men attacking him. Robbie, swearing and cursing, killed the axeman, then kicked a fallen man-at-arms in the face. Sir William lunged underhand and felt his sword scrape on broken mail and he twisted to stop the blade being trapped and yanked it back so that a gush of blood spilled through the metal rings of the wounded man's armor. That man fell, gasping and twitching, and more Englishmen came from the right, desperate to stop the Scottish attack that threatened to pierce clean through the Archbishop's line. "Douglas!" Sir William roared. "Douglas!" He was calling on his followers to come and support him, to shove and to gouge and to hack the last enemy down. He and his nephew had carved a bloody path deep into the Archbishop's ranks and it would take only a moment's fierce fighting to break the English center and then the real slaughter could begin. Sir William ducked as another axe flailed at him. Robbie killed that man, driving his sword through the axeman's throat, but Robbie immediately had to parry a spear thrust and in doing it he staggered back against his uncle. Sir William shoved his nephew upright and hammered his shield into an enemy's face. Where the hell were his men? "Douglas!" Sir William thundered again. "Douglas!"

And just then a sword or spear tangled his feet and he fell

and instinctively he covered himself with the shield. Men pounded past him and he prayed that they were his followers who were breaking the last English resistance and he waited for the enemy's screaming to begin, but instead there was an insistent tap on his helmet. The tapping stopped, then started again. "Sir William?" a gentle voice inquired.

The screaming had begun so Sir William could scarcely hear, but the gentle tapping on the crown of his helmet persuaded him it was safe to lower his shield. It took him a moment to see what was happening for his helmet had been wrenched askew when he fell and he had to pull it round. "God's teeth," he said when the world came into view.

"Dear Sir William," the kindly voice said, "I assume you yield? Of course you do. And is that young Robbie? My, how you've grown, young man! I remember you as a pup."

"Oh, God's teeth," Sir William said again, looking up at Lord Outhwaite.

"Can I give you a hand?" Lord Outhwaite asked solicitously, reaching down from his saddle. "And then we can talk ransoms."

"Jesus," Sir William said, "God damn it!" for he understood now that the feet pounding past had been English feet and that the screaming was coming from the Scots.

The English center had held after all, and for the Scots the battle had turned to utter disaster.

IT WAS THE archers again. The Scots had lost men all day and still they outnumbered their enemy, but they had no answer to the arrows and when the Scottish center broke down the wall and surged across its remains, so the Scottish left had retreated and exposed the flank of the King's sheltron to the English arrows.

It took a few moments for the bowmen to realize their advantage. They had joined the pursuit of the broken Scottish left and were unaware how close to victory was the Scottish

center, but then one of Lord Neville's men understood the
danger. "Archers!" His roar could be heard clear across the
Wear in Durham. "*Archers*!" Men broke off their plundering
and pulled arrows from the bags.

The bows began sounding again, each deep harp note
driving an arrow into the flank of the rampaging Scots.
David's sheltron had forced the central English battle back
across a pasture, they had stretched it thin and they were
closing on the Archbishop's great banner, and then the arrows began to bite and after the arrows came the men-at-
arms from the English right wing, the retainers of Lord Percy
and of Lord Neville, and some were already mounted on
their big horses that were trained to bite, rear and kick with
their iron-shod hooves. The archers, discarding their bows
yet again, followed the horsemen with axes and swords, and
this time their women came as well with knives unsheathed.

The Scottish King hacked at an Englishman, saw him fall,
then heard his standard-bearer shout in terror and he turned
to see the great banner falling. The standard-bearer's horse
had been hamstrung; it screamed as it collapsed and a rabble
of archers and men-at-arms clawed at man and beast,
snatched at the banner and hauled the standard-bearer down
to a ghastly death, but then the royal chaplain seized the
reins of the King's horse and dragged David Bruce out of the
mêlée. More Scotsmen gathered about their King, escorting
him away, and behind them the English were hacking down
from saddles, chopping with their swords, cursing as they
killed, and the King tried to turn back and continue the fight,
but the chaplain forced his horse away. "Ride, sir! Ride!" the
chaplain shouted. Frightened men blundered into the King's
horse that trampled on a clansman then stumbled on a
corpse. There were Englishmen in the Scottish rear now and
the King, seeing his danger, put back his spurs. An enemy
knight took a swing at him, but the King parried the blow
and galloped past the danger. His army had disintegrated

into groups of desperate fugitives. He saw the Earl of
Menteith try to mount a horse, but an archer seized his lordship's leg and hauled him back, then sat on him and put a
knife to his throat. The Earl shouted that he yielded. The
Earl of Fife was a prisoner, the Earl of Strathearn was dead,
the Earl of Wigtown was being assailed by two English
knights whose swords rang on his plate armor like black-
smiths' hammers. One of the big Scottish drums, its skins
split and tattered, rolled down the hill, going faster and
faster as the slope steepened, thumping hollow on the rocks
until at last it fell sideways and slid to a halt.

The King's great banner was in English hands now as
were the standards of a dozen Scottish lords. A few Scots
galloped north. Lord Robert Stewart, who had so nearly won
the day, was free and clear on the eastern side of the ridge
while the King plunged down the western side, going into
shadow because the sun was now lower than the hills toward
which he rode in desperate need of refuge. He thought of his
wife. Was she pregnant? He had been told that Lord Robert
had hired a witch to lay a spell on her womb so that the
throne would pass from Bruce to Stewart. "Sir! Sir!" One of
his men was screaming at him and the King came out of his
reverie to see a group of English archers already down in the
valley. How had they headed him off? He pulled on the
reins, leaned right to help the horse round and felt the arrow
thump into the stallion's chest. Another of his men was
down, tumbling along the stony ground that was tearing his
mail into bright shreds. A horse screamed, blood fanned
across the dusk and another arrow slammed into the King's
shield that was slung on his back. A third arrow was caught
in his horse's mane and the stallion was slowing, plunging
up and down as it labored for breath.

The King struck back with his spurs, but the horse could
not go faster. He grimaced and the gesture opened the
crusted wound on his cheek so that blood spilled from his

open visor down his ripped surcoat. The horse stumbled again. There was a stream ahead and a small stone bridge and the King marveled that anyone should make a masonry bridge over so slight a watercourse, and then the horse's front legs just collapsed and the King was rolling on the ground, miraculously free of his dying mount and without any broken bones and he scrambled up and ran to the bridge where three of his men waited on horseback, one with a riderless stallion. But even before the King could reach the three men the arrows flickered and hammered home, each one making the horses stagger sideways from the shock of its impact. The stallion screamed, tore itself free of the man's grasp and galloped eastward with blood dripping from its belly. Another horse collapsed with an arrow deep in its rump, two in its belly and another in its jugular. "Under the bridge!" the King shouted. There would be shelter under the arch, a place to hide, and when he had a dozen men he would make a break for it. Dusk could not be far off and if they waited for nightfall and then walked all night they might be in Scotland by dawn.

So four Scotsmen, one of them a King, huddled under the stone bridge and caught their breath. The arrows had stopped flying, their horses were all dead and the King dared to hope that the English archers had gone in search of other prey. "We wait here," he whispered. He could hear screams from the high ground, he could hear hooves on the slope, but none sounded close to the little low bridge. He shuddered, realizing the magnitude of the disaster. His army was gone, his great hopes were nothing, the Christmas feast would not be in London and Scotland lay open to its enemies. He peered northward. A group of clansmen splashed through the stream and suddenly six English horsemen appeared and drove their destriers off the high bank and the big swords hacked down and there was blood swirling downstream to run around the King's mailed feet and he shrank back into the shadows as the men-at-arms spurred westward to find more fugitives. Horses clattered over the bridge and the four Scotsmen said nothing, dared not even look at each other until the sound of the hooves had faded. A trumpet was calling from the ridge and its note was hateful: triumphant and scornful. The King closed his eyes because he feared he would shed tears.

"You must see a physician, sir," a man said and the King opened his eyes to see it was one of his servants who had spoken.

"This can't be cured," the King said, meaning Scotland.

"The cheek will mend, sir," the servant said reassuringly.

The King stared at his retainer as though the man had spoken in some strange foreign tongue and then, terribly and suddenly, his badly wounded cheek began to hurt. There had been no pain all day, but now it was agony and the King felt tears well from his eyes. Not from pain, but shame, and then, as he tried to blink the tears away there were shouts, falling shadows and the splash of boots as men jumped from the bridge. The attackers had swords and spears and they plunged under the bridge's arch like otter-hunters come to the kill and the King roared his defiance and leaped at the man who was in front and his rage was such that he forgot to draw his sword and instead punched the man with his armored fist and he felt the Englishman's teeth crunch under the blow, saw the blood spurt and he drove the man down into the stream, hammering him, and then he could not move because other men were pinioning him. The man beneath him, half drowned with broken teeth and bloodied lips, began to laugh.

For he had taken a prisoner. And he would be rich.

He had captured the King.

PART TWO

❧

England and Normandy, 1346–1347

The Winter Siege

I T WAS DARK in the cathedral. So dark that the bright colors painted on the pillars and walls had faded into blackness. The only light came from the candles on the side altars and from beyond the rood screen where flames shivered in the choir and black-robed monks chanted. Their voices wove a spell in the dark, twining and falling, surging and rising, a sound that would have brought tears to Thomas's eyes if he had possessed any tears left to shed. "*Libera me, Domine, de morte aeterna,*" the monks intoned as the candle smoke twisted up to the cathedral's roof. Deliver me, Lord, from everlasting death, and on the flagstones of the choir lay the coffin in which Brother Hugh Collimore lay undelivered, his hands crossed on his tunic, his eyes closed and, unknown to the prior, a pagan coin placed beneath his tongue by one of the other monks who feared the devil would take Collimore's soul if the ferryman who carried the souls of the departed across the river of the afterworld was not paid.

"*Requiem aeternam dona eis, Domine,*" the monks chanted, requesting the Lord to give Brother Collimore eternal rest, and in the city beneath the cathedral, in the small houses that clung to the side of the rock, there was weeping for so many Durham men had been killed in the battle, but the weeping was as nothing to the tears that would be shed when the news of the disaster returned to Scotland. The King was taken prisoner, and so was Sir William Douglas and the Earls of Fife and of Menteith and of Wigtown, and the Earl of Moray was dead as was the Constable of Scotland and the King's Marshal and the King's Chamberlain, all of them butchered, their bodies stripped naked and mocked by their enemies, and with them were hundreds of their countrymen, their white flesh laced bloody and food now for foxes and wolves and dogs and ravens. The gorestained Scottish standards were on the altar of Durham's cathedral and the remnants of David's great army were fleeing through the night and on their heels were the vengeful English going to ravage and plunder the lowlands, to take back what had been stolen and then to steal some more. "*Et lux perpetua luceat eis,*" the monks chanted, praying that eternal light would shine upon the dead monk, while on the ridge the other dead lay beneath the dark where the white owls shrieked.

"You must confide in me," the prior hissed at Thomas at the back of the cathedral. Small candles flickered on the scores of side altars where priests, many of them refugees from nearby villages sacked by the Scots, said Masses for the dead. The Latin of those rural priests was often execrable, a source of amusement to the cathedral's own clergy and to the prior who sat beside Thomas on a stone ledge. "I am your superior in God," the prior insisted, but still Thomas stayed silent and the prior became angry. "The King has commanded you! The bishop's letter says so! So tell me what you seek."

"I want my woman back," Thomas said, and he was glad it was dark in the cathedral for his eyes were red from crying. Eleanor was dead and Father Hobbe was dead and Brother Collimore was dead, all of them knifed and no one knew by whom, though one of the monks spoke of a dark man, a servant who had come with the foreign priest, and

Thomas was remembering the messenger he had seen in the dawn, and Eleanor had been alive then and they had not quarreled and now she was dead and it was his fault. His fault. The sorrow came to him, overwhelmed him and he howled his misery at the cathedral's nave.

"Be quiet!" said the prior, shocked at the noise.

"I loved her!"

"There are other women, hundreds of them." Disgusted, he made the sign of the cross. "What did the King send you to find? I order you to tell me."

"She was pregnant," Thomas said, gazing up into the roof, "and I was going to marry her." His soul felt as empty and dark as the space above him.

"I order you to tell me!" the prior repeated. "In the name of God, I order you!"

"If the King wishes you to know what I seek," Thomas spoke in French though the prior had been using English, "then the King will be pleased to tell you."

The prior stared angrily toward the rood screen. The French language, tongue of aristocrats, had silenced him, making him wonder who this archer was. Two men-at-arms, their mail clinking slightly, walked across the flagstones on their way to thank St. Cuthbert for their survival. Most of the English army was far to the north, resting through the dark hours before resuming their pursuit of the beaten enemy, but some knights and men-at-arms had come to the city where they guarded the valuable prisoners who had been placed in the bishop's residence in the castle. Perhaps, the prior thought, the treasure that Thomas of Hookton sought was no longer important; after all, a king had been captured along with half the earls of Scotland and their ransoms would wring that wretched country dry, yet he could not rid himself of the word *thesaurus*. A treasure, and the Church was ever in need of money. He stood. "You forget," he said coldly, "that you are my guest."

"I do not forget," Thomas said. He had been given space in the monks' guest quarters, or rather in their stables for there were greater men who needed the warmer rooms. "I do not forget," he said again, tiredly.

The prior now gazed up into the roof's high darkness. "Perhaps," he suggested, "you know more of Brother Collimore's murder than you pretend?" Thomas did not answer; the prior's words were nonsense and the prior knew it, for he and Thomas had both been on the battlefield when the old monk had been killed, and Thomas's grief over Eleanor's murder was heartfelt, but the prior was angry and frustrated and he spoke unthinkingly. Hopes of treasure did that to a man. "You will stay in Durham," the prior commanded, "until I give you permission to leave. I have given instructions that your horse is to be kept in my stables. You understand me?"

"I understand you," Thomas said tiredly, then he watched the prior walk away. More men-at-arms were entering the cathedral, their heavy swords clattering against pillars and tombs. In the shadows, behind one of the side altars, the Scarecrow, Beggar and Dickon watched Thomas. They had been shadowing him since the battle's end. Sir Geoffrey was wearing a fine coat of mail now, which he had taken from a dead Scotsman, and he had debated whether to join the pursuit, but instead had sent a sergeant and a half-dozen men with orders to take whatever they could when the pillage of Scotland began. Sir Geoffrey himself was gambling that Thomas's treasure, because it had interested a king, would be worthy of his own interest and so he had decided to follow the archer.

Thomas, oblivious of the Scarecrow's gaze, bent forward, eyes tight shut, thinking he would never be whole again. His back and arm muscles burned from a day of drawing a bow and the fingers of his right hand were scraped raw by the cord. If he closed his eyes he saw nothing but Scotsmen coming toward him and the bow making a dark line down memory's picture and the white of the arrows' feathers dwindling in their flight, and then that picture would vanish and he would see Eleanor writhing under the knife that had tortured her. They had made her speak. Yet what did she know? That Thomas had doubted the Grail, that he was a reluctant searcher, that he only wanted to be a leader of archers, and that he had let his woman and his friend go to their deaths.

A hand touched the back of his head and Thomas almost hurled himself aside in the expectation of something worse, a blade, perhaps, but then a voice spoke and it was Lord Outhwaite. "Come outside, young man," he ordered Thomas, "somewhere that the Scarecrow can't overhear us." He said that loudly and in English, then softened his tone and used French. "I've been looking for you." He touched Thomas's arm, encouraging him. "I heard about your girl and I was sorry. She was a pretty thing."

"She was, my lord."

"Her voice suggested she was well born," Lord Outhwaite said, "so her family will doubtless help you exact revenge?"

"Her father is titled, my lord, but she was his bastard."

"Ah!" Lord Outhwaite stumped along, helping his limping gait with the spear he had carried for most of the day. "Then he probably won't help, will he? But you can do it on your own. You seem capable enough." His lordship had taken Thomas into a cold, fresh night. A high moon flirted with silver-edged clouds while on the western ridge great fires burned to plume a veil of red-touched smoke above the city. The fires lit the battlefield for the men and women of Durham who searched the dead for plunder and knifed the Scottish wounded to make them dead so they could also be plundered. "I'm too old to join a pursuit," Lord Outhwaite said, staring at the distant fires, "too old and too stiff in the joints. It's a young man's hunt, and they'll pursue them all the way to Edinburgh. Have you ever seen Edinburgh Castle?"

"No, my lord." Thomas spoke dully, not caring if he ever saw Edinburgh or its castle.

"Oh, it's fine! Very fine!" Lord Outhwaite said enthusiastically. "Sir William Douglas captured it from us. He smuggled men past the gate inside barrels. Great big barrels. A clever man, eh? And now he's my prisoner." Lord Outhwaite peered at the castle as though he expected to see Sir William Douglas and the other high-born Scottish captives shinning down from the battlements. Two torches in slanting metal cressets lit the entrance where a dozen men-at-arms stood guard. "A rogue, our William, a rogue. Why is the Scarecrow following you?"

"I've no idea, my lord."

"I think you do." His lordship rested against a pile of stone. The area by the cathedral was heaped with stone and timber for the builders were repairing one of the great towers. "He knows you seek a treasure so he now seeks it too."

Thomas paid attention to that, looking sharply at his lordship, then looking back at the cathedral. Sir Geoffrey and his two men had come to the door, but they evidently dared not venture any closer for fear of Lord Outhwaite's displeasure. "How can he know?" Thomas asked.

"How can he not know?" Lord Outhwaite asked. "The monks know about it, and that's as good as asking a herald to announce it. Monks gossip like market wives! So the Scarecrow knows you might be the source of great wealth and he wants it. What is this treasure?"

"Just treasure, my lord, though I doubt it has great intrinsic worth."

Lord Outhwaite smiled. He said nothing for a while, but just stared across the dark gulf above the river. "You told me, did you not," he said finally, "that the King sent you in the company of a household knight and a chaplain from the royal household?"

"Yes, my lord."

"And they fell ill in London?"

"They did."

"A sickly place. I was there twice, and twice is more than enough! Noxious! My pigs live in cleaner conditions! But a royal chaplain, eh? No doubt a clever fellow, not a country priest, eh? Not some ignorant peasant tricked out with a phrase or two of Latin, but a rising man, a fellow who'll be a bishop before long if he survives his fever. Now why would the King send such a man?"

"You must ask him, my lord."

"A royal chaplain, no less," Lord Outhwaite went on as though Thomas had not spoken, then he fell silent. A scatter of stars showed between the clouds and he gazed up at them, then sighed. "Once," he said, "a long time ago, I saw a crystal vial of our Lord's blood. It was in Flanders and it liquefied in answer to prayer! There's another vial in Gloucestershire, I'm told, but I've not seen that one. I did once stroke the beard of St. Jerome in Nantes; I've held a hair from the tail of Balaam's ass; I've kissed a feather from the wing of St. Gabriel and brandished the very jawbone with which Samson slew so many Philistines! I have seen a sandal of St. Paul, a fingernail from Mary Magdalene and six fragments of the true cross, one of them stained by the very same holy blood that I saw in Flanders. I have glimpsed the bones of the fishes with which our Lord fed the five thousand, I have felt the sharpness of one of the arrow heads that felled St. Sebastian and smelled a leaf from the apple tree of the Garden of Eden. In my own chapel, young man, I have a knuckle bone of St. Thomas and a hinge from the box in which the frankincense was given to the Christ child. That hinge cost me a great deal of money, a great deal. So tell me,

Thomas, what relic is more precious than all those I have seen and all those I hope to see in the great churches of Christendom?"

Thomas stared at the fires on the ridge where so many dead lay. Was Eleanor in heaven already? Or was she doomed to spend thousands of years in purgatory? That thought reminded him that he had to pay for Masses to be said for her soul.

"You stay silent," Lord Outhwaite observed. "But tell me, young man, do you think I really possess a hinge from the Christ child's toy box of frankincense?"

"I wouldn't know, my lord."

"I sometimes doubt it," Lord Outhwaite said genially, "but my wife believes! And that's what matters: belief. If you believe a thing possesses God's power then it will work its power for you." He paused, his great shaggy head raised to the darkness as if he smelled for enemies. "I think you search for a thing of God's power, a great thing, and I believe that the devil is trying to stop you. Satan himself is stirring his creatures to thwart you." Lord Outhwaite turned an anxious face on Thomas. "This strange priest and his dark servant are the devil's minions and so is Sir Geoffrey! He is an imp of Satan if ever there was one." He threw a glance toward the cathedral's porch where the Scarecrow and his two henchmen had retreated into the shadows as a procession of cowled monks came into the night. "Satan is working mischief," Lord Outhwaite said, "and you must fight it. Do you have sufficient funds?"

After the talk of the devil the commonplace question about funds surprised Thomas. "Do I have funds, my lord?"

"If the devil fights you, young man, then I would help you and few things in this world are more helpful than money. You have a search to make, you have journeys to finish and you will need funds. So, do you have enough?"

"No, my lord," Thomas said.

"Then permit me to help you." Lord Outhwaite placed a bag of coins on the pile of stones. "And perhaps you would take a companion on your search?"

"A companion?" Thomas asked, still bemused.

"Not me! Not me! I'm much too old." Lord Outhwaite chuckled. "No, but I confess I am fond of Willie Douglas. The priest who I think killed your woman also killed Douglas's nephew, and Douglas wants revenge. He asks, no, he begs that the dead man's brother be permitted to travel with you."

"He's a prisoner, surely?"

"I suppose he is, but young Robbie's hardly worth ransoming. I suppose I might fetch a few pounds for him, but nothing like the fortune I intend to exact for his uncle. No, I'd rather Robbie traveled with you. He wants to find the priest and his servant and I think he could help you." Lord Outhwaite paused and when Thomas did not answer, he pressed his request. "He's a good young man, Robbie. I know him, I like him, and he's capable. A good soldier too, I'm told."

Thomas shrugged. At this moment he did not care if half Scotland traveled with him. "He can come with me, my lord," he said, "if I'm allowed to go anywhere."

"What do you mean? Allowed?"

"I'm not permitted to travel." Thomas sounded bitter. "The prior has forbidden me to leave the city and he's taken my horse." Thomas had found the horse, brought into Durham by Father Hobbe, tied at the monastery's gate.

Lord Outhwaite laughed. "And you will obey the prior?"

"I can't afford to lose a good horse, my lord," Thomas said.

"I have horses," Lord Outhwaite said dismissively, "including two good Scottish horses that I took today, and at dawn tomorrow the Archbishop's messengers will ride south to take news of this day to London and three of my men will accompany them. I suggest you and Robbie go with them. That will get the two of you safe to London and after that? Where will you go after that?"

"I'm going home, my lord," Thomas said, "to Hookton, to the village where my father lived."

"And will that murderous priest expect you to go there?"

"I can't say."

"He will search for you. Doubtless he considered waiting for you here, but that was too dangerous. Yet he'll want your knowledge, Thomas, and he'll torment you to find it. Sir Geoffrey will do the same. That wretched Scarecrow will do anything for money, but I suspect the priest is the more dangerous."

"So I keep my eyes open and my arrows sharp?"

"I would be cleverer than that," Lord Outhwaite said. "I have always found that if a man is hunting you then it's best that he finds you in a place of your own choosing. Don't be ambushed, but be ready to ambush him."

Thomas accepted the wisdom of the advice, but sounded dubious all the same. "And how will they know where I go?"

"Because I will tell them," Lord Outhwaite said, "or rather, when the prior complains that you have disobeyed him by leaving the city, I shall tell him and his monks will then inform anyone whose ears they can reach. Monks are garrulous creatures. So where would you like to face your enemies, young man? At your home?"

"No, my lord," Thomas said hastily, then thought for a few heartbeats. "At La Roche-Derrien," he went on.

"In Brittany?" Lord Outhwaite sounded surprised. "Is what you seek in Brittany?"

"I don't know where it is, my lord, but I have friends in Brittany."

"Ah, and I trust you will also see me as a friend." He pushed the bag of coins toward Thomas. "Take it."

"I shall repay you, my lord."

"You will repay me," his lordship said, standing, "by bringing me the treasure and letting me touch it just once before it goes to the King." He glanced at the cathedral where Sir Geoffrey lurked. "I think you had better sleep in the castle tonight. I have men there who can keep that wretched Scarecrow at bay. Come."

Sir Geoffrey Carr watched the two men go. He could not attack Thomas while Lord Outhwaite was with him, for Lord Outhwaite was too powerful; but power, the Scarecrow knew, came from money and it seemed there was treasure adrift in the world, treasure that interested the King and now interested Lord Outhwaite too.

So the Scarecrow, come hell or the devil to oppose him, intended to find it first.

THOMAS WAS NOT going to La Roche-Derrien. He had lied, naming the town because he knew it and because he did not mind if his pursuers went there, but he planned to be elsewhere. He would go to Hookton to see if his father had hidden the Grail there and afterward, for he did not expect to find it, he would go to France for it was there that the English army laid siege to Calais and it was there that his friends were, and there that an archer could find proper employment. Will Skeat's men were in the siege lines and Will's archers had wanted Thomas to be their leader and he knew he could do the job. He could lead his own band of men, be as feared as Will Skeat was feared. He thought about it as he rode southward, though he did not think consistently or well. He was too obsessed with the deaths of Eleanor and Father Hobbe, and torturing himself with the memory of his last look back at Eleanor and his remembrance of that glance meant that he saw the country through which he rode distorted by tears.

Thomas was supposed to ride south with the men carrying the news of the English victory to London, but he got no farther than York. He was supposed to leave York at dawn, but Robbie Douglas had vanished. The Scotsman's horse was still in the Archbishop's stables and his baggage was where he had dropped it in the yard, but Robbie was gone. For a moment Thomas was tempted to leave the Scot behind, but some vague sense of resented duty made him stay. Or perhaps it was that he did not much care for the company of the men-at-arms who rode with their triumphant news and so he let them go and went to look for his companion.

He found the Scot gaping up at the gilded bosses of the Minster's ceiling. "We're supposed to be riding south," Thomas said.

"Aye," Robbie answered curtly, otherwise ignoring Thomas.

Thomas waited. After a short while: "I said that we're supposed to be riding south."

"So we are," Robbie agreed, "and I'm not stopping you." He waved a magnanimous arm. "Ride on!"

"You're giving up the hunt for de Taillebourg?" Thomas asked. He had learned the priest's name from Robbie.

"No." Robbie still had his head back as he stared at the magnificence of the transept's ceiling. "I'll find him and then I'll gralloch the bastard."

Thomas did not know what gralloch meant, but decided the word was bad news for de Taillebourg. "So why the hell are you here?"

Robbie frowned. He had a shock of curling brown hair and a snub face that, at first glance, made him look boyish, though a second look would detect the strength in his jawline and the hardness of his eyes. He at last turned those eyes on Thomas. "What I can't stand," he said, "are those damned laddies! Those bastards!"

It took a couple of heartbeats before Thomas realized he meant the men-at-arms who had been their companions on the ride from Durham to York, the men who were now two hours south on the road to London. "What was wrong with them?"

"Did you hear them last night? Did you?" Robbie's indignation flared, attracting the attention of two men who were on a high trestle where they were painting the feeding of the five thousand on the nave's wall. "And the night before?" Robbie went on.

"They got drunk," Thomas said, "but so did we."

"Telling how they fought the battle!" Robbie said. "And to hear the bastards you'd think we ran away!"

"You did," Thomas said.

Robbie had not heard him. "You'd think we didn't fight at all! Boasting, they were, and we nearly won. You hear that?" He poked an aggressive finger into Thomas's chest. "We damn nearly won, and those bastards made us sound like cowards!"

"You lost," Thomas said.

Robbie stared at Thomas as though he could not believe his ears. "We drove you back halfway to bloody London! Had you running, we did! Pissing in your breeks! We damn nearly won, we did, and those bastards are gloating. Just gloating! I wanted to murder the pack of them!" A score of folk were listening. Two pilgrims, making their way on their knees to the shrine behind the high altar, were staring open-mouthed at Robbie. A priest was frowning nervously, while a child sucked its thumb and gazed aghast at the shock-headed man who was shouting so loudly. "You hear me?" Robbie yelled. "We damn nearly won!"

Thomas walked away.

"Where are you off to?" Robbie demanded.

"South," Thomas said. He understood Robbie's embarrassment. The messengers, carrying news of the battle, could not resist embellishing the story of the fight when they were entertained in castle or monastery and so a hard-fought, savage piece of carnage had become an easy victory.

No wonder Robbie was offended, but Thomas had small sympathy. He turned and pointed at the Scotsman. "You should have stayed at home."

Robbie spat in disgust, then became aware of his audience. "Had you running," he said hotly, then leaped over to catch up with Thomas. He grinned and there was a sudden and appealing charm in his face. "I didn't mean to shout at you," he said, "I was just angry."

"Me too," Thomas said, but his anger was at himself and it was mingled with guilt and grief that did not lessen as the two rode south. They took to the road in mornings heavy with dew, rode through autumn mists, hunched under the lash of rain, and for almost every step of the journey Thomas thought of Eleanor. Lord Outhwaite had promised to bury her and have Masses said for her soul and Thomas sometimes wished he was sharing her grave.

"So why is de Taillebourg chasing you?" Robbie asked on the day they rode away from York. They spoke in English for, though Robbie was from the noble house of Douglas, he spoke no French.

For a time Thomas said nothing, and just when Robbie thought he would not answer at all he gave a snort of derision. "Because," he said, "the bastard believes that my father possessed the Grail."

"The Grail!" Robbie crossed himself. "I heard it was in Scotland."

"In Scotland?" Thomas asked, astonished. "I know Genoa claims to have it, but Scotland?"

"And why not?" Robbie bristled. "Mind you," he relented, "I've heard there's one in Spain, too."

"Spain?"

"And if the Spanish have one," Robbie said, "then the French will have to have one as well, and for all I know the Portuguese too." He shrugged, then looked back to Thomas. "So did your father have another?"

Thomas did not know what to answer. His father had been wayward, mad, brilliant, difficult and tortured. He had been a great sinner and, for all that, he might well have been a saint as well. Father Ralph had laughed at the wider reaches of superstition, he had mocked the pig bones sold by pardoners as relics of the saints, yet he had hung an old, blackened and bent spear in his church's rafters and claimed it was the lance of St. George. He had never mentioned the Grail to Thomas, but since his death Thomas had learned that the history of his family was entwined with the Grail. In the end he elected to tell Robbie the truth. "I don't know," he said. "I simply don't know."

Robbie ducked under a branch that grew low across the road. "Are you telling me this is the real Grail?"

"If it exists," Thomas said and he wondered again if it did. He supposed it was possible, but wished it was not. Yet he had been charged with the duty of finding out and so he would seek his father's one friend and he would ask that man about the Grail and when he received the expected answer he would go back to France and join Skeat's archers. Will Skeat himself, his one-time commander and friend, was stranded in Caen, and Thomas had no knowledge whether Will still lived or, if he did, whether he could speak or understand or even walk. He could find out by sending a letter to Sir Guillaume d'Evecque, Eleanor's father, and Will could be given safe passage in return for the release of some minor French nobleman. Thomas would repay Lord Outhwaite with money plundered from the enemy and then, he told himself, he would find his consolation in the practice of his skill, in archery, in the killing of the King's enemies. Perhaps de Taillebourg would come and find him and Thomas would kill him like he would put down a rat. As for Robbie? Thomas had decided he liked the Scotsman, but he did not care whether he stayed or went.

Robbie only understood that de Taillebourg would seek

Thomas and so he would stay at the archer's side until he could kill the Dominican. He had no other ambition, just to avenge his brother: that was a family duty. "You touch a Douglas," he told Thomas, "and we'll fillet you. We'll skin you alive. It's a blood feud, see?"

"Even if the killer is the priest?"

"It's either him or his servant," Robbie said, "and the servant obeys the master: either way the priest's responsible, so he dies. I'll slit his bloody throat." He rode for a while in silence, then grinned. "And then I'll go to hell, but at least there'll be plenty of Douglases keeping the devil company." He laughed.

It took ten days to reach London and, once there, Robbie pretended to be unimpressed, as though Scotland had cities of this size in every other valley, but after a while he dropped the pretense and just stared in awe at the great buildings, crowded streets and serried market stalls. Thomas used Lord Outhwaite's coins so they could lodge in a tavern just outside the city walls beside the horse pond in Smithfield and close to the green where more than three hundred traders had their stalls. "And it's not even market day?" Robbie exclaimed, then snatched at Thomas's sleeve. "Look!" A juggler was spinning half a dozen balls in the air—that was nothing unusual for any county fair would show the same—but this man was standing on two swords, using them as stilts, with his bare feet poised on the swords' points. "How does he do it?" Robbie asked. "And look!" A dancing bear was shuffling to the tune of a flute just beneath the gibbet where two bodies hung. This was the place where London's felons were brought to be sent on their swift way to hell. Both corpses were encased in chains to hold the rotting flesh to their bones and the stench of the decaying corpses mingled with the smell of smoke and the reek of the frightened cattle who were bought and sold on the green, which stretched between London's wall and the Priory of St.

Bartholomew where Thomas paid a priest to say Masses for the souls of Eleanor and Father Hobbe.

Thomas, pretending to Robbie that he was far more familiar with London than was the truth, had chosen the tavern in Smithfield for no other reason than its sign was two crossed arrows. This was only his second visit to the city and he was as impressed, confused, dazzled and surprised as Robbie. They wandered the streets, gaping at churches and noblemen's houses, and Thomas used Lord Outhwaite's money to buy himself some new boots, calfskin leggings, an oxhide coat and a fine woolen cloak. He was tempted by a sleek French razor in an ivory case, but, not knowing the razor's value, feared he was being cheated; he reckoned he could steal himself a razor from a Frenchman's corpse when he reached Calais. Instead he paid a barber to shave him and then, dressed in his new finery, spent the cost of the unbought razor on one of the tavern's women and afterward lay with tears in his eyes because he was thinking of Eleanor.

"Is there a reason we're in London?" Robbie asked him that night.

Thomas drained his ale and beckoned the girl to bring more. "It's on our way to Dorset."

"That's as good a reason as any."

London was not really on the way from Durham to Dorchester, but the roads to the capital were so much better than those that wandered across the country and so it was quicker to travel through the great city. However, after three days, Thomas knew they must move on and so he and Robbie rode westward. They skirted Westminster and Thomas thought for an idle heartbeat of visiting John Pryke, the royal chaplain sent to accompany him to Durham who had fallen ill in London and now either lived or died in the abbey's hospital, but Thomas had no stomach to talk of the Grail and so he rode on.

The air became cleaner as they went deeper into the country. It was not reckoned safe to travel these roads, but Thomas's face was so grim that other travelers reckoned he was the danger rather than the prey. He was unshaven and he dressed, as he always had, in black, and the misery of the last days had put deep lines on his thin face. With Robbie's mass of unkempt hair, the two of them looked like any other vagabonds who wandered the roads, except these two were fearsomely armed. Thomas carried his sword, bow and arrow bag, while Robbie had his uncle's sword with the scrap of St. Andrew's hair encased in its hilt. Sir William had reckoned he would have small use for the sword in the next few years while his family attempted to find the vast ransom, and so he had lent it to Robbie with the encouragement to use it well.

"You think de Taillebourg will be in Dorset?" Robbie asked Thomas as they rode through a stinging rain shower.

"I doubt it."

"So why are we going?"

"Because he may go there eventually," Thomas said, "him and his damn servant." He knew nothing about the servant except what Robbie had told him: that the man was fastidious, elegant, dark in looks and mysterious, but Robbie had never heard his name. Thomas, finding it hard to believe that a priest would have killed Eleanor, had persuaded himself that the servant was the killer and so planned to make the man suffer in agony.

It was late afternoon when they ducked under the arch of Dorchester's east gate. A guard there, alarmed by their weapons, challenged them, but backed down when Thomas answered in French. It suggested he was an aristocrat and the guard sullenly let the two horsemen pass, then watched as they climbed East Street past All Saints' church and the county jail. The houses grew more prosperous as they neared the town's center and, close to St. Peter's church, the wool-merchants' homes might not have been out of place in London. Thomas could smell the shambles behind the houses where the butchers worked their trade, then he led Robbie into Cornhill, past the shop of the pewterer who had a stammer and a wall eye, then past the blacksmith where he had once bought some arrowheads. He knew most of these folk. The Dogman, a legless beggar who had come by his nickname because he lapped water from the River Cerne like a dog, was heaving down South Street on the wooden bricks strapped to his hands. Dick Adyn, brother of the town's jailer, was driving three sheep up the hill and paused to deliver a genial insult to Willie Palmer who was closing up his hosiery shop. A young priest hurried into an alley with a book wrapped in his arms and averted his eyes from a woman squatting in the gutter. A gust of wind blew woodsmoke low into the street. Dorcas Galton, brown hair drawn up into a bun, shook a rug out of an upstairs window and laughed aloud at something Dick Adyn said. They all spoke in the local accent, soft and broad and buzzing like Thomas's own, and he almost curbed the horse to speak with them, but Dick Adyn glanced at him and then looked swiftly away and Dorcas slammed the window shut. Robbie looked formidable, but Thomas's gaunt looks were even more frightening and none of the townsfolk recognized him as the bastard son of Hookton's last priest. They would know him if he introduced himself, but war had changed Thomas. It had given him a hardness that repelled strangers. He had left Dorset a boy, but come back as one of Edward of England's prized killers and when he left the town by the south gate a constable gave both him and Robbie good riddance and told them to stay away. "Be lucky the pair of you ain't in jail!" the man called, emboldened by his municipal coat of mail and ancient spear. Thomas stopped his horse, turned in the

saddle and just stared at the man who suddenly found reason
to duck back into the alley beside the gate. Thomas spat and
rode on.

"Your home town?" Robbie asked caustically.

"Not now," Thomas said and he wondered where home
was these days, and for some odd reason La Roche-Derrien
came unbidden to his thoughts and he found himself remembering Jeanette Chenier in her great house beside the River
Jaudy, and that recollection of an old love made him feel
guilty yet again for Eleanor. "Where's your home town?" he
asked Robbie rather than dwell on memories.

"I grew up close to Langholm."

"Where's that?"

"On the River Esk," Robbie said, "not far north of the border. It's a hard country, so it is. Not like this."

"This is a good countryside," Thomas said mildly. He
looked up at the high green walls of Maiden Castle where
the devil played on All Hallow's Eve and where the corncrakes now made their harsh song. There were ripe black-
berries in the hedgerows and, as the shadows lengthened,
fox cubs skittering at the edge of the fields. A few miles on
and the evening had almost shaded to night, but he could
smell the sea now and he imagined that he could hear it,
sucking and surging on the Dorset shingle. This was the
ghost time of day when the souls of the dead flickered at the
edges of men's sight and when good folk hurried home to
their fire and to their thatch and to their bolted doors. A dog
howled in one of the villages.

Thomas had thought to ride to Down Mapperley where
Sir Giles Marriott, the squire of Hookton among other villages, had his hall, but it was late and he did not think it wise
to arrive at the hall after dark. Besides, Thomas wanted to
see Hookton before he spoke with Sir Giles and so he turned
his tired horse toward the sea and led Robbie under the high

dark loom of Lipp Hill. "I killed my first men up on that hill," he boasted.

"With the bow?"

"Four of them," Thomas said, "with four arrows." That was not entirely true for he must have shot seven or eight arrows, maybe more, but he had still killed four of the raiders who had come across the Channel to pillage Hookton. And now he was deep in the twilight shadow of Hookton's sea valley and he could see the fret of breaking waves flashing white in the late dusk as he rode down beside the stream to the place where his father had preached and died.

No one lived there now. The raiders had left the village dead. The houses had been burned, the church roof had fallen and the villagers were buried in a graveyard choked by nettles, thorn and thistles. It was four and a half years since that raiding party had landed at Hookton led by Thomas's cousin, Guy Vexille, the Count of Astarac, and by Eleanor's father, Sir Guillaume d'Evecque. Thomas had killed four of the crossbowmen and that had been the beginning of his life as an archer. He had abandoned his studies at Oxford and, until this moment, had never returned to Hookton. "This was home," he told Robbie.

"What happened?"

"The French happened," Thomas said and gestured at the darkling sea. "They sailed from Normandy."

"Jesus." Robbie, for some reason, was surprised. He knew that the borderlands of England and Scotland were places where buildings were burned, cattle stolen, women raped and men killed, but he had never thought it happened this far south. He slid down from his horse and walked to a heap of nettles that had been a cottage. "There was a village here?"

"A fishing village," Thomas said and he strode down what was once the street to where the nets had been mended and the women had smoked fish. His father's house was a heap

of burned-out timbers, choked with bindweed now. The
other cottages were the same, their thatch and wattle reduced to ash and soil. Only the church to the west of the
stream was recognizable, its gaunt walls open to the sky.
Thomas and Robbie tied their horses to hazel saplings in the
graveyard, then took their baggage into the ruined church. It
was already too dark to explore, yet Thomas could not sleep
and so he went down to the beach and he remembered that
Easter morning when the Norman ships had grounded on the
shingle and the men had come shrieking in the dawn with
swords and crossbows, axes and fire. They had come for the
Grail. Guy Vexille believed it to be in his uncle's possession
and so the Harlequin had put the village of Hookton to the
sword. He had burned it, destroyed it and gone from it without the Grail.

The stream made its little noise as it twisted inside the
shingle Hook on its way to meet the great sound of the sea.
Thomas sat down on the Hook, swathed in his new cloak,
with the great black bow beside him. The chaplain, John
Pryke, had talked of the Grail in the same awed tones that
Father Hobbe had used when he spoke of the relic. The
Grail, Father Pryke said, was not just the cup from which
Christ had drunk wine at the Last Supper, but the vessel into
which Christ's dying blood had poured from the cross.
"Longinus," Father Pryke had said in his excitable manner,
"was the centurion beneath the cross and, when the spear
struck the dolorous blow, he raised the dish to catch the
blood!"

How, Thomas wondered, did the cup go from the upper
room where Christ had eaten his last meal into the possession of a Roman centurion? And, stranger still, how had it
reached Ralph Vexille? He closed his eyes, swaying back
and forward, ashamed of his disbelief. Father Hobbe had always called him Doubting Thomas. "You mustn't seek ex-

planations," Father Hobbe had said again and again, "because the Grail is a miracle. It transcends explanations."

"C'est une tasse magique," Eleanor had added, implicitly adding her reproof to Father Hobbe's.

Thomas so wanted to believe it was a magic cup. He wanted to believe that the Grail existed just beyond human sight, behind a veil of disbelief, a thing half visible, shimmering, wonderful, poised in light and glowing like pale fire. He wanted to believe that one day it would take on substance and that from its bowl, which had held the wine and the blood of Christ, would flow peace and healing. Yet if God wanted the world to be at peace and if He wanted sickness defeated, why did He hide the Grail? Father Hobbe's answer had been that mankind was not worthy to hold the cup, and Thomas wondered if that was true. Was anyone worthy? And perhaps, Thomas thought, if the Grail had any magic then it was to exaggerate the faults and virtues of those who sought it. Father Hobbe had become more saintlike in his pursuit and the strange priest and his dark servant more malevolent. It was like one of those crystal lenses that jewelers used to magnify their work, only the Grail was a crystal that magnified character. What, Thomas wondered, did it reveal of his own? He remembered his unease at the thought of marrying Eleanor, and suddenly he began to weep, to heave with sobs, to cry more than he had already cried since her murder. He rocked to and fro, his grief as deep as the sea that beat on the shingle, and it was made worse by the knowledge that he was a sinner, unshriven, his soul doomed to hell.

He missed his woman, he hated himself, he felt empty, alone and doomed, and so, in his father's dead village, he wept.

IT BEGAN to rain later, a steady rain that soaked through the new cloak and chilled Thomas and Robbie to the bone.

They had lit a fire that flickered feebly in the old church, hissing under the rain and giving them a small illusion of warmth. "Are there wolves here?" Robbie asked.

"Supposed to be," Thomas said, "though I never saw one."

"We have wolves in Eskdale," Robbie said, "and at night their eyes glow red. Like fire."

"There are monsters in the sea here," Thomas said. "Their bodies wash ashore sometimes and you can find their bones in the cliffs. Sometimes, even on calm days, men wouldn't come back from fishing and you'd know the monsters had taken them." He shivered and crossed himself.

"When my grandfather died," Robbie said, "the wolves circled the house and howled."

"Is it a big house?"

Robbie seemed surprised by the question. He considered it for a moment, then nodded. "Aye," he said. "My father's a laird."

"A lord?"

"Like a lord," Robbie said.

"He wasn't at the battle?"

"He lost a leg and an arm at Berwick. So we boys have to fight for him." He said he was the youngest of four sons. "Three now," he said, crossing himself and thinking of Jamie.

They half slept, woke, shivered, and in the dawn Thomas walked back to the Hook to watch the new day seep gray along the sea's ragged edge. The rain had stopped, though a cold wind shredded the wave-tops. The gray turned a leprous white, then silvery as the gulls called over the long shingle where, at the top of the Hook's bank, he found the weathered remnants of four posts. They had not been there when he left, but beneath one of them, half buried in stones, was a yellowish scrap of skull and he guessed this was one of the crossbowmen he had killed with his tall black bow on that Easter day. Four posts, four dead men and Thomas supposed that the four heads had been placed on the poles to gaze out to sea till the gulls pecked out their eyes and flensed the flesh back to the bare skulls.

He stared into the ruined village, but could see no one. Robbie was still inside the church from which a tiny wisp of smoke drifted, but otherwise Thomas was alone with the gulls. There were not even sheep, cattle or goats on Lipp Hill. He walked back inland, his feet crunching on the shingle, then realized he still held the broken curve of skull and he hurled it into the stream where the fishing boats had been flooded to rid them of rats and then, feeling hungry, he went and took the piece of hard cheese and dark bread from the saddlebag that he had dumped beside the church door. The walls of the church, now he could see them properly in the daylight, appeared lower than he remembered, probably because local folk had come with carts and taken the stones away for barns or sties or house walls. Inside the church there was only a tangle of thorns, nettles and a few gnarled lengths of charred timber that had long been overgrown by grass. "I was almost killed in here," he told Robbie, and he described how the raiders had beaten on the church door as he had kicked out the horn panes of the east window and jumped down into the graveyard. He remembered how his foot had crushed the silver Mass cup as he scrambled over the altar.

Had that silver cup been the Grail? He laughed aloud at the thought. The Mass cup had been a silver goblet on which was incised the badge of the Vexilles, and that badge, cut from the crushed cup, was now pinned to Thomas's bow. It was all that was left of the old goblet, but it had not been the Grail. The Grail was much older, much more mysterious and much more frightening.

The altar was long gone, but there was a shallow clay bowl in the nettles where it had stood. Thomas kicked the plants aside and picked up the bowl, remembering how his father would fill it with wafers before the Mass and cover it with a piece of linen cloth and then hurry it to the church, getting angry if any of the villagers did not take off their hats and bow to the sacrament as he passed. Thomas had kicked the bowl as he climbed onto the altar to escape the Frenchmen, and here it still was. He smiled ruefully, thought about keeping the bowl, but tossed it back into the nettles. Archers should travel light.

"Someone's coming," Robbie warned him, running to fetch his uncle's sword. Thomas picked up the bow and took an arrow from his bag, and just then he heard the thump of hooves and the baying of hounds. He went to the ruins of the door and saw a dozen great deerhounds splashing through the stream with tongues lolling between their fangs; he had no time to run from them, only to flatten himself against the wall as the hounds streaked for him.

"Argos! Maera! Back off now! Mind your goddamn manners!" the horseman bellowed at his hounds, reinforcing his commands with the crack of a whip over their heads, but the beasts surrounded Thomas and leaped up at him. Yet it was not in threat: they were licking his face and wagging their tails. "Orthos!" the huntsman snapped at one dog, then he stared hard at Thomas. He did not recognize him, but the hounds obviously knew him and that gave the huntsman pause.

"Jake," Thomas said.

"Sweet Jesus Christ!" Jake said. "Sweet Jesus! Look what the tide brought in. Orthos! Argos! Off and away, you bastards, off and away!" The whip cracked loud and the hounds, still excited, backed away. Jake shook his head. "It's Thomas, isn't it?"

"How are you, Jake?"

"Older," Jake Churchill said gruffly, then climbed down from the saddle, pushed through the hounds and greeted Thomas with an embrace. "It was your damned father who named these dogs. He thought it was a joke. It's good to see you, boy." Jake was gray-bearded, his face dark as a nut from the weather and his skin scarred from countless brushes with thorns. He was Sir Giles Marriott's chief huntsman and he had taught Thomas how to shoot a bow and how to stalk a deer and how to go hidden and silent through country. "Good Christ Almighty, boy," he said, "but you've fair grown up. Look at the size of you!"

"Boys do grow up, Jake," Thomas said, then gestured at Robbie. "He's a friend."

Jake nodded at the Scotsman, then hauled two of the hounds away from Thomas. The dogs, named for hounds from Greek and Latin myth, whined excitedly. "And what the hell are you two doing down here?" Jake wanted to know. "You should have come up to the hall like Christians!"

"We got here late," Thomas explained, "and I wanted to see the place."

"Nothing to see here," Jake said scornfully. "Nothing but hares here now."

"You're hunting hare now?"

"I don't bring ten brace of hounds to snaffle hares, boy. No, Lally Gooden's boy saw the pair of you sneaking in here last night and so Sir Giles sent me down to see what evil was brewing. We had a pair of vagabonds trying to set up home here in the spring and they had to be whipped on their way. And last week there was a pair of foreigners creeping about."

"Foreigners?" Thomas asked, knowing that Jake could well mean nothing more than that the strangers had come from the next parish.

"A priest and his man," Jake said, "and if he hadn't been a priest I'd have loosed the dogs on him. I don't like foreigners, don't see no point to them. Those horses of yours look hungry. So do the two of you. You want breakfast? Or are you going to stand there and spoil those damned hounds by patting them half to death?"

They rode back to Down Mapperley, following the hounds through the tiny village. Thomas remembered the place as big, twice the size of Hookton, and as a child he had thought it almost a town, but now he saw how small it was. Small and low, so that on horseback he towered above the thatched cottages that had seemed so palatial when he was a child. The dungheaps beside each cottage were as high as the thatch. Sir Giles Marriott's hall, just beyond the village, was also thatched, the moss-thick roof sweeping almost to the ground. "He'll be pleased to see you," Jake promised.

And so Sir Giles was. He was an old man now, a widower who had once been wary of Thomas's wildness, but now greeted him like a lost son. "You're thin, boy, too thin. Ain't good for a man to be thin. You'll have breakfast, the two of you? Pease pudding and small ale is what we've got. There was bread yesterday, but not today. When do we bake more bread, Gooden?" This was demanded of a servant.

"Today's Wednesday, sir," the servant said reprovingly.

"Tomorrow then," Sir Giles told Thomas. "Bread tomorrow, no bread today. It's bad luck to bake bread on Wednesday. It poisons you, Wednesday's bread. I must have eaten Monday's. You say you're Scottish?" This was to Robbie.

"I am, sir."

"I thought all Scotsmen had beards," Sir Giles said. "There was a Scotsman in Dorchester, wasn't there, Gooden? You remember him? He had a beard. He played the gittern and danced well. You must remember him."

"He was from the Scilly Isles," the servant said.

"That's what I just said. But he had a beard, didn't he?"

"He did, Sir Giles. A big one."

"There you are then," Sir Giles spooned some pease pudding into a mouth that only had two teeth left. He was fat, white-haired and red-faced and at least fifty years old. "Can't ride a horse these days, Thomas," he admitted. "Ain't good for anything now except sitting about the place and watching the weather. Did Jake tell you there be foreigners scuttling about?"

"He did, sir."

"A priest! Black and white robes like a magpie. He wanted to talk about your father and I said there was nothing to talk about. Father Ralph's dead, I said, and God rest his poor soul."

"Did the priest ask for me, sir?" Thomas asked.

Sir Giles grinned. "I said I hadn't seen you in years and hoped never to see you again, and then his servant asked me where he might look for you and I told him not to talk to his betters without permission. He didn't like that!" he chuckled. "So then the magpie asked about your father and I said I hardly knew him. That was a lie, of course, but he believed me and took himself off. Put some logs on that fire, Gooden. A man could freeze to death in his own hall if it was left to you."

"So the priest left, sir?" Robbie asked. It seemed unlike de Taillebourg just to accept a denial and meekly go away.

"He was frightened of dogs," Sir Giles said, still amused. "I had some of the hounds in here and if he hadn't been dressed like a magpie I'd have let them loose, but it don't do to kill priests. There's always trouble afterward. The devil comes and plays his games if you kill a priest. But I didn't like him and I told him I wasn't sure how long I could keep the dogs heeled. There's some ham in the kitchen. Would you like some ham, Thomas?"

"No, sir."

"I do hate winter." Sir Giles stared into the fire, which now blazed huge in his wide hearth. The hall had smoke-blackened beams supporting the huge expanse of thatch. At one end a carved timber screen hid the kitchens while the private rooms were at the other end, though since his wife had died Sir Giles no longer used the small chambers, but lived, ate and slept beside the hall fire. "I reckon this'll be my last winter, Thomas."

"I hope not, sir."

"Hope what you damned well like, but I won't last it through. Not when the ice comes. A man can't keep warm these days, Thomas. It bites into you, the cold does, bites into your marrow and I don't like it. Your father never liked it either." He was staring at Thomas now. "Your father always said you'd go away. Not to Oxford. He knew you didn't like that. Like whipping a destrier between the shafts, he used to say. He knew you'd run off and be a soldier. He always said you had wild blood in you." Sir Giles smiled, remembering. "But he also said you'd come home one day. He said you'd come back to show him what a fine fellow you'd become."

Thomas blinked back tears. Had his father really said that? "I came back this time," he said, "to ask you a question, sir. The same question, I think, that the French priest wanted to ask you."

"Questions!" Sir Giles grumbled. "I never did like questions. They need answers, see? Of course you want some ham! What do you mean, no? Gooden? Ask your daughter to unwrap that ham, will you?"

Sir Giles heaved himself to his feet and shuffled across the hall to a great chest of dark, polished oak. He raised the lid and, groaning with the effort of bending over, began to rummage through the clothes and boots that were jumbled inside. "I find now, Thomas," he went on, "that I don't need questions. I sit in the manor court every second week and I know whether they're guilty or innocent the moment they're

fetched into the hall! Mind you, we have to pretend otherwise, don't we? Now, where is it? Ah!" He found whatever
he sought and brought it back to the table. "There, Thomas,
damn your question and that's your answer." He pushed the
bundle across the table.

It was a small object wrapped in ancient sacking. Thomas
had an absurd premonition that this was the Grail itself and
was ridiculously disappointed when he discovered the bundle contained a book. The book's front cover was a soft
leather flap, four or five times larger than the pages, which
could be used to wrap the volume that, when Thomas
opened it, proved to be written in his father's hand. However, being by his father, nothing in it was straightforward.
Thomas leafed through the pages swiftly, discovering notes
written in Latin, Greek and a strange script which he thought
must be Hebrew. He turned back to the first page where only
three words were written and, reading them, felt his blood
run cold. "*Calix meus inebrians.*"

"Is it your answer?" Sir Giles asked.

"Yes, sir."

Sir Giles peered at the first page. "It's Latin that, isn't it?"

"Yes, sir."

"Thought it was. I looked, of course, but couldn't make
head nor tail of it and I didn't like to ask Sir John,"—Sir
John was the priest of St. Peter's in Dorchester—"or that
lawyer fellow, what's his name? The one who dribbles when
he gets excited. He speaks Latin, or he says he does. What
does it mean?"

" 'My cup makes me drunk,'" Thomas said.

" 'My cup makes me drunk'!" Sir Giles thought that was
splendidly funny. "Aye, your father's wits were well off the
wind. A good man, a good man, but dear me! " 'My cup
makes me drunk'!"

"It's from one of the psalms," Thomas said, turning to the

second page, which was written in the script he thought was Hebrew, though there was something odd about it. One of the recurrent symbols looked like a human eye and Thomas had never seen that in a Hebrew script before though, in all honesty, he had seen little Hebrew. "It's from the psalm, sir," he went on, "that begins by saying God is our shepherd."

"He's not my shepherd," Sir Giles grumbled. "I'm not some damned sheep."

"Nor me, sir," Robbie declared.

"I did hear"—Sir Giles looked at Robbie—"that the King of Scotland was taken prisoner."

"He was, sir?" Robbie asked innocently.

"Probably nonsense," Sir Giles replied, then he began telling a long tale about meeting a bearded Scotsman in London, and Thomas ignored the story to look through the pages of his father's book. He felt a kind of strange disappointment because the book suggested that the search for the Grail was justified. He wanted someone to tell him it was nonsense, to release him from the cup's thrall, but his father had taken it seriously enough to write this book. But his father, Thomas reminded himself, had been mad.

Mary, Gooden's daughter, brought in the ham. Thomas had known Mary since they were both children playing in puddles and he smiled a greeting at her, then saw that Robbie was gazing at her as though she was an apparition from heaven. She had dark long hair and a full mouth and Thomas was sure Robbie would be discovering more than a few rivals in Down Mapperley. He waited until Mary had gone, then held up the book. "Did my father ever talk to you about this, sir?"

"He talked of everything," Sir Giles said. "Talked like a woman, he did. Never stopped! I was your father's friend, Thomas, but I was never much of a man for religion. If he talked of it too much, I fell asleep. He liked that." Sir Giles paused to cut a slice of ham. "But your father was mad."

"You think this is madness, sir?" Thomas held up the book again.

"Your father was mad for God, but he was no fool. I never knew a man with so much common sense and I miss it. I miss the advice."

"Does that girl work here?" Robbie asked, gesturing at the screen behind which Mary had disappeared.

"All her life," Sir Giles said. "You remember Mary, Thomas?"

"I tried to drown her when we were both children," Thomas said. He turned the pages of his father's book again though he had no time now to tease any meanings from the tangled words. "You do know what this is, sir, don't you?"

Sir Giles paused, then nodded. "I know, Thomas, that many men want what your father claims to have possessed."

"So he did make that claim?"

Another pause. "He hinted at it," Sir Giles said heavily, "and I don't envy you."

"Me?"

"Because he gave me that book, Thomas, and he said that if anything happened to him I was to keep it until you were old enough and man enough to take up the task. That's what he said." Sir Giles stared at Thomas and saw his old friend's son flinch. "But if the two of you want to stay for a while," he said, "then you'd be welcome. Jake Churchill needs help. He tells me he's never seen so many fox cubs and if we don't kill some of the bastards then there'll be some rare massacres among the lambs next year."

Thomas glanced at Robbie. Their task was to find de Taillebourg and avenge the deaths of Eleanor, Father Hobbe and Robbie's brother, but it was unlikely, he thought, that the Dominican would come back here. Robbie, however, plainly wanted to stay: Mary Gooden had seen to that. And

Thomas was tired. He did not know where to seek the priest and so the chance to stay in this hall was welcome. It would be an opportunity to study the book and thus follow his father down the long, tortuous path of the Grail.

"We'll stay, sir," Thomas said.

For a while.

I T WAS THE FIRST TIME that Thomas had ever lived like a lord. Not a great lord, perhaps, not as an earl or a duke with scores of men to command, but still in privilege, ensconced in the manor—even if the manor was a thatched timber hall with a beaten earth floor—the days his to wile away as other people did life's hard work of cutting fire-wood, drawing water, milking cows, churning butter, pounding dough and washing clothes. Robbie was more used to it, but reckoned life was much easier in Dorset. "Back home," he said, "there's always some damn English raiders coming over the hill to steal your cattle or take your grain."

"Whereas you," Thomas said, "would never dream of riding south and stealing from the English."

"Why would I even think of such a thing?" Robbie asked, grinning.

So, as winter closed down on the land, they hunted Sir Giles Marriott's acres to make the fields safe for the lambing season and to bring back venison to Sir Giles's table; they drank in the Dorchester taverns and laughed at the mummers who came for the winter fair. Thomas found old friends and told them stories of Brittany, Normandy and Picardy, some of which were true, and he won the golden arrow at the fair's archery competition and he presented it to Sir Giles who hung it in the hall and declared it the finest trophy he had ever seen. "My son could shoot a good arrow. A very good arrow. I'd like to think he could have won this trophy himself."

Sir Giles's only son had died of a fever and his only daughter was married to a knight who held land in Devon and Sir Giles liked neither son-in-law nor daughter. "They'll inherit the property when I die," he told Thomas, "so you and Robbie may as well enjoy it now."

Thomas persuaded himself that he was not ignoring the search for the Grail because of the hours he spent poring over his father's book. The pages were thick vellum, expensive and rare, which showed how important these notes had been to Father Ralph, but even so they made small sense to Thomas. Much of the book was stories. One told how a blind man, caressing the cup, had received his sight but then, disappointed in the Grail's appearance, lost it again. Another told how a Moorish warrior had tried to steal the Grail and been turned into a serpent for his impiety. The longest tale in the book was about Perceval, a knight of antiquity who went on crusade and discovered the Grail in Christ's tomb. This time the Latin word used to describe the grail was *crater*, meaning bowl, whereas on other pages it was *calix*, a cup, and Thomas wondered if there was any significance in the distinction. If his father had possessed the Grail, would he not have known whether it was a cup or a bowl? Or perhaps there was no real difference. Whatever, the long tale told how the bowl had sat on a shelf of Christ's tomb in plain view of all who entered the sepulcher, both Christian pilgrims and their pagan enemies, yet not till Sir Perceval entered the grotto on his knees was the Grail actually seen by anyone, for Sir Perceval was a man of righteousness and thus worthy of having his eyes opened. Sir Perceval removed the bowl, bringing it back to Christendom where he planned to build a shrine worthy of the treasure, but, the tale laconically recorded, "he died." Thomas's father had written beneath this abrupt conclusion: "Sir Perceval was Count of Astarac and was known by another name. He married a Vexille."

"Sir Perceval!" Sir Giles was impressed. "He was a member of your family, eh? Your father never mentioned that to me. At least I don't think he did. I did sleep through a lot of his tales."

"He usually scoffed at stories like this," Thomas said.

"We often mock what we fear," Sir Giles observed sententiously. Suddenly he grinned. "Jake tells me you caught that old dog fox by the Five Marys." The Five Marys were ancient grave mounds that the locals claimed were dug by giants and Thomas had never understood why there were six of them.

"It wasn't there," Thomas said, "but back of the White Nothe."

"Back of White Nothe? Up on the cliffs?" Sir Giles stared at Thomas, then laughed. "You were on Holgate's land! You rascals!" Sir Giles, who had always complained mightily when Thomas had poached from his land, now found this predation on a neighbor hugely amusing. "He's an old woman, Holgate. So are you making head or tail of that book?"

"I wish I knew," Thomas said, staring at the name Astarac. All he knew was that Astarac was a fief or county in southern France and the home of the Vexille family before they were declared rebel and heretic. He had also learned that Astarac was close to the Cathar heartlands, close enough for the contagion to catch the Vexilles, and when, a hundred years before, the French King and the true Church had burned the heretics out of the land they had also forced the Vexilles to flee. Now it seemed that the legendary Sir Perceval was a Vexille? It seemed to Thomas that the further he penetrated the mystery the greater the entanglement. "Did my father ever talk to you of Astarac, sir?" He asked Sir Giles.

"Astarac? What's that?"

"Where his family came from."

"No, no, he grew up in Cheshire. That's what he always said."

But Cheshire had merely been a refuge, a place to hide from the Inquisition: was that where the Grail was now hidden? Thomas turned a page to find a long passage describing how a raiding column had tried to attack the tower of Astarac and had been repulsed by the sight of the Grail. "It dazzled them," Father Ralph had written, "so that 364 of them were cut down." Another page recorded that it was impossible for a man to tell a lie while he held his hand on the Grail, "or else he will be stricken dead." A barren woman would be granted the gift of children by stroking the Grail and if a man were to drink from it on Good Friday he would be vouchsafed a glimpse of "she whom he will take to wife in heaven." Another story related how a knight, carrying the Grail across a wilderness, was pursued by heathens and, when it seemed he must be caught, God sent a vast eagle that caught him, his horse and the precious Grail up into the sky, leaving the pagan warriors howling in frustrated rage.

One phrase was copied over and over in the pages of the book: "*Transfer calicem istem a me*," and Thomas could feel his father's misery and frustration reaching through the repeated phrase. "Take this cup from me," the words meant and they were the same words Christ had spoken in the Garden of Gethsemane as he pleaded with God the Father to spare him the pain of hanging on the tree. The phrase was sometimes written in Greek, a language Thomas had studied but never mastered fully; he managed to decipher most of the Greek text, but the Hebrew remained a mystery.

Sir John, the ancient vicar of St. Peter's, agreed that it was a strange kind of Hebrew. "I've forgotten all the Hebrew I ever learned," he told Thomas, "but I don't remember seeing a letter like that!" He pointed to the symbol that looked like a human eye. "Very odd, Thomas, very odd. It's almost Hebrew." He paused a while, then said plaintively, "If only poor Nathan was still here."

"Nathan?"

"He was before your time, Thomas. Nathan collected leeches and sent them to London. Physicians there prized Dorset leeches, did you know that? But, of course, Nathan was a Jew and he left with the others." The Jews had been expelled from England almost fifty years before, an event still green in the priest's memory. "No one has ever discovered where he found his leeches," Sir John went on, "and I sometimes wonder if he put a curse on them." He frowned at the book. "This belonged to your father?"

"It did."

"Poor Father Ralph," Sir John said, intimating that the book must have been the product of madness. He closed the volume and carefully wrapped the soft leather cover about the pages.

There was no sign of de Taillebourg, nor any news of Thomas's friends in Normandy. He wrote a difficult letter to Sir Guillaume which told how his daughter had died and begging for any news of Will Skeat whom Sir Guillaume had taken to Caen to be treated by Mordecai, the Jewish doctor. The letter went to Southampton and from there to Guernsey and Thomas was assured it would be sent on to Normandy, but no reply had come by Christmas and Thomas assumed the letter was lost. Thomas also wrote to Lord Outhwaite, assuring his lordship that he was being assiduous in his search and recounting some of the stories from his father's book.

Lord Outhwaite sent a reply that congratulated Thomas on what he had discovered, then revealed that Sir Geoffrey Carr had left for Brittany with half a dozen men. Rumor, Lord Outhwaite reported, claimed that the Scarecrow's debts were larger than ever, "which, perhaps, is why he has gone to Brittany." It would not just be hope of plunder that had taken the Scarecrow to La Roche-Derrien, but the law which said a debtor was not required to make repayments while he served the King abroad. "Will you follow the Scarecrow?" Lord Outhwaite inquired, and Thomas sent an answer saying he would be in La Roche-Derrien by the time Lord Outhwaite read these words, and then did nothing about leaving Dorset. It was Christmas, he told himself, and he had always enjoyed Christmas.

Sir Giles celebrated the twelve days of the feast in high style. He ate no meat from Advent Sunday, which was not a particular hardship for he loved eels and fish, but on Christmas Eve he ate nothing but bread, readying himself for the first feast of the season. Twelve empty hives were brought into the hall and decorated with sprigs of ivy and holly; a great candle, big enough to burn through the whole season, was placed on the high table and a vast log set to burn in the hearth, and Sir Giles's neighbors were invited to drink wine and ale, and eat beef, wild boar, venison, goose and brawn. The wassail cup, filled with mulled and spiced claret, was passed about the hall and Sir Giles, as he did every night of Christmas, wept for his dead wife and was drunkenly asleep by the time the candles burned out. On the fourth night of Christmas, Thomas and Robbie joined the hogglers as, disguised as ghosts and green men and wild men, they pranced about the parish extorting funds for the Church. They went as far as Dorchester, encroaching on two other parishes as they did, and got into a fight with the hogglers from All Saints' and they ended the night in the Dorchester jail from which they were released by an amused George Adyn who brought them a morning pot of ale and one of his wife's famous hog's puddings. The Twelfth Night feast was a boar that Robbie had speared, and after it was eaten, and when the guests were lying half drunk and satiated on the hall rushes, it began to snow. Thomas stood in the doorway and watched the flakes whirling in the light of a flickering torch.

"We must be away soon." Robbie had come to join him.

"Away?"

"We have work to do," the Scot said.

Thomas knew that was true, but he did not want to leave. "I thought you were happy enough here?"

"So I am," Robbie said, "and Sir Giles is more generous than I deserve."

"So?"

"It's Mary," Robbie said. He was embarrassed and did not finish.

"Pregnant?" Thomas guessed.

Robbie crossed himself. "It seems so."

Thomas stared at the snow. "If you give her enough money to make a dowry," he said, "she'll thrive."

"I've only got three pounds left," Robbie said. He had been given a purse by his uncle, Sir William, supposedly with enough money to last a year.

"That should be enough," Thomas said. The snow whirled in a gust of wind.

"It'll leave me with nothing!" Robbie protested.

"You should have thought of that before you ploughed the field," Thomas said, remembering how he had been in just this predicament with a girl in Hookton. He turned back to the hall where a harpist and flautist made music to the drunks. "We should go," he said, "but I don't know where."

"You said you wanted to go to Calais?"

Thomas shrugged. "You think de Taillebourg will seek us there?"

"I think," Robbie said, "that once he knows you have that book he'll follow you into hell itself."

Thomas knew Robbie was right, but the book was not proving to be of any great help. It never specifically said that

Father Ralph had possessed the Grail, nor described a place where a searcher might look for it. Thomas and Robbie had been looking. They had combed the sea caves in the cliffs near Hookton where they had found driftwood, limpets and seaweed. There had been no golden cup half hidden in the shingle. So where to go now? Where to look? If Thomas went to Calais then he could join the army, but he doubted de Taillebourg would seek him out in the heart of England's soldiery. Maybe, Thomas thought, he should go back to Brittany and he knew that it was not the Grail or the necessity to face de Taillebourg that attracted him to La Roche-Derrien, but the thought that Jeanette Chenier might have returned home. He thought of her often, thought of her black hair, of her fierce spirit and defiance, and every time he thought of her he suffered guilt because of Eleanor.

The snow did not last. It thawed and a hard rain came from the west to lash the Dorset coast. A big English ship was wrecked on the Chesil shingle and Thomas and Robbie took one of Sir Giles's wagons down to the beach and with the aid of Jake Churchill and two of his sons fought off a score of other men to rescue six packs of wool that they carried back to Down Mapperley and presented to Sir Giles who thereby made a year's income in one day.

And next morning the French priest came to Dorchester.

THE NEWS WAS BROUGHT by George Adyn. "I know as you said we should be watching for foreigners," he told Thomas, "and this one be real foreign. Dressed like a priest, he is, but who knows? Looks like a vagabond, he does. You say the word"—he winked at Thomas—"and we'll give the bugger a proper whipping and send him on up to Shaftesbury."

"What will they do with him there?" Robbie asked.

"Give him another whipping and send him back," George said.

"Is he a Dominican?" Thomas asked.

"How would I know? He's talking gibberish, he is. He don't talk proper, not like a Christian."

"What color is his gown?"

"Black, of course."

"I'll come and talk to him," Thomas said.

"He only jabbers away, he does. Your honor!" This was in greeting to Sir Giles, and Thomas then had to wait while the two men discussed the health of various cousins and nephews and other relatives, and it was close to midday by the time he and Robbie rode into Dorchester and Thomas thought, for the thousandth time, what a good town this was and how it would be a pleasure to live here.

The priest was brought out into the small jail yard. It was a fine day. Two blackbirds hopped along the top wall and an aconite was blooming in the yard corner. The priest proved to be a young man, very short, with a squashed nose, protuberant eyes and bristling black hair. He wore a gown so shabby, torn and stained that it was little wonder the constables had thought the man a vagrant; a misconception that made the little priest indignant. "Is this how the English treat God's servants? Hell is too good for you English! I shall tell the bishop and he will tell the Archbishop and he will inform the Holy Father and you will all be declared anathema! You will all be excommunicated!"

"See what I mean?" George Adyn asked. "Yaps away like a dog fox, but he don't make sense."

"He's speaking French," Thomas told him, then turned to the priest. "What's your name?"

"I want to see the bishop now. Here!"

"What's your name?"

"Bring me the local priest!"

"I'll punch your bloody ears out first," Thomas said. "Now what's your name?"

He was called Father Pascal, and he had just endured a

journey of exquisite discomfort, crossing the winter seas from Normandy, from a place south of Caen. He had traveled first to Guernsey and then on to Southampton from where he had walked, and he had done it all without any knowledge of English. It was a miracle to Thomas that Father Pascal had come this far. And it seemed even more of a miracle because Father Pascal had been sent to Hookton from Evecque, with a message for Thomas.

Sir Guillaume d'Evecque had sent him, or rather Father Pascal had volunteered to make the journey, and it was urgent for he was bringing a plea for help. Evecque was under siege. "It is terrible!" Father Pascal said. By now, calmed and placated, he was by the fire in the Three Cocks where he was eating goose and drinking bragget, a mixture of warmed mead and dark ale. "It is the Count of Coutances who is besieging him. The Count!"

"Why is that terrible?" Thomas inquired.

"Because the Count is his liege lord!" the priest exclaimed, and Thomas understood why Father Pascal said it was terrible. Sir Guillaume held his lands in fief to the Count and by making war on his own tenant the Count was declaring Sir Guillaume an outlaw.

"But why?" Thomas asked.

Father Pascal shrugged. "The Count says it is because of what happened at the battle. Do you know what happened at the battle?"

"I know," Thomas said, and because he was translating for Robbie he had to explain anyway. The priest referred to the battle that had been fought the previous summer by the forest at Crécy. Sir Guillaume had been in the French army, but in the middle of the fight he had seen his enemy, Guy Vexille, and had turned his men-at-arms against Vexille's troops.

"The Count says that is treason," the priest explained, "and the King has given his blessing."

Thomas said nothing for a while. "How did you know I was here?" he finally asked.

"You sent a letter to Sir Guillaume."

"I didn't think it reached him."

"Of course it did. Last year. Before this trouble started."

Sir Guillaume was in trouble, but his manor of Evecque, Father Pascal said, was built of stone and blessed with a moat and so far the Count of Coutances had found it impossible to break the wall or cross the moat, but the Count had scores of men while Sir Guillaume had a garrison of only nine. "There are some women too"—Father Pascal tore at a goose leg with his teeth—"but they don't count."

"Does he have food?"

"Plenty, and the well is good."

"So he can hold for a time?"

The priest shrugged. "Maybe? Maybe not? He thinks so, but what do I know? And the Count has a machine, a . . ." He frowned, trying to find the word.

"A trebuchet?"

"No, no, a springald!" A springald was like a massive crossbow that shot a huge dart. Father Pascal stripped the last morsel off the bone. "It is very slow and it broke once. But they mended it. It batters at the wall. Oh, and your friend is there," he mumbled, his mouth full.

"My friend?"

"Skeat, is that the name? He's there with the doctor. He can talk now, and he walks. He is much better, yes? But he cannot recognize people, not unless they speak."

"Unless they speak?" Thomas asked, puzzled.

"If he sees you," the priest explained, "he does not know you. Then you speak and he knows you." He shrugged again. "Strange, eh?" He drained his pot. "So what will you do, monsieur?"

"What does Sir Guillaume want me to do?"

"He wants you close by in case he needs to escape, but he's written a letter to the King explaining what happened in the battle. I sent the letter to Paris. Sir Guillaume thinks the King may relent so he waits for an answer, but me? I think Sir Guillaume is like this goose. Plucked and cooked."

"Did he say anything about his daughter?"

"His daughter?" Father Pascal was puzzled. "Oh! The bastard daughter? He said you would kill whoever killed her."

"I will, too."

"And that he wants your help."

"He can have it," Thomas said, "and we'll leave tomorrow." He looked at Robbie. "We're going back to war."

"Who am I fighting for?"

Thomas grinned. "Me."

* * *

THOMAS, ROBBIE and the priest left next morning. Thomas took a change of clothes, a full arrow bag, his bow, sword and mail coat and, wrapped in a piece of deerskin, his father's book that seemed like a heavy piece of baggage. In truth it was lighter than a sheaf of arrows, yet the duty its possession implied weighed on Thomas's conscience. He told himself he was merely riding to help Sir Guillaume, yet he knew he was continuing the quest for his father's secret.

Two of Sir Giles's tenants rode with them to bring back the mare that Father Pascal rode and the two stallions which Sir Giles had purchased from Thomas and Robbie. "You don't want to take them on a boat," Sir Giles said, "horses and boats don't mix."

"He paid us too much," Robbie remarked as they rode away.

"He doesn't want his son-in-law to get it," Thomas said. "Besides, he's a generous man. He gave Mary Gooden another three pounds as well. For her dowry. He's a lucky man."

Something in Thomas's tone caught Robbie's attention. " 'He' is? You mean she's found a husband?"

"A nice fellow. A thatcher in Tolpuddle. They'll be wed next week."

"Next week!" Robbie sounded aggrieved that his girl was marrying. It did not matter that he was abandoning her, it still cut his pride. "But why would he marry her?" he asked after a while. "Or doesn't he know she's pregnant?"

"He thinks the child is his," Thomas said, keeping a straight face, "and well it might be, I hear."

"Jesus!" Robbie swore when that made sense, then he turned to look back along the road and he smiled, remembering the good times. "He's a kind man," he said of Sir Giles.

"A lonely one," Thomas said. Sir Giles had not wanted them to leave, but accepted they could not stay.

Robbie sniffed the air. "There's more snow coming."

"Never!" It was a morning of gentle sunlight. Crocus and aconite were showing in sheltered spots and the hedgerows were noisy with chaffinches and robins. But Robbie had indeed smelled snow. As the day wore on, the skies became low and gray, the wind went into the east and hit their faces with a new bite and the snow followed. They found shelter in a verderer's house in the woods, crowding in with the man, his wife, five daughters and three sons. Two cows had a byre at one end of the house and four goats were tethered at the other. Father Pascal confided to Thomas that this was very like the house in which he had grown up, but he wondered if conventions in England were the same as in the Limousin. "Conventions?" Thomas asked.

"In our house," Father Pascal said, blushing, "the women pissed with the cows and the men with the goats. I would not want to do the wrong thing."

"It's the same here," Thomas assured him.

Father Pascal had proved a good companion. He had a fine singing voice and once they had shared their food with the verderer and his family the priest sang some French songs. Afterward, as the snow still fell and the smoke from the fire swirled thick under the thatch, he sat and talked with Thomas. He had been the village priest at Evecque and, when the Count of Coutances attacked, he had found refuge in the manor. "But I do not like being cooped up," he said, and so he had offered to carry Sir Guillaume's message to England. He had escaped from Evecque, he said, by first throwing his clothes across the moat and then swimming after them. "It was cold," he said, "I have never been so cold! I told myself it is better to be cold than to be in hell, but I don't know. It was terrible."

"What does Sir Guillaume want us to do?" Thomas asked him.

"He did not say. Perhaps, if the besiegers can be discouraged . . . ?" He shrugged. "The winter is not a good time for a siege, I think. Inside Evecque they are comfortable, they are warm, they have the harvest stored, and the besiegers? They are wet and cold. If you can make them more uncomfortable, who knows? Perhaps they will abandon the siege?"

"And you? What will you do?"

"I have no work left at Evecque," the priest said. Sir Guillaume had been declared a traitor and his goods pronounced forfeited so his serfs had been taken off to the Count of Coutances's estates, while his tenants, pillaged and raped by the besiegers, had mostly fled. "So perhaps I go to Paris? I cannot go to the Bishop of Caen."

"Why not?"

"Because he has sent men to help the Count of Coutances." Father Pascal shook his head in sad wonderment. "The bishop was impoverished by the English in the summer," he explained, "so he needs money, land and goods, and he hopes to get some from Evecque. Greed is a great provoker of war."

"Yet you're on Sir Guillaume's side?"

Father Pascal shrugged. "He is a good man. But now? Now I must look to Paris for preferment. Or maybe Dijon. I have a cousin there."

They struggled east for the next two days, riding across the dead heaths of the New Forest, which lay under a soft whiteness. At night the small lights of the forest villages glittered hard in the cold. Thomas feared they would reach Normandy too late to help Sir Guillaume, but that doubt was not reason enough to abandon the effort and so they struggled on. Their last few miles to Southampton were through a melting slush of mud and snow, and Thomas wondered how they were to reach Normandy, which was an enemy province. He doubted that any shipping would go there from Southampton because any English boat going close to the Normandy coast was liable to be snapped up by pirates. He knew plenty of boats would be going to Brittany, but that was a long walk from Caen. "We go through the islands, of course," Father Pascal said.

They spent one night in a tavern and next morning found space on the *Ursula*, a cog bound for Guernsey and carrying barrels of salt pork, kegs of nails, barrel staves, iron ingots, pots packed in sawdust, bolts of wool, sheaves of arrows and three crates of cattle horns. It was also carrying a dozen bowmen who were traveling to the garrison of the castle which guarded the anchorage at St. Peter Port. Come a bad west wind, the *Ursula*'s captain told them, and dozens of ships carrying wine from Gascony to England could be blown up-channel and St. Peter Port was one of their last harbors of refuge, though the French sailors knew it too and in bad weather their ships would swarm off the island trying to pick up a prize or two. "Does that mean they'll be waiting for us?" Thomas asked. The Isle of Wight was slipping astern and the ship was plunging into a winter-gray sea.

"Not waiting for us, they won't be, not us. They know the *Ursula*, they do," the captain, a toothless man with a face horribly scarred from the pox, grinned, "they do know her and they do love her." Which meant, presumably, that he had paid his dues to the men of Cherbourg and Carteret. However, he had paid no dues to Neptune or whatever spirit governed the winter sea for, though he claimed some special foreknowledge of winds and waves and asserted that both would be calm, the *Ursula* rolled like a bell swung on a beam: up and down, pitching hard over so that the cargo slid in the hold with a noise like thunder; and the evening sky was gray as death and then sleet began to seethe on the torn water. The captain, clinging to the steering oar with a grin, said it was nothing but a little blow that should not worry any good Christian, but others in his crew either touched the crucifix nailed to the single mast or else bowed their heads to a small shrine on the afterdeck where a crude wooden image was wrapped in bright ribbons. The image was supposed to be St. Ursula, the patron of ships, and Thomas said a prayer to her himself as he crouched in a small space under the foredeck, ostensibly sheltering there with the other passengers, but the overhead deck seams gaped and a mixture of rainwater and seawater continually slopped through. Three of the archers were sick and even Thomas, who had crossed the channel twice before and had been raised among fishermen and spent days aboard their small boats, was feeling ill. Robbie, who had never been to sea, looked cheerful and interested in everything that was happening aboard.

"It's these round ships," he yelled over the noise, "they roll!"

"You know about ships, do you?" Thomas asked.

"It seems obvious," Robbie said.

Thomas tried to sleep. He wrapped himself in his damp cloak, curled up and lay as still as the pitching boat would let him and, astonishingly, he did fall asleep. He woke a dozen times that night and each time he wondered where he was and when he remembered he wondered whether the night would ever end or whether he would ever be warm again.

Dawn was sickly gray and the cold bit into Thomas's bones, but the crew was altogether more cheerful for the wind had dropped and the sea was merely sullen, the long foam-streaked waves rising and falling sluggishly about a wicked group of rocks that appeared to be home for a myriad of seabirds. It was the only land in sight.

The captain stumped across the deck to stand beside Thomas. "The Casquets," he said, nodding at the rocks. "A lot of widows have been made on those old stones." He made the sign of the cross, spat over the gunwales for luck and then looked up to a widening rift in the clouds. "We're making good time," he said, "thanks be to God and to Ursula." He looked askance at Thomas. "So what takes you to the islands?"

Thomas thought of inventing some excuse, family perhaps, then thought the truth might elicit something more interesting. "We want to go on to Normandy," he said.

"They don't like Englishmen much in Normandy, not since our King paid them a visit last year."

"I was there."

"Then you'll know why they don't like us."

Thomas knew the captain was right. The English had killed thousands in Caen, then burned farms, mills and villages in a great swathe east and north. It was a cruel way to wage war, but it could persuade the enemy to come out of his strongholds and give battle. Doubtless that was why the Count of Coutances was laying Evecque's lands waste, in hope that Sir Guillaume would be enticed out of his stone walls to defend them. Except Sir Guillaume had only nine men and could not hope to face the Count in open battle. "We've business in Caen," Thomas admitted, "if we can ever reach the place."

The captain picked at a nostril, then flicked something into the sea. "Look for the troy frairs," he said.

"The what?"

"*Troy Frairs*," he said again. "It's a boat and that's her name. It's French. She ain't big, no larger than that little tub." He pointed to a small fishing boat, her hull tarred black, from which two men cast weighted nets into the broken sea about the Casquets. "A man called Ugly Peter runs the *Troy Frairs*. He might carry you to Caen, or maybe to Carteret or Cherbourg. Not that I told you that."

"Of course not," Thomas said. He supposed the captain meant that Ugly Peter commanded a boat called *Les Trois Frères*. He stared at the fishing boat and wondered what kind of life it was to drag sustenance from this hard sea. It was easier, no doubt, to smuggle wool into Normandy and wine back to the islands.

All morning they ran southward until at last they made landfall. A small island lay off to the east and a larger, Guernsey, to the west, and from both rose pillars of smoke from cooking fires that promised shelter and warm food, but though that promise fluttered in the sky, the wind backed and the tide turned and it took the rest of the day for the *Ursula* to beat down to the harbor where she anchored under the loom of the castle built on its rocky island. Thomas, Robbie and Father Pascal were rowed ashore and found respite from the cold wind in a tavern with a fire burning in a wide hearth beside which they ate fish stew and black bread washed down with a watery ale. They slept on straw-filled sacks that were home to lice.

It was four days before Ugly Peter, whose real name was Pierre Savon, put into the harbor, and another two before he was ready to leave again with a cargo of wool on which no duty would be paid. He was happy to take passengers, though only at a price which left Robbie and Thomas feeling robbed. Father Pascal was carried free on the grounds that he was a Norman and a priest which meant, according to Pierre the Ugly, that God loved him twice over and so was unlikely to sink *Les Trois Frères* so long as Father Pascal was aboard.

God must have loved the priest for he sent a gentle west wind, clear skies and calm seas so that *Les Trois Frères* seemed to fly her way to the River Orne. They went up to Caen on the tide, arriving in the morning, and once they were ashore Father Pascal offered Thomas and Robbie a blessing, then hitched up his shabby robe and began walking east to Paris. Thomas and Robbie, carrying heavy bundles of mail, weapons, arrows and spare clothing, went south through the city.

Caen looked no better than when Thomas had left it the previous year after it had been laid waste by English archers who, disregarding their King's orders to discontinue their attack, had swarmed over the river and hacked to death hundreds of men and women inside the city. Robbie stared in awe at the destruction on Île St. Jean, the newest part of Caen, which had suffered most from the English sack. Few of the burned houses had been rebuilt and there were ribs, skulls and long bones showing in the river's mud at the falling tide's margin. The shops were half bare, though a few countryfolk were in town selling food from carts and Thomas bought dried fish, bread and rock-hard cheese. Some looked askance at his bowstave, but he assured them he was a Scotsman and thus an ally of France. "They do have proper bows in Scotland, don't they?" he asked Robbie.

"Of course we do."

"Then why didn't you use them at Durham?"

"We just don't have enough," Robbie said, "and besides, we'd rather kill you bastards up close. Make sure you're

dead, see?" He stared open-mouthed at a girl carrying a pail
of milk. "I'm in love."

"If it's got tits you fall in love," Thomas said. "Now come
on." He led Robbie to Sir Guillaume's town house, the place
where he had met Eleanor, and though Sir Guillaume's crest
of three hawks was still carved in stone above the door there
was now a new banner flying over the house: a flag showing
a hump-backed boar with great tusks. "Whose flag is that?"
Thomas had crossed the small square to talk with a cooper
who was hammering an iron ring down the flanks of a new
barrel.

"It's the Count of Coutances," the cooper said, "and the
bastard's already raised our rents. And I don't care if you do
serve him." He straightened and frowned at the bowstave.
"Are you English?"

"*Écossais*," Thomas said.

"Ah!" The cooper was intrigued and leaned closer to
Thomas. "Is it true, monsieur," he asked, "that you paint
your faces blue in battle?"

"Always," Thomas said, "and our arses."

"*Formidable!*" the cooper said, impressed.

"What's he saying?" Robbie asked.

"Nothing." Thomas pointed at the oak which grew at the
center of the small square. A few shriveled leaves still clung
to the twigs. "I was hanged from that tree," he told Robbie.

"Aye, and I'm the Pope of Avignon." Robbie heaved up
his bundle. "Did you ask him where we could buy horses?"

"Expensive things, horses," Thomas said, "and I thought
we might save ourselves the bother of buying."

"We're footpads now?"

"Indeed," Thomas said. He led Robbie off the island
across the bridge where so many archers had died in the
frenzied attack, and then through the old city. That had been
less damaged than the Île St. Jean because no one had tried
to defend the narrow streets, while the castle, which had

never fallen to the English, had only suffered from cannon balls that had done little except chip the stones about the gate. A red and yellow banner flew from the castle rampart and men-at-arms, wearing the same colored livery, challenged Thomas and Robbie as they were leaving the old city. Thomas answered by saying they were Scottish soldiers seeking employment from the Count of Coutances. "I thought he'd be here," Thomas lied, "but we hear he's at Evecque."

"And getting nowhere," the guard commander said. He was a bearded man whose helmet had a great split that suggested he had taken it from a corpse. "He's been pissing at those walls for two months now and got nowhere, but if you want to die at Evecque, boys, then good luck to you."

They walked past the walls of the Abbaye aux Dames and Thomas had a sudden vision of Jeanette again. She had been his lover, but then had met Edward Woodstock, the Prince of Wales, and what chance did Thomas have after that? It had been here, in the Abbaye aux Dames, that Jeanette and the Prince had lived during the brief siege of Caen. Where was Jeanette now? Thomas wondered. Back in Brittany? Still seeking her infant son? Did she ever think of him? Or did she regret fleeing from the Prince of Wales in the belief that the Picardy battle would be lost? Perhaps, by now, she would be married again. Thomas suspected she had taken a small fortune in jewels when she had fled the English army, and a rich widow, scarce more than twenty years old, made an attractive bride.

"What happens"—Robbie interrupted his thoughts—"if they find out you're not Scottish?"

Thomas held up the two fingers of his right hand that drew the bowcord. "They cut those off."

"Is that all?"

"Those are the first things they cut off."

They walked on south through a country of small steep

hills, tight fields, thick woods and deep lanes. Thomas had never been to Evecque and, though it was not far from Caen, some of the peasants they asked had never heard of it, but when Thomas asked which way the soldiers had been going during the winter they pointed on southward. They spent their first night in a roofless hovel, a place that had evidently been abandoned when the English came in the summer and swept through Normandy.

They woke at dawn and Thomas put two arrows into a tree, just to keep in practice. He was cutting the steel heads out of the trunk when Robbie picked up the bow. "Can you teach me to use it?" he asked.

"What I can teach you," Thomas said, "will take ten minutes. But the rest will need a lifetime. I began shooting arrows when I was seven and after ten years I was beginning to get good at it."

"It can't be that difficult," Robbie protested, "I've killed a stag with a bow."

"That was a hunting bow," Thomas said. He gave Robbie one of the arrows and pointed to a willow that had stubbornly kept its leaves. "Hit the trunk."

Robbie laughed. "I can't miss!" The willow was scarcely thirty paces away.

"Go on, then."

Robbie drew the bow, glancing once at Thomas as he realized just how much strength was needed to bend the great yew stave. It was twice as stiff as the shorter hunting bows he had used in Scotland. "Jesus," he said softly as he hauled the string back to his nose and realized his left arm was trembling slightly with the tension of the weapon, but he peered down the arrow to check his aim and was about to loose when Thomas held up a hand. "You're not ready yet."

"I damn well am," Robbie said, though the words came out as grunts for the bow needed immense force to hold in the drawn position.

"You're not ready," Thomas said, "because there's four inches of the arrow sticking out in front of the bow. You have to pull it back until the arrow head touches your left hand."

"Oh, sweet Jesus," Robbie said and took a breath, nerved himself and pulled until the string was past his nose, past his eye and close by his right ear. The steel arrow head touched his left hand, but now he could no longer aim by looking down the arrow's shaft. He frowned as he realized the difficulty that implied, then compensated by edging the bow to the right. His left arm was shaking with the tension and, unable to keep the arrow drawn, he released, then twitched as the hemp string whipped along his inner left forearm. The arrow's feathers flashed white as they passed a foot from the willow's trunk. Robbie swore in amazement, then handed the bow to Thomas. "So the trick of it," he said, "is learning how to aim it?"

"The trick," Thomas said, "is not aiming at all. It's something that just happens. You look at the target and you let the arrow fly." Some archers, the lazy ones, only drew to the eye and that made them accurate, but their arrows lacked force. The good archers, the archers who drove down armies or brought down kings in shining armor, pulled the string all the way back. "I taught a woman to shoot last summer," Thomas said, taking back the bow, "and she became good. Really good. She hit a hare at seventy paces."

"A woman!"

"I let her use a longer string," Thomas said, "so the bow didn't need as much strength, but she was still good." He remembered Jeanette's delight when the hare tumbled in the grass, squealing, the arrow pinned through its haunches. Jeanette. Why was he thinking of her so much?

They walked on through a world edged white with frost. The puddles had frozen and the leafless hedgerows were outlined with a sharp white rime that faded as the sun climbed. They crossed two streams, then climbed through beechwoods toward a plateau which, when they reached it, proved to be a wild place of thin turf that had never been cut with a plough. A few gorse bushes broke the grass, but otherwise the road ran across a featureless plain beneath an empty sky. Thomas had thought that the heathland would be nothing but a narrow belt of high country and that they must soon drop into the wooded valleys again, but the road stretched on and he felt ever more like a hare on a chalk upland under the gaze of a buzzard. Robbie felt the same and the two of them left the road to walk where the gorse provided some intermittent cover.

Thomas kept looking ahead and behind. This was horse country, a firm-turfed upland where riders could go full gallop and where there were no woods or gullies in which two men on foot could hide. And the high ground seemed to extend forever.

At midday they reached a circle of standing stones, each about the height of a man and heavily encrusted with lichen. The circle was twenty yards across and one of the stones had fallen and they rested their backs against it while they took a meal of bread and cheese. "The devil's wedding party, eh?" Robbie said.

"The stones, you mean?"

"We have them in Scotland." Robbie twisted round and brushed fragments of snail shell from the fallen stone. "They're people who were turned into rocks by the devil."

"In Dorset," Thomas said, "folk say that God turned them into stone."

Robbie wrinkled his face at that idea. "Why would God do that?"

"For dancing on the sabbath."

"They'd just go to hell for that," Robbie said, then idly scratched at the turf with his heel. "We dig the stones up when we have the time. Look for gold, see?"

"You ever find any?"

"We do in the mounds sometimes. Pots anyway, and beads. Rubbish really. We throw it away as often as not. And we find elf stones, of course." He meant the mysterious stone arrow heads that were supposedly shot from elfin bowstrings. He stretched out, enjoying the feeble warmth of the sun that was now as high as it would climb in the midwinter sky. "I miss Scotland."

"I've never been."

"God's own country," Robbie said forcefully, and he was still talking about Scotland's wonders when Thomas fell gently asleep. He dozed, then was woken because Robbie had kicked him.

The Scot was standing on the fallen stone. "What is it?" Thomas asked.

"Company."

Thomas stood beside him and saw four horsemen a mile or more to the north. He dropped back to the turf, pulled upon his bundle and took out a single sheaf of arrows, then hooked the bowstring over the nocked tips of the stave. "Maybe they haven't seen us," he said optimistically.

"They have," Robbie commented, and Thomas climbed onto the stone again to see that the horsemen had left the road; they had stopped now and one of them stood in his stirrups to get a better look at the two strangers at the stone circle. Thomas could see they were wearing mail coats under their cloaks. "I can take three of them," he said, patting the bow, "if you manage the fourth."

"Ah, be kind to a poor Scotsman," Robbie said, drawing his uncle's sword, "leave me two. I have to make money, remember." He might have been facing a fight with four horsemen in Normandy, but he was still a prisoner of Lord Outhwaite and so bound to pay his ransom that had been set at a mere two hundred pounds. His uncle's was ten thousand and in Scotland the Douglas clan would be worrying how to raise it.

The horsemen still watched Thomas and Robbie, doubtless wondering who and what they were. The riders would not be fearful; after all they were mailed and armed and the two strangers were on foot and men on foot were almost certainly peasants and peasants were no threat to horsemen in armor. "A patrol from Evecque?" Robbie wondered aloud.

"Probably." The Count of Coutances would have men roaming the country looking for food. Or perhaps the horsemen were reinforcements riding to the Count's aid, but whoever they were they would regard any stranger in this countryside as prey for their weapons.

"They're coming," Robbie said as the four men spread into a line. The riders must have assumed the two strangers would try to escape and so were making the line to snare them. "The four horsemen, eh?" Robbie said. "I can never remember what the fourth one is."

"Death, war, pestilence and famine," Thomas said, putting the first arrow on the string.

"It's famine I always forget," Robbie said. The four riders were a half-mile away, swords drawn, cantering on the fine solid turf. Thomas was holding the bow low so they would not be ready for the arrows. He could hear the hoofbeats now and he thought of the four horsemen of the apocalypse, the dreadful quartet of riders whose appearance would presage the end of time and the last great struggle between heaven and hell. War would appear on a horse the color of blood, famine would be on a black stallion, pestilence would ravage the world on a white mount while death would ride the pale horse. Thomas had a sudden memory of his father sitting bolt upright, head back, intoning the Latin: "*et ecce equus pallidus.*" Father Ralph used to say the words to annoy his housekeeper and lover, Thomas's mother, who, though she knew no Latin, understood that the words were about death and hell and she thought, rightly as it turned out, that her priest lover was inviting hell and death to Hookton.

"Behold a pale horse," Thomas said. Robbie gave him a puzzled look. " 'I saw a pale horse,'" Thomas quoted, " 'and the name of its rider was Death, and Hell followed him.'"

"Is hell another of the riders?" Robbie asked.

"Hell is what these bastards are about to get," Thomas said and he brought up the bow and dragged back the cord and felt a sudden anger and hate in his heart for the four men, and then the bow sounded, the cord's note hard and deep, and before the sound had died he was already plucking a second arrow from where he had stuck a dozen point-down in the turf. He hauled the cord back and the four horsemen were still riding straight for them as Thomas aimed at the left-hand rider. He loosed, took a third arrow, and now the sound of the hooves on the frost-hardened turf was as loud as the Scottish drums at Durham and the second man from the right was thrashing left and right, falling back, an arrow jutting from his chest and the rider on the left was lying back on his saddle's cantle, and the other two, at last understanding their danger, were swerving to throw off Thomas's aim. Gobbets of earth and grass were thrown up from the horses' hooves as they slewed away. If the two unwounded riders had any sense, Thomas thought, they would ride away as though Hell and Death were on their heels, ride back the way they had come in a desperate bid to escape the arrows, but instead, with the rage of men who had been challenged by what they believed to be an inferior enemy, they curved back toward their prey and Thomas let the third arrow fly. The first two men were both out of it, one fallen from his saddle and the other lolling on his horse that just cropped the winter-pale turf; and the third arrow flew hard and straight at its victim, but his galloping horse tossed up its head and the arrow slid down the side of its skull, blood bright on the black hide: the horse twisted away from the pain and the rider, unready for the turn, was flailing for balance, but Thomas had no time to watch him for the fourth rider was inside the stone circle and closing on him. The man had a vast black cloak that billowed behind as he turned the pale gray horse and he shouted his defiance as he stretched out the sword to whip the point like a lance head into Thomas's chest, but Thomas had his fourth arrow on the cord and the man suddenly understood that he was a split second too late. "*Non!*" he shouted, and Thomas did not even draw the bow fully back, but let it fly off the half-string and the arrow still had enough force to bury itself in the man's head, splitting the bridge of his nose and driving deep into his skull. He twitched, his sword arm dropped, Thomas felt the wind as the man's horse thundered past him and then the rider fell back over the stallion's rump.

The third man, the one unseated from the black horse, had fallen in the stone circle's center and now approached Robbie. Thomas plucked an arrow from the turf. "No!" Robbie called. "He's mine."

Thomas relaxed the string.

"*Chien bâtard,*" the man said to Robbie. He was much older than the Scotsman and must have taken Robbie for a mere boy for he half smiled as he came fast forward to lunge his sword and Robbie stepped back, parried, and the blades rang like bells in the clear air. "*Bâtard!*" the man spat and attacked again.

Robbie stepped back once more, yielding ground until he had almost reached the stone ring, and his retreat worried Thomas who had stretched his string again, but then Robbie parried so fast and riposted so quickly that the Frenchman was going backward in a sudden and desperate hurry. "You English bastard," Robbie said. He swung his blade low and the man dropped his own blade to parry and Robbie just kicked it aside and lunged so that his uncle's blade sank into the man's neck. "Bastard English bastard," Robbie snarled, ripping the blade free in a spray of bright blood. "Bloody

English pig!" He freed the sword and swung it back to bury its edge in what was left of the man's neck.

Thomas watched the man fall. Blood was bright on the grass. "He wasn't English," Thomas said.

"It's just a habit when I fight," Robbie said. "It's the way my uncle trained me." He stepped toward his victim. "Is he dead?"

"You half cut off his head," Thomas said, "what do you think?"

"I think I'll take his money," Robbie said and knelt beside the dead man.

One of the first two men to be struck by Thomas's arrows was still alive. The breath bubbled in his throat and showed pink and frothy at his lips. He was the man lolling in his saddle and he moaned as Thomas spilled him down to the ground.

"Is he going to live?" Robbie had crossed to see what Thomas was doing.

"Christ, no," Thomas said and took out his knife.

"Jesus!" Robbie stepped back as the man's throat was cut. "Did you have to?"

"I don't want the Count of Coutances to know there are only two of us," Thomas said. "I want the Count of Coutances to be as scared as hell of us. I want him to think the devil's own horsemen are hunting his men."

They searched the four corpses and, after a lumbering chase, managed to collect the four horses. From the bodies and the saddlebags they took close to eighteen pounds of bad French silver coinage, two rings, three good daggers, four swords, a fine mail coat that Robbie claimed to replace his own, and a gold chain that they hacked in half with one of the captured swords. Then Thomas used the two worst swords to picket a pair of the horses beside the road and on the horses' backs he tied two of the corpses so that they hung in the saddle, bending sideways with vacant eyes and white skin laced with blood. The other two corpses, stripped of their mail, were placed on the road and in each of their dead mouths Thomas put sprigs of gorse. That gesture meant nothing, but to whoever found the bodies it would suggest something strange, even Satanic. "It'll worry the bastards," Thomas explained.

"Four dead men should give them a twitch," Robbie said.

"They'll be scared to hell if they think the devil's loose," Thomas said. The Count of Coutances would scoff if he knew there were only two young men come as reinforcements for Sir Guillaume d'Evecque, but he could not ignore four corpses and hints of weird ritual. And he could not ignore death.

To which end, when the corpses were arranged, Thomas took the big black cloak, the money and the weapons, the best of the stallions and the pale horse.

For the pale horse belonged to Death.

And with it Thomas could make nightmares.

A SINGLE SHORT BURST of thunder sounded as Thomas and Robbie neared Evecque. They did not know how close they were, but they were riding through country where all the farms and cottages had been destroyed which told Thomas that they must be within the manor's boundaries. Robbie, on hearing the rumble, looked puzzled for the sky immediately above them was clear, although there were dark clouds to the south. "It's too cold for thunder," he said.

"Maybe it's different in France?"

They left the road and followed a farm track that twisted through woods and petered out beside a burned building that still smoked gently. It made little sense to burn such steadings and Thomas doubted that the Count of Coutances had initially ordered the destruction, but Sir Guillaume's long defiance and the bloody-mindedness of most soldiers would ensure that the pillage and burning would happen anyway. Thomas had done the same in Brittany. He had listened to the screams and protests of families who had to watch their homes being burned and then he had touched the fire to the thatch. It was war. The Scots did it to the English, the English to the Scots, and here the Count of Coutances was doing it to his own tenant.

A second clap of thunder sounded and just after its echo

had died Thomas saw a great veil of smoke in the eastern sky. He pointed to it and Robbie, recognizing the smear of campfires and realizing the need for silence, just nodded. They left their horses in a thicket of hazel saplings and then climbed a long wooded hill. The setting sun was behind them, throwing their shadows long on the dead leaves. A woodpecker, red-headed and wings barred white, whirred loud and low above their heads as they crossed the ridge line to see the village and manor of Evecque beneath them.

Thomas had never seen Sir Guillaume's manor before. He had imagined it would be like Sir Giles Marriott's hall with one great barn-like room and a few thatched outbuildings, but Evecque was much more like a small castle. At the corner closest to Thomas it even had a tower: a square and not very tall tower, but properly crenellated and flying its banner of three stooping hawks to show that Sir Guillaume was not yet beaten. The manor's saving feature, though, was its moat, which was wide and thickly covered with a vivid green scum. The manor's high walls rose sheer from the water and had few windows, and those were nothing but arrow slits. The roof was thatched and sloped inward to a small courtyard. The besiegers, whose tents and shelters lay in the village to the north of the manor, had succeeded in setting fire to the roof at some point, but Sir Guillaume's few defenders must have managed to extinguish the flames for only one small portion of the thatch was missing or blackened. None of those defenders was visible now, though some of them must have been peering though the arrow slits that showed as small black specks against the gray stone. The only visible damage to the manor was some broken stones at one corner of the tower where it looked as though a giant beast had nibbled at the masonry, and that was probably the work of the springald that Father Pascal had mentioned, but the oversized crossbow had obviously broken again and irremediably for Thomas could see it lying in two gigantic pieces in the field beside the tiny stone village church. It had done very little damage before its main beam broke and Thomas wondered if the eastern, hidden side of the building had been hurt more. The manor's entrance must be on that far side and Thomas suspected the main siege works would also be there.

Only a score of besiegers was in sight, most doing nothing more threatening than sitting outside the village houses, though a half-dozen men were gathered around what looked like a small table in the churchyard. None of the Count's men was closer to the manor than a hundred and fifty paces, which suggested that the defenders had succeeded in killing some of their enemies with crossbows and the rest had learned to give the garrison a wide berth. The village itself was small, not much bigger than Down Mapperley, and, like the Dorset village, had a watermill. There were a dozen tents to the south of the houses and twice as many little turf shelters and Thomas tried to work out how many men could be sheltered in the village, tents and turf huts and decided the Count must now have about 120 men.

"What do we do?" Robbie asked.

"Nothing for now. Just watch."

It was a tedious vigil for there was little activity beneath them. Some women carried pails of water from the watermill's race, others were cooking on open fires or collecting clothes that had been spread out to dry over some bushes at the edge of the fields. The Count of Coutances's banner, showing the black boar on a white field spangled with blue flowers, flew on a makeshift staff outside the largest house in the village. Six other banners hung above the thatched rooftops, showing that other lords had come to share the plunder. A half-dozen squires or pages exercised some warhorses in the meadow behind the encampment, but otherwise Evecque's attackers were doing little except wait. Siege work was boring work. Thomas remembered the idle days outside La Roche-Derrien, though those long hours had been broken by the terror and excitement of the occasional assault. These men, unable to assault Evecque's walls because of the moat, could only wait and hope to starve the garrison into surrender or else tempt it into a sally by burning farms. Or perhaps they were waiting for a long piece of seasoned wood to repair the broken arm of the abandoned springald.

Then, just as Thomas was deciding that he had seen enough, the group of men who had been gathered about what he had thought was a low table beside the churchyard hedge suddenly ran back toward the church.

"What in God's name is that?" Robbie asked, and Thomas saw that it had not been a table they were crowding round, but a vast pot cradled in a heavy wooden frame.

"It's a cannon," Thomas said, unable to hide his awe, and just then the gun fired and the great metal pot and its huge wooden cradle both vanished inside a swelling burst of dirty smoke and, out of the corner of his eye, he saw a piece of stone fly away from the damaged corner of the manor. A thousand birds flew up from hedgerows, thatch and trees as the gun's booming thunder rolled up the hill and washed past him. That vast clap of sound was the thunder they had heard earlier in the afternoon. The Count of Coutances had managed to find a gun and was using it to nibble away at the manor. The English had used guns at Caen last summer, though not all the guns in their army, nor all the best efforts of the Italian gunners, had hurt Caen's castle. Indeed, as the smoke slowly cleared from the encampment, Thomas saw that this shot had made little impact on the manor. The noise seemed more violent than the missile itself, yet he supposed that if the Count's gunners could fire enough stones then eventually the masonry must give way and the tower collapse into the moat to make a rubble causeway across the water. Stone by stone, fragment by fragment, maybe three or four shots a day, and thus the besiegers would undermine the tower and make their rough path into Evecque.

A man rolled a small barrel out of the church, but another man waved him back and the barrel was taken back inside. The church had to be their powder store, Thomas thought, and the man had been sent back because the gunners had shot their last missile for the day and would not reload until morning. And that suggested an idea, but he pushed it away as impractical and stupid.

"Have you seen enough?" he asked Robbie.

"I've never seen a gun before," Robbie said, staring down at the distant pot as if hoping that it would be fired again, but Thomas knew it was unlikely that the gunners would discharge it again this evening. It took a long time to charge a cannon and, once the black powder was packed into its belly and the missile put into the neck, the gun had to be sealed with damp loam. The loam would confine the explosion that propelled the missile and it needed time to dry before the gun was fired, so it was unlikely that there would be another shot before morning. "It sounds more trouble than it's worth," Robbie said sourly when Thomas had explained it. "So you reckon they'll not fire again?"

"They'll wait till morning."

"I've seen enough then," Robbie said and they crawled back through the beeches until they were over the ridge, then went down to their picketed horses and rode into the falling night. There was a half-moon, cold and high, and the night was bitter, so bitter they decided they must risk a fire, though they did their best to hide it by taking refuge in a deep gully with rock walls where they made a crude roof of boughs covered in hastily cut turfs. The fire flickered through the holes in the roof to light the rock walls red, but Thomas doubted that any of the besiegers would patrol the woods in the dark. No one willingly went into deep trees at night for all kinds of beasts and monsters and ghosts stalked the woodlands, and that thought reminded Thomas of the summer journey he had made with Jeanette when they had slept night after night in the woods. It had been a happy time and the remembrance of it made him feel sorry for himself and then, as ever, guilty for Eleanor's sake and he held his hands to the small fire. "Are there green men in Scotland?" he asked Robbie.

"In the woods, you mean? There are goblins. Evil little bastards, they are." Robbie made the sign of the cross and, in case that was not sufficient, leaned over and touched the iron hilt of his uncle's sword.

Thomas was thinking of goblins and other creatures, things that waited in the night woods. Did he really want to go back to Evecque tonight? "Did you notice," he said to Robbie, "that no one in Coutances's camp seemed very disturbed that four of their horsemen hadn't returned? We didn't see anyone going looking for them, did we?"

Robbie thought about it, then shrugged. "Maybe the horsemen didn't come from the camp?"

"They did," Thomas said with a confidence he did not entirely feel and for a moment he guiltily wondered if the four horsemen had nothing to do with Evecque, then reminded himself that the riders had initiated the fight. "They must have come from Evecque," he said, "and they'll be worried there by now."

"So?"

"So will they have put more sentries on their camp tonight?"

Robbie shrugged. "Does it matter?"

"I'm thinking," Thomas said, "that I have to tell Sir Guillaume that we're here, and I don't know how to do that except by making a big noise."

"You could write a message," Robbie suggested, "and put it round an arrow?"

Thomas stared at him. "I don't have parchment," he said

patiently, "and I don't have ink, and have you ever tried shooting an arrow wrapped up in parchment? It would probably fly like a dead bird. I'd have to stand by the moat and it would be easier to throw the arrow from there."

Robbie shrugged. "So what do we do?"

"Make a noise. Announce ourselves." Thomas paused. "And I'm thinking that the cannon will break the tower down eventually if we don't do something."

"The cannon?" Robbie asked, then stared at Thomas. "Sweet Jesus," he said after a while as he thought of the difficulties. "Tonight?"

"Once Coutances and his men know we're here," Thomas said, "they'll double their sentries, but I'll bet the bastards are half asleep tonight."

"Aye, and wrapped up warm if they've any damn sense," Robbie said. He frowned. "But that gun looked like a rare great pot. How the hell do you break it?"

"I was thinking of the black powder in the church," Thomas said.

"Set fire to it?"

"There're plenty of campfires in the village," Thomas said and he wondered what would happen if they were captured in the enemy encampment, but it was pointless to worry about that. If the gun was to be made useless then it was best to strike before the Count of Coutances knew an enemy had come to harass him, and that made this night the ideal opportunity. "You don't have to come," Thomas told Robbie. "It's not as if your friends are inside the manor."

"Hold your breath," Robbie said scornfully. He frowned again. "What's going to happen afterward?"

"Afterward?" Thomas thought. "It depends on Sir Guillaume. If he gets no answer from the King then he'll want to break out. So he has to know we're here."

"Why?"

"In case he needs our help. He did send for us, didn't he?

Sent for me, anyway. So we go on making a noise. We make ourselves a nuisance. We give the Count of Coutances some nightmares."

"The two of us?"

"You and me," Thomas said, and the saying of it made him realize that Robbie had become a friend. "I think you and I can make trouble," he added with a smile. And they would begin this night. In this bitter and cold night, beneath a hard-edged moon, they would conjure the first of their nightmares.

THEY WENT ON FOOT and despite the bright half-moon it was dark under the trees and Thomas began to worry about whatever demons, goblins and specters haunted these Norman woods. Jeanette had told him that in Brittany there were *nains* and *gorics* that stalked the dark, while in Dorset it was the Green Man who stamped and growled in the trees behind Lipp Hill, and the fishermen spoke of the souls of the drowned men who would sometimes drag themselves on shore and moan for the wives they had left behind. On All Soul's Eve the devil and the dead danced on Maiden Castle, and on other nights there were lesser ghosts in and about the village and up on the hill and in the church tower and wherever a man looked, which was why no one left his house at night without a scrap of iron or a piece of mistletoe or, at the very least, a piece of cloth that had been touched by a holy wafer. Thomas's father had hated that superstition, but when his people had lifted their hands for the sacrament and he saw a scrap of cloth tied about their palms he had not refused them.

And Thomas had his own superstitions. He would only ever pick up the bow with his left hand; the first arrow to be shot from a newly strung bow had to be tapped three times against the stave, once for the Father, once for the Son and a third time for the Holy Spirit; he would not wear white clothes and he put his left boot on before his right. For a long time he had worn a dog's paw about his neck, then had thrown it away in the conviction it brought ill luck, but now, after Eleanor's death, he wondered if he should have kept it. Thinking of Eleanor, his mind slid back to the darker beauty of Jeanette. Did she remember him? Then he tried not to think of her, because thinking of an old love might bring ill luck and he touched the bole of a tree as he passed to cleanse away the thought.

Thomas was looking for the red glow of dying campfires beyond the trees that would tell him that they were close to Evecque, but the only light was the silver of the moon tangled in the high branches. *Nains* and *gorics*: what were they? Jeanette had never told him, except to say they were spirits that haunted the country. They must have something similar here in Normandy. Or perhaps they had witches? He touched another tree. His mother had firmly believed in witches and his father had instructed Thomas to say his paternoster if he ever got lost. Witches, Father Ralph had believed, preyed upon lost children, and later, much later, Thomas's father had told him that witches began their invocation of the devil by saying the paternoster backward and Thomas, of course, had tried it though he had never dared finish the whole prayer. *Olam a son arebil des*, the backward paternoster began, and he could say it still, even managing the difficult reversals of *temptationem* and *supersubstantialem*, though he was careful never to finish the whole prayer in case there was a stench of brimstone, a crack of flame and the terror of the devil descending on black wings with eyes of fire.

"What are you muttering?" Robbie asked.

"I'm trying to say *supersubstantialem* backward," Thomas said.

Robbie chuckled. "You're a strange one, Thomas."

"*Melait nats bus repus*," Thomas said.

"Is that French?" Robbie said. "Because I have to learn it."

"You will," Thomas promised him, then at last he glimpsed fires between the trees and they both went silent as they climbed the long slope to the crest among the beeches that overlooked Evecque.

No lights showed from the manor. A clean and cold moonlight glistened on the green-scummed moat that looked smooth as ice—perhaps it was ice?—and the white moon threw a black shadow into the damaged corner of the tower, while a glow of firelight showed on the manor's farther side, confirming Thomas's suspicion that there was a siege work opposite the building's entrance. He guessed that the Count's men had dug trenches from which they could douse the gateway with crossbow bolts as other men tried to bridge the moat where the drawbridge would be missing. Thomas remembered the crossbow bolts spitting from the walls of La Roche-Derrien and he shivered. It was bitter cold. Soon, Thomas thought, the dew would turn to frost, silvering the world. Like Robbie he was wearing a wool shirt beneath a leather jerkin and a coat of mail over which he had a cloak, yet still he was shivering and he wished he was back in the shelter of their gully where the fire burned.

"I can't see anyone," Robbie said.

Nor could Thomas, but he went on looking for the sentries. Maybe the cold was keeping everyone under a roof? He searched the shadows near the guttering campfires, watched for any movement in the darkness about the church and still saw no one. Doubtless there were sentinels in the siege works opposite the manor entrance, but surely they would be watching for any defender trying to sneak out of the back of the manor? Except who would swim a moat on a night this cold? And the besiegers were surely bored by now and their watchfulness would be low. He saw a silver-edged cloud sailing closer to the moon. "When the cloud covers the moon," he told Robbie, "we go."

"And God bless us both," Robbie said fervently, making the sign of the cross. The cloud seemed to move so slowly, then at last it veiled the moon and the glimmering landscape faded into gray and black. There was still a wan, faint light, but Thomas doubted the night would get any blacker and so he stood, brushed the twigs off his cloak and started toward the village along a track that had been beaten across the eastern slope of the ridge. He guessed the path had been made by pigs being taken to get fat on the beechmast in the woods and he remembered how Hookton's pigs had roamed the shingle eating fish heads and how his mother had always claimed it tainted the taste of their bacon. Fishy bacon, she had called it, and compared it unfavorably with the bacon of her native Weald in Kent. That, she had always said, had been proper bacon, nourished on beechmast and acorn, the best. Thomas stumbled on a tussock of grass. It was difficult to follow the track because the night suddenly seemed much darker, perhaps because they were on lower ground.

He was thinking of bacon and all the time they were getting closer to the village and Thomas was suddenly scared. He had seen no sentries, but what about dogs? One barking bitch in the night and he and Robbie could be dead men. He had not brought the bow, but suddenly wished he had—though what could he do with it? Shoot a dog? At least the path was easily visible now for it was lit by the campfires and the two of them walked confidently as though they belonged in the village. "You must do this all the time," Thomas said to Robbie softly.

"This?"

"When you raid across the border."

"Hell, we stay in the open country. Go after cattle and horses."

They were among the shelters now and stopped talking. A

sound of deep snoring came from one small turf hut and an unseen dog whined, but did not bark. A man was sitting in a chair outside a tent, presumably guarding whoever slept inside, but the guard himself was asleep. A small wind stirred the branches in an orchard by the church and the stream made a splashing noise as it plunged over the little weir beside the mill. A woman laughed softly in one of the houses where some men began to sing. The tune was new to Thomas and the deep voices smothered the sound of the churchyard gate, which squealed as he pushed it open. The church had a small wooden belfry and Thomas could hear the wind sighing on the bell. "Is that you, Georges?" a man called from the porch.

"*Non*." Thomas spoke more curtly than he intended, and the tone brought the man out from the black shadows of the porch's arch and Thomas, thinking he had initiated trouble, put his hand behind his back to grasp the hilt of his dagger.

"Sorry, sir." The man had mistaken Thomas for an officer, maybe even a lord. "I've been expecting a relief, sir."

"He's probably still sleeping," Thomas said.

The man stretched, yawning hugely. "The bastard never wakes up." The sentry was little more than a shadow in the dark, but Thomas sensed he was a big man. "And it's cold here," the man went on, "God, but it's cold. Did Guy and his men come back?"

"One of their horses threw a shoe," Thomas said.

"That's what it was! And I thought they'd found that ale shop in Saint-Germain. Christ and his angels, but that girl with the one eye! Have you seen her?"

"Not yet," Thomas said. He was still holding his dagger, one of the weapons that the archers called a misericord because it was used to put unhorsed and wounded men-at-arms out of their misery. The blade was slender and sufficiently flexible to slide between the joints of armor and seek out the life beneath, but he was reluctant to draw it. This sentry suspected nothing and his only offense was to want a long conversation. "Is the church open?" Thomas asked the sentry.

"Of course. Why not?"

"We have to pray," Thomas said.

"Must be a guilty conscience that makes men pray at night, eh?" The sentry was affable.

"Too many one-eyed girls," Thomas said. Robbie, not speaking French, stood to one side and stared at the great black shadow of the gun.

"A sin worth repenting," the man chuckled, then he drew himself up. "Would you wait here while I wake Georges? It won't take a moment."

"Take as long as you like," Thomas said grandly, "we shall be here till dawn. You can let Georges sleep if you want. The two of us will keep watch."

"You're a living saint," the man said, then he fetched his blanket from the porch before walking away with a cheerful goodnight. Thomas, when the man was gone, walked into the porch where he immediately kicked an empty barrel that rolled over with a great clatter. He swore and went still, but no one called from the village to demand an explanation for the noise.

Robbie crouched beside him. The dark was impenetrable in the porch, but they groped with their hands to discover a half-dozen empty barrels. They stank of rotten eggs and Thomas guessed they had once held black powder. He whispered to Robbie the gist of the conversation he had held with the sentry. "But what I don't know," he went on, "is whether he's going to wake Georges or not. I don't think so, but I couldn't tell."

"Who does he think we are?"

"Two men-at-arms probably," Thomas said. He pushed the empty barrels aside, then stood and groped for the rope that lifted the latch of the church door. He found it, then winced as the hinges squealed. Thomas could still see nothing, but the church had the same sour stench as the empty barrels. "We need some light," he whispered. His eyes slowly became accustomed to the gloom and he saw the faintest glimmer of light showing from the big eastern window over the altar. There was not even a small flame burning above the sanctuary where the wafers were kept, presumably because it was too dangerous with the gunpowder being stored in the nave. Thomas found the powder easily enough by bumping into the stack of barrels that were just inside the door. There were at least two score of them each about the size of a water pail, and Thomas guessed the cannon used one or maybe two barrels for each shot. Say three or four shots a day? So maybe there was two weeks' supply of powder here. "We need some light," he said again, turning, but Robbie made no response. "Where are you?" Thomas hissed the question, but again there was no answer and then he heard a boot thump hollow against one of the empty barrels in the porch and he saw Robbie's shadow flicker in the clouded moonlight of the graveyard.

Thomas waited. A campfire smoldered not far beyond the thorn hedge that kept cattle out of the village's graves and he saw a shadow crouch beside the dying flames and then there was a sudden flare of brightness, like summer lightning, and Robbie reeled back and then Thomas, dazzled and alarmed by the flare, could see nothing. He had gone to the church door and he expected to hear a shout from one of the men in the village, but instead he heard only the squeal of the gate and the Scotsman's footsteps. "I used an empty barrel," Robbie said, "except it wasn't as empty as I thought. Or else the powder gets into the wood."

He was standing in the porch and the barrel was in his hands; he had used it to scoop up some embers. The powder residue had flared, burning his eyebrows, and now fire leaped up the barrel's inside. "What do I do with it?" he asked.

"Christ!" Thomas imagined the church exploding. "Give it to me," he said, and he took the barrel, which was hot to the touch, and he ran with it into the church, his way lit by the flames, and he thrust the burning wood deep between two stacks of full barrels. "Now we get out," he said to Robbie.

"Did you look for the poor box?" Robbie said. "Only if we're going to smash the church, we might as well take the poor box."

"Come on!" Thomas snatched Robbie's arm and dragged him through the porch.

"It's a waste to leave it," Robbie said.

"There's no bloody poor box," Thomas said, "the village is full of soldiers, you idiot!"

They ran, dodging between graves and pounding past the bulbous cannon, which lay in its wooden firing cradle. They climbed a fence that filled a gap in the thorn hedge, then sprinted past the gaunt shape of the broken springald and the turf-roofed shelters, not caring if they made a noise, and two dogs began to bark, then a third howled at them and a man jumped up from beside the entrance of one of the big tents. "*Qui va là?*" he called, and began to wind his crossbow, but Thomas and Robbie were already past him and out in the open field where they stumbled on the uneven turf. The moon came from behind the cloud and Thomas could see his breath like a mist.

"*Halte!*" the man shouted.

Thomas and Robbie stopped. Not because the man had given them the order, but because a red light was filling the world. They turned and stared, and the sentry who had challenged them now forgot them as the night became scarlet.

Thomas was not sure what he had expected. A lance of flame to pierce the heavens? A great noise like thunder? Instead the noise was almost soft, like a giant's inrush of breath, and a soft blossoming flame spilled from the church windows as though the gates of hell had just been opened and the fires of death were filling the nave, but that great red glow only lasted an instant before the roof of the church lifted off and Thomas distinctly saw the black rafters splaying apart like butchered ribs. "Sweet Jesus Christ," he blasphemed.

"God in His heaven," Robbie said, wide-eyed.

Now the flames and smoke and air were boiling above the cauldron of the unroofed church, and still new barrels exploded, one after the other, each one pulsing a wave of fire and fumes into the sky. Neither Thomas nor Robbie knew it, but the powder had needed stirring because the heavier saltpeter found its way to the bottom of the barrels and the lighter charcoal was left at the top and that meant much of the powder was slow to catch the fire, but the explosions were serving to mix the remaining powder that pulsed bright and scarlet to spew a red cloud over the village.

Every dog in Evecque was barking or howling, and men, women and children were crawling from their beds to stare at the hellish glow. The noise of the explosions rolled across the meadows and echoed from the manor walls and startled hundreds of birds up from their roosts in the woodlands. Debris splashed in the moat, throwing up sharp-edged shards of thin ice that mirrored the fire so it seemed the manor was surrounded by a lake of sparkling flame.

"Jesus," Robbie said in awe, then the two of them ran on toward the beech trees at the high eastern side of the pastureland.

Thomas began to laugh as he stumbled up the path to the trees. "I'll go to hell for that," he said, stopping among the beeches and making the sign of the cross.

"For burning a church?" Robbie was grinning, his eyes reflecting the brightness of the fires. "You should see what we did to the Black Canons at Hexham! Christ, half Scotland will be in hell for that one."

They watched the fire for a few moments, then turned into

the darkness of the woods. Dawn was not far off. There was a lightness in the east where a wan gray, pale as death, edged the sky. "We have to go deeper into the forest," Thomas said, "we have to hide."

Because the hunt for the saboteurs was about to start and in the first light, as the smoke still made a great pall above Evecque, the Count of Coutances sent twenty horsemen and a pack of hounds to find the men who had destroyed his store of powder, but the day was cold, the ground hard with frost and the quarry's small scent faded early. Next day, in his petulance, the Count ordered his forces to make an attack. They had been readying gabions—great basketwork tubes woven from willow that were filled with earth and stones—and the plan was to fill the moat with the gabions and then swarm over the resultant bridge to assault the gatehouse. The gateway lacked its drawbridge which had been taken down early in the siege to leave an open and inviting archway which was blocked by nothing more than a low stone barricade.

The Count's advisers told him there were not enough gabions, that the moat was deeper than he thought, that the time was not propitious, that Venus was in the ascendant and Mars in the decline, and that he should, in brief, wait until the stars smiled on him and the garrison was hungrier and more desperate, but the Count had lost face and he ordered the assault anyway and his men did their best. They were protected so long as they held the gabions, for the earth-filled baskets were proof against any crossbow bolt, but once the gabions were thrown into the moat the attackers were exposed to Sir Guillaume's six crossbowmen who were sheltering behind the low stone wall that had been built across the manor's entrance arch where the drawbridge had once been. The Count had crossbowmen of his own and they were protected by pavises, full-length shields carried by a second man to protect the archer while he laboriously wound the

cord of the crossbow, but the men throwing the gabions had
no protection once their burdens were thrown and eight of
them died before the rest realized that the moat really was
too deep and that there were not nearly enough gabions. Two
pavise-holders and a crossbowman were badly wounded before the Count accepted he was wasting his time and called
the attackers back. Then he cursed Sir Guillaume on the
fourteen hump-backed devils of St. Candace before getting
drunk.

Thomas and Robbie survived. On the day after they had
burned the Count's powder Thomas shot a deer, and next
day Robbie discovered a rotting hare in a gap in a hedge and
when he pulled the body out discovered a snare that must
have been set by one of Sir Guillaume's tenants who had either been killed or chased off by the Count's men. Robbie
washed the snare in a stream and set it in another hedge and
next morning found a hare choking in the tightening noose.

They dared not sleep in the same place two nights running, but there was plenty of shelter in the deserted and
burned-out farms. They spent most of the next weeks in the
country south of Evecque where the valleys were deeper, the
hills steeper and the woods thicker. Here there were plenty
of hiding places and it was in that tangled landscape that
they made the Count's nightmare worse. Tales began to be
told in the besiegers' encampment of a tall man in black on a
pale horse and whenever the man on the pale horse appeared, someone would die. The death would be caused by a
long arrow, an English arrow, yet the man on the horse had
no bow, only a staff topped by a deer's skull, and everyone
knew what creature rode the pale horse and what a skull on a
pole denoted. The men who had seen the apparition told
their womenfolk in the Count's encampment and the womenfolk cried to the Count's chaplain and the Count said they
were dreaming, but the corpses were real enough. Four
brothers, come from distant Lyons to earn money by serving

in the siege, packed their belongings and went. Others threatened to follow. Death stalked Evecque.

The Count's chaplain said folk were touched by the moon and he rode into the dangerous south country, loudly chanting prayers and scattering holy water, and when the chaplain survived unscathed the Count told his men they had been fools, that there was no Death riding a pale horse, and next day two men died only this time they were in the east. The tales grew in the telling. The horseman was now accompanied by giant hounds whose eyes glowed, and the horseman did not even need to appear to explain any misfortune. If a horse tripped, if a man broke a bone, if a woman spilled food, if a crossbow string snapped, then it was blamed on the mysterious man who rode the pale horse.

The confidence of the besiegers plunged. There were mutterings of doom and six men-at-arms went south to seek employment in Gascony. Those who remained grumbled that they did the devil's work and nothing the Count of Coutances did seemed to restore his men's spirits. He tried cutting back trees to stop the mysterious archer shooting into the camp, but there were too many trees and not enough axes, and the arrows still came. He sent to the Bishop of Caen who wrote a blessing on a piece of vellum and sent it back, but that had no effect on the black-cloaked rider whose appearance presaged death, and so the Count, who fervently believed he did God's work and feared to fail in case he incurred God's wrath, now appealed to God for help.

He wrote to Paris.

LOUIS BESSIÈRES, Cardinal Archbishop of Livorno, a city he had only seen once when he traveled to Rome (on his return, he had made a detour so he would not be forced to see Livorno a second time), walked slowly down the Quai des Orfèvres on the Île de la Cité in Paris. Two servants went ahead of him, using staves to clear the way for the Cardinal who appeared not to be paying attention to the lean, hollow-cheeked priest who spoke to him so urgently. The Cardinal, instead, examined the wares on offer in the goldsmiths' shops lining the quai that was named for their trade: Goldsmith's Quay. He admired a necklace of rubies and even considered buying it, but then discovered a flaw in one of the stones. "So sad," he murmured, then moved to the next shop. "Exquisite!" he exclaimed of a salt cellar made in silver and emblazoned with four panels on which pictures of country life were enameled in blue, red, yellow and black. A man ploughed on one panel and broadcast seed on the next, a woman cut the harvest on the third while on the last panel the two sat at table admiring a glowing loaf of bread. "Quite exquisite," the Cardinal enthused, "don't you think it beautiful?"

Bernard de Taillebourg scarcely gave the salt cellar a glance. "The devil is at work against us, your eminence," he said angrily.

"The devil is always at work against us, Bernard," the Cardinal said reprovingly, "that is the devil's job. There would be something desperately amiss in the world if the devil were not at work against us." He caressed the salt cellar, running his fingers over the delicate curves of the panels, then decided the shape of the base was not quite right. Something crude there, he thought, a clumsiness in the design and, with a smile for the shopkeeper, he put it back on the table and strolled on. The sun shone; there was even some warmth in the winter air and a sparkle on the Seine. A legless man with wooden blocks on his stumps swung on short crutches across the road and held out a dirty hand toward the Cardinal whose servants rushed at the man with their staves. "No, no!" the Cardinal called and felt in his purse for some coins. "God's blessing on you, my son," he said. Cardinal Bessières liked giving alms, he liked the melting gratitude on the faces of the poor, and he especially liked their look of relief when he called off his servants a heart-beat before they used their staves. Sometimes the Cardinal paused just a fraction too long and he liked that too. But to-day was a warm, sunlit day stolen from a gray winter and so he was in a kindly mood.

Once past the Sabot d'Or, a tavern for scriveners, he turned away from the river into the tangle of alleys that twisted about the labyrinthine buildings of the royal palace. Parliament, such as it was, met here, and the lawyers scuttled the dark passages like rats, yet here and there, piercing the gloom, gorgeous buildings reared up to the sun. The Cardinal loved these alleys and had a fancy that shops magically disappeared overnight to be replaced by others. Had that laundry always been there? And why had he never noticed the bakery? And surely there had been a lute-makers' business beside the public privy? A furrier hung bear coats from a rack and the Cardinal paused to feel the pelts. De Taillebourg still yapped at him, but he scarcely listened.

Just past the furrier's was an archway guarded by men in blue and gold livery. They wore polished breastplates, plumed helmets and carried pikes with brightly polished blades. Few folk got past them, but the guards hastily stepped back and bowed as the Cardinal passed. He gave them a benevolent wave suggestive of a blessing, then followed a damp passage into a courtyard. This was all royal land now and the courtiers offered the Cardinal respectful bows for he was more than a cardinal, he was also Papal Legate to the throne of France. He was God's ambassador and Bessières looked the part for he was a tall man, strongly built and burly enough to overawe most men without his scarlet robes. He was good-looking and knew it, and vain, which he pretended he did not know, and he was ambitious, which he hid from the world but not from himself. After all, a cardinal archbishop had only one more throne to mount before he came to the crystal steps of the greatest throne of all and Bernard de Taillebourg seemed the unlikely instrument that might give Louis Bessières the triple crown for which he yearned.

And so the Cardinal wearily turned his attention to the Dominican as the two left the courtyard and climbed the stairs into the Sainte-Chapelle. "Tell me"—Bessières broke into whatever de Taillebourg had been saying—"about your servant. Did he obey you?"

De Taillebourg, so rudely interrupted, took a few seconds to adjust his thoughts, then he nodded. "He obeyed me in all things."

"He showed humility?"

"He did his best to show humility."

"Ah! So he still has pride?"

"It is ingrained in him," de Taillebourg said, "but he fought it."

"And he did not desert you?"

"No, your eminence."

"So he is back here in Paris?"

"Of course," de Taillebourg said curtly, then realized what tone he had used. "He is at the friary, your eminence," he added humbly.

"I wonder whether we should show him the undercroft again?" the Cardinal suggested as he walked slowly toward the altar. He loved the Sainte-Chapelle, loved the light that flooded between the high slender pillars. This was, he thought, as close to heaven as man came on earth: a place of supple beauty, overwhelming brightness and enchanting grace. He wished he had thought to order some singing, for the sound of eunuchs' voices piercing the high fanwork of the chapel's stones could take a man very close to ecstasy. Priests were running to the high altar, knowing what it was that the Cardinal had come to see. "I do find," he went on, "that a few moments in the undercroft compel a man to seek God's grace."

De Taillebourg shook his head. "He has been there already, your eminence."

"Take him again." There was a hardness in the Cardinal's voice now. "Show him the instruments. Show him a soul on the rack or under the fire. Let him know that hell is not confined to Satan's realm. But do it today. We may have to send you both away."

"Send us away?" De Taillebourg sounded surprised.

The Cardinal did not enlighten him. Instead he knelt before the high altar and took off his scarlet hat. He rarely, and only reluctantly, removed the hat in public for he was uncomfortably aware that he was going bald, but it was necessary now. Necessary and awe-inspiring, for one of the priests had opened the reliquary beneath the altar and brought out the purple cushion with its lace fringe and golden tassels, which he now presented to the Cardinal. And on the cushion lay the crown. It was so old, so fragile, so black and so very brittle that the Cardinal held his breath as he reached for it. The very earth seemed to stop in its motion, all sounds went silent, even heaven was still as he reached and then touched and then lifted the crown that was so light it seemed to have scarce any weight at all.

It was the crown of thorns.

It was the very crown that had been crammed onto Christ's head where it became imbued with his sweat and blood, and the Cardinal's eyes filled with tears as he raised it to his lips and kissed it gently. The twigs, woven into the spiky circlet, were spindly. They were frail as a wren's leg bones, yet the thorns were sharp still, as sharp as the day when they had been raked over the Savior's head to pour blood down His precious face, and the Cardinal lifted the crown high, using two hands, and he marveled at its lightness as he lowered it onto his thinning scalp to let it rest there. Then, hands clasped, he stared up at the golden cross on the altar.

He knew the clergy of Sainte-Chapelle disliked his coming here and wearing the crown of thorns. They had complained of it to the Archbishop of Paris and the Archbishop had whined to the King, but Bessières still came because he had the power to come. He had the Pope's delegated power and France needed the Pope's support. England was besieging Calais and Flanders was warring in the north and all of Gascony was now again swearing allegiance to Edward of England and Brittany was in revolt against its rightful French Duke and seethed with English bowmen. France was assailed and only the Pope could persuade the powers of Christendom to come to its aid.

And the Pope would probably do that, for the Holy Father was himself French. Clement had been born in the Limousin and had been Chancellor of France before being elected to the throne of St. Peter and installed in the great papal palace at Avignon. And there, in Avignon, Clement listened to the Romans who tried to persuade him to move the papacy back to their eternal city. They whispered and plotted, bribed and whispered again, and Bessières feared that Clement might one day give in to those wheedling voices.

But if Louis Bessières became Pope then there would be no more talk of Rome. Rome was a ruin, a pestilent sewer surrounded by petty states forever at war with each other, and God's Vicar on earth could never be safe there. But while Avignon was a good refuge for the papacy, it was not perfect because the city and its county of Venaissin both belonged to the kingdom of Naples, and the Pope, in Louis Bessières's view, should not be a tenant.

Nor should the Pope live in some provincial city. Rome had once ruled the world so the Pope had belonged in Rome, but in Avignon? The Cardinal, the thorns resting so lightly on his brow, stared up at the great blue and scarlet of the passion window above the altar; he knew which city deserved the papacy. Only one. And Louis Bessières was certain that, once he was Pope, he could persuade the King of France to yield the Île de la Cité to the Holy Father and so Cardinal Bessières would bring the papacy north and give it a new and glorious refuge. The palace would be his home, the Cathedral of Notre Dame would be his new St. Peter's and this glorious Sainte-Chapelle his private shrine where the crown of thorns would be his own relic. Perhaps, he thought, the thorns should be incorporated into the Pope's triple crown. He liked that idea, and he imagined praying here on his private island. The goldsmiths and the beggars, the lawyers and the whores, the laundries and the lute-makers would be sent across the bridges to the rest of Paris and the Île de la Cité would become a holy place. And then the Vicar of Christ would have the power of France always at his side and so the kingdom of God would spread and the infidel would be slain and there would be peace on earth.

But how to become Pope? There were a dozen men who wanted to succeed Clement, yet Bessières alone of those rivals knew of the Vexilles, and he alone knew that they had once owned the Holy Grail and might, perhaps, own it still.

Which was why Bessières had sent de Taillebourg to Scotland. The Dominican had returned empty-handed, but he had learned some things. "So you do not think the Grail is in England?" Bessières now asked him, keeping his voice low so that the Sainte-Chapelle's priests could not overhear their conversation.

"It may be hidden there," de Taillebourg sounded gloomy, "but it is not in Hookton. Guy Vexille searched the place when he raided it. We looked again and it is nothing but ruins."

"You still think Sir Guillaume took it to Evecque?"

"I think it possible, your eminence," de Taillebourg said. Then: "Not likely," he qualified the answer, "but possible."

"The siege goes badly. I was wrong about Coutances. I offered him a thousand fewer years in purgatory if he captured

Evecque by St. Timothy's Day, but he does not have the vigor to press a siege. Tell me about this bastard son."

De Taillebourg made a dismissive gesture. "He is nothing. He doubts the Grail even exists. All he wants is to be a soldier."

"An archer, you tell me?"

"An archer," de Taillebourg confirmed.

"I think you are wrong about him. Coutances writes to say that their work is being impeded by an archer. One archer who shoots long arrows of the English type."

De Taillebourg said nothing.

"One archer," the Cardinal pressed on, "who probably destroyed Coutances's whole stock of black powder. It was the only supply in Normandy! If we want more it will have to be brought from Paris."

The Cardinal lifted the crown from his head and placed it on the cushion. Then, slowly, reverently, he pressed his forefinger against one of the thorns and the watching priests leaned forward. They feared he was trying to steal one of the thorns, but the Cardinal was only drawing blood. He winced as the thorn broke his skin, then he lifted his finger to his mouth and sucked. There was a heavy gold ring on the finger and hidden beneath the ruby, which was cunningly hinged, was a thorn he had stolen eight months before. Sometimes, in the privacy of his bed chamber, he scratched his forehead with the thorn and imagined being God's deputy on earth. And Guy Vexille was the key to that ambition. "What you will do," he ordered de Taillebourg when the taste of the blood was gone, "is show Guy Vexille the undercroft again to remind him what hell awaits him if he fails us. Then go with him to Evecque."

"You'd send Vexille to Evecque?" De Taillebourg could not hide his surprise.

"He is ruthless and he is cruel," the Cardinal said as he stood and put on his hat, "and you tell me he is ours. So we shall spend money and we shall give him black powder and enough men to crush Evecque and bring Sir Guillaume to the undercroft." He watched as the crown of thorns was taken back to its reliquary. And soon, he thought, in this chapel, in this place of light and glory, he would have a greater prize. He would have a treasure to bring all Christendom and its riches to his throne of gold. He would have the Grail.

THOMAS AND ROBBIE were both filthy; their clothes were caked with dirt; their mail coats were snagged with twigs, dead leaves and earth; and their hair was uncut, greasy and matted. At night they shivered, the cold seeping into the marrow of their souls, but by day they had never felt so alive for they played a game of life and death in the small valleys and tangled woods about Evecque. Robbie, clad in a swathing black cloak and carrying the skull on its pole, rode the white horse to lead Coutances's men into ambush where Thomas killed. Sometimes Thomas merely wounded, but he rarely missed for he was shooting at close range, forced to it by the thickness of the woods, and the game reminded him of the songs the archers liked to sing and the tales their women told about the army's campfires. They were the songs and tales of the common folk, ones never sung by the troubadours, and they told of an outlaw called Robin Hood. It was either Hood or Hude, Thomas was not sure for he had never seen it written down, but he knew Hood was an English hero who had lived a couple of hundred years before and his enemies had been England's French-speaking nobility. Hood had fought them with an English weapon, the war bow, and today's nobility doubtless thought the stories were subversive which was why no troubadour sung them in the great halls. Thomas had sometimes thought he might write them down himself, except no one ever wrote in English. Every book Thomas had ever seen was in Latin or French. But why should the Hood songs not be put between covers?

Some nights he told the Hood tales to Robbie as the two of them shivered in whatever poor shelter they had found, but the Scotsman thought the stories dull things. "I prefer the tales of King Arthur," he said.

"You have those in Scotland?" Thomas asked, surprised.

"Of course we do!" Robbie said. "Arthur was Scots."

"Don't be so bloody daft!" Thomas said, offended.

"He was a Scotsman," Robbie insisted, "and he killed the bloody English."

"He was English," Thomas said, "and he'd probably never heard of the bloody Scots."

"Go to hell," Robbie snarled.

"I'll see you there first," Thomas spat and thought that if he ever did write the Hood tales he would have the legendary bowman go north and spit a few Scots on some honest English arrows.

They were both ashamed of their tempers next morning. "It's because I'm hungry," Robbie said, "I'm always short-tempered when I'm hungry."

"And you're always hungry," Thomas said.

Robbie laughed, then heaved the saddle onto his white horse. The beast shivered. Neither horse had eaten well and they were both weak so Thomas and Robbie were being cautious, not wanting to be trapped in open country where the Count's better horses could outrun their two tired destriers. At least the weather had turned less cold, but then great bands of rain swept in from the western ocean and for a week it poured down and no English bow could be drawn in such weather. The Count of Coutances would doubtless be beginning to believe that his chaplain's holy water had driven the pale horse from Evecque and so spared his men, but his enemies were also spared for no more powder had come for the cannon and now the meadows about the moated house were so waterlogged that trenches flooded and the besiegers were wading through mud. Horses developed hoof rot and men stayed in their shelters shivering with fever.

At every dawn Thomas and Robbie rode first to the woods south of Evecque and there, on the side of the manor where the Count had no entrenchments and only a small sentry post, they stood at the edge of the trees and waved. They had received an answering wave on the third morning that they signaled the garrison, but after that there was nothing until the week of the rain. Then, on the morning after they had argued about King Arthur, Thomas and Robbie waved to the manor and this time they saw a man appear on the roof. He raised a crossbow and shot high into the air. The quarrel was not aimed at the sentry post and if the men on guard there even saw its flight they did nothing, but Thomas watched it fall into the pasture where it splashed in a puddle and skidded through the wet grass.

They did not ride out that day. Instead they waited until evening, until the darkness had fallen, and then Thomas and Robbie crept to the pasture and, on hands and knees, searched the thick wet grass and old cowdung. It seemed to take them hours, but at last Robbie found the bolt and discovered there was a waxed packet wrapped about the short shaft. "You see?" Robbie said when they were back in their shelter and shivering beside a feeble fire. "It can be done." He gestured at the message wrapped about the quarrel. To make the bolt fly the message had been whipped to the shaft with cotton cord that had shrunk and Thomas had to cut it free, then he unwrapped the waxed parchment and held it close to the fire so he could read the message, which had been written with charcoal. "It's from Sir Guillaume," Thomas said, "and he wants us to go to Caen."

"Caen?"

"And we're to find a"—Thomas frowned and held the let-

ter with its crabbed handwriting even closer to the flames—
"we're to find a shipmaster called Pierre Villeroy."

"I wonder if that's Ugly Peter," Robbie put in.

"No," Thomas said, peering close at the parchment, "this
man's ship is called the *Pentecost*, and if he's not there we're
to look for Jean Lapoullier or Guy Vergon." Thomas was
holding the message so close to the fire that it began to
brown and curl as he read the last words aloud. "Tell
Villeroy I want the *Pentecost* ready by St. Clement's Day
and he must provision for ten passengers going to Dunkirk.
Wait with him, and we shall meet you in Caen. Set a fire in
the woods tonight to show you have received this."

That night they did set a fire in the woods. It blazed
briefly, then rain came and the fire died, but Thomas was
sure the garrison would have seen the flames.

And by dawn, wet, tired and filthy, they were back in
Caen.

THOMAS AND ROBBIE searched the city's quays but
there was no sign of Pierre Villeroy or of his ship, the *Pentecost*, but a tavern-keeper reckoned Villeroy was not far away.
"He carried a cargo of stone to Cabourg," the man told
Thomas, "and he reckoned he should be back today or tomorrow, and the weather won't have held him up." He
looked askance at the bowstave. "Is that a goddamn bow?"
He meant an English bow.

"Hunting bow from Argentan," Thomas said carelessly
and the lie satisfied the tavern-keeper for there were some
men in every French community who could use the long
hunting bow, but they were very few and never enough to
coalesce into the kind of army that turned hillsides red with
noble blood.

"If Villeroy's back today," the man said, "he'll be drinking
in my tavern tonight."

"You'll point him out to me?" Thomas asked.

"You can't miss Pierre," the man laughed, "he's a giant! A giant with a bald head, a beard you could breed mice in and a poxed skin. You'll recognize Pierre without me."

Thomas reckoned that Sir Guillaume would be in a hurry when he reached Caen and would not want to waste time coaxing horses onto the *Pentecost*, therefore he spent the day haggling about prices for the two stallions and that night, flush with money, he and Robbie returned to the tavern. There was no sign of a big-bearded giant with a bald head, but it was raining, they were both chilled and reckoned they might as well wait and so they ordered eel stew, bread and mulled wine. A blind man played a harp in the tavern's corner, then began singing about sailors and seals and the strange sea beasts that rose from the ocean floor to howl at the waning moon. Then the food arrived and just as Thomas was about to taste it a stocky man with a broken nose crossed the tavern floor and planted himself belligerently in front of Thomas. He pointed at the bow. "That's an English bow," the man said flatly.

"It's a hunting bow from Argentan," Thomas said. He knew it was dangerous to carry such a distinctive weapon and last summer, when he and Jeanette had walked from Brittany to Normandy, he had disguised the bowstave as a pilgrim's staff, but he had been more careless on this visit. "It's just a hunting bow," he repeated casually, then flinched because the eel stew was so hot.

"What does the bastard want?" Robbie asked.

The man heard him. "You're English."

"Do I sound English?" Thomas asked.

"So how does he sound?" The man pointed to Robbie. "Or has he lost his tongue now?"

"He's Scottish."

"Oh, I'm sure, and I'm the goddamn Duke of Normandy."

"What you are," Thomas said mildly, "is a goddamn nuisance," and he heaved the bowl of soup into the man's face and kicked the table into his groin. "Get out!" he told Robbie.

"Christ, I love a fight!" Robbie said. A half-dozen of the scalded man's friends were charging across the floor and Thomas hurled a bench at their legs, tripping two, and Robbie swung his sword at another man.

"They're English!" the scalded man shouted from the floor. "They're Goddamns!" The English were hated in Caen.

"He's calling you English," Thomas told Robbie.

"I'll piss down his throat," Robbie snarled, kicking the scalded man in the head, then he punched another man with the hilt of his sword and was screaming his Scottish war cry as he advanced on the survivors.

Thomas had snatched up their baggage and his bowstave and pulled open a door. "Come on!" he shouted.

"Call me English, you tosspots!" Robbie challenged. His sword was holding the attackers at bay, but Thomas knew they would summon their courage and charge home and Robbie would almost certainly have to kill one to escape and then there would be a hue and cry and they would be lucky not to end dangling at rope ends from the castle battlements, so he just dragged Robbie backward through the tavern door. "Run!"

"I was enjoying that," Robbie insisted and tried to head back into the tavern, but Thomas pulled him hard away and then shoulder-charged a man coming into the alley.

"Run!" Thomas shouted again and pushed Robbie toward the Île's center. They dodged into an alley, sprinted across a small square and finally went to ground in the shadows of the porch of St. Jean's church. Their pursuers searched for a few minutes, but the night was cold and the patience of the hunters limited.

"There were six of them," Thomas said.

"We were winning!" Robbie said truculently.

"And tomorrow," Thomas said, "when we're supposed to be finding Pierre Villeroy or one of the others, you'd rather be in Caen's jail?"

"I haven't punched a man since the fight at Durham," Robbie said, "not properly."

"What about the hoggling fight in Dorchester?"

"We were too drunk. Doesn't count." He started to laugh. "Anyway, you started it."

"I did?"

"Aye," Robbie said, "you chucked the eel stew right in his face! All that stew."

"I was only trying to save your life," Thomas pointed out. "Christ! You were talking English in Caen! They hate the English!"

"So they should," Robbie said, "so they should, but what am I supposed to do here? Keep my mouth shut? Hell! It's my language too. God knows why it's called English."

"Because it is English," Thomas said, "and King Arthur spoke it."

"Sweet Jesus!" Robbie said, then laughed again. "Hell, I hit that one fellow so hard he won't know what day it is when he wakes up."

They found shelter in one of the many houses that were still abandoned after the savagery of the English assault in the summer. The house's owners were either far away, or more likely their bones were in the big common grave in the churchyard or mired in the river's bed.

Next morning they went down to the quays again. Thomas remembered wading through the strong current as the crossbowmen fired from the moored ships. The quarrels had spat up small fountains of water and, because he dared not get his bowstring wet, he had not been able to shoot back. Now he and Robbie walked down the quays to discover the *Pentecost* had magically appeared in the night. She was as big a ship as any that made it upriver, a ship capable of crossing to England with a score of men and horses aboard, but she was high and dry now as the falling tide stranded her on the mud. Thomas and Robbie gingerly crossed the narrow gangplank to hear a monstrous snoring coming from a small fetid cabin in the stern. Thomas fancied the deck itself vibrated every time the man drew breath and he wondered how any creature who made such a sound would react to being woken, but just then a waif of a girl, pale as a dawn mist and thin as an arrow, climbed from the cabin hatch and put some clothes on the deck and a finger to her lips. She looked very fragile and, as she pulled up her robe to tug on stockings, showed legs like twigs. Thomas doubted she could have been more than thirteen years old.

"He's sleeping," she whispered.

"So I hear," Thomas said.

"Sh!" She touched her finger to her lips again then hauled a thick woolen shirt over her night-gown, put her thin feet into huge boots and wrapped herself in a big leather coat. She pulled a greasy woolen hat over her fair hair and picked up a bag that appeared to be made of ancient frayed sail-cloth. "I'm going to buy food," she said quietly, "and there's a fire to be made in the forepeak. You'll find a flint and steel on the shelf. Don't wake him!"

With that warning she tiptoed off the ship, swathed in her great coat and boots, and Thomas, appalled at the depth and loudness of the snoring, decided discretion was the best course. He went to the forepeak where he found an iron brazier standing on a stone slab. A fire was already laid in the brazier and, after opening the hatch above to serve as a chimney, he struck sparks from the flint. The kindling was damp, but after a while the fire caught and he fed it scraps of wood so that by the time the girl came back there was a respectable blaze. "I'm Yvette," she said, apparently incurious as to who Thomas and Robbie were, "Pierre's wife," she explained, then fetched out a huge blackened pan onto which she broke twelve eggs. "Do you want to eat too?" she asked Thomas.

"We'd like to."

"You can buy some eggs from me," she said, nodding at her sailcloth bag, "and there's some ham and bread in there. He likes his ham."

Thomas looked at the eggs whitening on the fire. "Those are all for Pierre?"

"He's hungry in the morning," she explained, "so why don't you cut the ham? He likes it thick." The ship suddenly creaked and rolled slightly on the mud. "He's awake," Yvette said, taking a pewter plate from the shelf. There was a groan from the deck, then footsteps and Thomas backed out of the forepeak and turned to find the biggest man he had ever seen.

Pierre Villeroy was a foot taller than Thomas's bow. He had a chest like a hogshead, a smoothly bald pate, a face terribly scarred by the childhood pox and a beard in which a hare could have become lost. He blinked at Thomas. "You've come to work," he grunted.

"No, I brought you a message."

"Only we've got to start soon," Villeroy said in a voice that seemed to rumble from some deep cavern.

"A message from Sir Guillaume d'Evecque," Thomas explained.

"Have to use the low tide, see?" Villeroy said. "I've three tubs of moss in the hold. I've always used moss. My father did. Others use shredded hemp, but I don't like it, don't like it at all. Nothing works half as well as fresh moss. It holds, see? And mixes better with the pitch." His ferocious face suddenly creased into a gap-toothed smile. "*Mon caneton!*" he declared as Yvette brought out his plate heaped with food.

Yvette, his duckling, provided Thomas and Robbie with

two eggs apiece, then produced two hammers and a pair of strange iron instruments that looked like blunt chisels. "We're caulking the seams," Villeroy explained, "so I'll heat the pitch and you two can ram moss between the planks." He scooped a mess of egg yolk into his mouth with his fingers. "Have to do it while the ship's high and dry between tides."

"But we've brought you a message," Thomas insisted.

"I know you have. From Sir Guillaume. Which means he wants the *Pentecost* for a voyage and what Sir Guillaume wants he gets because he's been good to me, he has, but the *Pentecost* ain't no good to him if she sinks, is she? Ain't no good down on the seabed with all the drowned mariners, is she? She has to be caulked. My darling and I almost drowned ourselves yesterday, didn't we, my duckling?"

"She was taking on water," Yvette agreed.

"Gurgling away, it was," Villeroy declared loudly, "all the way from Cabourg to here, so if Sir Guillaume wants to go somewhere then you two had better start work!" He beamed at them above his vast beard, which was now streaked with egg yolk.

"He wants to go to Dunkirk," Thomas said.

"Planning on making a run for it, is he?" Villeroy mused aloud. "He'll be over that moat and on his horses and up and away before the Count of Coutances knows what year it is."

"Why Dunkirk?" Yvette wondered.

"He's joining the English, of course," Villeroy said without out a trace of any resentment for that presumed betrayal by Sir Guillaume. "His lord has turned against him, the bishops is pissing down his gullet and they do say the King has a finger in the pie, so he might as well change sides now. Dunkirk? He'll be joining the siege of Calais." He scooped more eggs and ham into his mouth. "So when does Sir Guillaume want to sail?"

"St. Clement's Day," Thomas said.

"When's that?"

None of them knew. Thomas knew which day of the month was the feast of St. Clement, but he did not know how many days away that was, and that ignorance gave him an excuse to avoid what he was certain would be a disgustingly messy, cold and wet job. "I'll find out," he said, "and be back to help you."

"I'll come with you," Robbie volunteered.

"You stay here," Thomas said sternly, "Monsieur Villeroy has a job for you."

"A job?" Robbie had not understood the earlier conversation.

"It's nothing much," Thomas reassured him, "you'll enjoy it!"

Robbie was suspicious. "So where are you going?"

"To church, Robbie Douglas," Thomas said, "I'm going to church."

THE ENGLISH HAD CAPTURED Caen the previous summer, then occupied the city just long enough to rape its women and plunder its wealth. They had left Caen battered, bleeding and shocked, but Thomas had stayed when the army marched away. He had been sick and Dr. Mordecai had treated him in Sir Guillaume's house and later, when Thomas had been well enough to walk, Sir Guillaume had taken him to the Abbaye aux Hommes to meet Brother Germain, the head of the monastery's scriptorium and as wise a man as any Thomas had ever met. Brother Germain would certainly know when St. Clement's Day was, but that was not the only reason Thomas was going to the abbey. He had realized that if any man could understand the strange script in his father's notebook it was the old monk, and the thought that perhaps this morning he would find an answer to the Grail's mystery gave Thomas a pang of excitement. That surprised him. He often doubted the Grail's existence and even more frequently wished the cup would pass from him, but now, suddenly, he felt the thrill of the hunt. More, he was suddenly overwhelmed with the solemnity of the quest, so much so that he stopped walking and stared into the shimmering light reflected from the river and tried to recall his vision of fire and gold in the northern English night. How stupid to doubt, he thought suddenly. Of course the Grail existed! It was just waiting to be found and so bring happiness to a broken world.

"Mind out!" Thomas was startled from his reverie by a man pushing a barrow of oyster shells who barged past him. A small dog was tied to the barrow and it lunged at Thomas, snapping ineffectually at his ankles before yelping as the rope dragged it onward. Thomas was hardly aware of man or dog. Instead he was thinking that the Grail must hide itself from the unworthy by giving them doubts. To find it, then, all he had to do was believe in it and, perhaps, to request a little help from Brother Germain.

A porter accosted Thomas in the abbey's gateway, then immediately suffered a coughing fit. The man doubled over, gasped for breath, then straightened slowly and blew his nose onto his fingers. "I've caught my death," he wheezed, "that's what it is, I've caught my death." He hawked up a gob of mucus and spat it toward the beggars by the gate. "The scriptorium's that way," he said, "past the cloister."

Thomas made his way to the sunlit room where a score of monks stood at tall, sloping desks. A small fire burned in a central hearth, ostensibly to keep the ink from freezing, but the high room was still cold enough for the monks' breath to mist above their parchments. They were all copying books and the stone chamber clicked and scratched with the sound of the quills. Two novice monks were pounding powder for paints at a side table, another was scraping a lambskin and a fourth was sharpening goose quills, all of them nervous of Brother Germain who sat on a dais where he worked at his own manuscript. Germain was old and small, fragile and bent, with wispy white hair, milky myopic eyes and a bad-tempered expression. His face had been just three inches from his work until he heard Thomas's footsteps, then he abruptly looked up and, though he could not see well, he did at least observe that his unannounced visitor had a sword at his side. "What business does a soldier have in God's house?" Brother Germain snarled. "Come to finish what the English started last summer?"

"I have business with you, brother," Thomas said. The scratching of the quills had abruptly ceased as the monks tried to overhear the conversation.

"Work!" Brother Germain snapped at the monks. "Work! You are not translated to heaven yet! You have duties, attend to them!" Quills rattled in ink pots and the scratching and pounding and scraping began again. Brother Germain looked alarmed as Thomas stepped up onto the dais. "Do I know you?" he snarled.

"We met last summer. Sir Guillaume brought me to see you."

"Sir Guillaume!" Brother Germain, startled, laid his quill down. "Sir Guillaume? I doubt we'll see him again! Ha! Mewed up by Coutances, that's what I hear, and a good thing. You know what he did?"

"Coutances?"

"Sir Guillaume, you fool! He turned against the King in Picardy! Turned against the King. He made himself a traitor. He was always a fool, always risking his neck, but now he'll be lucky to keep his head. What's that?"

Thomas had unwrapped the book and now placed it on the desk. "I was hoping, brother," he said humbly, "that you could make some sense of—"

"You want me to read it, eh? Never learned yourself and now you think I have nothing better to do than read some nonsense so you can determine its value?" Folk who could not read sometimes came into possession of books and brought them to the monastery to have them valued, hoping against hope that some collection of pious advice might turn out to be a rare book of theology, astrology or philosophy. "What did you say your name was?" Brother Germain demanded.

"I didn't," Thomas said, "but I'm called Thomas."

The name held no apparent memories for Brother Germain, but nor was he interested any longer for he was immersed in the book, mouthing words under his breath, turning pages with long white fingers, lost in wonder, and then he leafed back to the first page and read the Latin aloud. " '*Calix meus inebrians*.' " He breathed the words as if they were sacred, then made the sign of the cross and turned to the next page which was in the strange Hebrew script and he became even more excited. " 'To my son,' " he said aloud, evidently translating, " 'who is the son of the Tirshatha and the grandson of Hachaliah.' " He turned his short-sighted eyes on Thomas. "Is that you?"

"Me?"

"Are you the grandson of Hachaliah?" Germain asked and, despite his bad eyesight, he must have detected the puzzlement on Thomas's face. "Oh, never mind!" he said impatiently. "Do you know what this is?"

"Stories," Thomas said. "Stories of the Grail."

"Stories! Stories! You're like children, you soldiers. Mindless, cruel, uneducated and greedy for stories. You know what this script is?" He poked a long finger at the strange letters which were dotted with the eye-like symbols. "You know what it is?"

"It's Hebrew, isn't it?"

" 'It's Hebrew, isn't it?' " Brother Germain mocked Thomas with mimicry. "Of course it's Hebrew, even a fool educated at the university in Paris would know that, but it's their magical script. It's the lettering the Jews use to work their charms, their dark magic." He peered close at one of the pages. "There, you see? The devil's name, Abracadabra!" He frowned for a few seconds. "The writer claims Abracadabra can be raised to this world by invoking his name above the Grail. That seems plausible." Brother Germain made the sign of the cross again to ward off evil, then peered up at Thomas. "Where did you get this?" He asked the question sharply, but did not wait for an answer. "You're him, aren't you?"

"Him?"

"The Vexille that Sir Guillaume brought to me," Brother Germain said accusingly and made the sign of the cross again. "You're English!" He made that sound even worse. "Who will you take this book to?"

"I want to understand it first," Thomas said, confused by the question.

"Understand it! You?" Brother Germain scoffed. "No, no. You must leave it with me, young man, so I can make a copy of it and then the book itself must go to Paris, to the Dominicans there. They sent a man to ask about you."

"About me?" Thomas was even more confused now.

"About the Vexille family. It seems one of your foul brood fought at the King's side this summer, and now he has submitted to the Church. The Inquisition have had . . ." Brother German paused, evidently seeking the right word, ". . . conversations with him."

"With Guy?" Thomas asked. He knew Guy was his cousin, knew Guy had fought on the French side in Picardy and he knew Guy had killed his father in search of the Grail, but he knew little more.

"Who else? And now, they do say, Guy Vexille is reconciled to the Church," Brother Germain said as he turned the pages. "Reconciled to the Church indeed! Can a wolf lay down with lambs? Who wrote this?"

"My father."

"So you are Hachaliah's grandson," Brother Germain said with reverence, then he closed his thin hands over the book. "Thank you for bringing it to me," he said.

"Can you tell me what the Hebrew passages say?" Thomas asked, baffled by Brother Germain's last words.

"Tell you? Of course I can tell you, but it will mean nothing. You know who Hachaliah was? You are familiar with the Tirshatha? Of course not. The answers would be wasted on you! But I thank you for bringing me the book." He drew a scrap of parchment toward him, took up his quill and dipped it in the ink. "If you take this note to the sacristan he will give you a reward. Now I have work." He signed the note and held it toward Thomas.

Thomas reached for the book. "I can't leave it here," he said.

"Can't leave it here! Of course you can! Such a thing belongs to the Church. Besides, I must make a copy." Brother Germain folded his hands over the book and hunched over it. "You will leave it," he hissed.

Thomas had thought of Brother Germain as a friend, or at least not as an enemy, and even the old monk's harsh words about Sir Guillaume's treachery had not altered that opinion, Germain had said that the book must go to Paris, to the Dominicans, but Thomas now understood that Germain was allied with those men of the Inquisition who, in turn, had Guy Vexille on their side. And Thomas understood too that those formidable men were seeking the Grail with an avidity he had not appreciated until this moment, and their path to the Grail lay through him and this book. Those men were his enemies, and that meant that Brother Germain was also his foe and it had been a terrible mistake to bring the book to the abbey. He felt a sudden fear as he reached for the book. "I have to leave," he insisted.

Brother Germain tried to hold onto the book, but his twig-like arms could not compete with Thomas's bow-given strength. He nevertheless clutched it stubbornly, threatening to tear its soft leather cover. "Where will you go?" Brother Germain demanded, then tried to trick Thomas with a false promise. "If you leave it," he said, "I shall make a copy and send the book to you when it is finished."

Thomas was going north to Dunkirk so he named a place in the other direction. "I'm going to La Roche-Derrien," he lied.

"An English garrison?" Brother Germain still tried to pull the book away, then yelped as Thomas slapped his hands. "You can't take that to the English!"

"I am taking it to La Roche-Derrien," Thomas said, finally retrieving the book. He folded the soft leather cover over the pages, then half drew his sword because several of the younger monks had slipped from their high stools and looked as though they wanted to stop him, but the sight of the blade dissuaded them from any violence. They just watched as he walked away.

The porter was coughing still, then leaned against the arch and fought for breath while tears streamed from his eyes. "At least it ain't leprosy," he managed to say to Thomas, "I know it ain't leprosy. My brother had leprosy and he didn't cough. Not much anyway."

"When is St. Clement's Day?" Thomas remembered to ask.

"Day after tomorrow, and God love me if I live to see it."

No one followed Thomas, but that afternoon, while he and Robbie were standing up to their crotches in flooding cold river water and pounding thick moss into the *Pentecost*'s planking, a patrol of soldiers in red and yellow livery asked Pierre Villeroy if he had seen an Englishman dressed in mail and a black cloak.

"That's him down there," Villeroy said, pointing to Thomas, then laughed. "If I see an Englishman," he went on, "I'll piss down the bastard's throat till he drowns."

"Bring him to the castle instead," the patrol's leader said, then led his men to question the crew on the next boat.

Villeroy waited till the soldiers were out of earshot. "For that," he said to Thomas, "you owe me two more rows of caulking."

"Jesus Christ!" Thomas swore.

"Now He was a properly skilled carpenter," Villeroy observed through a mouthful of Yvette's apple pie, "but He was also the Son of God, wasn't he? So he didn't have to do menial jobs like caulking, so it's no damn good asking for His help. Just bang the moss in hard, boy, bang it in hard."

SIR GUILLAUME had held the manor from its attackers for close on three months and did not doubt he could hold it indefinitely so long as the Count of Coutances did not bring more gunpowder to the village, but Sir Guillaume knew that his time in Normandy was ended. The Count of Coutances was his liege lord, Sir Guillaume held land of him as the Count held land of the King, and if a man was declared a traitor by his liege lord, and if the King supported the declaration, then a man had no future unless he was to find another lord who owed fealty to a different King. Sir Guillaume had written to the King and he had appealed to friends who had influence at court, but no reply had come. The siege had continued, and so Sir Guillaume must leave the manor. That saddened him for Evecque was his home. He knew every inch of its pastures, knew where to find the shed deer antlers, knew where the young hares lay trembling in the long grass, and knew where the pike brooded like demons in the deeper streams. It was home, but a man declared a traitor had no home and so, on the eve of St. Clement's, when his besiegers were sunk in a damp winter gloom, he made his escape.

He had never doubted his ability to escape. The Count of Coutances was a dull, unimaginative, middle-aged man whose experience of war had always been in the service of greater lords. The Count was averse to risk and given to a blustery temper whenever the world escaped his understanding, which happened frequently. The Count certainly did not understand why great men in Paris were encouraging him to besiege Evecque, but he saw the chance of enriching himself and so he obeyed them, even though he was wary of Sir Guillaume. Sir Guillaume was in his thirties and had spent half his life fighting, usually on his own account, and in Normandy he was called the lord of the sea and of the land because he fought on both with enthusiasm and effectiveness. He had been handsome once, hard-faced and golden-haired, but Guy Vexille, Count of Astarac, had taken one eye and had left scars that made Sir Guillaume's face even harder. He was a formidable man, a fighter, but in the hierarchy of kings, princes, dukes and counts he was a lesser being and his lands made it tempting to declare him a traitor.

There were twelve men, three women and eight horses inside the manor, which meant every horse but one had to carry two riders. After nightfall, when rain was softly falling across Evecque's waterlogged fields, Sir Guillaume ordered planks, put across the gap where the drawbridge should have been, and then the horses, blindfolded, were led one by one across the perilous bridge. The besiegers, huddled from the cold and rain, saw and heard nothing, even though the sentries in the forwardmost works had been placed to guard against just such an attempt to escape.

The horses' blindfolds were taken off, the fugitives mounted and then rode northward. They were challenged just once by a sentry who demanded to know who they were. "Who the hell do you think we are?" Sir Guillaume retorted, and the savagery in his voice persuaded the sentry not to ask any more questions. By dawn they were in Caen and the Count of Coutances was still none the wiser. It was only when one of the sentries saw the planks spanning the moat that the besiegers realized their enemy was gone, and even then the Count wasted time by searching the manor. He found furniture, straw and cooking pots, but no treasures.

An hour later a hundred black-cloaked men arrived at Evecque. Their leader carried no banner and their shields had no badges. They looked battle-hardened, like men who earned their living by renting their lances and swords to whoever paid the most, and they curbed their horses beside the makeshift bridge over Evecque's moat and two of them, one a priest, crossed into the courtyard. "What's been taken?" the priest demanded curtly.

The Count of Coutances turned angrily on the man who wore Dominican robes. "Who are you?"

"What have your men plundered here?" the priest, gaunt and angry, asked again.

"Nothing," the Count assured him.

"Then where's the garrison?"

"The garrison? Escaped."

Bernard de Taillebourg spat in his rage. Guy Vexille, next to him, gazed up at the tower which now flew the Count's banner. "When did they escape?" he asked. "And where did they go?"

The Count bridled at the tone. "Who are you?" he demanded, for Vexille wore no badge on his black surcoat.

"Your equal," Vexille said coldly, "and my lord the King will want to know where they have gone."

No one knew, though a few questions eventually elicited that some of the besiegers had been aware of horsemen going northward in the cold night and that surely meant that Sir Guillaume and his men had ridden to Caen. And if the Grail had been hidden in Evecque then that would have gone north as well and so de Taillebourg ordered his men to remount their tired horses.

They reached Caen in the early afternoon, but by then the *Pentecost* was halfway down the river to the sea, blown northward by a fitful wind that barely gave headway against the last of the flooding tide. Pierre Villeroy grumbled at the futility of trying to stem the tide, but Sir Guillaume insisted for he expected his enemies to appear at any moment. He had only two men-at-arms with him now, for the rest had not wanted to follow their lord to a new allegiance. Even Sir Guillaume had little enthusiasm for that enforced loyalty. "You think I want to fight for Edward of England?" he grumbled to Thomas. "But what choice do I have? My own lord turned against me. So I'll swear fealty to your Edward and at least I'll live." That was why he was going to Dunkirk, so that he could make the small journey to the English siege lines about Calais and make his obeisance to King Edward.

The horses had to be abandoned on the quay, so all Sir Guillaume brought aboard the *Pentecost* was his armor, some clothes and three leather bags of money that he dumped on the deck before offering Thomas an embrace. And then Thomas had turned to his old friend, Will Skeat, who had glanced at him without recognition and then looked away. Thomas, about to speak, checked himself. Skeat was wearing a sallet and his hair, white as snow now, hung lank beneath its battered metal brim. His face was thinner than ever, deep-lined, and with a vague look as though he had just woken and did not know where he was. He also looked old. He could not have been more than forty-five, yet he looked sixty, though at least he was alive. When Thomas had last seen him he had been dreadfully wounded with a sword cut through the scalp which had laid his brain open and it had been a miracle he had lived long enough to reach Normandy and the skilled attentions of Mordecai, the Jewish doctor who was now being helped across the precarious gangplank.

Thomas took another step toward his old friend who again glanced at him without recognition. "Will?" Thomas said, puzzled. "Will?"

And at the sound of Thomas's voice light came into Skeat's eyes. "Thomas!" he exclaimed. "By God, it is you!" He stepped toward Thomas, stumbling slightly, and the two men embraced. "By God, Thomas, it's grand to hear an English voice. I've heard nowt but foreign jabber all winter. Good God, boy, you look older."

"I am older," Thomas said. "But how are you, Will?"

"I'm alive, Tom, I'm alive, though I sometimes wonder if

it wouldn't have been better to die. Weak as a kitten, I am."
His speech was slightly slurred, as if he had drunk too much,
but he was plainly sober.

"I shouldn't call you plain Will now, should I," Thomas
asked, "for you're Sir William now."

"Sir William! Me?" Skeat laughed. "You're full of crap,
boy, just like you always were. Always too clever for your
own good, eh, Tom?" Skeat did not remember the battle in
Picardy, did not remember the King knighting him before
the first French charge. Thomas had sometimes wondered
whether that act had been pure desperation to raise the
archers' spirits for the King had surely seen how hugely his
little, sick army was outnumbered and he could not have believed his men would survive. But survive they did, and win,
though the cost to Skeat had been terrible. He took off his
sallet to scratch his pate and one side of his scalp was revealed as a wrinkled horror of lumpy scar, pink and white.
"Weak as a kitten," Skeat said again, "and I haven't pulled a
bow in weeks."

Mordecai insisted that Skeat had to rest. Then he greeted
Thomas as Villeroy let go the mooring lines and used a
sweep to shove the *Pentecost* into the river's current. Mordecai grumbled about the cold, about the privations of the
siege and about the horrors of being aboard a ship, then he
smiled his wise old smile. "You look good, Thomas. For a
man who was once hanged you look indecently good. How's
your urine?"

"Clear and sweet."

"Your friend Sir William, now—" Mordecai jerked his
head toward the forecabin where Skeat had been bedded
down in a pile of sheepskins—"his urine is very murky. I
fear you did me no favors by sending him to me."

"He's alive."

"I don't know why."

"And I sent him to you because you're the best."

"You flatter me." Mordecai staggered slightly because the ship had rocked in a small river wave that no one else had noticed, yet he looked alarmed; had he been a Christian he would doubtless have warded off imminent danger by the sign of the cross. Instead he looked worriedly at the ragged sail as though he feared it might collapse and smother him. "I do detest ships," he said plaintively. "Unnatural things. Poor Skeat. He seems to be recovering, I admit, but I cannot boast that I did anything except wash the wound and stop people putting charms of moldy bread and holy water on his scalp. I find religion and medicine mix uneasily. Skeat lives, I think, because poor Eleanor did the right thing when he was wounded." Eleanor had put the broken piece of skull on the exposed brain, made a poultice of moss and spider web, then bandaged the wound. "I was sorry about Eleanor."

"Me too," Thomas said. "She was pregnant. We were going to marry."

"She was a dear thing, a dear thing."

"Sir Guillaume must be angry?"

Mordecai rocked his head from side to side. "When he received your letter? That was before the siege, of course." He frowned, trying to remember. "Angry? I don't think so. He grunted, that was all. He was fond of Eleanor, of course, but she was a servant's child, not . . ." He paused. "Well, it's sad. But as you say, your friend Sir William lived. The brain is a strange thing, Thomas. He understands, I think, though he cannot remember. His speech is slurred, and that might have been expected, but strangest of all is that he does not recognize anyone with his eyes. I will walk into a room and he'll ignore me, then I speak and he knows me. We have all got into the habit of speaking as we get near him. You'll get used to it." Mordecai smiled. "But it is good to see you."

"So you travel to Calais with us?" Thomas asked.

"Dear me, no! Calais?" He shuddered. "But I couldn't

stay in Normandy. I suspect that the Count of Coutances, cheated of Sir Guillaume, would love to make an example of a Jew, so from Dunkirk I shall travel south again. To Montpellier first, I think. My son is studying medicine there. And from Montpellier? I might go to Avignon."

"Avignon?"

"The Pope is very hospitable to Jews," Mordecai said, reaching out for the gunwale as the *Pentecost* shivered under a small wind gust, "and we need hospitality."

Mordecai had intimated that Sir Guillaume's reaction to Eleanor's death was callous, but that was not evident when Sir Guillaume spoke of his lost daughter with Thomas as the *Pentecost* cleared the river's mouth and the cold waves stretched to the gray horizon. Sir Guillaume, his ravaged face hard and grim, looked close to tears as he heard how Eleanor had died. "Do you know anything more about the men who killed her?" he asked when Thomas had finished his tale. Thomas could only repeat what Lord Outhwaite had told him after the battle, about the French priest called de Taillebourg and his strange servant.

"De Taillebourg," Sir Guillaume said flatly, "another man to kill, eh?" He made the sign of the cross. "She was illegitimate"—he spoke of Eleanor, not to Thomas, but to the wind, instead—"but she was a sweet girl. All of my children are dead now." He gazed at the ocean, his dirty long yellow hair stirring in the breeze. "We have so many men to kill, you and I"—he spoke to Thomas now—"and the Grail to find."

"Others are looking for it," Thomas said.

"Then we must find it before them," Sir Guillaume growled. "But we go to Calais first, I make my allegiance to Edward and then we fight. By God, Thomas, we fight." He turned and scowled at his two men-at-arms as if reflecting on how his fortunes and following had been shrunk by fate, then he saw Robbie and grinned. "I like your Scotsman."

"He can fight," Thomas said.

"That's why I like him. And he wants to kill de Taille-bourg too?"

"Three of us want to kill him."

"Then God help the bastard because we'll serve his tripes to the dogs," Sir Guillaume growled. "But he'll have to be told you're in the Calais siege lines, eh? If he's to come looking for us he has to know where you are."

To reach Calais the *Pentecost* needed to go east and north, but once clear of the land she merely wallowed instead of sailing. A small south-west wind had taken her clear of the river mouth, but then, long before she was out of sight of the Norman shore, the breeze faded and the big ragged sail flapped and slatted and banged on the yard. The ship rolled like a barrel in a long dull swell that came from the west where dark clouds heaped like some gloom-laden range of hills. The winter day faded early, the last of its cold light a sullen glint beneath the clouds. A few spots of fire showed on the darkening land. "The tide will take us up the sleeve," Villeroy said gloomily, "then float us down again. Then up and down and up and down till God or St. Nicholas sends us wind."

The tide took them up the English Channel as Villeroy had predicted, then drifted them down again. Thomas, Robbie and Sir Guillaume's two men-at-arms took it in turns to go down into the stone-filled bilge and hand up pails of water. "Of course she leaks," Villeroy told a worried Mordecai, "all ships leak. She'd leak like a sieve if I didn't caulk her every few months. Bang in the moss and pray to St. Nick. It keeps us all from drowning."

The night was black. The few lights ashore flickered in a damp haze. The sea broke feebly against the hull, and the sail hung uselessly. For a time a fishing boat lay close, a lantern burning on its deck, and Thomas listened to the low chant as the men hauled a net, then they unshipped oars and rowed eastward until their tiny glimmering light vanished in the haze. "A west wind will come," Villeroy said, "it always does. West from the lost lands."

"The lost lands?" Thomas asked.

"Out there," Villeroy said, pointing into the black west. "If you go as far as a man can sail you'll find the lost lands and you'll see a mountain taller than the sky where Arthur sleeps with his knights." Villeroy made the sign of the cross. "And on the clifftops under the mountain you can see the souls of the drowned sailors calling for their womenfolk. It's cold there, always cold, cold and fog-smothered."

"My father saw those lands once," Yvette put in.

"He said he did," Villeroy commented, "but he was a rare drinker."

"He said the sea was full of fish," Yvette went on as if her husband had not spoken, "and the trees were very small."

"Cider, he drank," Villeroy offered. "Whole orchards went down his gullet, but he could sail a boat, your father. Drunk or sober, he was a seaman."

Thomas was staring into the western darkness, imagining a voyage to the land where King Arthur and his knights slept under the fog and where the souls of the drowned called for their lost lovers. "Time to bail ship," Villeroy said to him, and Thomas went down into the bilge and scooped the water into buckets until his arms were aching with tiredness, and then he went to the forepeak and slept in the cocoon of sheepskins that Villeroy kept there because, he said, it was colder at sea than on land and a man should drown warm.

Dawn came slow, seeping into the east like a gray stain. The steering oar creaked in its ropes, doing nothing as the ship rocked on the windless swell. The Norman coast was still in sight, a gray-green slash to the south, and as the winter light grew Thomas saw three small ships rowing out from the coast. The three headed up channel until they were east of the *Pentecost*; Thomas assumed they were fishermen and he wished that Villeroy's boat had oars and so could make some progress in this frustrating stillness. There was a pair of great sweeps lashed to the deck, but Yvette said they were only useful in port. "She's too heavy to row for long," she said, "especially when she's full."

"Full?"

"We carry cargo," Yvette said. Her man was sleeping in the stern cabin, his snores seeming to vibrate the whole ship. "Up and down the coast we go," Yvette said, "with wool and wine, bronze and iron, building stone and hides."

"You like it?"

"I love it." She smiled at him and her young face, which was strangely wedgelike, took on a beauty as she did so. "My mother now," she went on, "she was going to have me put into the bishop's service. Cleaning and washing, cooking and cleaning till your hands are fair worn away by work, but Pierre told me I could live free as a bird on his boat and so we do, so we do."

"Just the two of you?" The *Pentecost* seemed a large ship for just two, even if one of them was a giant.

"No one else will sail with us," Yvette said. "It's bad luck to have a woman on a boat. My father always said that."

"He was a fisherman?"

"A good one," Yvette said, "but he drowned all the same. He was caught on the Casquets on a bad night." She looked up at Thomas earnestly. "He did see the lost lands, you know."

"I believe you."

"He sailed ever so far north and then west, and he said the men from the north lands know the fishing grounds of the lost lands well and there's fish as far as you can see. He said you could walk on the sea it was so thick with fish, and one day he was creeping through the fog and he saw the land and he saw the trees like bushes and he saw the dead souls on shore. They were dark, he said, like they'd been scorched by hell's fires, and he took fright and he turned and sailed away. It took him two months to get there and a month and a half to come home and all his fish had gone bad because he wouldn't go ashore and smoke them."

"I believe you," Thomas said again, though he was not really sure that he did.

"And I think if I drown," Yvette said, "then me and Pierre will go to the lost lands together and he won't have to sit on the cliffs and call for me." She spoke very matter-of-factly, then went to ready some breakfast for her man whose snoring had just ceased.

Sir Guillaume emerged from the forecabin. He blinked at the winter daylight, then strolled aft and pissed across the stern rail while he stared at the three boats which had rowed out from the river and were now a mile or so east of the *Pentecost*. "So you saw Brother Germain?" he asked Thomas.

"I wish I hadn't."

"He's a scholar," Sir Guillaume said, pulling up his trews and tying the waist knot, "which means he doesn't have balls. Doesn't need to. He's clever, mind you, clever, but he was never on our side, Thomas."

"I thought he was your friend."

"When I had power and money, Thomas," Sir Guillaume said, "I had many friends, but Brother Germain was never one of them. He's always been a good son of the Church and I should never have introduced you to him."

"Why not?"

"Once he learned you were a Vexille he reported our conversation to the bishop and the bishop told the Archbishop and the Archbishop told the Cardinal and the Cardinal spoke to whoever gives him his crumbs, and suddenly the Church got excited about the Vexilles and the fact that your family had once owned the Grail. And it was just about then that Guy Vexille reappeared so the Inquisition took hold of him." He paused, gazing at the horizon, then made the sign of the cross. "That's who your de Taillebourg is, I'd wager my life on it. He's a Dominican and most Inquisitors are hounds of God." He turned his one eye on Thomas. "Why do they call them the hounds of God?"

"It's a joke," Thomas said, "from the Latin. *Domini canis*: the hound of God."

"Doesn't make me laugh," Sir Guillaume said gloomily. "If one of those bastards gets hold of you it's red-hot pokers in the eyes and screams in the night. And I hear they got hold of Guy Vexille and I hope they hurt him."

"So Guy Vexille is a prisoner?" Thomas was surprised. Brother Germain had said his cousin was reconciled with the Church.

"That's what I heard. I heard he was singing psalms on the Inquisition's rack. And doubtless he told them that your father had possessed the Grail, and how he sailed to Hook-ton to find it and how he failed. But who else went to Hook-ton? Me, that's who, so I think Coutances was told to find me, arrest me and haul me to Paris. And meanwhile they sent men to England to find out what they could."

"And to kill Eleanor," Thomas said bleakly.

"Which they'll pay for," Sir Guillaume said.

"And now," Thomas said, "they've sent men here."

"What?" Sir Guillaume asked, startled.

Thomas pointed at the three fishing boats which now were rowing directly toward the *Pentecost*. They were too far away for him to see who or what was on board, but something about their deliberate approach alarmed him. Yvette, coming aft with bread, ham and cheese, saw Thomas and Sir Guillaume staring and she joined them, then uttered a curse that only a fisherman's daughter would ever have learned and ran to the stern cabin and shouted for her man to get on deck.

Yvette's eyes were accustomed to the sea and she knew

these were no fishing boats. They had too many men aboard for a start and after a while Thomas could see those men for himself and his eyes, which were more used to looking for enemies among the green leaves, saw that some of them wore mail and he knew that no man went to sea in mail unless he was intent on killing.

"They'll have crossbows." Villeroy was on deck now, tying the neck cords of a swathing leather cloak and looking from the approaching boats up to the clouds as if he might see a breath of wind coming from the heavens. The sea was still heaving in great swells, but the water was smooth as beaten brass and there were no wind-driven ripples streaking the swells' long flanks. "Crossbows," Villeroy repeated gloomily.

"You want me to surrender?" Sir Guillaume asked Villeroy. His voice was sour, suggesting the question was nothing but sarcasm.

"Ain't for me to tell your lordship what to do"—Villeroy sounded just as sarcastic—"but your men could fetch some of the bigger stones out of the bilge."

"What will that achieve?" Sir Guillaume asked.

"I'll drop 'em on the bastards when they try to board. Those little boats? A stone'll go straight through their bottoms and then yon bastards will be trying to swim with mail strapped to their chests." Villeroy grinned. "Hard to swim when you're wrapped in iron."

The stones were fetched, and Thomas readied his arrows and bow. Robbie had donned his mail coat and had his uncle's sword at his side. Sir Guillaume's two men-at-arms were with him in the waist of the boat, the place where any boarding attempt would be made for there the gunwale was closest to the sea. Thomas went to the higher stern where Will Skeat joined him and though he did not recognize Thomas he did see the bow and held out a hand.

"It's me, Will," Thomas said.

"I know it's you," Skeat said. He lied and was embarrassed. "Let me try the bow, boy."

Thomas gave him the great black stave and watched in sadness as Skeat failed to draw it even halfway. Skeat thrust the weapon back to Thomas with a look of embarrassment. "I'm not what I was," he muttered.

"You'll be back, Will."

Skeat spat over the gunwale. "Did the King really knight me?"

"He did."

"Sometimes I think I can remember the battle, Tom, then it fades. Like a fog." Skeat stared at the three approaching boats, which had spread into a line. Their oarsmen were pulling hard and Thomas could see crossbowmen standing in the bows and stern of each craft. "Have you ever shot an arrow from a boat?" Skeat asked.

"Never."

"You're moving and they're moving. It makes it hard. But take it slow, lad, take it slow."

A man shouted from the closest boat, but the pursuers were still too far away and whatever the man said was lost in the air. "St. Nicholas, St. Ursula," Villeroy prayed, "send us wind, and send us plenty of it."

"He's having a go at us," Skeat said because a crossbowman in the bows of the central boat had raised his weapon. He seemed to cock it high in the air, then he shot and the bolt banged with astonishing force low into the *Pentecost*'s stern. Sir Guillaume, ignoring the threat, climbed onto the rail and took hold of the backstay to keep his balance. "They're Coutances's men," he told Thomas, and Thomas saw that some of the men in the nearest boat were wearing the green and black livery that had been the uniform of Evecque's besiegers. More crossbows twanged and two of the bolts thudded into the stern planks and two others whipped past Sir

Guillaume to slap into the impotent sail, but most splashed into the sea. It might have been calm, but the crossbowmen were still having a hard time aiming their weapons from the small boats.

And the three attacking boats were small. Each held eight or ten oarsmen and about the same number of archers or men-at-arms. The three craft had plainly been chosen for their speed under oars, but they were dwarfed by the *Pentecost* which would make any attempt to board the bigger vessel very perilous, though one of the three boats seemed determined to come alongside Villeroy's ship. "What they're going to do," Sir Guillaume said, "is let those two boats shower us with quarrels while this bastard"—he gestured at the boat that was pulling hard to close on the *Pentecost*— "puts her men on board."

More crossbow bolts thumped into the hull. Two more quarrels pierced the sail and another hit the mast just above a weathered crucifix that was nailed to the tarred timber. The figure of Christ, white as bone, had lost its left arm and Thomas wondered if that was a bad omen, then tried to forget it as he drew the big bow and shot off an arrow. He only had thirty-four shafts left, but this was not the time to stint on them and so, while the first was still in the air, he loosed a second and the crossbowmen had not finished winding their cords back as the first arrow slashed a rower's arm and the second drove a splinter up from the boat's bow, then a third arrow hissed above the oarsmen's heads to splash into the sea. The rowers ducked, then one gasped and fell forward with an arrow in his back, and the next instant a man-at-arms was struck in the thigh and fell onto two of the oarsmen and there was sudden chaos aboard the boat which slewed sharply away with its oars clattering against each other. Thomas lowered the big bow.

"Taught you well," Will Skeat said fervently. "Ah, Tom, you always were a lethal bastard."

The boat pulled away. Thomas's arrows had been far more accurate than the crossbow bolts for he had been shooting from a much larger and more stable ship than the narrow and overburdened rowboats. Only one of the men aboard those smaller ships had been killed, but the frequency of Thomas's first arrows had put the fear of God into the rowers who could not see where the missiles came from, but only hear the hiss of feathers and the cries of the wounded. Now the other two boats overtook the third and the crossbowmen leveled their weapons.

Thomas took an arrow from the bag and worried what would happen when he had no more shafts, but just then a swirl of ripples showed that a wind was coming across the water. An east wind, of all things, the most unlikely of all winds in this sea, but it came from the east nonetheless and the *Pentecost*'s big brown sail filled and slackened, then filled again, and suddenly she was turning away from her pursuers and the water was gurgling down her flanks. Coutances's men pulled hard on their oars. "Down!" Sir Guillaume shouted and Thomas dropped behind the rail as a volley of crossbow bolts punched into the *Pentecost*'s hull or flew high to tear the ragged sail. Villeroy shouted at Yvette to man the steering oar, then he sheeted down the mainsail before diving into the stern cabin to fetch a huge and evidently ancient crossbow that he cocked with a long iron lever. He loaded a rusty bolt into the groove, then shot it at the nearest pursuer. "Bastards," he roared. "Your mothers were goats! They were whoring goats! Poxed whoring goats! Bastards!" He cocked the weapon again, loaded another corroded missile and shot it away, but the bolt plunged into the sea. The *Pentecost* was gathering speed and already out of crossbow range.

The wind filled and the *Pentecost* drew farther away from her pursuers. The three rowboats had first gone up channel in the expectation that the flooding tide and a possible western wind would bring the *Pentecost* to them, but with the wind coming from the east the oarsmen could not keep up with their quarry and so the three boats fell astern and finally abandoned the chase. But just as they gave up, so two new pursuers appeared in the mouth of the River Orne. Two ships, both of them large and equipped with big square sails like the *Pentecost*'s mainsail, were coming out to sea. "The one in front is the *Saint-Esprit*," Villeroy said. Even at this distance from the river mouth he could distinguish the two boats, "and the other is the *Marie*. She sails like a pregnant pig, but the *Saint-Esprit* will catch us."

"The *Saint-Esprit*?" Sir Guillaume sounded appalled. "Jean Lapoullier?"

"Who else?"

"I thought he was a friend!"

"He was your friend," Villeroy said, "so long as you had land and money, but what do you have now?"

Sir Guillaume brooded on the truth of that question for a while. "So why are you helping me?"

"Because I'm a fool," Villeroy said cheerfully, "and because you'll pay me damn well."

Sir Guillaume grunted at that truism. "Not if we sail in the wrong direction," he added after a while.

"The right direction," Villeroy pointed out, "is away from the *Saint-Esprit* and downwind, so we'll stand on west."

They stood on westward all day. They made good speed, but still the big *Saint-Esprit* slowly closed the gap. In the morning she had been a blur on the horizon; by midday Thomas could see the little platform at her masthead where, Villeroy told him, crossbowmen would be stationed; and by mid-afternoon he could see the black and white eyes painted on her bows. The east wind had increased all through the day until it was blowing strong and cold, whipping the wavetops into white streamers. Sir Guillaume suggested going north, maybe as far as the English shore, but Villeroy

claimed not to know that coastline and said he was unsure
where he could find shelter there if the weather turned bad.
"And this time of year it can turn fast as a woman's temper,"
Villeroy added, and as if to prove him right they ran into violent sleet squalls that hissed on the sea and buffeted the
ship and cut visibility down to a few yards. Sir Guillaume
again urged a northward course, suggesting they turn while
the ship was hidden inside the squall, but Villeroy stubbornly refused and Thomas guessed that the huge man
feared being accosted by English ships that loved nothing
better than capturing French vessels.

Another squall crashed past them, the rain bouncing up a
hand's breadth from the deck and the sleet making a slushy
white coating on the eastern flank of every halyard and
sheet. Villeroy feared that his sail would split, but dared not
shorten the canvas because whenever the squalls passed,
leaving the sea white and frantic, the *Saint-Esprit* was always in sight and always a little closer. "She's a quick one,"
Villeroy said grudgingly, "and Lapoullier knows how to sail
her."

Yet the short winter day was passing and night would offer
a chance for the *Pentecost* to escape. The pursuers knew that
and they must have been praying that their ship would be
given a little extra speed; as dusk fell, she was closing the gap
inch by inch, yet still the *Pentecost* kept her lead. They were
out of sight of land now, two ships on a seething and darkening ocean, and then, when the night was almost complete, the
first flame arrow streaked out from the *Saint-Esprit*'s bow.

It was shot from a crossbow. The flames seared the night,
arcing up and then plunging to fall in the *Pentecost*'s wake.
"Send him an arrow back," Sir Guillaume growled.

"Too far," Thomas said. A good crossbow would always
outrange a yew stave, though in the time it took to reload the
crossbow the English archer would have run within range

and loosed half a dozen arrows. But Thomas could not do that in this gathering darkness, nor did he dare waste arrows. He could only wait and watch as a second fire bolt slashed up against the clouds. It too fell behind.

"They don't fly as well," Will Skeat said.

"What's that, Will?" Thomas had not heard clearly.

"They wrap the shaft in cloth and it slows them down. You ever shot a fire arrow, Tom?"

"Never."

"Takes fifty paces off the range," Skeat said, watching a third arrow plunge into the sea, "and plays hell with accuracy."

"That one was closer," Sir Guillaume said.

Villeroy had put a barrel on the deck and he was filling it with seawater. Yvette, meanwhile, had nimbly climbed the rigging to perch herself on the crosstrees where the one yard hung from the masthead and now she hauled up canvas pails of water which she used to soak the sail.

"Can we use fire arrows?" Sir Guillaume asked. "That thing must have the range." He nodded at Villeroy's monstrous crossbow. Thomas translated the question for Will Skeat whose French was still rudimentary.

"Fire arrows?" Skeat's face wrinkled as he thought. "You have to have pitch, Tom," he said dubiously, "and you must soak it into the wool and then bind the woolen cloth onto the arrow real hard, but fray the edges a little to get the fire burning nicely. Fire has to be deep in the cloth, not just on the edge because that won't last, and when it's burning hard and deep you send the arrow off before it eats through the shaft."

"No," Thomas translated for Sir Guillaume, "we can't."

Sir Guillaume cursed, then turned away as the first fire arrow thumped into the *Pentecost*, but the bolt struck low on the stern, so low that the next heave of a wave extinguished the flames with an audible hiss. "We must be able to do something!" Sir Guillaume raged.

"We can be patient," Villeroy said. He was standing at the stern oar.

"I can use your bow?" Sir Guillaume asked the big sailor and, when Villeroy nodded, Sir Guillaume cocked the huge crossbow and sent a quarrel back toward the *Saint-Esprit*. He grunted as he pulled on the lever to cock the weapon again, astonished at the strength needed. A crossbow drawn by a lever was usually much weaker than the bows armed with a wormscrew and ratchet, but Villeroy's bow was massive. Sir Guillaume's bolts must have struck the pursuing ship, but it was too dark to tell if any damage had been done. Thomas doubted it for the *Saint-Esprit*'s bows were high and her gunwales stout. Sir Guillaume was merely driving metal into planks, but the *Saint-Esprit*'s fiery missiles were beginning to threaten the *Pentecost*. Three or four enemy crossbows were firing now and Thomas and Robbie were busy dousing the burning bolts with water, then a flaming quarrel hit the sail and creeping fire began to glow on the canvas, but Yvette succeeded in extinguishing it just as Villeroy pushed the steering oar hard over. Thomas heard the oar's long shank creak under the strain and felt the ship lurch as she turned southward. "The *Saint-Esprit* was never quite as quick off the wind," Villeroy said, "and she wallows in a cross sea."

"And we're quicker?" Thomas asked.

"We'll find out," Villeroy said.

"Why didn't we try to find out earlier?" Sir Guillaume snarled the question.

"Because we didn't have sea room," Villeroy answered placidly as a flaming bolt seared over the stern deck like a meteor. "But we're well clear of the cape now." He meant they were safely to the west of the Norman peninsula and south of them now were the rock-studded sea reaches between Normandy and Brittany. The turn meant that the range suddenly shortened as the *Saint-Esprit* held on westward and Thomas shot a clutch of arrows at the dim figures of armored men in the pursuing ship's waist. Yvette had come down to the deck and was hauling on ropes and, when she was satisfied with the new set of the sail, she clambered back up to her eyrie just as two more fire bolts thumped into the canvas and Thomas saw the flames leap up the sail as Yvette dragged up buckets. Thomas sent another arrow high into the night so that it plunged down onto the enemy deck and Sir Guillaume was shooting the heavier crossbow bolts as fast as he could, but neither man was rewarded with a cry of pain. Then the range opened again and Thomas unstrung his bow. The *Saint-Esprit* was turning to follow the *Pentecost* south and, for a few heartbeats, she seemed to disappear in the dark, but then another fire arrow climbed from her deck and in its sudden light Thomas saw she had made the turn and was again in the *Pentecost*'s wake. Villeroy's sail was still burning, giving the *Saint-Esprit* a mark she could not fail to follow and the pursuing bowmen sent three arrows together, their flames flickering hungrily in the night, and Yvette heaved desperately on the buckets, but the sail was ablaze now and the ship was slowing as the canvas lost its force and then, blessedly, there was a seething hiss and a squall came lashing in from the east.

The sleet pelted down with an extraordinary violence, rattling on the charred sail and drumming on the deck, and Thomas thought it would last forever, but it stopped as suddenly as it had begun and all on board the *Pentecost* stared astern, waiting for the next fire bolt to climb from the *Saint-Esprit*'s deck, but when the flame finally seared into the sky it was a long way off, much too far away for its light to illuminate the *Pentecost* and Villeroy grunted. "They reckoned we'd turn back west in that squall," he said with amusement, "but they were being too clever for their own good." The *Saint-Esprit* had tried to head off the *Pentecost*, thinking Villeroy would put his ship straight downwind again, but the pursuers had made the wrong guess and they were now a long way to the north and west of their quarry.

More fire arrows burned in the dark, but now they were being shot in all directions in hope that the small light of one would glint a dull reflection from the *Pentecost*'s hull, but Villeroy's ship was drawing ever farther away, pulled by the remnants of her scorched sail. If it had not been for the squall, Thomas thought, they would surely have been overhauled and captured, and he wondered whether the hand of God was somehow sheltering him because he possessed the book of the Grail. Then guilt assailed him; the guilt of doubting the Grail's existence; of wasting Lord Outhwaite's money instead of spending it on the pursuit of the Grail; then the greater guilt and pity of Eleanor and Father Hobbe's wasteful deaths, and so he dropped to his knees on the deck and stared up at the one-armed crucifix. Forgive me, Lord, he prayed, forgive me.

"Sails cost money," Villeroy said.

"You shall have a new sail, Pierre," Sir Guillaume promised.

"And let's pray that what's left of this one will get us somewhere," Villeroy said sourly. Off to the north a last fire arrow etched red across the black, and then there was no more light, just the endless dark of a broken sea in which the *Pentecost* survived under her tattered sail.

Dawn found them in a mist and with a fitful breeze that fluttered a sail so weakened that Villeroy and Yvette doubled it on itself so that the wind would have more than charred holes to blow upon, and when they reset it the *Pentecost* limped south and west and everyone on board thanked God for the mist because it hid them from the pirates that haunted the gulf between Normandy and Brittany. Villeroy was not sure where they were, though he was certain enough that the Norman coast was to the east and that all the land in that direction was in fealty to the Count of Coutances and so they held on south and west with Yvette perched in the bows to keep a lookout for the frequent reefs. "They breed rocks, these waters," Villeroy grumbled.

"Then go into deeper water," Sir Guillaume suggested.

The big man spat overboard. "Deeper water breeds English pirates out of the isles."

They pushed on south, the wind dying and the sea calming. It was still cold, but there was no more sleet and, when a feeble sun began to burn off the shredding mists, Thomas sat beside Mordecai in the bow. "I have a question for you," he said.

"My father told me never to get on board a ship," Mordecai responded. His long face was pale and his beard, which he usually brushed so carefully, was tangled. He was shivering despite a makeshift cloak of sheepskins. "Did you know," he went on, "that Flemish sailors claim that you can calm a storm by throwing a Jew overboard?"

"Do they really?"

"So I'm told," Mordecai said, "and if I was on board a Flemish ship I might welcome drowning as an alternative to this existence. What is that?"

Thomas had unwrapped the book that his father had bequeathed him. "My question," he said, ignoring Mordecai's question, "is who is Hachaliah?"

"Hachaliah?" Mordecai repeated the name, then shook his head. "Do you think the Flemings carry Jews aboard their ships as a precaution? It would seem a sensible, if cruel, thing to do. Why die when a Jew can die?"

Thomas opened the book to the first page of Hebrew

script where Brother Germain had deciphered the name Hachaliah. "There," he said, giving the book to the doctor, "Hachaliah."

Mordecai peered at the page. "Grandson of Hachaliah," he translated aloud, "and son of the Tirshatha. Of course! It's a confusion about Jonah and the great fish."

"Hachaliah is?" Thomas asked, staring at the page of strange script.

"No, dear boy!" Mordecai said. "The superstition about Jews and storms is a confusion about Jonah, a mere ignorant confusion." He looked back at the page. "Are you the son of the Tirshatha?"

"I'm the bastard son of a priest," Thomas said.

"And did your father write this?"

"Yes."

"For you?"

Thomas nodded. "I think so."

"Then you are the son of the Tirshatha and the grandson of Hachaliah," Mordecai said, then smiled. "Ah! Of course! Nehemiah. My memory is almost as bad as poor Skeat's, eh? Fancy forgetting that Hachaliah was the father of Nehemiah."

Thomas was still none the wiser. "Nehemiah?"

"And he was the Tirshatha, of course he was. Extraordinary, isn't it, how we Jews prosper in foreign states and then they tire of us and we get blamed for every little accident. Then time passes and we are restored to our offices. The Tirshatha, Thomas, was the Governor of Judaea under the Persians. Nehemiah was the Tirshatha, not the King, of course, just Governor for a time under the rule of Artaxerxes." Mordecai's erudition was impressive, but hardly enlightening. Why would Father Ralph identify himself with Nehemiah who must have lived hundreds of years before Christ, before the Grail? The only answer that Thomas could conjure up was the usual one of his father's madness.

Mordecai was turning the parchment pages and winced when one cracked. "How people do yearn," he said, "for miracles." He prodded a page with a finger stained by all the medicines he had pounded and stirred. " 'A golden cup in the Lord's hand that made all the earth drunk,' now what on earth does that mean?"

"He's talking about the Grail," Thomas said.

"I had understood that, Thomas," Mordecai chided him gently, "but those words were not written about the Grail. It refers to Babylon. Part of the lamentations of Jeremiah." He turned another page. "People like mystery. They want nothing explained, because when things are explained then there is no hope left. I have seen folk dying and known there is nothing to be done, and I am asked to go because the priest will soon arrive with his dish covered by a cloth, and everyone prays for a miracle. It never happens. And the person dies and I get blamed, not God or the priest, but I!" He let the book fall on his lap where the pages stirred in the small wind. "These are just stories of the Grail, and some odd scriptures that might refer to it. A book, really, of meditations." He frowned. "Did your father truly believe the Grail existed?"

Thomas was about to give a vigorous affirmative, but paused, remembering. For much of the time his father had been a wry, amused and clever man, but there had been other times when he had been a wild, shrieking creature, struggling with God and desperate to make sense of the sacred mysteries. "I think," Thomas said carefully, "that he did believe in the Grail."

"Of course he did," Mordecai said suddenly, "how stupid of me! Of course your father believed in the Grail because he believed that he possessed it!"

"He did?" Thomas asked. He was utterly confused now.

"Nehemiah was more than the Tirshatha of Judaea," the doctor said, "he was cupbearer to Artaxerxes. He says so at

the beginning of his writings. 'I was the King's cupbearer.'
There." He pointed to a line of Hebrew script. " 'I was the
King's cupbearer.' Your father's words, Thomas, taken from
Nehemiah's story."

Thomas stared at the writing and knew that Mordecai was
right. That was his father's testimony. He had been cupbearer to the greatest King of all, to God Himself, to Christ,
and the phrase confirmed Thomas's dreams. Father Ralph
had been the cupbearer. He had possessed the Grail. It did
exist. Thomas shivered.

"I think"—Mordecai spoke gently—"that your father believed he possessed the Grail, but it seems unlikely."

"Unlikely!" Thomas protested.

"I am merely a Jew," Mordecai said blandly, "so what can
I know of the savior of mankind? And there are those who
say I should not even speak of such things, but so far as I understand Jesus was not rich. Am I right?"

"He was poor," Thomas said.

"So I am right, he was not a rich man, and at the end of his
life he attends a *seder*."

"A *seder*?"

"The Passover feast, Thomas. And at the *seder* he eats
bread and drinks wine, and the Grail, tell me if I am wrong,
was either the bread dish or the wine goblet, yes?"

"Yes."

"Yes," Mordecai echoed and glanced off to his left where
a small fishing boat rode the broken swell. There had been
no sign of the *Saint-Esprit* all morning, and none of the
smaller boats they passed showed any interest in the *Pentecost*. "Yet if Jesus was poor," Mordecai said, "what kind of
seder dish would he use? One made of gold? One ringed
with jewels? Or a piece of common pottery?"

"Whatever he used," Thomas said, "God could trans-
form."

"Ah yes, of course, I was forgetting," Mordecai said. He sounded disappointed, but then he smiled and gave Thomas the book. "When we reach wherever we are going," he said, "I can write down translations of the Hebrew for you and I hope it helps."

"Thomas!" Sir Guillaume bellowed from the stern. "We need fresh arms to bail water!"

The caulking had not been finished and the *Pentecost* was taking water at an alarming rate and so Thomas went down into the bilge and handed up the pails to Robbie who jettisoned the water over the side. Sir Guillaume had been pressing Villeroy to go north and east again in an attempt to run past Caen and make Dunkirk, but Villeroy was unhappy with his small sail and even more unhappy with the leaking hull. "I have to put in somewhere soon," he growled, "and you have to buy me a sail."

They dared not call into Normandy. It was well known throughout the province that Sir Guillaume had been declared a traitor and if the *Pentecost* was searched—and it was probable on this smuggling coast that she would be—then Sir Guillaume would be discovered. That left Brittany and Sir Guillaume was eager to make Saint-Malo or Saint-Brieuc, but Thomas protested from the bilge that he and Will Skeat would be considered enemies by the Breton authorities who, in those towns, held allegiance to Duke Charles who was struggling against the English-backed rebels who reckoned Duke Jean was Brittany's true ruler. "So where would you go?" Sir Guillaume demanded. "England?"

"We'll never make England," Villeroy said unhappily, looking at his sail.

"The islands?" Thomas suggested, thinking of Guernsey or Jersey.

"The islands!" Sir Guillaume liked that idea.

This time it was Villeroy who objected. "Can't do it," he

said bluntly and explained that the *Pentecost* was a Guernsey boat and he had been one of the men who helped capture her. "I take her into the isles," he said, "and they'll take her back and me with her."

"For God's sake!" Sir Guillaume snarled. "Then where do we go?"

"Can you make Tréguier?" Will Skeat asked and everyone was so astonished he had spoken that for a few heartbeats no one responded.

"Tréguier?" Villeroy asked after a while, then nodded. "Like as not," he said.

"Why Tréguier?" Sir Guillaume demanded.

"It was in English hands last I heard," Skeat said.

"Still is," Villeroy put in.

"And we've got friends there," Skeat went on.

And enemies, Thomas thought. Tréguier was not just the closest Breton port in English hands, but also the harbor closest to La Roche-Derrien where Sir Geoffrey Carr, the Scarecrow, had gone. And Thomas had told Brother Germain that he was headed for the same small town, and that would surely mean de Taillebourg would hear of it and follow. And perhaps Jeanette was there too, and suddenly, though Thomas had been saying for weeks that he would not go back, he desperately wanted to reach La Roche-Derrien.

For it was there in Brittany he possessed friends, old lovers and enemies he wanted to kill.

PART THREE

Brittany, Spring 1347

The King's Cupbearer

JEANETTE CHENIER, Comtesse d'Armorique, had lost her husband, her parents, her fortune, her house, her son and her royal lover, and all before she was twenty years old.

Her husband had been lost to an English arrow and had died in agony, weeping like a child.

Her parents had died of the bloody flux and their bed-clothes had been burned before they were buried near the altar of St. Renan's church. They had left Jeanette, their only remaining child, a small fortune in gold, a wine-shipping business and the great merchant's house on the river in La Roche-Derrien.

Jeanette had spent much of the fortune on equipping ships and men to fight the hated English who had killed her husband, but the English won and thus the fortune vanished.

Jeanette had begged help from Charles of Blois, Duke of Brittany and her dead husband's kinsman, and that was how she had lost her son. The three-year-old Charles, named for the duke, had been snatched from her. She was called a whore because she was a merchant's daughter and thus unworthy to be an aristocrat and Charles of Blois, to show Jeanette how much he despised her, had raped her. Her son, now the Count of Armorica, was being raised by one of Charles of Blois's loyal supporters to ensure that the boy's extensive lands stayed sworn to the house of Blois. So

Jeanette, who had lost her fortune in the attempt to make Duke Charles the undisputed ruler of Brittany, learned a new hatred and found a new lover, Thomas of Hookton. She fled north with him to the English army in Normandy and there she had caught the eye of Edward of Woodstock, Prince of Wales, and so Jeanette had abandoned Thomas. But then, fearing that the English would be crushed by the French in Picardy and that the victorious French would punish her for her choice of lover, she had fled again. She had been wrong about the battle, the English had won, but she could not go back. Kings, and the sons of Kings, did not reward fickleness and so Jeanette Chenier, dowager Countess of Armorica, had gone back to La Roche-Derrien to find she had lost her house.

When she had left La Roche-Derrien she had been deeply in debt and Monsieur Belas, a lawyer, had taken the house to pay those debts. Jeanette, on her return, possessed money enough to pay all she owed, for the Prince of Wales had been generous with jewels, but Belas would not move from the house. The law was on his side. Some of the English who occupied La Roche-Derrien showed sympathy for Jeanette, but they did not interfere with the decision of the court and it would not have mattered overmuch if they had, for everyone knew the English could not stay in the small town for long. Duke Charles was gathering a new army in Rennes and La Roche-Derrien was the most isolated and remote of all the English strongholds in Brittany, and when Duke Charles snapped up the town he would reward Monsieur Belas, his agent, and scorn Jeanette Chenier whom he called a whore because she was not nobly born.

So Jeanette, unable to claim back her house, found another, much smaller, close to La Roche-Derrien's southern gate and she confessed her sins to the priest at St. Renan's church, who said she had been wicked beyond man's measure and perhaps beyond God's measure as well; the priest promised her absolution if she would sin with him and he hoisted up his robes and reached for her, then cried aloud as Jeanette kicked him. She continued to take mass at St. Renan's, for it was her childhood church and her parents were buried beneath the painting of Christ emerging from the tomb with a golden light about His head, and the priest dared not refuse her the sacrament and dared not meet her eyes.

Jeanette had lost her servants when she fled north with Thomas, but she hired a fourteen-year-old girl to be her kitchen maid and the girl's idiot brother to draw water and collect firewood. The Prince's jewels, Jeanette reckoned, would last her a year and something would turn up by then. She was young, she was truly beautiful, she was filled with anger, her child was still a hostage and she was inspired by hatred. Some in the town feared she was mad because she was much thinner than when she had left La Roche-Derrien, but her hair was still raven-black, her skin as smooth as the rare silk that only the wealthiest could afford and her eyes were big and bright. Men came and begged her favors, but were told they could not speak to her again unless they brought her the shriveled heart of Belas the lawyer and the shriveled prick of Charles of Blois. "Bring them both to me in reliquaries," she told them, "but bring me my son alive." Her anger repelled men and some of them spread the tale that she was moon-touched, perhaps a witch. The priest of St. Renan's confided to the other clergy in the town that Jeanette had tried to tempt him and he spoke darkly of bringing in the Inquisition, but the English would not permit it for the King of England refused to let the torturers of God work their dark arts in his possessions. "There's enough grumbling," Dick Totesham, commander of the English garrison in La Roche-Derrien said, "without bringing in damned friars to stir up trouble."

Totesham and his garrison knew that Charles of Blois was

raising an army that would attack La Roche-Derrien before marching on to besiege the other English strongholds in Brittany, and so they worked hard to make the town's walls higher and to build new ramparts outside the old. Local farm laborers were whipped to the work. They were forced to push barrowloads of clay and rock, they drove timbers into the soil to make palisades and they dug ditches. They hated the English for forcing them to work without pay, but the English did not care for they had to defend themselves and Totesham pleaded with Westminster to send him more men and on the feast of St. Felix, in the middle of January, a troop of Welsh archers landed at Tréguier, which was the small harbor an hour and a half's walk upriver from La Roche-Derrien, but the garrison's only other reinforcements were a few knights and men-at-arms who were down on their luck and came to the small town in hope of plunder and prisoners. Some of those knights came from as far away as Flanders, lured by false rumors of the riches to be had in Brittany, and another six men-at-arms arrived from northern England, led by a malevolent, raw-faced man who carried a whip and a heavy load of grudges, and they were La Roche-Derrien's last reinforcements before the *Pentecost* came to the river.

La Roche-Derrien's garrison was small, but Duke Charles's army was large and grew even larger. Spies in English pay told of Genoese crossbowmen arriving at Rennes in companies a hundred strong, and of men-at-arms riding from France to swear fealty to Charles of Blois. His army swelled and the King of England, apparently careless of his garrisons in Brittany, sent them no help. Which meant that La Roche-Derrien, smallest of all the English fortress towns in Brittany and the one closest to the enemy, was doomed.

THOMAS FELT STRANGELY unsettled as the *Pentecost* slipped between the low rocky outcrops that marked the mouth of the River Jaudy. Was it a failure, he wondered, to be coming back to this small town? Or had God sent him because it was here that the enemies of the Grail would be seeking him? That was how Thomas thought of the mysterious de Taillebourg and his servant. Or perhaps, he told himself, he was merely nervous of seeing Jeanette again. Their history was too tangled, there was too much hate mixed with the love, yet he did want to see her and he was worried she would not want to see him. He tried and failed to conjure a picture of her face as the incoming tide carried the *Pentecost* into the river's mouth, where guillemots spread their ragged black wings to dry above rocks fretted with white foam. A seal raised its glistening head, stared indignantly at Thomas and then went back to the depths. The riverbanks came closer, bringing the smell of land. There were boulders and pale grass and small wind-bent trees, while in the shallows there were sinuous fish traps made from woven willow stakes. A small girl, scarce more than six years old, used a stone to knock limpets from the rocks. "It's a poor supper, that," Will Skeat remarked.

"It is, Will, it is."

"Ah, Tom!" Skeat smiled, recognizing the voice. "You never had limpets for supper!"

"I did!" Thomas protested. "And for breakfast too."

"A man who speaks Latin and French? Eating limpets?" Skeat grinned. "You can write, ain't that so, Tom?"

"Good as a priest, Will."

"I reckon we should send a letter to his lordship," Skeat said, meaning the Earl of Northampton, "and ask for my men to be shipped here, only he won't do that without money, will he?"

"He owes you money," Thomas said.

Skeat frowned at Thomas. "He does?"

"Your men have been serving him these last months. He has to pay for that."

Skeat shook his head. "The Earl was never slow to pay for

good soldiers. He'll be keeping their purses full, I'll be
bound, and if I want them here I'll have to persuade him to
let them go and I'll have to pay their passages too." Skeat's
men were contracted to fight for the Earl of Northampton
who, after campaigning in Brittany, had joined the King in
Normandy and now served him near Calais. "I'll have to pay
passage for men and horses, Thomas," Skeat went on, "and
unless things have changed since I got slapped about the
head that won't be cheap. Won't be cheap. And why would
the Earl want them to leave Calais? They'll have a bellyful
of fighting come springtime."

The question was a good one, Thomas thought, for there
surely would be some vicious fighting near Calais when the
winter ended. So far as Thomas knew the town had not
fallen, but the English had surrounded it and the French
King was said to be raising a great army that would attack
the besiegers in springtime.

"There'll be plenty of fighting here come spring," Thomas
said, nodding at the riverbank, which was very close now.
The fields beyond the banks were fallow, but at least the
barns and farmhouses still stood for these lands fed La
Roche-Derrien's garrison and so they had been spared the
pillage, rape and fire that had crackled across the rest of the
dukedom.

"There'll be fighting here," Skeat agreed, "but more in
Calais. Maybe you and I should go there, Tom?"

Thomas said nothing. He feared Skeat could no longer
command a band of men-at-arms and archers. His old friend
was too prone to forgetfulness or to sudden bouts of vague-
ness and melancholy, and those attacks were made worse by
the times when Skeat seemed like his old self—except he
never was *quite* like the old Will Skeat who had been so
swift in war, savage in decision and clever in battle. Now he
repeated himself, became confused and was too frequently
puzzled—as he was now by a guardboat flying England's

red cross on its white field that pulled downstream toward the *Pentecost*. Skeat frowned at the small craft. "Is he an enemy?"

"Flying our flag, Will."

"He is?"

A mail-clad man stood up in the rowboat's bows and hailed the *Pentecost*. "Who are you?"

"Sir William Skeat!" Thomas shouted back, using the name that would be most welcome in Brittany.

There was a pause, maybe of incredulity. "Sir William Skeat?" the man called back. "Will Skeat, you mean?"

"The King knighted him," Thomas told the man.

"I keep forgetting that myself," Skeat said.

The portside oarsmen backed water so that the guard boat turned in the tide alongside the *Pentecost*. "What are you carrying?" the man asked.

"Empty!" Thomas shouted.

The man stared up at the ragged, scorched, doubled sail. "You had trouble?"

"Off Normandy."

"Time those bastards were killed once and for all," the man grumbled, then gestured upriver to where Tréguier's houses smeared the sky with their woodsmoke. "Tie up outboard of the *Edward*," he ordered them. "There's a harbor fee you'll have to pay. Six shillings."

"Six shillings?" Villeroy exploded when he was told. "Six bloody shillings! Do they think we pull money off the seabed in nets?"

Thus Thomas and Will Skeat came back to Tréguier where the cathedral had lost its tower after Bretons who supported Charles of Blois had fired crossbows at the English from its summit. In retaliation the English had pulled the tower down and shipped the stone to London. The little harbor town was scantily populated now for it had no walls and Charles of Blois's men sometimes raided the warehouses behind the quay. Small ships could go all the way upriver to La Roche-Derrien, but the *Pentecost* drew too much water and so she tied herself alongside the English cog and then a dozen men in red-crossed jupons came aboard to take the harbor fee and look for contraband or else a healthy bribe to persuade them to ignore whatever they might discover, but they found neither goods nor bribe. Their commander, a fat man with a weeping ulcer on his forehead, confirmed that Richard Totesham still commanded at La Roche-Derrien. "He be there," the fat man said, "and Sir Thomas Dagworth commands in Brest."

"Dagworth!" Skeat sounded pleased. "He's a good one, he is. So's Dick Totesham," he added to Thomas, then looked puzzled as Sir Guillaume emerged from the forecabin.

"It's Sir Guillaume," Thomas said in a low voice.

"'Course it is," Skeat said.

Sir Guillaume dropped the saddlebags on the deck and the chink of coins drew an expectant gaze from the fat man. Sir Guillaume met his gaze and half drew his sword.

"Reckon I be going," the fat man said.

"Reckon you do," Skeat said with a chuckle.

Robbie heaved his baggage onto the deck, then stared across the waist of the *Edward* to where four girls were gutting herrings and chucking the offal into the air where gulls snatched it in mid flight. The girls strung the gutted fish on long poles that would be placed in the smokers at the quay's end. "Are they all as pretty as that?" Robbie asked.

"Prettier," Thomas said, wondering how the Scot could see the girl's faces under their bonnets.

"I'm going to like Brittany," Robbie said.

There were debts to be paid before they could leave. Sir Guillaume paid off Villeroy and added enough cash to buy a new sail. "You might do well," he advised the big man, "to avoid Caen for a while."

"We'll go on down to Gascony," Villeroy said. "There's

always trade in Gascony. Maybe we'll even poke on down to Portugal?"

"Perhaps," Mordecai spoke shyly, "you would let me come?"

"You?" Sir Guillaume turned on the doctor. "You hate goddamn ships."

"I have to go south," Mordecai said wearily, "to Montpellier first of all. The farther south a man is, the friendlier the people. I would rather suffer a month of sea and cold than meet Duke Charles's men."

"Passage to Gascony"—Sir Guillaume offered Villeroy a gold coin—"for a friend of mine."

Villeroy glanced at Yvette, who shrugged, and that persuaded the big man to agree. "You're welcome, doctor," he said.

So they said farewell to Mordecai and then Thomas and Robbie, Will Skeat and Sir Guillaume and his two men-at-arms went ashore. A boat was going upstream to La Roche-Derrien, but not till later in the day and so the two men-at-arms were left with the baggage and Thomas led the others along the narrow track that followed the river's western bank. They wore mail and carried weapons for the local peasantry were not friendly to the English, but the only men they passed were a dozen drab laborers pitch-forking dung from two carts. The men paused to watch the soldiers pass, but said nothing. "And by this time tomorrow," Thomas commented, "Charles of Blois will know we've arrived."

"He'll be quaking in his boots," Skeat said with a grin.

It began to rain as they reached the bridge which led into La Roche-Derrien. Thomas stopped under the arch of the protective barbican on the bank opposite the town and pointed upstream to the ramshackle quay where he and Skeat's other archers had sneaked into La Roche-Derrien on the night it first fell to the English. "Remember that place, Will?" he asked.

" 'Course I remember," Skeat said, though he looked vague and Thomas did not say more.

They crossed the stone bridge and hurried down the street to the house by the tavern that had always been Richard Totesham's headquarters and Totesham himself was just sliding out of his saddle as they arrived. He turned and scowled at the newcomers, then recognized Will Skeat and stared at his old friend as though he had seen a ghost. Skeat looked blankly back and his lack of recognition troubled Totesham. "Will?" the garrison commander asked. "Will? Is it you, Will?"

A look of astonished delight animated Skeat's face. "Dick Totesham! Of all the folk to meet!"

Totesham was puzzled that Skeat should be surprised to meet him in a garrison he commanded, but then he saw the emptiness in his old friend's eyes and frowned. "Are you well, Will?"

"I had a bash on the head," Skeat said, "but a doctor cobbled me together again. Things get blurred here and there, just blurred."

The two clasped hands. They were both men who had been born penniless and become soldiers, then earned the trust of their masters and gained the profits of prisoners ransomed and property plundered until they were wealthy enough to raise their own bands of men, which they hired to the King or to a noble and so became richer still as they ravaged more enemy lands. When the troubadours sang of battle they named the King as the fighting hero, and extolled the exploits of dukes, earls, barons and knights, but it was men like Totesham and Skeat who did most of England's fighting.

Totesham clapped Skeat good-naturedly on the shoulder. "Tell me you've brought your men, Will."

"God knows where they are," Skeat said. "I haven't laid eyes on them in months."

"They're outside Calais," Thomas put in.

"Dear God." Totesham made the sign of the cross. He was a squat man, gray-haired and broad-faced, who held La Roche-Derrien's garrison together by sheer force of character, but he knew he had too few men. Far too few men. "I've a hundred and thirty-two men under orders," he told Skeat, "and half of those are sick. Then there's fifty or sixty mercenaries who might or might not stay till Charles of Blois arrives. Of course the townsfolk will fight for us, or most of them will."

"They will?" Thomas interrupted, astonished at the claim. When the English had captured the town the previous year the town's people had fought bitterly to defend their walls, and when they had lost they had been subjected to rape and plunder, yet now they supported the garrison?

"Trade's good," Totesham explained. "They've never been so rich! Ships to Gascony, to Portugal, to Flanders and to England. Making money, they are. They don't want us to leave, so yes, some will fight for us and it'll help, but it's not like having trained men."

The other English troops in Brittany were a long way to the west so when Charles of Blois came with his army, Totesham would have to hold the small town for two or three weeks before he could expect any relief and, even with the inhabitants' help, he doubted he could do it. He had sent a petition to the King at Calais begging that more men be sent to La Roche-Derrien. "We are far from help," his clerk had written to Totesham's dictation, "and our enemies gather close about." Totesham, seeing Will Skeat, had assumed that Skeat's men had arrived in answer to his petition and he could not hide his disappointment. "You'll write to the King yourself?" Totesham asked Will.

"Tom here can write for me."

"Ask for your men to be sent," Totesham urged. "I need three or four hundred more archers, but your fifty or sixty would help."

"Tommy Dagworth can't send you any?" Skeat asked.

"He's as hard pressed as I am. Too much land to hold, too few men and the King won't hear of us surrendering a single acre to Charles of Blois."

"So why doesn't he send reinforcements?" Sir Guillaume asked.

"Because he ain't got men to spare," Totesham said, "which is no reason for us not to ask."

Totesham took them inside his house where a fire blazed in a big hearth and his servants brought jugs of mulled wine and plates of bread and cold pork. A baby lay in a wooden cradle by the fire and Totesham blushed when he admitted it was his. "Newly married," he told Skeat, then ordered a maid to take the baby away before it began crying. He flinched when Skeat took off his hat to reveal his scarred, thick-ridged scalp, then he insisted on hearing Will's story, and when it was told he thanked Sir Guillaume for the help the Frenchman had given his friend. Thomas and Robbie got a cooler welcome, the latter because he was Scottish and the former because Totesham remembered Thomas from the previous year. "You were a bloody nuisance," Totesham said bluntly, "you and the Countess of Armorica."

"Is she here?" Thomas asked.

"She came back, aye." Totesham sounded guarded.

"We can go back to her house, Will," Thomas said to Skeat.

"No you can't," Totesham said firmly. "She lost the house. It was sold to pay her debts and she's been screaming about it ever since, but it was sold fair and square. And the lawyer who bought it has paid us a quittance to be left in peace and I don't want him disturbed, so the two of you can find yourself space at the Two Foxes. Then come and have supper." This invitation was to Will Skeat and to Sir Guillaume and pointedly not to Thomas or Robbie.

Thomas did not mind. He and Robbie found a room to

share in the tavern called the Two Foxes and afterward, as
Robbie had his first taste of Breton ale, Thomas went to St.
Renan's church, which was one of the smallest in La Roche-
Derrien, but also one of the wealthiest because Jeanette's father had endowed it. He had built a bell tower and paid to
have fine pictures painted on its walls, though by the time
Thomas reached St. Renan's it was too dark to see the Savior walking on Galilee's water or the souls tumbling down to
their fiery hell. The only light in the church came from some
candles burning on the altar where a silver reliquary held St.
Renan's tongue, but Thomas knew there was another treasure beneath the altar, something almost as rare as a saint's
silent tongue, and he wanted to consult it. It was a book, a
gift from Jeanette's father, and Thomas had been astonished
to find it there, not just because the book had survived the
fall of the town—though in truth not many soldiers would
seek books for plunder—but because there was any book in
a small church in a Breton town. Books were rare and that
was St. Renan's treasure: a bible. Most of the New Testament was missing, evidently because some soldiers had
taken those pages to use in the latrines, but all of the Old
Testament remained. Thomas threaded his way through the
black-dressed old ladies who knelt and prayed in the nave
and he found the book beneath the altar and blew off the dust
and cobwebs, then put it beside the candles. One of the
women hissed that he was being impious, but Thomas ignored her.

He turned the stiff pages, sometimes stopping to admire a
painted capital. There was a bible in St. Peter's church in
Dorchester and his father had possessed one, and Thomas
must have seen a dozen in Oxford, but he had seen few others and, as he searched the pages, he marveled at the time it
must take to copy such a vast book. More women protested
his annexation of the altar and so, to placate them, he went a
few steps away and sat cross-legged with the heavy book on

his lap. He was now too far from the candles and found it hard to read the script, which was mostly ill done. The capitals were pretty, suggesting they had been done by a skilled hand, but most of the writing was cramped and his task was made no easier by his ignorance of where to look in the huge book. He began at the end of the Old Testament, but did not find what he wanted and so he leafed back, the huge pages crackling as he turned them. He knew what he sought was not in the Psalms so he turned those pages fast, then slowed again, seeking words out of the ill-written script and then, suddenly, the names jumped from the page. " '*Neemias Athersatha filius Achelai*, Nehemiah the Governor, son of Hachaliah.' " He read the whole passage, but did not find what he sought, and so he leafed still farther back, page by stiff page, knowing he was close, and there, at last, it was.

"*Ego enim eram pincerna regis.*"

He stared at the phrase, then read it aloud. " '*Ego enim eram pincerna regis.*' "

"For I was the King's cupbearer."

Mordecai had thought Father Ralph's book was a plea to God to make the Grail true, but Thomas did not agree. His father did not want to be the cupbearer. No, the notebook was a way of confessing and of hiding the truth. His father had left a trail for him to follow. Go from Hachaliah to the Tirshatha and realize that the Governor was also the cupbearer: *ego enim eram pincerna regis*. "Was," Thomas thought. Did that mean his father had lost the Grail? It was more likely that he knew Thomas would only read the book after his death. But Thomas was certain of one thing: the words confirmed that the Grail did exist and his father had been its reluctant keeper. I was the King's cupbearer; let this cup pass from me; the cup makes me drunk. The cup existed and Thomas felt a shiver go though his body. He stared at the candles on the altar and his eyes blurred with tears. Eleanor had been right. The Grail existed and it was waiting to be found and to put the world right and to bring God to man and man to God and peace on earth. It existed. It was the Grail.

"My father," a woman said, "gave that book to the church."

"I know he did," Thomas said, then he closed the bible and he turned to look at Jeanette and he was almost frightened to see her in case she was less beautiful than he remembered, or perhaps he feared the sight of her would engender hatred because she had abandoned him, but instead he felt tears in his eyes when he saw her face. "*Merle*," he said softly, using her nickname. It meant Blackbird.

"Thomas." Her voice was toneless, then she flicked her head toward an old woman dressed and veiled in black. "Madame Verlon," Jeanette said, "who is nervous of life, told me that an English soldier was stealing the bible."

"So you came to fight the soldier?" Thomas asked. A candle guttered to his right, its flame flickering as fast as a small bird's heart.

Jeanette shrugged. "The priest here is a coward and would not challenge an English archer, so who else would come?"

"Madame Verlon can rest safe," Thomas said as he put the bible back under the altar.

"She also said"—Jeanette's voice had a quaver in it—"that the man stealing the bible had a big black bow." Which was why, she implied, she had come herself instead of sending for help. She had guessed it was Thomas.

"At least you did not have to come far," Thomas said, gesturing to the side door which led into the yard of Jeanette's father's house. He was pretending not to know that she had lost the house.

Her head jerked back. "I do not live there," she said curtly, "not now."

A dozen women were listening and they stepped nervously back as Thomas came toward them. "Then perhaps, madame," he said to Jeanette, "you will let me escort you home?"

She nodded abruptly. Her eyes seemed very bright and big in the candlelight. She was thinner, Thomas thought, or perhaps that was the darkness in the church shadowing her cheeks. She had a bonnet tied under her chin and a great black cloak that swept on the flagstones as she followed him to the western door. "You remember Belas?" she asked him.

"I remember the name," Thomas said. "Wasn't he a lawyer?"

"He is a lawyer," Jeanette said, "and a thing of bile, a creature of slime, a cheat. What was that English word you taught me? A tosspot. He is a tosspot. When I came home he had bought the house, claiming it was sold to pay my debts. But he had bought the debts! He promised to look after my business, waited till I was gone, then took my house. And now I am back he won't let me pay what I owed. He says it is paid. I said I would buy the house from him for more than he paid, but he just laughs at me."

Thomas held the door for her. Rain was spitting in the street. "You don't want the house," he told her, "not if Charles of Blois comes back. You should be gone by then."

"You're still telling me what to do, Thomas?" she asked and then, as if to soften the harshness of her words, she took his arm. Or perhaps she put her hand through his elbow because the street was steep and slippery. "I will stay here, I think."

"If you hadn't escaped from him," Thomas said, "Charles was going to marry you to one of his men-at-arms. If he finds you here he'll do that. Or worse."

"He already has my child. He has already raped me. What more can he do? No"—she clutched Thomas's arm fiercely—"I shall stay in my little house by the south gate and when he rides into the town I will sink a crossbow quarrel in his belly."

"I'm surprised you haven't put a quarrel into Belas's belly."

"You think I would hang for a lawyer's death?" Jeanette asked and gave a short, hard laugh. "No, I shall save my death for the life of Charles of Blois and all Brittany and France will know he was killed by a woman."

"Unless he returns your child?"

"He won't!" she said fiercely. "He answered no appeals." She meant, Thomas was sure, that the Prince of Wales, maybe the King as well, had written to Charles of Blois, but the appeals had achieved nothing, and why should they? England was Charles's most bitter enemy. "It's all about land, Thomas," she said wearily, "land and money." She meant that her son, who at three years old was the Count of Armorica, was the rightful heir to great swathes of western Brittany that were presently under English occupation. If the child were to give fealty to Duke Jean, who was Edward of England's candidate to rule Brittany, then the claim of Charles of Blois to sovereignty of the duchy would be seriously weakened and so Charles had taken the child and would keep him till he was of an age to swear fealty.

"Where is Charles?" Thomas asked. It was one of the ironies of Jeanette's life that her son had been named after his great-uncle in an attempt to win his favor.

"He is in the Tower of Roncelets," Jeanette said, "which is south of Rennes. He is being raised by the Lord of Roncelets." She turned on Thomas. "It's almost a year since I've seen him!"

"The Tower of Roncelets," Thomas said, "it's a castle?"

"I've not seen it. A tower, I suppose. Yes, a castle."

"You're sure he's there?"

"I'm sure of nothing," Jeanette said wearily, "but I received a letter which said Charles was there and I have no reason to doubt it."

"Who wrote the letter?"

"I don't know. It was not signed." She walked in silence for a few paces, her hand warm on his arm. "It was Belas," she said finally. "I don't know that for sure, but it must be. He was goading me, tormenting me. It is not enough that he has my house and Charles of Blois has my child, Belas wants me to suffer. Or else he wants me to go to Roncelets knowing that I would be given back to Charles of Blois. I'm sure it was Belas. He hates me."

"Why?"

"Why do you think?" she asked scornfully. "I have something he wants, something all men want, but I won't give it to him."

They walked on through dark streets. Singing sounded from some taverns, and somewhere a woman screamed at her man. A dog barked and was silenced. The rain pattered on thatch, dripped from the eaves and made the muddy street slippery. A red glow slowly appeared ahead, growing as they came closer until Thomas saw the flames of two braziers warming the guards on the south gate and he remembered how he and Jake and Sam had opened that gate to let in the English army. "I promised you once," he said to Jeanette, "that I would fetch Charles back."

"You and I, Thomas," Jeanette said, "made too many promises." She still sounded weary.

"I should start keeping some of mine," Thomas said. "But to reach Roncelets I need horses."

"I can afford horses," Jeanette said, stopping by a dark doorway. "I live here," she went on, then looked into his face. He was tall, but she was very nearly the same height. "The Count of Roncelets is famous as a warrior. You mustn't die to keep a promise you should never have made."

"It was made, though," Thomas said.

She nodded. "That is true."

There was a long pause. Thomas could hear a sentry's footsteps on the wall. "I—" he began.

"No," she said hastily.

"I didn't . . ."

"Another time. I must get used to your being here. I'm tired of men, Thomas. Since Picardy . . ." She paused and Thomas thought she would say no more, but then she shrugged. "Since Picardy I have lived like a nun."

He kissed her forehead. "I love you," he said, meaning it, but surprised all the same that he had spoken the thought aloud.

For a heartbeat she did not speak. The reflected light from the two braziers glinted red in her eyes. "What happened to that girl?" she asked. "That little pale thing who was so protective of you?"

"I failed to protect her," Thomas said, "and she died."

"Men are such bastards," she said, then turned and pulled the rope that lifted the latch of the door. She paused for a moment. "But I'm glad you're here," she said without looking back, and then the door was shut, the bolt slid home and she was gone.

SIR GEOFFREY CARR had begun to think his foray to Brittany was a mistake. For a long time there had been no sign of Thomas of Hookton and once the archer arrived he had made little effort to discover any treasure. It was mysterious and all the time Sir Geoffrey's debts were growing. But then, at last, the Scarecrow discovered what plans Thomas of Hookton was hatching. That new knowledge took Sir Geoffrey to Maître Belas's house.

Rain poured on La Roche-Derrien. It was one of the wettest winters in memory. The ditch beyond the strengthened town wall was flooded so it looked like a moat, and many of the River Jaudy's water meadows resembled lakes. The streets of the town were sticky with mud, men's boots were thick with it and women went to market wearing awkward wooden pattens that slipped treacherously on the steeper streets and still thick mud was smeared on the hems of their dresses and cloaks. The only good things about such rain was the protection it offered against fire and, for the English, the knowledge that it would make any siege of the town difficult. Siege engines, whether catapults, trebuchets or guns, needed a solid base, not a quagmire, and men could not assault through a marsh. Richard Totesham was said to be praying for more rain and giving thanks every morning that dawned gray, heavy and damp.

"A wet winter, Sir Geoffrey," Belas greeted the Scarecrow, then gave his visitor a covert inspection. A raw and ugly face, he thought, and while Sir Geoffrey's clothes were of a fine quality, they had also been made for a fatter man which suggested that either the Englishman had recently lost weight or, more likely, the clothes had been taken from a man he had killed in battle. A coiled whip hung at his belt, which seemed a strange accoutrement, but the lawyer never presumed to understand soldiers. "A very wet winter," Belas went on, waving the Scarecrow into a chair.

"It's a pissing wet winter," Sir Geoffrey snarled to cover his nervousness, "nothing but rain, cold and chilblains." He was nervous because he was not certain that this thin and watchful lawyer was as sympathetic to Charles of Blois as tavern rumor suggested, and he had been forced to leave Beggar and Dickon in the courtyard below and he felt vulnerable without their protective company, especially as the lawyer had a great hulking attendant who was dressed in a leather jerkin and had a long sword at his side.

"Pierre protects me," Belas said. He had seen Sir Geoffrey glancing at the big man. "He protects me from the enemies all honest lawyers make. Please, Sir Geoffrey, sit yourself." He gestured again at a chair. A small fire burned in the hearth, the smoke vanishing up a newly made chimney. The lawyer had a face as hungry as a stoat and pale as a grass-snake's belly. He was wearing a black gown and a black cloak edged with black fur and a black hat with flaps that covered his ears, though he now pushed one flap up so he could hear the Scarecrow's voice. "*Parlez-vous français?*" he asked.

"No."

"*Brezoneg a ouzit?*" the lawyer inquired and, when he saw the dumb incomprehension on the Scarecrow's face, shrugged. "You don't speak Breton?"

"I just told you, didn't I? I don't talk French."

"French and Breton are not the same language, Sir Geoffrey."

"They're not bloody English," Sir Geoffrey said belligerently.

"Indeed they are not. Alas, I do not speak English well, but I learn fast. It is, after all, the language of our new masters."

"Masters?" the Scarecrow asked. "Or enemies?"

Belas shrugged. "I am a man of, how do you say? of affairs. A man of affairs. It is not possible, I think, to be such and not to make enemies." He shrugged again, as if he spoke of trivialities, then he leaned back in his chair. "But you come on business, Sir Geoffrey? You have property to convey, perhaps? A contract to make?"

"Jeanette Chenier, Countess of Armorica," Sir Geoffrey said bluntly.

Belas was surprised, but did not show it. He was alert, though. He knew well enough that Jeanette wanted revenge and he was ever watchful for her machinations, but now he pretended indifference. "I know of the lady," he admitted.

"She knows you. And she don't like you, *Monsieur* Belas," Sir Geoffrey said, making his pronunciation of the name sound like a sneer. "She don't like you one small bit. She'd like to have your collops in a skillet and kindle a fierce fire under them."

Belas turned to the papers on his desk as though his visitor was being tedious. "I told you, Sir Geoffrey, that a lawyer inevitably makes enemies. It is nothing to worry about. The law protects me."

"Piss on the law, Belas." Sir Geoffrey spoke flatly. His eyes, curiously pale, watched the lawyer, who pretended to be busy sharpening a quill. "Suppose the lady got her son back?" the Scarecrow went on. "Suppose the lady takes her son to Edward of England and has the boy swear fealty to Duke Jean? The law won't stop them chopping off your collops then, will it? One, two, snip, snip and stoke the fire, lawyer."

"Such an eventuality," Belas said in apparent boredom, "could have no possible repercussions for me."

"So your English ain't bad, eh?" Sir Geoffrey sneered. "I don't pretend to know the law, monsieur, but I know folk. If the Countess gets her son then she'll go to Calais and see the King."

"So?" Belas asked, still pretending carelessness.

"Three months"—Sir Geoffrey held up three fingers— "four, maybe, before your Charles of Blois can get here. And she might be in Calais in four weeks' time and back here with the King's piece of parchment inside eight weeks, and by then she'll be valuable. Her son has what the King wants and he'll give her what she wants, and what she wants is your collops. She'll bite them off with her little white teeth and then she'll skin you alive, monsieur, and the law won't help you. Not against the King, it won't."

Belas had been pretending to read a parchment, which he now released so that it rolled up with a snap. He stared at the Scarecrow, then shrugged. "I doubt, Sir Geoffrey, that what you describe is likely to happen. The Countess's son is not here."

"But suppose, monsieur, just suppose, that a party of men is readying themselves to go to Roncelets and fetch the little tosspot?"

Belas paused. He had heard a rumor that just such a raid was being planned, but he had doubted the rumor's truth for such tales had been told a score of times and come to nothing. Yet something in Sir Geoffrey's tone suggested that this time there might be some meat on the bone. "A party of men," Belas responded flatly.

"A party of men," the Scarecrow confirmed, "that plans to ride to Roncelets and watch until the little darling is taken out for his morning piddle and then they'll snatch him, bring him back here and put your collops in the frying pan."

Belas unrolled the parchment and pretended to read it again. "It is hardly surprising, Sir Geoffrey," he said carelessly, "that Madame Chenier conspires for the return of her son. It is to be expected. But why should you bother me with it? What harm can it do me?" He dipped the newly sharpened quill in his ink pot. "And how do you know about this planned raid?"

"Because I ask the right questions, don't I?" the Scarecrow answered.

In truth the Scarecrow had heard rumors that Thomas planned a raid on Rostrenen, but other men in the town had sworn that Rostrenen had been picked over so often that a sparrow would die of starvation there now. So what, the Scarecrow had wondered, was Thomas really doing? Sir Geoffrey was certain that Thomas was riding to find the treasure, the same treasure that had taken him to Durham, but why would it be at Rostrenen? What was there? Sir Geoffrey had accosted one of Richard Totesham's deputies in a tavern and bought the man ale and asked about Rostrenen and the man had laughed and shaken his head. "You don't want to ride on that nonsense," he told Sir Geoffrey.

"Nonsense?"

"They ain't going to Rostrenen. They're going to Roncelets. Well, we don't know that for certain," the man had continued, "but the Countess of Armorica is up to her pretty neck in the whole business, so that means it must be Roncelets. And you want my advice, Sir Geoffrey? Stay out of it. They don't call Roncelets the wasp's nest for nothing."

Sir Geoffrey, more confused than ever, asked more questions and slowly he came to understand that the *thesaurus* Thomas sought was not thick golden coins, nor leather bags filled with jewels, but instead was land: the Breton estates of the Count of Armorica, and if Jeanette's little son swore allegiance to Duke Jean, then the English cause in Brittany was advanced. It was a treasure in its way, a political treasure: not so satisfying as gold, but it was still valuable. Quite what the land had to do with Durham the Scarecrow did not know. Perhaps Thomas had gone there to find some deeds? Or a grant made by a previous duke? Some lawyer's nonsense, and it did not matter; what mattered was that Thomas was riding to seize a boy who could bring political muscle to the King of England, and Sir Geoffrey had then wondered how he could benefit from the child and for a time he had toyed with the wild idea of kidnapping the boy and taking him to Calais himself, but then he had realized there was a far safer profit to be made by simply betraying Thomas. Which was why he was here, and Belas, he suspected, was interested, but the lawyer was also pretending that the raid on Roncelets was none of his business and so the Scarecrow decided it was time to force the lawyer's hand. He stood and pulled down his rain-soaked jerkin. "You ain't interested, monsieur?" he asked. "So be it. You know your business better than I do, but I know how many are going to Roncelets and I know who leads them and I can tell you when they're going." The quill was no longer moving and drips of ink were falling from its tip to blot the parchment, but Belas did not notice as the Scarecrow's harsh voice ground on. "Of course they ain't told Mr. Totesham what they're doing, on account that officially he'd disapprove, which he might or he might not, I wouldn't know, so he thinks they're going to burn some farms near Rostrenen, which maybe they will and maybe they won't, but whatever they say and whatever Master Totesham might believe, I know they're going to Roncelets."

"How do you know?" Belas asked quietly.

"I know!" Sir Geoffrey said harshly.

Belas put down the pen. "Sit," he ordered the Scarecrow, "and tell me what you want."

"Two things," Sir Geoffrey said as he sat again. "I came to this damned town to make money, but we're having thin pickings, monsieur, thin pickings." Very thin, for English troops had been pillaging Brittany for months and there were no farms within a day's ride that had not been burned and robbed, while to ride further afield was to risk strong enemy patrols. Beyond the walls of its fortresses Brittany was a wilderness of ambush, danger and ruin and the Scarecrow had quickly discovered that it would be a hard landscape in which to make a fortune.

"So money is the first thing you want," Belas said acidly. "And the second?"

"Refuge," Sir Geoffrey said.

"Refuge?"

"When Charles of Blois takes the town," the Scarecrow said, "then I want to be in your courtyard."

"I cannot think why," Belas said dryly, "but of course you will be welcome. And as for money?" He licked his lips. "Let us first see how good your information is."

"And if it is good?" the Scarecrow asked.

Belas considered for a moment. "Seventy *écus*?" he suggested. "Eighty, perhaps?"

"Seventy *écus*?" The Scarecrow paused to convert it into pounds, then spat. "Just ten pounds! No! I want a hundred pounds and I want them in English-struck coin."

They settled on sixty English pounds, to be paid when Belas had proof that Sir Geoffrey was telling him the truth, and that truth was that Thomas of Hookton was leading men to Roncelets and they were leaving on the eve of Valentine's Feast which was just over two weeks away.

"Why so long?" Belas wanted to know.

"He wants more men. He's only got half a dozen now and he's trying to persuade others to go with him. He's telling them there's gold to be had at Roncelets."

"If you want money," Belas asked acidly, "why don't you ride with him?"

"Because I'm seeing you instead," Sir Geoffrey answered.

Belas leaned back in his chair and steepled his pale, long fingers. "And that is all you want?" he asked the Englishman. "Some money and refuge?"

The Scarecrow stood, bending his head under the room's low beams. "You pay me once," he said, "and you'll pay me again."

"Perhaps," Belas said evasively.

"I give you what you want," Sir Geoffrey said, "and you'll pay me." He went to the door, then stopped because Belas had called him back.

"Did you say Thomas of Hookton?" Belas asked and there was an undeniable interest in his voice.

"Thomas of Hookton," the Scarecrow confirmed.

"Thank you," Belas said, and he looked down at a scroll he had just unrolled and it seemed he found Thomas's name written there for his finger checked and he smiled. "Thank you," he said again and, to Sir Geoffrey's astonishment, the lawyer took a small purse from a chest beside his desk and pushed it toward the Scarecrow. "For that news, Sir Geoffrey, I do thank you."

Sir Geoffrey, back down in the courtyard, found he had been given ten pounds of English gold. Ten pounds for just mentioning Thomas's name? He suspected there was much more to learn about Thomas's plans, but at least he had gold in his pocket now, so the visit to the lawyer had been profitable and there was the promise of more lawyer's gold to come.

But it was still bloody raining.

THOMAS PERSUADED Richard Totesham that instead of writing another plea to the King they should appeal to the Earl of Northampton who was now among the leaders of the army besieging Calais. The letter reminded his lordship of his great victory in capturing La Roche-Derrien and stressed that achievement might all be for naught if the garrison was not reinforced. Richard Totesham dictated most of the words and Will Skeat put a cross beside his name at the foot of the letter which claimed, truthfully enough, that Charles of Blois was assembling a new and mighty army in Rennes.

"Master Totesham," Thomas wrote, "who sends your lordship humble greetings, reckons that Charles's army already numbers a thousand men-at-arms, two times that number in crossbowmen and other men besides, while in our garrison we have scarce a hundred healthy men, while your kinsman, Sir Thomas Dagworth, who is a week's march away, can raise no more than six or seven hundred men."

Sir Thomas Dagworth, the English commander in Brittany, was married to the Earl of Northampton's sister and Totesham was hoping that family pride alone would persuade the Earl to avoid a defeat in Brittany, and if Northampton were to send Skeat's archers, just the archers and not the men-at-arms, it would double the number of bowmen on La Roche-Derrien's walls and give Totesham a chance to resist a siege. Send the archers, the letter pleaded, with their bows, their arrows, but without their horses and Totesham would send them back to Calais when Charles of Blois was repulsed. "He won't believe that," Totesham grumbled, "he'll know I'll want to keep them, so make sure he knows it's a solemn promise. Tell him I swear on Our Lady and on St. George that the archers will go back."

The description of Charles of Blois's army was real enough. Spies in English pay sent the news which, in truth, Charles was eager for his enemies to learn for the more La Roche-Derrien's garrison was outnumbered the lower its hopes would be. Charles already had close to four thousand men, more were coming every week, and his engineers had hired nine great siege engines to hurl boulders at the walls of the English towns and fortresses in his duchy. La Roche-Derrien would be attacked first and few men gave it a hope of lasting longer than a month.

"It is not true, I trust," Totesham said sourly to Thomas when the letter was written, "that you have designs on Roncelets?"

"On Roncelets?" Thomas pretended not to have heard of the place. "Not Roncelets, sir, but Rostrenen."

Totesham gazed at Thomas with dislike. "There's nothing at Rostrenen," the garrison commander said icily.

"I hear there's food there, sir," Thomas said.

"Whereas"—Totesham continued as if Thomas had not spoken—"the Countess of Armorica's son is said to be held at Roncelets."

"Is he, sir?" Thomas asked disingenuously.

"And if it's a swiving you want,"—Totesham ignored Thomas's lies—"then I can recommend the brothel behind St. Brieuc's chantry."

"We're riding to Rostrenen," Thomas insisted.

"And none of my men will ride with you," Totesham said, meaning none that took his wages, though that still left the mercenaries.

Sir Guillaume had agreed to ride with Thomas, though he was uncomfortable about the prospects for success. He had bought horses for himself and his two men but he reckoned they were of poor quality. "If it comes to a chase out of Roncelets," he said, "we'll be trounced. So take a lot of men to put up a decent fight."

Thomas's first instinct had been to ride with just a handful of others, but a few men on bad horses would be easy bait. More men made the expedition safer.

"And why are you going anyway?" Sir Guillaume demanded. "Just to get into the widow's skirts?"

"Because I made a promise to her," Thomas said, and it was true, though Sir Guillaume's reason had the more truth. "And because," Thomas went on, "I need to let our enemies know that I'm here."

"You mean de Taillebourg?" Sir Guillaume asked. "He knows already."

"You think so?"

"Brother Germain will have told him," Sir Guillaume said confidently, "in which case I reckon your Dominican is already in Rennes. He'll come for you in good time."

"If I raid Roncelets," Thomas said, "they'll hear of me. Then, I can be sure they'll come."

By Candlemas he knew he could rely on Robbie, on Sir Guillaume and his two men-at-arms and he had found seven other men who had been lured by the rumors of Roncelets' wealth or by the prospect of Jeanette's good opinion. Robbie wanted to leave straightaway, but Will Skeat, like Sir Guillaume, advised Thomas to take a larger party. "This ain't like northern England," Skeat said, "you can't run for the border. You get caught, Tom, and you'll need a dozen good men to lock shields and break heads. Reckon I ought to come with you."

"No," Thomas said hastily. Skeat had his lucid moments, but too often was vague and forgetful, though now he tried to help Thomas by recommending other men to go on the raid. Most turned the invitation down: the Tower of Roncelets was too far off, they claimed, or the Lord of Roncelets was too powerful and the odds against the raiders too great.

Some were frightened of offending Totesham who, fearing to lose any of his garrison, had decreed that no raids should go farther than a day's ride from the town. His caution meant there was little plunder to be had and it was only the poorest mercenaries who, desperate for anything they could turn into cash, offered to ride with Thomas.

"Twelve men is enough," Robbie insisted. "Sweet Christ, but I've been on enough raids into England. My brother and I once took a herd of cattle from Lord Percy with just three other men and Percy had half the county searching for us. Go in fast and come out quicker. Twelve men is enough."

Thomas was almost convinced by Robbie's fervent words, but he worried that the odds were still too uneven and the horses too badly conditioned to allow them to go swiftly in and come out quicker. "I want more men," he told Robbie.

"If you go on dithering," Robbie told him, "the enemy will hear about you. They'll be waiting for us."

"They won't know where to wait," Thomas said, "or what to think." He had spread a score of rumors about the raid's purpose and hoped that the enemy would be thoroughly confused. "But we'll go soon," he promised Robbie.

"Sweet God, but who's left to ask?" Robbie demanded. "Let's ride now!"

But that same day a ship came to Tréguier and three more Flemish men-at-arms rode into the garrison. Thomas found them that night in a tavern by the river's edge. The three complained how they had been in the English lines at Calais, but there was too little fighting there and thus few prospects of wealthy prisoners. They wanted to try their luck in Brittany and so they had come to La Roche-Derrien. Thomas spoke to their leader, a gaunt man with a twisted mouth and with two fingers missing from his right hand, who listened, grunted an acknowledgment and said he would think about it. Next morning all three Flemings came to the Two Foxes tavern and said they were willing to ride.

"We came here to fight," their leader, who was called Lodewijk, said, "so we go."

"So let's leave!" Robbie urged Thomas.

Thomas would have liked to recruit still more men, but he knew he had waited long enough. "We'll go," he told Robbie, then he went to find Will Skeat and made the older man promise to keep an eye on Jeanette. She liked and trusted Skeat and Thomas was confident enough to leave his father's notebook in her keeping. "We shall be back," he told her, "in six or seven days."

"God be with you," Jeanette said. She clung to Thomas for an instant. "God be with you," she said again, "and bring me my son."

And next dawn, in a mist that pearled their long mail coats, the fifteen horsemen rode.

LODEWIJK—HE INSISTED it was Sir Lodewijk though
his two companions sniggered whenever he did—refused to speak French, claiming that the language made his
tongue sour. "It is a people of filth," Lodewijk maintained,
"the French. Filth. The word is good, *ja*? Filth?"

"The word is good," Thomas agreed.

Jan and Pieter, Sir Lodewijk's companions, spoke only in
guttural Flemish spiced with a handful of English curses
they must have learned near Calais.

"What's happening in Calais?" Thomas asked Sir
Lodewijk as they rode south.

"Nothing. The town is . . . what you say?" Sir Lodewijk
made a circling motion with his hand.

"Surrounded."

"*Ja*, the town is goddamn surrounded. By the English, *ja*?
And by . . ." He paused, uncertain of the word he wanted,
then pointed to a stretch of waterlogged ground that lay east
of the road. "By that."

"Marshes."

"*Ja*! By bloody marshes. And the goddamn bloody
French, they are on . . ." Again he was lost for words, so
jabbed his mailed finger at the lowering sky.

"Higher ground?" Thomas guessed.

"*Ja*! Bloody high ground. Not so bloody high, I think, but

higher. And they . . ." He put a hand over his eyes, as if shading them.

"Stare?"

"*Ja*! They stare at each other. So nothing is happens but they and we gets bloody wet. Pissing wet, *ja*?"

They got wet later that morning when the rains swept in from the ocean. Great curtains of gray lashed the deserted farmlands and upland heaths where the trees were permanently bent toward the east. When Thomas had first come to Brittany this had been a productive land of farms, orchards, mills and grazing, but now it was blasted naked. The fruit trees, untended, were thick with bullfinches, the fields were choked with weeds and the pastures tangled with couch grass. Here and there a few folk still tried to scratch a living, but they were constantly being forced to La Roche-Derrien to work on the ramparts and their harvests and livestock were forever being stolen by English patrols. If any such Bretons were aware of the fifteen horsemen they took care to hide themselves and so it seemed as though Thomas and his companions rode through a deserted country.

They rode with one spare horse. They should have had more because only the three Flemings were mounted on good stallions. Sea voyages usually had a bad effect on horses, but Sir Lodewijk made it plain their journey had been unusually quick. "Bloody winds, *ja*?" He whirled his hand and made a whooshing noise to suggest the strength of the winds which had brought the destriers through in such fine fettle. "Quick! Bloody quick!"

The Flemings were not only well mounted, but well equipped. Jan and Pieter had fine mail hauberks while Sir Lodewijk had his chest, both thighs and one arm protected by good plate that was strapped over a leather-backed mail habergeon. The three wore black surcoats with a broad white stripe running down front and back, and all had undecorated shields, though Sir Lodewijk's horse's trapper displayed a badge showing a knife dripping blood. He tried to explain the device, but his English could not cope and Thomas was left with the vague impression that it was the mark of a trading guild in Bruges. "The butchers?" he suggested to Robbie. "Is that what he said? Butchers?"

"Bloody butchers don't make war. Except on pigs," Robbie said. He was in a fine mood. Raiding was in his blood and he had heard stories in La Roche-Derrien's taverns of the plunder that could be stolen if a man was willing to break Richard Totesham's rule and ride farther than a day's journey from the town. "The trouble in the north of England," he told Thomas, "is that if it's worth stealing then it's behind big bloody walls. We scratch up some cattle now and then, and a year ago I stole a fine horse off my Lord Percy, but there's not any gold and silver to be had. Nothing that you'd call real plunder. The Mass vessels are all wood or pewter or clay, and the poor boxes are poorer than the poor. And ride too far south and the bastards will be waiting for you on the way home. I hate bloody English archers."

"I'm a bloody English archer."

"You're different," Robbie said, and he meant it for he was puzzled by Thomas. Most archers were country born, the sons of yeomen or smiths or bailiffs, while a few were the sons of laborers, but none in Robbie's experience was well born, which Thomas plainly was for he spoke French and Latin, he was confident in the company of lords and other archers deferred to him. Robbie might look like a wild Scottish fighter, but he was the son of a gentleman and nephew to the Knight of Liddesdale, and thus he regarded archers as inferior beings who, in a properly arranged universe, could be ridden down and slaughtered like game, but he liked Thomas. "You're just bloody different," he said. "Mind you, when my ransom's paid and I'm safe home, I'll come back and kill you."

Thomas laughed, but it was forced laughter. He was nervous. He put the nervousness down to being in the unfamiliar position of leading a raid. This was his idea, and it had been his promises that brought most of these men on the long ride. He had claimed that Roncelets, being so far from any English stronghold, lay in unplundered country. Snatch the child, he had promised them, and they could then pillage as much as they wished or at least until the enemy woke up and organized a pursuit, and that promise had persuaded men to follow him and the responsibility of it weighed on Thomas. He also resented worrying. His ambition, after all, was to be the leader of a war band like Will Skeat had been before his injury, and what hope did he have of being a good leader if he fretted over a little raid like this? Yet fret he did, and he worried most of all that he might not have anticipated everything that could go wrong; and the men who had joined him gave him small consolation for, except for his friends and the newly arrived Flemings, they were the poorest and least well equipped of all the adventurers who had come to La Roche-Derrien in search of wealth. One of them, a quarrelsome man-at-arms from western Brittany, became drunk on the first day and Thomas discovered he had two water skins filled with a fierce apple spirit. He broke both skins, whereupon the enraged Breton drew his sword and attacked Thomas, but he was too drunk to see properly and a knee to his groin and a thump over the head put him down hard. Thomas took the man's horse and left him groaning in the mud, which meant he was down to fourteen men. "That will have helped," Sir Guillaume said cheerfully.

Thomas said nothing. He deserved to be mocked, he thought.

"No, I mean it! You knock a man down one day and you might do it again. You know why some men are bad leaders?"

"Why?"

"They want to be liked."

"That's bad?" Thomas asked.

"Men want to admire their leaders, they want to fear
them, and above all they want them to be successful. What
does being liked have to do with any of that? If the leader is
a good man he will be liked and if he's not, he won't, and if
he is a good man and a bad leader then he is better off dead.
You see? I am full of wisdom." Sir Guillaume laughed. He
might be down on his luck, his manor lost and fortune gone,
but he was riding to a fight and that cheered him. "The good
thing about this rain," he said, "is that the enemy won't expect you to be riding in it. It's stay-at-home weather."

"They'll know we've left La Roche-Derrien," Thomas
said. He was certain that Charles of Blois had as many spies
in the town as the English had in Rennes.

"He won't know yet," Sir Guillaume said. "We're traveling faster than any message can go. Anyway, while they
know we've left La Roche-Derrien, they don't know where
we're going."

They rode south in hope that the enemy would think they
were planning to scavenge the farms near Guingamp, then
late in the first day they turned eastward and climbed into a
high, empty country. The hazels were in blossom and rooks
were calling from the bare elm tops, signs that the year was
turning away from winter. They camped in a deserted farm,
sheltered by low scorched stone walls, and before the last
glimmer of dusk faded they had a good augury when Robbie, rooting about in the ruins of the barn, discovered a
leather bag half buried beside the broken wall. The exorbi-
tant rain had washed the earth away above the bag which
held a small silver plate and three handfuls of coins. Whoever had buried the money must have thought the coins too
heavy to carry or else had feared being robbed during their
exile from the house.

"We, how do you say?" Sir Lodewijk made a chopping
motion with his hand as if he cut up a pie.

"Share?"

"*Ja*! We share?"

"No," Thomas said. That had not been the agreement. He would have preferred to have shared, for that was how Will Skeat had treated spoils, but the men who rode with him wanted to keep whatever they found.

Sir Lodewijk bridled. "It is how we do it, *ja*? We share."

"We don't share," Sir Guillaume said harshly, "it's been agreed." He spoke in French and Sir Lodewijk reacted as though he had been struck, but he understood well enough and just turned and walked away.

"Tell your Scottish friend to watch his back," Sir Guillaume said to Thomas.

"Lodewijk's not so bad," Thomas said, "you just don't like him because he's Flemish."

"I hate the Flemish," Sir Guillaume agreed, "they're dull, stupid porkwits. Like the English."

The small argument with the Flemings did not fester. Next morning Sir Lodewijk and his companions were cheerful and, because their horses were much fresher and fitter than any others, they volunteered, with much broken English and elaborate hand signals, to ride ahead as scouts and all day their black and white surcoats appeared and reappeared far ahead and each time they waved the main party on, signaling that there was no danger. The deeper they went into enemy territory the greater the risk, but the Flemings' watchfulness meant that they made good progress. They were weaving a path either side of the main highway that ran east and west along Brittany's spine, a road flanked by deep woods, which hid the raiders from the few people who traveled on the road. They saw only two drovers with their skinny cattle and a priest leading a band of pilgrims who walked barefoot, waved tattered branches and sang a dirge. No pickings there.

Next day they went south again. They were now entering

a country where the farms had escaped English raiders and so the people were unafraid of horsemen and the pastures were filled with ewes and their newborn lambs, many of which had been torn to bloody scraps because the men of Brittany were too busy hunting each other and so the foxes thrived and the lambs died. Shepherds' dogs barked at the gray-mailed men, and now Thomas no longer had the Flemings ride ahead, but instead he and Sir Guillaume led the horsemen and, if challenged, they answered in French, claiming to be supporters of Charles of Blois. "Where's Roncelets?" they constantly asked and at first found no one who knew, but as the morning wore on they discovered a man who had at least heard of the place, then another who said his father had once been there and he thought it was beyond the ridge, the forest and the river, and then a third who gave them precise directions. The tower, he said, was no more than a half-day's journey away at the far end of a long wooded ridge that ran between two rivers. He showed them where to ford the nearer river, told them to follow the ridge crest southward and then bowed his head in thanks for the coin Thomas gave him.

They crossed the river, climbed the ridge and rode south. Thomas knew they must be close to Roncelets when they stopped for the third night, but he did not press on for he reckoned it would be better to come to the tower in the dawn and so they camped under beech trees, shivering because they dared not light a fire, and Thomas slept badly because he was listening to the strange things crackle and rustle deep in the woods and he feared those noises might be made by patrols sent out by the Lord of Roncelets. Yet no patrols found them. Thomas doubted there were any patrols except in his imagination, yet still he could not sleep and so, very early, while the others snored, he blundered through the trees to where the ridge's flank fell steeply away and he stared into the night in hope of seeing a glimmer of light cast from the battlements of the Tower of Roncelets. He saw nothing, but he heard sheep bleating piteously farther down the slope and he guessed that a fox had got among the lambs and was slaughtering them.

"The shepherd's not doing his job." Someone spoke in French and Thomas turned, thinking it was one of Sir Guillaume's men-at-arms, but saw, in the small moonlight, that it was Sir Lodewijk.

"I thought you wouldn't use French?" Thomas said.

"There are times when I do," Sir Lodewijk said and he strolled to stand beside Thomas and then, smiling, he rammed a makeshift club into Thomas's belly and when Thomas gasped and bent over the Fleming slammed the broken branch over his head and then kicked him in the chest. The attack was sudden, unexpected and overwhelming. Thomas was fighting for breath, half doubled over, staggering, and he tried to straighten and claw at Sir Lodewijk's eyes, but the club hit him a resounding blow on the side of the head and Thomas was down.

The Flemings' three horses had been tied to trees a small way from the others. No one had thought that strange and no one had remarked that the beasts had been left saddled and no one woke as the horses were untethered and led away. Sir Guillaume alone stirred when Sir Lodewijk collected his pieces of plate armor. "Is it dawn?" he asked.

"Not yet," Sir Lodewijk answered in soft French, then carried his armor and weapons out to the wood's edge where Jan and Pieter were lashing Thomas's wrists and ankles. They slung him belly down on a horse's back, tied him to the beast's girth strap and then took him eastward.

Sir Guillaume woke properly twenty minutes later. The birds were filling the trees with song and the sun was a hint of light in the misted east.

Thomas had vanished. His mail coat, his arrow bag, his sword, his helmet, his cloak, his saddle and his big black bow were all still there, but Thomas and the three Flemings were gone.

THOMAS WAS TAKEN to the Tower of Roncelets, a foursquare, unadorned fortress that reared from an outcrop of rock high above a river bend. A bridge, made of the same gray stone as the tower, carried the high road to Nantes across the river and no merchant could move his goods across the bridge without paying dues to the Lord of Roncelets whose banner of two black chevrons on a yellow field flew from the tower's high ramparts. His men wore the black and yellow stripes as a livery and were inevitably called *guêpes*, wasps. This far east in Brittany the folk spoke French rather than Breton and their tower was nicknamed the Guêpier, the wasp's nest, though on this late winter's morning most of the soldiers in the village wore plain black liveries rather than the waspish stripes of the Lord of Roncelets. The newcomers were quartered in the little cottages that lay between the Guêpier and the bridge and it was in one of those cottages that Sir Lodewijk and his two companions rejoined their comrades. "He's up in the castle"—Sir Lodewijk jerked his head toward the tower—"and God help him."

"No trouble?" a man asked.

"No trouble at all," Sir Lodewijk said. He had drawn a knife and was cutting off the white stripes that had been sewn onto his surcoat. "He made it easy for us. A stupid bloody Englishman, eh?"

"So why do they want him?"

"God knows and who cares? All that matters is that they've got him and the devil will have him soon." Sir Lodewijk yawned hugely. "And there's a dozen more of them out in the woods so we're riding out to find them."

Fifty horsemen rode westward from the village. The

sound of their hooves and their curb chains and creaking
leather armor was loud, but quickly faded when they rode
into the ridge's thick woods. A pair of kingfishers, startling
blue, whipped up the river and vanished in shadows. Long
weeds waved in the current where a flash of silver showed
that the salmon were returning. A girl carried a pail of milk
down the village street and wept because in the night she
had been raped by one of the black-liveried soldiers and she
knew it was futile to complain for no one would protect her
or even make a protest on her behalf. The village priest saw
her, understood why she was weeping, and reversed his
course so he would not have to face her. The black and yellow flag on the Guêpier's ramparts flapped in a small gust of
wind, then hung limp. Two young men with hooded falcons
perched on their arms rode out of the tower and turned
south. The great door grated shut behind them and the sound
of the heavy locking bar dropping into its brackets could be
heard throughout the village.

Thomas heard it too. The sound shuddered through the
rock on which the Guêpier was built and reverberated up the
winding stair to the long, bare room where he had been
taken. Two windows lit the chamber, but the wall was so
thick and the embrasures so deep that Thomas, who was
chained between the windows, could not see through either
of them. An empty hearth stood on the opposite wall, the
stones of its chimney hood stained black. The floor's wide
wooden boards were scarred and worn by too many nail-
studded boots and Thomas guessed this had been a barrack
room. It probably still was, but now it was needed as his
prison and so the men-at-arms had been ordered out and
Thomas carried in and manacled to the iron ring set into the
wall between the two windows. The manacles encircled his
wrists and held them behind his back and were connected to
the iron ring in the wall by three feet of chain. He had tested

the ring, seeing if he could shift it or perhaps snap a link of the chain, but all he did was hurt his wrists. A woman laughed somewhere in the tower. Feet sounded on the circular stairs beyond the door, but no one came into the room and the footsteps faded.

Thomas wondered why the iron ring should have been cemented into the wall. It seemed an odd thing to have so high up the tower where no horse would ever need to be tied. Maybe it had been placed there when the castle had been built. He had watched once as men hauled stones to the top of a church tower and they had used a pulley attached to a ring like this one. It was better to think of the ring and of stones and of masons making the tower than to reflect on his idiocy in being so easily captured, or to wonder what was about to happen to him, though of course he did wonder about that and nowhere in his imagination was the answer comforting. He tugged on the ring again, hoping that it had been there a long time and that the mortar that bedded it would have been weakened, but all he did was break the skin of his wrists on the manacles' sharp edges. The woman laughed again and a child's voice sounded.

A bird flew in one of the windows, fluttered for a few heartbeats and then vanished again, evidently rejecting the room as a nesting site. Thomas closed his eyes and softly recited the prayer of the Grail, the same prayer that Christ had uttered in Gethsemane: "*Pater, si vis, transfer calicem istum a me.*" Father, if you're willing, take this cup from me. Thomas repeated the prayer over and over, suspecting it was a waste of breath. God had not spared his own son the agony of Golgotha so why would He spare Thomas? Yet what hope did he have without prayer? He wanted to weep for his own naïveté in thinking he could ride here and somehow snatch the child from this stronghold that stank of woodsmoke, horse dung and rancid fat. It had all been so stupid and he knew he had not done it for the Grail, but to impress Jeanette. He was a fool, such a damned fool, and like a fool he had walked into his enemy's trap and he knew he would not be ransomed. What value did he have? So why was he even alive? Because they wanted something from him and just then the door to the room opened and Thomas opened his eyes.

A man in a monk's black robe carried two trestles into the room. He had untonsured hair, suggesting he was a lay servant to a monastery. "Who are you?" Thomas asked.

The man, who was short and had a slight limp, gave no answer, but just placed the two trestles in the center of the floor and, a moment later, brought in five planks that he laid across the trestles to make a table. A second untonsured man, similarly robed in black, entered the room and stared at Thomas. "Who are you?" Thomas asked again, but the second man was as silent as the first. He was a big man with bony ridges over his eyes and sunken cheeks and he inspected Thomas as if he were appraising a bullock at slaughter time.

"Are you going to make the fire?" the first man asked.

"In a minute," the second man said and he pulled a short-bladed knife from a sheath at his belt and walked toward Thomas. "Stay still," he growled, "and you don't get hurt."

"Who are you?"

"No one you know and no one you'll ever know," the man said, then he seized the neck of Thomas's woolen jerkin and, with one savage cut, slit it down the front. The blade touched, but did not break Thomas's skin. Thomas pulled back, but the man simply followed him, slashing and tugging at the torn cloth until Thomas's chest was naked, then he slit down the sleeves and pulled the jerkin away so that Thomas was naked from the waist up. Then the man pointed at Thomas's right foot, "lift it," he ordered. Thomas hesitated and the man sighed. "I can make you do it," he said, "and that will hurt, or you can do it yourself and it won't hurt."

He pulled off both of Thomas's boots, then cut the waist of his breeches.

"No!" Thomas protested.

"Don't waste your breath," the man said, and he sawed and tugged and ripped with the blade until he had cut through the breeches and could pull them away to leave Thomas shivering and naked. Then the man scooped up the boots and torn clothes and carried them out of the room.

The other man was carrying things into the room and placing them on the table. There was a book and a pot, presumably of ink, because the man placed two goose feathers beside the book and a small ivory-handled knife to trim the quills. Then he put a crucifix on the table, two large candles like those that would grace the altar of a church, three pokers, a pair of pincers and a curious instrument that Thomas could not see properly. Last of all he put two chairs behind the table and a wooden bucket within Thomas's reach. "You know what that's for, don't you?" he asked, knocking the bucket with his foot.

"Who are you? Please!"

"Don't want you to make a mess on the floor, do we?"

The bigger man came back into the room carrying some kindling and a basket of logs. "At least you'll be warm," he said to Thomas with evident amusement. He had a small clay pot filled with glowing embers that he used to light the kindling, then he piled on the smaller logs and held his hands to the growing flames. "Nice and warm," he said, "and that's a blessing in winter. Never known a winter like it! Rain! We should be building an ark."

A long way off a bell tolled twice. The fire began to crackle and some of the smoke seeped out into the room, perhaps because the chimney was cold. "What he really likes," the big man who had laid the fire said, "is a brazier."

"Who?" Thomas asked.

"He always likes a brazier, he does, but not on a wooden floor. I told him."

"Who?" Thomas demanded.

"Don't want to burn the place down! Not a brazier, I told him, not on a wooden floor, so we had to use the hearth." The big man watched the fire for a while. "That seems to be burning proper, don't it?" He heaped a half-dozen larger logs on the fire and then backed away. He gave Thomas a casual look, shook his head as if the prisoner was beyond help and then both men left the room.

The firewood was dry and so the flames blazed high, fast and fierce. More smoke billowed into the room and gusted out of the windows. Thomas, in a sudden spurt of rage, dragged at the manacles, heaving with all his archer's strength to pull the iron ring from the wall, but all he achieved was to cut the iron gyves further into his bleeding wrists. He stared up at the ceiling, which was simply planks over beams, presumably the floor of the chamber above. He had heard no footsteps up there, but then there came the sound of feet just beyond the door and he stepped back to the wall.

A woman and a small child came in. Thomas crouched to hide his nakedness and the woman laughed at his modesty. The child laughed too and it took Thomas a few seconds to realize that the boy was Jeanette's son, Charles, who was gazing at him with interest, curiosity, but no recognition. The woman was tall, fair-haired, very pretty and very pregnant. She wore a pale blue dress that was belted above her swollen belly and was trimmed with white lace and little loops of pearls. Her hat was a blue spire with a brief veil that she pushed away from her eyes to see Thomas better.

Thomas drew up his knees to hide himself, but the woman brazenly crossed the room to stare down at him. "Such a pity," she said.

"A pity?" Thomas asked.

She did not elaborate. "Are you really English?" she demanded and looked peeved when Thomas did not answer. "They're making a rack downstairs, Englishman. Windlasses and ropes to stretch you. Have you ever seen a man after he's been racked? He flops. It's amusing, but not, I think, for the man himself."

Thomas still ignored her, looking instead at the small boy who had a round face, black hair and the fierce dark eyes of Jeanette, his mother. "You remember me, Charles?" Thomas asked, but the boy just stared at him blankly. "Your mother sends you greetings," Thomas said and saw the surprise on the boy's face.

"Mama?" Charles, who was almost four, asked.

The woman snatched at Charles's hand and dragged him away as though Thomas carried a contagion. "Who are you?" she asked angrily.

"Your mother loves you, Charles," Thomas told the wide-eyed boy.

"Who are you?" the woman insisted, and then turned as the door was pushed open.

A Dominican priest came in. He was gaunt, thin and tall with short gray hair and a fierce face. He frowned when he saw the woman and child. "You should not be here, my lady," he said harshly.

"You forget, priest, who rules here," the pregnant woman retorted.

"Your husband," the priest said firmly, "and he will not want you here, so you will leave." The priest held the door open and the woman, whom Thomas assumed to be the Lady of Roncelets, hesitated for a heartbeat and stalked out. Charles looked back once, then was dragged out of the room just before another Dominican entered, this one a younger man, small and bald, with a towel folded over one arm and a bowl of water in his hands. He was followed by the two robed servants who walked with folded hands and downcast eyes to stand beside the fire. The first priest, the gaunt one, closed the door, then he and his fellow priest walked to the table.

"Who are you?" Thomas asked the gaunt priest, though he suspected he knew the answer. He was trying to remember that misted morning in Durham when he had seen de Taillebourg fight Robbie's brother. He thought it was the same man, the priest who had murdered Eleanor or else ordered her death, but he could not be certain.

The two priests ignored him. The smaller man put the water and towel on the table, then both men knelt. "In the name of the Father and of the Son and of the Holy Ghost," the older priest said, making the sign of the cross, "amen." He stood, opened his eyes and looked down at Thomas who was still crouching on the pitted floorboards. "You are Thomas of Hookton," he said formally, "bastard son of Father Ralph, priest of that place?"

"Who are you?"

"Answer me, please," the Dominican said.

Thomas stared up into the man's eyes and recognized the terrible strength in the priest and knew that he dared not give in to that strength. He had to resist from the very first and so he said nothing.

The priest sighed at this display of petty obstinacy. "You are Thomas of Hookton," he declared, "Lodewijk says so. In which case, greetings, Thomas. My name is Bernard de Taillebourg and I am a friar of the Dominican order and, by the grace of God and at the pleasure of the Holy Father, an Inquisitor of the faith. My brother in Christ"—here de Taillebourg gestured at the younger priest, who had settled at the table where he opened the book and picked up one of the quills—"is Father Cailloux, who is also an Inquisitor of the faith."

"You are a bastard," Thomas said, staring at de Taillebourg, "you're a murdering bastard."

He might have spared his breath for de Taillebourg showed no reaction. "You will stand, please," the priest demanded.

"A motherless murdering bastard," Thomas said, making no move.

De Taillebourg made a small gesture and the two servants ran forward and took Thomas by his arms and dragged him upright and, when he threatened to collapse, the bigger one slapped him hard in the face, stinging the bruise left by the blow Sir Lodewijk had given him before dawn. De Taillebourg waited till the men were back beside the fire. "I am charged by Cardinal Bessières," he said tonelessly, "to discover the whereabouts of a relic and we are informed that you can assist us in this matter, which is deemed to be of such importance that we are empowered by the Church and by Almighty God to ensure that you tell us the truth. Do you understand what that means, Thomas?"

"You killed my woman," Thomas said, "and one day, priest, you're going to roast in hell and the devils will dance on your shriveled arse."

De Taillebourg again showed no reaction. He was not using his chair, but standing tall and arrow-thin behind the table on which he rested the tips of his long, pale fingers. "We know," he said, "that your father might have possessed the Grail, and we know that he gave you a book in which he wrote his account of that most precious thing. I tell you that we know of these matters so that you do not waste our time or your pain by denying them. Yet we shall need to know more and that is why we are here. You understand me, Thomas?"

"The devil will piss in your mouth, priest, and shit in your nostrils."

De Taillebourg looked faintly pained as if Thomas's crudity was tiresome. "The Church grants us the authority to question you, Thomas," he continued in a mild voice, "but in her infinite mercy she also commands that we do not shed blood. We may use pain, indeed it is our duty to employ pain, but it must be pain without bloodshed. This means we may employ fire"—his long pale fingers touched one of the pokers on the table—"and we may crush you and we may stretch you and God will forgive us for it will be done in His name and in His most holy service."

"Amen," Brother Cailloux said and, like the two servants, made the sign of the cross. De Taillebourg pushed all three of the pokers to the edge of the table and the smaller servant ran across the room, took the irons and plunged them into the fire.

"We do not employ pain lightly," de Taillebourg said, "or wantonly, but with prayerful regret and with pity and with a tearful concern for your immortal soul."

"You're a murderer," Thomas said, "and your soul will sear in hell."

"Now," de Taillebourg continued, apparently oblivious to Thomas's insults, "let us start with the book. You told Brother Germain in Caen that your father wrote it. Is that true?"

And so it began. A gentle questioning at first to which Thomas gave no answers for he was consumed by a hatred for de Taillebourg, a hatred fed by the memory of Eleanor's pale and blood-laced body, yet the questioning was insistent and unceasing, and the threat of an awful pain was in the three pokers that heated in the fire, and so Thomas persuaded himself that de Taillebourg knew some things and there could be very little harm in telling him others. Besides,

the Dominican was so very reasonable and so very patient.
He endured Thomas's anger, he ignored the abuse, he expressed again and again an unwillingness to employ torture
and said he only wanted the truth, however inadequate and
so, after an hour, Thomas began to answer the questions.
Why suffer, he asked himself, when he did not possess what
the Dominican wanted? He did not know where the Grail
was, he was not even certain that the Grail existed and so,
hesitantly at first, and then more willingly, he talked.

There was a book, yes, and much of it was in strange languages and scripts and Thomas claimed to have no idea
what those mysterious passages meant. As for the rest he admitted a knowledge of Latin and agreed he had read those
parts of the book, but he dismissed them as vague, repetitive
and unhelpful. "They were just stories," he said.

"What kind of stories?"

"A man received his sight after looking at the Grail and
then, when he was disappointed in its appearance, he lost his
sight again."

"God be praised for that," Father Cailloux interjected,
then dipped the quill in ink and wrote down the miracle.

"What else?" de Taillebourg asked.

"Stories of soldiers winning battles because of the Grail,
stories of healings," Thomas said.

"Do you believe them?"

"The stories?" Thomas pretended to think, then nodded.
"If God has given us the Grail, father," he said, "then it will
surely work miracles."

"Did your father possess the Grail?"

"I don't know."

So de Taillebourg asked him about Father Ralph and
Thomas told how his father had walked the stony beach at
Hookton wailing for his sins and sometimes preaching to the
wild things of the sea and the sky.

"Are you saying he was mad?" de Taillebourg asked.

"He was mad with God," Thomas said.

"Mad with God," de Taillebourg repeated, as though the words intrigued him. "Are you suggesting he was a saint?"

"I think many saints must have been like him," Thomas replied cautiously, "but he was also a great mocker of superstitions."

"What do you mean?"

"He was very fond of St. Guinefort," Thomas said, "and called on him whenever some minor problem occurred."

"Is it mockery to do that?" de Taillebourg asked.

"St. Guinefort was a dog," Thomas said.

"I know what St. Guinefort was," de Taillebourg said testily, "but are you saying God could not use a dog to effect His sacred purposes?"

"I am saying that my father did not believe a dog could be a saint, and so he mocked."

"Did he mock the Grail?"

"Never," Thomas answered truthfully, "not once."

"And in his book"—de Taillebourg suddenly reverted to the earlier subject—"did he say how the Grail came to be in his possession?"

For the last few moments Thomas had been aware that there was someone standing on the other side of the door. De Taillebourg had closed it, but the latch had been silently lifted and the door pushed gently ajar. Someone was there, listening, and Thomas assumed it was the Lady of Roncelets. "He never claimed that the Grail was in his possession," he countered, "but he did say that it was once owned by his family."

"Once owned," de Taillebourg said flatly, "by the Vexilles."

"Yes," Thomas replied and he was sure the door moved a fraction.

Father Cailloux's pen scratched on the parchment. Everything Thomas said was being written down and he remem-

bered a wandering Franciscan preacher at a fair in Dorchester shouting at the people that every sin they ever committed was being recorded in a great book in heaven and
when they died and went to the judgment before God the
book would be opened and their sins read out, and George
Adyn had made the crowd laugh by calling out that there
was not enough ink in Christendom to record what his
brother was doing with Dorcas Churchill in Puddletown.
The sins, the Franciscan had angrily retorted, were recorded
in letters of fire, the same fire that would roast adulterers in
the depths of hell.

"And who is Hachaliah?" de Taillebourg asked.

Thomas was surprised by the question and hesitated.
Then he tried to look puzzled. "Who?"

"Hachaliah," de Taillebourg repeated patiently.

"I don't know," Thomas said.

"I think you do," de Taillebourg declared softly.

Thomas stared at the priest's strong, bony face. It reminded him of his father's face for it had the same grim de-
termination, a hard-jawed inwardness which hinted that this
man would not care what others thought of his behavior because he justified himself only to God. "Brother Germain
mentioned the name," Thomas said cautiously, "but what it
means I don't know."

"I don't believe you," de Taillebourg insisted.

"Father," Thomas said firmly, "I do not know what it
means. I asked Brother Germain and he refused to tell me.
He said it was beyond someone of my wits to understand."

De Taillebourg stared at Thomas in silence. The fire
roared hollow in the chimney and the big servant shifted the
pokers as one of the logs collapsed. "The prisoner says he
doesn't know," de Taillebourg dictated to Father Cailloux
without taking his gaze from Thomas. The servants put more
logs on the fire and de Taillebourg let Thomas stare at the

pokers and worry about them for a moment before he resumed his questioning. "So," the Dominican asked, "where is the book now?"

"In La Roche-Derrien," Thomas said promptly.

"Where in La Roche-Derrien?"

"With my baggage," Thomas said, "which I left with an old friend, Will Skeat." That was not true. He had left the book in Jeanette's keeping, but he did not want to expose her to danger. Will Skeat, even with a damaged memory, could look after himself better than the Blackbird. "Sir William Skeat," Thomas added.

"Does Sir William know what the book is?" de Taillebourg asked.

"He can't even read! No, he doesn't know."

There were other questions then, scores of them. De Taillebourg wanted to know the story of Thomas's life, why he had abandoned Oxford, why he had become an archer, when he had last made confession, what had he been doing in Durham? What did the King of England know of the Grail? What did the Bishop of Durham know? The questions went on and on until Thomas was faint from hunger and from standing, yet de Taillebourg seemed indefatigable. As evening came on and the light from the two windows paled and darkened he still persisted. The two servants had long looked rebellious while Father Cailloux kept frowning and glancing at the windows as if to suggest that the time for a meal was long past, but de Taillebourg did not know hunger. He just pressed and pressed. With whom had Thomas traveled to London? What had he done in Dorset? Had he searched for the Grail in Hookton? Brother Cailloux filled page after page with Thomas's answers and, as the evening wore on, he had to light the candles so he could see to write. The flames of the fire cast shadows from the table legs and Thomas was swaying with fatigue when at last de Taillebourg nodded. "I shall think and pray about all your answers tonight, Thomas," he said, "and in the morning we shall continue."

"Water," Thomas croaked, "I need water."

"You shall be given food and drink," de Taillebourg said.

One of the servants removed the pokers from the fire. Father Cailloux closed the book and gave Thomas a glance which seemed to have some sympathy. A blanket was fetched and with it came a meal of smoked fish, beans, bread and water, and one of Thomas's hands was unmanacled so he could eat it. Two guards, both in plain black surcoats, watched him eat, and when he was done they snapped the manacles back about his wrist and he sensed a pin being pushed through the clasp to secure it. That gave him hope and when he was left alone he tried to reach the pin with his fingers, but both the gyves were deep bracelets and he could not reach the clasp. He was trapped.

He lay back against the wall, huddled in the blanket and watching the dying fire. No heat crossed the room and Thomas shivered uncontrollably. He contorted his fingers as he tried to reach the clasp of the manacles, but it was impossible and he suddenly moaned involuntarily as he anticipated the pain. He had been spared torture this day, but did that mean he had escaped it altogether? He deserved to, he thought, for he had mostly told the truth. He had told de Taillebourg that he did not know where the Grail was, that he was not even certain it existed, that he had rarely heard his father speak of it and that he would rather be an archer in the King of England's army than a seeker of the Grail. Again he felt a terrible shame that he had been captured so easily. He should have been on his way back to La Roche-Derrien by now, riding home to the taverns and the laughter and the ale and the easy company of soldiers. There were tears in his eyes and he was ashamed of that too. Laughter sounded from deep in the castle and he thought he could hear the sound of a harp playing.

Then the door opened.

He could only see that a man had come into the room. The visitor was wearing a swathing black cloak that made him appear a sinister shadow as he crossed to the table where he stopped and stared down at Thomas. The fire's dying timbers were behind the man, edging his tall cloaked figure with red, but illuminating Thomas. "I am told," the man said, "that he did not burn you today?"

Thomas said nothing, just huddled under the blanket.

"He likes burning people," the visitor said. "He does like it. I have watched him. He shudders as the flesh bubbles." He went to the fire, picked up one of the pokers and thrust it into the smoldering embers before piling new logs over the dying flames. The dry wood burned quickly and, in the flaring light, Thomas could see the man for the first time. He had a narrow, sallow face, a long nose, a strong jaw and black hair swept back from a high forehead. It was a good face, intelligent and hard, then it was shadowed as the man turned away from the fire. "I am your cousin," he said.

A stab of hatred coursed through Thomas. "You're Guy Vexille?"

"I am the Count of Astarac," Vexille said. He walked slowly toward Thomas. "Were you at the battle by the forest of Crécy?"

"Yes."

"An archer?"

"Yes."

"And at the battle's end," Guy Vexille said, "you shouted three words in Latin."

"*Calix meus inebrians,*" Thomas said.

Guy Vexille perched on the edge of the table and gazed at Thomas for a long time. His face was in shadow so Thomas could see no expression, only the faint glimmer of his eyes. " '*Calix meus inebrians,*' " Vexille said at last. "It is the secret motto of our family. Not the one we show on our crest. You know what that is?"

"No."

" '*Pie repone te,*' " Guy Vexille said.

" 'In pious trust,' " Thomas translated.

"You're strangely well educated for an archer," Vexille said. He stood and paced up and down as he spoke. "We display '*pie repone te,*' but our real motto is '*calix meus inebrians.*' We are the secret guardians of the Grail. Our family has held it for generations, we were entrusted with it by God, and your father stole it."

"You killed him," Thomas said.

"And I am proud of that," Guy Vexille said, then suddenly stopped and turned to Thomas. "Were you the archer on the hill that day?"

"Yes."

"You shoot well, Thomas."

"That was the first day I ever killed a man," Thomas said, "and it was a mistake."

"A mistake?"

"I killed the wrong one."

Guy Vexille smiled, then went back to the fire and pulled out the poker to see its tip was a dull red. He pushed it back into the heat. "I killed your father," he said, "and I killed your woman in Durham and I killed the priest who was evidently your friend."

"You were de Taillebourg's servant?" Thomas asked, astonished. He had hated Guy Vexille because of his father's death. Now he had two more deaths to add to that hatred.

"I was indeed his servant," Vexille confirmed. "It was the penance put on me by de Taillebourg, the punishment of humility. But now I am a soldier again and charged with recovering the Grail."

Thomas hugged his knees under the blanket. "If the Grail has so much power," he asked, "then why is our family so powerless?"

Guy Vexille thought about the question for a moment, then shrugged. "Because we squabbled," he said, "because we were sinners, because we were not worthy. But we shall change that, Thomas. We shall recover our strength and our virtue." Guy Vexille stooped to the fire and took the poker from the flames and swept it like a sword so that it made a hissing sound and its red-hot tip seared an arc of light in the dim room. "Have you thought, Thomas," he asked, "of helping me?"

"Helping you?"

Vexille paced close to Thomas. He still swung the poker in great scything cuts so that the light trailed like a falling star to leave wispy lines of smoke in the dark room. "Your father," he went on, "was the elder brother. Did you know that? If you were legitimate, you would be Count of Astarac." He dropped the poker's tip so that it was close to Thomas's face, so close that Thomas could feel the scorching heat. "Join me," Guy Vexille said intensely, "tell me what you know, help me retrieve the book and go with me on the quest for the Grail." He crouched so that his face was at the same height as Thomas's. "Bring glory to our family, Thomas," he said softly, "such glory that you and I could rule all Christendom and, with the power of the Grail, lead a crusade against the infidel that will leave them writhing in agony. You and I, Thomas! We are the Lord's anointed, the Grail guardians, and if we join hands then for generations men will talk of us as the greatest warrior saints that the Church ever knew." His voice was deep, even, almost musical. "Will you help me, Thomas?"

"No," Thomas said.

The poker came close to Thomas's right eye, so close that it loomed like a great sullen sun, but Thomas did not twitch away. He did not think his cousin would plunge the poker into his eye, but he did think Guy Vexille wanted him to flinch and so he stayed still.

"Your friends got away today," Vexille said. "Fifty of us rode to catch them and somehow they avoided us. They went deep into the trees."

"Good."

"But all they can do is retreat to La Roche-Derrien and they'll be trapped there. Come the spring, Thomas, we shall close that trap." Thomas said nothing. The poker cooled and went dark, and Thomas at last dared to blink. "Like all the Vexilles," Guy said, taking the poker away and standing, "you are as brave as you are foolish. Do you know where the Grail is?"

"No."

Guy Vexille stared at him, judging that answer, then shrugged. "Do you think the Grail exists, Thomas?"

Thomas paused, then gave the answer he had denied to de Taillebourg through all the long day. "Yes."

"You're right," Vexille said, "you're right. It does exist. We had it and your father stole it and you are the key to finding it."

"I know nothing of it!" Thomas protested.

"But de Taillebourg won't believe that," Vexille said, dropping the poker onto the table. "De Taillebourg wants the Grail as a starving man wants bread. He dreams of it. He moans in his sleep and he weeps for it." Vexille paused, then smiled. "When the pain becomes too much to bear, Thomas, and it will, and when you are wishing that you were dead, and you will, then tell de Taillebourg that you repent and that you will become my liege man. The pain will stop then, and you will live."

It had been Vexille, Thomas realized, who had been listening outside the door. And tomorrow he would listen again. Thomas closed his eyes. *Pater*, he prayed, *si vis, transfer calicem istem a me.* He opened his eyes again. "Why did you kill Eleanor?" he asked.

"Why not?"

"That is a ridiculous answer," Thomas snarled.

Vexille's head snapped back as if he had been struck. "Because she knew we existed," he said, "that's why."

"Existed?"

"She knew we were in England, she knew what we wanted," Guy Vexille said. "She knew we had spoken to Brother Collimore. If the King of England had learned that we were searching for the Grail in his kingdom then he would have stopped us. He would have imprisoned us. He would have done to us what we are doing to you."

"You think Eleanor could have betrayed you to the King?" Thomas asked, incredulous.

"I think it was better that no one knew why we were there," Guy Vexille said. "But do you know what, Thomas? That old monk could tell us nothing except that you existed. All that effort, that long journey, the killings, the Scottish weather, just to learn about you! He didn't know where the Grail was, couldn't imagine where your father might have hidden it, but he did know about you and we have been seeking you ever since. Father de Taillebourg wants to question you, Thomas, he wants to make you cry with pain until you tell him what I suspect you cannot tell him, but I don't want your pain. I want your friendship."

"And I want you dead," Thomas said.

Vexille shook his head sadly, then stooped so that he was near to Thomas. "Cousin," he said quietly, "one day you will kneel to me. One day you will place your hands between my hands and you will pledge your allegiance and we shall exchange the kiss of lord and man, and thus you will become my liege man and we shall ride together, beneath the cross, to glory. We shall be as brothers, I promise it." He kissed his fingers then laid the tips on Thomas's cheek and the touch of them was almost like a caress. "I promise it, brother," Vexille whispered, "now goodnight."

"God damn you, Guy Vexille," Thomas snarled.

"*Calix meus inebrians*," Guy Vexille said, and went.

THOMAS LAY SHIVERING in the dawn. Every footstep in the castle made him cringe. Beyond the deep windows cockerels crowed and birds sang and he had an impression, for what reason he did not know, that there were thick woods outside the Tower of Roncelets and he wondered if he would ever see green leaves again. A sullen servant brought him a breakfast of bread, hard cheese and water and, while he ate, the manacles were unpinned and a wasp-liveried guard watched him, but the gyves were again fixed onto his wrists as soon as he had finished. The bucket was carried away to be emptied and another put in its place.

Bernard de Taillebourg arrived shortly after and, while his servants revived the fire and Father Cailloux settled himself at the makeshift table, the tall Dominican greeted Thomas politely. "Did you sleep well? Was your breakfast adequate? It's colder today, isn't it? I've never known a winter as wet. The river flooded in Rennes for the first time in years! All those cellars under water."

Thomas, cold and frightened, did not respond and de Taillebourg did not take offense. Instead he waited as Father Cailloux dipped a quill in the ink, then ordered the taller servant to take Thomas's blanket away. "Now," he said when his prisoner was naked, "to business. Let us talk about your father's notebook. Who else is aware of the book's existence?"

"No one," Thomas said, "except Brother Germain and you know about him."

De Taillebourg frowned. "But, Thomas, someone must have given it to you! And that person is surely aware of it! Who gave it to you?"

"A lawyer in Dorchester," Thomas lied glibly.

"A name, please, give me a name."

"John Rowley," Thomas said, making the name up.

"Spell it, please," de Taillebourg said and after Thomas had obeyed the Inquisitor paced up and down in apparent frustration. "This Rowley must have known what the book was, surely?"

"It was wrapped in a cloak of my father's and in a bundle of other old clothes. He didn't look."

"He might have done."

"John Rowley," Thomas said, spinning his invention, "is old and fat. He won't go searching for the Grail. Besides, he thought my father was mad, so why would he be interested in a book of his? All Rowley's interested in is ale, mead and mutton pies."

The three pokers were heating in the fire again. It had started to rain and gusts of cold wind sometimes blew drops through the open windows. Thomas remembered his cousin's warning in the night that de Taillebourg liked to inflict pain, yet the Dominican's voice was mild and reasonable and Thomas sensed he had survived the worst. He had endured a day of de Taillebourg's questioning and his answers seemed to have satisfied the stern Dominican who was now reduced to filling in the gaps of Thomas's story. He wanted to know about the lance of St. George and Thomas told how the weapon had hung in Hookton's church and how it had been stolen and how he had taken it back at the battle outside the forest of Crécy. Did Thomas believe it was the real lance? de Taillebourg asked and Thomas shook his head. "I don't know," he said, "but my father believed it was."

"And your cousin stole the lance from Hookton's church?"

"Yes."

"Presumably," de Taillebourg mused, "so that no one would realize he sailed to England to search for the Grail. The lance was a disguise." He thought about that and Thomas, not feeling the need to comment, said nothing. "Did the lance have a blade?" de Taillebourg asked.

"A long one."

"Yet, surely, if this was the lance that killed the dragon," de Taillebourg observed, "the blade would have melted in the beast's blood?"

"Would it?" Thomas asked.

"Of course it would!" de Taillebourg insisted, staring at Thomas as though he were mad. "Dragon's blood is molten! Molten and fiery." He shrugged as if to acknowledge that the lance was irrelevant to his quest. Father Cailloux's pen scratched as he tried to keep up with the interrogation and the two servants stood by the fire, scarcely bothering to hide their boredom as de Taillebourg looked for a new subject to explore. He chose Will Skeat for some reason and asked about his wound and about his memory lapses. Was Thomas really sure Skeat could not read?

"He can't read!" Thomas said. He sounded now as though he were reassuring de Taillebourg and that was a measure of his confidence. He had begun the previous day with insults and hate, but now he was eagerly helping the Dominican toward the end of the interrogation. He had survived.

"Skeat can't read," de Taillebourg said as he paced up and down. "I suppose that's not surprising. So he won't be looking at the notebook you left in his keeping?"

"I'll be lucky if he doesn't use its pages to wipe his arse. That's the only use Will Skeat has for paper or parchment."

De Taillebourg gave a dutiful smile then stared up at the ceiling. He was silent for a long time, but at last shot Thomas a puzzled look. "Who is Hachaliah?"

The question took Thomas by surprise and he must have shown it. "I don't know," he managed to say after a pause.

De Taillebourg watched Thomas. The room was suddenly tense; the servants were fully awake and Father Cailloux was no longer writing, but gazing at Thomas. De Taillebourg smiled. "I'm going to give you one last chance, Thomas," he said in his deep voice. "Who is Hachaliah?"

Thomas knew he must brazen it out. Get past this, he thought, and the interrogation would be done. "I'd never heard of him," he said, doing his best to sound guileless, "before Brother Germain mentioned his name."

Why de Taillebourg seized on Hachaliah as the weak point of Thomas's defenses was a mystery, but it was a shrewd seizure for if the Dominican could prove that Thomas knew who Hachaliah was then he could prove that Thomas had translated at least one of the Hebrew passages in the book. He could prove that Thomas had lied through the whole interrogation and he would open whole new areas of revelation. So de Taillebourg pressed hard and when Thomas continued with his denials the priest beckoned to the servants. Father Cailloux flinched.

"I told you," Thomas said nervously, "I really don't know who Hachaliah is."

"But my duty to God," de Taillebourg said, taking the first of the red-hot pokers from the tall servant, "is to make sure you are not telling lies." He looked at Thomas with what appeared to be sympathy, "I don't want to hurt you, Thomas. I just want the truth. So tell me, who is Hachaliah?"

Thomas swallowed. "I don't know," he said, then repeated it in a louder voice, "I don't know!"

"I think you do," de Taillebourg said, and so the pain began.

"In the name of the Father," de Taillebourg prayed as he placed the iron against the bare flesh of Thomas's leg, "and of the Son and of the Holy Ghost." The two servants held Thomas down and the pain was worse than he could have believed and he tried to twist away from it, but he could not move and his nostrils were filled with the stench of burning flesh and still he would not answer the question for he thought that by revealing his lies he would open himself to more punishment. Somewhere in his shrieking head he believed that if he persisted in the lie then de Taillebourg must believe him and he would cease to use the fire, but in a competition of patience between torturer and prisoner the prisoner has no chance. A second poker was heated and its tip traced down Thomas's ribs. "Who is Hachaliah?" de Taillebourg asked.

"I've told you—"

The red-hot iron was put to his chest and drawn down to his belly to leave a line of burning, puckered, raw flesh and the wound was instantly cauterized so it left no blood and Thomas's scream echoed from the high ceiling. The third poker was waiting and the first was being reheated so that the pain did not need to stop, and then Thomas was turned onto his burned belly and the strange device which he had not been able to recognize when it was first put on the table was placed over a knuckle of his left hand and he knew it was an iron vice, screw-driven, and de Taillebourg tightened the screw and the pain made Thomas jerk and scream again. He lost consciousness, but Father Cailloux brought him back to his senses with the towel and cold water.

"Who is Hachaliah?" de Taillebourg asked.

Such a stupid question, Thomas thought. As if the answer was important! "I don't know!" He moaned the words and prayed that de Taillebourg would believe him, but the pain came again and the best moments, other than pure oblivion, were when Thomas drifted in and out of consciousness and it seemed that the pain was a dream—a bad dream, but still only a dream—and the worst moments were when he realized it was not a dream and that his world was reduced to agony, pure agony, and then de Taillebourg would apply more pain, either tightening a screw to shatter a finger or else placing the hot iron on his flesh.

"Tell me, Thomas," the Dominican said gently, "just tell me and the pain will end. It will end if you just tell me. Please, Thomas, you think I enjoy this? In the name of God, I hate it so tell me, please, tell me."

So Thomas did. Hachaliah was the father of the Tirshatha, and the Tirshatha was the father of Nehemiah.

"And Nehemiah," de Taillebourg asked, "was what?"

"Was the cup bearer to the King," Thomas sobbed.

"Why do men lie to God?" de Taillebourg asked. He had put the finger-vice back on the table and the three pokers were all in the fire. "Why?" he asked again. "The truth is always discovered, God ensures that. So, Thomas, after all, you did know more than you claimed and we shall have to discover your other lies, but let us talk first, though, about Hachaliah. Do you think this citation from the book of Esdras is your father's way of proclaiming his possession of the Grail?"

"Yes," Thomas said, "yes, yes, yes." He was hunched against the wall, his broken hands manacled behind him, his body a mass of pain, but perhaps the hurt would end if he confessed all.

"But Brother Germain tells me that the Hachaliah entry in your father's book," de Taillebourg said, "was written in Hebrew. Do you know Hebrew, Thomas?"

"No."

"So who translated the passage for you?"

"Brother Germain."

"And Brother Germain told you who Hachaliah was?" de Taillebourg asked.

"No," Thomas whimpered. There was no point in lying for the Dominican would doubtless check with the old monk, but the answer opened a new question that, in turn, would reveal other areas where Thomas had lied. Thomas knew that, but it was too late to resist now.

"So who did tell you?" de Taillebourg asked.

"A doctor," Thomas said softly.

"A doctor," de Taillebourg repeated. "That doesn't help me, Thomas. You want me to use the fire again? What doctor? A doctor of theology? A physician? And if you asked this mysterious doctor to explain the significance of the passage, was he not curious why you wished to know?" •

So Thomas confessed it was Mordecai, and admitted that Mordecai had looked at the notebook and de Taillebourg thumped the table in the first display of temper he had shown in all the long hours of questioning. "You showed the book to a Jew?" He hissed the question, his voice incredulous. "To a Jew? In the name of God and of all the precious saints, what were you thinking? To a Jew! To a man of the race that killed our dear Savior! If the Jews find the Grail, you fool, they will raise the Antichrist! You will suffer for that betrayal! You must suffer!" He crossed the room, snatched a poker from the fire, and brought it back to where Thomas huddled against the wall. "To a Jew!" de Taillebourg shouted and he scored the poker's glowing tip down Thomas's leg. "You foul thing!" he snarled over Thomas's screams. "You are a traitor to God, a traitor to Christ, a traitor to the Church! You are no better than Judas Iscariot!"

The pain went on. The hours went on. It seemed to Thomas that there was nothing left but pain. He had lied when there had been no pain and so now all his previous answers were being checked against the measure of agony he could endure without losing consciousness.

"So where is the Grail?" de Taillebourg demanded.

"I don't know," Thomas said and then, louder, "I don't know!" He watched the red-hot iron come to his skin and by now he was shrieking before it even touched.

The screaming did no good because the torture went on. And on. And Thomas talked, telling all he knew, and he was even tempted to do as Guy Vexille had suggested and beg de Taillebourg to let him swear allegiance to his cousin, but then, somewhere in the red horror of his torment, he thought of Eleanor and kept silent.

On the fourth day, when he was quivering, when even a twitch of de Taillebourg's hand was enough to make him whimper and beg for mercy, the Lord of Roncelets came into the room. He was a tall man with short bristling black hair and a broken nose and two missing front teeth. He was wearing his own waspish livery, the two black chevrons on yellow, and he sneered at Thomas's scarred and broken body. "You didn't bring the rack upstairs, father." He sounded disappointed.

"It wasn't necessary," de Taillebourg said.

The Lord of Roncelets prodded Thomas with a mailed foot. "You say the bastard's an English archer?"

"He is."

"Then cut off his bow fingers," Roncelets said savagely.

"I cannot shed blood," de Taillebourg said.

"By God, I can." Roncelets pulled a knife from his belt.

"He is my charge!" de Taillebourg snapped. "He is in God's hands and you will not touch him. You will not shed his blood!"

"This is my castle, priest," Roncelets growled.

"And your soul is in my hands," de Taillebourg retorted.

"He's an archer! An English archer! He came here to snatch the Chenier boy! That's my business!"

"His fingers have been shattered by the vice," de Taillebourg said, "so he's an archer no longer."

Roncelets was placated by that news. He prodded Thomas again. "He's a piece of piss, priest, that's what he is. A piece of feeble piss." He spat on Thomas, not because he hated Thomas in particular, but because he detested all archers who had dethroned the knight from his rightful place as king of the battlefield. "What will you do with him?" he asked.

"Pray for his soul," de Taillebourg said curtly and when the Lord of Roncelets was gone he did exactly that. It was evident he had finished his questioning for he produced a small vial of holy oil and he gave Thomas the final rites of the church, touching the oil to his brow and to his burned breast and then he said the prayers for the dying. "*Sana me, Domine*," de Taillebourg intoned, his fingers gentle on Thomas's brow, "*quoniam conturbata sunt ossa mea*." Heal me, Lord, for my bones are twisted with pain. And when that was said and done Thomas was carried down the castle stairs into a dungeon sunk into a pit in the rock crag on which the Guêpier was built. The floor was the bare black stone, as damp as it was cold. His manacles were removed as he was locked in the cell and he thought he must go mad for his body was all pain and his fingers were shattered and he was no longer an archer for how could he draw a bow with broken hands? Then the fever came and he wept as he shivered and sweated and at night, when he was half sleeping, he gibbered in his nightmares; and he wept again when he woke for he had not endured the torture, but had told de Taillebourg everything. He was a failure, lost in the dark, dying.

Then, one day, he did not know how many days it was since he had been taken down to the Guêpier's cellars, de Taillebourg's two servants came and fetched him. They put a rough woolen shirt on him, pulled dirty woolen breeches over his soiled legs and then they carried him up to the castle yard and threw him into the back of an empty dung cart. The tower's gate creaked open and, accompanied by a score of men-at-arms in the Lord of Roncelets's livery and dazzled by the pale sunlight, Thomas left the Guêpier. He was hardly aware of what was happening, he just lay on the dirty boards, hunched in pain, the stink of the cart's usual cargo sour in his nostrils, wanting to die. The fever had not gone and he was shaking with weakness. "Where are you taking me?" he asked, but no one answered; maybe no one even heard him for his voice was so feeble. It rained. The cart rumbled northward and the villagers crossed themselves and Thomas drifted in and out of a stupor. He thought he was dying and he supposed they were taking him to the graveyard and he tried to call out to the cart's driver that he still lived, but instead it was Brother Germain who answered him in a querulous voice, saying he should have left the book with him in Caen. "It's your own fault," the old monk said and Thomas decided he was dreaming.

He was next aware of a trumpet calling. The cart had stopped and he heard the flapping of cloth and looked up and saw that one of the horsemen was waving a white banner. Thomas wondered if it was his winding sheet. They wrapped a baby when it came into the world and they wrapped a corpse when it went out and he sobbed because he did not want to be buried, and then he heard English voices and he knew he was dreaming as strong hands lifted him from the remnants of dung. He wanted to scream, but he was too weak, and then all sense left him and he was unconscious.

When he woke it was dark and he was in another cart, a clean one this time, and there were blankets over him and a straw mattress beneath him. The cart had a leather cover on wooden half-hoops to keep out the rain and sunlight. "Will you bury me now?" Thomas asked.

"You're talking nonsense," a man said and Thomas recognized Robbie's voice.

"Robbie?"

"Aye, it's me."

"Robbie?"

"You poor bastard," Robbie said and stroked Thomas's forehead. "You poor, poor bastard."

"Where am I?"

"You're going home, Thomas," Robbie said, "you're going home."

To La Roche-Derrien.

HE HAD BEEN RANSOMED. A week after his disappearance and two days after the rest of the raiding party had returned to La Roche-Derrien a messenger had come to the garrison under a flag of truce. He brought a letter from Bernard de Taillebourg that was addressed to Sir William Skeat. Surrender Father Ralph's book, the letter said, and Thomas of Hookton will be delivered back to his friends. Will Skeat had the message translated and read to him, but he knew nothing of any book so he asked Sir Guillaume if he had any idea what the priest wanted and Sir Guillaume spoke to Robbie who, in turn, talked to Jeanette and next day an answer went back to Roncelets.

Then there was a fortnight's delay because Brother Germain had to be fetched from Normandy to Rennes. De Taillebourg insisted on that precaution because Brother Germain had seen the book and he could confirm that what was exchanged for Thomas was indeed Father Ralph's notebook.

"And so it was," Robbie said.

Thomas stared up at the ceiling. He vaguely felt it had been wrong to exchange him for the book, even if he was grateful to be alive, to be home and among his friends.

"It was the right book," Robbie went on with indecent relish, "but we added some stuff to it." He grinned at Thomas. "We copied it all out first, of course, and then we added some rubbish to mislead them. To confuse them, see? And that shriveled old monk never noticed. He just pawed at the book like a starving dog given a bone."

Thomas shuddered. He felt as if he had been stripped of

pride, strength and even manhood. He had been utterly humiliated, reduced to a shivering, whining, twitching thing.
Tears ran down his face though he made no sound. His
hands hurt, his body hurt, everything hurt. He did not even
know where he was, only that he had been brought back to
La Roche-Derrien and carried up a steep flight of stairs to
this small chamber under a roof's steep rafters where the
walls were roughly plastered and a crucifix hung at the head
of the bed. A window screened with opaque horn let in a
dirty brown light.

Robbie went on telling him about the false entries they
had added to Father Ralph's book. It had been his idea, he
said, and Jeanette had copied out the book first, but after that
Robbie had let his imagination run wild. "I put some of it in
Scots," he boasted, "how the Grail is really in Scotland.
Have the bastards searching the heather, eh?" He laughed,
but could see that Thomas was not listening. He went on
talking anyway, and then another person came into the room
and wiped the tears from Thomas's face. It was Jeanette.

"Thomas?" she asked, "Thomas?"

He wanted to tell her that he had seen and spoken to her
son, but he could not find the words. Guy Vexille had said
Thomas would want to die while he was being tortured and
that had been true, but Thomas was surprised to find it was
still true. Take a man's pride, he thought, and you leave him
with nothing. The worst memory was not the pain, nor the
humiliation of begging for the pain to stop, but the gratitude
he had felt toward de Taillebourg when the pain did stop.
That was the most shameful thing of all.

"Thomas?" Jeanette asked again. She knelt by the bed and
stroked his face. "It's all right," she said softly, "you're safe
now. This is my house. No one will hurt you here."

"I might," a new voice said and Thomas shook with fear,
then turned to see that it was Mordecai who had spoken.
Mordecai? The old doctor was supposed somewhere in the

warm south. "I might have to reset your finger and toe
bones," the doctor said, "and that will be painful." He put his
bag on the floor. "Hello, Thomas. I do hate boats. We waited
for the new sail and then when they'd finished sewing it up
they decided there wasn't enough caulking between the
planks and when that was corrected they decided the rigging
needed work and so the wretched boat is still sitting there.
Sailors! All they ever do is talk about going to sea. Still, I
shouldn't complain, it gave me the time to concoct some
new material for your father's notebook and I rather enjoyed
doing that! Now I hear you need me. My dear Thomas, what
have they done to you?"

"Hurt me," Thomas said and they were the first words he
had spoken since he had come to Jeanette's house.

"Then we must mend you," Mordecai said very calmly.
He peeled the blanket back from Thomas's scarred body and,
though Jeanette flinched, Mordecai just smiled. "I've seen
worse come from the Dominicans," he said, "much worse."

So Thomas was again tended by Mordecai and time was
measured by the clouds passing beyond the opaque window
and the sun climbing ever higher in the sky and the noise of
birds plucking straw from the thatch to make their nests.
There were two days of awful pain when Mordecai brought
a bone-setter to rebreak and splint Thomas's fingers and
toes, but that pain went after a week and the burns on his
body healed and the fever passed. Day after day Mordecai
peered at his urine and declared it was clearing. "You have
the strength of an ox, young Thomas."

"I have the stupidity of one," Thomas said.

"Just brashness," Mordecai said, "just youth and brashness."

"When they . . ." Thomas began and flinched from remembering what de Taillebourg had done. "When they
talked to me," he said instead, "I told them you had seen the
notebook."

"They can't have liked that," Mordecai said. He had taken a spool of cord from a pocket of his gown and now looped one end of the line around a spur of wood that protruded from an untrimmed rafter. "They can't have liked the thought of a Jew being curious about the Grail. They doubtless thought I wanted to use it as a pisspot?"

Thomas, despite the impiety, smiled. "I'm sorry, Mordecai."

"For telling them about me? What choice did you have? Men always talk under torture, Thomas, that is why torture is so useful. It is why torture will be used so long as the sun goes on circling the earth. And you think I am in more danger now than I was? I'm Jewish, Thomas, Jewish. Now, what do I do with this?" He was speaking of the cord, which now hung from the rafter and which he evidently wished to attach to the floor, but there was no obvious anchor point.

"What is it?" Thomas asked.

"A remedy," Mordecai said, staring helplessly at the cord, then at the floor. "I was ever unpractical with matters like this. A hammer and nail, you think?"

"A staple," Thomas suggested.

Jeanette's idiot servant boy was sent out with careful instructions and managed to find the staple that Mordecai asked Thomas to hammer into the floorboard, but Thomas held up his crooked right hand with its fingers bent like claws and said he could not do it, so Mordecai clumsily banged the staple in himself and then tightened the cord and tied it off so that it stretched taut from floor to ceiling. "What you must do," he said, admiring his handiwork, "is pluck it like a bowcord."

"I can't," Thomas said in panic, holding up his crooked hands again.

"What are you?" Mordecai asked.

"What am I?"

"Ignore the specious answers. I know you're an Englishman and I assume you're a Christian, but what are you?"

"I was an archer," Thomas said bitterly.

"And you still are," Mordecai said harshly, "and if you are not an archer then you are nothing. So pluck that cord! And keep on plucking it until your fingers can close on it. Practice. Practice. What else do you have to do with your time?"

So Thomas practiced and after a week he could tighten two fingers opposite the thumb and make the cord reverberate like a harp string, and after another week he could bend the fingers of both hands about the cord and he plucked it so vigorously that it finally broke under the strain. His strength was coming back and the burns had healed to leave puckered welts where the poker had scored his skin, but the wounds in his memory did not heal. He would not talk of what had been done to him for he did not want to remember it, instead he practiced plucking the cord until it snapped and then he learned to grip a quarterstaff and fought mock battles in the house yard with Robbie. And, as the days had lengthened out of winter, he went for walks beyond the town. There was a windmill on a slight hill that lay not far from the town's eastern gate and at first he could hardly manage the climb because his toes had been broken in the vice and his feet felt like unyielding lumps, but by the time April had filled the meadows with cowslips he was walking confidently. Will Skeat often went with him and though the older man never said much his company was easy. If he did talk it was to grumble about the weather or complain because the food was strange or, more likely, because he had heard nothing from the Earl of Northampton. "You think we should write to his lordship again, Tom?"

"Maybe the first letter didn't reach him?"

"I never did like things written down," Skeat said, "it ain't natural. Can you write to him?"

"I can try," Thomas said, but though he could pluck a

bowcord and hold a quarterstaff or even a sword he could not manage the quill. He tried but his letters were scratchy and uncontrolled and in the end one of Totesham's clerks wrote the letter, though Totesham himself did not think the message would do any good.

"Charles of Blois will be here before we get any reinforcements," he said. Totesham was awkward with Thomas, who had disobeyed him by riding to Roncelets, but Thomas's punishment had been far more than Totesham would have wanted and so he felt sorry for the archer. "You want to carry the letter to the Earl?" he asked Thomas.

Thomas knew he was being offered an escape, but he shook his head. "I'll stay," he said, and the letter was entrusted to a shipmaster who was sailing the next day.

The letter was a futile gesture and Totesham knew it for his garrison was almost certainly doomed. Each day brought news of the reinforcements reaching Charles of Blois, and the enemy's raiding parties were now coming within sight of La Roche-Derrien's walls and harassing the forage parties that searched the countryside for any cattle, goats and sheep that could be driven back to the town to be slaughtered and salted down. Sir Guillaume enjoyed such foraging raids. Since losing Evecque he had become fatalistic and so savage that already the enemy had learned to be wary of the blue jupon with its three yellow hawks. Yet one evening, coming home from a long day that had yielded only two goats, he was grinning when he came to see Thomas. "My enemy has joined Charles," he said, "the Count of Coutances, God damn his rotten soul. I killed one of his men this morning and I only wish it had been the Count himself."

"Why's he here?" Thomas asked. "He's not a Breton."

"Philip of France is sending men to help his nephew," Sir Guillaume said, "so why won't the King of England send men to oppose him? He thinks Calais is more important?"

"Yes."

"Calais," Sir Guillaume said in disgust, "is the arsehole of France." He picked a shred of meat from between his teeth. "And your friends were out riding today," he went on.

"My friends?"

"The wasps."

"Roncelets," Thomas said.

"We fought half a dozen of the bastards in some be-nighted village," Sir Guillaume said, "and I put a lance clean through a black and yellow belly. He was coughing after-ward."

"Coughing?"

"It's the wet weather, Thomas," Sir Guillaume explained, "it gives men a cough. So I left him alone, killed another of the bastards, then went back and cured his cough. I cut his head off."

Robbie rode with Sir Guillaume and, like him, amassed coins taken from dead enemy patrols, though Robbie also rode in hope of meeting Guy Vexille. He knew that name now because Thomas had told him that it was Guy Vexille who had killed his brother just before the battle outside Durham and Robbie had gone to St. Renan's church, put his hand on the altar's cross and sworn revenge. "I shall kill Guy Vexille and de Taillebourg," he vowed.

"They're mine," Thomas insisted.

"Not if I get to them first," Robbie promised.

Robbie had found himself a brown-eyed Breton girl called Oana who hated to leave his side and she came with him whenever he walked with Thomas. One day, as they set out for the windmill, she appeared with Thomas's big black bow.

"I can't use that!" Thomas said, frightened of it.

"Then what bloody use are you?" Robbie asked and he patiently encouraged Thomas to draw the bow and praised him as his strength returned. The three of them would take the bow to the windmill and Thomas would drive arrows into the wooden tower. The shots were feeble at first for he could scarcely pull the cord halfway and the more power he exerted the more treacherous his fingers seemed to be and the more wayward his aim, but by the time the swallows and swifts had magically reappeared above the town's roofs he could pull the cord all the way back to his ear and put an arrow through one of Oana's wooden bracelets at a hundred paces.

"You're cured," Mordecai told him when Thomas told him that news.

"Thanks to you," Thomas said, though he knew it was not only Mordecai, any more than it was the friendship of Will Skeat or of Sir Guillaume or of Robbie Douglas that had helped him recover. Bernard de Taillebourg had wounded Thomas, but those bloodless wounds of God had not just been to his body, but to his soul, and it was on a dark spring night when the lightning was flickering in the east that Jeanette had climbed to her attic. She had not left Thomas until the town's cockerels greeted the new dawn and if Mordecai understood why Thomas was smiling the next day he said nothing, but he noted that from that moment on Thomas's recovery was swift.

Thereafter Thomas and Jeanette talked every night. He told her of Charles and of the look on the boy's face when Thomas had mentioned his mother; Jeanette wanted to know everything about that look and she worried that it meant nothing and that her son had forgotten her, but eventually she believed Thomas when he said the boy had almost wept when he heard news of her. "You told him I loved him?" she asked.

"Yes," Thomas said, and Jeanette lay silent, tears in her eyes, and Thomas tried to reassure her, but she shook her head as if there was nothing Thomas could say that would console her. "I'm sorry," he said.

"You tried," Jeanette said.

They wondered how the enemy had known Thomas was

coming and Jeanette said that she was sure that Belas the lawyer had had a hand in it. "I know he writes to Charles of Blois," she said, "and that horrid man, what did you call him? *Épouvantail*?"

"The Scarecrow."

"Him," Jeanette confirmed, "*l'épouvantail*. He talks to Belas."

"The Scarecrow talks to Belas?" Thomas asked, surprised.

"He lives there now. He and his men live in the storehouses." She paused. "Why does he even stay in the town?" Others of the mercenaries had slipped away to find employment where there was some hope of victory rather than stay and endure the defeat that Charles of Blois threatened.

"He can't go home," Thomas said, "because he has too many debts. He's protected from his creditors so long as he's here."

"But why La Roche-Derrien?"

"Because I'm here," Thomas said. "He thinks I can lead him to treasure."

"The Grail?"

"He doesn't know that," Thomas said, but he was wrong because the next day, while he was alone at the windmill and shooting arrows at a wand he had planted a hundred and fifty paces away, the Scarecrow and his six men-at-arms came riding out of the town's eastern gate. They turned off the Pontrieux road, filed through a gap in the hedge and spurred up the shallow slope toward the mill. They were all in mail and all with swords except for Beggar who, dwarfing his horse, carried a morningstar.

Sir Geoffrey reined in close to Thomas, who ignored him to shoot an arrow that just brushed the wand. The Scarecrow let the coils of his whip ripple to the ground. "Look at me," he ordered Thomas.

Thomas still ignored him. He took an arrow from his belt

and put it on the string, then jerked his head aside as he saw the whip snake toward him. The metal tip touched his hair, but did no damage. "I said look at me," Sir Geoffrey snarled.

"You want an arrow in your face?" Thomas asked him.

Sir Geoffrey leaned forward on his saddle's pommel, his raw red face twisted with a spasm of anger. "You are an archer"—he pointed his whip handle at Thomas—"and I am a knight. If I chop you down there's not a judge alive who would condemn me."

"And if I put an arrow through your eye," Thomas said, "the devil will thank me for sending him company."

Beggar growled and spurred his horse forward, but the Scarecrow waved the big man back. "I know what you want," he said to Thomas.

Thomas hauled the string back, instinctively corrected for the small wind rippling the meadow's grass, and released. The arrow made the wand quiver. "You have no idea what I want," he told Sir Geoffrey.

"I thought it was gold," the Scarecrow said, "and then I thought it was land, but I never understood why gold or land would take you to Durham." He paused as Thomas shot another arrow that hissed a hand's breadth past the distant wand. "But now I know," he finished, "now at last I know."

"What do you know?" Thomas asked derisively.

"I know you went to Durham to talk with the churchmen because you're seeking the greatest treasure of the Church. You're looking for the Grail."

Thomas let the bowcord slacken, then looked up at Sir Geoffrey. "We're all looking for the Grail," Thomas said, still derisive.

"Where is it?" Sir Geoffrey growled.

Thomas laughed. He was surprised the Scarecrow knew about the Grail, but he supposed that gossip in the garrison had probably let everyone in La Roche-Derrien know. "The best questioners of the Church asked me that," he said, holding up one crooked hand, "and I didn't tell them. You think I'll tell you?"

"I think," the Scarecrow said, "that a man searching for the Grail doesn't lock himself into a garrison that only has a month or two to live."

"Then maybe I'm not looking for the Grail," Thomas said and shot another arrow at the wand, but this shaft was warped and the arrow wobbled in flight and went wide. Above him the great sails of the mill, furled about their spars and tethered by ropes, creaked as a wind gust tried to turn them.

Sir Geoffrey coiled the whip. "You failed the last time you rode out. What happens if you ride again? What happens if you ride after the Grail? And you must be going soon, before Charles of Blois gets here. So when you ride you're going to need help." Thomas, incredulous, realized that the Scarecrow had come to offer him help, or perhaps Sir Geoffrey was asking for help. He was in La Roche-Derrien for only one reason, treasure, and he was no nearer to it now than he had been when he first accosted Thomas outside Durham. "You daren't fail again," the Scarecrow went on, "so next time take some real fighters with you."

"You think I'd take you?" Thomas asked, astonished.

"I'm an Englishman," the Scarecrow said indignantly, "and if the Grail exists I want it in England. Not in some scab of a foreign place."

The sound of a sword scraping from its scabbard made the Scarecrow and his men turn in their saddles. Jeanette and Robbie had come to the meadow with Oana at Robbie's side; Jeanette had her crossbow cocked and Robbie, as though he did not have a care in the world, was now slashing the tops from thistles with his uncle's sword. Sir Geoffrey turned back to Thomas. "What you don't need is a damned Scotchman," he said angrily, "nor a damned French bitch. If you look for the Grail, archer, look for it with loyal Englishmen! It's what the King would want, isn't it?"

Again Thomas did not answer. Sir Geoffrey hung the whip on a hook attached to his belt, then jerked his reins. The seven men cantered down the hill, going close to Robbie as if tempting him to attack them, but Robbie ignored them. "What did that bastard want?"

Thomas shot at the wand, brushing it with the arrow's feathers. "I think," he said, "that he wanted to help me find the Grail."

"Help you!" Robbie exclaimed. "Help you find the Grail? Like hell. He wants to steal it. That bastard would steal the milk from the Virgin Mary's tits."

"Robbie!" Jeanette said, shocked, then aimed her crossbow at the wand.

"Watch her," Thomas said to Robbie. "She'll close her eyes when she shoots. She always does."

"Damn you," Jeanette said, then, unable to help it, closed her eyes as she pulled the trigger. The bolt slapped out of the groove and miraculously clipped the top six inches from the wand. Jeanette looked at Thomas triumphantly. "I can shoot better than you with my eyes closed," she said.

Robbie had been on the town's walls and had seen the Scarecrow accost Thomas and so he had come to help, but now, with Sir Geoffrey gone, they sat in the sun with their backs against the mill's wooden skirt. Jeanette was staring at the town's wall which still showed the scars where the English-made breach had been repaired with a lighter-colored stone. "Are you really nobly born?" she asked Thomas.

"Bastard born," Thomas said.

"But to a nobleman?"

"He was the Count of Astarac," Thomas said, then laughed because it was strange to think that Father Ralph, mad Father Ralph who had preached to the gulls on Hookton's beach, had been a count.

"So what's the badge of Astarac?" Jeanette asked.

"A yale," Thomas told her, "holding a cup," and he

showed her the faded silver patch on his black bowstave that was engraved with the strange creature that had horns, cloven hooves, claws, tusks and a lion's tail.

"I'll have a banner made for you," Jeanette said.

"A banner? Why?"

"A man should display his badge," Jeanette said.

"And you should leave La Roche-Derrien," Thomas retorted. He kept trying to persuade her to leave the town, but she insisted she would stay. She doubted now she would ever get her son back and so she was determined to kill Charles of Blois with one of her crossbow's bolts, which were made of dense yew heartwood tipped with iron heads and fledged, not with feathers, but with stiff pieces of leather inserted into slits cut crosswise into the yew and then bound up with cord and glue. That was why she practiced so assiduously, for the chance to cut down the man who had raped her and taken her child.

Easter came before the enemy arrived. The weather was warm now. The hedgerows were full of nestlings and the meadows echoed with the shriek of partridges and on the day after Easter, when folk ate up the remnants of the feast that had broken their Lenten fast, the dreaded news at last arrived from Rennes.

That Charles of Blois had marched.

MORE THAN four thousand men left Rennes under the white ermine banner of the Duke of Brittany. Two thousand of them were crossbowmen, most wearing the green and red livery of Genoa and bearing the city's badge of the Holy Grail on their right arms. They were mercenaries, hired and prized for their skill. A thousand infantrymen marched with them, the men who would dig the trenches and assault the broken walls of the English fortresses, and then there were over a thousand knights or men-at-arms, most of them French, who formed the hard armored heart of Duke

Charles's army. They marched toward La Roche-Derrien, but the real aim of the campaign was not to capture the town, which was of negligible value, but rather to draw Sir Thomas Dagworth and his small army into a pitched battle in which the knights and men-at-arms, mounted on their big armored horses, would be released to smash their way through the English ranks.

A convoy of heavy carts carried nine siege machines, which needed the attentions of over a hundred engineers who understood how to assemble and work the giant devices that could hurl boulders the size of beer barrels farther than a bow could drive an arrow. A Florentine gunner had offered six of his strange machines to Charles, but the Duke had turned them down. Guns were rare, expensive and, he believed, temperamental, while the old mechanical devices worked well enough if they were properly greased with tallow and Charles saw no reason to abandon them.

Over four thousand men left Rennes, but far more arrived in the fields outside La Roche-Derrien. Country folk who hated the English joined the army to gain revenge for all the cattle, harvests, property and virginity their families had lost to the foreigners. Some were armed with nothing more than mattocks or axes, but when the time came to assault the town such angry men would be useful.

The army came to La Roche-Derrien and Charles of Blois heard the last of the town's gates slam shut. He sent a messenger to demand the garrison's surrender, knowing the request was futile, and while his tents were pitched he ordered other horsemen to patrol westward on the roads leading to Finisterre, the world's end. They were there to warn him when Sir Thomas Dagworth's army marched to relieve the town, if indeed it did march. His spies had told Charles that Dagworth could not even raise a thousand men. "And how many of those will be archers?" he asked.

"At most, your grace, five hundred." The man who answered was a priest, one of the many who served in Charles's retinue. The Duke was known as a pious man and liked to employ priests as advisers, secretaries and, in this case, as a spymaster. "At most five hundred," the priest repeated, "but in truth, your grace, far fewer."

"Fewer? How so?"

"Fever in Finisterre," the priest answered, then smiled thinly. "God is good to us."

"Amen to that. And how many archers are in the town garrison?"

"Sixty healthy men, your grace"—the priest had Belas's latest report—"just sixty."

Charles grimaced. He had been defeated by English archers before, even when he had so outnumbered them that defeat had seemed impossible, and, as a result, he was properly wary of the long arrows, but he was also an intelligent man and he had given the problem of the English war bow a deal of thought. It was possible to defeat the weapon, he thought, and on this campaign he would show how it could be done. Cleverness, that most despised of soldierly qualities, would triumph, and Charles of Blois, styled by the French as the Duke and ruler of Brittany, was undeniably a clever man. He could read and write in six languages, spoke Latin better than most priests and was a master of rhetoric. He even looked clever with his thin, pale face and intense blue eyes, fair beard and moustache. He had been fighting his rivals for the dukedom almost all his adult life, but now, at last, he had gained the ascendancy. The King of England, besieging Calais, was not reinforcing his garrisons in Brittany while the King of France, who was Charles's uncle, had been generous with men, which meant that Duke Charles at last outnumbered his enemies. By summer's end, he thought, he would be master of all his ancestral domains, but then he cautioned himself against over-confidence. "Even five hundred archers," he observed, "even five hundred and sixty archers can be dangerous." He had a precise voice, pedantic and dry, and the priests in his entourage often thought he sounded very like a priest himself.

"The Genoese will swamp them with bolts, your grace," a priest assured the Duke.

"Pray God they do," Charles said piously, though God, he thought, would need some help from human cleverness.

Next morning, under a late spring sun, Charles rode around La Roche-Derrien, though he kept far enough away so that no English arrow could reach him. The defenders had hung banners from the town walls. Some of the flags displayed the English cross of St. George, others the white ermine badge of the Montfort Duke that was so similar to Charles's own device. Many of the flags were inscribed with insults aimed at Charles. One showed the Duke's white ermine with an English arrow through its bleeding belly, and another was evidently a picture of Charles himself being trampled under a great black horse, but most of the flags were pious exhortations inviting God's help or displaying the cross to show the attackers where heaven's sympathies were supposed to lie. Most besieged towns would also have flaunted the banners of their noble defenders, but La Roche-Derrien had few nobles, or at least few who displayed their badges, and none to match the ranks of the aristocrats in Charles's army. The three hawks of Evecque were displayed on the wall, but everyone knew Sir Guillaume had been dispossessed and had no more than three or four followers. One flag showed a red heart on a pale field and a priest in Charles's entourage thought it was the badge of the Douglas family in Scotland, but that was a nonsense for no Scotsman would be fighting for the English. Next to the red heart was a brighter banner showing a blue and white sea of wavy lines. "Is that . . ." Charles began to ask, then paused, frowning.

"The badge of Armorica, your grace," the Lord of Roncelets answered. Today, as Duke Charles circled the town, he was accompanied by his great lords so that the defenders would see their banners and be awed. Most were lords of Brittany; the Viscount Rohan and the Viscount Morgat rode close behind the Duke, then came the lords of Châteaubriant and of Roncelets, Laval, Guingamp, Rougé, Dinan, Redon and Malestroit, all of them mounted on high-stepping destriers, while from Normandy the Count of Coutances and the lords of Valognes and Carteret had brought their retainers to do battle for the nephew of their King.

"I thought Armorica was dead," one of the Norman lords remarked.

"He has a son," Roncelets answered.

"And a widow," the Count of Guingamp said, "and she's the traitorous bitch flying the banner."

"A pretty traitorous bitch, though," the Viscount Rohan said, and the lords laughed for they all knew how to treat unruly but pretty widows.

Charles grimaced at their unseemly laughter. "When we take the town," he ordered coldly, "the dowager Countess of Armorica will not be hurt. She will be brought to me." He had raped Jeanette once and he would rape her again, and when that pleasure was done he would marry her off to one of his men-at-arms who would teach her to mind her manners and to curb her tongue. Now he reined in his horse to watch as more banners were hung from the ramparts, all of them insults to him and his house. "It's a busy garrison," he said dryly.

"Busy townspeople," the Viscount Rohan snarled. "Busy goddamn traitors."

"Townsfolk?" Charles seemed puzzled. "Why would the townsfolk support the English?"

"Trade," Roncelets answered curtly.

"Trade?"

"They're becoming rich," Roncelets growled, "and they like it."

"They like it enough to fight against their lord?" Charles asked in disbelief.

"A disloyal rabble," Roncelets said dismissively.

"A rabble," Charles said, "that we shall have to impoverish." He spurred on, only checking his horse when he saw another nobleman's banner, this one showing a yale flourishing a chalice. So far he had not seen a single banner that promised a great ransom if its lord was captured, but this badge was a mystery. "Whose is that?" he asked.

No one knew, but then a slim young man on a tall black horse answered from the rear of the Duke's entourage. "The badge of Astarac, your grace, and it belongs to an impostor." The man who had answered had come from France with a hundred grim horsemen liveried in plain black and he was accompanied by a Dominican with a frightening face. Charles of Blois was glad to have the black-liveried men in his army, for they were all hard and experienced soldiers, but he did feel somewhat nervous of them. They were somehow too hard, too experienced.

"An impostor?" he repeated and spurred on. "Then we do not need to worry ourselves about him."

There were three gates on the town's landward side and a fourth, opening onto the bridge, facing the river. Charles planned to besiege each of those gates so that the garrison would be trapped like foxes with their earths stopped. "The army," he decreed when the lords returned to the ducal tent, which had been raised close to the windmill that stood on the slight hill to the east of the town, "will be divided into four parts, and one part will face each gate." The lords listened and a priest copied down the pronouncement so that history would have a true record of the Duke's martial genius.

Each of the four divisions of Charles's army would outnumber any relief force that Sir Thomas Dagworth could gather, but, to make himself even more secure, Charles ordered that the four encampments were to surround themselves with earthworks so that the English would be forced to attack across ditches, banks, palisades and thorn hedges. The obstacles would conceal Charles's men from the archers and give his Genoese crossbowmen cover while they rewound their weapons. The ground between the four encampments was to be cleared of hedges and other obstacles to leave a bare wilderness of grass and marsh.

"The English archer," Charles told his lords, "is not a man who will fight face to face. He kills from a distance and he hides behind hedges, thus frustrating our horses. We shall turn that tactic against him." The tent was big, white and airy, and the smell inside was of trampled grass and men's sweat. From beyond the canvas walls came the sound of dull thudding as the engineers used wooden mallets to assemble the biggest of the great siege engines.

"Our men," Charles further decreed, "will stay within their own defenses. We shall thus make four fortresses that will stand at the four gates of the town and if the English send a relief force then those men will have to attack our fortresses. Archers cannot kill men they cannot see." He paused to make sure those simple words were understood. "Archers," he said again, "cannot kill men they cannot see. Remember that! Our crossbows will be behind banks of earth, we will be screened by hedges and hidden by palisades, and the enemy will be out in the open where they can be cut down."

There were growls of agreement for the Duke made sense. Archers could not kill invisible men. Even the fierce Dominican who had come with the soldiers in black looked impressed.

The midday bells rang from the town. One, the loudest, was cracked and gave a harsh note. "La Roche-Derrien," the

Duke continued, "does not matter. Whether it falls or not is of little consequence. What matters is that we draw our enemy's army out to attack us. Dagworth will probably come to protect La Roche-Derrien. When he arrives we shall crush him and once he is broken then only the English garrisons will be left and we shall take them one by one until, at summer's end, all Brittany is ours." He spoke slowly and simply, knowing it was best to spell out the campaign for these men who, though they were tough as rams, were not renowned as thinkers. "And when Brittany is ours," he went on, "there will be gifts of land, of manors and of strongholds." A much louder growl of approbation sounded and the listening men grinned for there would be more than land, manors and castles as the rewards of victory. There would be gold, silver and women. Lots of women. The growl turned into laughter as the men realized they were all thinking the same thing.

"But it is here"—Charles's voice called his audience to order—"that we make our victory possible, and we do it by denying the English archer his targets. An archer cannot kill men he cannot see!" He paused again, looking at his audience and he saw them nodding as the simple truth of that assertion at last penetrated their skulls. "We shall all be in our own fortress, one of four fortresses, and when the English army comes to relieve the siege they will attack one of those fortresses. That English army will be small. Fewer than a thousand men! Suppose, then, that it begins by attacking the fort I shall make here. What will the rest of you do?"

He waited for an answer and, after a while, the Lord of Roncelets, as uncertain as a schoolboy giving a response to his master, frowned and made a suggestion. "Come to help your grace?"

The other lords nodded and smiled agreement.

"No!" Charles said angrily. "No! No! No!" He waited, making sure they had understood the simple word. "If you leave your fortress," he explained, "then you offer the English archer a target. It is what he wants! He will want to tempt us from behind our walls to cut us down with his arrows. So what do we do? We stay behind our walls. *We stay behind our walls.*" Did they understand that? It was the key to victory. Keep the men hidden and the English must lose. Sir Thomas Dagworth's army would be forced to assault earth walls and thorn hedges and the crossbowmen would spit them on quarrels and when the English were so thinned that only a couple of hundred remained on their feet the Duke would release his men-at-arms to slaughter the remnant. "You do not leave your fortresses," he insisted, "and any man who does will forfeit my generosity." That threat sobered the Duke's listeners. "If even one of your men leaves the sanctuary of the walls," Charles continued, "we shall make sure that you will not share in the distribution of land at the end of the campaign. Is that plain, gentlemen? Is that plain?"

It was plain. It was simple.

Charles of Blois would make four fortresses to oppose the four gates of the town and the English, when they came, would be forced to assault those newly made walls. And even the smallest of the Duke's four forts would have more defenders than the English had attackers, and those defenders would be sheltered, and their weapons would be lethal, and the English would die and so Brittany would pass to the House of Blois.

Cleverness. It would win wars and make reputations. And once Charles had shown how to defeat the English here he would defeat them through all France.

Because Charles dreamed of a crown heavier than Brittany's ducal coronet. He dreamed of France, but it must begin here, in the flooded fields about La Roche-Derrien, where the English archer would be taught his place.

In hell.

THE NINE SIEGE engines were all trebuchets, the largest
of them capable of throwing a stone weighing twice the
weight of a grown man for almost three hundred paces. All
nine had been made at Regensburg in Bavaria and the senior
engineers who accompanied the gaunt machines were all
Bavarians who understood the intricacies of the weapons.
The two biggest had throwing beams over fifty feet long and
even the two smallest, which were placed on the far bank of
the Jaudy to threaten the bridge and its barbican, had beams
thirty-six feet long.

The biggest two, which were named Hellgiver and Widowmaker, were placed at the foot of the hill on which the
windmill stood. In essence each was a simple machine,
merely a long beam mounted on an axle like a giant's balance or a child's seesaw, only one end of the seesaw was
three times longer than the other. The shorter end was
weighted with a huge wooden box that was filled with lead
weights, while the longer end, which actually threw the missile, was attached to a great windlass which drew it down to
the ground and so raised the ten tons of lead counterweights.
The stone missile was placed in a leather sling some fifteen
feet long, which was attached to the longer arm. When the
beam was released so that the counterweight slammed
down, the longer end whipped up into the sky and the sling
whipped even faster and the boulder was released from the
sling's leather cradle to curve through the sky and crash
down onto its target. That much was simple. What was hard
was to keep the mechanism greased with tallow, to construct
a winch strong enough to haul the long beam down to the
ground, to make a container strong enough to thump down
again and again and not spill the ten tons of lead weights
and, trickiest of all, to fashion a device strong enough to
hold the long beam down against the weight of the lead yet

capable of releasing the beam safely. These were the matters on which the Bavarians were experts and for which they were paid so generously.

There were many who said that the Bavarians' expertise was redundant. Guns were much smaller and hurled their missiles with greater force, but Duke Charles had applied his intelligence to the comparison and decided on the older technology. Guns were slow and prone to explosions that killed their expensive gunners. They were also painfully slow because the gap between the missile and the gun's barrel had to be sealed to contain the powder's force and so it was necessary to pack the cannon ball about with wet loam, and that needed time to dry before the powder could be ignited, and even the most skillful gunners from Italy could not fire a weapon more than three or four times a day. And when a gun fired it spat a ball weighing only a few pounds. While it was true that the small ball flew with a velocity so great that it could not even be seen, nevertheless the older trebuchets could throw a missile of twenty or thirty times the weight three or four times in every hour. La Roche-Derrien, the Duke decided, would be hammered the old-fashioned way, and so the little town was surrounded by the nine trebuchets. As well as Hellgiver and Widowmaker, there was Stone-Hurler, Crusher, Gravedigger, Stonewhip, Spiteful, Destroyer and Hand of God.

Each trebuchet was constructed on a platform made of wooden beams and protected by a palisade that was tall and stout enough to stop any arrow. Some of the peasants who had joined the army were trained to stand close to the palisades and be ready to throw water over any fire arrows that the English might use to burn the fences down and so expose the trebuchets' engineers. Other peasants dug the ditches and threw up the earthen banks that formed the Duke's four fortresses. Where possible they used existing ditches or incorporated the thick blackthorn hedges into the defenses.

They made barriers of sharpened stakes and dug pits to break horses' legs. The four parts of the Duke's army ringed themselves with such defenses and, day after day, as the walls grew and the trebuchets took shape from the pieces transported on the wagons, the Duke had his men practice forming their lines of battle. The Genoese crossbowmen manned the half-finished walls while behind them the knights and men-at-arms paraded on foot. Some men grumbled that such practices were a waste of time, but others saw how the Duke intended to fight and they approved. The English archers would be baffled by the walls, ditches and palisades and the crossbows would pick them off one by one, and finally the enemy would be forced to attack across the earth walls and the flooded ditches to be slaughtered by the waiting men-at-arms.

After a week of back-breaking work the trebuchets were assembled and their counterpoise boxes had been filled with great pigs of lead. Now the engineers had to demonstrate an even subtler skill, the art of dropping their great stones one after the other onto the exact same spot of the wall so that the ramparts would be battered away and a path opened into the town. Then, once the relieving army was defeated, the Duke's men could assault La Roche-Derrien and put its treasonous inhabitants to the sword.

The Bavarian engineers selected their first stones carefully, then trimmed the length of the slings to affect the range of their machines. It was a fine spring morning. Kestrels soared, buttercups dotted the fields, trout were rising to the mayflies, the wild garlic was blossoming white and pigeons flew through the new leaves of the green woods. It was the loveliest time of the year and Duke Charles, whose spies told him that Sir Thomas Dagworth's English army had yet to leave western Brittany, anticipated triumph. "The Bavarians," he told one of his attendant priests, "may begin."

The trebuchet named Hellgiver shot first. A lever was pulled that extracted a thick metal pin from a staple attached to the long arm of Hellgiver's beam. Ten tons of lead dropped with a crash that could be heard in Tréguier, the long arm whipped up and the sling whirled at the arm's end with the sound of a sudden gale and a boulder arched into the sky. It seemed to hang for a moment, a great stone lump in the kestrel-haunted sky, and then, like a thunderbolt, it fell.

The killing had begun.

THE FIRST STONE, thrown by Hellgiver, crashed through the roof of a dyer's house close to St. Brieuc's church and took off the heads of an English man-at-arms and the dyer's wife. A joke went through the garrison that the two bodies were so crushed together by the boulder that they would go on coupling throughout eternity. The stone which killed them, a rock about the size of a barrel, had missed the eastern ramparts by no more than twenty feet and the Bavarian engineers made adjustments to the sling and the next stone thumped just short of the wall, spewing up filth and sewage from the ditch. The third boulder hit the wall plumb and then a monstrous thump announced that Widowmaker had just shot its first missile and one after the other Stone-Hurler, Crusher, Gravedigger, Stonewhip, Spiteful, Destroyer and Hand of God added their contributions.

Richard Totesham did his best to blunt the assault of the trebuchets. It was evident that Charles was attempting to make four breaches, one on each side of the town, and so Totesham ordered vast bags to be sewn and stuffed with straw and the bags were placed to cushion the walls, which were further protected by baulks of timber. Those precautions served to slow the process of making the breaches, but the Bavarians were sending some of their missiles deep into the town and nothing could be done to shield the houses from those plunging boulders. Some townsfolk argued that Totesham should construct a trebuchet of his own and try to break the enemy's machines, but he doubted there was time and instead a giant crossbow was fashioned from ships' spars that had been brought upstream from Tréguier before the siege began. Tréguier was now deserted for, lacking walls, its inhabitants had either come to La Roche-Derrien for shelter, fled to sea in their ships or gone over to Charles's camp.

Totesham's springald was thirty feet in width and shot a bolt eight feet long propelled by a cord made from braided leather. It was cocked by means of a ship's windlass. It took four days to make the weapon and the very first time they tried to use it the spar-arm broke. It was a bad omen, and there was an even worse one next morning when a horse drawing a cart of night soil broke free from its harness and kicked a child in the head. The child died. Later that day a stone from one of the smaller trebuchets across the river plunged into Richard Totesham's house and brought down half the upper floor and very nearly killed his baby. Over a score of mercenaries tried to desert the garrison that night and some must have got clean away, others joined Charles's army and one, who had been carrying a message for Sir Thomas Dagworth concealed in a boot, was caught and beheaded. Next morning his severed head, with the letter fixed between his teeth, was hurled into the town by the trebuchet called the Hand of God and the spirits of the garrison plummeted even further.

"I am not sure," Mordecai told Thomas, "whether omens can be trusted."

"Of course they can."

"I should like to hear your reasons. But show me your urine first."

"You said I was cured," Thomas protested.

"Eternal vigilance, dear Thomas, is the price of health. Piss for me."

Thomas obeyed, Mordecai held the liquid up to the sun, then dipped a finger in it and dabbed it onto his tongue. "Splendid!" he said. "Clear, pure and not too saline. That is a good omen, is it not?"

"That's a symptom," Thomas said, "not an omen."

"Ah." Mordecai smiled at the correction. They were in the small back yard behind Jeanette's kitchen where the doctor watched the house-martins bringing mud to their new nests beneath the eaves. "Enlighten me, Thomas," he said with another smile, "on the matter of omens."

"When our Lord was crucified," Thomas said, "there was darkness in daytime and a curtain in the temple was torn in two."

"You are saying that omens are secreted at the very heart of your faith?"

"And yours too, surely?" Thomas asked.

Mordecai flinched as a boulder crunched down somewhere in the town. The sound reverberated, then there was another splintering crash as a weakened roof or floor gave way. Dogs howled and a woman screamed. "They're doing it deliberately," Mordecai said.

"Of course," Thomas said. Not only was the enemy sending boulders to fall on the tight small houses of the town, but they sometimes used the trebuchets to lob the rotting corpses of cattle or pigs or goats to splatter their filth and stench through the streets.

Mordecai waited till the woman had stopped screaming. "I don't think I believe in omens," he said. "We suffer some bad luck in the town and everyone assumes we are doomed, but how do we know there is not some ill fortune afflicting the enemy?"

Thomas said nothing. Birds squabbled in the thatch, oblivious that a cat was stalking just below the roof ridge.

"What do you want, Thomas?" Mordecai asked.

"Want?"

"What do you want?"

Thomas grimaced and held out his right hand with its crooked fingers. "For these to be straight."

"And I want to be young again," Mordecai said impatiently. "Your fingers are mended. They are misshapen, but mended. Now tell me what you want."

"What I want," Thomas said, "is to kill the men who killed Eleanor. To bring Jeanette's son back. Then to be an archer. Just that. An archer." He wanted the Grail too, but he did not like to talk of that with Mordecai.

Mordecai tugged at his beard. "To kill the men who killed Eleanor?" he mused aloud. "I think you'll do that. Jeanette's son? Maybe you will do that too, though I don't understand why you wish to please her. You don't want to marry Jeanette, do you?"

"Marry her!" Thomas laughed. "No."

"Good."

"Good?" Thomas was offended now.

"I have always enjoyed talking with alchemists," Mordecai said, "and I have often seen them mix sulfur and quicksilver. There is a theory that all metals are composed of those two substances, did you know? The proportions vary, of course, but my point, dear Thomas, is that if you put quicksilver and sulfur into a vessel, then heat it, the result is very often calamitous." He mimed an explosion with his hands. "That, I think, is you and Jeanette. Besides, I cannot see her married to an archer. To a king? Yes. To a duke? Maybe. To a count or an earl? Certainly. But to an archer?"

He shook his head. "There is nothing wrong with being an archer, Thomas. It's a useful skill in this wicked world." He sat silent for a few heartbeats. "My son is training to be a doctor."

Thomas smiled. "I sense a reproof."

"A reproof?"

"Your son will be a healer and I'm a killer."

Mordecai shook his head. "Benjamin is training to be a physician, but he would rather be a soldier. He wants to be a killer."

"Then why—" Thomas stopped because the answer was obvious.

"Jews cannot carry weapons," Mordecai said, "that is why. No, I meant no reproof. I think, as soldiers go, Thomas, that you are a good man." He paused and frowned because another stone from one of the bigger trebuchets had slammed into a building not far away and, as the echoing crash subsided, he waited for the screams. None came. "Your friend Will is a good man, too," Mordecai went on, "but I fear he's no longer an archer."

Thomas nodded. Will Skeat was cured, but not restored. "It would have been better, I sometimes think—" Thomas began.

"If he had died?" Mordecai finished the thought. "Wish death on no man, Thomas, it comes soon enough without a wish. Sir William will go home to England, no doubt, and your Earl will look after him."

The fate of all old soldiers, Thomas thought. To go home and die on the charity of the family they served. "Then I'll go to the siege of Calais when all this is over," Thomas said, "and see if Will's archers need a new leader."

Mordecai smiled. "You won't look for the Grail?"

"I don't know where it is," Thomas said.

"And your father's book?" Mordecai asked. "It didn't help?"

Thomas had been poring over the copy Jeanette had made. He thought his father must have used some kind of code, though try as he might he could not pierce the code's workings. Or else, in its ramblings, the book was merely a symptom of Father Ralph's troubled mind. Yet Thomas was sure of one thing. His father had believed he possessed the Grail. "I will look for the Grail," Thomas said, "but I sometimes think the only way to seek it is *not* to search for it." He looked up, startled, as there was a sudden scrabbling sound on the roof. The cat had made a rush and almost lost its footing as birds scattered upward.

"Another omen?" Mordecai suggested, looking up at the escaping birds. "Surely a good one?"

"Besides," Thomas said, "what do you know of the Grail?"

"I am a Jew. What do I know of anything?" Mordecai asked innocently. "What would happen, Thomas, if you found the Grail?" He did not wait for an answer. "Do you think," he went on instead, "that the world will become a better place? Is it just lacking the Grail? Is that all?" There was still no answer. "It's a thing like Abracadabra, is that it?" Mordecai said sadly.

"The devil?" Thomas was shocked.

"Abracadabra isn't the devil!" Mordecai answered, equally shocked. "It's simply a charm. Some foolish Jews believe if you write it in the form of a triangle and hang it about your neck then you'll not suffer from the ague! What nonsense! The only cure for an ague is a warm poultice of cow dung, but folk will put their trust in charms and, I fear, in omens too, yet I do not think God works through the one or reveals Himself through the other."

"Your God," Thomas said, "is a very long way away."

"I rather fear he is."

"Mine is close," Thomas said, "and He does show Himself."

"Then you're fortunate," Mordecai said. Jeanette's distaff and spindle were on the bench beside him and he put the distaff under his left arm and tried to spin some thread from the wool bundled about its head, but he could make nothing of it. "You are fortunate," he said again, "and I hope that when Charles's troops break in that your God stays close. As for the rest of us, I suppose we're doomed?"

"If they break in," Thomas said, "then either take refuge in a church or try and escape by the river."

"I can't swim."

"Then the church is your best hope."

"I doubt that," Mordecai said, putting down the distaff. "What Totesham should do," he said sadly, "is surrender. Let us all leave."

"He won't do that."

Mordecai shrugged. "So we must die."

Yet, the very next day, he was given a chance to escape when Totesham said that anyone who did not want to suffer the privations of the siege could leave the town by the southern gate, but no sooner was it thrown open than a force of Charles's men-at-arms, all in mail and with their faces hidden by their helmets' gray visors, blocked the road. No more than a hundred folk had decided to go, all of them women and children, but Charles's men-at-arms were there to say they would not be allowed to abandon La Roche-Derrien. It was not in the besiegers' interest to have fewer mouths for the garrison to feed and so the gray men barred the road and Totesham's soldiers shut the town gate and the women and children were stranded all day.

That evening the trebuchets ceased their work for the first time since the stone had killed the dyer's wife and her lover and, in the strange silence, a messenger came from Charles's encampment. A trumpeter and a white flag announced that he wanted a truce and Totesham ordered an English trumpeter to respond to the Breton and for a white banner to be waved above the southern gate. The Breton messenger waited until a man of rank came to the walls, then he gestured at the women and children. "These folk," he said, "cannot be allowed to pass through our lines. They will starve here."

"This is the pity your master has for his people?" Totesham's envoy responded. He was an English priest who spoke Breton and French.

"He has such pity for them," the messenger answered, "that he would free them of England's chains. Tell your master that he has until this evening's angelus to surrender the town, and if he does he will be permitted to march out with all his weapons, banners, horses, families, servants and possessions."

It was a generous offer but the priest did not even consider it. "I will tell him," the priest said, "but only if you tell your master that we have food for a year and weapons enough to kill all of you twice over."

The messenger bowed, the priest returned the compliment and the parley was over. The trebuchets began their work again and, at nightfall, Totesham ordered the town gates opened and the fugitives were allowed back inside to the jeers of those who had not fled.

Thomas, like every man in La Roche-Derrien, served time on the ramparts. It was tedious work for Charles of Blois took great care to ensure that none of his forces strayed within bowshot of the English archers, but there was some diversion to be had in watching the great trebuchets. They were cranked down so slowly that it seemed the vast beams were hardly moving, but gradually, almost imperceptibly, the big wooden box with its lead weights would rise from behind the protective palisade and the long arm would sink out of sight. Then, when the long arm was winched as low as it could go, nothing would happen for a long time, presumably because the engineers were loading the sling and then, just when it seemed nothing ever would happen, the counterweight would drop, the palisade would quiver, startled birds flash up from the grass and the long arm would slash up, judder, the sling would whip about and a stone arc into the air. The sound would come then, the monstrous crash of the falling counterweight, followed a heartbeat later by the thump of the stone onto the broken ramparts. More straw-filled bags would be thrown onto the growing breach, but the missiles still did their damage and so Totesham ordered his men to begin making new walls behind the growing breaches.

Some men, including Thomas and Robbie, wanted to make a sally. Put together sixty men, they argued, and let them stream out of the town at first light. They could easily overrun one or two of the trebuchets, soak the machines in oil and pitch and throw burning brands into the tangle of ropes and timber, but Totesham refused. His garrison was too small, he argued, and he did not want to lose even a half-dozen men before he needed to fight Charles's men in the breaches.

He lost men anyway. By the third week of the siege Charles of Blois had finished his own defensive works and the four portions of his army were all protected behind earth walls, hedges, palisades and ditches. He had scoured the land between his encampments of any obstacles so that when a relieving army came its archers would have nowhere to hide. Now, with his own encampments fortified and the trebuchets biting ever bigger holes in La Roche-Derrien's walls, he sent his crossbowmen forward to harass the ramparts. They came in pairs, one man with the crossbow and his partner holding a pavise, a shield so tall, wide and stoutly made that it could protect both men. The pavises were painted, some with holy imprecations, but most with insults in French, English and, in some cases, because the crossbowmen were Genoese, Italian. Their quarrels battered the wall, whistled about the defenders' heads and smacked into the thatch of the houses beyond the walls. Sometimes the Genoese would shoot fire arrows and Totesham had six squads of men who did nothing except chase down fires in thatch and, when they were not extinguishing flames, they hauled water out of the River Jaudy and soaked the thatch roofs that were nearest the ramparts and thus most in danger from the crossbowmen.

The English archers shot back, but the crossbowmen were mostly hidden behind their pavises and, when they did shoot, they exposed themselves for only a heartbeat. Some died all the same, but they were also bringing down archers on the town's walls. Jeanette often joined Thomas on the southern rampart and loosed her bolts from a crenellation by the gate. A crossbow could be fired from a kneeling position so she did not expose much of her body to danger, while Thomas had to stand to loose an arrow. "You shouldn't be here," he told her every time and she would mimic his words, then stoop to rewind her bow.

"Do you remember," she asked him, "the first siege?"

"When you were shooting at me?"

"Let's hope I'm more accurate now," she said, then propped the bow on the wall, aimed and pulled the trigger. The bolt smacked into a pavise that was already stuck with feathered English arrows. Beyond the crossbowmen was the earth wall of the closest encampment above which showed the ungainly beams of two trebuchets and, beyond them, the gaudy flags of some of Charles's lords. Jeanette recognized the banners of Rohan, Laval, Malestroit, and Roncelets, and the first sight of that wasplike banner had filled her with anger and then she had cried for the thought of her son in Roncelets's distant tower. "I wish they'd assault now," she said, "and I could put a bolt in Roncelets as well as Blois."

"They won't attack until they've defeated Dagworth," Thomas said.

"You think he's coming?"

"I think that's why they're here," Thomas said, nodding toward the enemy, then he stood, drew the bow and launched an arrow at a crossbowman who had just stepped out from behind his shield. The man ducked back a heartbeat before Thomas's arrow hissed past him. Thomas crouched again. "Charles knows he can pluck us whenever he wants," he said, "but what he really wants is to crush Dagworth."

For when Sir Thomas Dagworth was crushed there would be no English field army left in Brittany and the fortresses would inevitably fall, one by one, and Charles would have his duchy.

Then, a month after Charles had arrived, when the hedges about his four fortresses were white with hawthorn blossom and the petals were blowing from the apple trees and the banks of the river were thick with iris and the poppies were a brilliant red in the growing rye, there was a drift of smoke in the southwestern sky. The watchers on La Roche-Derrien's walls saw scouts riding from the enemy encampment and they knew that the smoke must come from campfires which meant that an army was coming. Some feared it might be reinforcements for the enemy, but they were reassured by others who claimed, truly, that only friends would be approaching from the southwest. What Richard Totesham and the others who knew the truth did not reveal was that any relieving force would be small, much smaller than Charles's army, and that it was coming toward a trap that Charles had made.

For Charles's ploy had worked and Sir Thomas Dagworth
had taken the bait.

CHARLES OF BLOIS summoned his lords and commanders to the big tent beside the mill. It was Saturday and the
enemy force was now a short march away and, inevitably,
there were hotheads in his ranks who wanted to strap on
their plate armor, hoist up their lances and clatter off on
horseback to be killed by the English archers. Fools
abounded, Charles thought, then dashed their hopes by making it clear that no one except the scouts was to leave any of
the four encampments. "No one!" He pounded the table, almost upsetting the ink pot belonging to the clerk who copied
down his words. "No one will leave! Do you all understand
that?" He looked from face to face and thought again what
fools his lords were. "We stay behind our entrenchments,"
he told them, "and they will come to us. They will come to
us and they will be killed."

Some of the lords looked disgruntled, for there was little
glory in fighting behind earth walls and damp ditches when
a man could be galloping on a destrier, but Charles of Blois
was firm and even the richest of his lords feared his threat
that any man who disobeyed him would not share in the distribution of land and wealth that would follow the conquest
of Brittany.

Charles picked up a piece of parchment. "Our scouts have
ridden close to Sir Thomas Dagworth's column," he said in
his precise voice, "and we now have an accurate estimate of
their numbers." Knowing that every man in the tent wanted
to hear the enemy's strength, he paused, because he wanted
to invest this announcement with drama, but he could not
help smiling as he revealed the figures. "Our enemies," he
said, "threaten us with three hundred men-at-arms and four
hundred archers."

There was a pause as the numbers were understood, then came an explosion of laughter. Even Charles, usually so pallid, unbending and stern, joined in. It was risible! It was actually impertinent! Brave, perhaps, but utterly foolhardy. Charles of Blois had four thousand men and hundreds of peasant volunteers who, though not actually encamped inside his earthworks, could be relied on to help massacre an enemy. He had two thousand of the finest crossbowmen in Europe, he had a thousand armored knights, many of them champions of great tournaments, and Sir Thomas Dagworth was coming with seven hundred men? The town might contribute another hundred or two hundred, but even at their most hopeful the English could not muster more than a thousand men and Charles had four times that number. "They will come, gentlemen," he told his excited lords, "and they will die here."

There were two roads on which they might approach. One came from the west and it was the most direct route, but it led to the far side of the River Jaudy and Charles did not think Dagworth would use that road. The other curled about the besieged town to approach from the southeast and that road led straight toward the largest of Charles's four encampments, the eastern encampment where he was in personal command and where the largest trebuchets pounded La Roche-Derrien's walls.

"Let me tell you, gentlemen"—Charles stilled the amusement of his commanders—"what I believe Sir Thomas will do. What I would do if I were so unfortunate as to be in his shoes. I believe he will send a small but noisy force of men to approach us on the Lannion road" —that was the road that came from the west, the direct route—"and he will send them during the night to tempt us into believing that he will attack our encampment across the river. He will expect us to reinforce that encampment

and then, in the dawn, his real attack will come from the
east. He hopes that most of our army will be stranded
across the river and that he can come in the dawn and destroy the three encampments on this bank. That, gentlemen, is what he will probably attempt and it will fail. It
will fail because we have one clear, hard rule and it will not
be broken! No one leaves an encampment! No one! Stay
behind your walls! We fight on foot, we make our battle
lines and we let them come to us. Our crossbowmen will
cut down their archers, then we, gentlemen, shall destroy
their men-at-arms. But no one leaves the encampments!
No one! We do not make ourselves targets for their bows.
Do you understand?"

The Lord of Châteaubriant wanted to know what he was
supposed to do if he was in his southern encampment and
there was a fight going on in another of the forts. "Do I just
stand and watch?" he asked, incredulous.

"You stand and watch," Duke Charles said in a steely
voice. "You do not leave your encampment. You understand? Archers cannot kill what they cannot see! Stay hidden!"

The Lord of Roncelets pointed out that the skies were
clear and the moon nearly full. "Dagworth is no fool," he
went on, "and he'll know we've made these fortresses and
cleared the land to deny them cover. So why won't he attack
at night?"

"At night?" Charles asked.

"That way our crossbowmen can't see their targets, but
the English will have enough moonlight to see their way
across our entrenchments."

It was a good point that Charles acknowledged by nodding brusquely. "Fires," he said.

"Fires?" a man asked.

"Build fires now! Big fires! When they come, light the fires. Turn night into day!"

His men laughed, liking the idea. Fighting on foot was not how lords and knights made their reputations, but they all understood that Charles had been thinking how to defeat the dreaded English archers and his ideas made sense even if they offered little chance for glory, but then Charles offered them a consolation. "They will break, gentlemen," he said, "and when they do I shall have my trumpeter give seven blasts. Seven! And when you hear the trumpet, you may leave your encampments and pursue them." There were growls of approval, for the seven trumpet blasts would release the armored men on their huge horses to slaughter the remnants of Dagworth's force.

"Remember!" Charles pounded the table once more to get his men's attention. "Remember! You do not leave your encampment until the trumpet sounds! Stay behind the trenches, stay behind the walls, let the enemy come to you and we shall win." He nodded to show he was finished. "And now, gentlemen, our priests will hear confessions. Let us cleanse our souls so that God can reward us with victory."

Fifteen miles away, in the roofless refectory of a plundered and abandoned monastery, a much smaller group of men gathered. Their commander was a gray-haired man from Suffolk, stocky and gruff, who knew he faced a formidable challenge if he was to relieve La Roche-Derrien. Sir Thomas Dagworth listened to a Breton knight tell what his scouts had discovered: that Charles of Blois's men were still in the four encampments placed opposite the town's four gates. The largest encampment, where Charles's great banner of a white ermine flew, was to the east. "It is built around the windmill," the knight reported.

"I remember that mill," Sir Thomas said. He ran his fingers through his short gray beard, a habit when he was thinking. "That's where we must attack," he said, so softly that he could have been talking to himself.

"It's where they're strongest," a man warned him.

"So we shall distract them." Sir Thomas stirred himself from his reverie. "John"—he turned to a man in a tattered mail coat—"take all the camp servants. Take the cooks, clerks, grooms, anyone who isn't a fighter. Then take all the carts and all the draught horses and make an approach on the Lannion road. You know it?"

"I can find it."

"Leave before midnight. Lots of noise, John! You can take my trumpeter and a couple of drummers. Make 'em think the whole army's coming from the west. I want them sending men to the western encampment well before dawn."

"And the rest of us?" the Breton knight asked.

"We'll march at midnight," Sir Thomas said, "and go east till we reach the Guingamp road." That road approached La Roche-Derrien from the southeast. Since Sir Thomas's small force had marched from the west he hoped that the Guingamp road was the very last one Charles would expect him to use. "It'll be a silent march," he ordered, "and we go on foot, all of us! Archers in front, men-at-arms behind, and we'll attack their eastern fort in the darkness." By attacking in the dark Sir Thomas hoped he could cheat the crossbowmen of their targets and, better still, catch the enemy asleep.

So his plans were made: he would make a feint in the west and attack from the east. And that was exactly what Charles of Blois expected him to do.

Night fell. The English marched, Charles's men armed themselves and the town waited.

* * *

THOMAS COULD HEAR the armorers in Charles's camp.
He could hear their hammers closing the rivets of the plate
armor and hear the scrape of stones on blades. The campfires in the four fortresses did not die down as they usually
did, but were fed to keep them bright and high so that their
light glinted off the iron straps that fastened the frames of
the big trebuchets outlined against the fires' glow. From the
ramparts Thomas could see men moving about in the nearest enemy encampment. Every few minutes a fire would
glow even brighter as the armorers used bellows to fan the
flames.

A child cried in a nearby house. A dog whined. Most of
Totesham's small garrison was on the ramparts and a good
many of the townspeople were there too. No one was quite
sure why they had gone to the walls for the relief army had
to be a long way off still, yet few people wanted to go to
bed. They expected something to happen and so they
waited for it. The day of judgment, Thomas thought, would
feel like this, as men and women waited for the heavens to
break and the angels to descend and for the graves to open
so that the virtuous dead could rise into the sky. His father,
he remembered, had always wanted to be buried facing the
west, but on the eastern edge of the graveyard, so that
when he rose from the dead he would be looking at his
parishioners as they came from the earth. "They will need
my guidance," Father Ralph had said, and Thomas had
made sure it had been done as he wished. Hookton's
parishioners, buried so that if they sat up they would look
eastward toward the glory of Christ's second coming,
would find their priest in front of them, offering them reassurance.

Thomas could have done with some reassurance this
night. He was with Sir Guillaume and his two men-at-arms
and they watched the enemy's preparations from a bastion

on the town's southeast corner, close to where the tower of
St. Barnabé's church offered a vantage point. The remnants
of Totesham's giant springald had been used to make a rick-
ety bridge from the bastion to a window in the church tower
and once through the window there was a ladder that
climbed past a gaping hole torn by one of the Widowmaker's
stones to the tower parapet. Thomas must have made the
journey a half-dozen times before midnight because, from
the parapet, it was just possible to see over the palisade into
the largest of Charles's camps. It was while he was on the
tower that Robbie came to the rampart beneath. "I want you
to look at this," Robbie called up to him, and flourished a
newly painted shield. "You like it?"

Thomas peered down and, in the moonlight, saw something red. "What is it?" he asked. "A blood smear?"

"You blind English bastard," Robbie said, "it's the red
heart of Douglas!"

"Ah. From up here it looks like something died on the
shield."

But Robbie was proud of his shield. He admired it in the
moonlight. "There was a fellow painting a new devil on the
wall in St. Goran's church," he said, "and I paid him to do
this."

"I hope you didn't pay him too much," Thomas said.

"You're just envious." Robbie propped the shield against
the parapet before edging over the makeshift bridge to the
tower. He vanished through the window then reappeared at
Thomas's side. "What are they doing?" he asked, gazing
eastward.

"Jesus," Thomas blasphemed, because something was at
last happening. He was staring past the great black shapes of
Hellgiver and Widowmaker into the eastern encampment
where men, hundreds of men, were forming a battle line.
Thomas had assumed that any fight would not start until

dawn, yet now it looked as though Charles of Blois was readying to fight in the night's black heart.

"Sweet Jesus," Sir Guillaume, summoned to the tower's top, echoed Thomas's surprise.

"The bastards are expecting a fight," Robbie said, for Charles's men were lining shoulder to shoulder. They had their backs to the town and the moon glinted off the espaliers that covered the knights' shoulders and touched the blades of spears and axes white.

"Dagworth must be coming," Sir Guillaume said.

"At night?" Robbie asked.

"Why not?" Sir Guillaume retorted, then shouted down to one of his men-at-arms to go and tell Totesham what was happening. "Wake him up," he snarled when the man wanted to know what he should do if the garrison commander was asleep. "Of course he's not asleep," he added to Thomas. "Totesham might be a bloody Englishman, but he's a good soldier."

Totesham was not asleep, but nor had he been aware that the enemy was formed for battle and, after he had negotiated the precarious bridge to St. Barnabé's tower, he gazed at Charles's troops with his customary sour expression. "Reckon we'll have to lend a hand," he said.

"I thought you didn't approve of sorties beyond the wall?" Sir Guillaume, who had chafed under that restriction, observed.

"This is the battle that saves us," Totesham said. "If we lose this fight then the town falls, so we must do what we can to win it." He sounded bleak, then he shrugged and turned back to the tower's ladder. "God help us," he said softly as he climbed down into the shadows. He knew Sir Thomas Dagworth's relieving army would be small and he feared it would be much smaller than he dared imagine, but when it attacked the enemy encampment the garrison had to be ready to help. He did not want to alert the enemy to the likelihood of a sortie from the battered gates and so he did not sound the church bells to gather his troops, but rather sent men through all the streets to summon the archers and men-at-arms to the market square outside St. Brieuc's church. Thomas went back to Jeanette's house and pulled on his mail habergeon, which Robbie had brought back from the Roncelets raid, then he strapped his sword belt in place, fumbling with the buckle because his fingers were still clumsy at such finicky things. He hung the arrow bag on his left shoulder, slid the black bow out of its linen cover, put a spare bowcord in his sallet, then pulled the sallet onto his head. He was ready.

And so, he saw, was Jeanette. She had her own habergeon and helmet and Thomas gaped at her. "You can't join the sortie!" he said.

"Join the sortie?" She sounded surprised. "When you all leave the town, Thomas, who will guard the walls?"

"Oh." He felt foolish.

She smiled, stepped to him and gave him a kiss. "Now go," she said, "and God go with you."

Thomas went to the marketplace. The garrison was gathering there, but they were desperately few in number. A tavernkeeper rolled a barrel of ale into the square, tapped it and let men help themselves. A smith was sharpening swords and axes in the light of a cresseted torch that burned outside the porch of St. Brieuc's and his stone rang on long steel blades, the sound strangely mournful in the night. It was warm. Bats flickered about the church and dipped into the tangled moon-cast shadows of a house ruined by a trebuchet's direct hit. Women were bringing food to the soldiers and Thomas remembered how, just the year before, these same women had screamed as the English scrambled into the town. It had been a night of rape, robbery and murder, yet now the townsfolk did not want their occupiers to leave and the market square was becoming ever more crowded as men from the town brought makeshift weapons to help the foray. Most were armed with the axes they used to chop their firewood, though a few had swords or spears, and some townsmen even possessed leather or mail armor. They far outnumbered the garrison and would at least make the sally seem formidable.

"Christ Jesus." A sour voice spoke behind Thomas. "What in Christ's name is that?"

Thomas turned and saw the lanky figure of Sir Geoffrey Carr staring at Robbie's shield, which was propped against the steps of a stone cross in the market's center. Robbie also turned to look at the Scarecrow who was leading his six men.

"Looks like a squashed turd," the Scarecrow said. His voice was slurred and it was evident he had spent the evening in one of the town's many taverns.

"It's mine," Robbie said.

Sir Geoffrey kicked the shield. "Is that the bloody heart of Douglas, boy?"

"It's my badge," Robbie said, exaggerating his Scottish accent, "if that's what you mean." Men all about had stopped to listen.

"I knew you were a Scot," the Scarecrow said, sounding even more drunk, "but I didn't know you were a damned Douglas. And what the hell is a Douglas doing here?" The Scarecrow raised his voice to appeal to the assembled men. "Whose side is bloody Scotland on, eh? Whose side? And the goddamn Douglases have been fighting us since they were spawned from the devil's own arsehole!" The Scarecrow staggered, then pulled the whip from his belt and let its coils ripple down. "Sweet Jesus," he shouted, "but his goddamn family has impoverished good Englishmen. They're goddamn thieves! Spies!"

Robbie dragged his sword free and the whip lashed up, but Sir Guillaume shoved Robbie out of the way before the clawed tip could slash his face, then Sir Guillaume's sword was drawn and he and Thomas were standing beside Robbie on the steps of the cross. "Robbie Douglas," Sir Guillaume shouted, "is my friend."

"And mine," Thomas said.

"Enough!" A furious Richard Totesham pushed through the crowd. "Enough!"

The Scarecrow appealed to Totesham. "He's a damned Scot!"

"Good God, man," Totesham snarled, "we've got Frenchmen, Welshmen, Flemings, Irishmen and Bretons in this garrison. What the hell difference does it make?"

"He's a Douglas!" the Scarecrow insisted drunkenly. "He's an enemy!"

"He's my friend!" Thomas bellowed, inviting to fight anyone who wished to side with Sir Geoffrey.

"Enough!" Totesham's anger was big enough to fill the whole marketplace. "We have fight enough on our hands without behaving like children! Do you vouch for him?" he demanded of Thomas.

"I vouch for him." It was Will Skeat who answered. He pushed through the crowd and put an arm about Robbie's shoulders. "I vouch for him, Dick."

"Then Douglas or not," Totesham said, "he's no enemy of mine." He turned and walked away.

"Sweet Jesus!" The Scarecrow was still angry. He had been impoverished by the house of Douglas and he was still poor—the risk he had taken in pursuing Thomas had not paid off because he had found no treasure—and now all his enemies seemed united in Thomas and Robbie. He staggered again, then spat at Robbie. "I burn men who wear the heart of Douglas," he said, "I burn them!"

"He does too," Thomas said softly.

"Burns them?" Robbie asked.

"At Durham," Thomas said, his gaze on Sir Geoffrey's eyes, "he burned three prisoners."

"You did what?" Robbie demanded.

The Scarecrow, drunk as he was, was suddenly aware of the intensity of Robbie's anger, and aware too that he had not gained the sympathy of the men in the marketplace, who preferred Will Skeat's opinion to his. He coiled the whip, spat at Robbie, and stalked uncertainly away.

Now it was Robbie who wanted a fight. "Hey, you!" he shouted.

"Leave it be," Thomas said. "Not tonight, Robbie."

"He burned three men?" Robbie demanded.

"Not tonight," Thomas repeated, and he pushed Robbie hard back so that the Scotsman sat on the steps of the cross.

Robbie was staring at the retreating Scarecrow. "He's a dead man," he said grimly. "I tell you, Thomas, that bastard is a dead man."

"We're all dead men," Sir Guillaume said quietly, for the enemy was ready for them and in overwhelming numbers.

And Sir Thomas Dagworth was nearing their trap.

JOHN HAMMOND, a deputy to Sir Thomas Dagworth, led the feint that came from the west along the Lannion road. He had sixty men, as many women, a dozen carts and thirty horses and he used them to make as much noise as possible once they were within sight of the westernmost of Duke Charles's encampments.

Fires outlined the earthworks and firelight showed in the tiny slits between the timbers of the palisade. There seemed to be a lot of fires in the encampment, and even more blazed up once Hammond's small force began to bang pots and pans, clatter staves against trees and blow their trumpets. The drummers beat frantically, but no panic showed on the earthen ramparts. A few enemy soldiers appeared there, stared for a while down the moonlit road where Hammond's men and women were shadows under the trees, then turned and went away. Hammond ordered his people to make even more noise and his six archers, the only real soldiers in his decoy force, went closer to the camp and shot their arrows over the palisades, but still there was no urgent response. Hammond expected to see men streaming over the river that Sir Thomas's spies had said was bridged with boats, but no one appeared to be moving between the enemy encampments. The feint, it seemed, had failed.

"If we stay here," a man said, "they'll goddamn crucify us."

"They goddamn will," Hammond agreed fervently. "We'll go back down the road a bit," he said, "just a bit. Back into deeper shadow."

The night had begun badly with the failure of the feint assault, but Sir Thomas's men, the real attackers, had made better progress than they expected and arrived off the eastern flank of Duke Charles's encampment not long after the decoy group began its noisy diversion three miles to the west. Sir Thomas's men crouched at the edge of a wood and stared across the felled land to the shape of the nearest earthworks. The road, pale in the moonlight, ran empty to a big wooden gate where it was swallowed up by the makeshift fort.

Sir Thomas had divided his men into two parties that would attack either side of the wooden gate. There was to be nothing subtle in the assault, just a rush through the dark then a swarming attack over the earth wall and kill whoever was discovered on its farther side. "God give you joy," Sir Thomas said to his men as he walked down their line, then he drew his sword and waved his party on. They would approach as silently as they could and Sir Thomas still hoped he would achieve surprise, but the firelight on the other side of the defenses looked unnaturally bright and he had a sinking feeling that the enemy was ready for him. Yet none showed on the embanked wall and no crossbow quarrels hissed in the dark, and so he dared to let his hopes rise and then he was at the ditch and splashing through its muddy bottom. There were archers to left and right of him, all scrambling up the bank to the palisade. Still no crossbows shot, no trumpet sounded and no enemy showed. The archers were at the fence now and it proved more flimsy than it looked for the logs were not buried deeply enough and they could be kicked over without much effort. The defenses were not formidable, and were not even defended for no enemy challenged as Sir Thomas's men-at-arms splashed through the ditch, their swords bright in the moonlight. The archers finished demolishing the palisade and Sir Thomas stepped over the fallen timbers and ran down the bank into Charles's camp.

Except he was not inside the camp, but rather on a wide open space that led to another bank and another ditch and another palisade. The place was a labyrinth! But still no bolts flew in the dark and his archers were running ahead again, though some cursed as they tripped in holes dug to trap horses' hooves. The fires were bright beyond the next palisade. Where were the sentries? Sir Thomas hefted his shield with its device of a wheatsheaf and looked to his left to see that his second party was across the first bank and streaming over the grass toward the second. His own archers pulled at the new palisade and, like the first, it tumbled easily. No one was speaking, no one was shouting orders, no one was calling on St. George for help, they were just doing their job, but surely the enemy must hear the falling timbers? But the second palisade was down and Sir Thomas jostled with the archers through the new gap and there was a meadow in front and a hedge beyond it, and beyond that hedge were the enemy tents and the high windmill with its furled sails and the monstrous shapes of the two biggest trebuchets, all of them lit by the bright fires. So close now! And Sir Thomas felt a fierce surge of joy for he had achieved surprise and the enemy was surely his, and just at that moment the crossbows sounded.

The bolts flickered in from his right flank, from an earth bank that ran between the second earthwork and the hedge. Archers were falling, cursing. Sir Thomas turned toward the crossbowmen who were hidden, and then more bolts came from the thick hedge in front and he knew he had surprised no one, that the enemy had been waiting for him, and his men were screaming now, but at least the first archers were shooting back. The long English arrows flashed in the moonlight, but Sir Thomas could see no targets and he realized the archers were shooting blindly. "To me!" he shouted. "Dagworth! Dagworth! Shields!" Maybe a dozen men-at-arms heard and obeyed him, making a cluster who overlapped their shields and then ran clumsily toward the hedge. Break through that, Sir Thomas thought, and at least some of the crossbowmen would be visible. Archers were shooting to their front and their side, confused by the enemy's bolts. Sir Thomas snatched a glance across the road and saw his other men were being similarly assailed. "We have to get through the hedge," he shouted, "through the hedge! Archers! Through the hedge!" A crossbow bolt slammed into his shield, half spinning him round. Another hissed overhead. An archer was twisting on the grass, his belly pierced by a quarrel.

Other men were shouting now. Some called on St. George, others cursed the devil, some screamed for their wives or mothers. The enemy had massed his crossbows and was pouring the bolts out of the darkness. An archer reeled back, a quarrel in his shoulder. Another screamed pitiably, hit in the groin. A man-at-arms fell to his knees, crying Jesus, and now Sir Thomas could hear the enemy shouting orders and insults. "The hedge!" he roared. Get through the

hedge, he thought, and maybe his archers would have clear
targets at last. "Get through the hedge!" he bellowed, and
some of his archers found a gap closed up with nothing but
hurdles and they kicked the wicker barriers down and
streamed through. The night seemed alive with bolts, fierce
with them, and a man shouted at Sir Thomas to look behind.
He turned and saw the enemy had sent scores of crossbowmen to cut off his retreat and that new force was pushing Sir
Thomas's men on into the heart of the encampment. It had
been a trap, he thought, a goddamned trap. Charles had
wanted him to come into the encampment, he had obliged
and now Charles's men were curling about him. So fight, he
told himself, fight!

"Through the hedge!" Sir Thomas thundered. "Get
through the damned hedge!" He dodged between the bodies
of his men, pounded through the gap and looked for an enemy to kill, but instead he saw that Charles's men-at-arms
were formed in a battle line, all armored, visors down and
shields up. A few archers were shooting at them now, the
long arrows smacking into shields, bellies, chests and legs,
but there were too few archers and the crossbowmen, still
hidden by hedges or walls or pavises, were killing the English bowmen. "Rally on the mill!" Sir Thomas shouted for
that was the most prominent landmark. He wanted to collect
his men, form them into ranks and start to fight properly, but
the crossbows were closing on him, hundreds of them, and
his frightened men were scattering into the tents and shelters.

Sir Thomas swore out of sheer frustration. The survivors
of the other assault party were with him now, but all of his
men were entangled in the tents, tripping on ropes, and still
the crossbow bolts slammed through the dark, ripping the
canvas as they hurtled into Sir Thomas's dying force. "Form
here! Form here!" he yelled, choosing an open space between three tents, and maybe twenty or thirty men ran to

him, but the crossbowmen saw them and poured their bolts
down the dark alleys between the tents, and then the enemy
men-at-arms came, shields up, and the English archers were
scattering again, trying to find a vantage point to catch their
breath, find some protection and look for targets. The great
banners of the French and Breton lords were being brought
forward and Sir Thomas, knowing he had blundered into this
trap and been comprehensively beaten, just felt a surge of
anger. "Kill the bastards," he bawled and he led his men at
the nearest enemy, the swords rang in the dark, and at least,
now that it was hand to hand, the crossbowmen could not
shoot at the English men-at-arms. The Genoese were hunting the hated English archers instead, but some of the bowmen had found a wagon park and, sheltered by the vehicles,
were at last fighting back.

But Sir Thomas had no shelter and no advantage. He had
a small force and the enemy a great one, and his men were
being forced backward by sheer pressure of numbers.
Shields crashed on shields, swords hammered on helmets,
spears came under the shields to tear through men's boots, a
Breton flailed an axe, beating down two Englishmen and letting in a rush of men wearing the white ermine badge who
shrieked their triumph and cut down still more men. A man-
at-arms screamed as axes hacked through the mail covering
his thighs, then another axe battered in his helmet and he
was silent. Sir Thomas staggered backward, parrying a
sword blow, and saw some of his men running into the dark
spaces between the tents to find refuge. Their visors were
down and they could hardly see where they were going or
the enemy who came to kill them. He slashed his sword at a
man in a pig-snout helmet, backswung the blade into a
shield striped yellow and black, took a step back to make
space for another blow and then his feet were tangled by a
tent's guy ropes and he fell backward onto the canvas.

The knight in the pig-snout helmet stood over him, his

plate mail shining in the moon and his sword at Sir Thomas's throat.

"I yield," Sir Thomas said hurriedly, then repeated his surrender in French.

"And you are?" the knight asked.

"Sir Thomas Dagworth," Sir Thomas said bitterly and he held up his sword to his enemy who took the weapon and then pushed up his snouted visor.

"I am the Viscount Morgat," the knight said, "and I accept your surrender." He bowed to Sir Thomas, handed back his sword and held out a hand to help the Englishman to his feet. The fight was still going on, but it was sporadic now as the French and Bretons hunted down the survivors, killed the wounded who were not worth ransoming and hammered their own wagons with crossbow bolts to kill the English bowmen who still sheltered there.

The Viscount Morgat escorted Sir Thomas to the windmill where he presented him to Charles of Blois. A great fire burned a few yards away and in its light Charles stood beneath the furled sails with his jupon smeared with blood for he had helped to break Sir Thomas's band of men-at-arms. He sheathed his sword, still bloody, and took off his plumed helmet and stared at the prisoner who had twice defeated him in battle. "I commiserate with you," Charles said coldly.

"And I congratulate your grace," Sir Thomas said.

"The victory belongs to God," Charles said, "not to me," yet all the same he felt a sudden exhilaration because he had done it! He had defeated the English field army in Brittany and now, as certain as blessed dawn follows darkest night, the duchy would fall to him. "The victory is God's alone," he said piously, and he remembered it was now very early on Sunday morning and he turned to a priest to tell the man to have a Te Deum sung in thanks for this great victory.

And the priest nodded, eyes wide, even though the Duke had not yet spoken, and then he gasped and Charles saw there was an unnaturally long arrow in the man's belly, then another white-fledged shaft hammered into the windmill's flank and a raucous, almost bestial, growl sounded from the dark.

For though Sir Thomas was captured and his army was utterly defeated, the battle, it seemed, was not quite finished.

RICHARD TOTESHAM watched the fight between Sir Thomas's men and Charles's forces from the top of the eastern gate tower. He could not see a great deal from that vantage point for the palisades atop the earthworks, the two great trebuchets and the windmill obscured much of the battle, but it was abundantly clear that no one was coming from the other three French encampments to help Charles in his largest fortress. "You'd think they'd be helping each other," he said to Will Skeat who was standing next to him.

"It's you, Dick!" Will Skeat exclaimed.

"Aye, it's me, Will," Totesham said patiently. He saw that Skeat was dressed in mail and had a sword at his side, and he put a hand on his old friend's shoulder. "Now, you're not going to be fighting tonight, Will, are you?"

"If there's going to be a scrap," Skeat said, "then I'd like to help."

"Leave it to the young ones, Will," Totesham urged, "leave it to the young ones. You stay and guard the town for me. Will you do that?"

Skeat nodded and Totesham turned back to stare into the enemy's camp. It was impossible to tell which side was winning for the only troops he could see belonged to the enemy and they had their backs to him, though once in a while a fly-

ing arrow would flash a reflection of the firelight as proof
that Sir Thomas's men still fought, but Totesham reckoned it
was a bad sign that no troops were coming from the other
fortresses to help Charles of Blois. It suggested the Duke did
not need help, which in turn suggested that Sir Thomas Dagworth did and so Totesham leaned over the inner parapet.
"Open the gate!" he shouted.

It was still dark. Dawn was two hours or more away, yet
the moon was bright and the fires in the enemy camp threw a
garish light. Totesham hurried down the stairs from the ramparts while men pulled away the stone-filled barrels that had
formed a barricade inside the gateway, then lifted the great
locking bar that had not been disturbed in a month. The
gates creaked open and the waiting men cheered. Totesham
wished they had kept silent for he did not want to alert the
enemy that the garrison was making a sortie, but it was too
late now and so he found his own troop of men-at-arms and
led them to join the stream of soldiers and townsmen who
poured through the gate.

Thomas went to the attack alongside Robbie and Sir Guillaume and his two men. Will Skeat, despite his promise to
Totesham, had wanted to come with them, but Thomas had
pushed him onto the ramparts and told him to watch the fight
from there. "You ain't fit enough, Will," Thomas had insisted.

"If you say so, Tom," Skeat had agreed meekly, then
climbed the steps. Thomas, once he was through the gate,
looked back and saw Skeat on the gate tower. He raised a
hand, but Skeat did not see him or, if he did, could not recognize him.

It felt strange to be outside the long-locked gates. The air
was fresher, lacking the stench of the town's sewage. The attackers followed the road which ran straight for three hundred paces before vanishing beneath the palisade which

protected the timber platforms on which Hellgiver and Widowmaker were mounted. That palisade was higher than a tall
man and some of the archers were carrying ladders to get
across the obstacle, but Thomas reckoned the palisades had
been made in a hurry and would probably topple to a good
heave. He ran, still clumsy on his twisted toes. He expected
the crossbows to start at any moment, but no bolts came
from Charles's earthworks; the enemy, Thomas supposed,
were occupied with Dagworth's men.

Then the first of Totesham's archers reached the palisade
and the ladders went up, but, just as Thomas had reckoned, a
whole length of the heavy fence collapsed with a crash when
men put their weight on the ladders. The banks and palisades had not been built to keep men out, but to shelter the
crossbowmen, but those crossbowmen still did not know
that a sortie had come from the town and so the bank was
undefended.

Four or five hundred men crossed the fallen palisade.
Most were not trained soldiers, but townsmen who had been
enraged by the enemy's missiles crashing into their houses.
Their women and children had been maimed and killed by
the trebuchets and the men of La Roche-Derrien wanted revenge, just as they wanted to keep the prosperity brought by
the English occupation, and so they cheered as they
swarmed into the enemy camp. "Archers!" Totesham roared
in a huge voice. "Archers, to me! Archers!"

Sixty or seventy archers ran to obey him, making a line
just to the south of the platforms where the two biggest trebuchets were set. The rest of the sortie were charging at the
enemy who were no longer formed in their battle line, but
had scattered into small groups who were so intent on com-
pleting their victory over Sir Thomas Dagworth that they
had not been watching behind them. Now they turned,
alarmed, as a feral roar announced the garrison's arrival.
"Kill the bastards!" a townsman shouted in Breton.

"Kill!" an English voice roared.

"No prisoners!" another man bellowed, and though Totesham, fearful for lost ransoms, called out that prisoners must be taken, no one heard him in the savage roar that the attackers made.

Charles's men-at-arms instinctively formed a line, but Totesham, ready for it, had gathered his archers and now he ordered them to shoot: the bows began their devil's music and the arrows hissed through the dark to bury themselves in mail and flesh and bone. The bowmen were few, but they shot at close range, they could not miss, and Charles's men cowered behind their shields as the missiles whipped home, but the arrows easily pierced shields and the men-at-arms broke and scattered to find shelter among the tents. "Hunt them down! Hunt them down!" Totesham released his archers to the kill.

Less than a hundred of Sir Thomas Dagworth's men were still fighting and most of those were the archers who had gone to ground in the wagon park. Some of the others were prisoners, many were dead, while most were trying to escape across the earthworks and palisades, but those men, hearing the great roar behind them, turned back. Charles's men were scattered: many were still hunting down the remnants of the first attack and those who had tried to resist Totesham's sortie were either dead or fleeing into shadows. Totesham's men now struck the heart of the encampment with the savagery of a tempest. The townsmen were filled with rage. There was no subtlety in their assault, just a lust for vengeance as they swarmed past the two great trebuchets. The first huts they encountered were the shelters of the Bavarian engineers who, wanting no part of the hand-to-hand slaughter that was finishing off the survivors of Sir Thomas Dagworth's assault, had stayed by their billets and now died there. The townsmen had no idea who their victims were, only that they were the enemy, and so they were chopped down with axes, mattocks and hammers. The chief engineer tried to protect his eleven-year-old son, but they died together under a frenzy of blows, and meanwhile the English and Fleming men-at-arms were streaming past.

Thomas had shot his bow with the other archers, but now he sought Robbie whom he had last seen by the two big trebuchets. Widowmaker had been winched down ready to launch its first missile in the dawn and Thomas stumbled over a stout metal spike that protruded a yard from the beam and acted as an anchor for the sling. He cursed, because the metal had hurt his shins, then he climbed onto the trebuchet's frame and shot an arrow above the heads of the men slaughtering the Bavarians. He had been aiming at the enemy still clustered at the foot of the windmill and he saw a man fall there before the gaudy shields came up. He shot again, and realized that his wounded hands were doing what they had always done and were doing it well, and so he plucked a third arrow from the bag and drove it into a firelit shield painted with a white ermine, then the English men-at-arms and their allies were climbing the hill and obscuring his aim so he jumped down from the trebuchet and resumed his search for Robbie.

The enemy was defending the mill stoutly and most of Totesham's men had veered away into the tents where they had more hope of finding plunder. The townsmen, their Bavarian tormentors killed, were following with bloody axes. A man in plate armor stepped from behind a tent and cut at a man with a sword, folding him at the belly, and Thomas did not think, but put an arrow on the cord, drew and loosed. The arrow went through the slit in the enemy's visor as cleanly as if Thomas had been shooting on the butts at home and moon-glossed blood, glistening like a jewel, oozed from the visor slits as the man fell backward onto the canvas.

Thomas ran on, stepping over bodies, edging past half-fallen tents. This was no place for a bow, everything was too cramped, and so he slung the yew stave on his shoulder and drew his sword. He ducked into a tent, stepped over a fallen bench, heard a scream and twisted, sword raised, to see a woman on the ground, half hidden by bedding, shaking her head at him. He left her there, went out into the firelit night and saw an enemy aiming a crossbow at the English men-at-arms who attacked the mill. He took two steps and stabbed the man in the small of the back so that his victim arched his wounded spine and twisted and shook. Thomas, dragging the sword free, was so appalled by the noise the dying man made that he hacked the blade down again and again, chopping at the fallen, twitching man to make him silent.

"He's dead! Christ, man, he's dead!" Robbie shouted at him, then snatched at Thomas's sleeve and pulled him toward the mill and Thomas took the bow from his shoulder and shot two men wearing the white ermine badge on their jupons. They had been trying to escape, running down the back side of the hill. A dog streaked across the shoulder of the slope, something red and dripping in its jaws. There were two great bonfires on the hill, flanking the mill, and a man-at-arms fell backward into one, driven there by the strike of an English arrow. Sparks exploded upward as he fell, then he began to scream as his flesh roasted inside his armor. He tried to scramble out of the flames, but a townsman thrust him back with the butt of a spear and laughed at the man's desperate squeals. The clash of swords, shields and axes was huge, filling the night, but in the strange chaos there was a peaceful area at the back of the windmill. Robbie had seen a man duck through a small doorway there and he pulled Thomas that way. "He's either hiding or running away!" Robbie shouted. "He must have money!"

Thomas was not sure what Robbie was talking about, but he followed anyway; he just had time to sling his bow again and draw the sword a second time before Robbie smashed the door down with his mail-clad shoulder and plunged into the darkness. "Come here, you English bastard!" he shouted.

"You want to be killed?" Thomas roared at him. "You're fighting for the goddamn English!"

Robbie swore at that reminder, then Thomas saw a shadow to his right, only a shadow, and he swung his sword that way. It clanged against another sword and Robbie was screaming in the dusty dark and the man was shouting at them in French and Thomas pulled back, but Robbie just slammed his sword down once, twice, and the blade chopped through bone and flesh and there was a crash as an armored man fell onto the upper millstone. "What the hell was he saying to me?" Robbie wanted to know.

"He was trying to surrender." A voice spoke from across the mill and Thomas and Robbie both spun toward the sound, their swords banging against the wooden tangle of joists, beams, cogwheels and axles, and then the unseen man called out again. "Whoa, boys, whoa! I'm English." There was a thump as an arrow struck the outside wall. The furled sails tugged against their tethers and made the wooden machinery squeal and shudder. More arrows thumped into the boards. "I'm a prisoner," the man said.

"You're not now," Thomas said.

"I suppose not." The man climbed over the millstones and pushed open the door and Thomas saw he was middle-aged with gray hair. "What's happening?" the man asked.

"We're gralloching the devils," Robbie said.

"Pray God you are." The man turned and offered his hand to Robbie. "I'm Sir Thomas Dagworth, and I thank you both." He drew his sword and ducked out into the moonlit night, and Robbie stared at Thomas.

"Did you hear that?"

"He said thank you," Thomas said.

"Aye, but he said he was Sir Thomas Dagworth!"

"Then maybe he was?"

"So what the hell was he doing in here?" Robbie asked, before taking hold of the man he had killed and, with much effort and the clank of armor against stone and timber, dragged him to the door where the fires offered light. The man had discarded his helmet and Robbie's sword had split his skull, but under the gore there was the glint of gold and Robbie dragged a chain from beneath the man's breastplate. "He must have been an important fellow," Robbie said, admiring the gold chain, then he grinned at Thomas. "We'll split it later, eh?"

"Split it?"

"We're friends, aren't we?" Robbie asked, then pushed the gold under his habergeon before shoving the corpse back into the mill. "Valuable armor that," he said. "We'll come back when it's over and hope no bastard has stolen it."

There was tangled, bloody horror in the encampment now. Survivors of Sir Thomas Dagworth's attack still fought, notably the archers in the wagon park, but as the town's garrison swept through the tents they released prisoners or brought other survivors out of the dark places where they had been hiding. Charles's crossbowmen, who could have stemmed the garrison's attack, were mostly fighting against the English archers in the wagon park. The Genoese were using their huge pavises as shelters, but the new attackers came from behind and the crossbowmen had nowhere to hide as the long arrows hissed through the night. The war bows sang their devil's melody, ten arrows flying to every quarrel shot, and the crossbowmen could not endure the slaughter. They fled.

The victorious archers, reinforced now by the men who

had been among the wagons, turned back to the shelters and tents where a deadly game of hide and seek was being played in the dark avenues between the canvas walls, but then a Welsh archer discovered that the enemy could be flushed out if the tents were set on fire. Soon there were smoke and flames spewing all across the encampment and enemy soldiers were running from the fires onto the arrows and blades of the incendiarists.

Charles of Blois had retreated from the windmill, reckoning his position on the hill made him conspicuous, and he had tried to rally some knights in front of his own sumptuous tent, but an overwhelming rush of townsmen had swept those knights underfoot and Charles watched, appalled, as butchers, coopers, wheelwrights and thatchers massacred their betters with axes, cleavers and reaping hooks. He had hastily retreated into his tent, but now one of his retainers unceremoniously pulled him toward the back entrance. "This way, your grace."

Charles shook off the man's hand. "Where can we go?" he asked plaintively.

"We'll go to the southern camp, sir, and bring men back to help."

Charles nodded, reflecting that he should have ordered that himself and regretting his insistence that none of his men leave their encampments. Well over half his army was in the other three camps, all of them close by and all of them eager to fight and more than capable of sweeping this disorganized horde aside, yet they were obeying his orders and standing tight while his encampment was put to the sword. "Where's my trumpeter?" he demanded.

"Sir? I'm here, your grace! I'm here." The trumpeter had miraculously survived the fight and stayed close to his lord.

"Sound the seven blasts," Charles ordered.

"Not here!" a priest snapped and, when Charles looked offended, made a hasty explanation. "It will attract the enemy, your grace. After two blasts they'll be onto us like hounds!"

Charles acknowledged the wisdom of the advice with a curt nod. A dozen knights were with him now and they made a formidable force in this night of fractured battle. One of them peered from the tent and saw flames searing the sky and knew the Duke's tents would be fired soon. "We must go, your grace," he insisted, "we must find our horses."

They left the tent, hurrying across the patch of beaten grass where the Duke's sentinels usually stood, and then an arrow flickered from the dark to glance off a breastplate. Shouts were suddenly loud and a rush of men came from the right and so Charles retreated to his left, which took him back up the slope toward the firelit windmill, and then a shout announced that he had been seen and the first arrows slashed up the hill. "Trumpeter!" Charles shouted. "Seven blasts! Seven blasts!"

Charles and his men, barred from reaching their horses, now had their backs against the mill's apron, which was stuck with scores of white-feathered arrows. Another arrow spitted a man in the midriff, drilling through his mail, piercing his belly and the mail on his back to pin him to the mill's boards, then an English voice roared at the archers to stop shooting. "It's their Duke!" the man roared, "it's their Duke! We want him alive! Stop shooting! Bows down!"

The news that Charles of Blois was cornered at the mill prompted a growl from the attackers. The arrows stopped flying and Charles's battered, bleeding men-at-arms who were defending the hill stared down the slope to see, just beyond the light of the mill's two fires, a mass of dark creatures prowling like wolves. "God help us," a priest said in a scared voice.

"Trumpeter!" Charles of Blois snapped.

"Sir," the trumpeter acknowledged. He had found his instrument's mouthpiece mysteriously plugged by earth. He must have fallen, though he did not remember doing so. He shook the last of the soil out of the silver mouthpiece, then put the trumpet to his mouth and the first blast sounded sweet and loud in the night. The Duke drew his sword. He only had to defend the mill long enough for his reinforcements to come from the other camps and sweep this impertinent rabble into hell. The second trumpet note rang out.

Thomas heard the trumpet, turned and saw the flash of silver by the mill, then he saw the reflection of flamelight rippling off the instrument's bell as the trumpeter raised it to the moon for the third time. Thomas had heard no order to stop shooting arrows and so he hauled his bow's cord back, twitched his left hand up a fraction and released. The arrow whipped over the heads of the English men-at-arms and struck the trumpeter just as he took breath for the third blast and the air hissed and bubbled out of his pierced lung as he spilled sideways onto the turf. The dark prowling things at the hill's base saw the man fall and suddenly charged.

No help came to Charles from the three remaining fortresses. They had heard two trumpet blasts, but only two, and they reckoned Charles must be winning; besides, they had his strict and constantly repeated orders to stay where they were on pain of losing out when the conquered lands were distributed among the victors. So they did stay, watching the smoke boil out of the flames and wondering what happened in the large eastern encampment.

Chaos was happening. This fight, Thomas reckoned, was like the attack on Caen: unplanned, disordered and utterly brutal. The English and their allies had been keyed up, nervous, expecting defeat, while Charles's men had been expecting victory—indeed they had gained the early victory—but now the English nervousness was being turned into a maddened, bloody, vicious assault and the French and Bretons were being harried into terror. A ragged clash sounded as the English men-at-arms slammed into Charles's men defending the windmill. Thomas wanted to join that fight, but Robbie suddenly pulled at his mail sleeve. "Look!" Robbie was pointing back into the burning tents.

Robbie had seen three horsemen in plain black surcoats and with them, on foot, a Dominican. Thomas saw the white and black robes and followed Robbie through the tents, trampling over a collapsed spread of blue and white canvas, past a fallen standard, running between two fires and then across an open space that whirled with smoke and burning scraps of flying cloth. A woman with a dress half torn away screamed and ran across their path and a man scattered fire with his boots as he pursued her into a turf-roofed hut. For a moment they lost sight of the priest, then Robbie saw the black and white robes again: the Dominican was trying to mount an unsaddled horse that the men in black surcoats held for him. Thomas drew his bow, let the arrow fly and saw it bury itself up to its feathers in the horse's breast; the beast reared up, yellow hooves flailing, and the Dominican fell backward. The men in black surcoats galloped away from the bow's threat and the priest, abandoned, turned and saw his pursuers and Thomas recognized de Taillebourg, God's torturer. Thomas screamed a challenge and drew the bow again, but de Taillebourg ran toward some remaining tents. A Genoese crossbowman suddenly appeared, saw them, raised his weapon and Thomas let the cord go. The arrow slashed the man's throat, spilling blood down his red and green tunic. The woman screamed inside the shelter, then was abruptly silenced as Thomas followed Robbie to where the Inquisitor had disappeared among the tents. The door flap of one was still swinging and Robbie, sword drawn, thrust the canvas aside and ducked into what proved to be a chapel.

De Taillebourg was standing at the altar with its white Easter frontal. A crucifix stood on the altar between two flickering candles. The camp outside was an uproar of screams and pain and arrows, of horses whimpering and men shouting, but it was oddly calm in the makeshift chapel.

"You bastard," Thomas said, drawing his sword and advancing on the Dominican, "you goddamn stinking turd-faced piece of priestly shit."

Bernard de Taillebourg had one hand on the altar. He raised the other to make the sign of the cross. "*Dominus vo-biscum,*" he said in his deep voice. An arrow scraped over the tent's roof with a high-pitched scratching sound and another whipped through a side wall and span down behind the altar.

"Is Vexille with you?" Thomas demanded.

"God's blessings on you, Thomas," de Taillebourg said. He was fierce-faced, stern, eyes hard, and he made the sign of the cross toward Thomas, then stepped back as Thomas raised the sword.

"Is Vexille with you?" Thomas demanded again.

"Can you see him?" the Dominican asked, peering about the chapel, then smiled. "No, Thomas, he's not here. He's gone into the dark. He rode to fetch help and you cannot kill me."

"Give me a reason," Robbie said, "because you killed my brother, you bastard."

De Taillebourg looked at the Scotsman. He did not recognize Robbie, but he saw the anger and offered him the same blessing he had given Thomas. "You cannot kill me," he said after he had made the sign of the cross, "because I am a priest, my son, I am God's anointed, and your soul will be damned through all time if you so much as touch me."

Thomas's response was to lunge his sword at de Taille-bourg's belly, forcing the priest hard back against the altar. A man screamed outside, the sound faltering and fading, ending in a sob. A child wept inconsolably, her breath coming in great gasps, and a dog barked frantically. The light of the burning tents was lurid on the chapel's canvas walls. "You are a bastard," Thomas said, "and I don't mind killing you for what you did to me."

"What I did!" De Taillebourg's anger flared like the fires outside. "I did nothing!" He spoke in French now. "Your cousin begged me to spare you the worst and so I did. One day, he said, you would be on his side! One day you would join the side of the Grail! One day you would be on God's side and so I spared you, Thomas. I left you your eyes! I did not burn your eyes!"

"I'll enjoy killing you," Thomas said, though in truth he was nervous of attacking a priest. Heaven would be watching and the recording angel's pen would be writing letters of fire in a great book.

"And God loves you, my son," de Taillebourg said gently, "God loves you. And God chastises whom he loves."

"What's he saying?" Robbie interrupted.

"He's saying that if we kill him," Thomas said, "our souls are damned."

"Till another priest undamns them," Robbie said. "There ain't a sin done on earth that some priest won't absolve if the price is right. So stop talking to the bastard and just kill him." He advanced on de Taillebourg, sword raised, but Thomas held him back.

"Where's my father's book?" Thomas asked the priest.

"Your cousin has it," de Taillebourg replied. "I promise you, your cousin has it."

"Then where is my cousin?"

"I told you, he rode away to fetch help," de Taillebourg said, "and now you must go too, Thomas. You must leave me here to pray."

Thomas almost obeyed, but then he remembered his pathetic gratitude to this man when he had ceased the torture, and the memory of that gratitude was so shaming, so painful, that he suddenly shuddered and, almost without thinking, swung the sword at the priest.

"No!" de Taillebourg shouted, his left arm cut to the bone where he had tried to defend himself from Thomas's sword.

"Yes," Thomas said, and the rage was consuming him, filling him, and he cut again and Robbie was beside him, stabbing with his sword, and Thomas swung a third time, but so lavishly that his blade got tangled with the tent roof.

De Taillebourg was swaying now. "You can't kill me!" he shouted. "I'm a priest!" He screamed that last word and was still screaming as Robbie chopped Sir William Douglas's sword into his neck. Thomas disentangled his own blade. De Taillebourg, the front of his robes soaked with blood, was staring at him with astonishment, then the priest tried to speak and could not, and the blood was spreading through the weave of his robes with an extraordinary swiftness. He fell to his knees, still trying to speak, and Thomas's sword blow took him on the other side of his neck, and more blood spurted out to slash drops across the white altar frontal. De Taillebourg looked up, this time with puzzlement on his face, then Robbie's last blow killed the Dominican, tearing his windpipe out of his neck. Robbie had to leap back to avoid the spray of blood. The priest twitched and in his death throes his left hand pulled the blood-drenched frontal off the altar, spilling candles and cross. He made a rattling noise, twitched and was still.

"That did feel good," Robbie said in the sudden dark as the candles went out. "I hate priests. I've always wanted to kill one."

"I had a friend who was a priest," Thomas said, making the sign of the cross, "but he was murdered, either by my cousin or by this bastard." He stirred de Taillebourg's body with his foot, then stooped and wiped his sword blade clean on the hem of the priest's robes.

Robbie went to the tent door. "My father reckons that hell is full of priests," he said.

"Then there's one more on his way down there now," Thomas said. He picked up his bow and he and Robbie went back into the dark where the screams and arrows laced the night. So many tents and huts were now aflame that it might as well have been daylight and in the lurid glare Thomas saw a crossbowman kneeling between two picketed and terrified horses. The crossbow was aimed up the hill to where so many English were fighting. Thomas put an arrow on his cord, drew, and at the very last second, just as he was about to put the arrow through the crossbowman's spine, he recognized the blue and white wavy pattern on the jupon and he jerked his aim aside so that his arrow hit the crossbow instead and knocked it out of Jeanette's hands. "You'll get killed!" he shouted at her angrily.

"That's Charles!" She pointed up the hill, equally angry with him.

"The only crossbows are with the enemy," he said to her. "You want to be shot by an archer?" He picked up her bow by its crank and tossed it into the shadows. "And what are you goddamn doing here?"

"I came to kill him!" she said, pointing again at Charles of Blois who, with his retainers, was warding off a desperate assault. He had eight surviving knights with him and they were all fighting savagely even though they were hugely outnumbered and every one of them was wounded. Thomas led Jeanette up the slope just in time to see a tall English man-at-arms hack at Charles who caught the blow on his shield and slid his own sword under its rim to stab the Englishman in the thigh. Another man attacked and was slashed down by an axe, a third pulled one of Charles's re-

tainers away from the mill and hacked at his helmet. There
seemed to be a score of Englishmen trying to reach Charles,
smashing their shields into his retainers' weapons, thrusting
swords and chopping with big war axes.

"Give him room!" an authoritative voice shouted. "Give
him room! Back away! Back away! Let him yield!"

The attackers reluctantly moved back. Charles had his visor up and there was blood on his pale face and more blood
on his sword. A priest was on his knees beside him.

"Yield!" a man shouted at the Duke, who seemed to understand because he impulsively shook his head in refusal,
but then Thomas put an arrow on his cord, drew and
pointed it at Charles's face. Charles saw the threat and hesitated.

"Yield!" another man shouted.

"Only to a man of rank!" Charles called in French.

"Who has rank here?" Thomas called in English, then
again in French. One of Charles's remaining men-at-arms
slowly collapsed, first to his knees, then onto his belly with a
crash of plate armor.

A knight stepped out of the English ranks. He was a Breton, one of Totesham's deputies, and he announced his
name to prove to Charles that he was a man of noble birth
and then he held out his hand and Charles of Blois, nephew
to the King of France and claimant of the Duchy of Brittany, stepped awkwardly forward and held out his sword. A
huge cheer went up, then the men on the hill divided to let
the Duke and his captor walk away. Charles expected to be
given his sword back and looked surprised when the Breton
did not make the offer, then the defeated Duke walked
stiffly down the hill, ignoring the triumphant English, but
suddenly checked for a black-haired figure had stepped into
his path.

It was Jeanette. "Remember me?" she asked.

Charles looked her up and down and flinched as though he had been struck when he recognized the badge on her jupon. Then he flinched again when he saw the anger in her eyes. He said nothing.

Jeanette smiled. "Rapist," she said, then spat through his open visor. The Duke jerked his head away, but too late, and Jeanette spat into his face again. He shivered with anger. She was daring him to strike her, but he restrained himself and Jeanette, unable to do the same, spat a third time. "*Ver*," she said scornfully and walked away to an ironic cheer.

"What's *ver*?" Robbie asked.

"Worm," Thomas said, then smiled at Jeanette. "Well done, my lady."

"I was going to kick his goddamn balls," she said, "but I remembered he was wearing armor."

Thomas laughed, then stepped aside as Richard Totesham ordered a half-dozen men-at-arms to escort Charles back into La Roche-Derrien. Short of capturing the King of France, he was as valuable a captive as any to be had in the war. Thomas watched him walk away. Charles of Blois would now be joining the King of Scotland as England's prisoner and both men would have to raise a fortune if they wished to be ransomed.

"It isn't finished!" Totesham shouted. He had seen the crowd of jeering men following the captured Duke and hurried to pull them away. "It isn't done! Finish the job!"

"Horses!" Sir Thomas Dagworth called. "Take their horses!"

The fight in Charles's encampment was won, but not ended. The assault from the town had hit like a storm and driven clean through the center of Duke Charles's carefully prepared battle line and what was left of his force was now split into small groups. Scores were already dead, and others were fleeing into the darkness. "Archers!" a shout went up.

"Archers to me!" Dozens of archers ran to the back of the encampment, where the escaping French and Bretons were trying to reach the other fortresses, and the bows cut the fugitives down mercilessly.

"Clean them out!" Totesham shouted. "Clean them out!" A rough kind of organization had emerged in the shambles as the garrison and the townsmen, augmented by the survivors of Sir Thomas Dagworth's force, hunted through the burning encampment to drive any survivors back to where the archers waited. It was slow work, not because the enemy was making any real resistance, but because men were constantly stopping to pillage tents and shelters. Women and children were pulled out into the moonlight and their men were killed. Prisoners worth a huge ransom were slaughtered in the confusion and darkness. The Viscount Rohan was chopped down, as were the lords of Laval and of Châteaubriant, of Dinan and of Redon.

A gray light glimmered in the east, the first hint of dawn. Whimpering sounded in the burned camp.

"Finish them off?" Richard Totesham had at last found Sir Thomas Dagworth. The two men were on the encampment's ramparts from where they stared at the southern enemy fortress.

"Can't leave them sitting there," Sir Thomas said, then held out a hand. "Thanks, Dick."

"For doing my job?" Totesham responded, embarrassed. "So let's scour the bastards out of the other camps, eh?"

A trumpet called the English to assemble.

CHARLES OF BLOIS had told his men that an archer could not shoot a man he could not see, and that was true, but the men of the southern encampment, who formed the second largest portion of Charles's army, were crowding onto their outer rampart in an effort to see what was happening in the eastern encampment about the windmill. They had lit fires to give their own crossbowmen illumination, but those fires now served to outline them as they stood on the earth bank, which had no palisade, and the English archers, given such a target, could not miss. Those archers were in the cleared ground between the encampments, shadowed by the loom of the long earthworks, and their arrows flickered out of the night to strike the watching French and Bretons. Crossbowmen tried to shoot back, but they made the easiest targets for few of them possessed mail, and then, with a roar, the English men-at-arms were charging over the defenses and the killing began again. Townsmen, eager for plunder, followed the charge and the archers, seeing the earthwork stripped of defenders, ran to catch up.

Thomas paused on the earth rampart to shoot a dozen arrows into the panicked enemy who had made this encampment where the English siege camp had stood the previous year. He had lost sight of Sir Guillaume and, though he had told Jeanette to go back to the town, she was still with him, but now armed with a sword she had taken from a dead Breton. "You shouldn't be here!" he snarled at her.

"Wasps!" she called back, and pointed to a dozen men-at-arms wearing the black and yellow surcoats of the Lord of Roncelets.

The enemy here made small resistance. They had been unaware of the disaster that had overcome Charles, and they had been surprised by the sudden assault from the darkness. The surviving crossbowmen now retreated panicking into the tents and the English again snatched brands from the great fires and hurled them onto the canvas roofs to flare bright and garish in the predawn darkness. The English and Welsh archers had slung their bows and were grimly working their way through the tent lines with axes, swords and clubs. It was another slaughter, fuelled by the prospect of plunder, and some of the French and Bretons, rather than face the screaming mass of maddened men, took to their horses and fled east toward the thin gray light that now leaked a touch of red along the horizon.

Thomas and Robbie headed for the men wearing Roncelets's waspish stripes. Those men had attempted to make a stand beside a trebuchet that had the name Stonewhip painted on its big frame, but they had been outflanked by archers and now they were trying to escape and in the chaos they did not know which way to go. Two of them ran at Thomas and he skewered one with his sword while Robbie stunned the other with a massive blow to his helmet, then a rush of archers swept the men in black and yellow aside and Thomas scabbarded his wet sword and unslung his bow before running into a big unburned tent that stood beside a pole flying the black and yellow banner and there, between a bed and an open chest, was the Lord of Roncelets himself. He and a squire were scooping coins from the chest into small bags and they turned as Thomas and Robbie entered and the Lord of Roncelets snatched up a sword from the bed just as Thomas dragged back the bowcord. The squire lunged at Robbie, but Thomas loosed the arrow and the squire jerked back as if tugged by a massive rope and the blood from the wound in his forehead pattered red on the tent roof. The squire jerked a few times and then was still, and the Lord of Roncelets was still three paces from Thomas when the second arrow was placed on the string. "Come on, my lord," Thomas said, "give me a reason to send you to the devil."

The Lord of Roncelets looked like a fighter. He had short bristly hair, a broken nose and missing teeth, but there was no belligerence in him now. He could hear the screams of defeat all about him, he could smell the burning flesh of the men trapped among the tents and he could see the arrow on Thomas's bow that was aimed at his face and he simply held out his sword in instant surrender. "You have rank?" he asked Robbie. He had not recognized Thomas and, anyway, presumed that any man carrying a bow had to be a commoner.

Robbie did not understand the question, which had been asked in French, and so Thomas answered for him. "He's a Scottish lord," Thomas said, exaggerating Robbie's status.

"Then I yield to him," Roncelets said angrily and threw his sword at Robbie's feet.

"God," Robbie said, not understanding the exchange, "but he scared quick!"

Thomas gently released the bowcord's tension and held up the crooked fingers of his right hand. "It's a good job you surrendered," he told Roncelets. "Remember you wanted to cut these off?" He could not help smiling as first recognition, then abject fear showed on Roncelets's face. "Jeanette!" Thomas shouted, his small victory gained. "Jeanette!" Jeanette came through the tent flap and with her, of all people, was Will Skeat. "What the hell are you doing here?" Thomas demanded angrily.

"You wouldn't keep an old friend from a scrap, would you, Tom?" Skeat asked with a grin and Thomas thought he could see his friend's true character in that grin.

"You're an old fool," Thomas grumbled, then he picked up the Lord of Roncelets's sword and gave it to Jeanette. "He's our prisoner," he said, "yours as well."

"Ours?" Jeanette was puzzled.

"He's the Lord of Roncelets," Thomas said, and he could not help another smile, "and I've no doubt we can squeeze a ransom from him. And I don't mean that cash"—he pointed at the open chest—"that's ours anyway."

Jeanette stared at Roncelets and it slowly dawned on her that if the Lord of Roncelets was her prisoner then her son was as good as returned to her. She laughed suddenly, then gave Thomas a kiss. "So you do keep your promises, Thomas."

"And you keep good guard of him," Thomas said, "because his ransom is going to make us all rich. Robbie, you, me and Will. We're all going to be wealthy." He grinned at Skeat. "You'll stay with her, Will? Look after him?"

"I'll stay," Will agreed.

"Who is she?" the Lord of Roncelets asked Thomas.

"The Countess of Armorica," Jeanette answered for him and laughed again when she saw the shock on his face.

"Take him back to the town now," Thomas told them, and he ducked outside the tent where he found two townsmen searching for plunder among the nearest tents. "You two!" he snapped at them, "you're going to help guard a prisoner. Take him back to the town and you'll be well rewarded. Guard him well!" Thomas pulled the two men into the tent. He reckoned the Lord of Roncelets could not escape if Jeanette, Skeat and the two men were watching him. "Just guard him," he told them, "and take him to your old house." This last was to Jeanette.

"My old house?" she was puzzled.

"You wanted to kill someone tonight," Thomas said, "and you can't kill Charles of Blois, so why don't you go and murder Belas?" He laughed at the look on her face, then he and Robbie slammed down the chest lid and covered it with blankets from the bed in hope of hiding it for a few moments and then they went back to the fight.

All through the flame-lit battle Thomas had caught glimpses of men in plain black surcoats and he knew that Guy Vexille must be nearby, but he had not seen him. Now there were shouts and the clash of blades from the encampment's southern edge and Thomas and Robbie ran to see what the commotion was. They saw that a group of horsemen in black surcoats was fighting off a score of English men-at-arms. "Vexille!" Thomas shouted. "Vexille!"

"It's him?" Robbie asked.

"It's his men, anyway," Thomas said. He guessed his cousin had been in the eastern encampment with de Taille-bourg and that he had come here in hope of bringing a relief force to Charles's aid, but he had been too late and now his men were fighting a rearguard battle to protect other men who were fleeing.

"Where is he?" Robbie demanded.

Thomas could not see his cousin. He shouted again. "Vex-ille! Vexille!"

And there he was. The Harlequin, Count of Astarac, ar-mored in plate, visor lifted, mounted on a black destrier and carrying a plain black shield. He saw Thomas and raised his sword in an ironic salute. Thomas unslung his bow, but Guy Vexille saw the threat, turned away and his horsemen closed protectively about him. "Vexille!" Thomas yelled and he ran toward his cousin. Robbie called a warning and Thomas ducked as a horseman swung a blade at him, then he pushed against the horse, smelling leather and sweat, and another horseman banged into him, almost throwing him off his feet. "Vexille!" he bellowed. He could see Guy Vexille again, only now his cousin was turning back, spurring toward him, and Thomas drew the bowcord, but Vexille held up his right hand to show he had scabbarded his sword and the gesture made Thomas lower the black bow.

Guy Vexille, his visor raised and his handsome face lit by the fires, smiled. "I have the book, Thomas."

Thomas said nothing, but just raised the bow again.

Guy Vexille shook his head in reproof. "No need for that, Thomas. Join me."

"In hell, you bastard," Thomas said. This was the man who had killed his father, had killed Eleanor, had killed Fa-ther Hobbe, and Thomas drew the arrow fully back and Vex-ille took a small knife that had been concealed in his shield hand and calmly leaned forward and cut the bowcord. The

broken string made the bow jump violently in Thomas's
hand and the arrow spewed away harmlessly. The cord had
been cut so swiftly that Thomas had been given no time to
react.

"One day you'll join me, Thomas," Vexille said, then he
saw that the English archers had at last noticed his men and
were beginning to take their toll and so he turned his horse,
shouted at his men to retreat and spurred away.

"Jesus!" Thomas swore in frustration.

"*Calix meus inebrians!*" Guy Vexille shouted, then he was
lost among the horsemen galloping south. A flight of English arrows followed them, but none struck Vexille.

"Bastard!" Robbie swore at the retreating figure.

A woman's scream sounded from the burning tents.

"What did he say to you?" Robbie asked.

"He wanted me to join him," Thomas said bitterly. He
threw away the slashed cord and took the spare from under
his sallet. His clumsy fingers fumbled as he restrung the
bow, but he managed to do it on the second try. "And he said
he's got the book."

"Aye, well, much good that will bloody do him," Robbie
commented. The fight had died and he knelt by a black-
dressed corpse and began searching for coins. Sir Thomas
Dagworth was shouting for men to assemble at the encampment's western edge to assault the next fortress where some
of the defenders, realizing that the battle was lost, were already running away. Church bells were ringing in La Roche-
Derrien, celebrating that Charles of Blois had entered the
town as a prisoner.

Thomas stared after his cousin. He was ashamed because
one small part of him, one small and treacherous part, had
been tempted to take the offer. Join his cousin, be back in a
family, look for the Grail and harness its power. The shame
was sour, like the shame of the gratitude he had felt toward

de Taillebourg when the torture ceased. "Bastard!" he yelled uselessly. "*Bastard.*"

"Bastard!" It was Sir Guillaume's voice that cut across Thomas's. Sir Guillaume, with his two men-at-arms, was prodding a prisoner in the back with a sword. The captive wore plate armor and the sword scraped on it with every prod. "Bastard!" Sir Guillaume bawled again, then saw Thomas. "It's Coutances! Coutances!" He pulled off his prisoner's helmet. "Look at him!"

The Count of Coutances was a melancholy-looking man, bald as an egg, who was doing his best to appear dignified. Sir Guillaume poked him again. "I tell you, Thomas"—he spoke in French—"that this bastard's wife and daughters will have to whore themselves to raise this ransom! They'll be swiving every man in Normandy to buy this gutless bastard back!" He jabbed the Count of Coutances again. "I'm going to squeeze you witless!" Sir Guillaume roared and then, exultant, marched his prisoner onward.

The woman screamed again.

There had been many women screaming that night, but something about this sound cut through Thomas's awareness and he turned, alarmed. The scream sounded a third time and Thomas began to run. "Robbie!" he shouted. "To me!"

Thomas ran across the remnants of a burning tent, his boots throwing up sparks and embers. He swerved round a smoking brazier, almost tripped on a wounded man who was vomiting into an upturned helmet, ran down an alley between armorers' huts where anvils, bellows, hammers, tongs and barrels full of rivets and mail rings were spilled on the grass. A man in a farrier's apron with blood streaming from a head wound staggered into his path and Thomas shoved him aside to run toward the black and yellow standard that still flew outside the Lord of Roncelets's burning tent. "Jeanette!" he called. "Jeanette!"

But Jeanette was a prisoner. She was being held by a huge man who had pressed her spine against the windlass of the trebuchet called Stonewhip that stood just beyond the Lord of Roncelets's tent. The man heard Thomas shouting and looked round, grinning. It was Beggar, all beard and rotted teeth, and he shoved Jeanette hard as she struggled to escape him.

"Hold her, Beggar!" Sir Geoffrey Carr shouted. "Hold the bitch!"

"The pretty ain't going anywhere," Beggar said, "going nowhere, darling," and he tried to haul up her coat of mail, but it was too heavy and awkward and Jeanette was struggling too frantically.

The Lord of Roncelets, still without his sword, was sitting on Stonewhip's frame. He had a red mark on his face, suggesting he had been struck, and Sir Geoffrey Carr with five other men-at-arms was standing over him. The Scarecrow stared defiantly at Thomas. "He's my prisoner!" he insisted.

"He belongs to us," Thomas said, "we took him."

"Listen, boy," the Scarecrow said, his voice still slurred by drink, "I am a knight and you are a turd. You understand me?" He staggered slightly as he stepped toward Thomas. "I am a knight," he said again, louder, "and you are nothing!" His red face, made lurid by the flames, was twisted in derision. "You are nothing!" he shouted again, then whipped round to make sure that his men were guarding the Lord of Roncelets. Such a wealthy captive would solve all Sir Geoffrey's problems and he was determined to hold onto him and take the ransom for himself. "She can't take a captive," he said, pointing his sword at Jeanette, "because she's got tits, and you can't take him because you're a turd. But I'm a knight! A *knight*!" He spat the word at Thomas who, goaded by the insults, drew his bow. The new string was slightly too long and he could feel the lack of power in the black stave because of it, but he reckoned there was enough strength for his purpose. "Beggar!" the Scarecrow shouted, "if he looses that bow, kill the bitch."

"Kill the pretty," Beggar said. He was drooling spittle, which ran down his big beard as he stroked the mail rings above Jeanette's breasts. She still fought, but he had her bent painfully back across the windlass and she could hardly move.

Thomas kept the bow drawn. The trebuchet's long beam, he saw, had been winched down to the ground though the engineers must have been interrupted before they could load a stone because the great leather sling was empty. A heap of stones stood off to the right and a sudden movement there made Thomas see there was a wounded man leaning against the boulders. The man was trying to stand, but could not. There was blood on his face. "Will?" Thomas asked.

"Tom!" Will Skeat tried to push himself upright again. "It's you, Tom!"

"What happened?" Thomas asked.

"Not what I was, Tom," Skeat said. The two townsmen who had been helping to guard the Lord of Roncelets were dead at Skeat's feet, and Skeat himself seemed to be dying. He was white-faced, feeble and every breath was a struggle. There were tears on his face. "I tried to fight," he said pitiably, "I did try, but I'm not what I was."

"Who attacked you?" Thomas asked, but Skeat seemed unable to answer.

"Will was just trying to protect me," Jeanette shouted, then she screamed as Beggar thrust her back so hard that at last she was forced onto the top of the windlass and Beggar could push her mail skirts up. He gabbled excitedly just as Sir Geoffrey roared in anger.

"It's the Douglas bastard!"

Thomas loosed the cord. With a new bowcord he liked to shoot a couple of arrows to discover how the new hemp would behave, but he had no time for such niceties now, he just loosed the arrow and it sliced through the tangles of Beggar's beard to cut his throat, the broad arrow head slitting his gullet as cleanly as a butcher's knife, and Jeanette screamed as the blood spurted across her jupon and face. The Scarecrow bellowed in rage and ran at Thomas who rammed the horn-tipped bowstave into the red face then let the weapon fall as he drew his sword. Robbie ran past him and thrust his uncle's sword at the Scarecrow's belly, but even drunk Sir Geoffrey was quick and he managed to parry the blow and strike back. Two of his men-at-arms were running to help—the others were guarding the Lord of Roncelets—and Thomas saw the two men coming. He went to his left, hoping to put the big frame of Stonewhip between himself and the men wearing Sir Geoffrey's badge of the black axe, but Sir Geoffrey almost cut him off and Thomas gave a desperate backswing with his newly drawn sword that slammed against the Scarecrow's blade with a force that numbed Thomas's arm. The blow rocked the Scarecrow back, then he recovered and leaped forward and Thomas was desperately defending himself as the Scarecrow rained blows down on him. Thomas was no swordsman and he was being beaten down to his knees and Robbie could not help him because he was fending off Sir Geoffrey's two followers, and then there was an almighty crash, a bang that sounded as though the gates of hell had just opened, and the ground shook as the Scarecrow screamed in utter agony. His howl, trailing blood, seared into the sky.

Jeanette had pulled the lever that released the long beam. Ten tons of counterweight had thumped to the ground and the thick metal pin that held the sling had jerked up between Sir Geoffrey's legs and torn a bloody hole from his crotch to his belly. He should have been hurled halfway to the town by the trebuchet's beam, but instead the pin had been trapped in his entrails and he was caught on the beam's end where he writhed in agony, his blood pouring down to the ground.

His men, seeing their master dying, stepped back. Why fight for a man who could offer no reward? Robbie gaped up as the Scarecrow twisted and jerked, and somehow the dying man managed to tear himself free of the great iron stake and he fell, trailing intestines and spraying blood. He hit the ground with a thump, bounced bloodily, yet still he lived. His eyes were twitching and his mouth was drawn back in a snarl. "Goddamn Douglas," he managed to gasp before Robbie stepped to him, lifted his uncle's sword, and rammed it down once, straight between the Scarecrow's eyes.

The Lord of Roncelets had watched it all happen with disbelief. Now Jeanette was holding a sword to his face, daring him to run away, and he dumbly shook his head to show that he had no intention of risking his life among the drunken, screaming, savage men who had come out of the night to destroy the greatest army the duchy of Brittany had ever raised.

Thomas crossed to Sir William Skeat, but his old friend was dead. He had been wounded in the neck and he had bled to death on the stone pile. He looked strangely peaceful. A first shaft of the new day's sun cut across the world's edge to light the bright blood at the top of Stonewhip's beam as Thomas closed his mentor's eyes. "Who killed Will Skeat?" Thomas demanded of Sir Geoffrey's men and Dickon, the young one, pointed at the wreckage of mail, flesh, entrails and bone that had been the Scarecrow.

Thomas inspected the dents in his sword. He must learn to use one, he thought, or else he would die by the sword, then he looked up at Sir Geoffrey's men. "Go and help the attack on the next fort," he told them. They stared at him. "Go!" he snapped and, startled, they ran westward.

Thomas pointed his sword at the Lord of Roncelets. "Take him back to town," he told Robbie, "and guard him well."

"What about you?" Robbie asked.

"I'm going to bury Will," Thomas said. "He was a friend."
He thought he must shed some tears for Will Skeat, but there
were none. Not now, anyway. He sheathed the sword, then
smiled at Robbie. "You can go home, Robbie."

"I can?" Robbie seemed puzzled.

"De Taillebourg's dead. Roncelets will pay your ransom
to Lord Outhwaite. You can go to Eskdale, go home, go back
to killing Englishmen."

Robbie shook his head. "Guy Vexille lives."

"He's mine to kill."

"And mine," Robbie said. "You forget he killed my
brother. I'm staying till he's dead."

"If you can ever find him," Jeanette said softly.

The sun was lighting the smoke of the burning encampments and casting long shadows across the ground where the
last of Charles's army abandoned their earthworks and fled
toward Rennes. They had come in their great splendor and
now they scuttled away in abject defeat.

Thomas went to the engineers' tents and found a pickaxe,
a mattock and a shovel. He dug a grave beside Stonewhip
and tipped Skeat into the damp soil and tried to say a prayer,
but he could not think of one, and then he remembered the
coin for the ferryman and so he went to the Lord of Roncelets's tent and pulled the charred canvas away from the
chest and took a piece of gold and went back to the grave.
He jumped down beside his friend and put the coin under
Skeat's tongue. The ferryman would find it and know from
the gold that Sir William Skeat was a special man. "God
bless you, Will," Thomas said, then he scrambled out of the
grave and he filled it in, though he kept pausing in hope that
Will's eyes would open, but of course they did not and
Thomas at last wept as he shoveled earth onto his friend's
pale face. The sun was up by the time he finished and
women and children were coming from the town to look for

plunder. A kestrel flew high and Thomas sat on the chest of coins and waited for Robbie to return from the town.

He would go south, he thought. Go to Astarac. Go and find his father's notebook and solve its mystery. The bells of La Roche-Derrien were ringing for the victory, a huge victory, and Thomas sat among the dead and knew he would have no peace until he had found his father's burden. *Calix meus inebrians. Transfer calicem istem a me. Ego enim eram pincerna regis.*

Whether he wanted the job or not he was the King's cup-bearer, and he would go south.

Historical Note

The novel begins with the battle of Neville's Cross. The
name of the battle is derived from the stone cross that
Lord Neville erected to mark the victory, though it is possible there was another cross already on the site which
Lord Neville's memorial replaced. The battle, fought by a
large Scottish army against a small scratch force hastily
assembled by the Archbishop of York and the northern
lords, was a disaster for the Scots. Their King, David II,
was captured as described in *Vagabond*, trapped under a
bridge. He managed to knock out some of his captor's
teeth, but then was subdued. He spent a long time at Bam-
burgh Castle recovering from his facial wound, then was
taken to London and put into the Tower with most of the
other Scottish aristocracy captured that day, including Sir
William Douglas, the Knight of Liddesdale. The two Scottish Earls who had previously sworn fealty to Edward
were decapitated, then quartered, and the parts of their
body displayed around the realm as a warning against
treachery. Later that year Charles of Bloiš, nephew to the
King of France and would-be Duke of Brittany, joined
David II in the Tower of London. It was a remarkable double by the English who would, in another decade, add the
King of France himself to the haul.

The Scots invaded England at the request of the French to whom they were allied, and it is probable that David II truly believed England's army was all in northern France. But England had foreseen just this kind of trouble and certain northern lords were charged with staying at home and being ready to raise forces if the Scots ever marched. The backbone of those forces was, of course, the archer, and this is the great age of English (and, to a lesser extent, Welsh) archery. The weapon used was the longbow (a name that was coined much later) which was a yew bow at least six feet in length with a draw weight of over a hundred pounds (more than double the weight of modern competition bows). It is a mystery why England alone could field armies of lethal archers who did, indeed, become kings of the European battlefield, but the likeliest answer is that mastery of the longbow was an English enthusiasm, practiced as a sport in hundreds of villages. Eventually laws were passed making archery practice obligatory, presumably because the enthusiasm was fading. It was, certainly, an extraordinarily difficult weapon to use, requiring immense strength, and the French, though they tried to introduce the weapon into their ranks, never mastered the longbow. The Scots were accustomed to these archers and had learned never to attack them on horseback, but in truth there was no answer to the longbow until firearms were deployed on the battlefield.

Prisoners were important. A great man like Sir William Douglas would only be released on payment of a vast ransom, though Sir William was given early parole to help negotiate the ransom of the King of Scotland and when he failed he dutifully returned to his imprisonment in the Tower of London. The ransoms for men like Charles of Blois and King David II were massive and might take years to negotiate and raise. In David's case the ransom was £66,000, a sum that has to be multiplied at least a hundred times to get even a rough approximation of its modern value. The Scots were allowed to pay it in ten installments and twenty noblemen had to be surrendered as hostages for the payment before David was released in 1357 by which time, ironically, his sympathies had become entirely pro-English. Sir Thomas Dagworth was officially the captor of Charles of Blois and he sold him to Edward III for the much smaller sum of £3,500, but doubtless it was better to have that money in hand than wait while a larger ransom was collected in France and Brittany. King David's captor had been an Englishman called John Coupland who also sold his prisoner to Edward, in Coupland's case for a knighthood and land.

Charles's defeat at La Roche-Derrien is one of the great unsung English triumphs of the period. Charles had faced archers before and had worked out, rightly as it happened, that the way to defeat them was to make them attack well-protected positions. What the archer could not see he could not kill. The tactic worked against Sir Thomas Dagworth's assault, but then came Richard Totesham's frenetic sortie from the town and, because Charles had insisted that the four parts of his army stay behind their protective earthworks, he was overwhelmed and the other parts of his army were then defeated in turn. His defeat and capture were an immense shock to his allies, the French, who were failing to relieve the siege of Calais. I must record my debt to Jonathan Sumption whose book, *Trial by Battle*, the first volume of his superb history of the Hundred Years War, was of particular use to me. The errors in the novel are entirely mine, of course, though in the interests of lightening my post bag may I gently point out that Durham Cathedral only possessed two towers in 1347 and that I placed the Hachaliah reference in the book of Esdras, instead of in Nehemiah, because I was using the Vulgate and not the King James Bible.

Here's an exciting excerpt from
Thomas of Hookton's next adventure

HERETIC

by Bernard Cornwell

available October 2003

Prologue

Calais, 1347

The road came from the southern hills and crossed the marshes by the sea. It was a bad road. A summer's persistent rain had left it a strip of glutinous mud that baked hard when the sun came out, but it was the only road that led from the heights of Sangatte to the harbors of Calais and Gravelines. At Nieulay, a hamlet of no distinction whatever, it crossed the River Ham on a stone bridge. The Ham was scarcely worth the title of river. It was a slow stream that oozed through fever-ridden marshlands until it vanished among the coastal mudflats. It was so short that a man could wade from its source to the sea in little more than an hour, and it was so shallow that a man could cross it at low tide without getting his waist wet. It drained the swamps where reeds grew thick and herons hunted frogs among the marsh grass, and it was fed by a maze of smaller streams where the villagers from Nieulay and Hammes and Guines set their wicker eel traps.

Nieulay and its stone bridge might have expected to slumber through history, except that the town of Calais lay just two miles to the north and, in the summer of 1347, an army of thirty thousand Englishmen was laying siege to the port and their encampment lay thick between the town's formidable walls and the marshes. The road which came from the heights and crossed the Ham at Nieulay was the only route a

French relief force might use and in the height of the summer, when the inhabitants of Calais were close to starvation, Philip of Valois, King of France, brought his army to Sangatte.

Twenty thousand Frenchmen lined the heights, their banners thick in the wind blowing from the sea. The oriflamme was there, the sacred war pennant of France. It was a long flag with three pointed tails, a blood-red ripple of precious silk, and if the flag looked bright that was because it was new. The old oriflamme was in England, a trophy taken on the wide green hill between Wadicourt and Crécy the previous summer. But the new flag was as sacred as the old, and about it were the standards of France's great lords; the banners of Bourbon, of Montmorency and of the Count of Armagnac. Lesser flags flew among the noble standards, but all proclaimed that the greatest warriors of Philip's kingdom were come to give battle to the English. Yet between them and the enemy were the River Ham and the bridge at Nieulay that was defended by a stone tower around which the English had dug trenches that they had filled with archers and men-at-arms. Beyond that force was the river, then the marshes, and on the higher ground close to Calais's high wall and its double moat was a makeshift town of wooden houses and tents where the English army lived. And such an army as had never been seen in France. The besieger's encampment was bigger than Calais itself. As far as the eye could see were streets lined with canvas, with timber houses, with paddocks for horses, and between them were men-at-arms and archers. The oriflamme might as well have stayed unfurled.

"We can take the tower, sire," Sir Geoffrey de Charny, as hard a soldier as any in Philip's army, gestured down the hill to where the English garrison of Nieulay was isolated on the French side of the river.

"To what end?" Philip asked. He was a weak man, hesitant in battle, but his question was pertinent. If the tower did fall and the bridge of Nieulay was thus delivered into his hands, what would it serve? The bridge merely led to an even greater English army that was already arraying itself on the firm ground at the edge of its encampment.

The citizens of Calais, starved and despairing, had seen the French banners on the southern crest and they had responded by hanging their own flags from their ramparts. They displayed images of the Virgin, pictures of Saint Denis of France and, high on the citadel, the blue and yellow royal standard to tell Philip that his subjects still lived, still fought, but the brave display could not hide that they had been besieged for eleven months. They needed help.

"Take the tower, sire," Sir Geoffrey urged, "and then attack across the bridge! Good Christ, if the Goddamns see us win one victory they might lose heart!" A growl of agreement came from the assembled lords.

The King was less optimistic. It was true that Calais's garrison still held out, and that the English had hardly damaged its walls, let alone found a way to cross the twin moats, but nor had the French been able to carry any supplies to the beleaguered town. The people there did not need encouragement, they needed food. A puff of smoke showed beyond the encampment and a few heartbeats later the sound of a cannon rolled across the marshes. The missile must have struck the wall, but Philip was too far away to see its effect.

"A victory here will encourage the garrison," the lord of Montmorency urged, "and put despair in the English hearts."

But why should the English lose heart if the tower of Nieulay fell? Philip thought it would merely fill them with a resolve to defend the road on the far side of the bridge, but he also understood that he could not keep his rough hounds leashed when a hated enemy was in sight and so he gave his permission. "Take the tower," he instructed, "and God give you victory."

The King stayed where he was as the lords gathered men and armed themselves. The wind from the sea brought the smell of salt, but also a scent of decay which probably came from rotting weed on the long tidal flats. It made Philip melancholy. His new astrologer had refused to attend the King for weeks, pleading that he had a fever, but the King had learned that the man was in fine health which meant that he must have seen some great disaster in the stars and simply feared to tell the King. Gulls cried beneath the clouds. Far out to sea a grubby sail bellied toward England, while another ship was anchoring off the English held beaches and was ferrying men ashore in small boats to swell the enemy ranks. The King looked back to the road and saw a group of around forty or fifty English knights riding toward the bridge. The King made the sign of the cross again, praying that the knights would be trapped by his attack. He hated the English. Hated them.

The Duke of Bourbon had delegated the organization of the assault to Sir Geoffrey de Charny and Edouard de Beaujeu, and that was good. The King trusted both men to be sensible. He did not doubt they could carry the tower, though he still did not know what good it would do, but he supposed it was better than letting his wilder noblemen carry their lances in a wild charge across the bridge to utter defeat in the marshlands. He knew they would love nothing better than to make such an attack. They thought war was a game and every defeat only made them more eager to play again. Fools, he thought, and he made the sign of the cross and he wondered what dire prophecy the astrologer was hiding from him. What we need, he thought, is a miracle. Some great sign from God. Then he twitched in alarm because a nakerer had just beaten his great kettle-drum. A trumpet sounded.

The music did not presage the advance. Rather the musicians were warming their instruments, ready for the attack.

Edouard de Beaujeu was on the right where he had assembled over a thousand crossbowmen and as many men-at-arms, and he plainly intended to assault the English from one flank while Sir Geoffrey de Charny and at least five hundred men-at-arms charged straight down the hill at the English entrenchments. Sir Geoffrey was striding along the line shouting at the knights and men-at-arms to dismount. They did so reluctantly. They believed that the essence of war was the cavalry charge, but Sir Geoffrey knew that horses were no use against a stone tower protected by entrenchments and so he was insisting they fight on foot. "Shields and swords," he told them, "no lances! On foot! On foot!" Sir Geoffrey had learned the hard way that horses were pitiably vulnerable to English arrows, while men on foot could advance at the crouch behind stout shields. Some of the higher-born men were refusing to dismount, but he ignored them. Even more French men-at-arms were hurrying to join the charge. The small band of English knights had crossed the bridge now and looked as if they intended to ride straight up the road to challenge the whole French battle line, but instead they checked their horses and gazed up at the horde on the ridge. The King, watching them, saw that they were led by a great lord. He could tell that by the size of the man's banner, while at least a dozen of the other knights carried the square flags of bannerets on their lances. A rich group, he thought, worth a small fortune in ransoms. He hoped they would ride to the tower and so trap themselves.

The Duke of Bourbon trotted his horse back to Philip. The duke was in plate armor that had been scoured with sand, vinegar and wire until it shone white. His helmet, still hanging from his saddle's pommel, was crested with feathers dyed blue. He had refused to dismount from his destrier that had a steel chanfron to protect its face and a trapper of gleaming mail to shield its body from the English archers who were no doubt stringing their bows in the entrench-

ments. "The oriflamme, sire," the Duke said, and it was supposed to be a request, but somehow sounded like an order.

"The oriflamme?" The King pretended not to understand.

"May I have the honor, sire, of carrying it to battle."

The King sighed. "You outnumber the enemy ten to one,"
he said, "you hardly need the oriflamme. Let it stay here.
The enemy will have seen it." And the enemy would know
what the unfurled oriflamme meant. It instructed the French
to take no prisoners, to kill everyone, though doubtless any
wealthy English knight would still be captured rather than
killed, for a corpse yielded no ransom. Still, the unfurled
triple-tongued flag should put terror into English hearts. "It
will remain here," the King insisted.

The Duke began to protest, but just then a trumpet
sounded and the crossbowmen started down the hill. They
were in green and red tunics with the Grail badge of Genoa
on their left arms, and each was accompanied by a foot soldier holding a pavise, a huge shield that would protect the
crossbowman while he reloaded his clumsy weapon. A half
mile away, beside the river, Englishmen were running from
the tower to the earth entrenchments that had been dug so
many months before that they were now thickly covered
with grass and weeds. "You will miss your battle," the King
said to the Duke who, forgetting the scarlet banner, wheeled
his great armored war horse toward Sir Geoffrey's men.

"Montjoie Saint Denis!" The Duke shouted France's war
cry and the nakerers thumped their big drums and a dozen
trumpeters blared their challenge at the sky. There were
clicks as helmet visors were lowered. The crossbowmen
were already at the foot of the slope, spreading right to en-
velop the English flank. Then the first arrows flew. English
arrows, white-feathered, fluttering across the green land and
the King, leaning forward in his saddle, saw that there were
too few archers on the enemy side. Usually, whenever the
damned English gave battle, their archers outnumbered their

knights and men-at-arms by at least three to one, but the out-post of Nieulay seemed mostly to be garrisoned by men-at-arms. "God speed you!" the King called to his soldiers. He was suddenly enthused because he could scent victory.

The trumpets sounded again and now the gray metallic tide of men-at-arms swept down the slope. They roared their war cry and the sound was rivalled by the drummers who were hammering their taut goatskins and the trumpeters who were playing as if they could defeat the English with sound alone. "God and Saint Denis!" the King shouted.

The crossbow quarrels were flying now. Each short iron bolt was fitted with leather vanes and they made a hiss as they streaked toward the earthworks. Hundreds of bolts flew, then the Genoese stepped behind the huge shields to work the ratchets that bent back their steel-reinforced bows. Some English arrows thumped into the pavises, but then the archers turned toward Sir Geoffrey's attack. They put bodkin-headed arrows on their strings, arrows that were tipped with three or four inches of narrow shafted steel that could pierce mail as if it were linen. They drew and shot, drew and shot and the arrows thumped into shields and the French closed ranks. One man was pierced in the thigh and stumbled and the men-at-arms flowed around him and closed up again. An English archer, standing to loose his bow, was hit in the shoulder by a crossbow bolt and his arrow flew crazily into the air.

"Montjoie Saint Denis!" The men-at-arms bellowed their challenge as the charge reached the flat ground at the foot of the slope and the arrows hammered into shields with sicken-ing force, but the French held their tight formation, shield overlapping shield, and the crossbowmen edged closer to aim at the English archers who were forced to stand high in their trenches to loose their weapons. A bolt went clean through an iron sallet to pierce an English skull. The man toppled sideways, blood spilling down his face. A volley of

arrows whipped from the tower's top and the answering
crossbow bolts rattled on the stones as the English men-at-
arms, seeing that their arrows had not checked the enemy,
stood with unsheathed swords to meet the charge.

"Saint George!" they shouted, then the French attackers
were at the first entrenchment and stabbing down at the English beneath them. Some Frenchmen found narrow causeways piercing the trench and they streamed through to attack
the defenders from the rear. Archers in the two rearmost
trenches had easy targets, but so did the Genoese crossbowmen who stepped from behind their pavises to rain iron on
the enemy. Some of the English, sensing the slaughter to
come, were leaving their entrenchments to run toward the
Ham. Edouard de Beaujeu, leading the crossbowmen, saw
the fugitives and shouted at the Genoese to drop their crossbows and join the attack. They drew swords or axes and
swarmed at the enemy. "Kill!" Edouard de Beaujeu shouted.
He was mounted on a destrier and, his sword drawn, he
spurred the big stallion forward. "Kill!"

The Englishmen in the forward trench were doomed.
They struggled to protect themselves from the mass of
French men-at-arms, but the swords, axes and spears slashed
down. Some men tried to yield, but the oriflamme was flying
and that meant no prisoners and the French swamped the
slick mud at the trench's bottom with English blood. The defenders from the rearward trenches were all running now,
but the handful of French horsemen, those too proud to fight
on foot, spurred across the narrow causeways, shoved
through their own men-at-arms and screamed the war cry as
they drove their big horses into the fugitives beside the river.
Stallions wheeled as swords chopped. An archer lost his
head beside the river that turned sudden red. A man-at-arms
screamed as he was trampled by a destrier, then stabbed with
a lance. An English knight held his hands in the air, offering
a gauntlet as a token of surrender, and he was ridden down

from behind, his spine pierced with a sword, then another horseman cut an axe into his face. "Kill them!" the Duke of Bourbon shouted, his sword wet, "kill them all!" He saw a group of archers escaping toward the bridge and shouted at his followers. "With me! With me! Montjoie Saint Denis!"

The archers, nearly thirty of them, had fled toward the bridge, but when they reached the straggle of reed-thatched houses beside the river they heard the hoofbeats and turned in alarm. For a heartbeat it seemed they would panic again, but one man checked them. "Shoot the horses, boys," he said, and the bowmen hauled on their cords, loosed, and the white-fledged arrows slammed into the destriers. The Duke of Bourbon's stallion staggered sideways as two arrows drove through its mail and leather armor, then it fell as another two horses went down, hooves flailing, and the other riders instinctively turned away, looking for easier pickings. The Duke's squire yielded his own horse to his master, then died as a second English volley hissed from the village. The Duke, rather than waste time trying to mount his squire's horse, lumbered away in his precious plate armor that had protected him from the arrows. Ahead of him, around the base of Nieulay's tower, the survivors from the English trenches had formed a shield wall that was now surrounded by vengeful Frenchmen. "No prisoners!" a French knight shouted, "no prisoners!" The Duke called for his men to help him into the saddle.

Two of the Duke's men-at-arms dismounted to help their master onto the new horse, and just then they heard the thunder of hooves and they turned to see a group of English knights charging from the village. "Sweet Jesus!" The Duke was half in and half out of the saddle, his sword scabbarded, and he began to fall backwards as the men helping him drew their own swords. Where the hell had these English come from? Then his other men-at-arms, desperate to protect their lord, slammed down their visors and turned to meet the chal-

lenge. The Duke sprawled on the turf and heard the clash of
armored horsemen.

The English were the group of men the French King had
seen, and they had paused in the village to watch the slaughter in the entrenchments and had been about to ride back
across the bridge when the Duke of Bourbon's men had
come close. Too close. A challenge that could not be ignored
and so the English lord led his household knights in a charge
that tore into the Duke of Bourbon's men. The Frenchmen
had not been ready for the attack, and the English came in
proper array, knee to knee, and the long ash lances, carried
upright as they charged, suddenly dropped to the killing position and tore through mail and leather. The English leader
was wearing a blue surcoat slashed with a diagonal white
band on which three red stars were blazoned. Yellow lions
occupied the blue field that turned suddenly black with enemy blood as he rammed his sword up into the unprotected
armpit of a French man-at-arms. The man shook with pain,
tried to backswing his sword, but then another Englishman
hammered a mace into his visor that crumpled under the
blow and sprang blood from a dozen rents. A hamstrung
horse screamed and toppled. "Stay close!" the Englishman
in the gaudy surcoat was shouting at his men, "stay close!"
His horse reared up and flailed its hooves at an unhorsed
Frenchman. That man went down, helmet and skull crushed
by a horseshoe and then the rider saw the Duke standing
helpless beside a horse and he recognized the value of the
man's shining plate armor and so spurred at him. The Duke
fended the sword blow with his shield, swung his own blade
that jarred on the enemy's leg armor and suddenly the horseman was gone.

Another Englishman had pulled his leader's horse away.
A mass of French horsemen was coming down the hill. The
King had sent them in hope of capturing the English lord
and his men, and still more Frenchmen, unable to join the at-

tack on the tower because too many of their fellows were assembling to help kill the garrison's remnant, were now
charging the bridge. "Back!" the English leader called, but
the village street and the narrow bridge were blocked by
fugitives and threatened by Frenchmen. He could cut his
way through, but that would mean killing his own archers
and losing some of his knights in the chaotic panic and so instead he looked across the road and saw a path running beside the river. It might lead to the beach, he thought, and
there, perhaps, he could turn and ride east to rejoin the English lines.

The English knights slashed their spurs back. The path
was narrow, only two horsemen could ride abreast, and on
one side was the River Ham and on the other a stretch of
boggy swamp, but the path itself was firm and the English
rode it until they reached a stretch of higher ground where
they could assemble. But they could not escape. The small
piece of higher ground was almost an island, reachable only
by the path and surrounded by a morass of reeds and mud.
They were trapped.

A hundred French horsemen were ready to follow along
the path, but the English had dismounted and made a shield
wall, and the thought of hacking their way through that steel
barrier persuaded the French to turn back to the tower where
the enemy was more vulnerable. Archers were still shooting
from its ramparts, but the Genoese crossbowmen were re-
plying, and now the French slammed into the English men-
at-arms drawn up at the tower's foot.

The French attacked on foot. The ground was slippery because of the summer's rain and the mailed feet churned it to
mud as the leading men-at-arms bellowed their war cry and
threw themselves onto the outnumbered English. Those English had locked their shields and they thrust them forward
to meet the charge. There was a clash of steel on wood, a
scream as a blade slid under a shield's edge and found flesh.

The men in the second English rank, the rear rank, flailed with maces and swords over their comrades' heads. "Saint George!" a shout went up, "Saint George!" and the men-at-arms heaved forward to throw the dead and dying off their shields. "Kill the bastards!"

"Kill them!" Sir Geoffrey de Charny yelled, and the French came back, stumbling in their mail and plate across the wounded and dead, and this time the English shields were not touching rim to rim and the French found gaps. Swords crashed onto plate armor, thrust through mail, beat in helmets. A few last defenders were trying to escape across the river, but the Genoese crossbowmen pursued them and it was a simple matter to hold an armored man down in the water until he drowned, then pillage his body. A few English fugitives stumbled away on the farther bank, going to where an English battle line of archers and men-at-arms was forming to repel any attack across the Ham.

Back at the tower a Frenchman with a battle axe swung repeatedly at an Englishman, cracking open the espalier that protected his right shoulder, slashing through the mail beneath, then beating the man down to a crouch and still the blows came until the axe had laid open the enemy's chest and there was a splay of white ribs among the mangled flesh and torn armor. Blood and mud made a paste underfoot. For every Englishman there were three enemies, and the tower door had been left unlocked to give the men outside a place where they could retreat, but instead it was the French who forced their way inside. The last defenders outside the tower were cut down and killed, while inside the attackers began fighting up the stairs.

The steps turned to the right as they climbed. That meant the defenders could use their right arms without much encumbrance while the attackers were forever balked by the big central pillar of the stairs, but a French knight with a short spear made the first rush and he disemboweled an Englishman with the blade and then another defender killed the knight with a sword thrust over the dying man's head. Visors were up here, for it was dark in the tower, and a man could not see with his eyes half covered with steel and so the English stabbed at French eyes. Men-at-arms pulled the dead off the steps, leaving a trail of bloody guts behind and then two more men charged up, slipping on offal, and they parried English blows, thrust their swords up into groins, and still more Frenchmen pushed into the tower. A terrible scream filled the stairwell, then another bloodied body was hauled down and out of the way and another three steps were clear and the French shoved on up again. "Montjoie Saint Denis!"

An Englishman with a blacksmith's hammer came down the steps and he beat at French helmets, killing one man by crushing his skull and driving the others back until a knight had the wit to seize a crossbow and sidle up the stairs until he had a clear view and the bolt went through the Englishman's mouth to lift off the back of his skull and the French rushed again, screaming hate and victory, trampling the dying man under their blood-spattered feet and carrying their swords up to the very top of the tower where a dozen men tried to push them back down the steps, but still more French were thrusting up the stairs and they forced the leading attackers onto the swords of the defenders and the next men clambered over the dying and the dead to rout the last of the garrison. Men were hacked down. One archer lived long enough to have his fingers chopped off, then his eyes prized out and he was still screaming as he was thrown off the tower onto the waiting swords below.

The French cheered. The tower was a charnel house, slick with blood, but the banner of France would fly from its ramparts. The entrenchments had become graves for the English. Victorious men stripped the clothes from the dead to search for coins, and just then a trumpet called.

There were still some Englishmen on the French side of the river. There were horsemen trapped on a patch of firmer ground.

So the killing was not done.